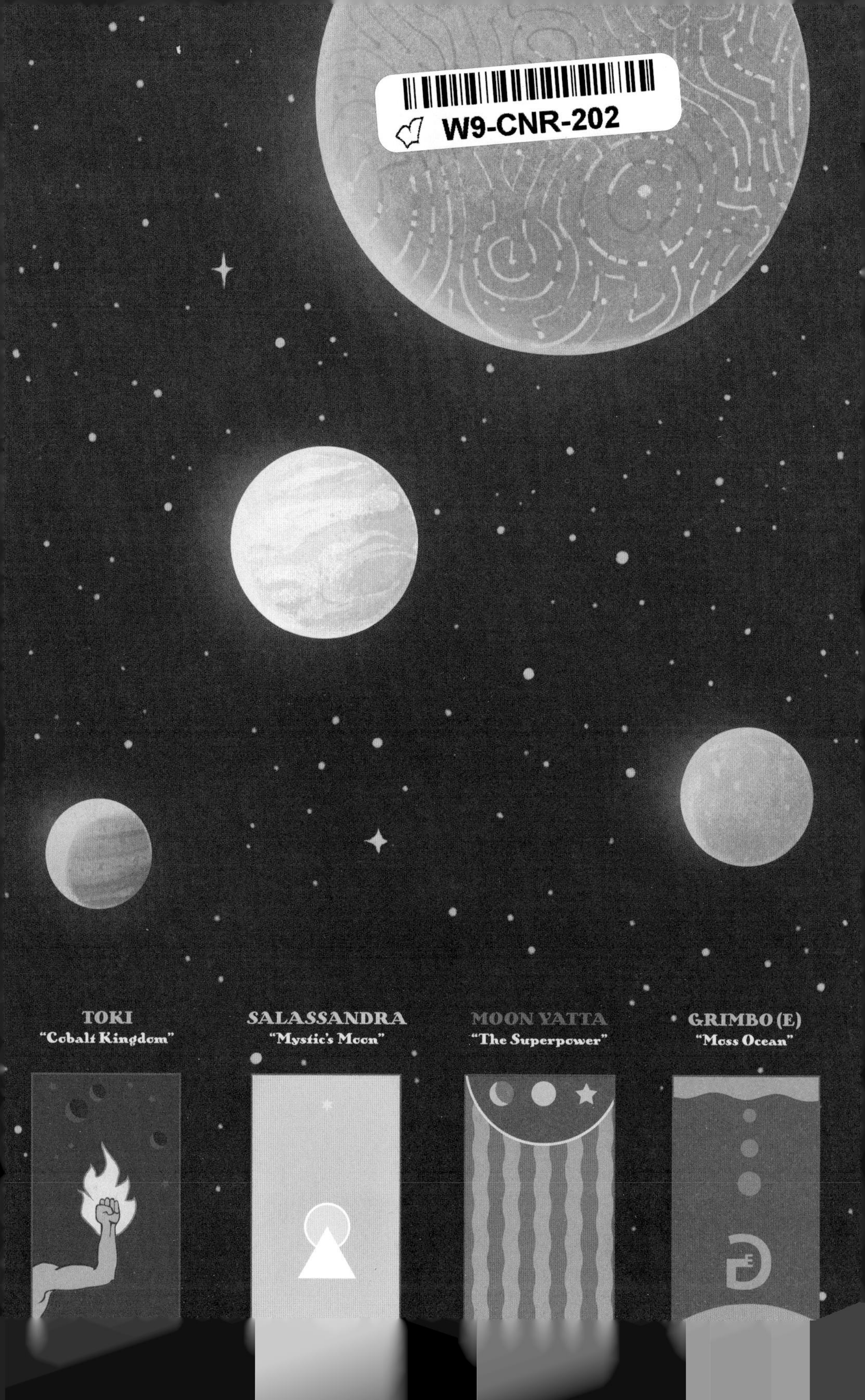
TOKI
"Cobalt Kingdom"
SALASSANDRA
"Mystic's Moon"
MOON YATTA
"The Superpower"
GRIMBO (E)
"Moss Ocean"

5 Worlds

BOOK 1

THE SAND WARRIOR

Mark
SIEGEL

Alexis
SIEGEL

Xanthe
BOUMA

Boya
SUN

Matt
ROCKEFELLER

Random House 🏠 New York

"One by one the five great Beacons
went dark and the Gods were gone;
And none would ever again light the
shining Beacons, save a Warrior of
Sand, crowned with living fire. . . ."
—FROM THE HOURS OF PRINCE FELID

Chapter 1

RUNAWAY SAND

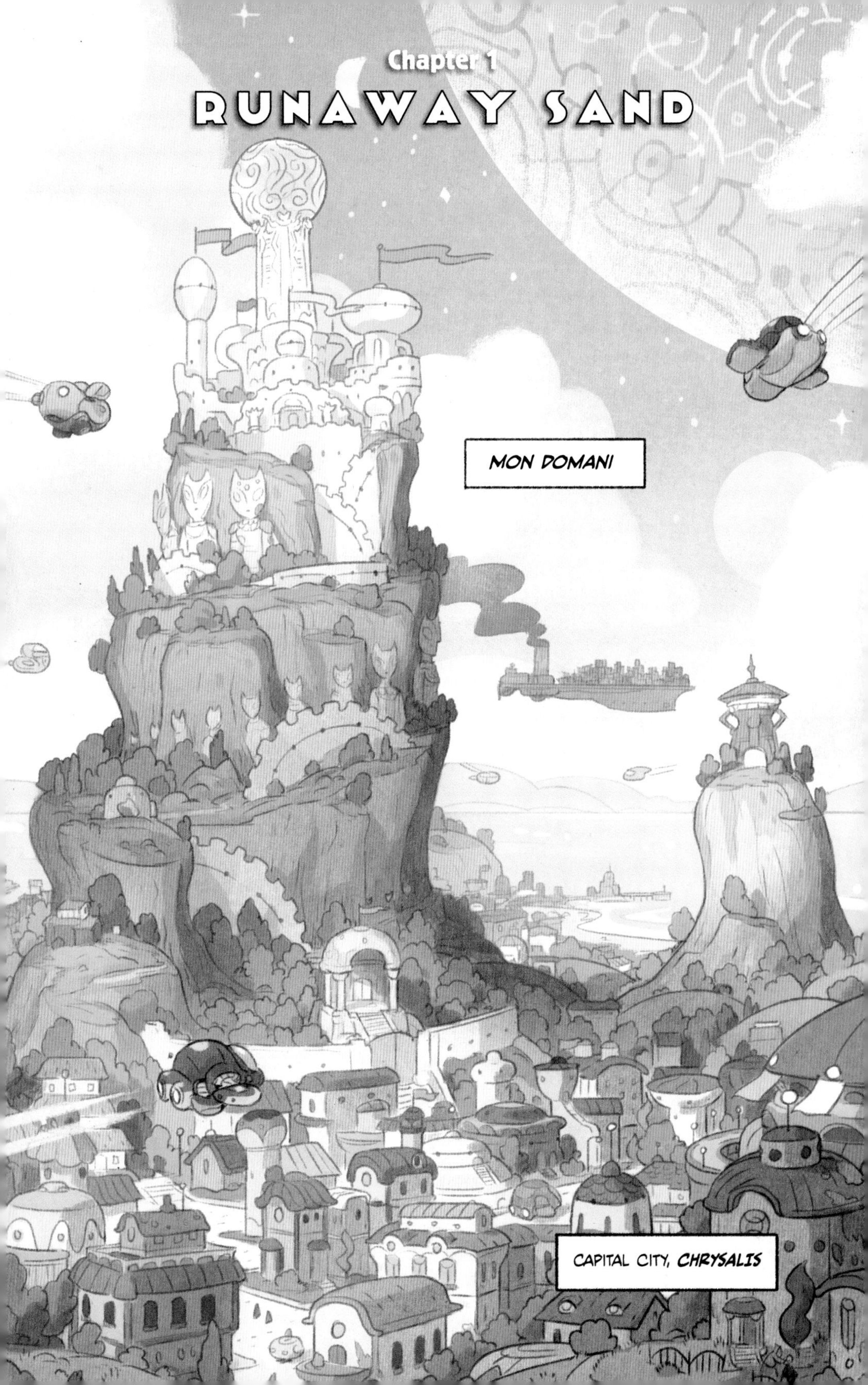
MON DOMANI
CAPITAL CITY, CHRYSALIS

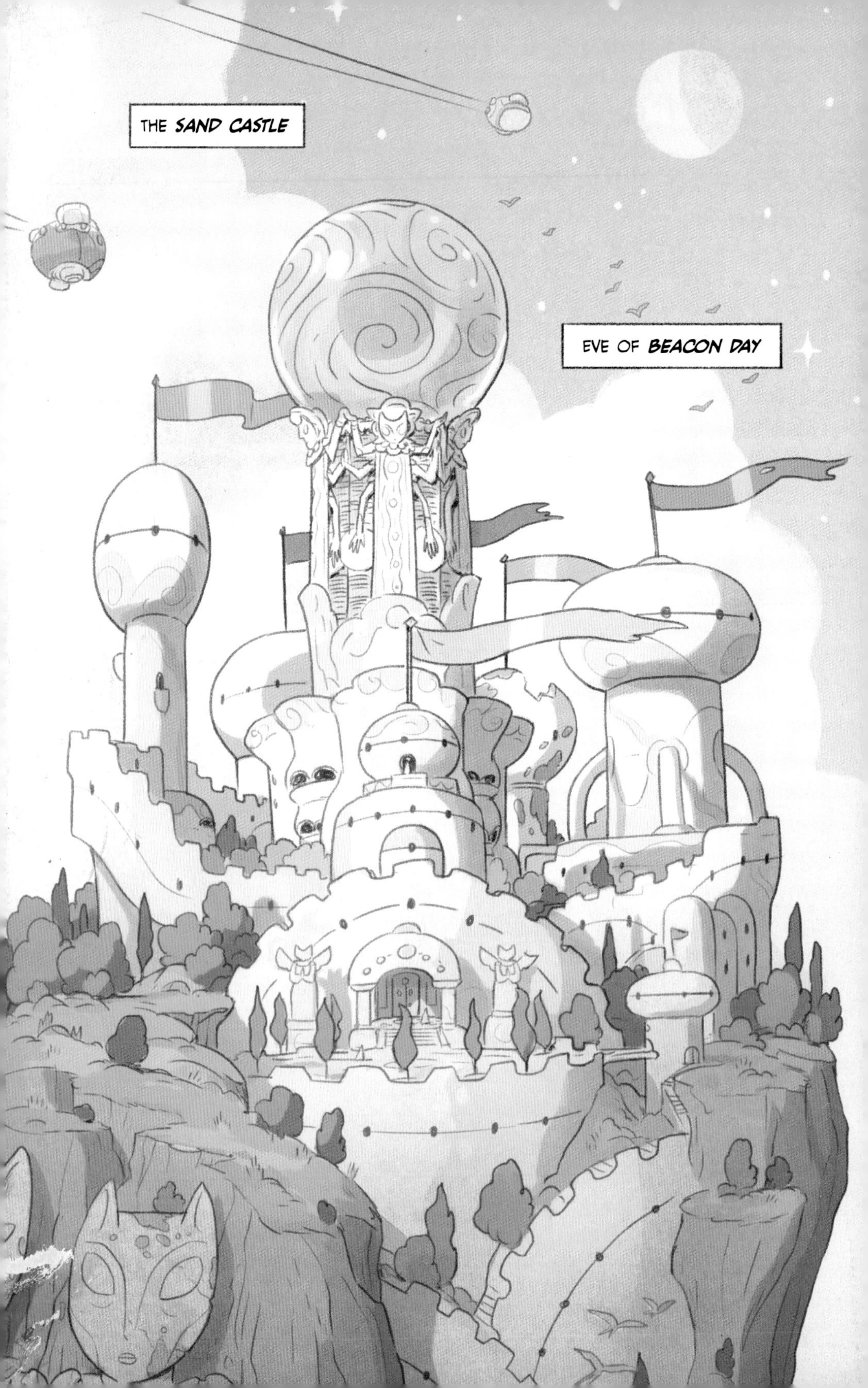
THE SAND CASTLE
EVE OF BEACON DAY

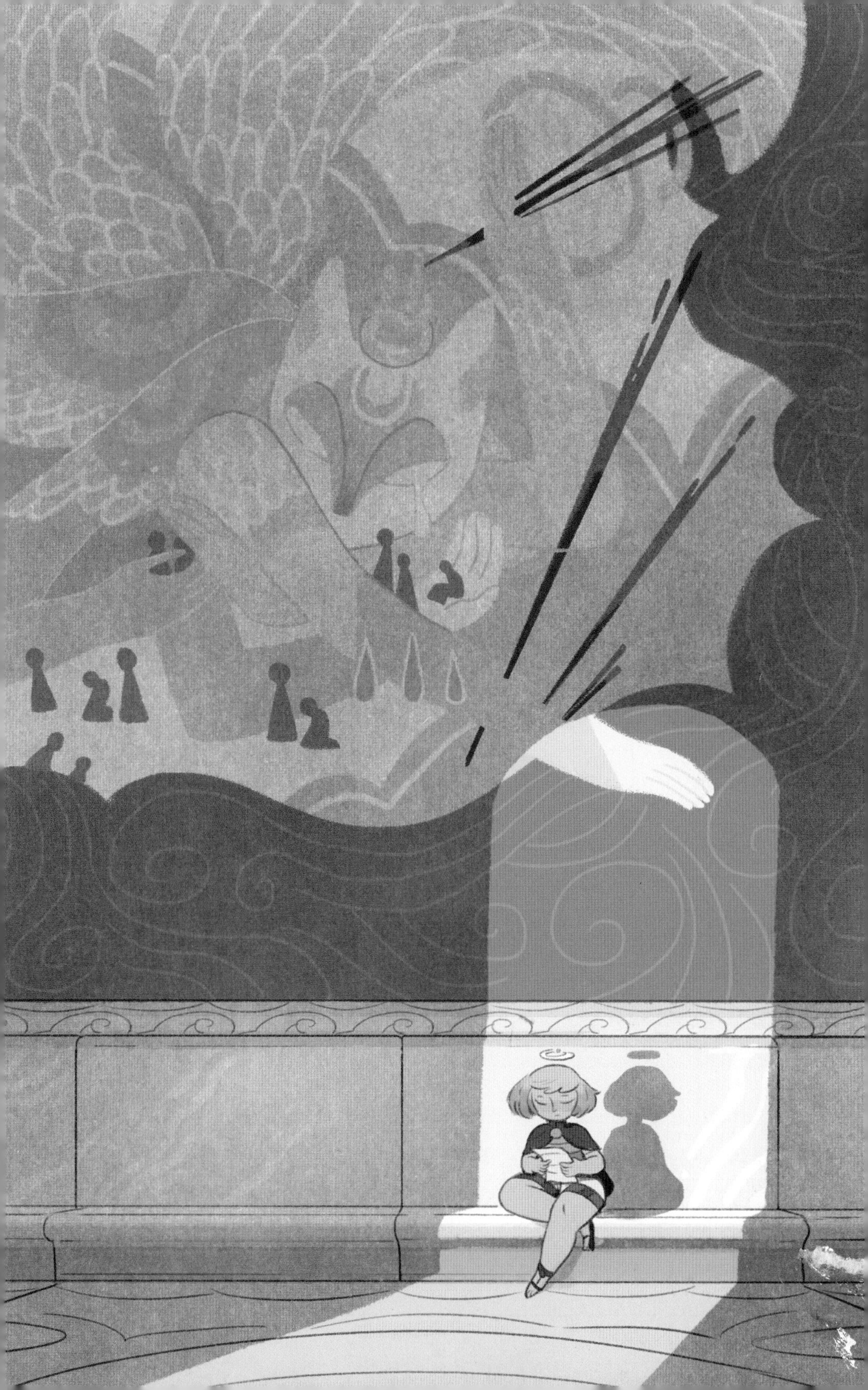

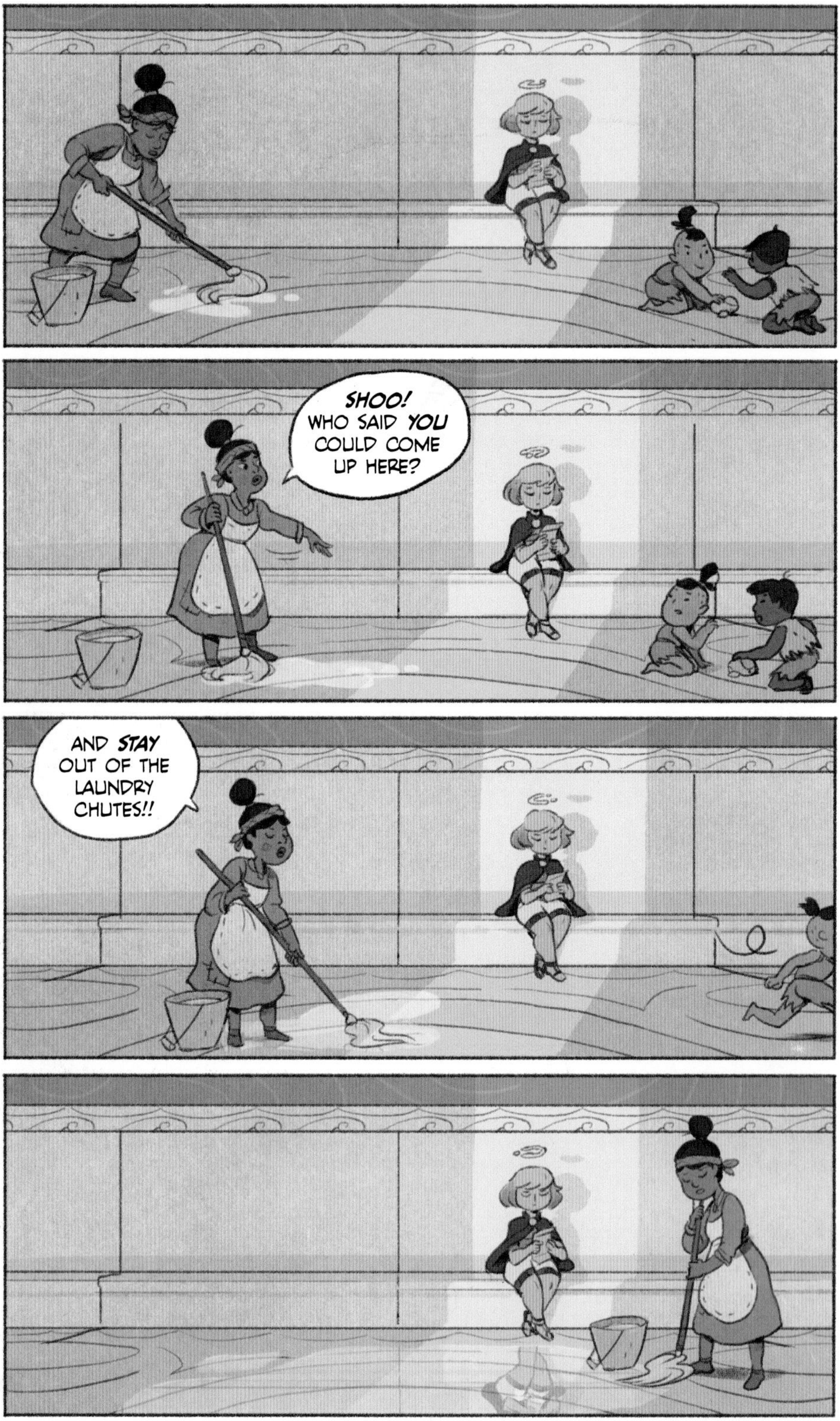
SHOO! WHO SAID YOU COULD COME UP HERE?
AND STAY OUT OF THE LAUNDRY CHUTES!!

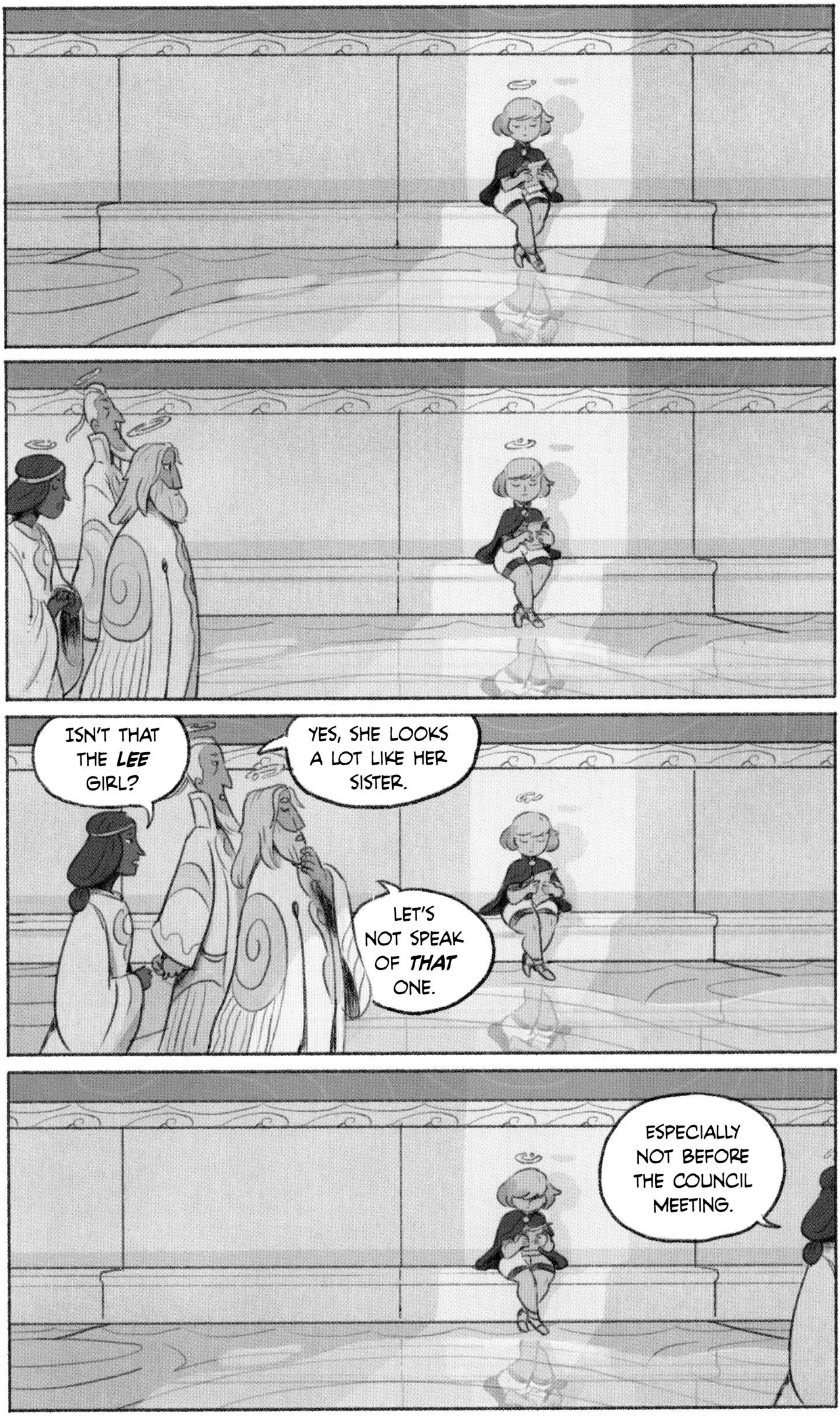
ISN'T THAT THE LEE GIRL?
YES, SHE LOOKS A LOT LIKE HER SISTER.
LET'S NOT SPEAK OF THAT ONE.
ESPECIALLY NOT BEFORE THE COUNCIL MEETING.

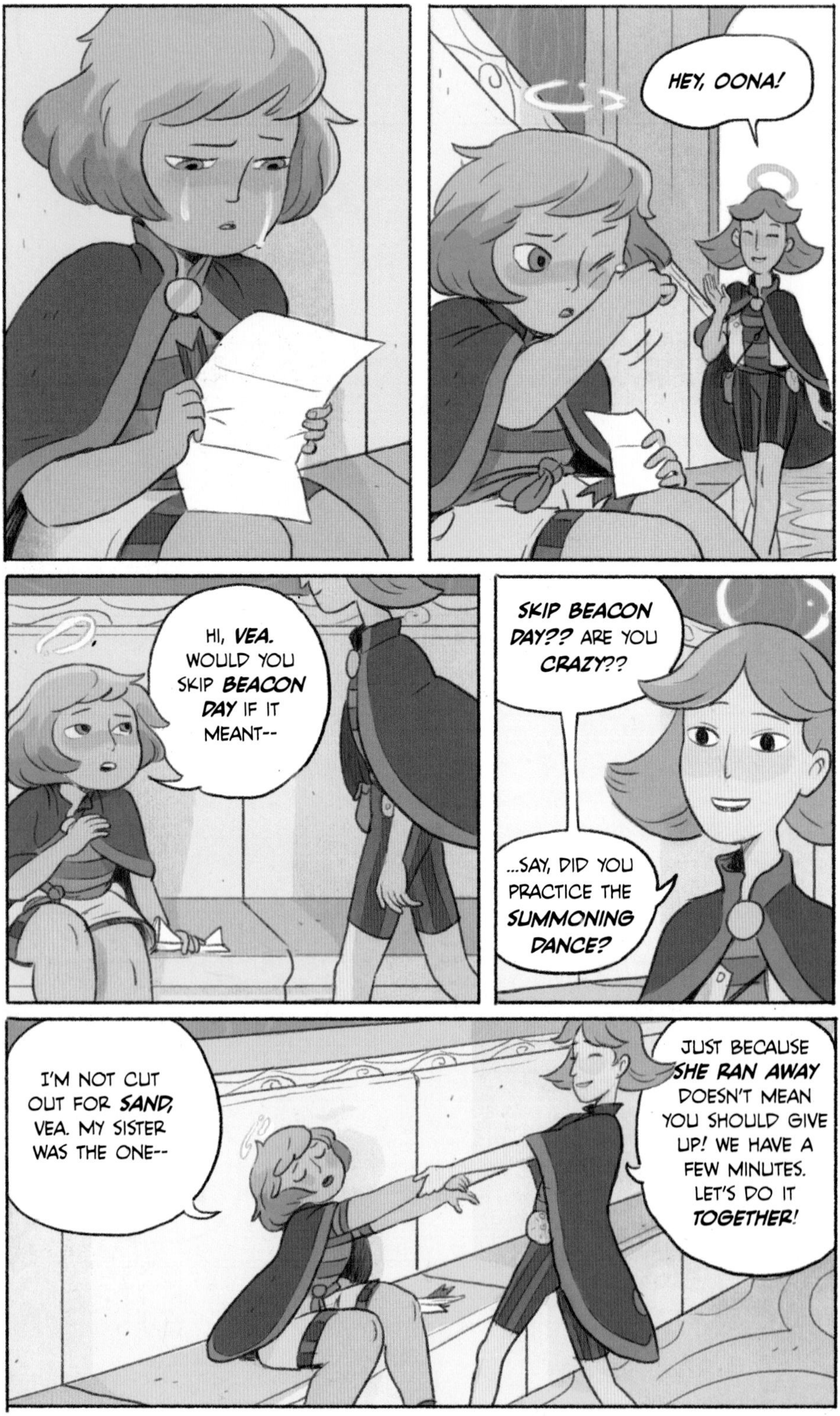
HEY, OONA!
HI, VEA. WOULD YOU SKIP BEACON DAY IF IT MEANT--
SKIP BEACON DAY?? ARE YOU CRAZY??
...SAY, DID YOU PRACTICE THE SUMMONING DANCE?
I'M NOT CUT OUT FOR SAND, VEA. MY SISTER WAS THE ONE--
JUST BECAUSE SHE RAN AWAY DOESN'T MEAN YOU SHOULD GIVE UP! WE HAVE A FEW MINUTES. LET'S DO IT TOGETHER!

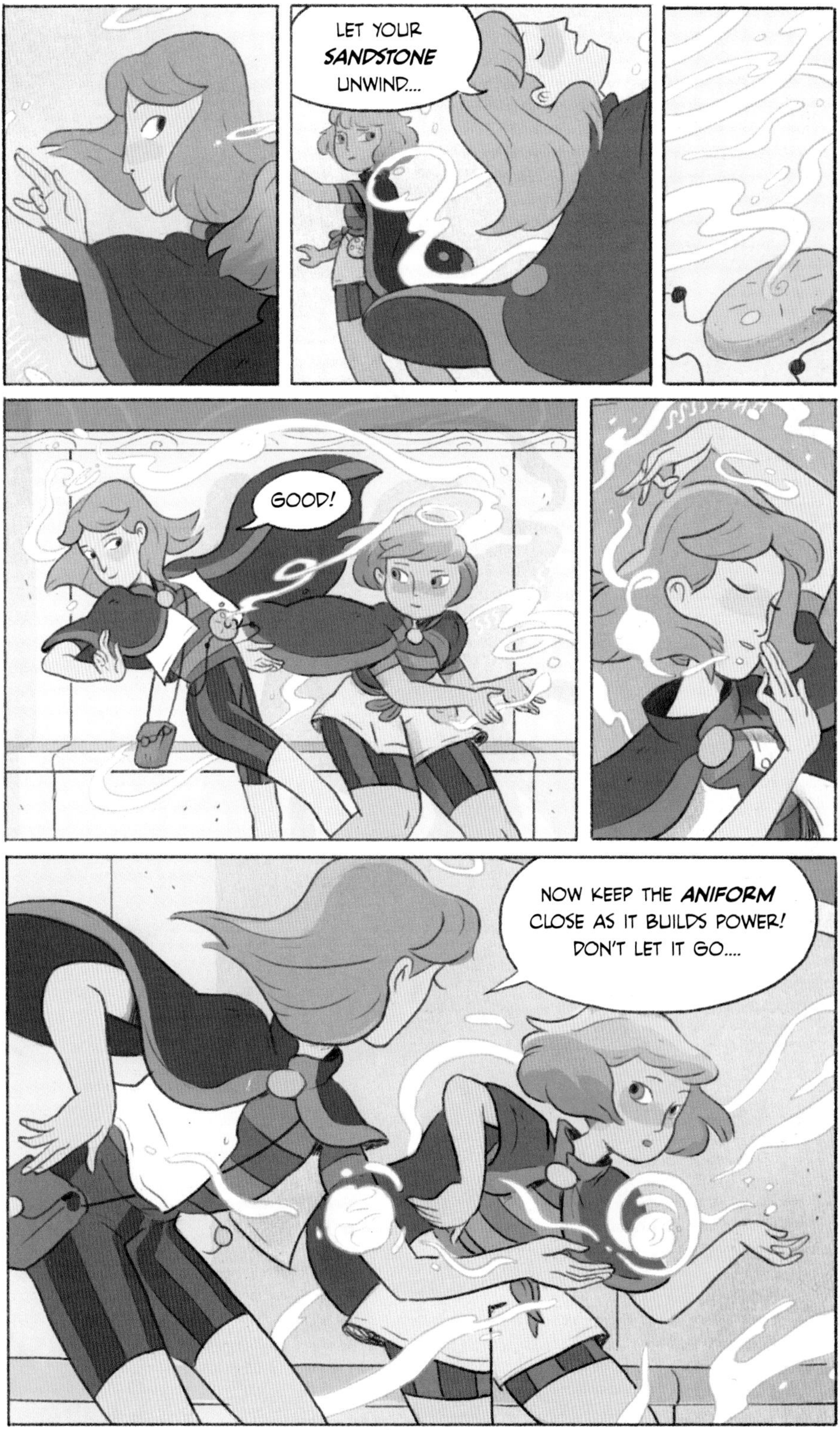
LET YOUR **SANDSTONE** UNWIND....
GOOD!
NOW KEEP THE **ANIFORM** CLOSE AS IT BUILDS POWER! DON'T LET IT GO....

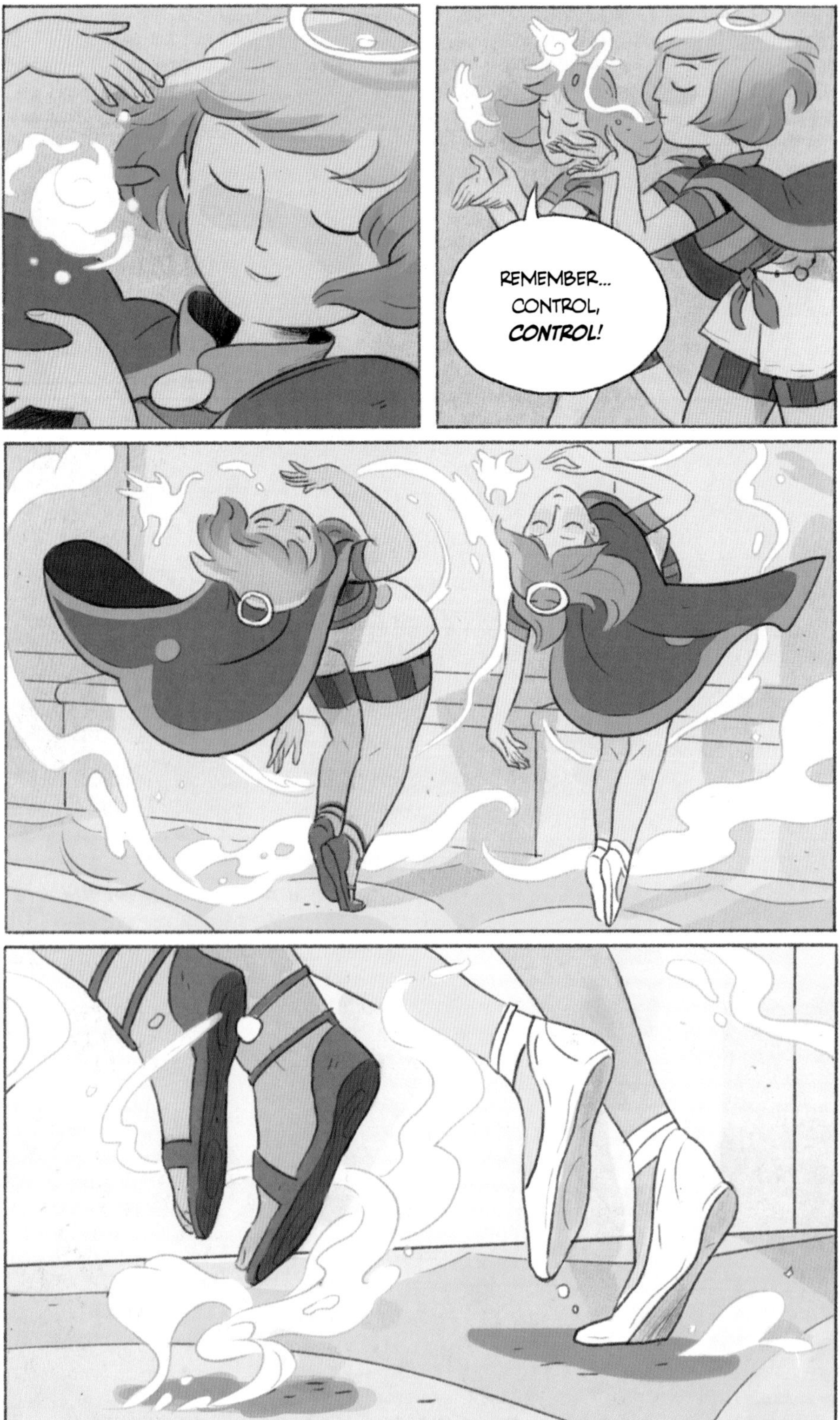
REMEMBER... CONTROL, CONTROL!

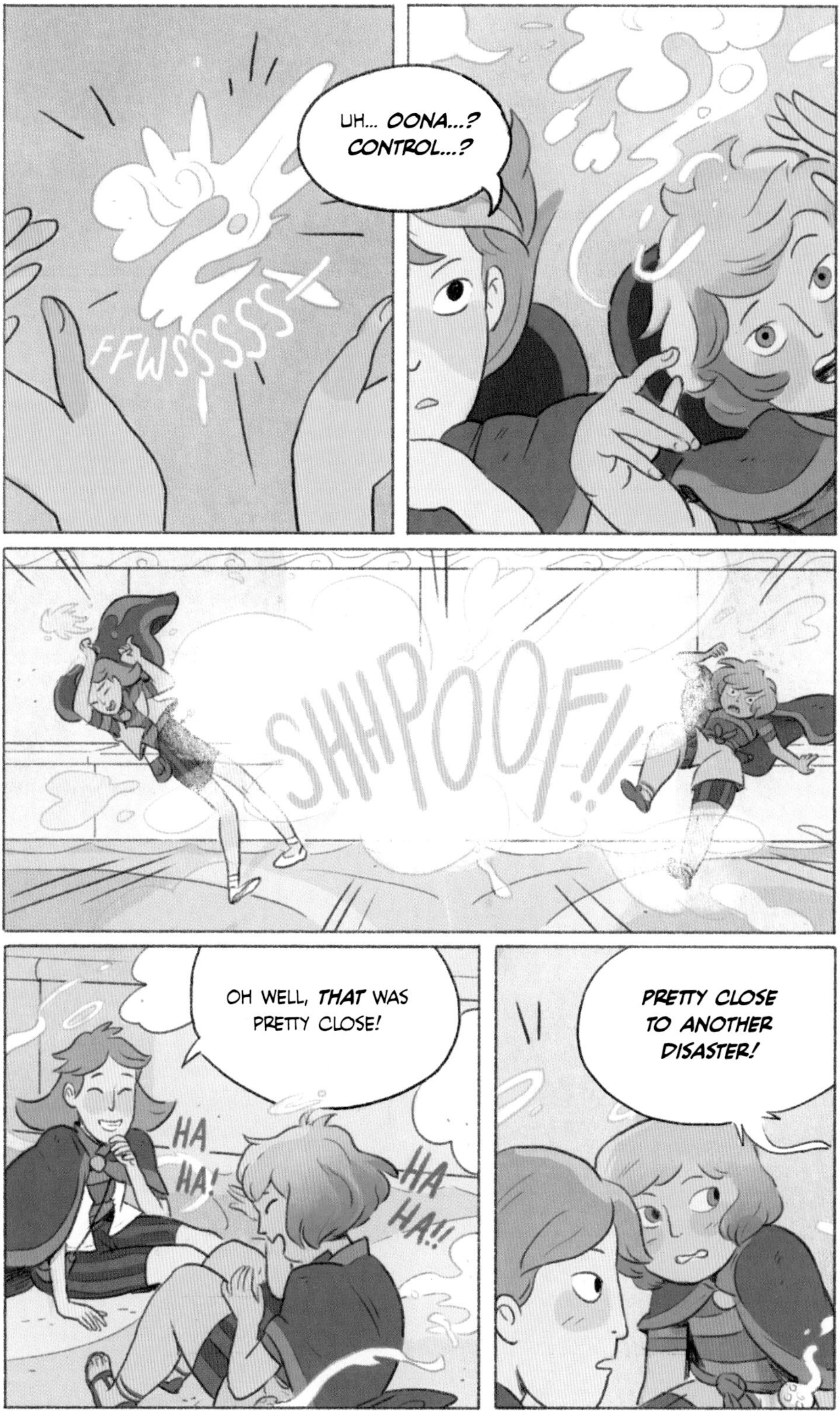
FFWSSSSS
UH... OONA...? CONTROL...?
SHHPOOF!!!
OH WELL, THAT WAS PRETTY CLOSE!
HA HA!
HA HA!!
PRETTY CLOSE TO ANOTHER DISASTER!

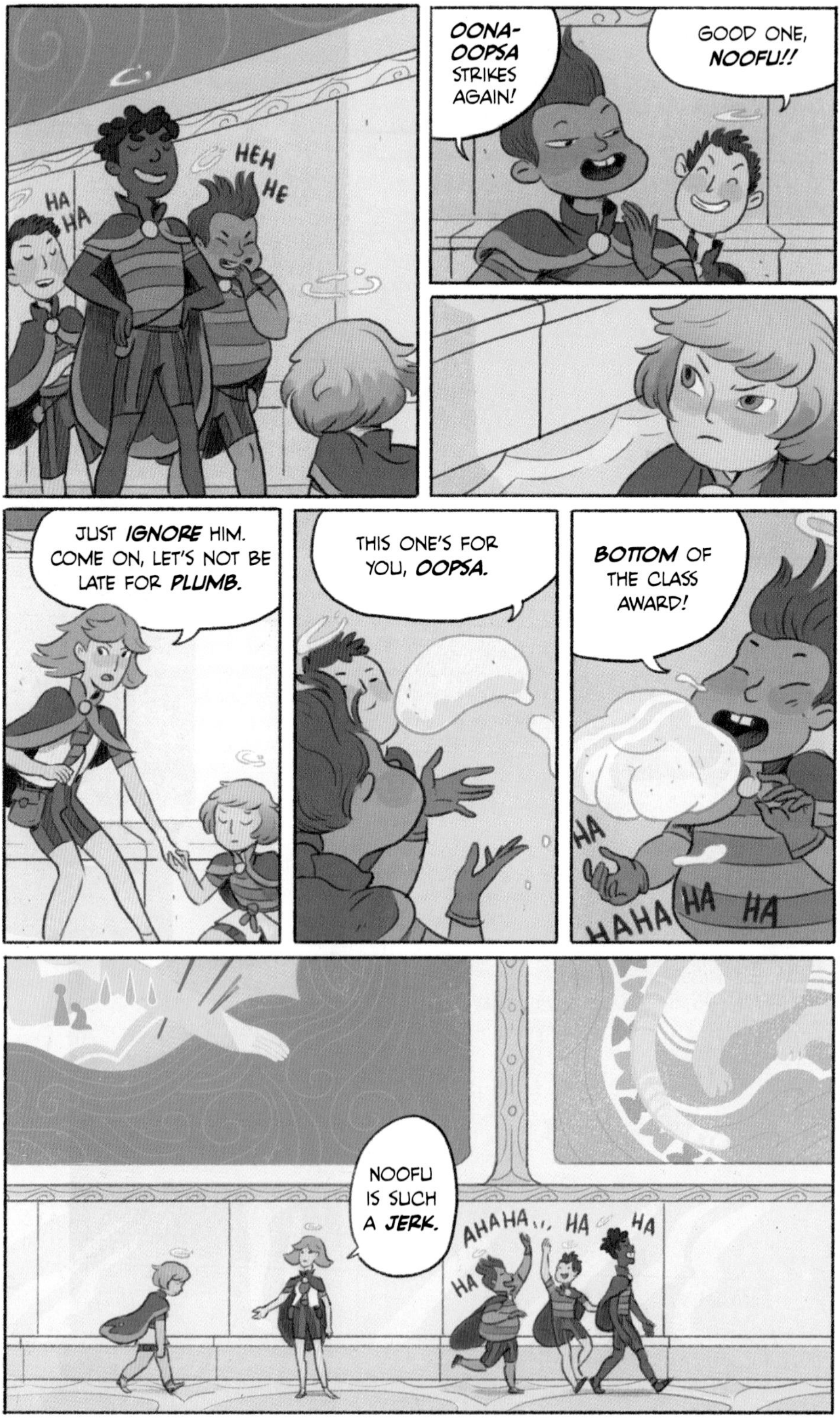
HA HA
HEH HE
OONA-OOPSA STRIKES AGAIN!
GOOD ONE, NOOFU!!
JUST IGNORE HIM. COME ON, LET'S NOT BE LATE FOR PLUMB.
THIS ONE'S FOR YOU, OOPSA.
BOTTOM OF THE CLASS AWARD!
HA
HAHA HA HA
NOOFU IS SUCH A JERK.
AHAHA... HA HA
HA

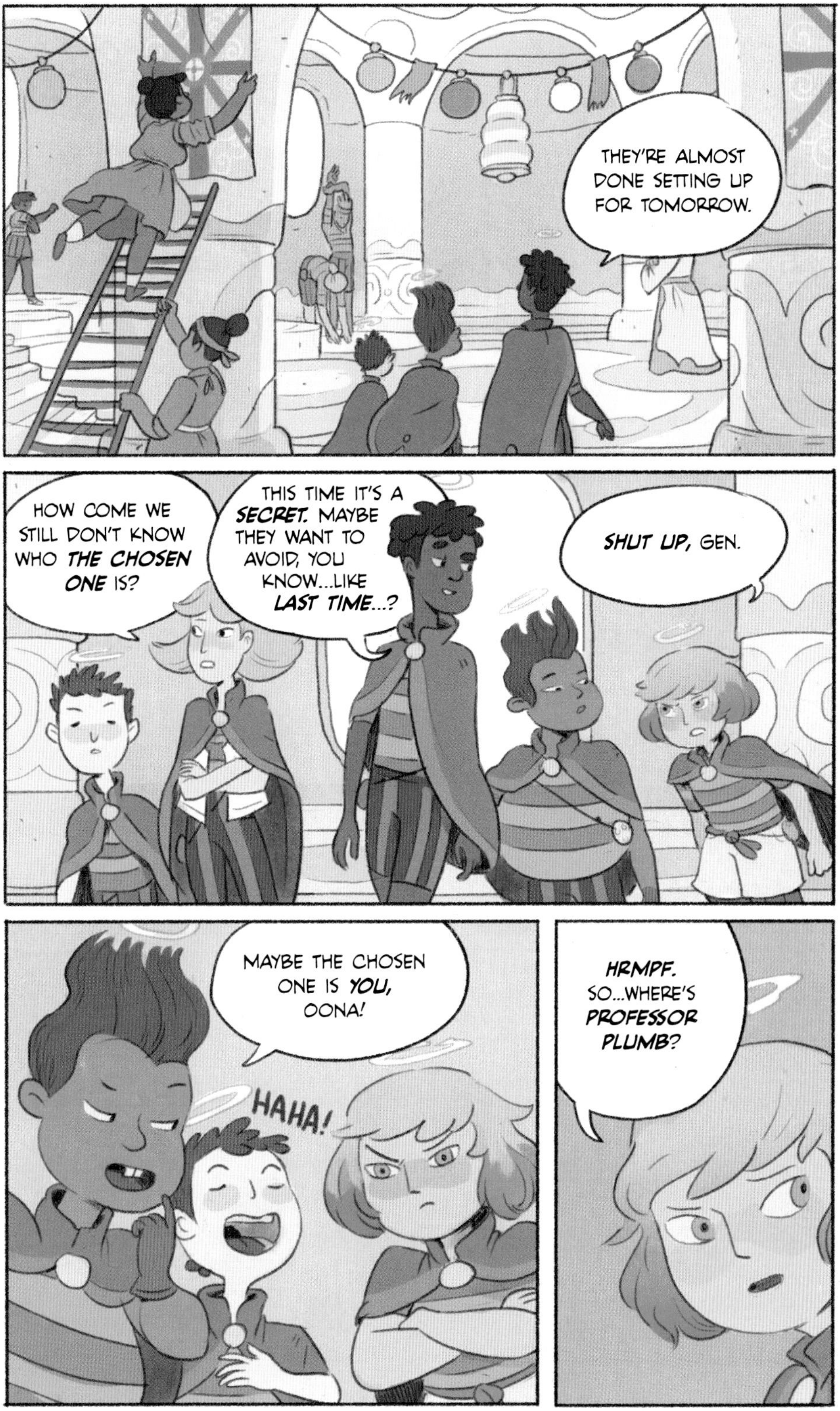
THEY'RE ALMOST DONE SETTING UP FOR TOMORROW.
HOW COME WE STILL DON'T KNOW WHO THE CHOSEN ONE IS?
THIS TIME IT'S A SECRET. MAYBE THEY WANT TO AVOID, YOU KNOW...LIKE LAST TIME...?
SHUT UP, GEN.
MAYBE THE CHOSEN ONE IS YOU, OONA!
HAHA!
HRMPF. SO...WHERE'S PROFESSOR PLUMB?

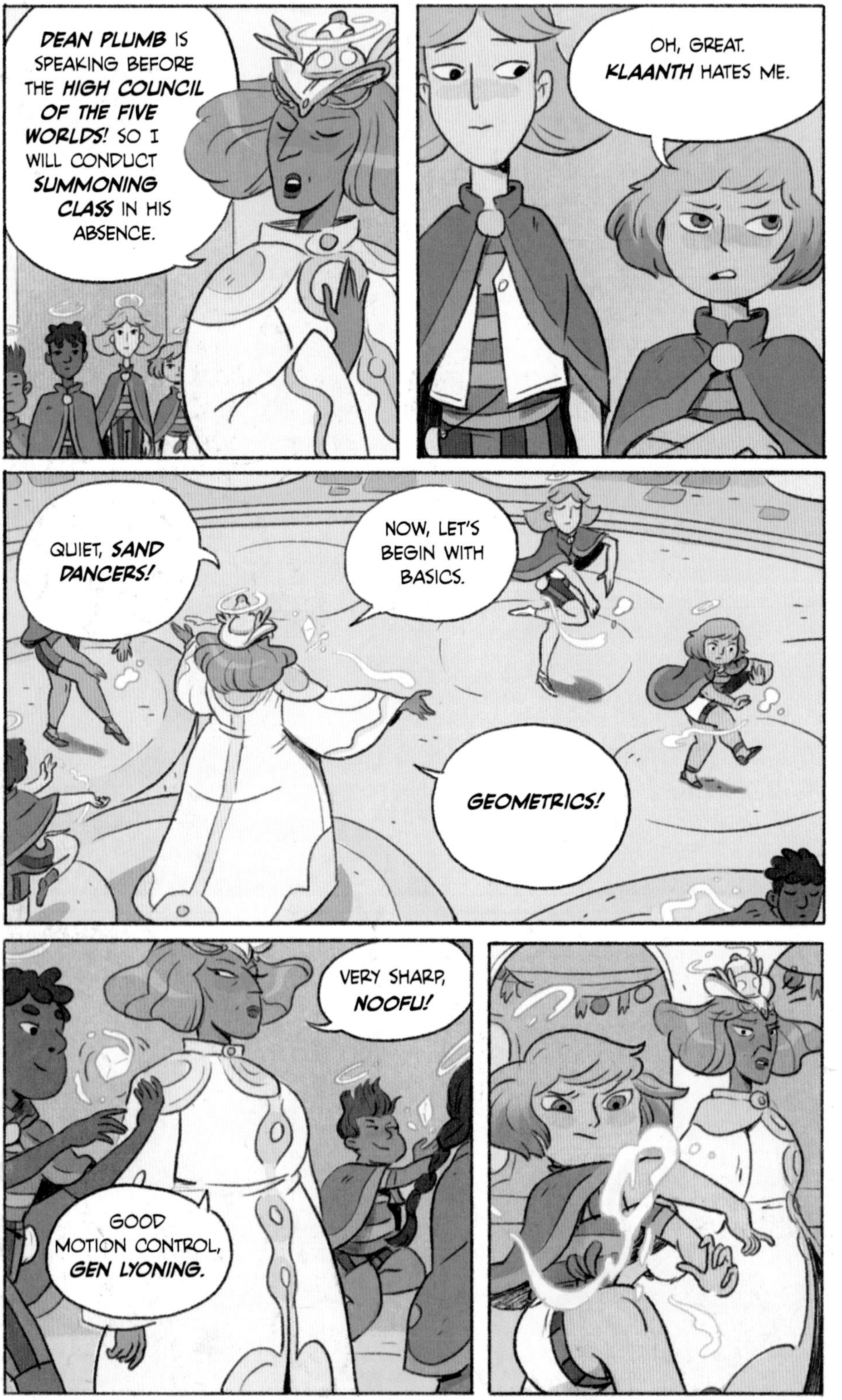
DEAN PLUMB IS SPEAKING BEFORE THE HIGH COUNCIL OF THE FIVE WORLDS! SO I WILL CONDUCT SUMMONING CLASS IN HIS ABSENCE.
OH, GREAT. KLAANTH HATES ME.
QUIET, SAND DANCERS!
NOW, LET'S BEGIN WITH BASICS.
GEOMETRICS!
VERY SHARP, NOOFU!
GOOD MOTION CONTROL, GEN LYONING.

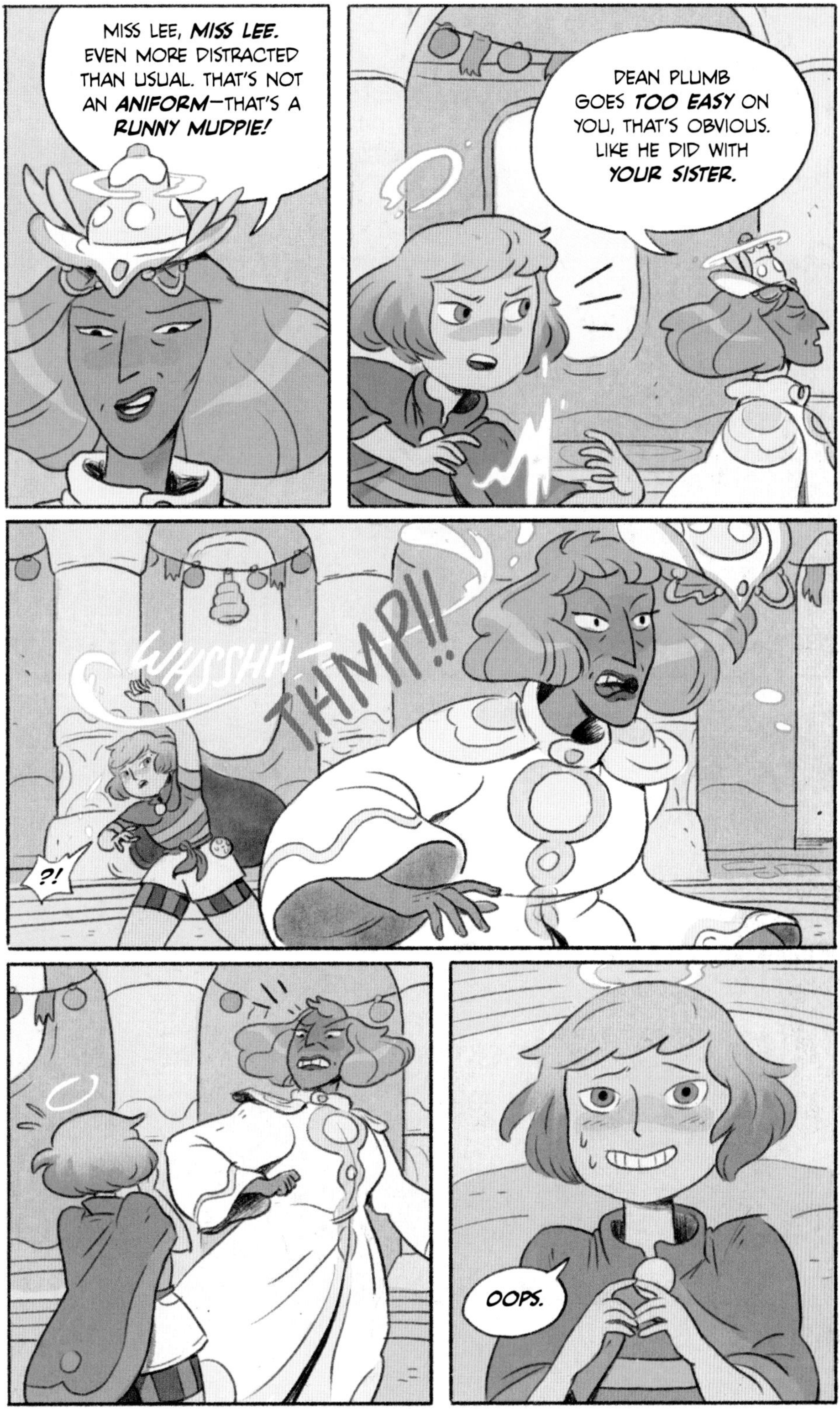
MISS LEE, MISS LEE. EVEN MORE DISTRACTED THAN USUAL. THAT'S NOT AN ANIFORM—THAT'S A RUNNY MUDPIE!
DEAN PLUMB GOES TOO EASY ON YOU, THAT'S OBVIOUS. LIKE HE DID WITH YOUR SISTER.
WHSSHH—THMP!!
?!
OOPS.

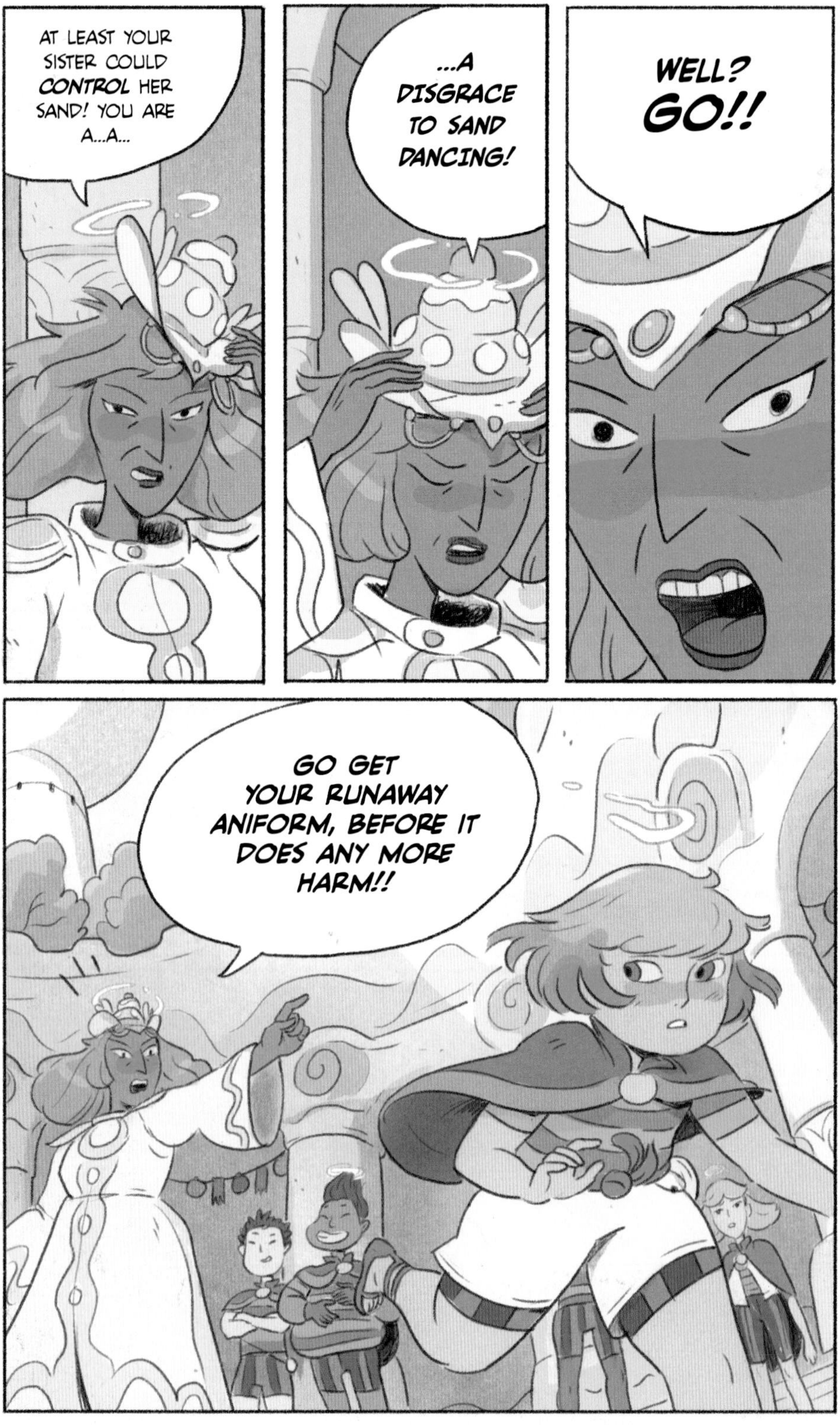
AT LEAST YOUR SISTER COULD CONTROL HER SAND! YOU ARE A...A...
...A DISGRACE TO SAND DANCING!
WELL? GO!!
GO GET YOUR RUNAWAY ANIFORM, BEFORE IT DOES ANY MORE HARM!!

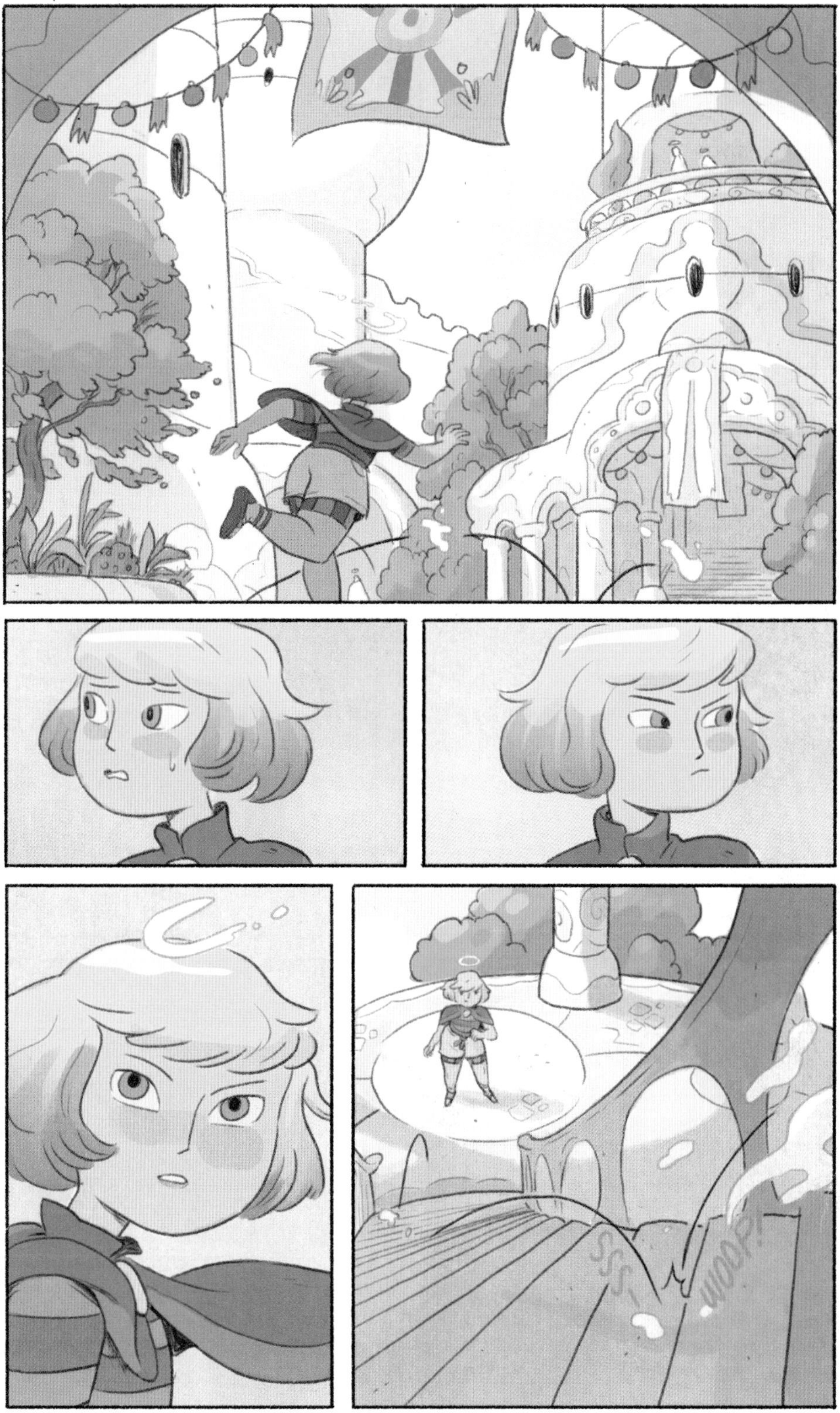
SS!
WOOP!

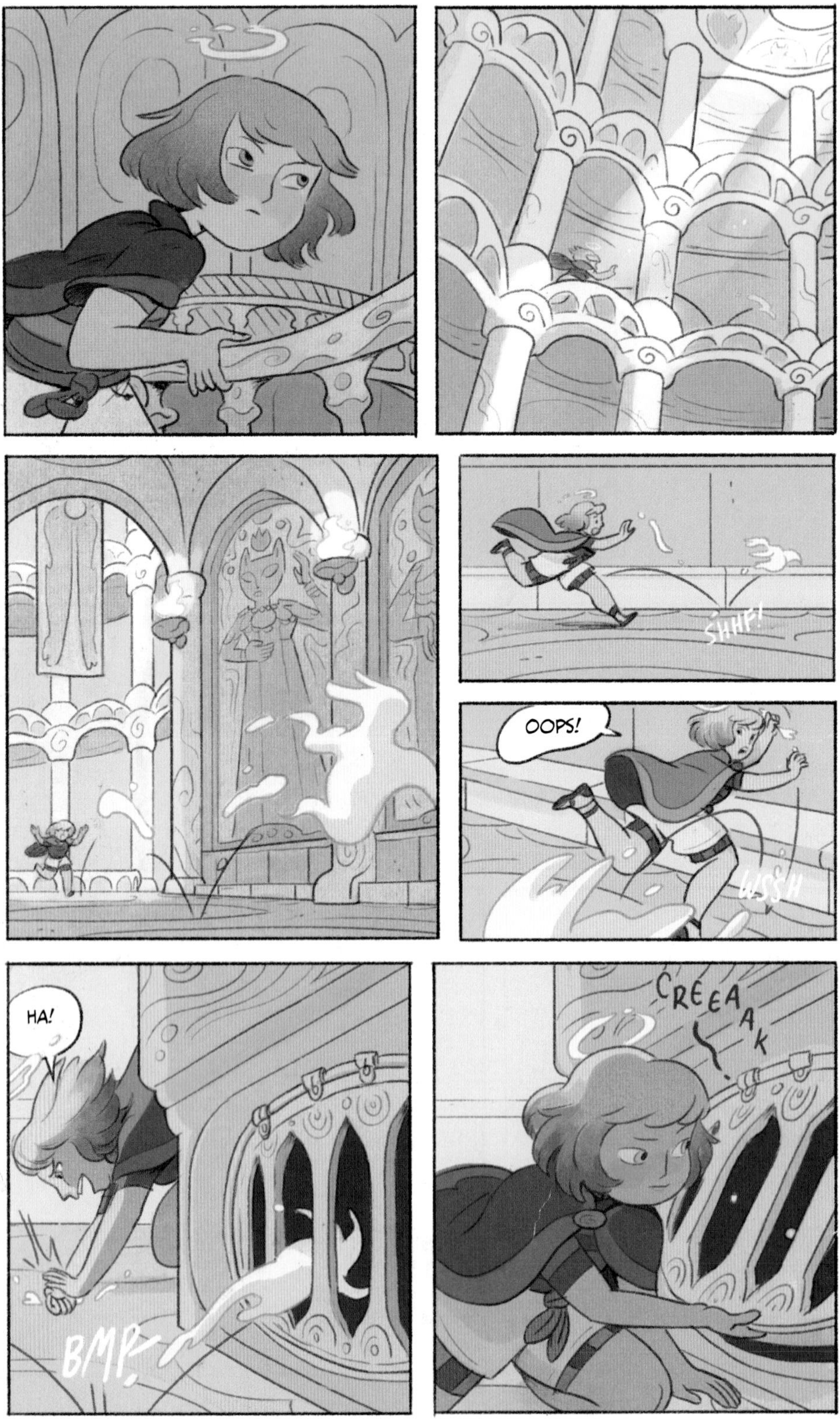
SHHF!
OOPS!
WSSH
HA!
BMP
CREEAAK

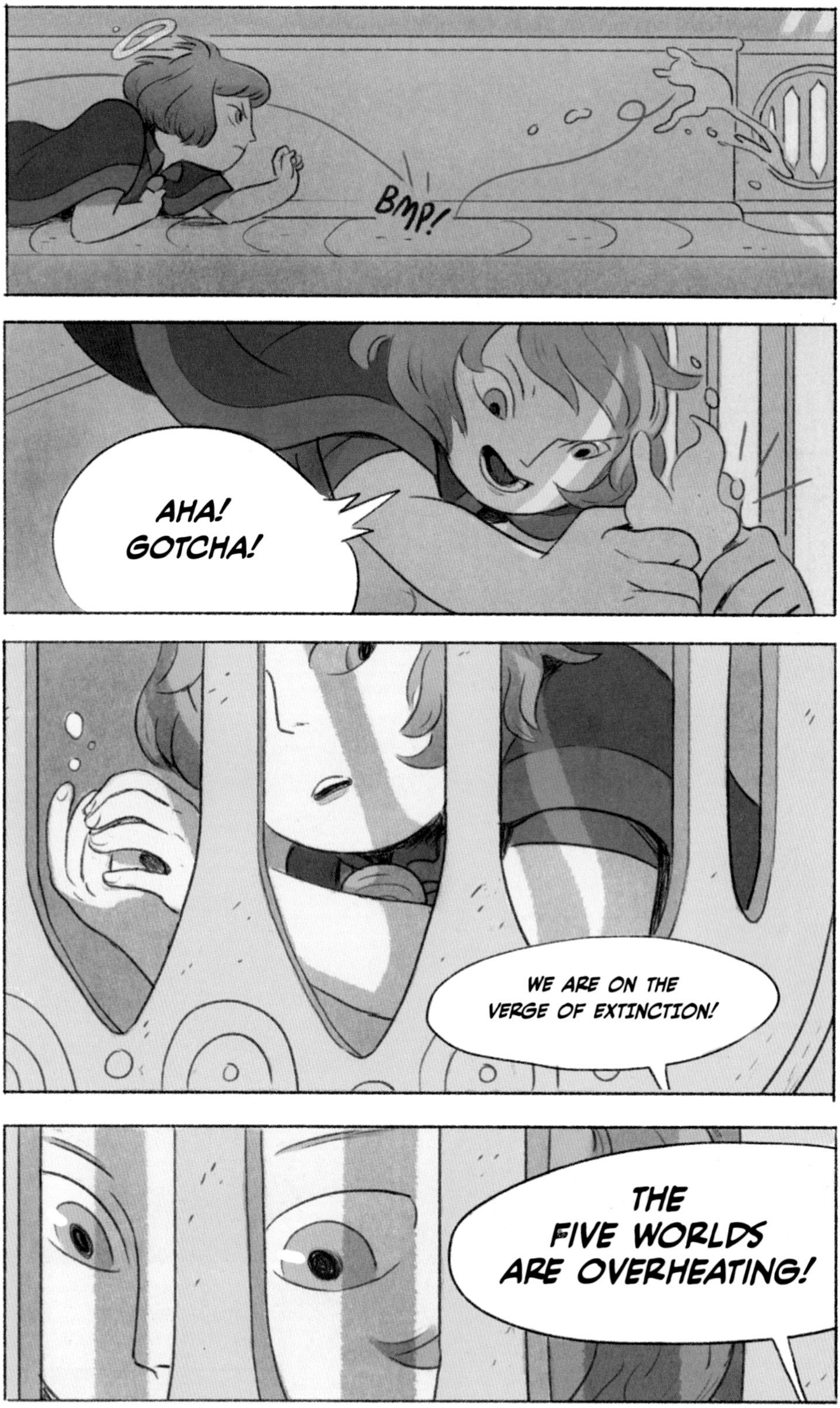
BMP!
AHA! GOTCHA!
WE ARE ON THE VERGE OF EXTINCTION!
THE FIVE WORLDS ARE OVERHEATING!

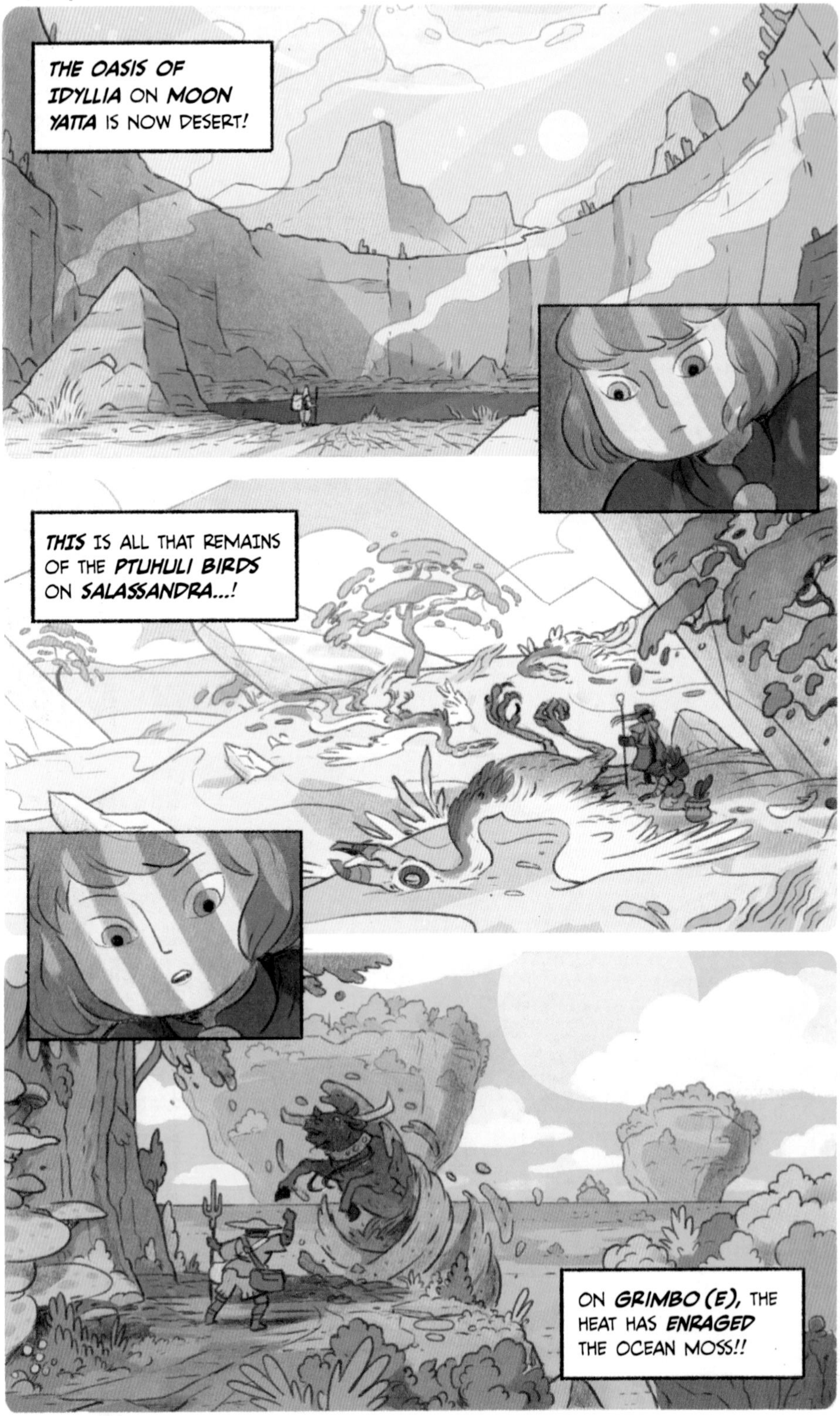
THE OASIS OF IDYLLIA ON MOON YATTA IS NOW DESERT!
THIS IS ALL THAT REMAINS OF THE PTUHULI BIRDS ON SALASSANDRA...!
ON GRIMBO (E), THE HEAT HAS ENRAGED THE OCEAN MOSS!!

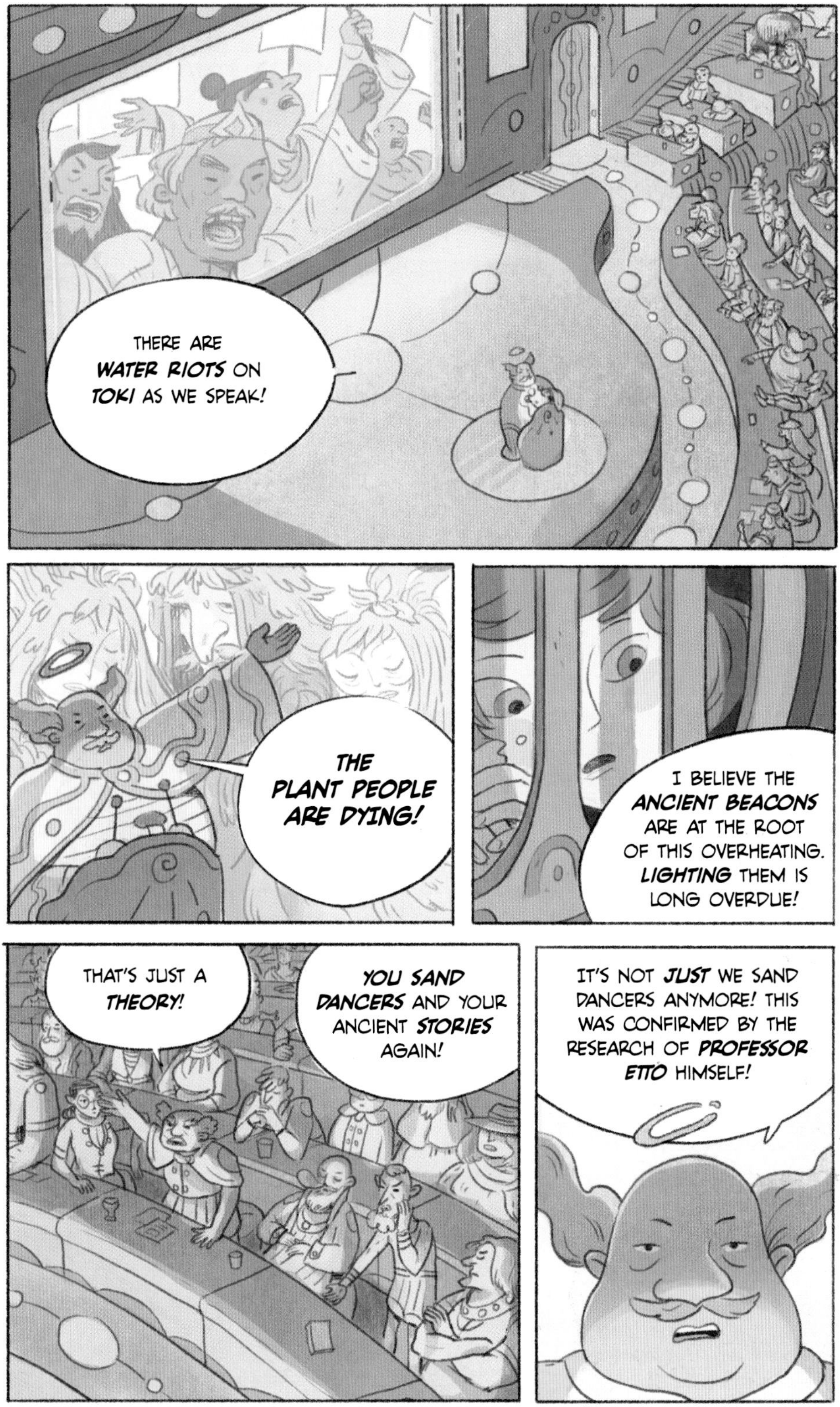
THERE ARE WATER RIOTS ON TOKI AS WE SPEAK!
THE PLANT PEOPLE ARE DYING!
I BELIEVE THE ANCIENT BEACONS ARE AT THE ROOT OF THIS OVERHEATING. LIGHTING THEM IS LONG OVERDUE!
THAT'S JUST A THEORY!
YOU SAND DANCERS AND YOUR ANCIENT STORIES AGAIN!
IT'S NOT JUST WE SAND DANCERS ANYMORE! THIS WAS CONFIRMED BY THE RESEARCH OF PROFESSOR ETTO HIMSELF!

IN THE GOLDEN AGE, WHEN THE *FELID GODS* LIVED AMONG US, THE *BEACONS* SHONE BRIGHT ON EACH OF OUR WORLDS--A TIME OF *BALANCE AND HARMONY!*

⌇ ETTO'S THEOREM ⌇

ON

OFF

OVERLOADING

RELEASING HIGHER CORE ENERGY

BACKUP OVERHEATING

PLANETARY TO SOLAR ILLUMINATION

MODULATING PLANETARY EVOLUTION

DWINDLING RESOURCE

BUT WHEN THE GREAT *FELID QUEEN* FELL TO THE EVIL *MIMIC,* THE *BEACONS WENT DARK!* NOW, A THOUSAND YEARS LATER, OUR WORLDS ARE *DYING!*

THE *SAND DANCERS' PROPHECY* TELLS US THAT ONLY BY *RELIGHTING* THE ANCIENT BEACONS--

THE BEACONS *CANNOT* BE LIT! MANY HAVE TRIED!

NOT LEAST OF THEM *YOUR* PEOPLE!

THE PROPHECY OF THE *SAND WARRIOR* IS NOT UNIVERSALLY ACCEPTED!

NOT THE *SAND CASTLE VERSION,* ANYWAY.

WE *MUST* SET ASIDE OUR DIFFERENCES AND COME TOGETHER AS *ONE GALAXY!*

SECRETLY I HAVE TRAINED *THE GREATEST SAND DANCER YET.* HE IS TRULY *THE CHOSEN ONE,* AND HE *WILL* LIGHT OUR WHITE BEACON!

I AM ASKING YOU TO *LET HIM LIGHT EVERY ONE OF THE FIVE BEACONS* AND AVERT *THE EXTINC-TION OF THE FIVE WORLDS!*

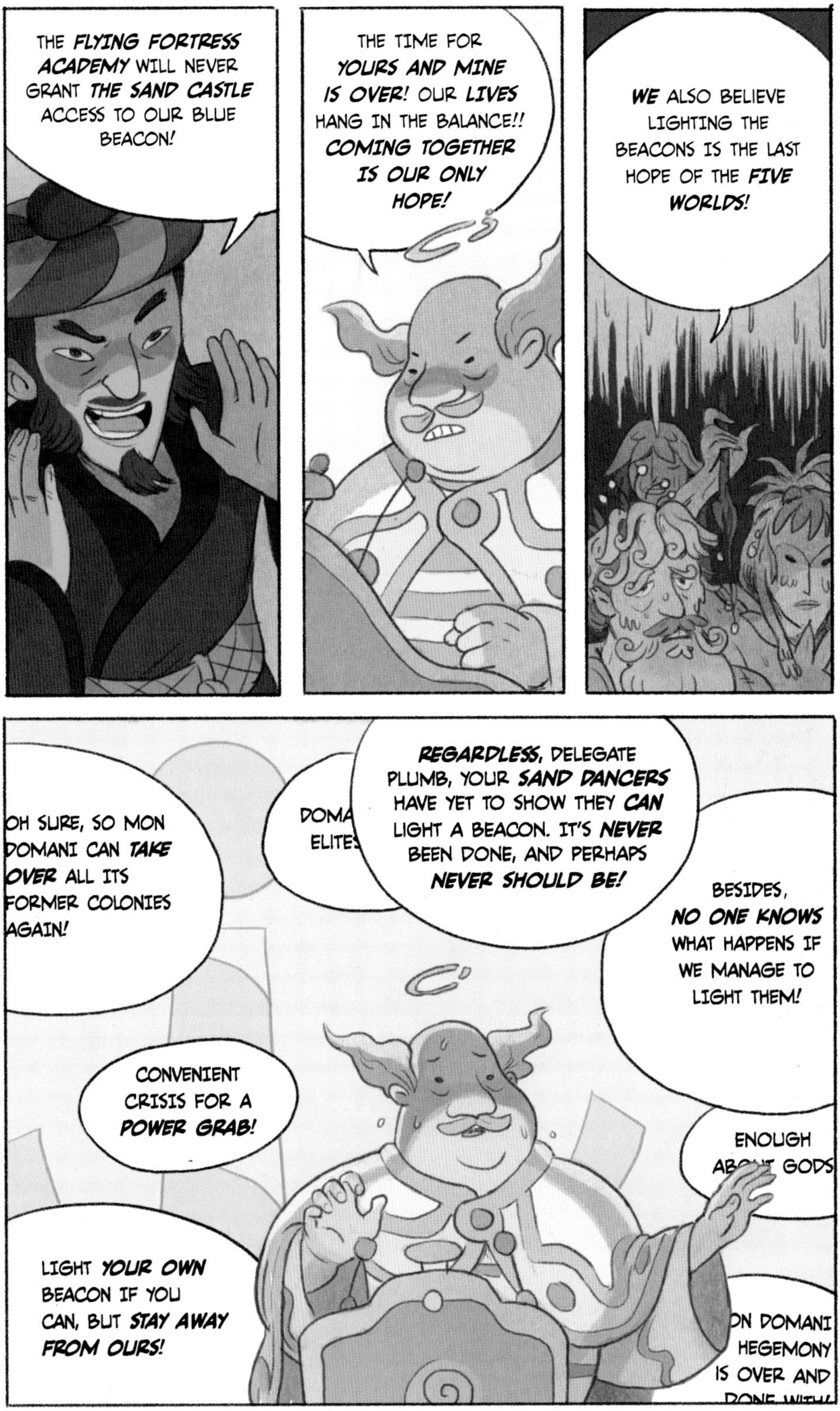
THE FLYING FORTRESS ACADEMY WILL NEVER GRANT THE SAND CASTLE ACCESS TO OUR BLUE BEACON!
THE TIME FOR YOURS AND MINE IS OVER! OUR LIVES HANG IN THE BALANCE!! COMING TOGETHER IS OUR ONLY HOPE!
WE ALSO BELIEVE LIGHTING THE BEACONS IS THE LAST HOPE OF THE FIVE WORLDS!
OH SURE, SO MON DOMANI CAN TAKE OVER ALL ITS FORMER COLONIES AGAIN!
DOMA ELITES
REGARDLESS, DELEGATE PLUMB, YOUR SAND DANCERS HAVE YET TO SHOW THEY CAN LIGHT A BEACON. IT'S NEVER BEEN DONE, AND PERHAPS NEVER SHOULD BE!
BESIDES, NO ONE KNOWS WHAT HAPPENS IF WE MANAGE TO LIGHT THEM!
CONVENIENT CRISIS FOR A POWER GRAB!
ENOUGH GODS
LIGHT YOUR OWN BEACON IF YOU CAN, BUT STAY AWAY FROM OURS!
ON DOMANI HEGEMONY IS OVER AND

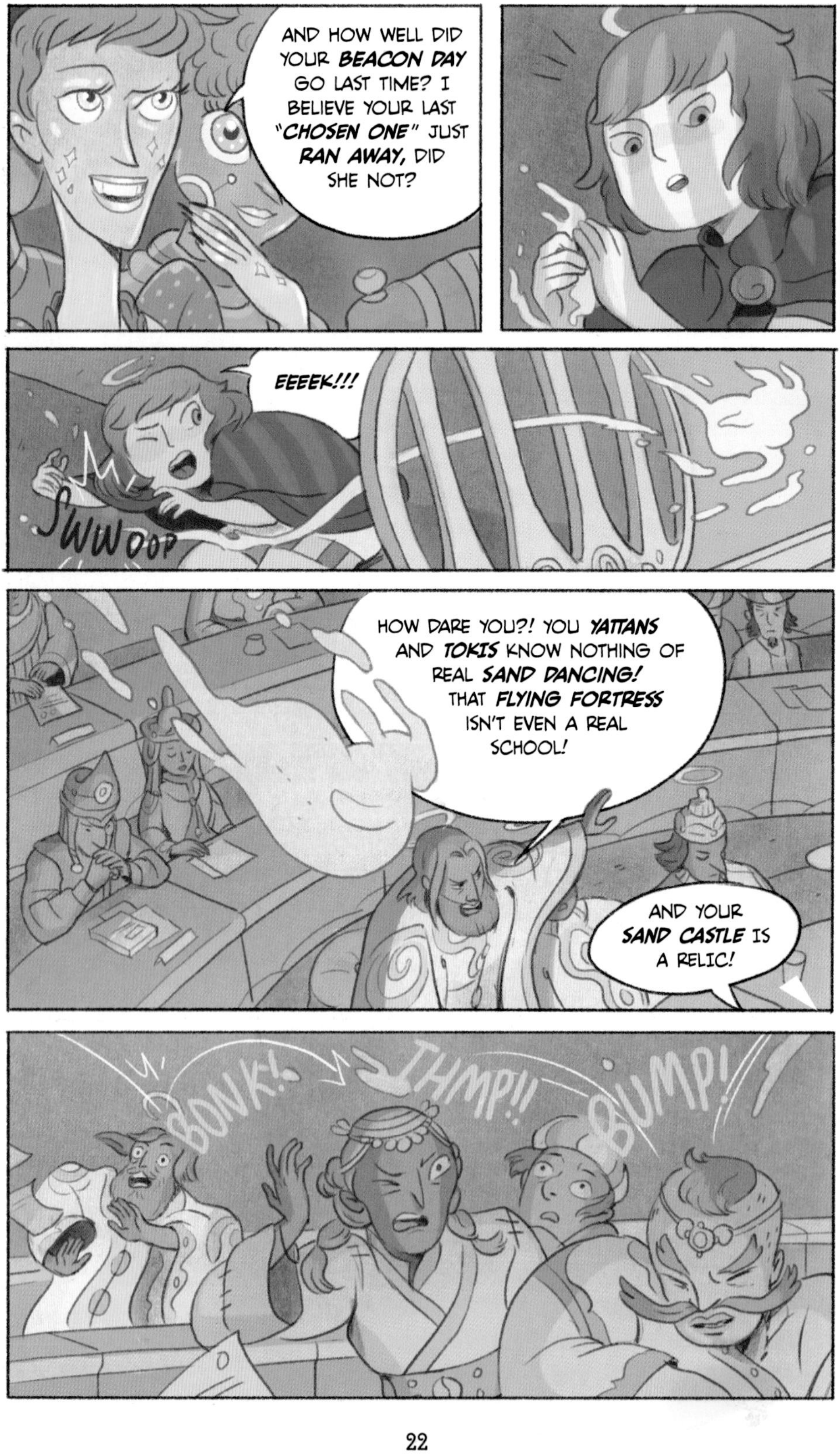
AND HOW WELL DID YOUR BEACON DAY GO LAST TIME? I BELIEVE YOUR LAST "CHOSEN ONE" JUST RAN AWAY, DID SHE NOT?
EEEEK!!!
SWWOOP
HOW DARE YOU?! YOU YATTANS AND TOKIS KNOW NOTHING OF REAL SAND DANCING! THAT FLYING FORTRESS ISN'T EVEN A REAL SCHOOL!
AND YOUR SAND CASTLE IS A RELIC!
BONK!
THMP!!
BUMP!

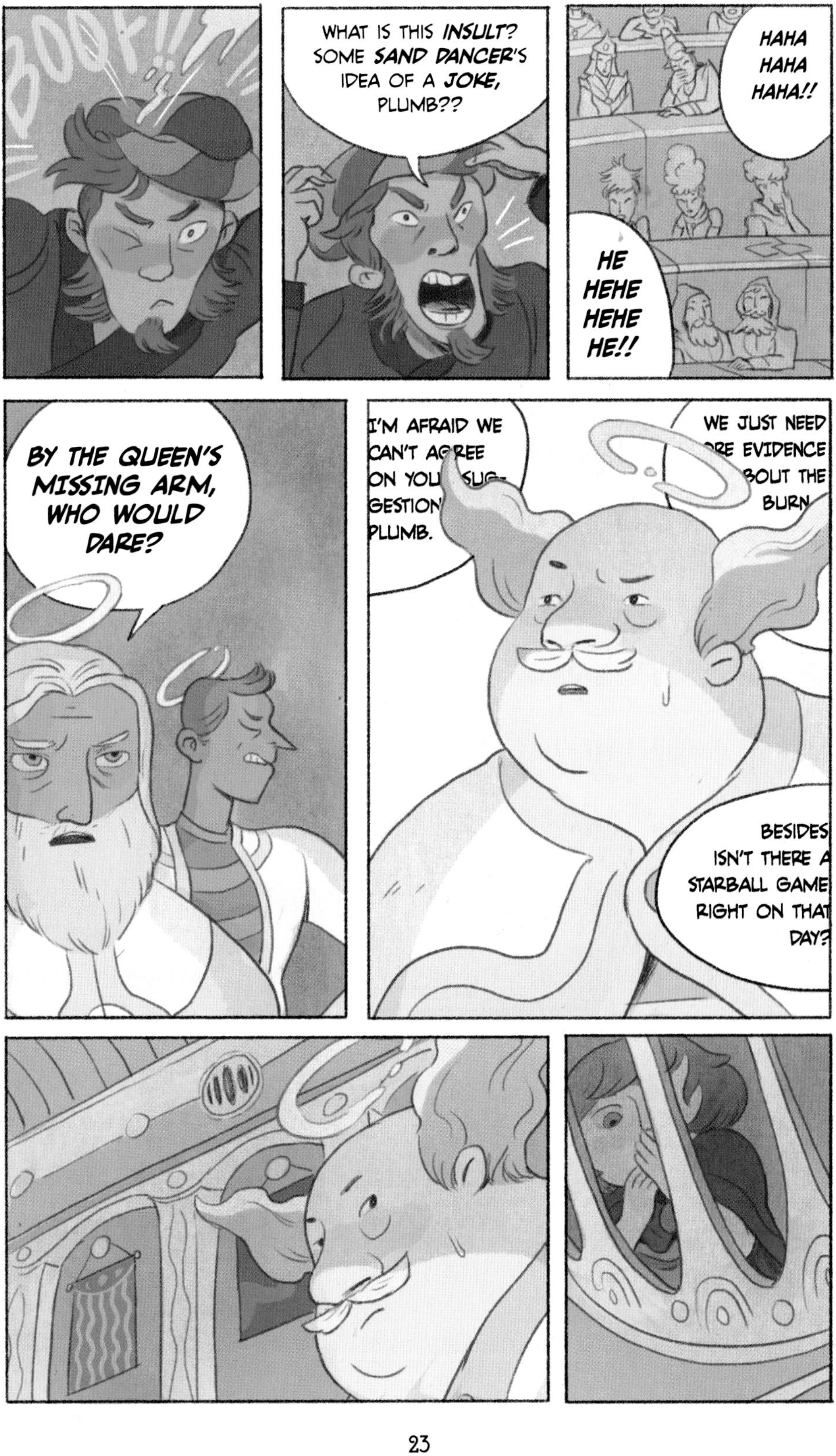
BOOF!!!
WHAT IS THIS INSULT? SOME SAND DANCER'S IDEA OF A JOKE, PLUMB??
HAHA HAHA HAHA!!
HE HEHE HEHE HE!!
BY THE QUEEN'S MISSING ARM, WHO WOULD DARE?
I'M AFRAID WE CAN'T AGREE ON YOU SUG- GESTION PLUMB.
WE JUST NEED ORE EVIDENCE BOUT THE BURN
BESIDES ISN'T THERE A STARBALL GAME RIGHT ON THAT DAY?

Chapter 2

THE BOY IN THE MASK

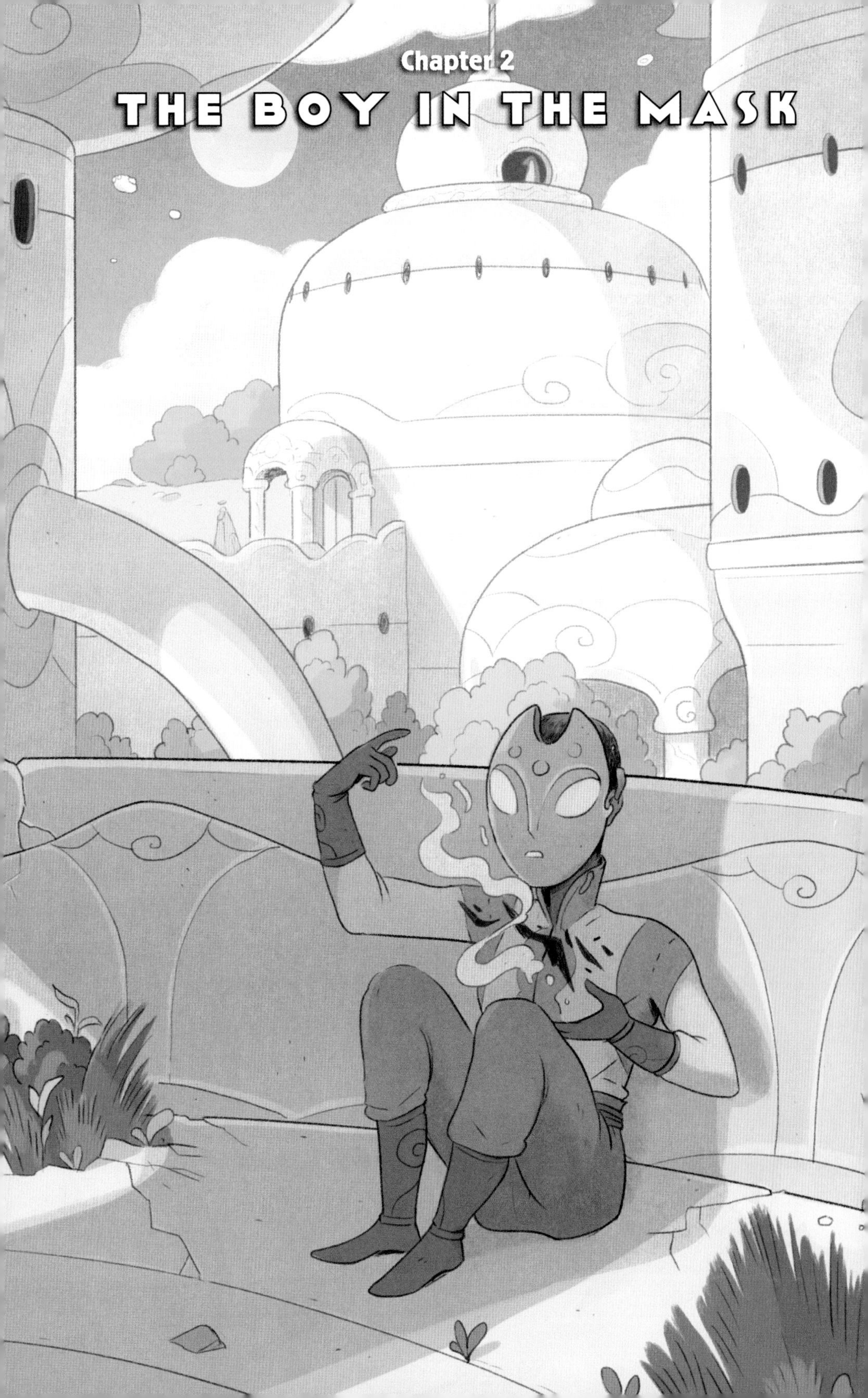

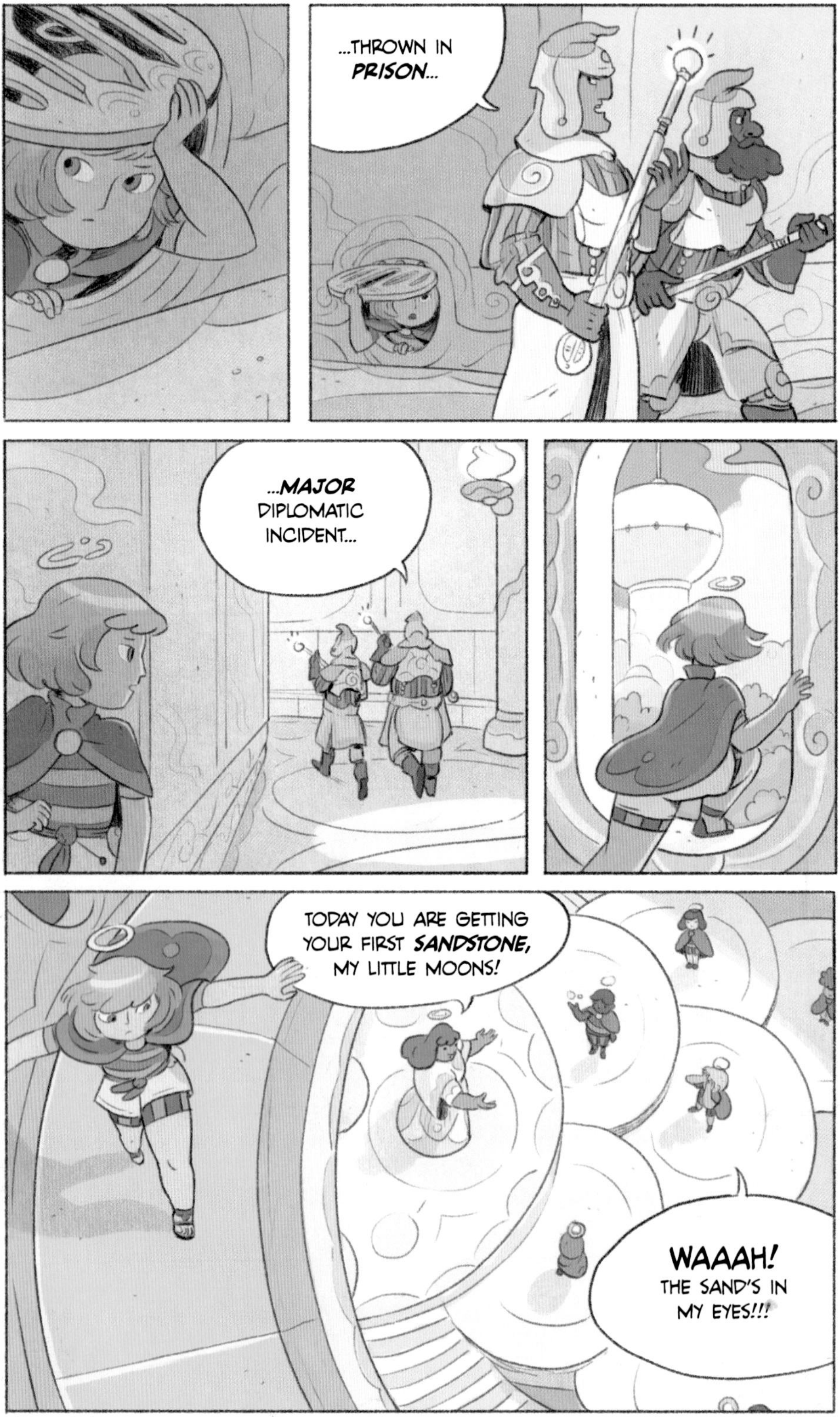
...THROWN IN PRISON...
...MAJOR DIPLOMATIC INCIDENT...
TODAY YOU ARE GETTING YOUR FIRST SANDSTONE, MY LITTLE MOONS!
WAAAH! THE SAND'S IN MY EYES!!!

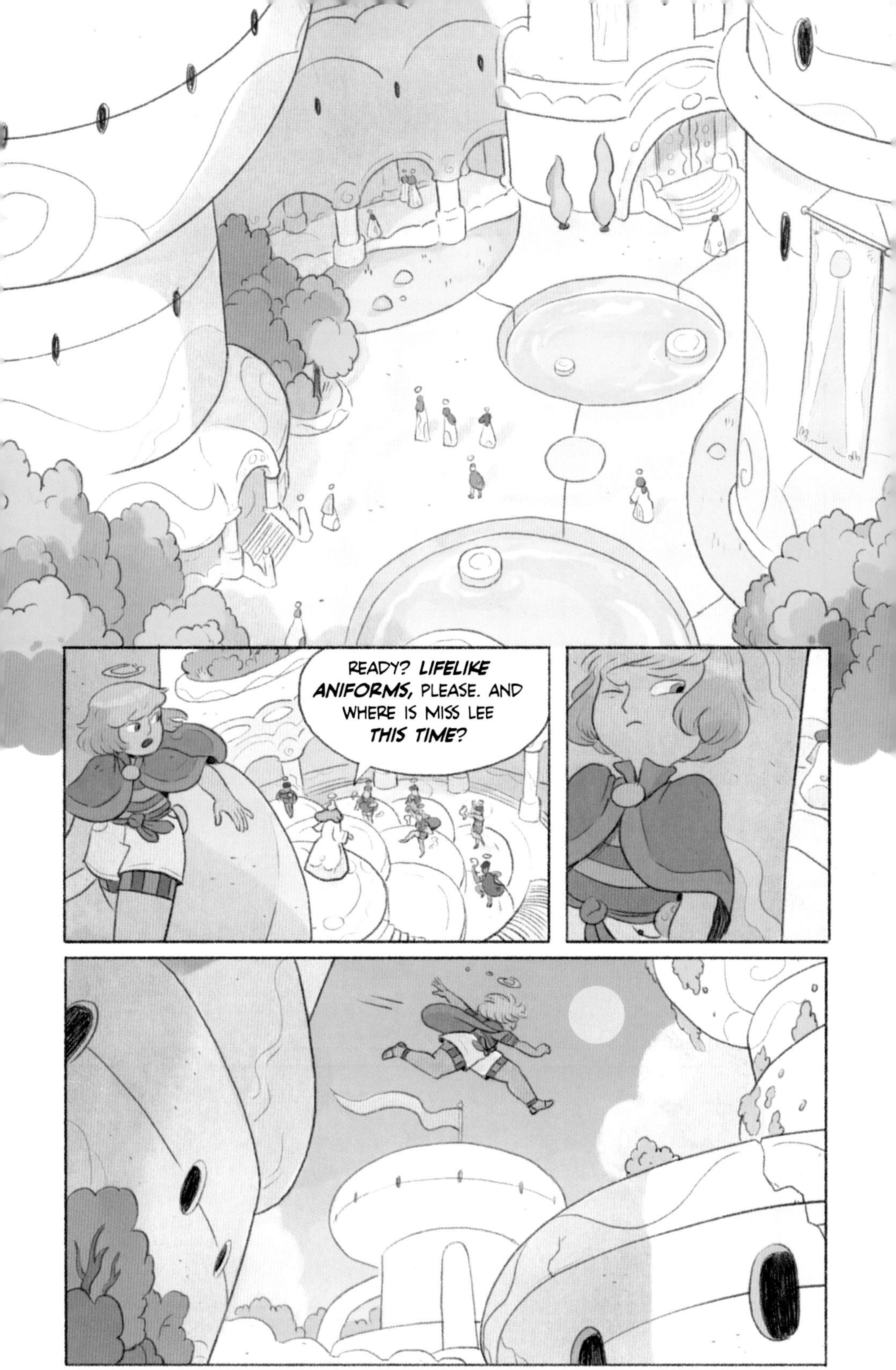
READY? LIFELIKE ANIFORMS, PLEASE. AND WHERE IS MISS LEE THIS TIME?

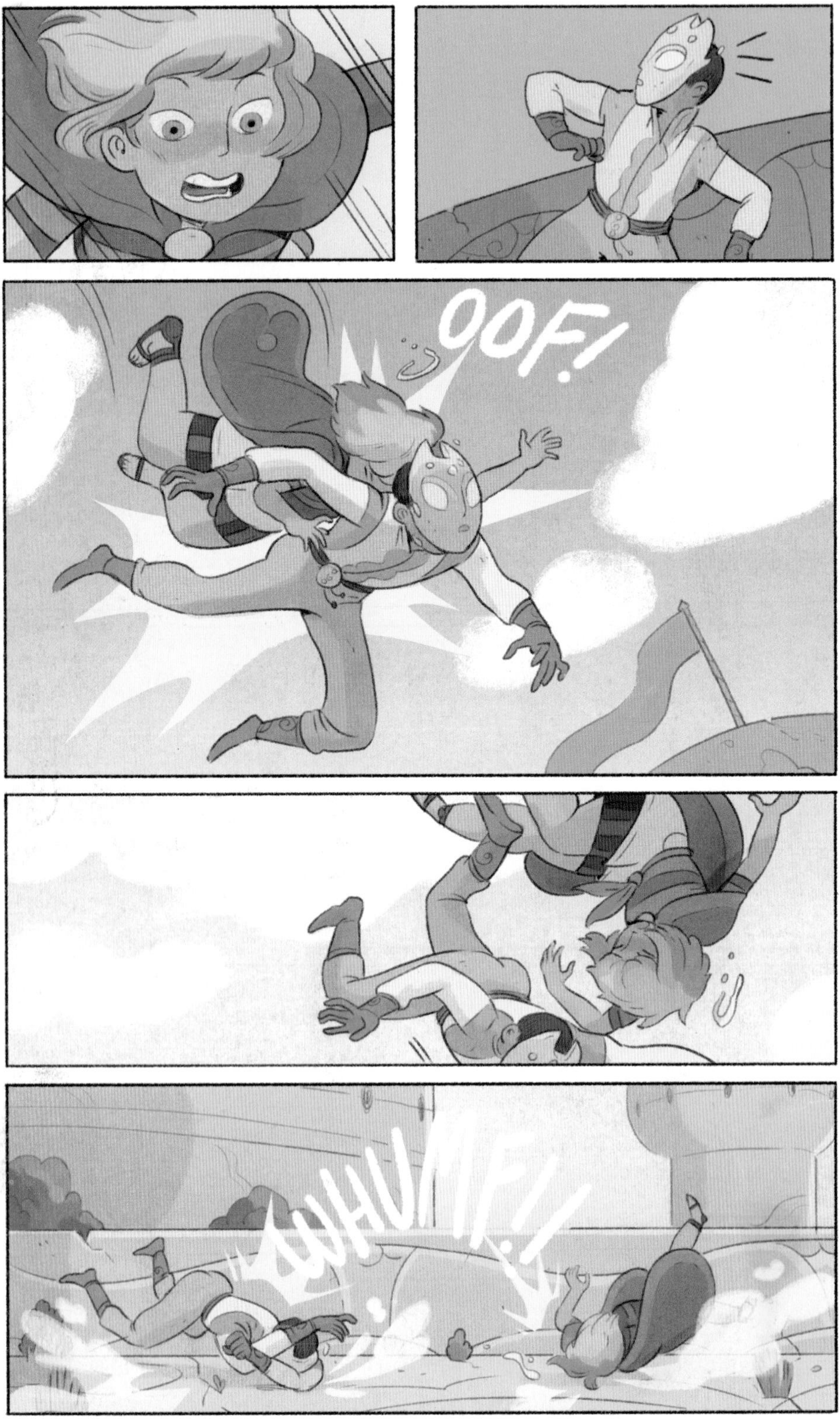
OOF!
WHUMF!!

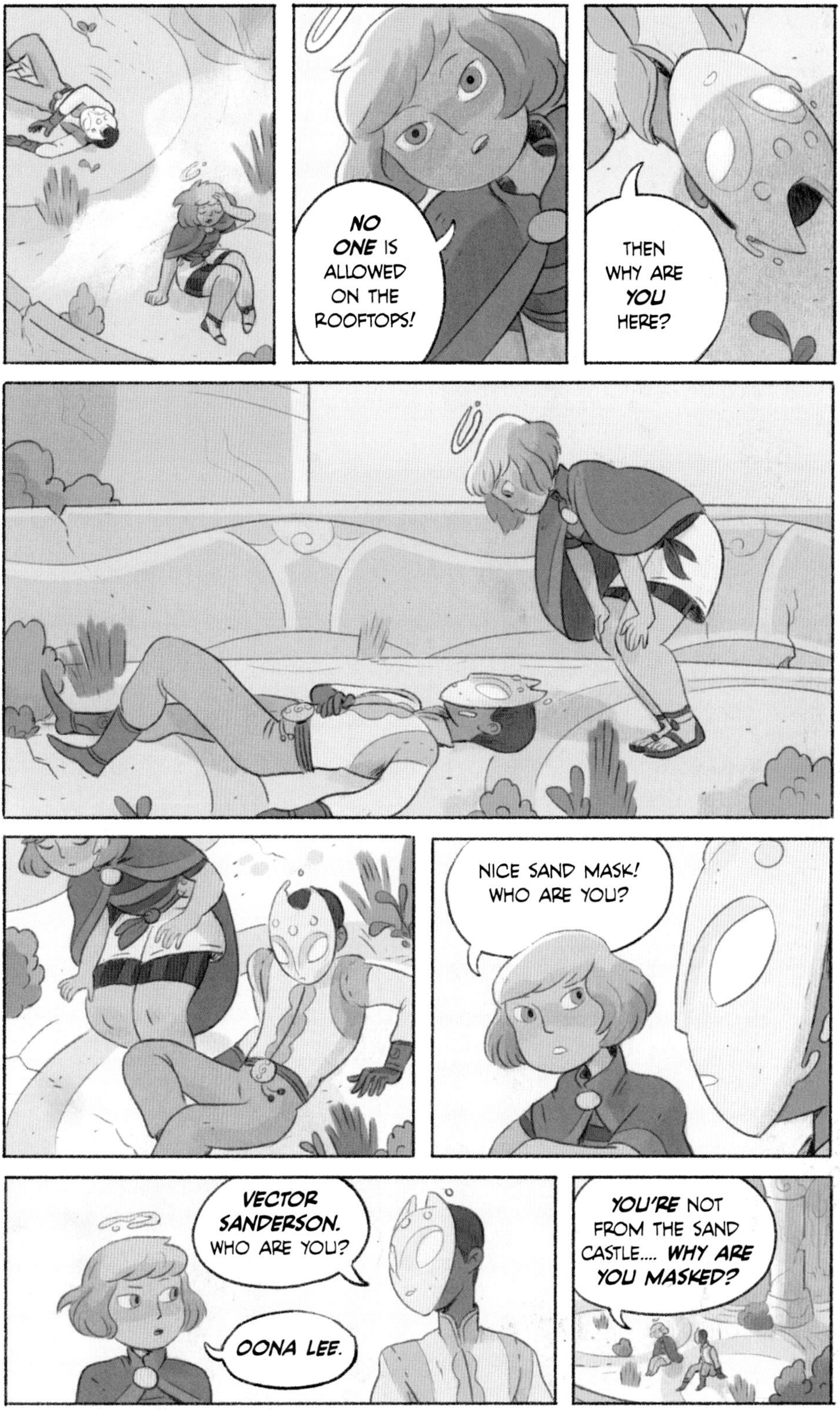
NO ONE IS ALLOWED ON THE ROOFTOPS!
THEN WHY ARE YOU HERE?
NICE SAND MASK! WHO ARE YOU?
VECTOR SANDERSON. WHO ARE YOU?
OONA LEE.
YOU'RE NOT FROM THE SAND CASTLE.... WHY ARE YOU MASKED?

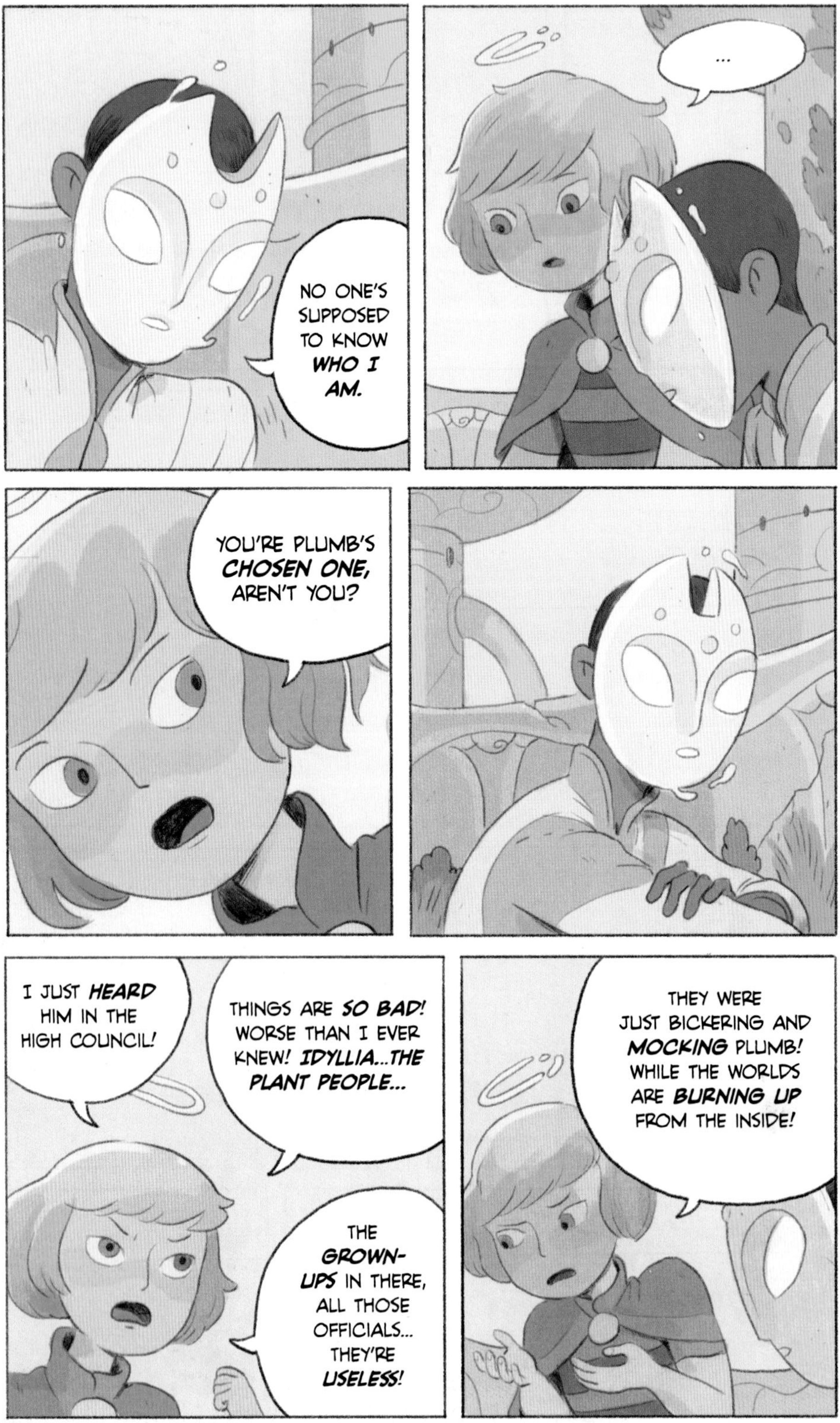
NO ONE'S SUPPOSED TO KNOW ***WHO I AM.***
...
YOU'RE PLUMB'S ***CHOSEN ONE,*** AREN'T YOU?
I JUST ***HEARD*** HIM IN THE HIGH COUNCIL!
THINGS ARE ***SO BAD!*** WORSE THAN I EVER KNEW! ***IDYLLIA...THE PLANT PEOPLE...***
THE ***GROWN-UPS*** IN THERE, ALL THOSE OFFICIALS... THEY'RE ***USELESS!***
THEY WERE JUST BICKERING AND ***MOCKING*** PLUMB! WHILE THE WORLDS ARE ***BURNING UP*** FROM THE INSIDE!

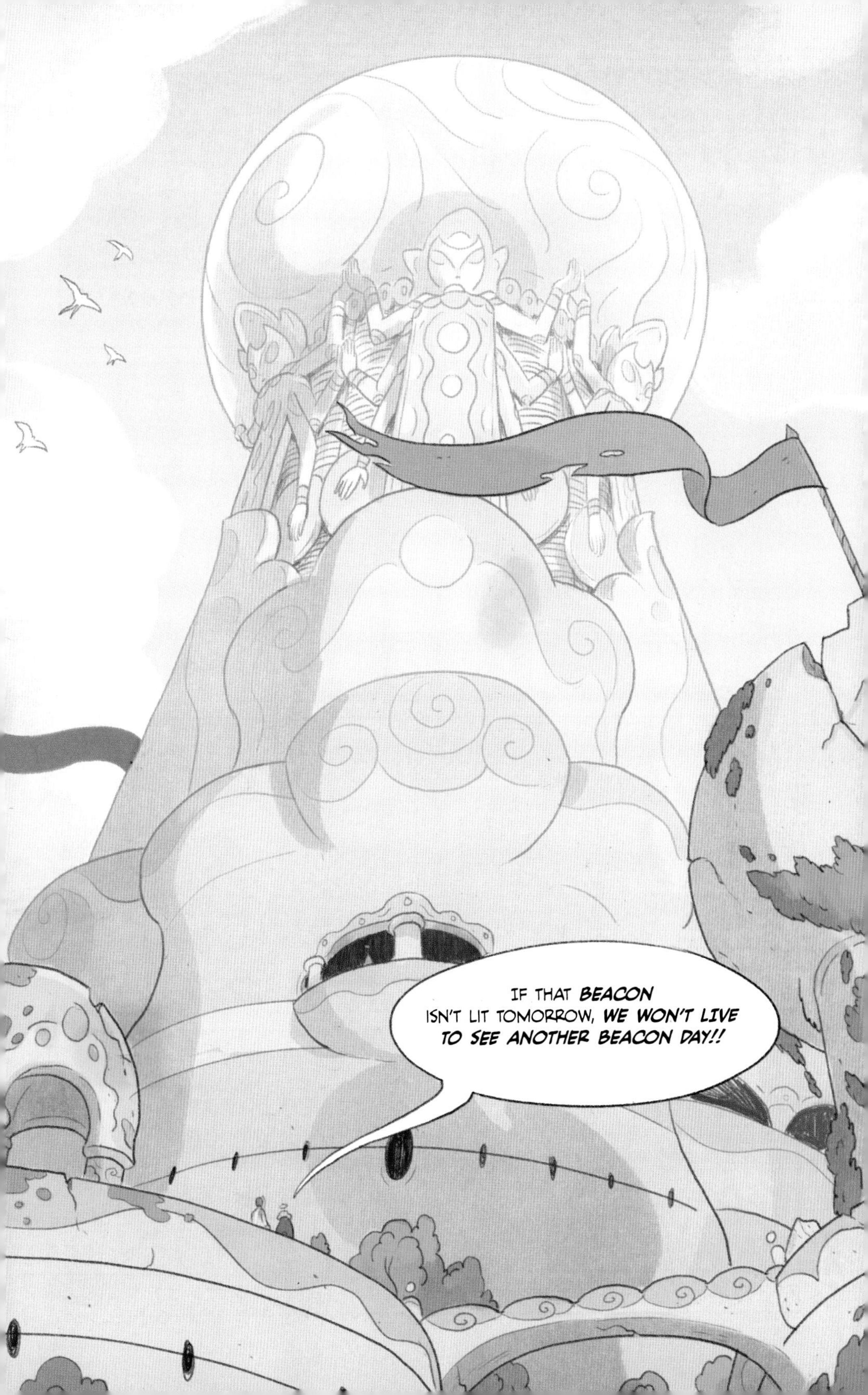
IF THAT **BEACON** ISN'T LIT TOMORROW, ***WE WON'T LIVE TO SEE ANOTHER BEACON DAY!!***

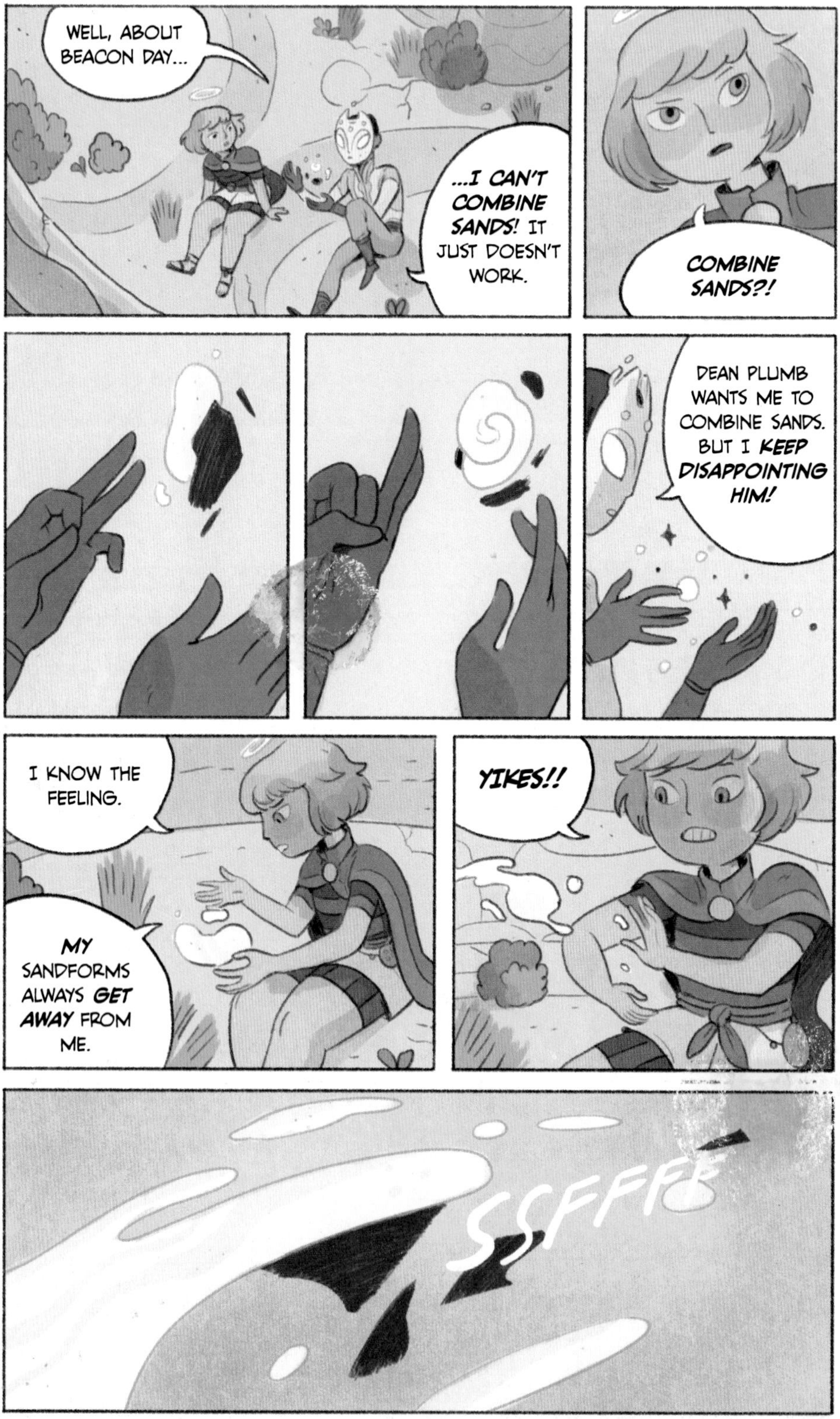
WELL, ABOUT BEACON DAY...
...I CAN'T COMBINE SANDS! IT JUST DOESN'T WORK.
COMBINE SANDS?!
DEAN PLUMB WANTS ME TO COMBINE SANDS. BUT I KEEP DISAPPOINTING HIM!
I KNOW THE FEELING.
MY SANDFORMS ALWAYS GET AWAY FROM ME.
YIKES!!
SSFFFF

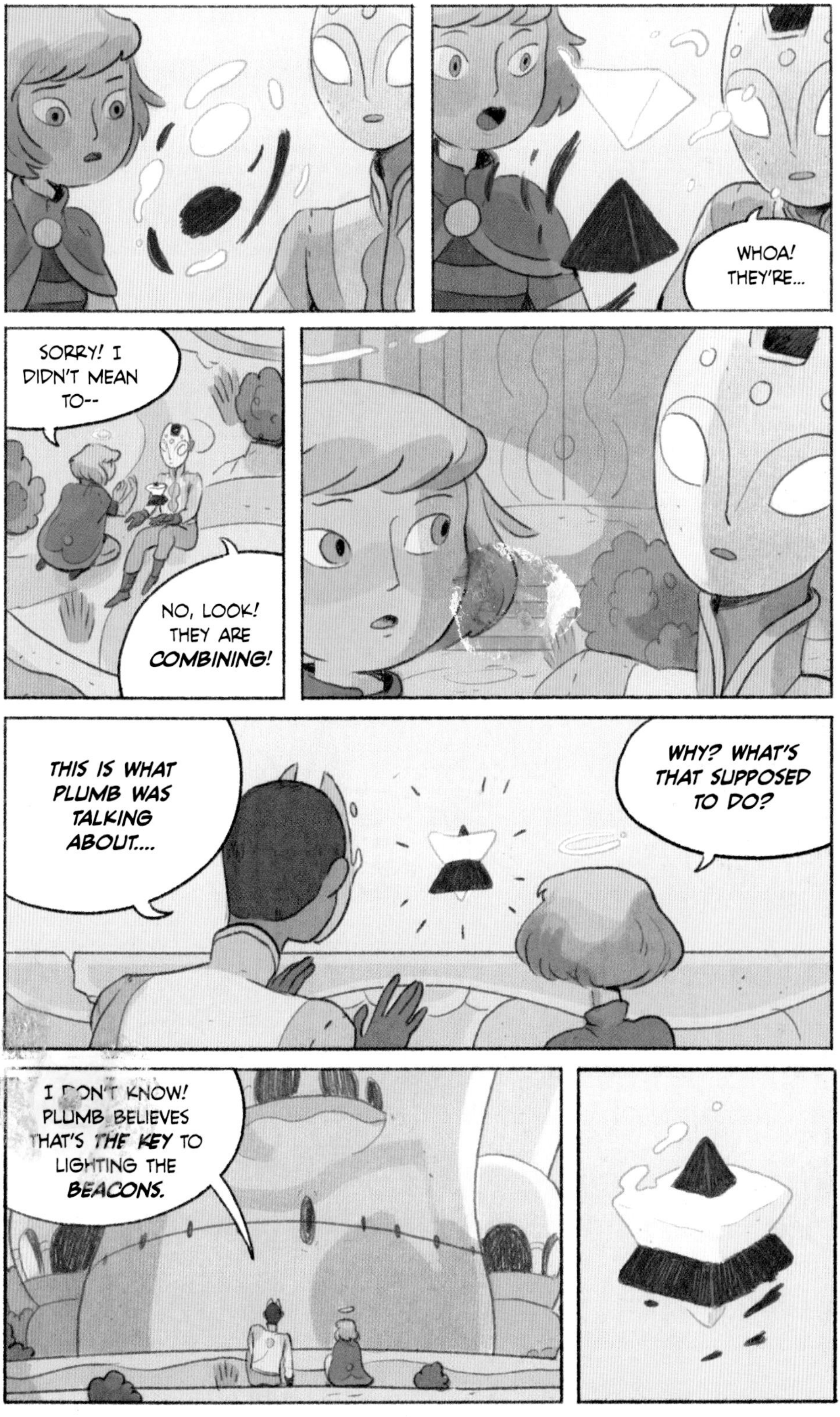
WHOA! THEY'RE...
SORRY! I DIDN'T MEAN TO--
NO, LOOK! THEY ARE COMBINING!
THIS IS WHAT PLUMB WAS TALKING ABOUT....
WHY? WHAT'S THAT SUPPOSED TO DO?
I DON'T KNOW! PLUMB BELIEVES THAT'S THE KEY TO LIGHTING THE BEACONS.

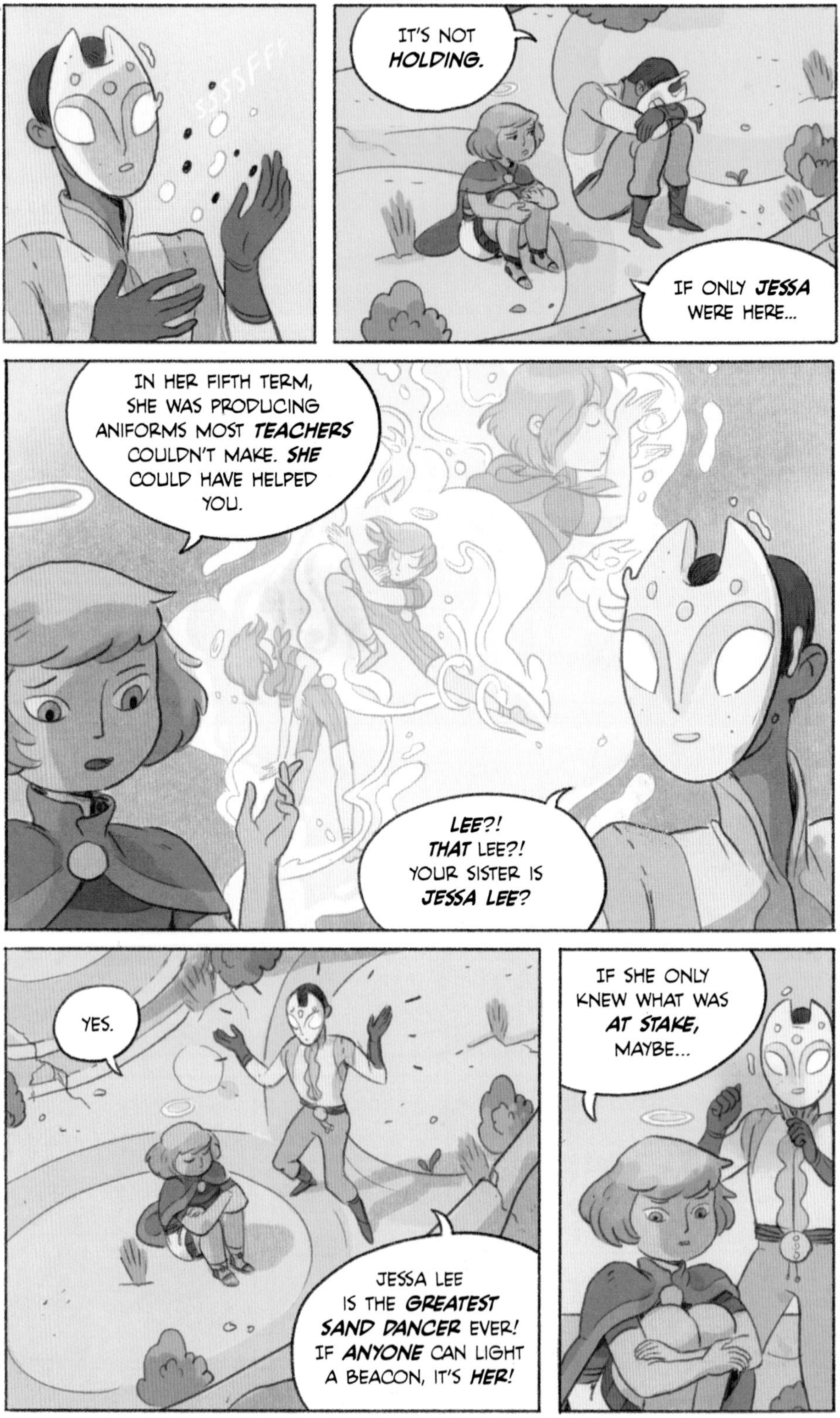
IT'S NOT HOLDING.
IF ONLY JESSA WERE HERE...
IN HER FIFTH TERM, SHE WAS PRODUCING ANIFORMS MOST TEACHERS COULDN'T MAKE. SHE COULD HAVE HELPED YOU.
LEE?! THAT LEE?! YOUR SISTER IS JESSA LEE?
YES.
JESSA LEE IS THE GREATEST SAND DANCER EVER! IF ANYONE CAN LIGHT A BEACON, IT'S HER!
IF SHE ONLY KNEW WHAT WAS AT STAKE, MAYBE...

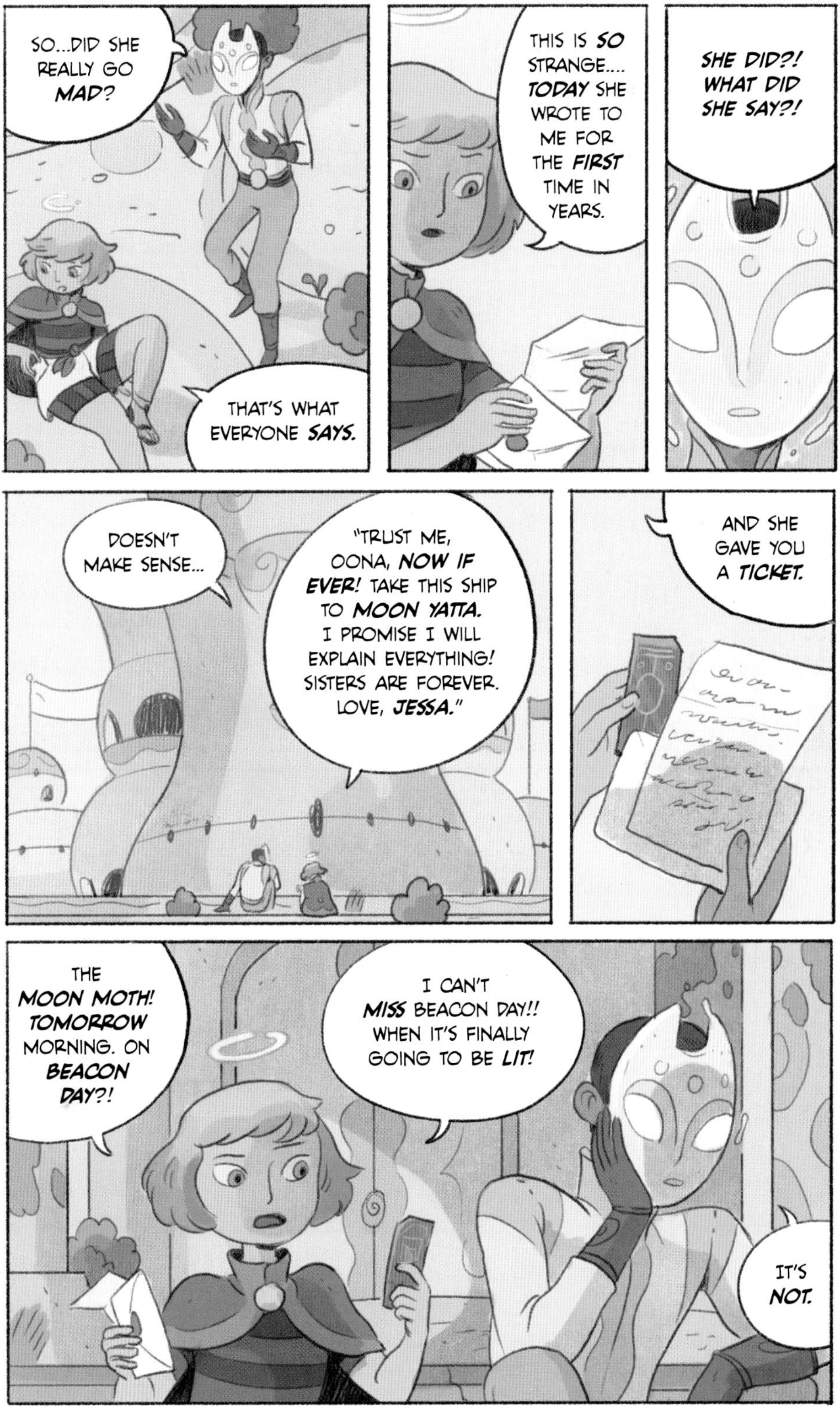
SO...DID SHE REALLY GO MAD?
THAT'S WHAT EVERYONE SAYS.
THIS IS SO STRANGE.... TODAY SHE WROTE TO ME FOR THE FIRST TIME IN YEARS.
SHE DID?! WHAT DID SHE SAY?!
DOESN'T MAKE SENSE...
"TRUST ME, OONA, NOW IF EVER! TAKE THIS SHIP TO MOON YATTA. I PROMISE I WILL EXPLAIN EVERYTHING! SISTERS ARE FOREVER. LOVE, JESSA."
AND SHE GAVE YOU A TICKET.
THE MOON MOTH! TOMORROW MORNING. ON BEACON DAY?!
I CAN'T MISS BEACON DAY!! WHEN IT'S FINALLY GOING TO BE LIT!
IT'S NOT.

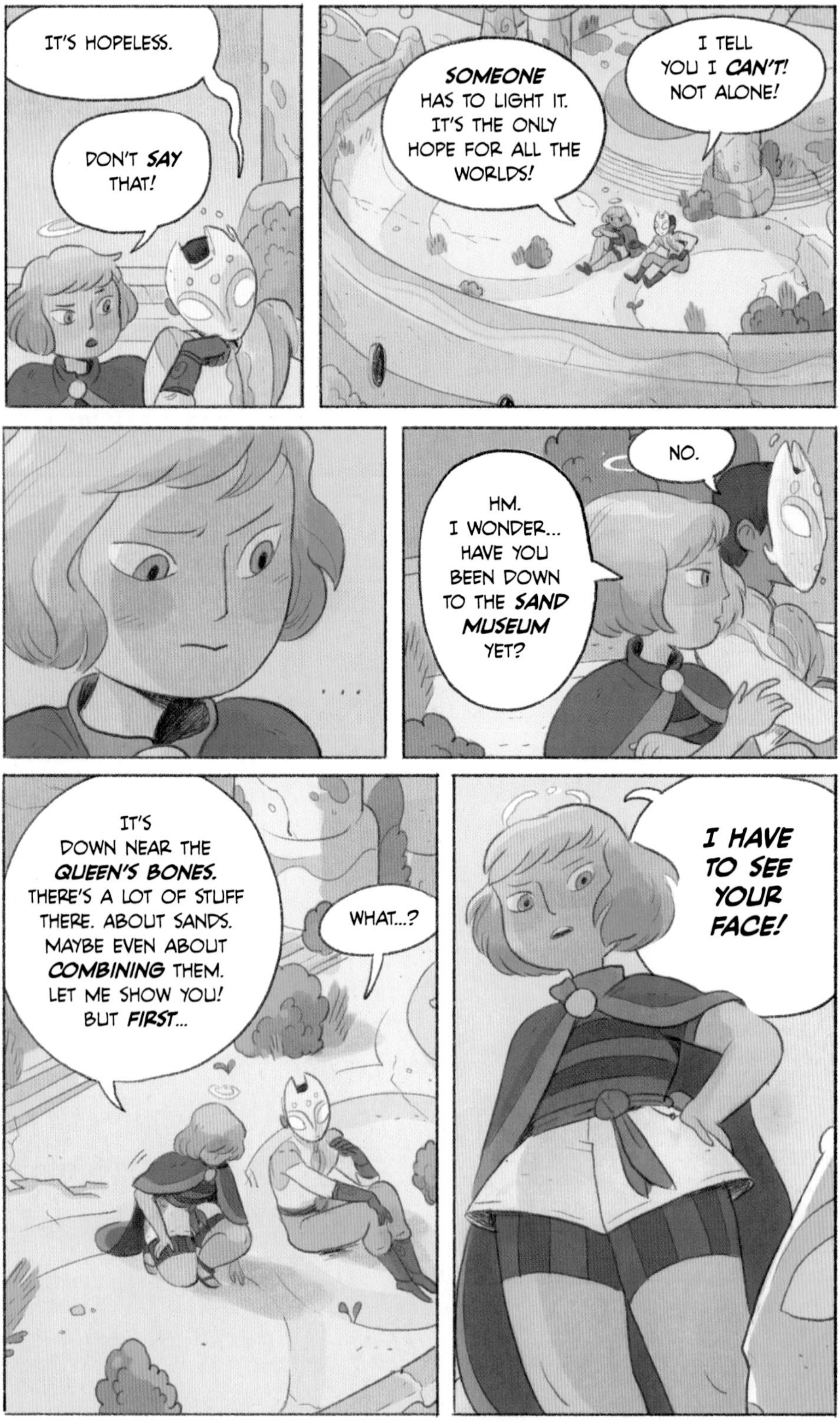
IT'S HOPELESS.
DON'T SAY THAT!
SOMEONE HAS TO LIGHT IT. IT'S THE ONLY HOPE FOR ALL THE WORLDS!
I TELL YOU I CAN'T! NOT ALONE!
...
HM. I WONDER... HAVE YOU BEEN DOWN TO THE SAND MUSEUM YET?
NO.
IT'S DOWN NEAR THE QUEEN'S BONES. THERE'S A LOT OF STUFF THERE. ABOUT SANDS. MAYBE EVEN ABOUT COMBINING THEM. LET ME SHOW YOU! BUT FIRST...
WHAT...?
I HAVE TO SEE YOUR FACE!

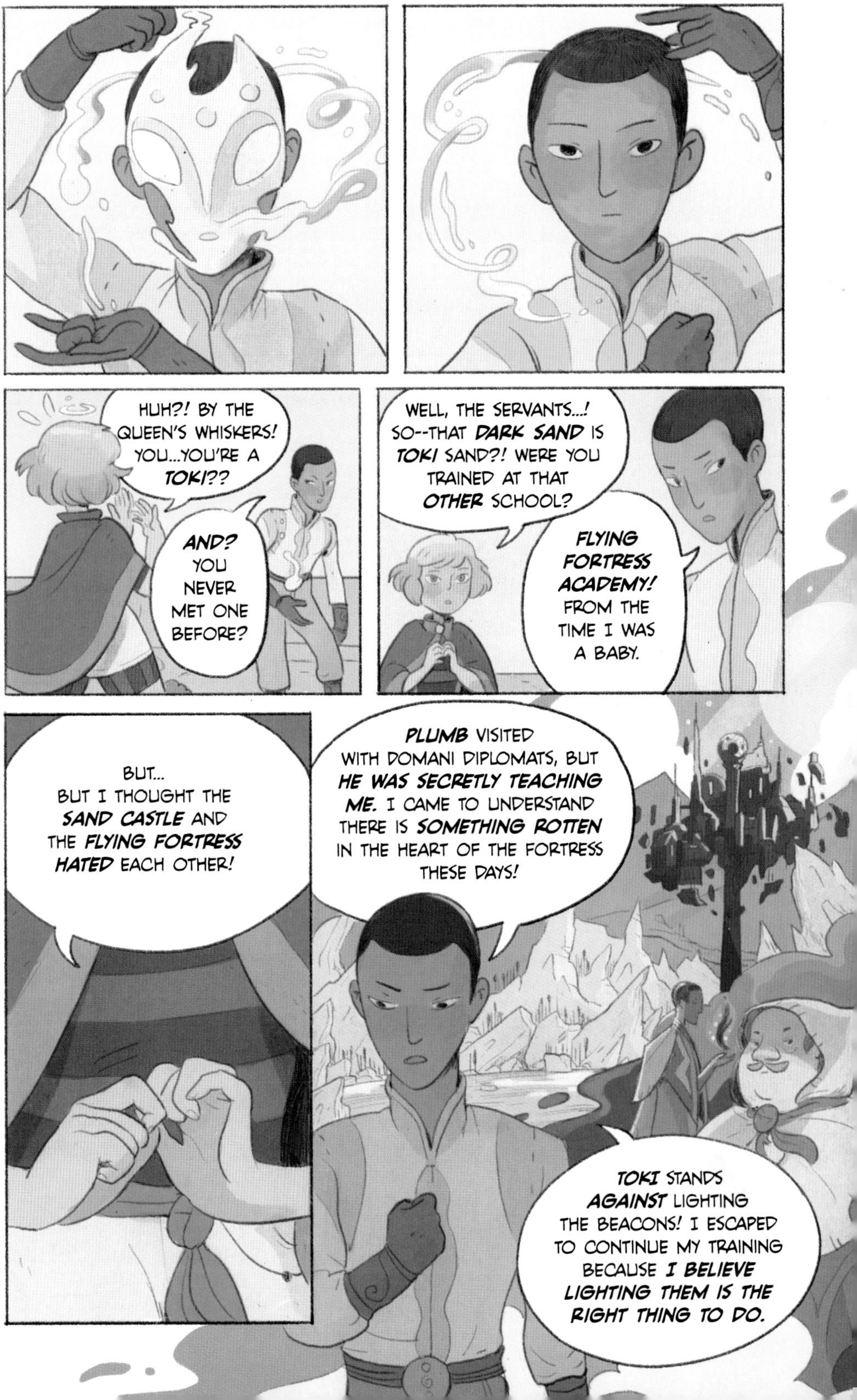
HUH?! BY THE QUEEN'S WHISKERS! YOU...YOU'RE A TOKI??
AND? YOU NEVER MET ONE BEFORE?
WELL, THE SERVANTS...! SO--THAT DARK SAND IS TOKI SAND?! WERE YOU TRAINED AT THAT OTHER SCHOOL?
FLYING FORTRESS ACADEMY! FROM THE TIME I WAS A BABY.
BUT... BUT I THOUGHT THE SAND CASTLE AND THE FLYING FORTRESS HATED EACH OTHER!
PLUMB VISITED WITH DOMANI DIPLOMATS, BUT HE WAS SECRETLY TEACHING ME. I CAME TO UNDERSTAND THERE IS SOMETHING ROTTEN IN THE HEART OF THE FORTRESS THESE DAYS!
TOKI STANDS AGAINST LIGHTING THE BEACONS! I ESCAPED TO CONTINUE MY TRAINING BECAUSE I BELIEVE LIGHTING THEM IS THE RIGHT THING TO DO.

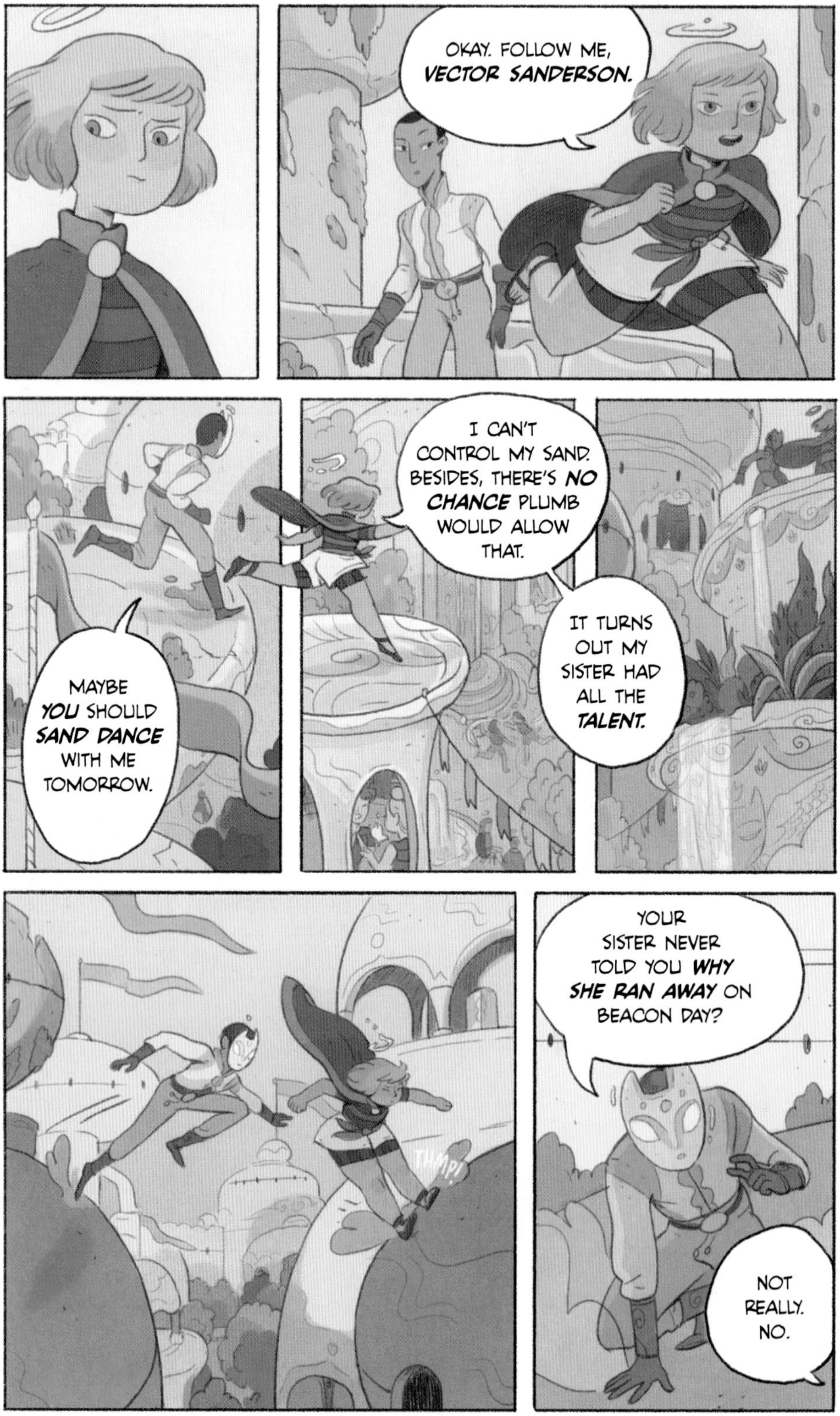
OKAY. FOLLOW ME, VECTOR SANDERSON.
MAYBE YOU SHOULD SAND DANCE WITH ME TOMORROW.
I CAN'T CONTROL MY SAND. BESIDES, THERE'S NO CHANCE PLUMB WOULD ALLOW THAT.
IT TURNS OUT MY SISTER HAD ALL THE TALENT.
THMP!
YOUR SISTER NEVER TOLD YOU WHY SHE RAN AWAY ON BEACON DAY?
NOT REALLY. NO.

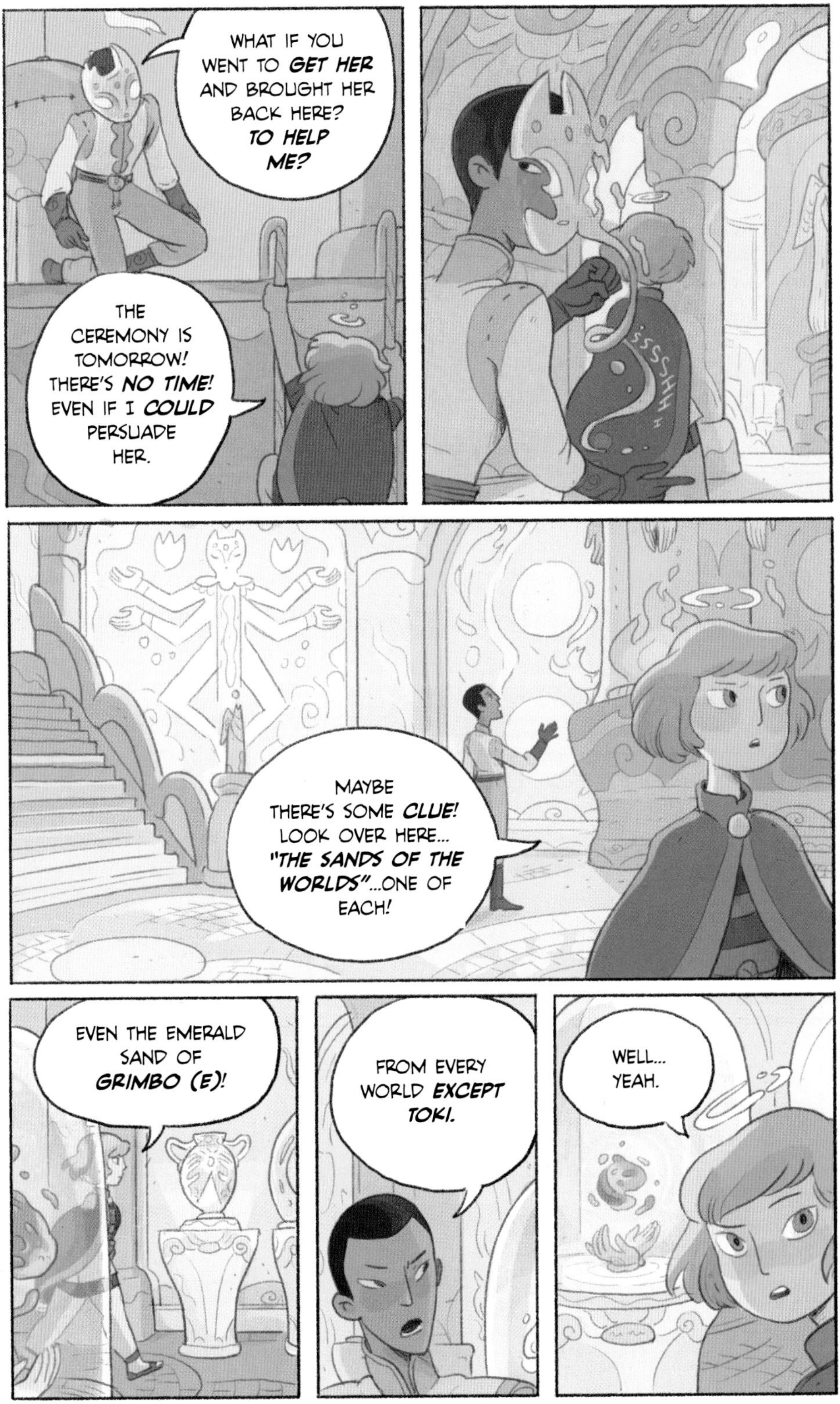
WHAT IF YOU WENT TO GET HER AND BROUGHT HER BACK HERE? TO HELP ME?
THE CEREMONY IS TOMORROW! THERE'S NO TIME! EVEN IF I COULD PERSUADE HER.
HSSSSS
MAYBE THERE'S SOME CLUE! LOOK OVER HERE... "THE SANDS OF THE WORLDS"...ONE OF EACH!
EVEN THE EMERALD SAND OF GRIMBO (E)!
FROM EVERY WORLD EXCEPT TOKI.
WELL... YEAH.

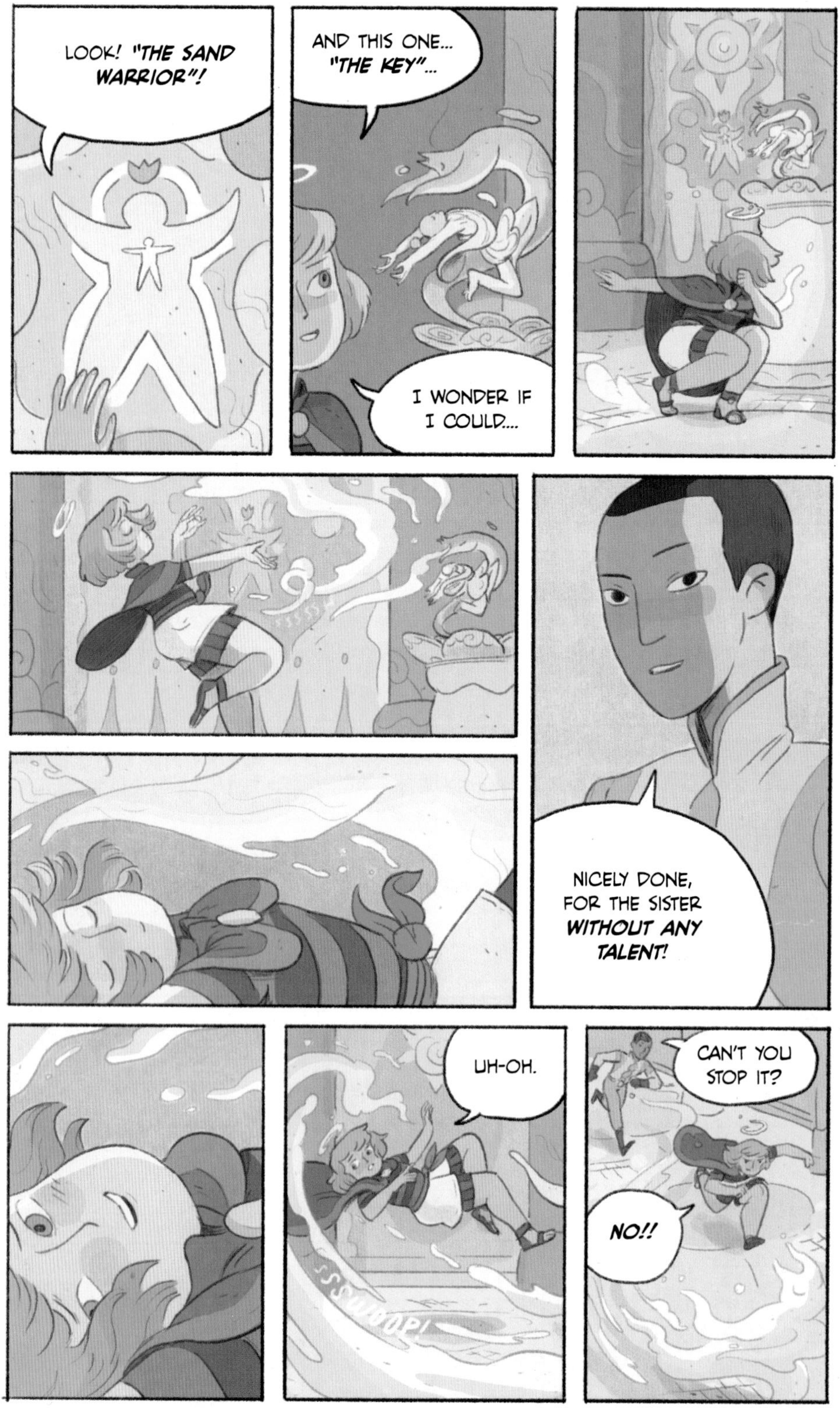

LOOK! "**THE SAND WARRIOR**"!
AND THIS ONE... "**THE KEY**"...
I WONDER IF I COULD...
NICELY DONE, FOR THE SISTER **WITHOUT ANY TALENT!**
UH-OH.
SSSWOOOP!
CAN'T YOU STOP IT?
NO!!

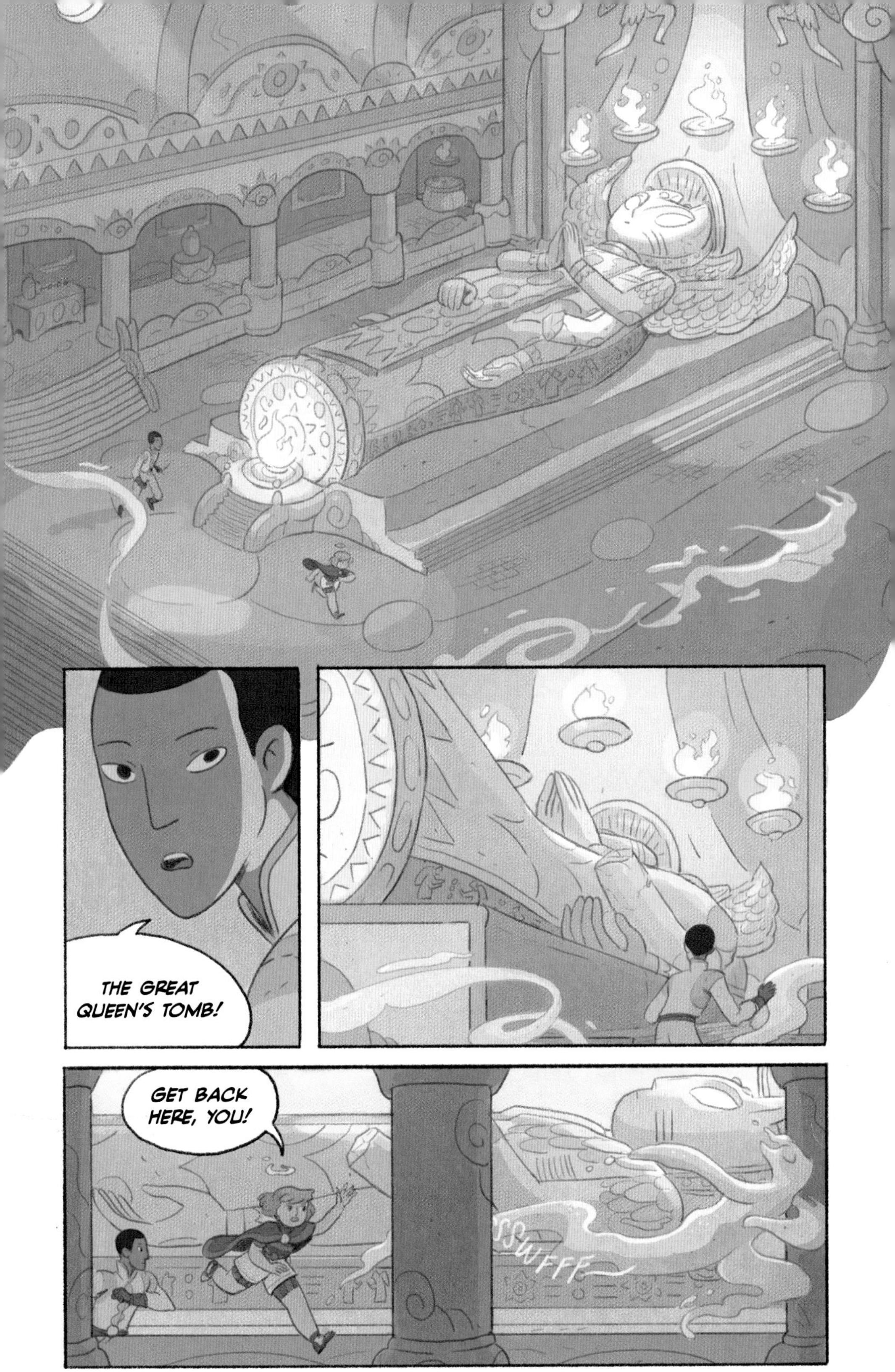
THE GREAT QUEEN'S TOMB!
GET BACK HERE, YOU!
SSWFFF

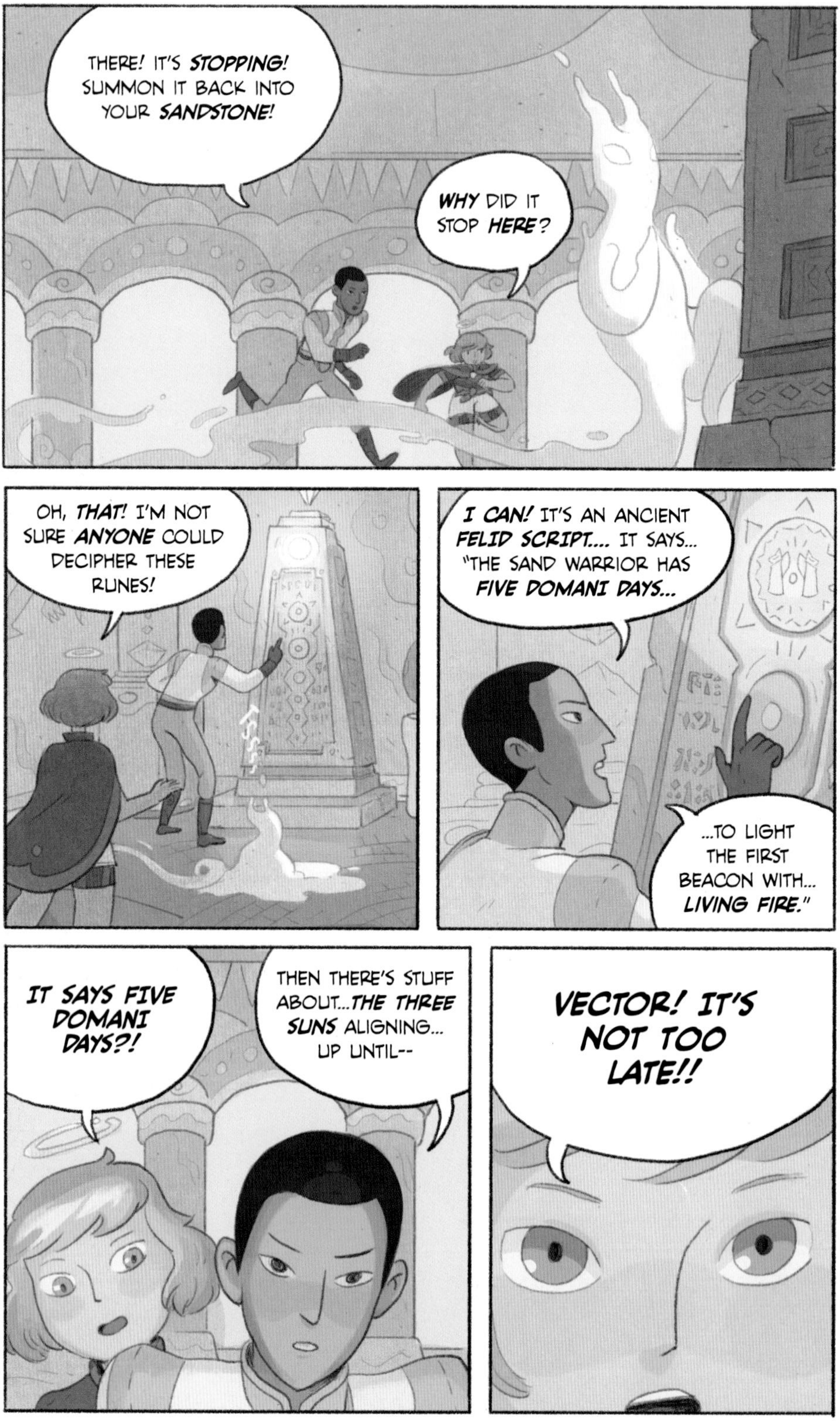
THERE! IT'S STOPPING! SUMMON IT BACK INTO YOUR SANDSTONE!
WHY DID IT STOP HERE?
OH, THAT! I'M NOT SURE ANYONE COULD DECIPHER THESE RUNES!
I CAN! IT'S AN ANCIENT FELID SCRIPT.... IT SAYS... "THE SAND WARRIOR HAS FIVE DOMANI DAYS...
...TO LIGHT THE FIRST BEACON WITH... LIVING FIRE."
IT SAYS FIVE DOMANI DAYS?!
THEN THERE'S STUFF ABOUT...THE THREE SUNS ALIGNING... UP UNTIL--
VECTOR! IT'S NOT TOO LATE!!

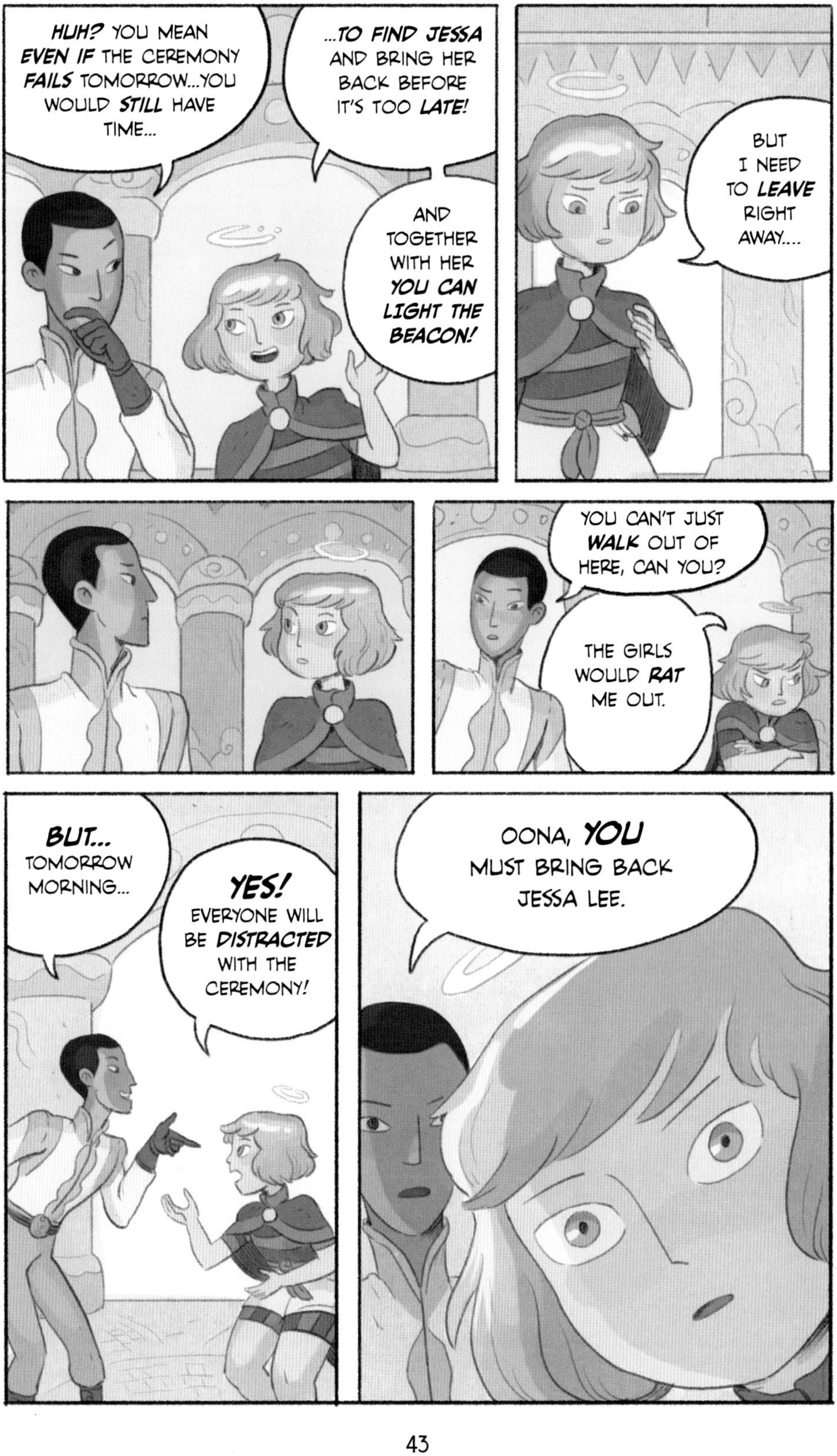
HUH? YOU MEAN EVEN IF THE CEREMONY FAILS TOMORROW...YOU WOULD STILL HAVE TIME...
...TO FIND JESSA AND BRING HER BACK BEFORE IT'S TOO LATE!
AND TOGETHER WITH HER YOU CAN LIGHT THE BEACON!
BUT I NEED TO LEAVE RIGHT AWAY....
YOU CAN'T JUST WALK OUT OF HERE, CAN YOU?
THE GIRLS WOULD RAT ME OUT.
BUT... TOMORROW MORNING...
YES! EVERYONE WILL BE DISTRACTED WITH THE CEREMONY!
OONA, YOU MUST BRING BACK JESSA LEE.

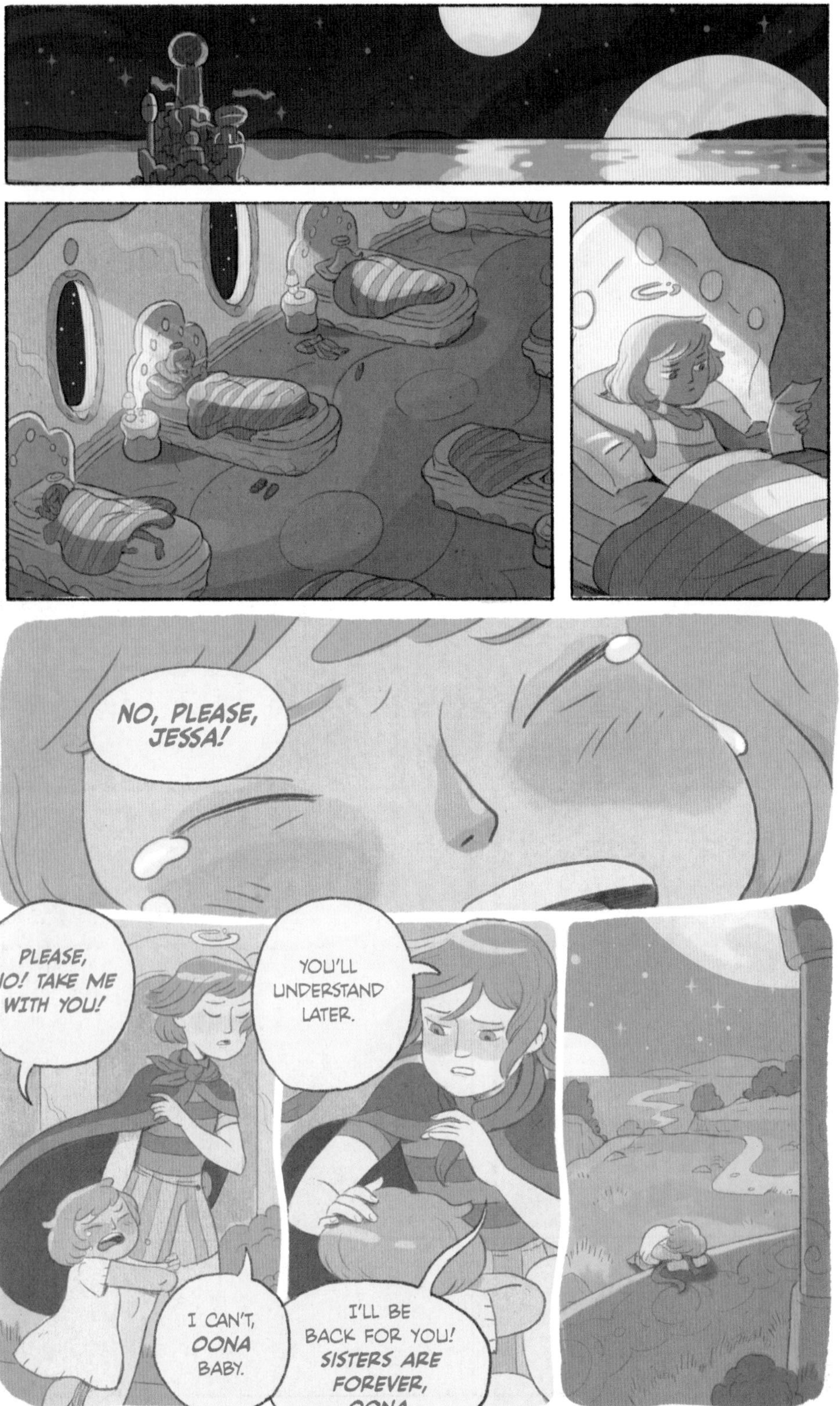
NO, PLEASE, JESSA!
PLEASE, NO! TAKE ME WITH YOU!
YOU'LL UNDERSTAND LATER.
I CAN'T, OONA BABY.
I'LL BE BACK FOR YOU! SISTERS ARE FOREVER, OONA.

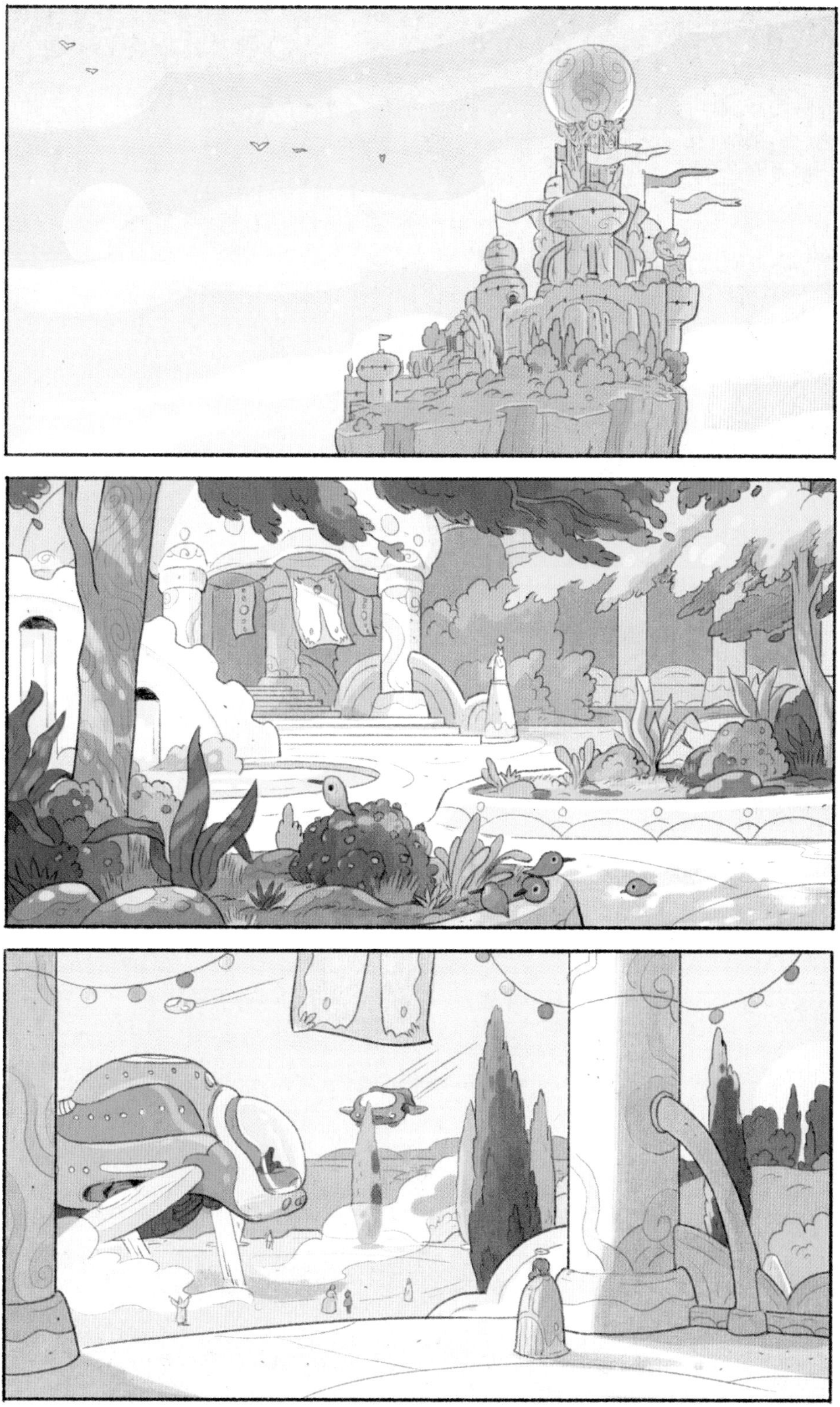

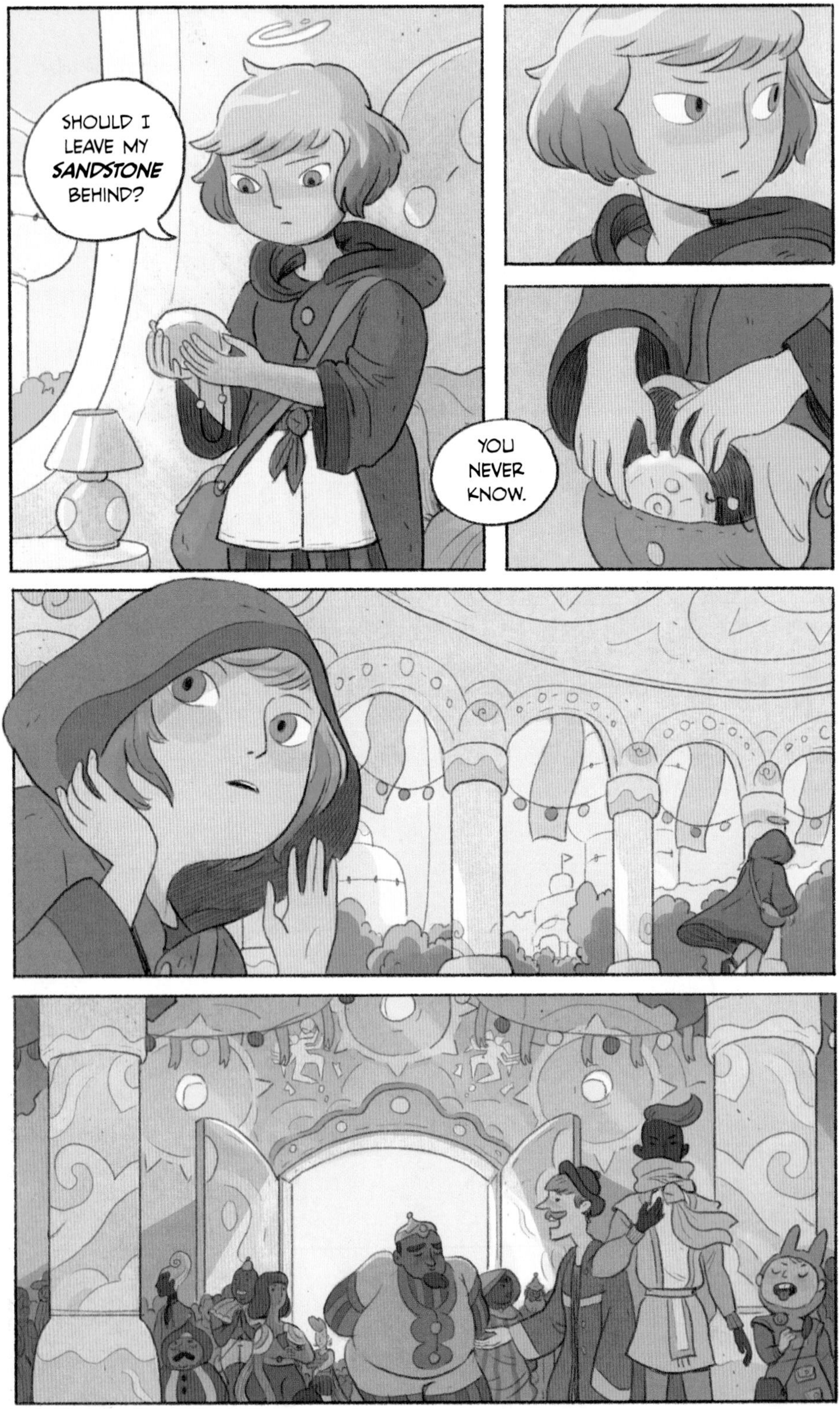
SHOULD I LEAVE MY *SANDSTONE* BEHIND?
YOU NEVER KNOW.

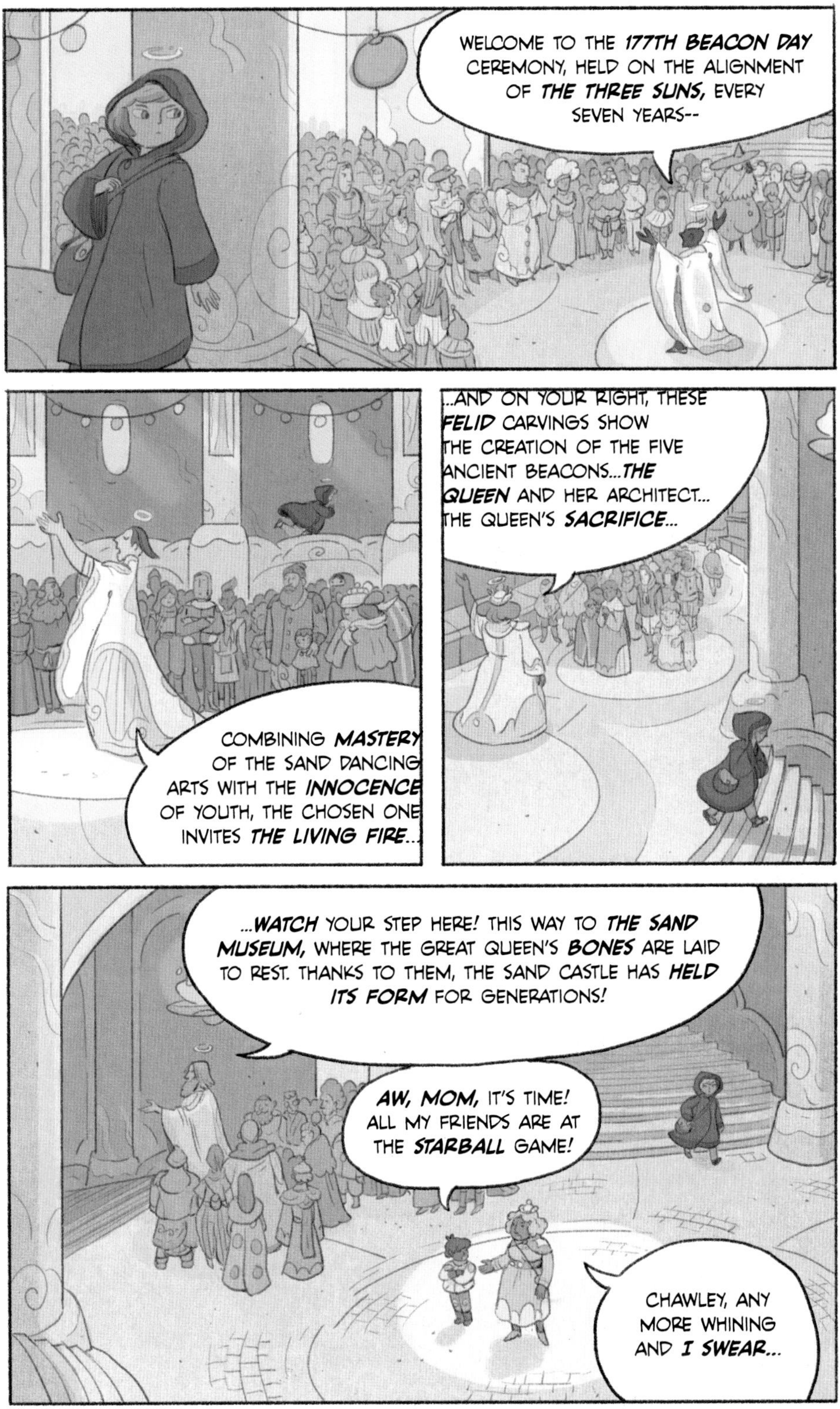
WELCOME TO THE 177TH BEACON DAY CEREMONY, HELD ON THE ALIGNMENT OF THE THREE SUNS, EVERY SEVEN YEARS--
COMBINING MASTERY OF THE SAND DANCING ARTS WITH THE INNOCENCE OF YOUTH, THE CHOSEN ONE INVITES THE LIVING FIRE...
...AND ON YOUR RIGHT, THESE FELID CARVINGS SHOW THE CREATION OF THE FIVE ANCIENT BEACONS...THE QUEEN AND HER ARCHITECT... THE QUEEN'S SACRIFICE...
...WATCH YOUR STEP HERE! THIS WAY TO THE SAND MUSEUM, WHERE THE GREAT QUEEN'S BONES ARE LAID TO REST. THANKS TO THEM, THE SAND CASTLE HAS HELD ITS FORM FOR GENERATIONS!
AW, MOM, IT'S TIME! ALL MY FRIENDS ARE AT THE STARBALL GAME!
CHAWLEY, ANY MORE WHINING AND I SWEAR...

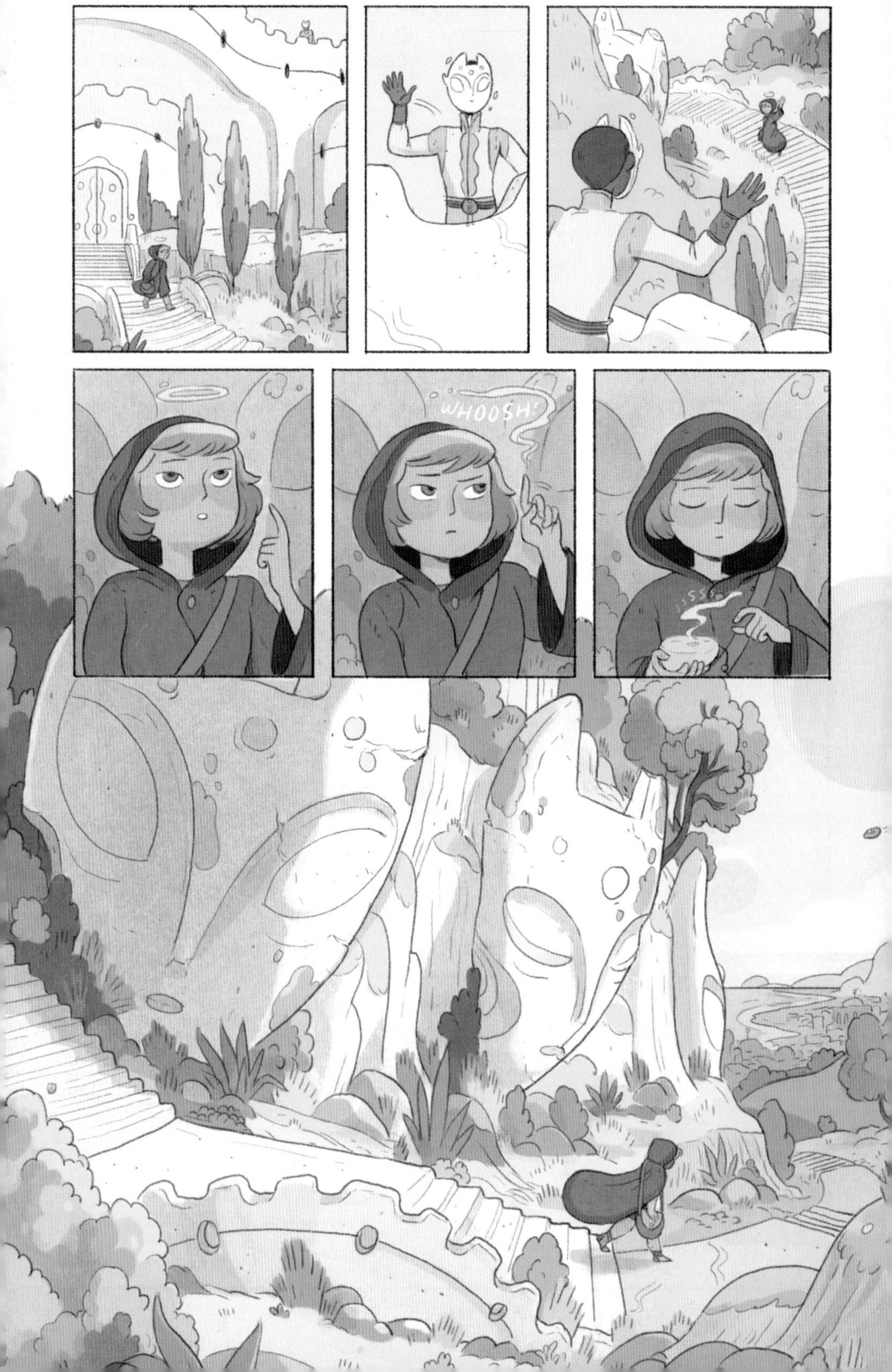
WHOOSH!
SSS

Chapter 3

COLLISION AT STARBALL STADIUM

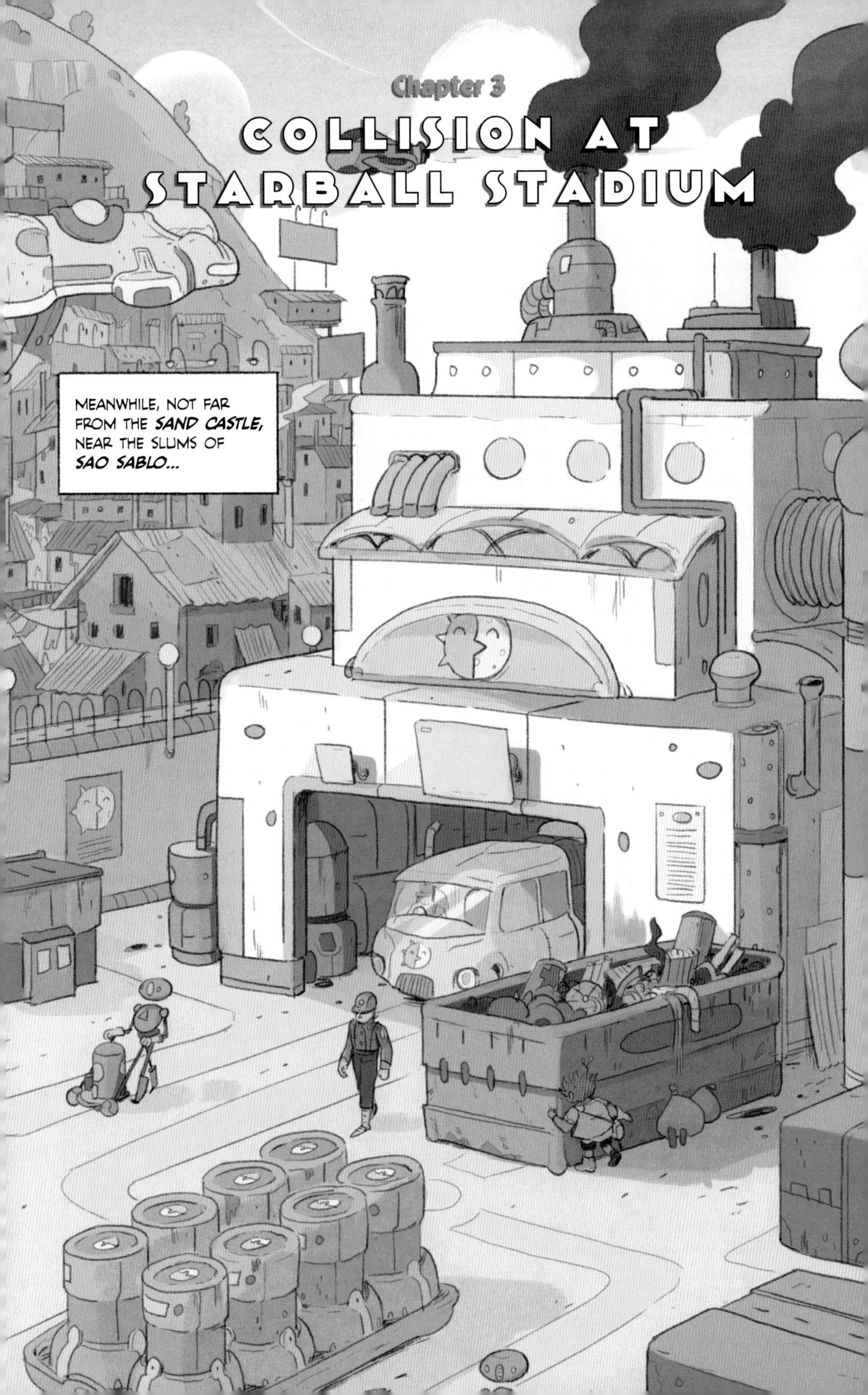
MEANWHILE, NOT FAR FROM THE *SAND CASTLE,* NEAR THE SLUMS OF *SAO SABLO...*

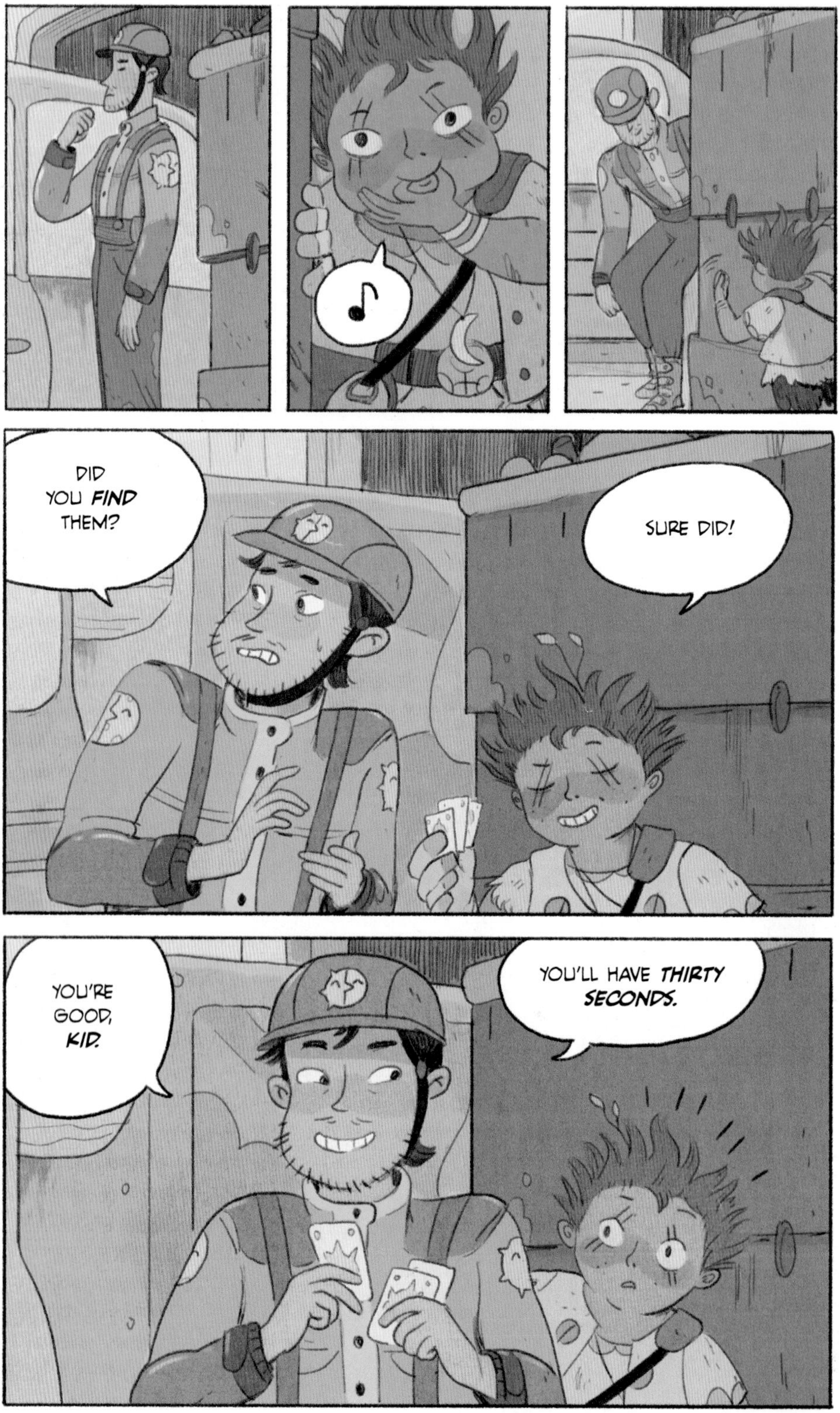
♪
DID YOU *FIND* THEM?
SURE DID!
YOU'RE GOOD, *KID.*
YOU'LL HAVE *THIRTY SECONDS.*

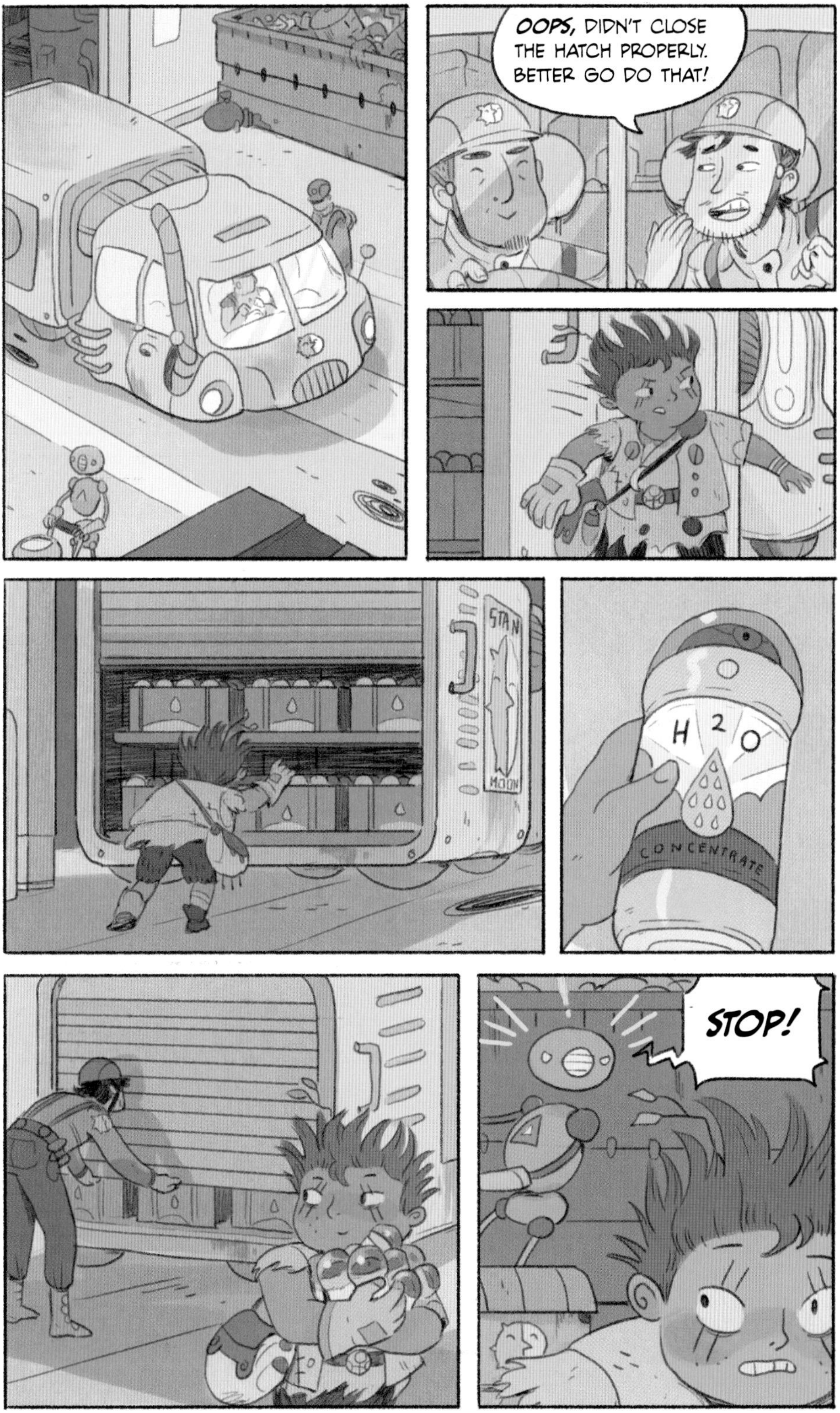
OOPS, DIDN'T CLOSE THE HATCH PROPERLY. BETTER GO DO THAT!
STAN MOON
H2O
CONCENTRATE
STOP!

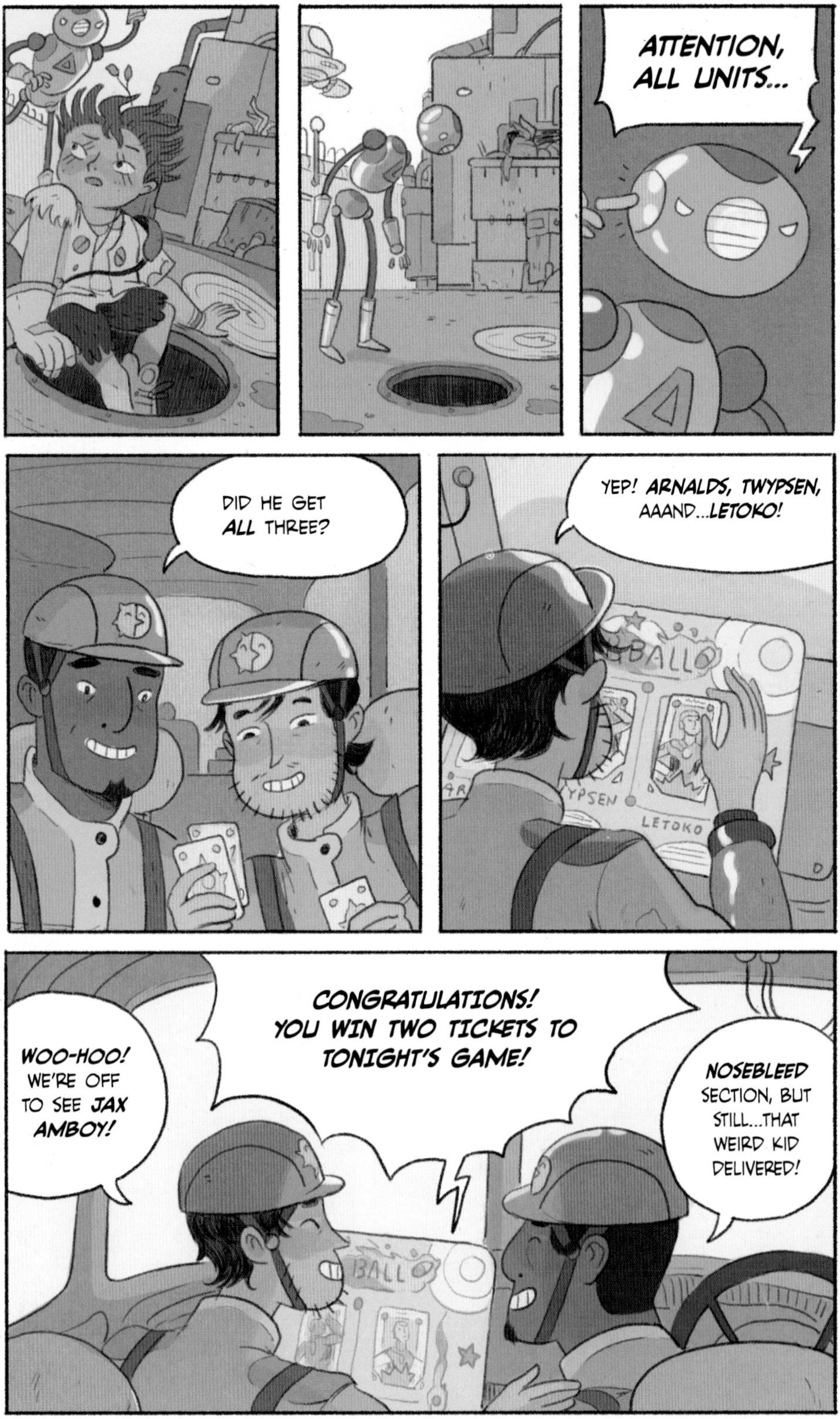
ATTENTION, ALL UNITS...
DID HE GET ALL THREE?
YEP! ARNALDS, TWYPSEN, AAAND...LETOKO!
BALL
TYPSEN
LETOKO
WOO-HOO! WE'RE OFF TO SEE JAX AMBOY!
CONGRATULATIONS! YOU WIN TWO TICKETS TO TONIGHT'S GAME!
NOSEBLEED SECTION, BUT STILL...THAT WEIRD KID DELIVERED!
BALL

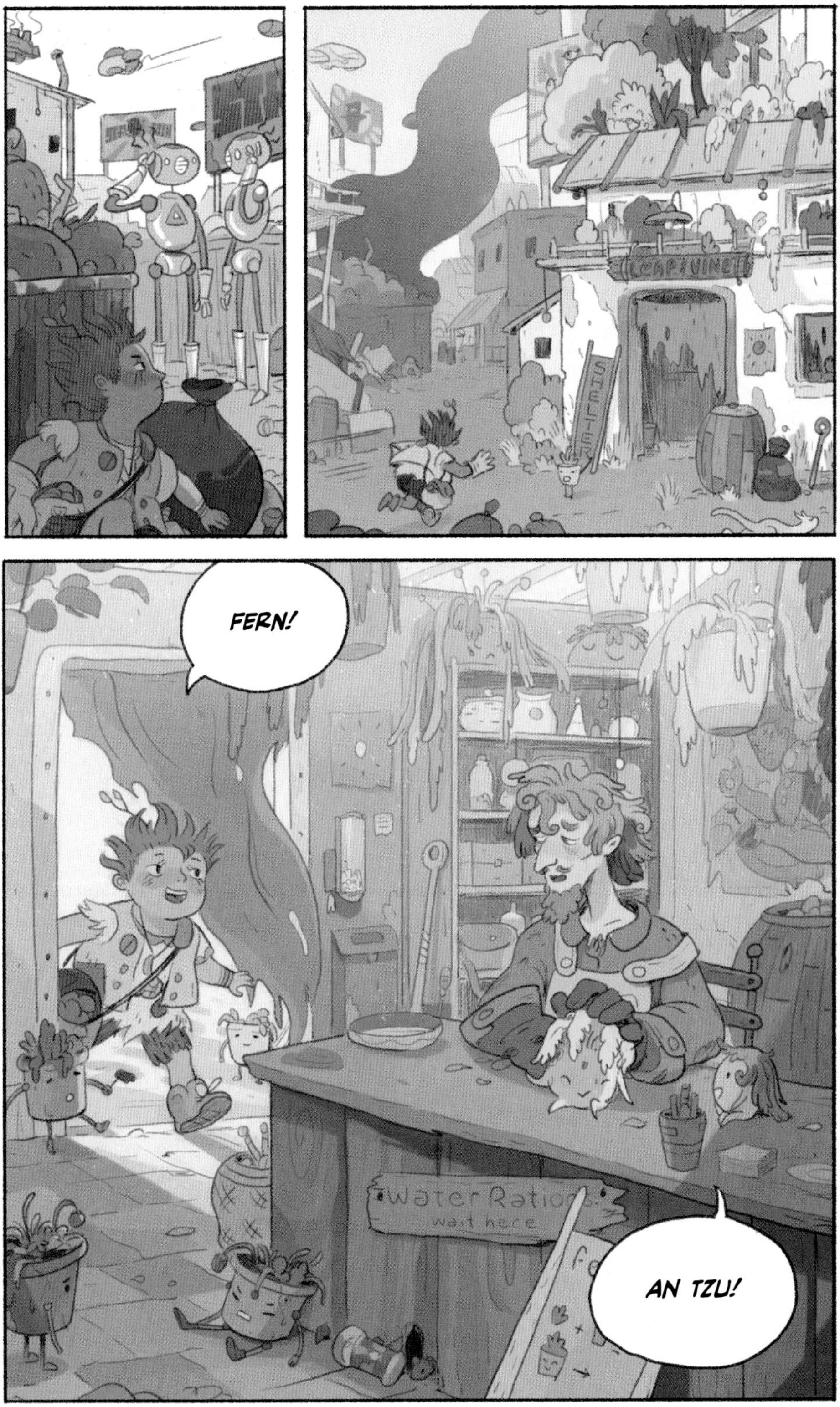
SHELTER
FERN!
wait here
AN TZU!

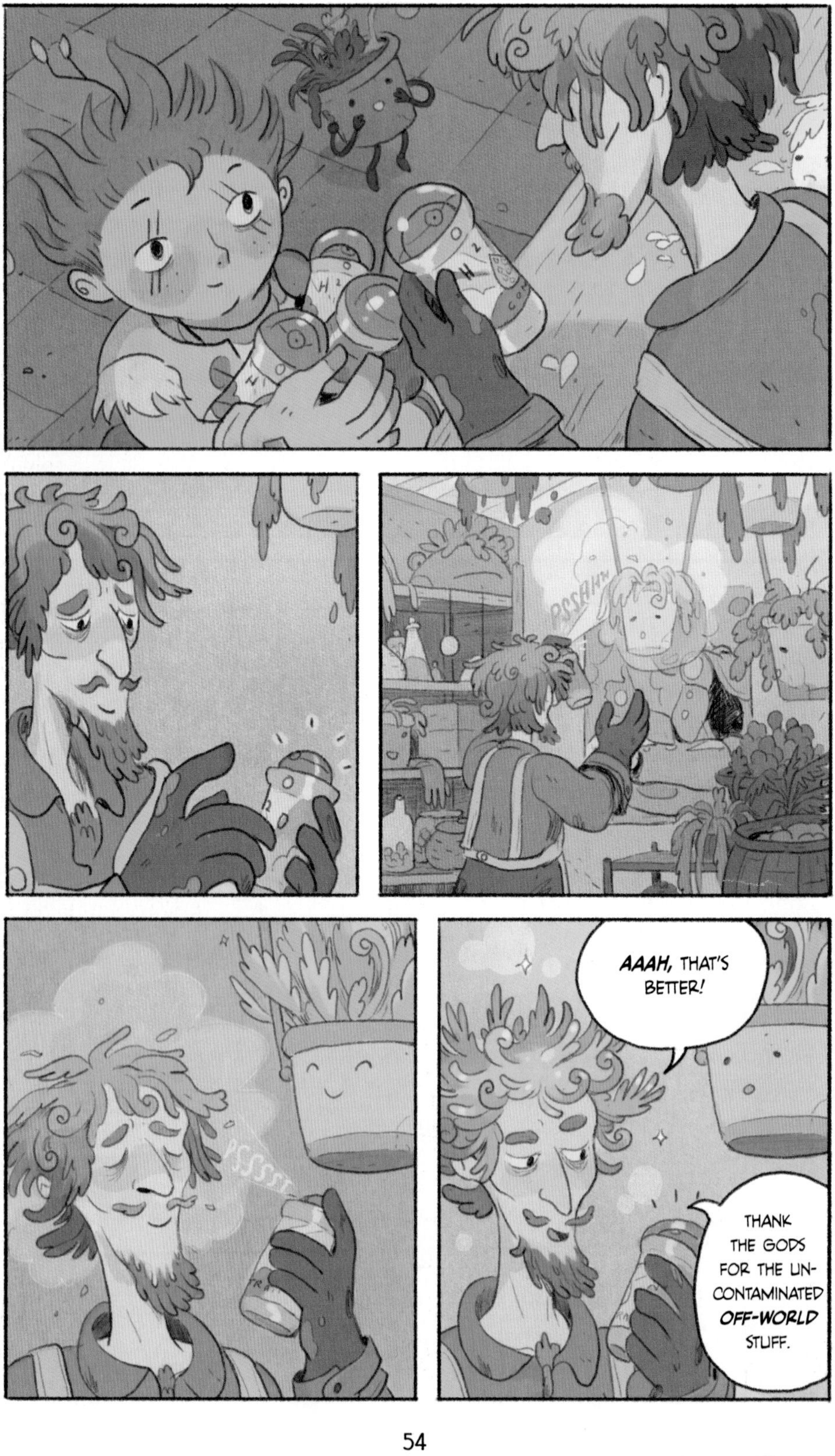
AAAH, THAT'S BETTER!
THANK THE GODS FOR THE UN-CONTAMINATED **OFF-WORLD** STUFF.

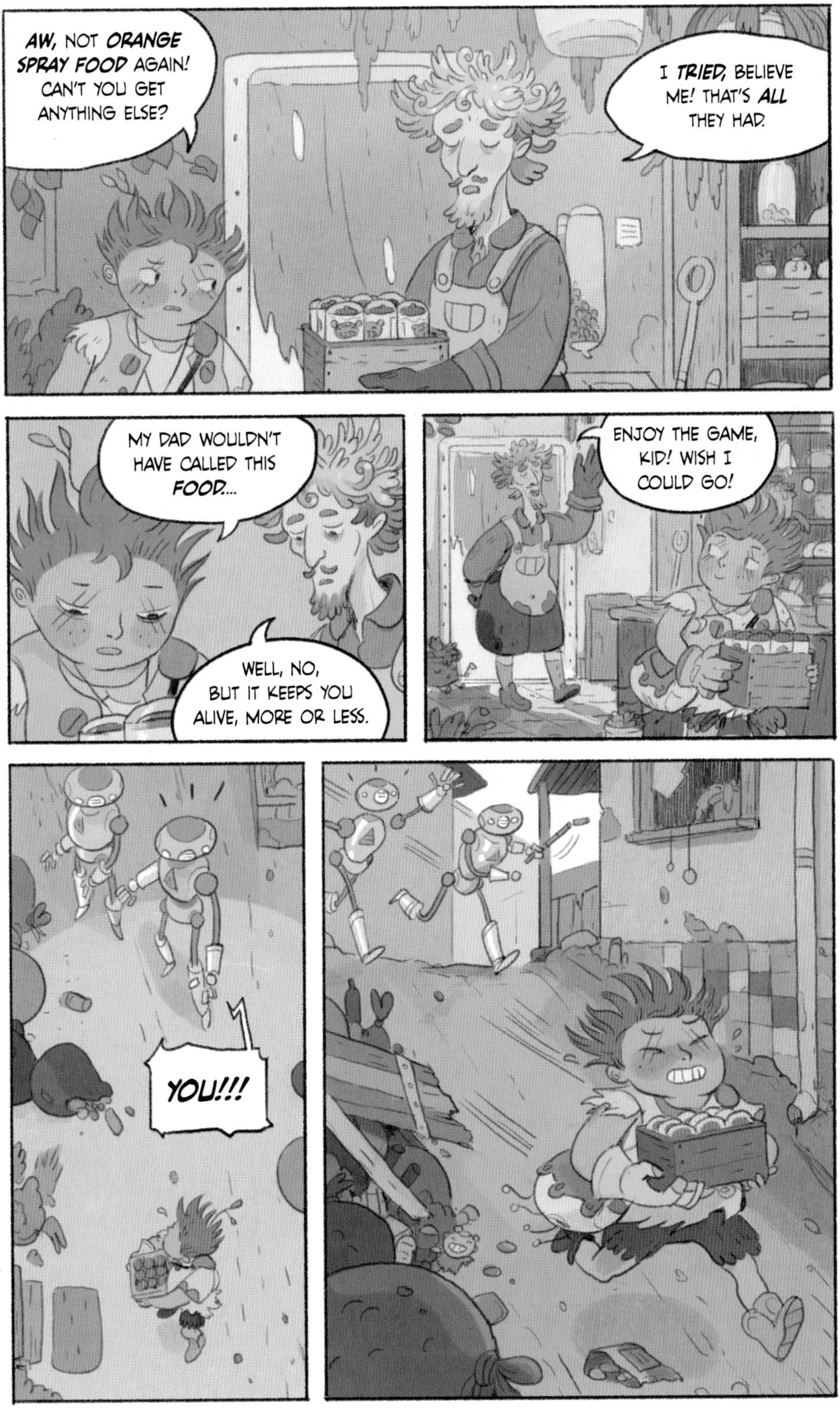
AW, NOT ORANGE SPRAY FOOD AGAIN! CAN'T YOU GET ANYTHING ELSE?
I TRIED, BELIEVE ME! THAT'S ALL THEY HAD.
MY DAD WOULDN'T HAVE CALLED THIS FOOD...
WELL, NO, BUT IT KEEPS YOU ALIVE, MORE OR LESS.
ENJOY THE GAME, KID! WISH I COULD GO!
YOU!!!

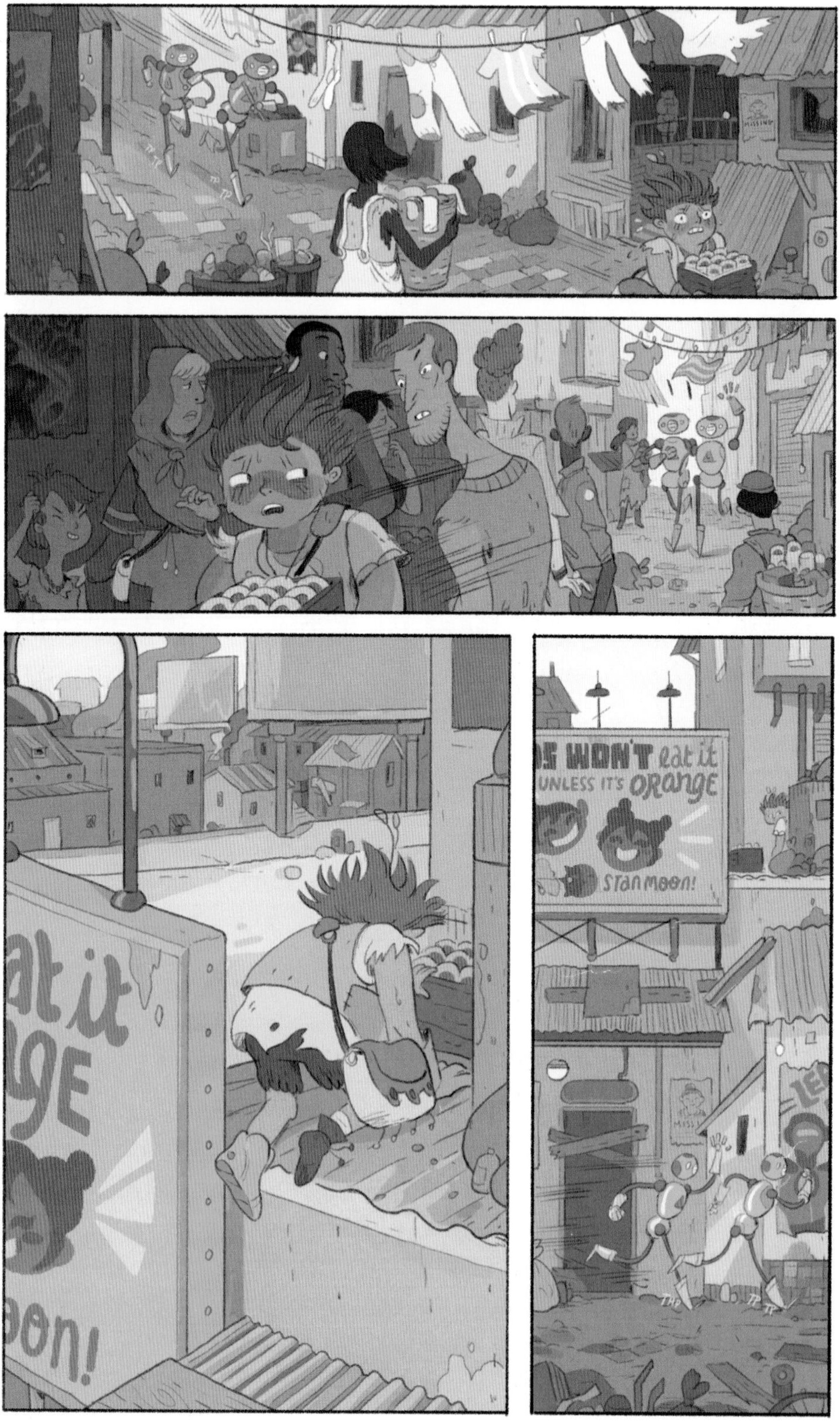
MISSING
WON'T eat it
UNLESS IT'S ORANGE
Stan Moon!
THP
TP TP

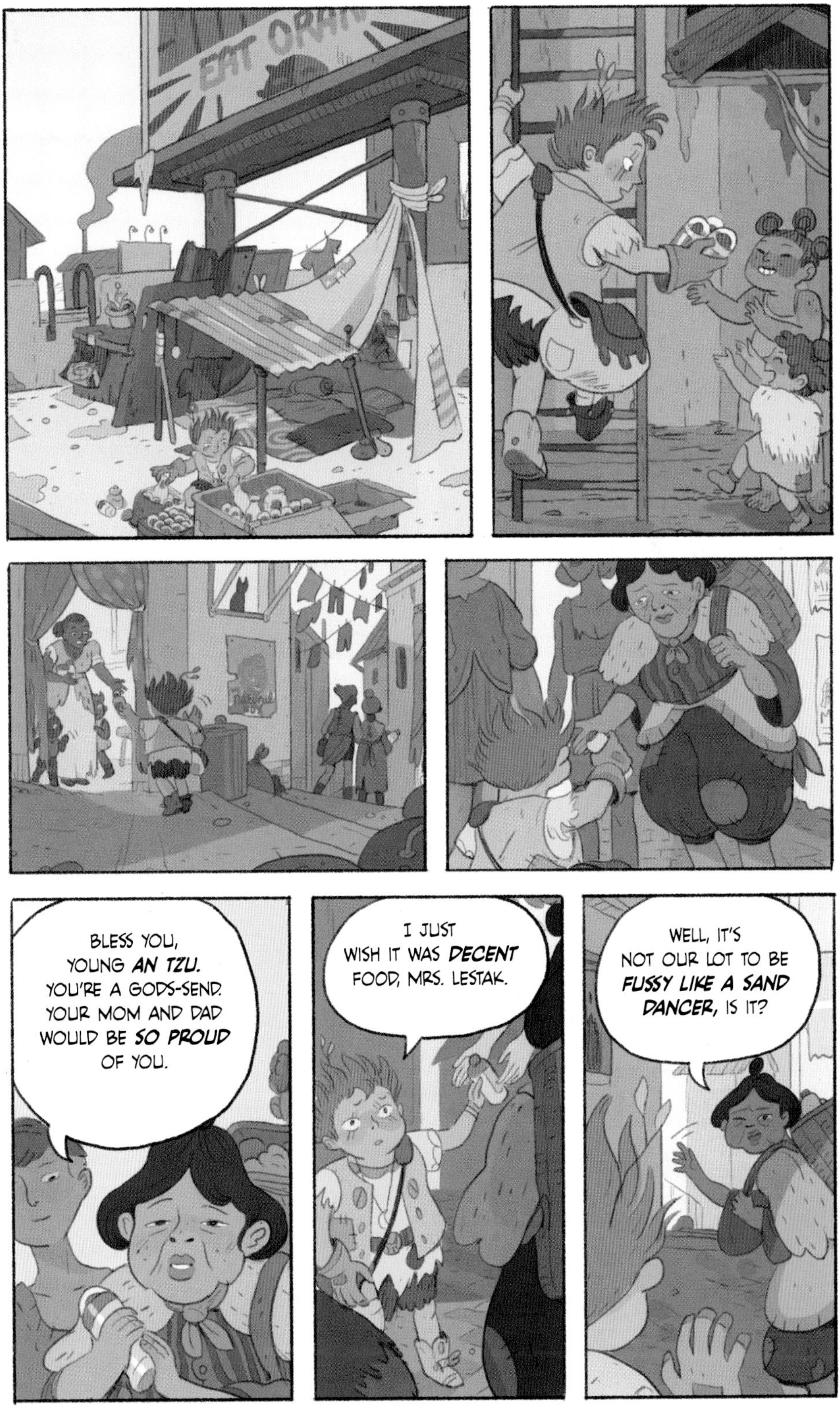
BLESS YOU, YOUNG AN TZU. YOU'RE A GODS-SEND. YOUR MOM AND DAD WOULD BE SO PROUD OF YOU.
I JUST WISH IT WAS DECENT FOOD, MRS. LESTAK.
WELL, IT'S NOT OUR LOT TO BE FUSSY LIKE A SAND DANCER, IS IT?

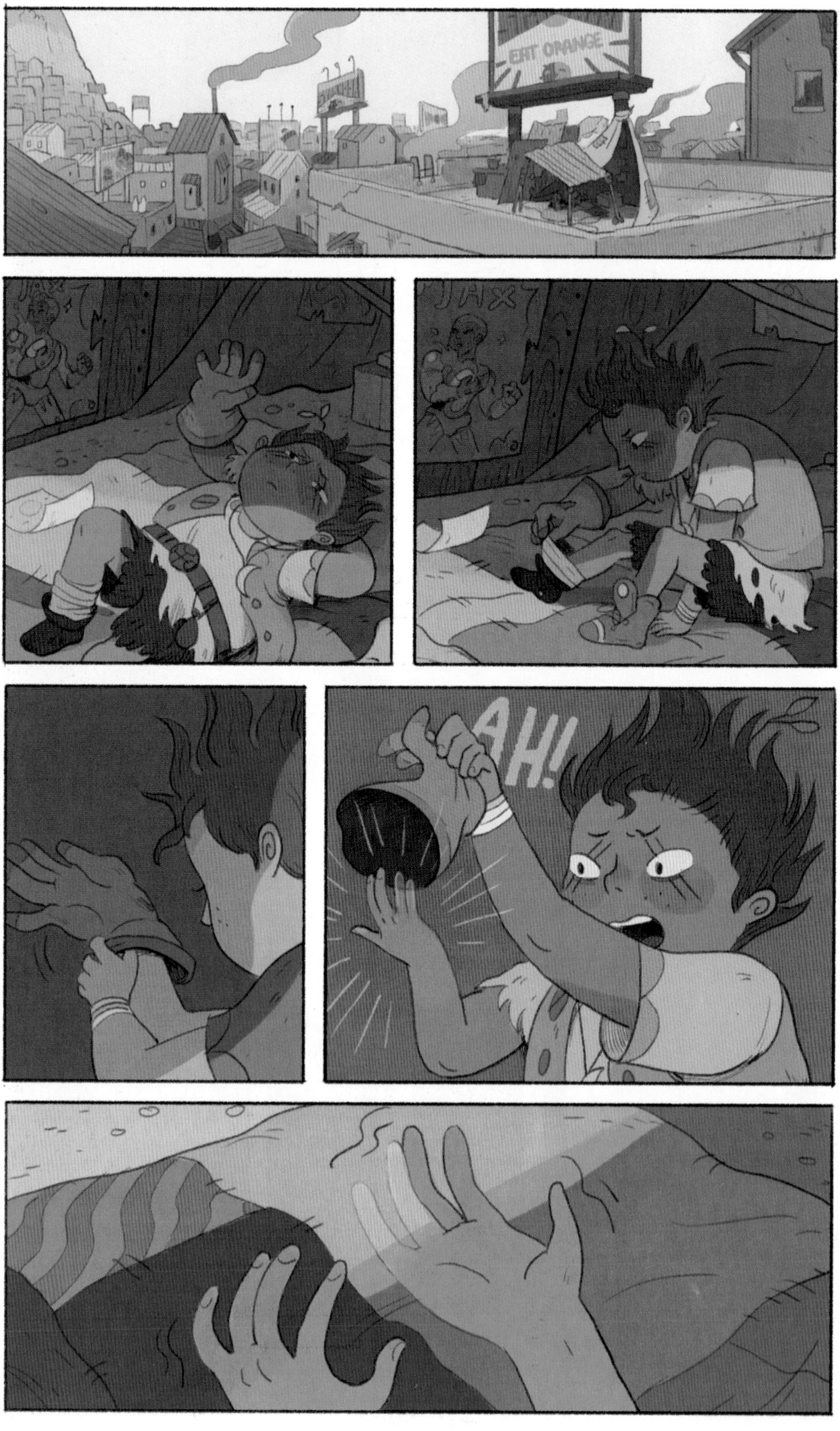
EAT ORANGE
AH!

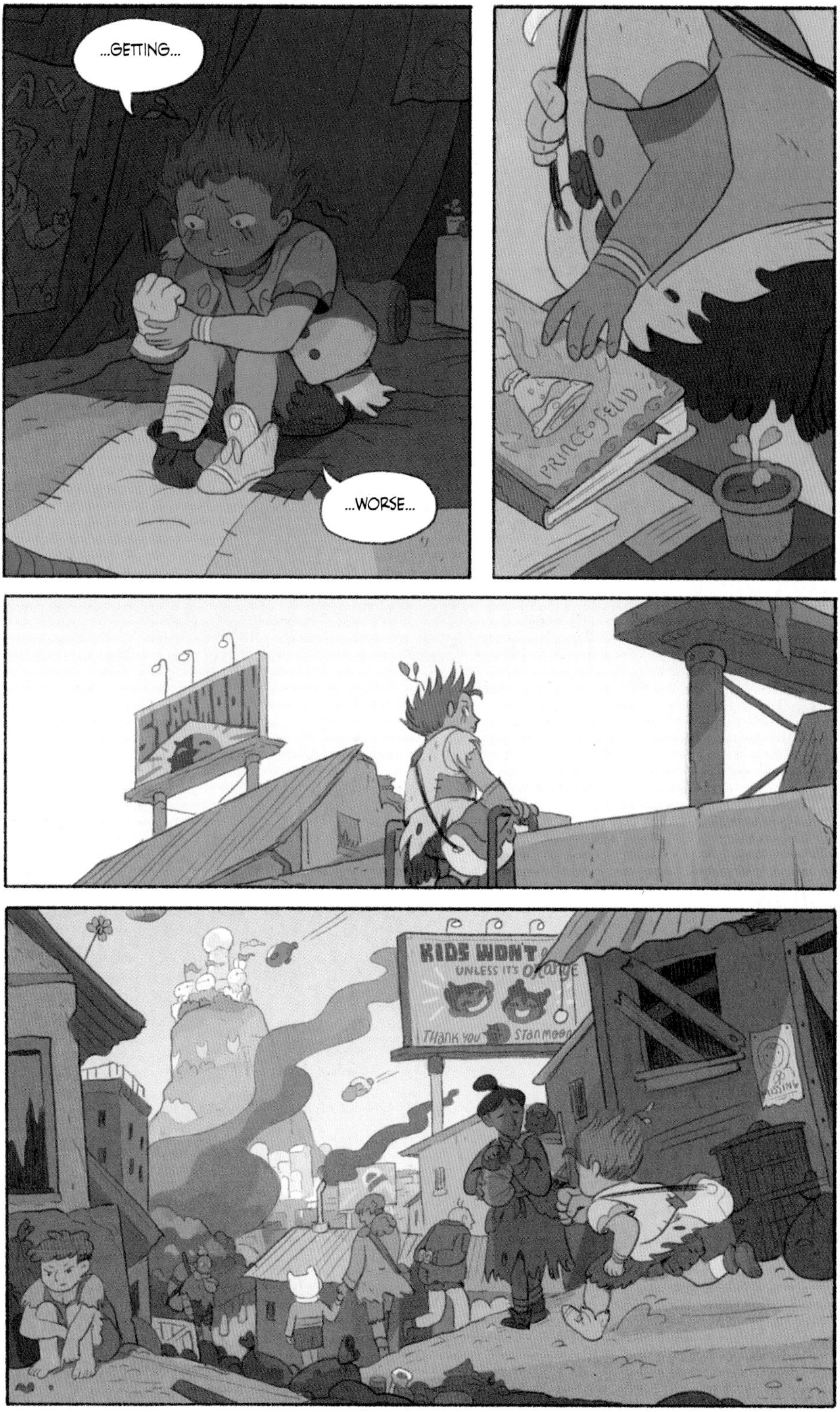
...GETTING...
...WORSE...
KIDS WON'T
UNLESS IT'S
THANK YOU
STANMOON

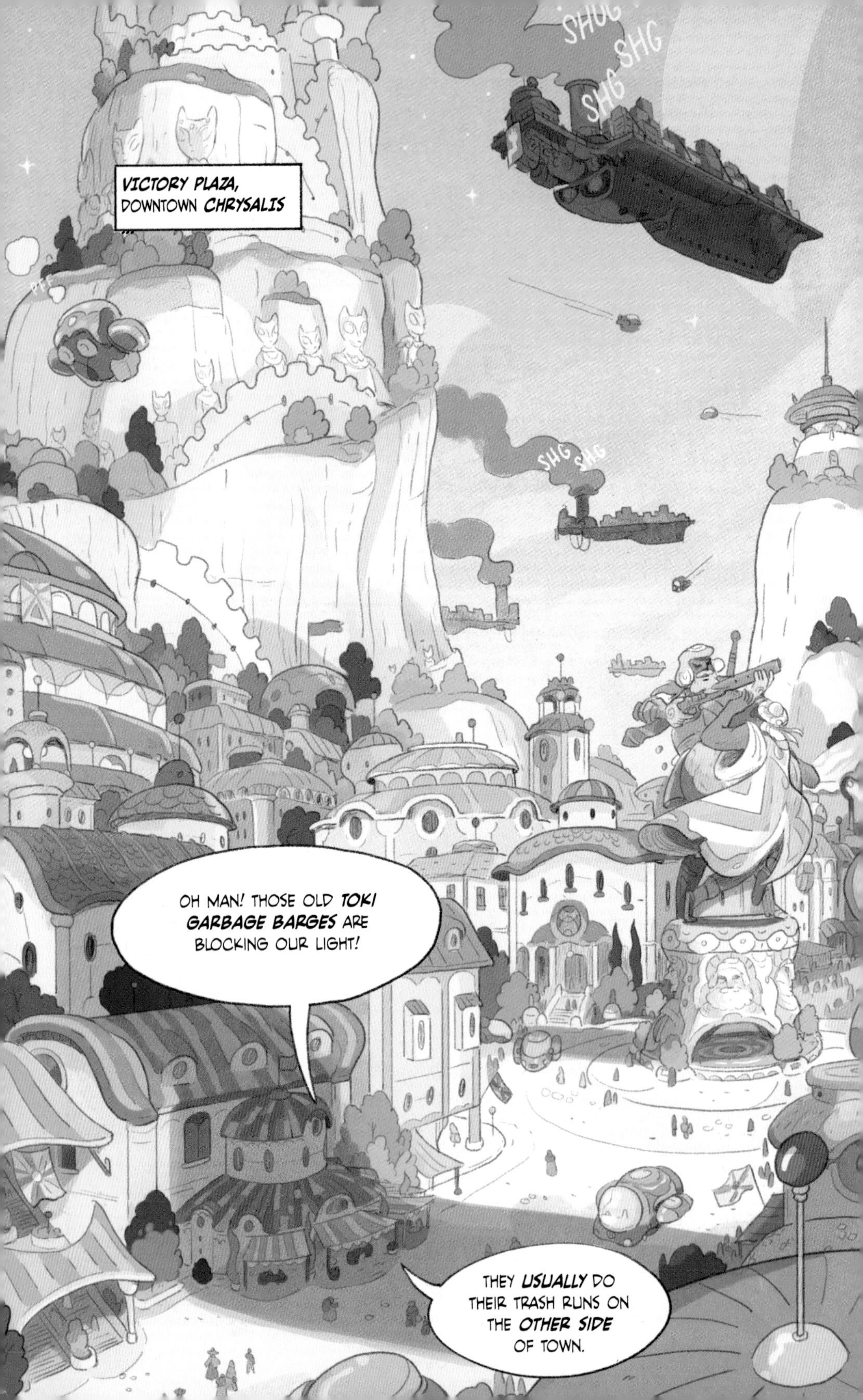

VICTORY PLAZA, DOWNTOWN CHRYSALIS
SHUG SHG SHG
SHG SHG
OH MAN! THOSE OLD TOKI GARBAGE BARGES ARE BLOCKING OUR LIGHT!
THEY USUALLY DO THEIR TRASH RUNS ON THE OTHER SIDE OF TOWN.

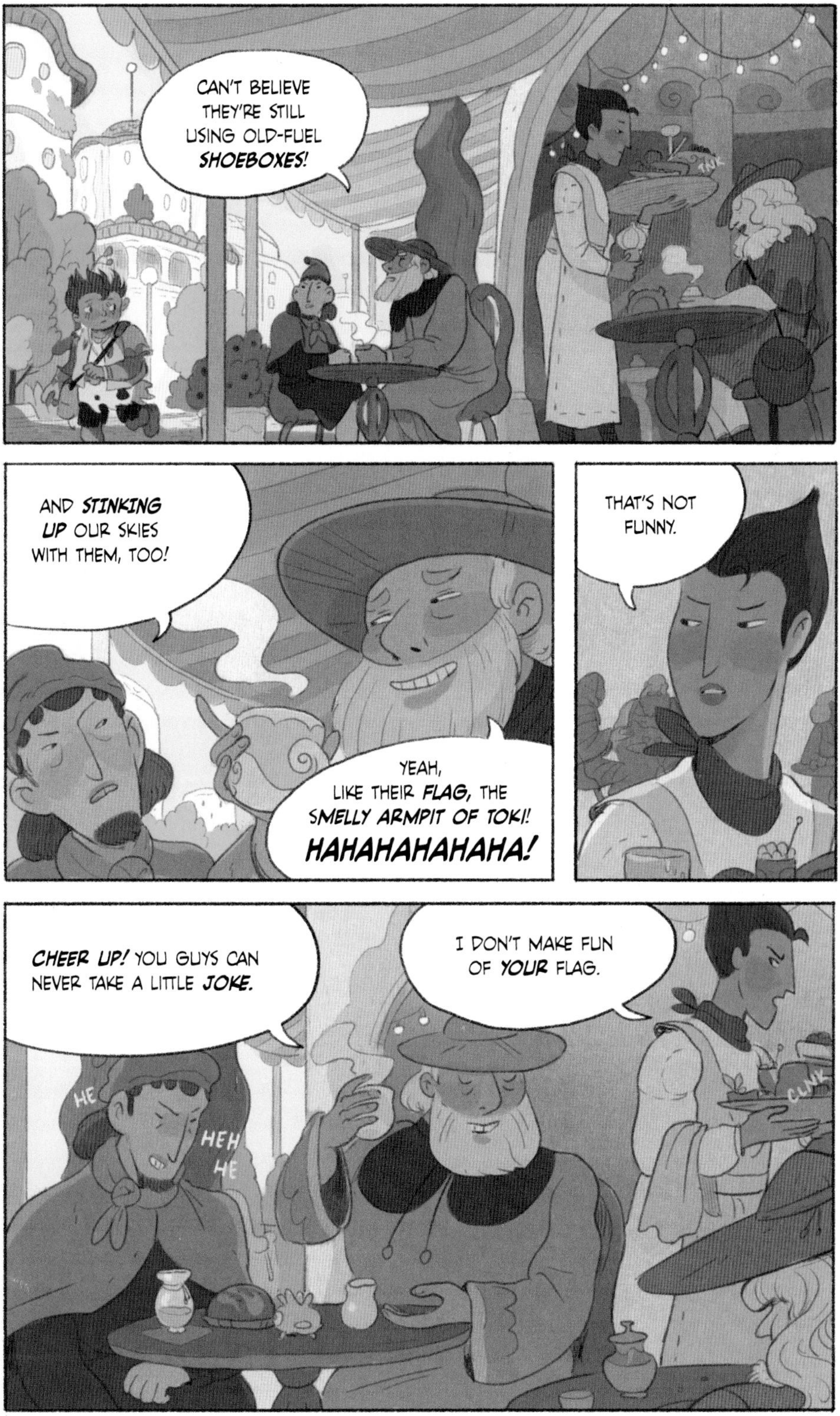
CAN'T BELIEVE THEY'RE STILL USING OLD-FUEL SHOEBOXES!
TINK
AND STINKING UP OUR SKIES WITH THEM, TOO!
YEAH, LIKE THEIR FLAG, THE SMELLY ARMPIT OF TOKI! HAHAHAHAHAHA!
THAT'S NOT FUNNY.
CHEER UP! YOU GUYS CAN NEVER TAKE A LITTLE JOKE.
I DON'T MAKE FUN OF YOUR FLAG.
HE
HEH
HE
CLNK

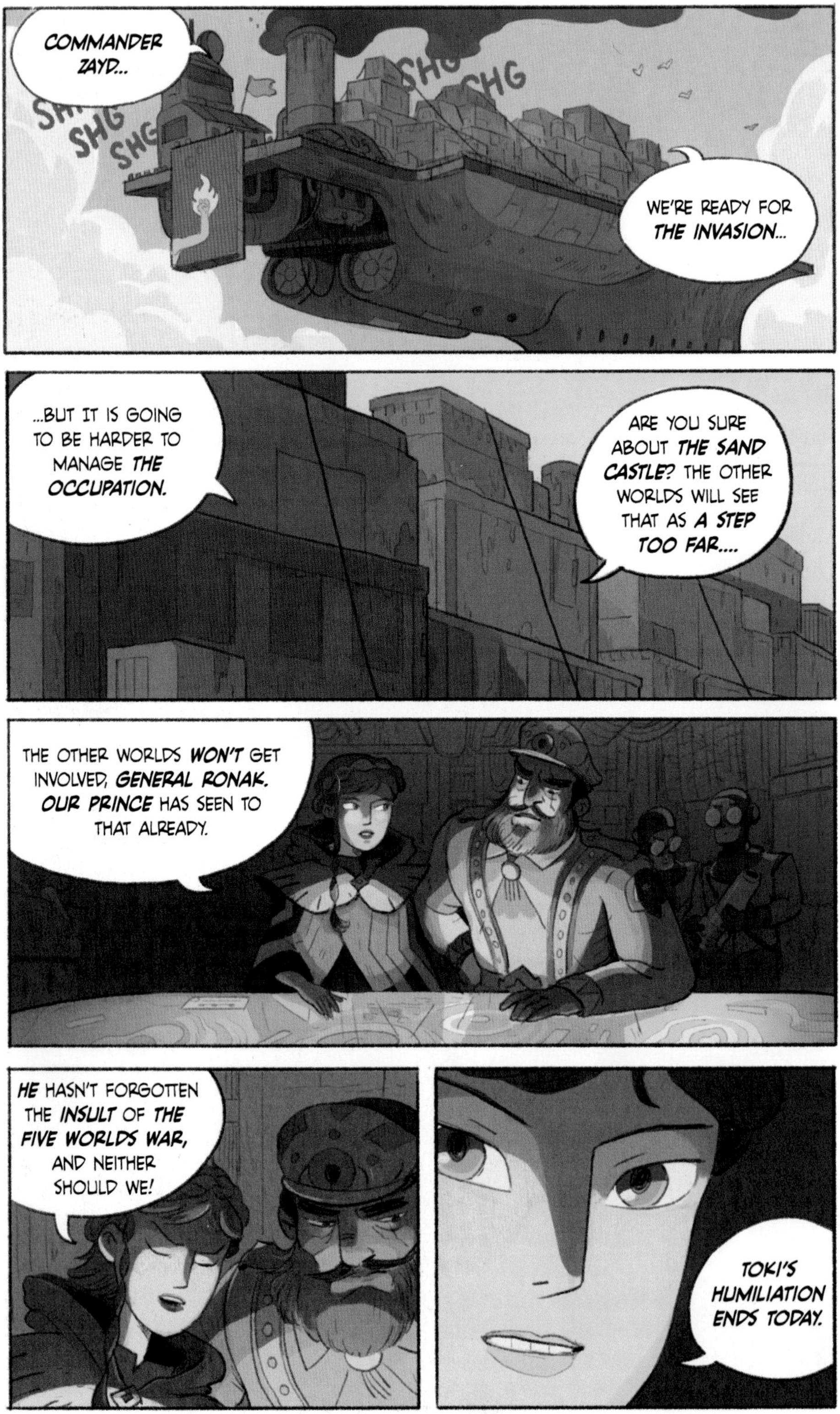
COMMANDER ZAYD...
SHG SHG SHG
SHG SHG
WE'RE READY FOR THE INVASION...
...BUT IT IS GOING TO BE HARDER TO MANAGE THE OCCUPATION.
ARE YOU SURE ABOUT THE SAND CASTLE? THE OTHER WORLDS WILL SEE THAT AS A STEP TOO FAR....
THE OTHER WORLDS WON'T GET INVOLVED, GENERAL RONAK. OUR PRINCE HAS SEEN TO THAT ALREADY.
HE HASN'T FORGOTTEN THE INSULT OF THE FIVE WORLDS WAR, AND NEITHER SHOULD WE!
TOKI'S HUMILIATION ENDS TODAY.

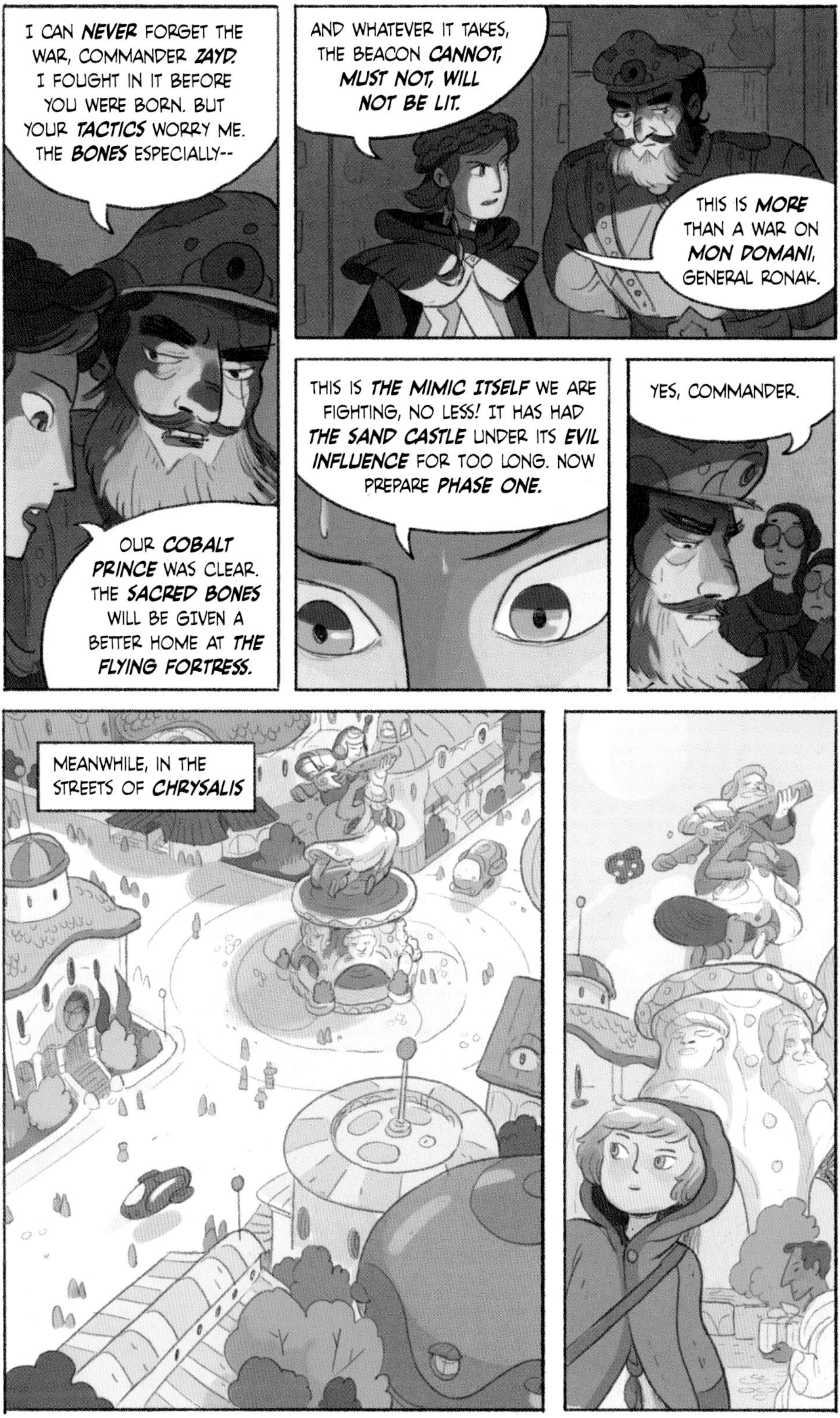
I CAN NEVER FORGET THE WAR, COMMANDER ZAYD. I FOUGHT IN IT BEFORE YOU WERE BORN. BUT YOUR TACTICS WORRY ME. THE BONES ESPECIALLY--
OUR COBALT PRINCE WAS CLEAR. THE SACRED BONES WILL BE GIVEN A BETTER HOME AT THE FLYING FORTRESS.
AND WHATEVER IT TAKES, THE BEACON CANNOT, MUST NOT, WILL NOT BE LIT.
THIS IS MORE THAN A WAR ON MON DOMANI, GENERAL RONAK.
THIS IS THE MIMIC ITSELF WE ARE FIGHTING, NO LESS! IT HAS HAD THE SAND CASTLE UNDER ITS EVIL INFLUENCE FOR TOO LONG. NOW PREPARE PHASE ONE.
YES, COMMANDER.
MEANWHILE, IN THE STREETS OF CHRYSALIS

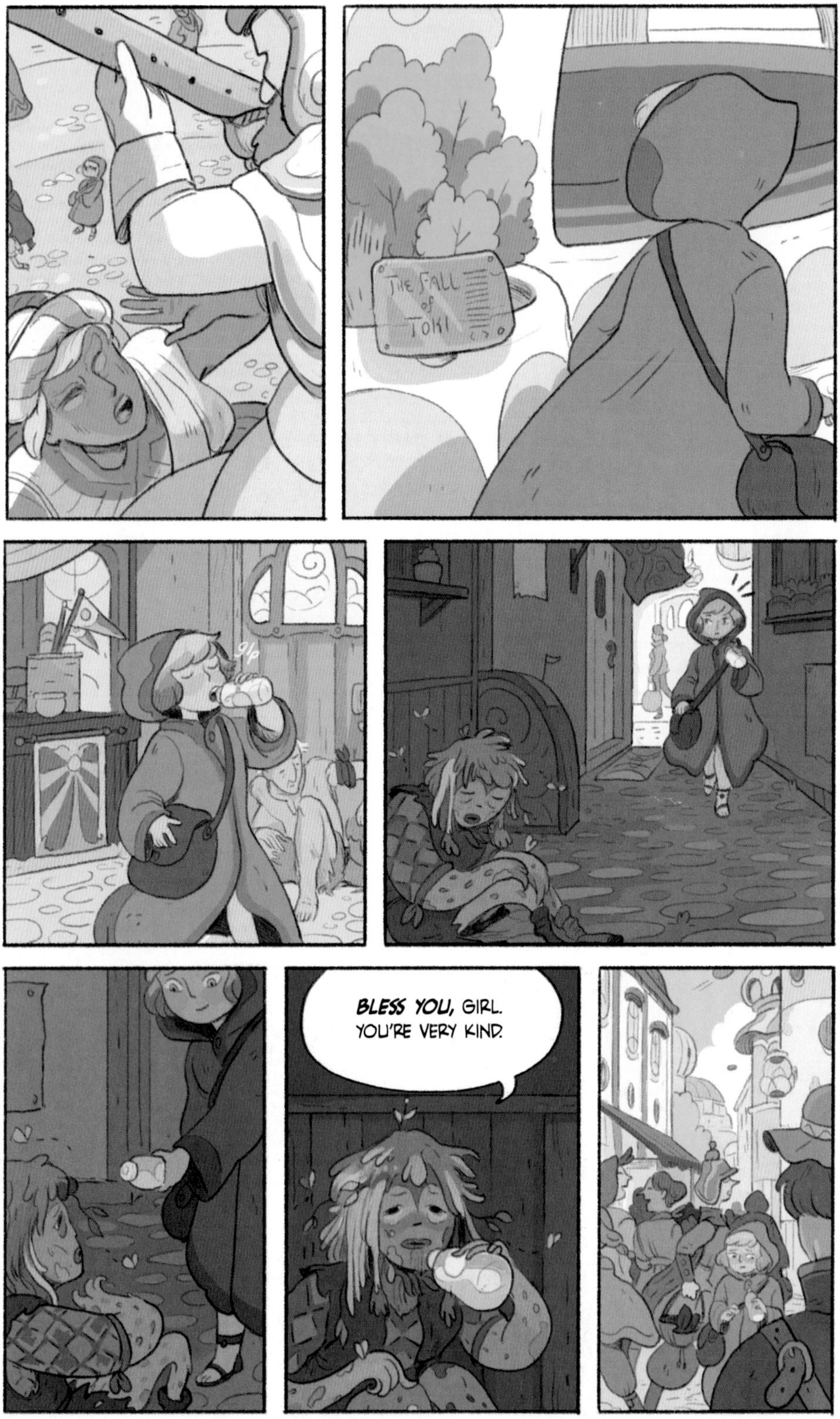
THE FALL of TOKI
glp
BLESS YOU, GIRL.
YOU'RE VERY KIND.

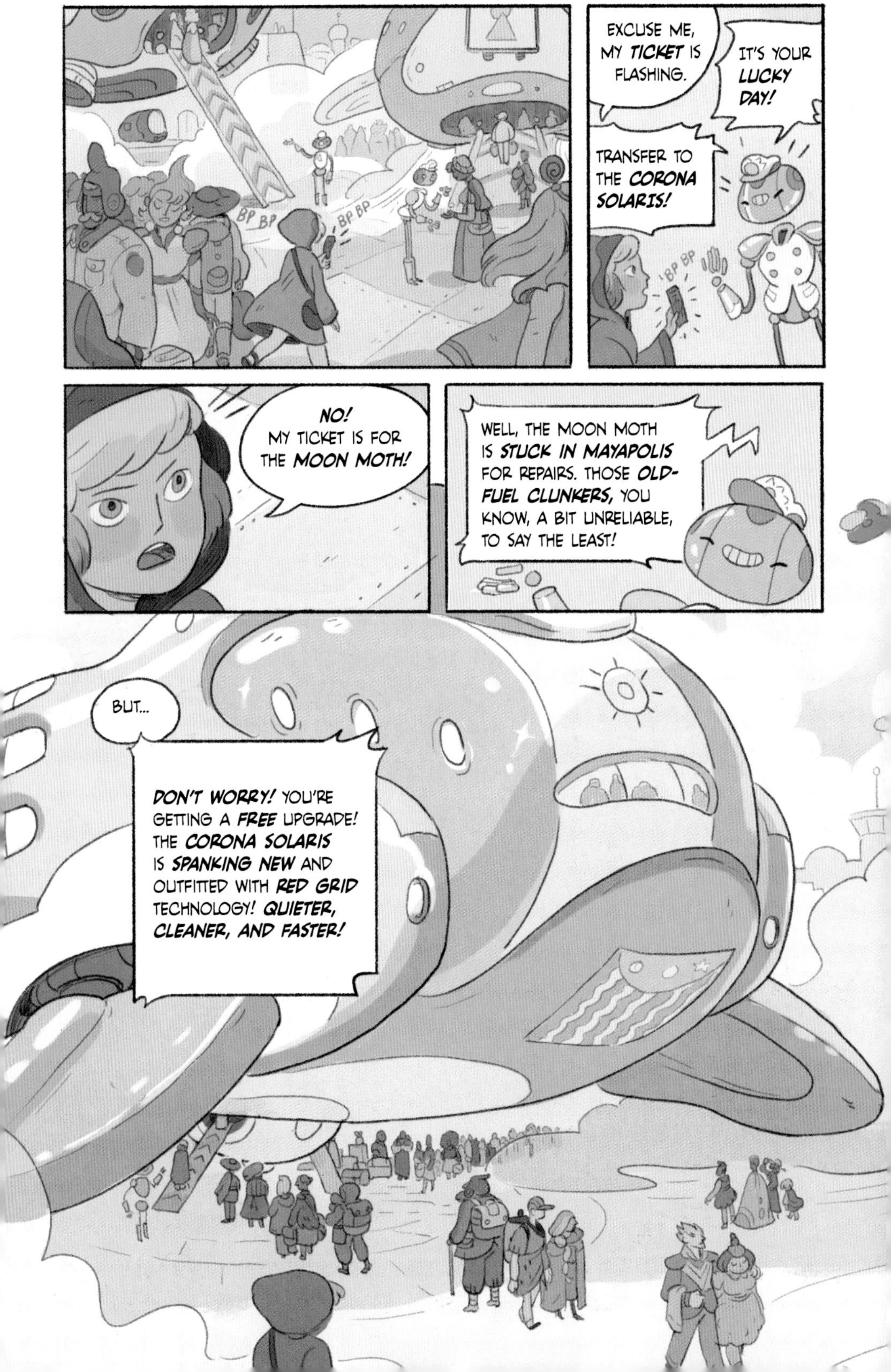
BP BP
BP BP
EXCUSE ME, MY TICKET IS FLASHING.
IT'S YOUR LUCKY DAY!
TRANSFER TO THE CORONA SOLARIS!
BP BP
NO! MY TICKET IS FOR THE MOON MOTH!
WELL, THE MOON MOTH IS STUCK IN MAYAPOLIS FOR REPAIRS. THOSE OLD-FUEL CLUNKERS, YOU KNOW, A BIT UNRELIABLE, TO SAY THE LEAST!
BUT...
DON'T WORRY! YOU'RE GETTING A FREE UPGRADE! THE CORONA SOLARIS IS SPANKING NEW AND OUTFITTED WITH RED GRID TECHNOLOGY! QUIETER, CLEANER, AND FASTER!

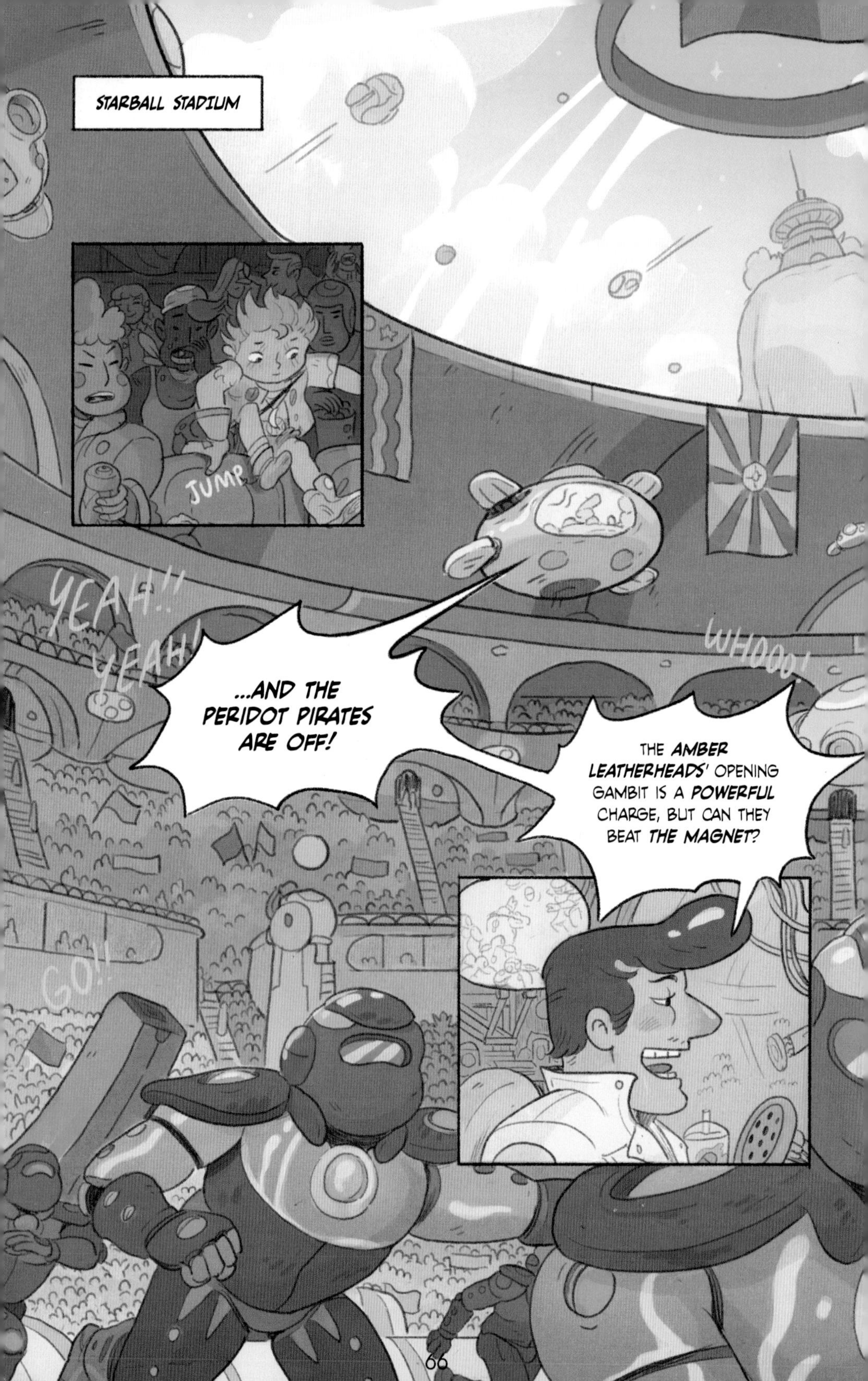
STARBALL STADIUM
JUMP
YEAH!!
YEAH!
WHOOO!
...AND THE PERIDOT PIRATES ARE OFF!
THE AMBER LEATHERHEADS' OPENING GAMBIT IS A POWERFUL CHARGE, BUT CAN THEY BEAT THE MAGNET?
GO!!

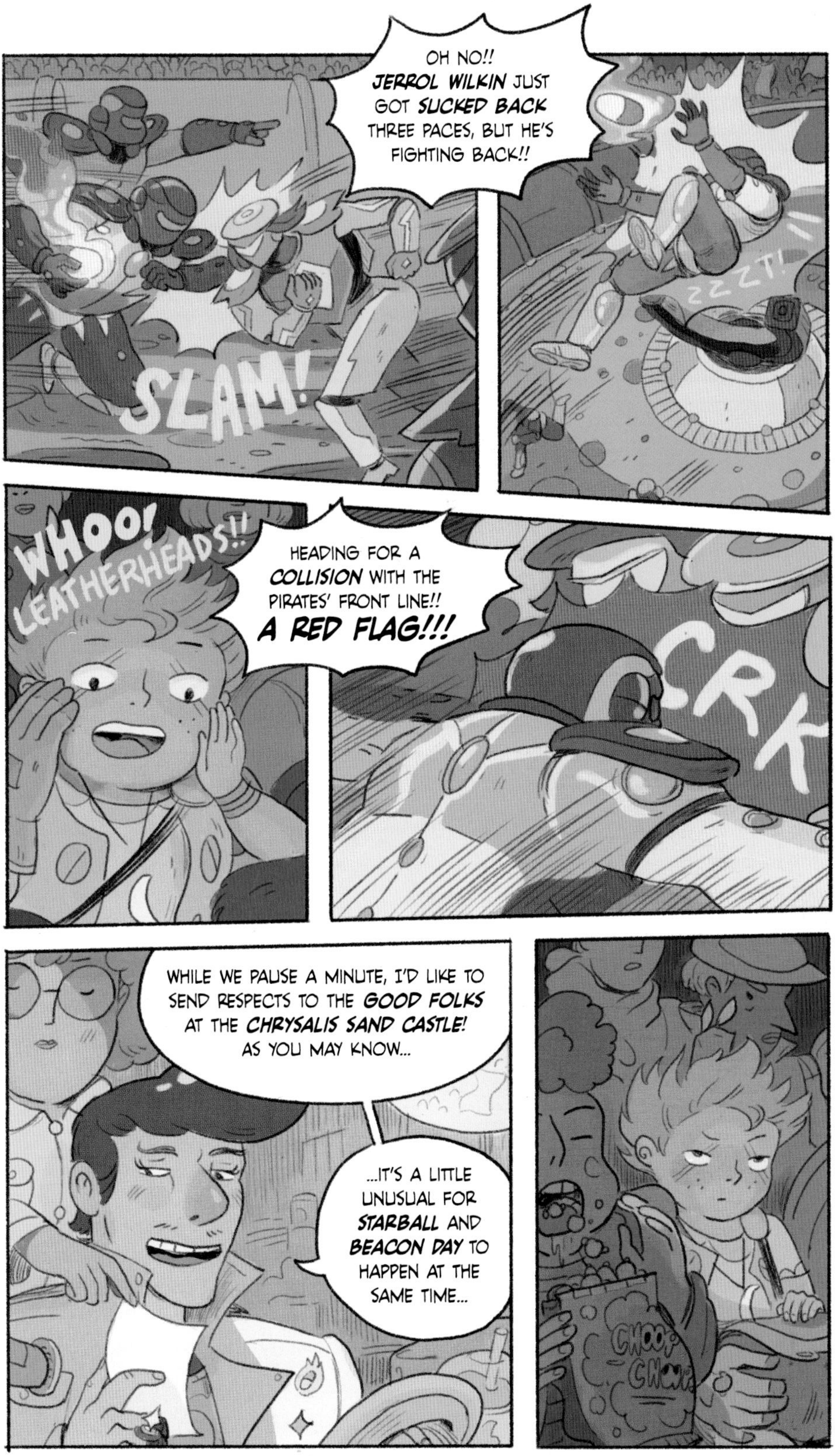
OH NO!! JERROL WILKIN JUST GOT SUCKED BACK THREE PACES, BUT HE'S FIGHTING BACK!!
SLAM!
ZZZT!
WHOO! LEATHERHEADS!!
HEADING FOR A COLLISION WITH THE PIRATES' FRONT LINE!! A RED FLAG!!!
CRK
WHILE WE PAUSE A MINUTE, I'D LIKE TO SEND RESPECTS TO THE GOOD FOLKS AT THE CHRYSALIS SAND CASTLE! AS YOU MAY KNOW...
...IT'S A LITTLE UNUSUAL FOR STARBALL AND BEACON DAY TO HAPPEN AT THE SAME TIME...

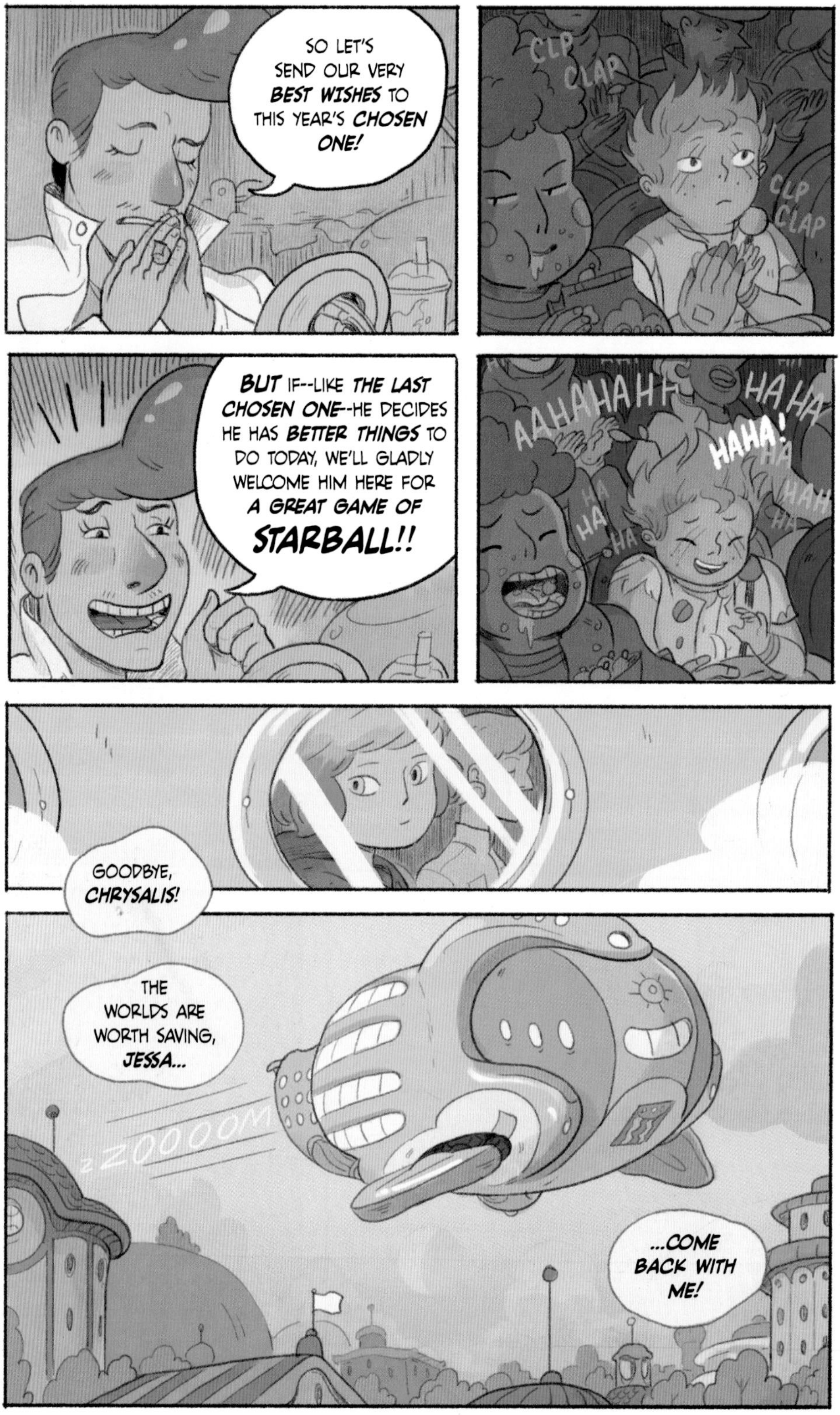

SO LET'S SEND OUR VERY BEST WISHES TO THIS YEAR'S CHOSEN ONE!
CLP CLAP
CLP CLAP
BUT IF--LIKE THE LAST CHOSEN ONE--HE DECIDES HE HAS BETTER THINGS TO DO TODAY, WE'LL GLADLY WELCOME HIM HERE FOR A GREAT GAME OF STARBALL!!
AAHAHAHH
HA HA
HAHA!
HA HA
GOODBYE, CHRYSALIS!
THE WORLDS ARE WORTH SAVING, JESSA...
zZOOOOM
...COME BACK WITH ME!

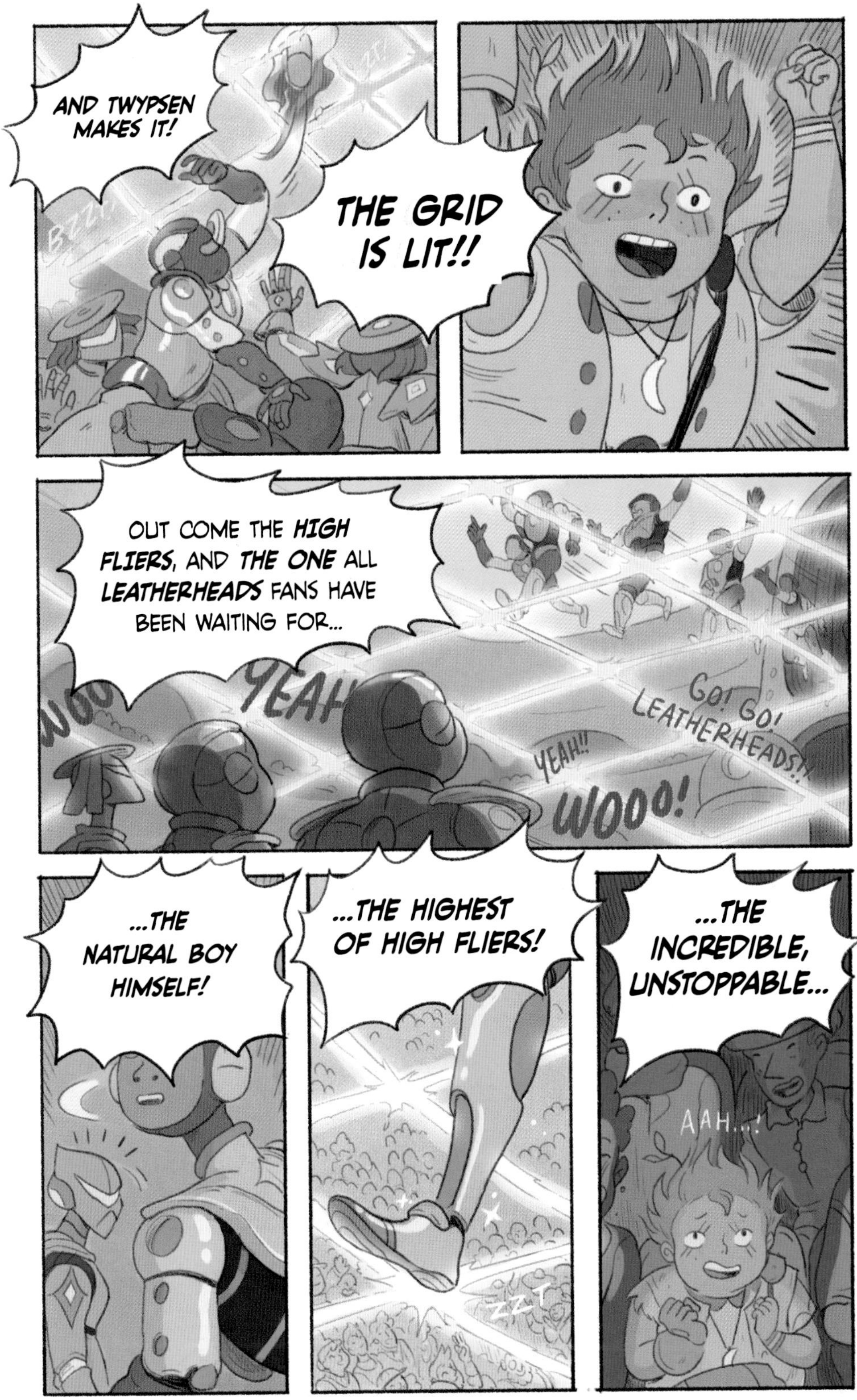
AND TWYPSEN MAKES IT!
BZZT!
THE GRID IS LIT!!
OUT COME THE HIGH FLIERS, AND THE ONE ALL LEATHERHEADS FANS HAVE BEEN WAITING FOR...
WOO
YEAH
GO! GO! LEATHERHEADS!!
YEAH!!
WOOO!
...THE NATURAL BOY HIMSELF!
...THE HIGHEST OF HIGH FLIERS!
ZZT
...THE INCREDIBLE, UNSTOPPABLE...
AAH...!

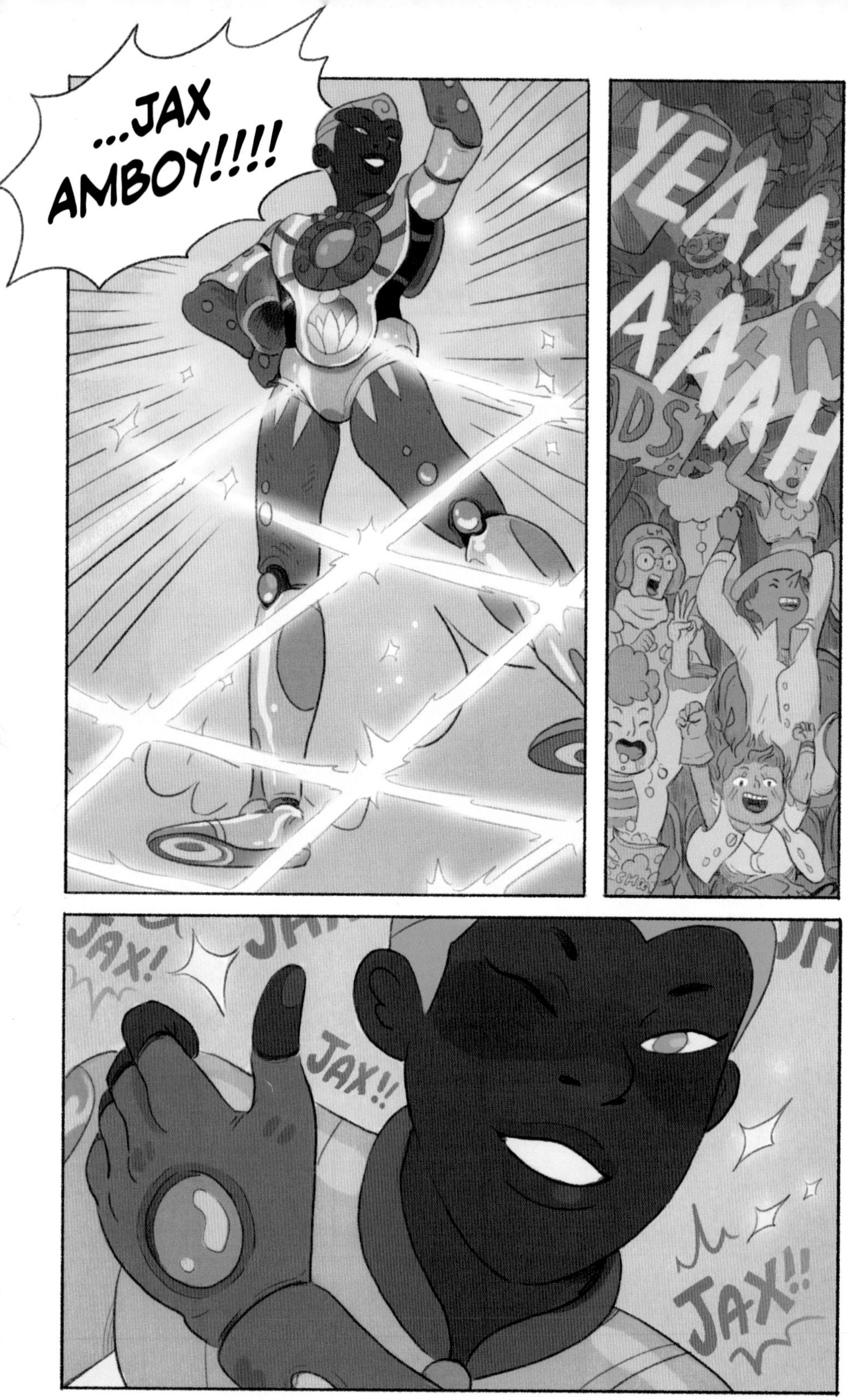
...JAX AMBOY!!!!
JAX!
JAX!!
JAX!!

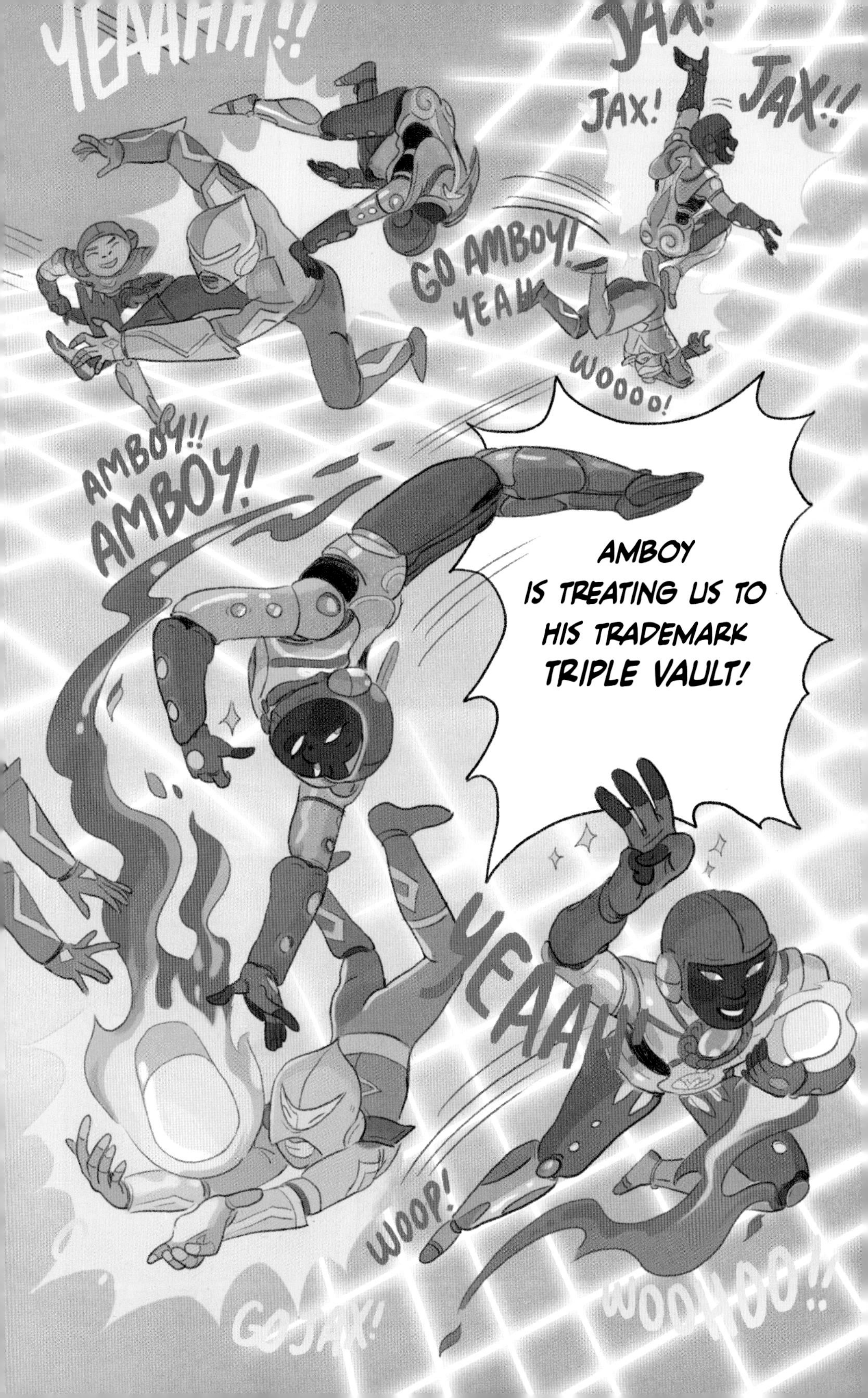
YEAAHH!!
JAX!
JAX!
JAX!!
GO AMBOY!
YEAH
WOOOO!
AMBOY!!
AMBOY!
AMBOY IS TREATING US TO HIS TRADEMARK TRIPLE VAULT!
YEAAH
WOOP!
GO JAX!
WOOHOO!!

LADIES AND GENTLEMEN, FOR THOSE OF YOU WHO CAN TEAR YOUR EYES AWAY FROM *THE STARBALL GAME* FOR A MOMENT...

...ON THE LEFT WE NOW HAVE A BEAUTIFUL VIEW OF DOWNTOWN *CHRYSALIS...*

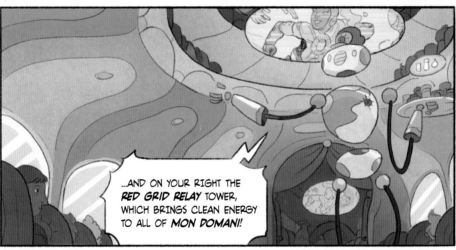

...AND ON YOUR RIGHT THE *RED GRID RELAY* TOWER, WHICH BRINGS CLEAN ENERGY TO ALL OF *MON DOMANI!*

BIP BIP BIP

IN FACT, IT POWERS *THIS VERY SHIP!*

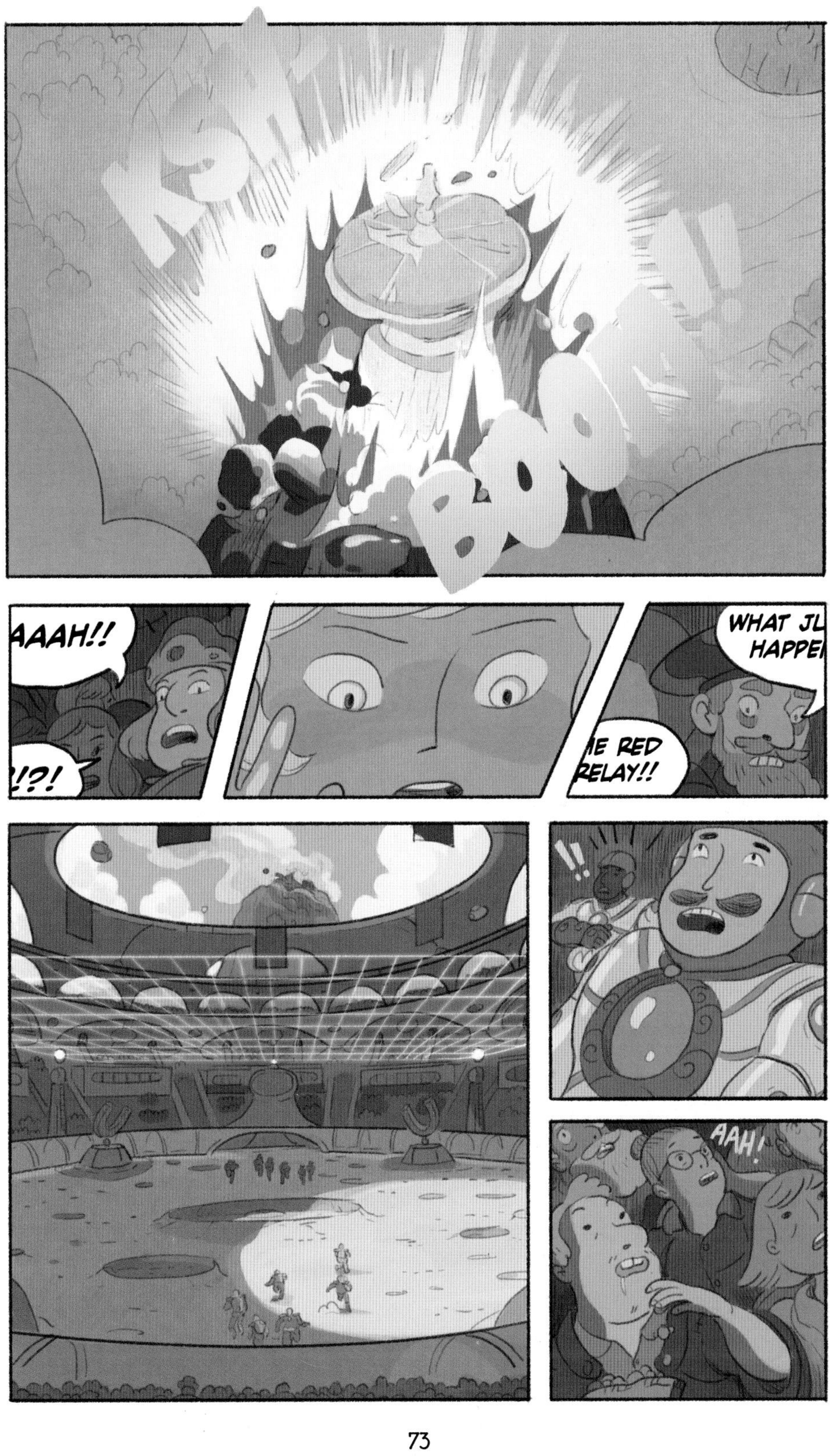
KSH
BOO
AAAH!!
!?!
WHAT JU
HAPPEN
IE RED
RELAY!!
!!
AAH!

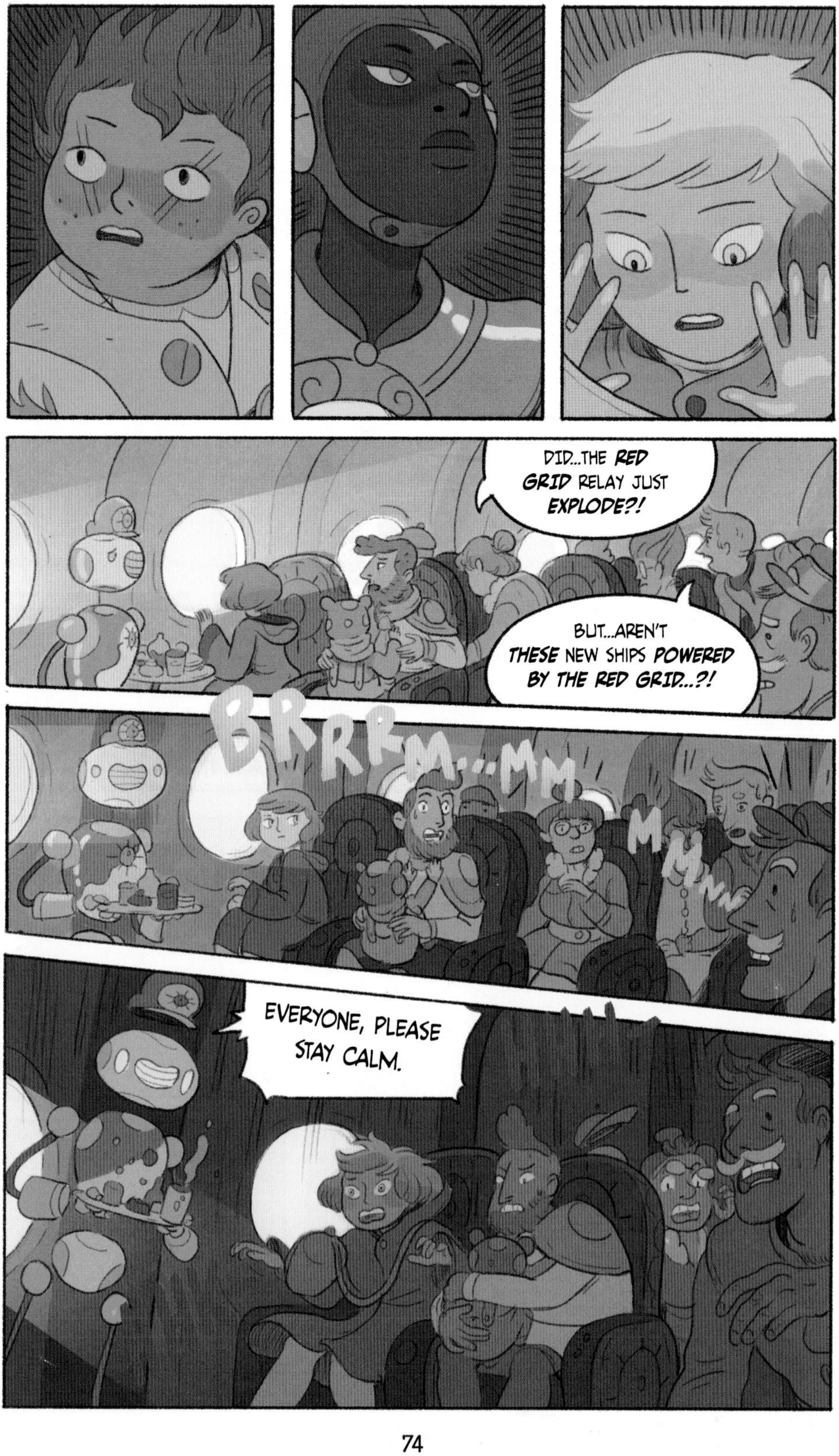
DID...THE RED GRID RELAY JUST EXPLODE?!
BUT...AREN'T THESE NEW SHIPS POWERED BY THE RED GRID...?!
BRRRM...MM
MMMnn
EVERYONE, PLEASE STAY CALM.

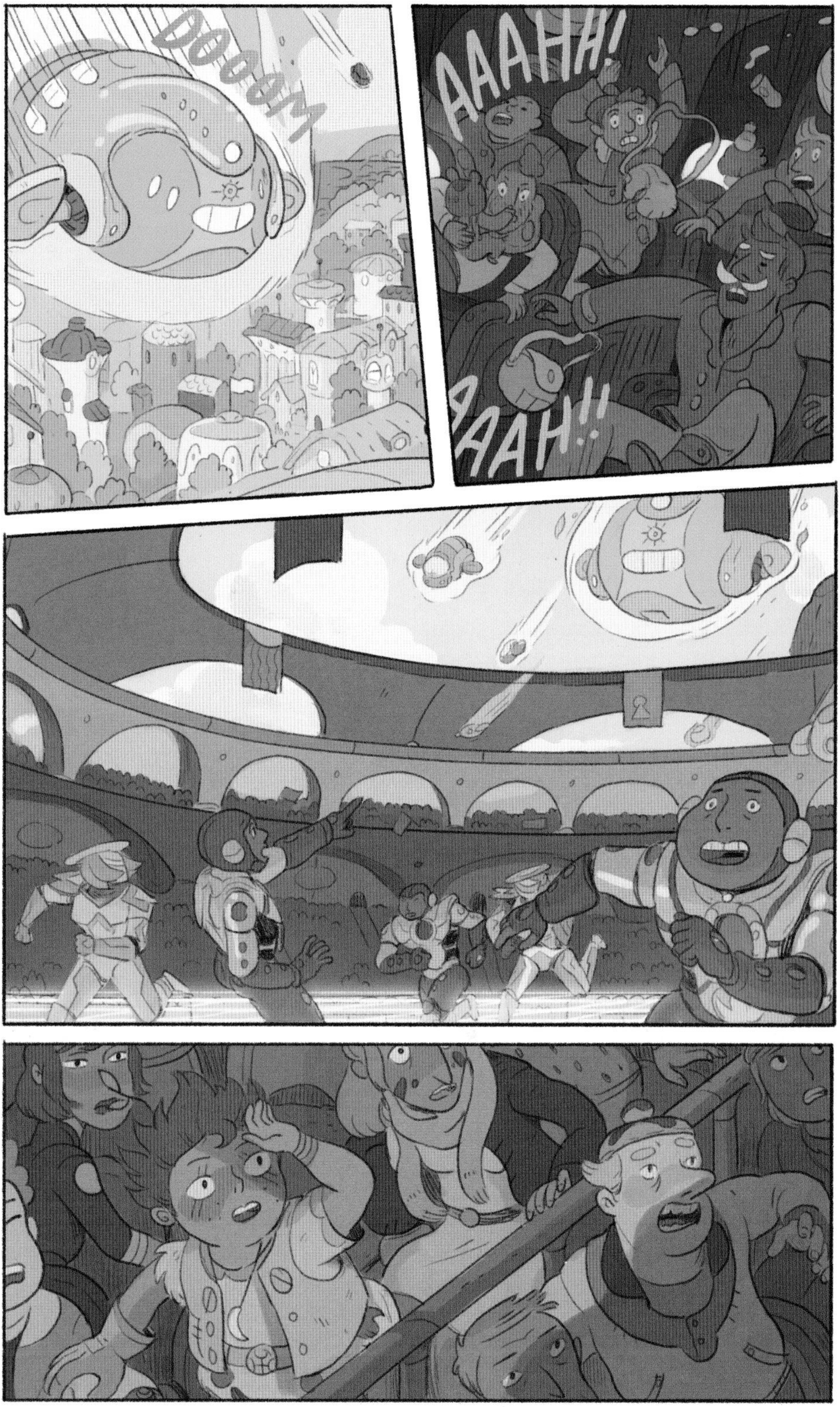
DOOOM
AAAHH!
AAAH!!

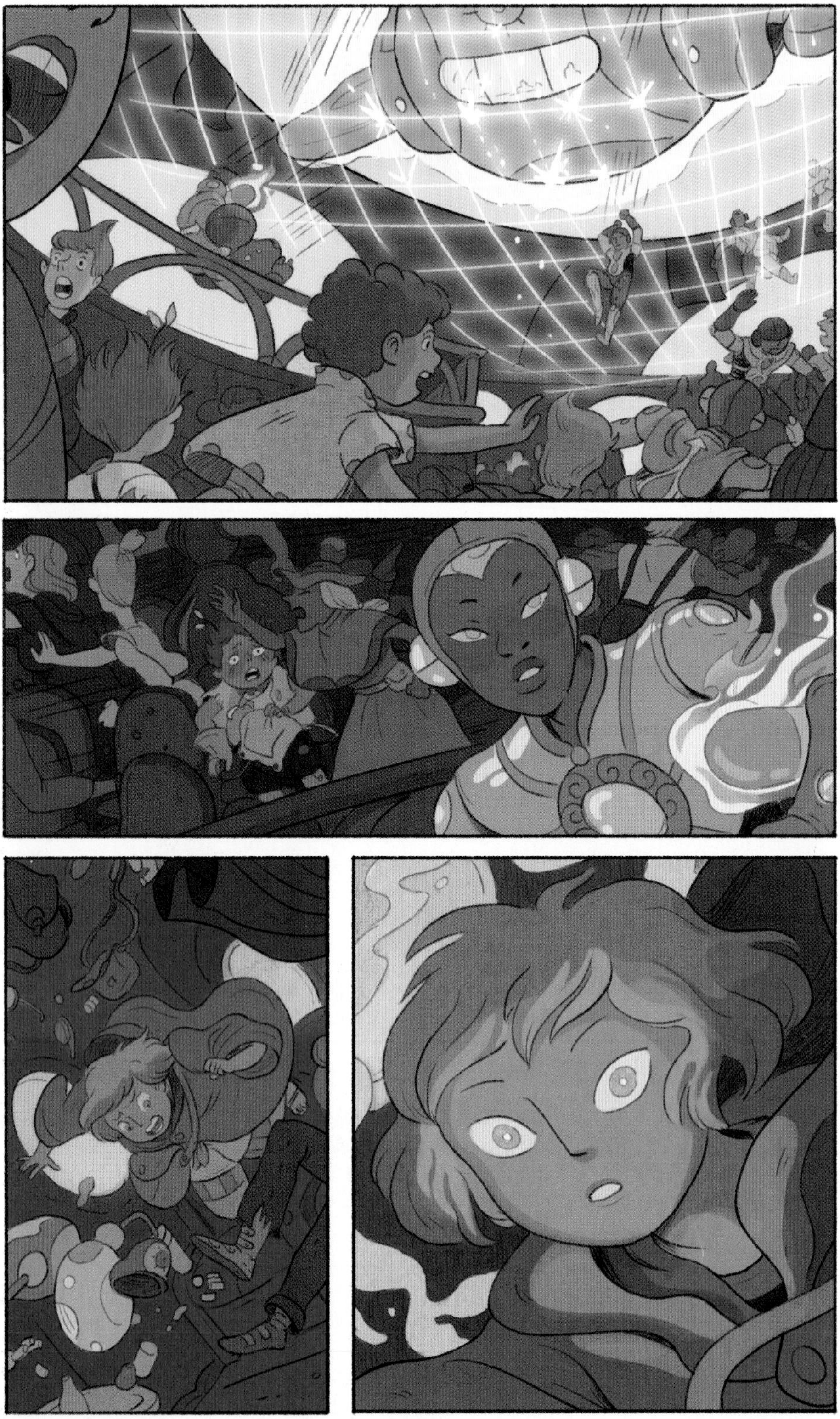

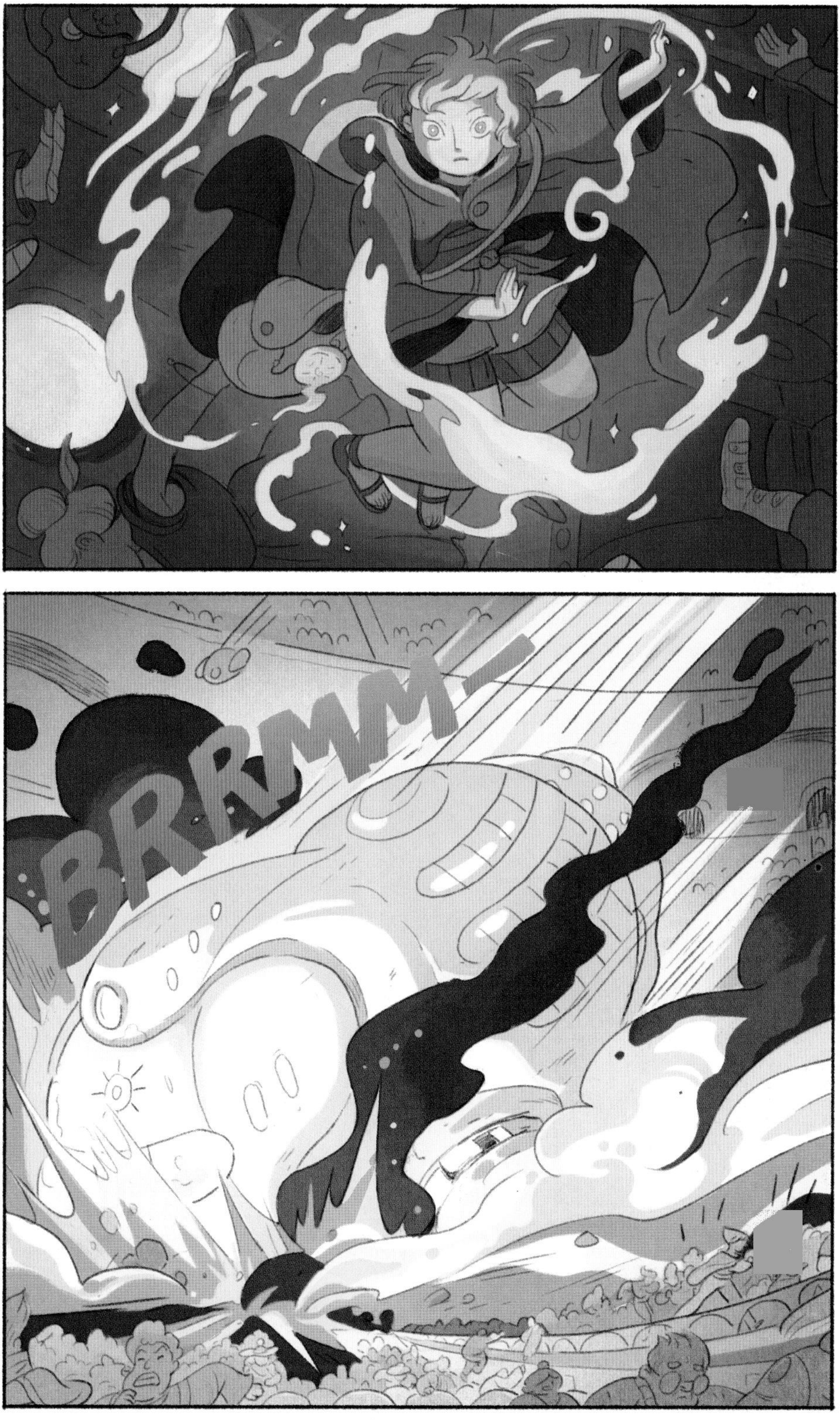
BRRMM—

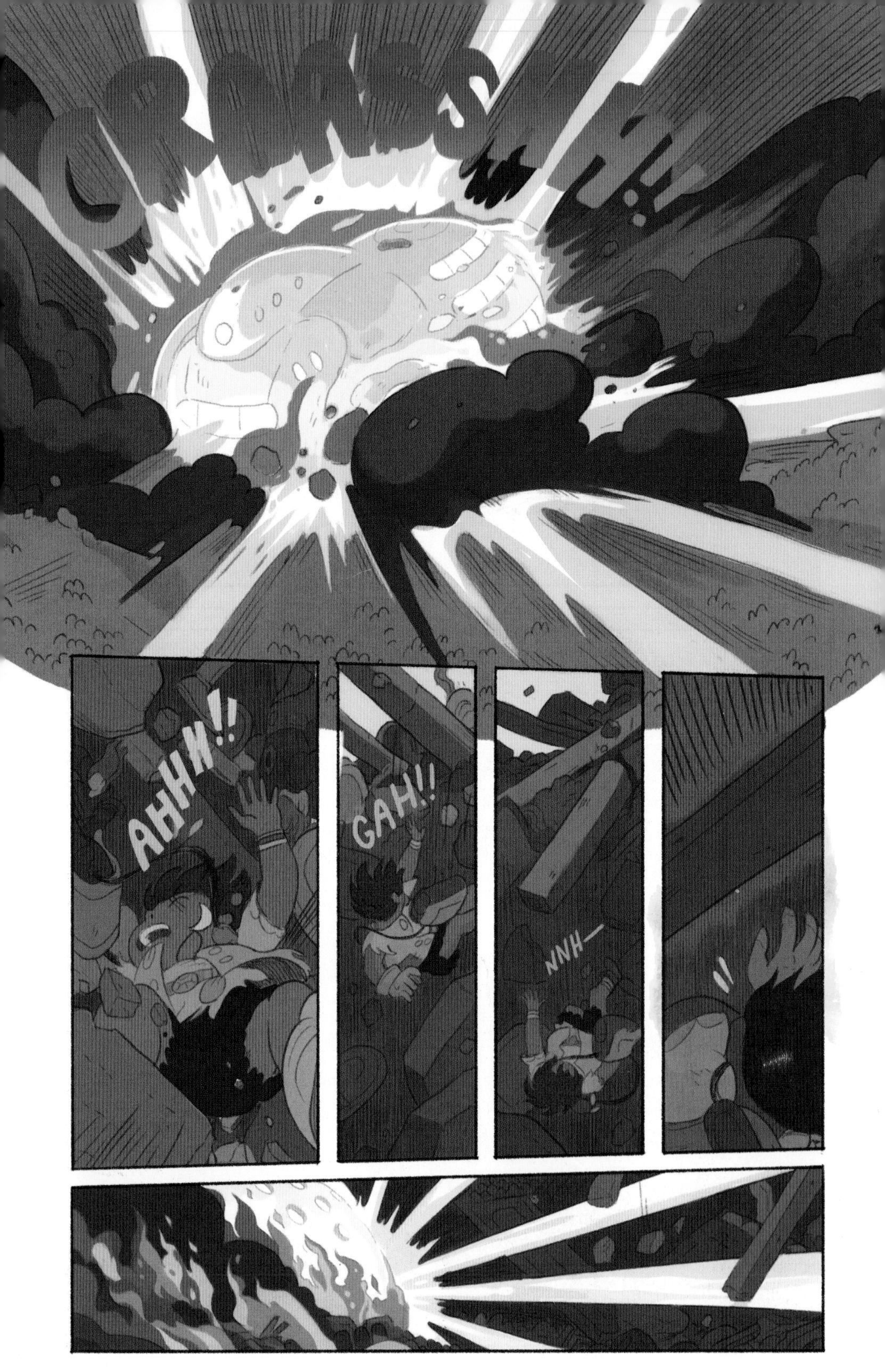
CRASH
AHHH!!
GAH!!
NNH—
!!

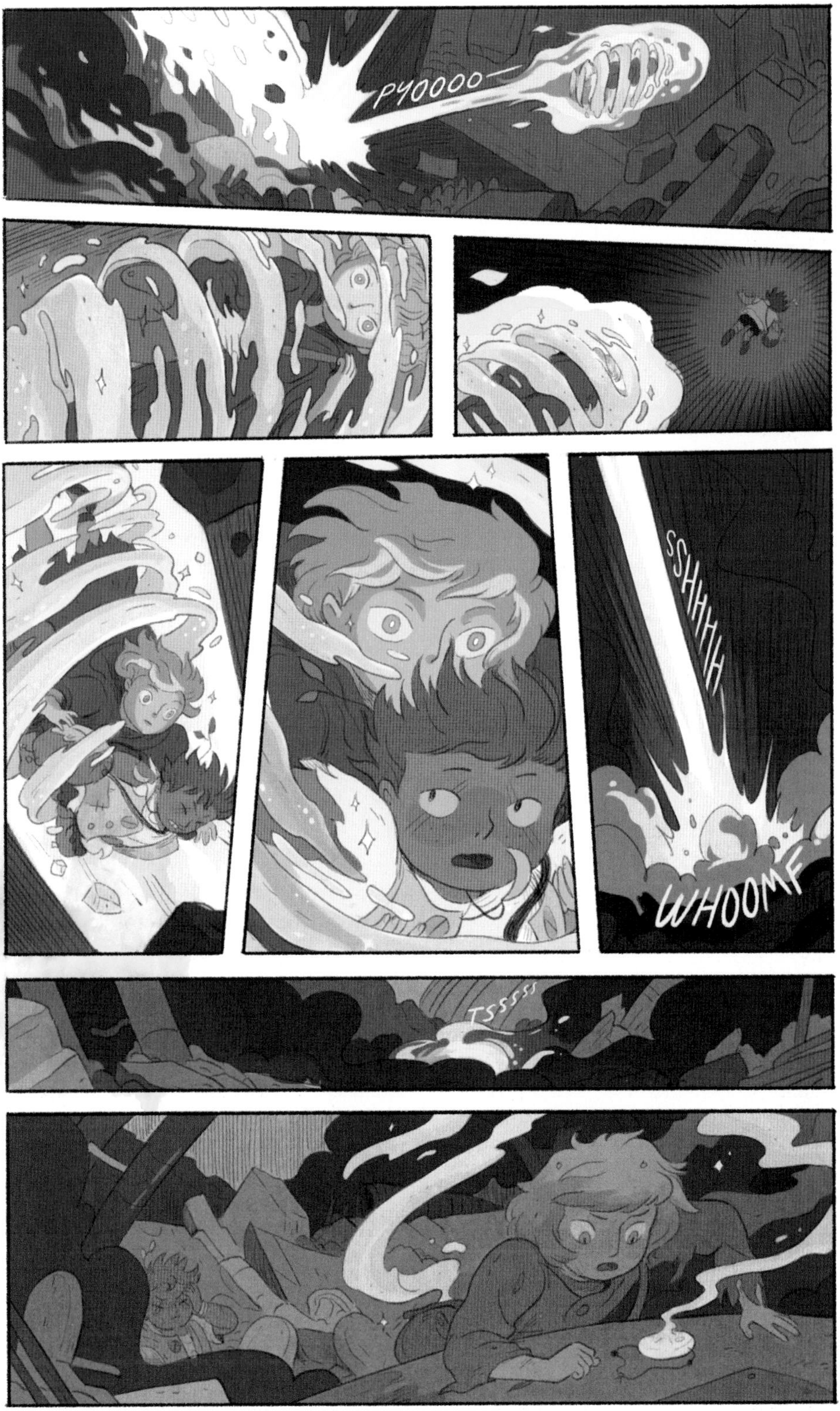
PYOOOO—
SHHHHH
WHOOMF
TSSSSS

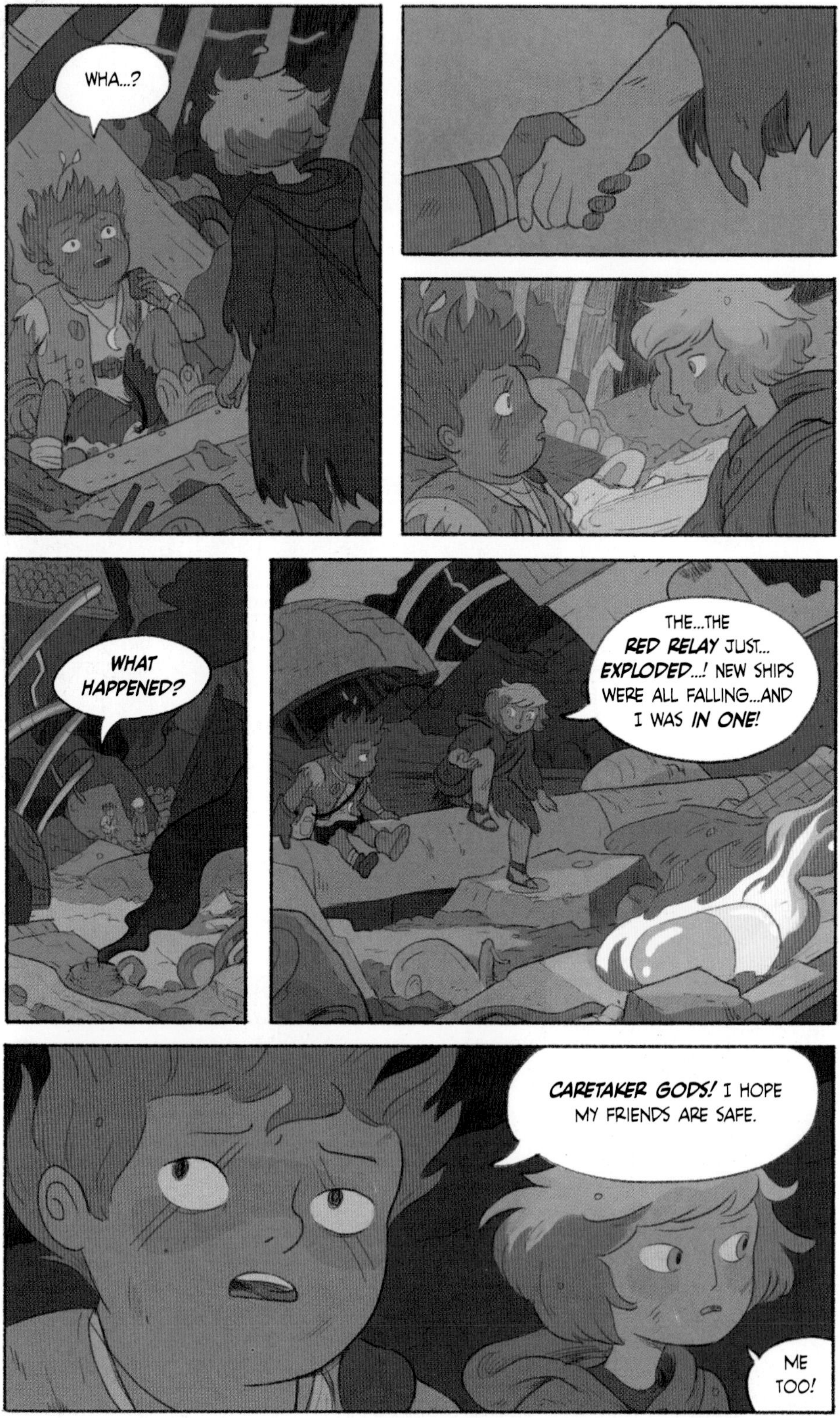
WHA...?
WHAT HAPPENED?
THE...THE RED RELAY JUST... EXPLODED...! NEW SHIPS WERE ALL FALLING...AND I WAS IN ONE!
CARETAKER GODS! I HOPE MY FRIENDS ARE SAFE.
ME TOO!

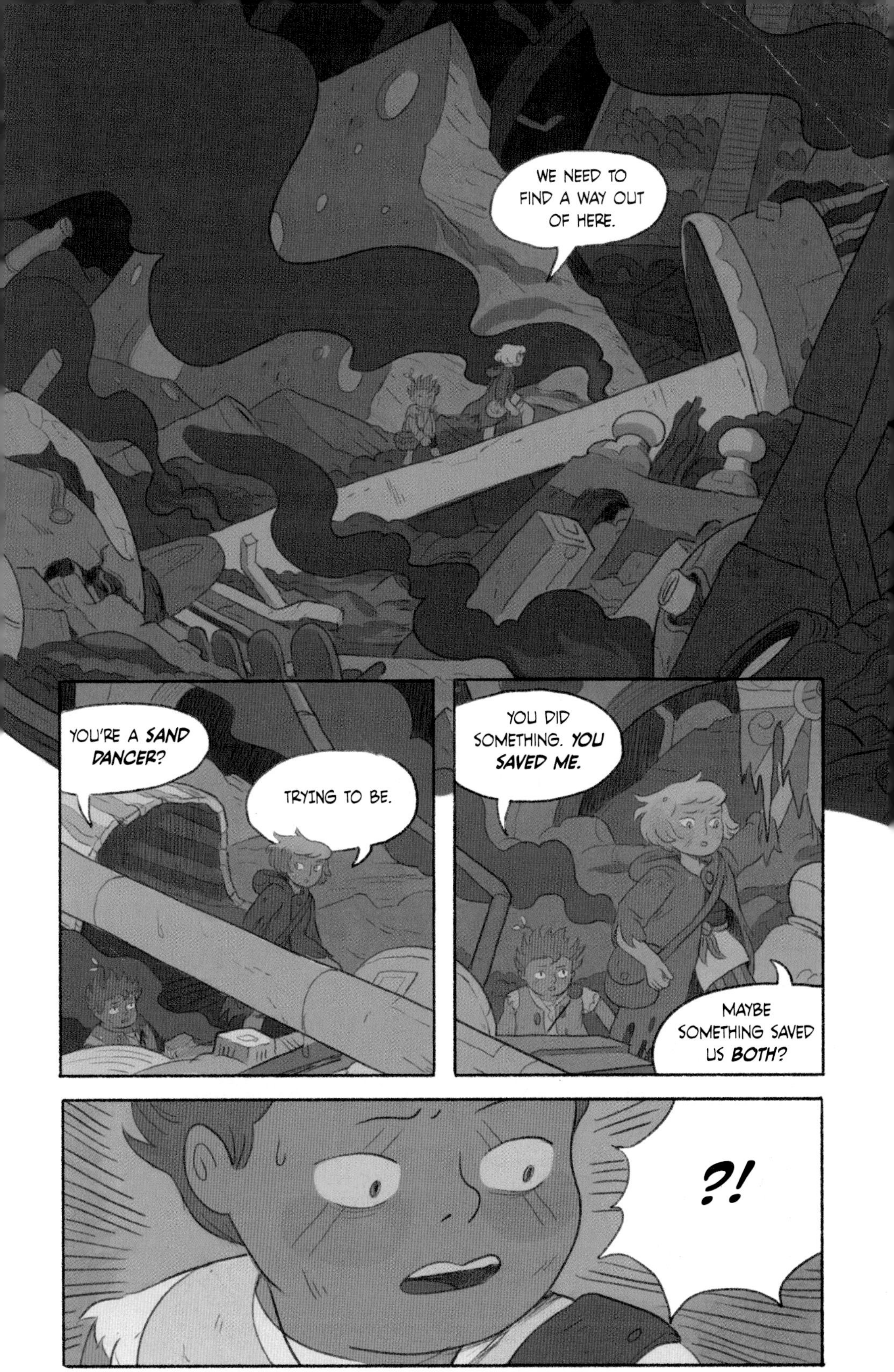
WE NEED TO FIND A WAY OUT OF HERE.
YOU'RE A SAND DANCER?
TRYING TO BE.
YOU DID SOMETHING. YOU SAVED ME.
MAYBE SOMETHING SAVED US BOTH?
?!

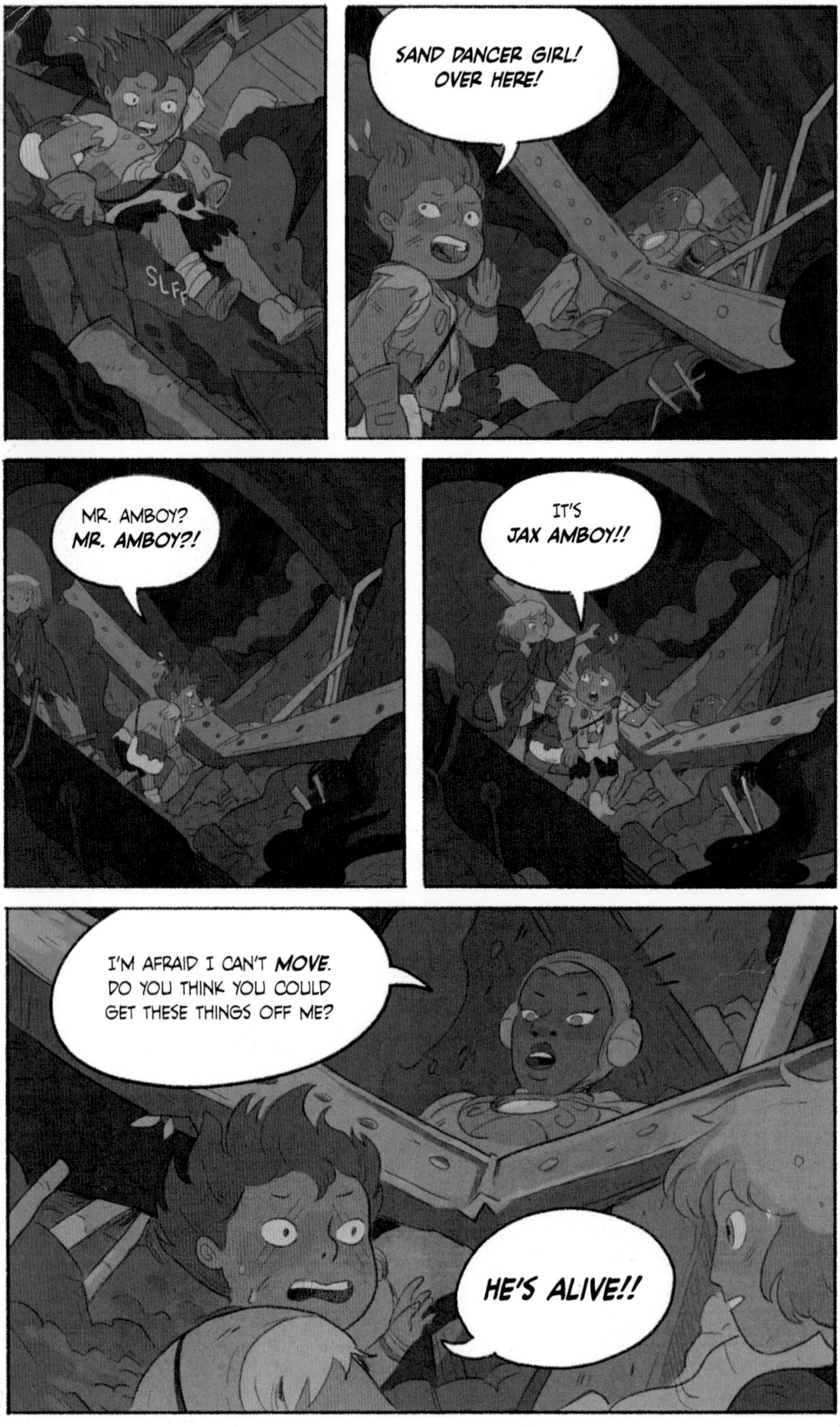
SLFF
SAND DANCER GIRL! OVER HERE!
MR. AMBOY? MR. AMBOY?!
IT'S JAX AMBOY!!
I'M AFRAID I CAN'T MOVE. DO YOU THINK YOU COULD GET THESE THINGS OFF ME?
HE'S ALIVE!!

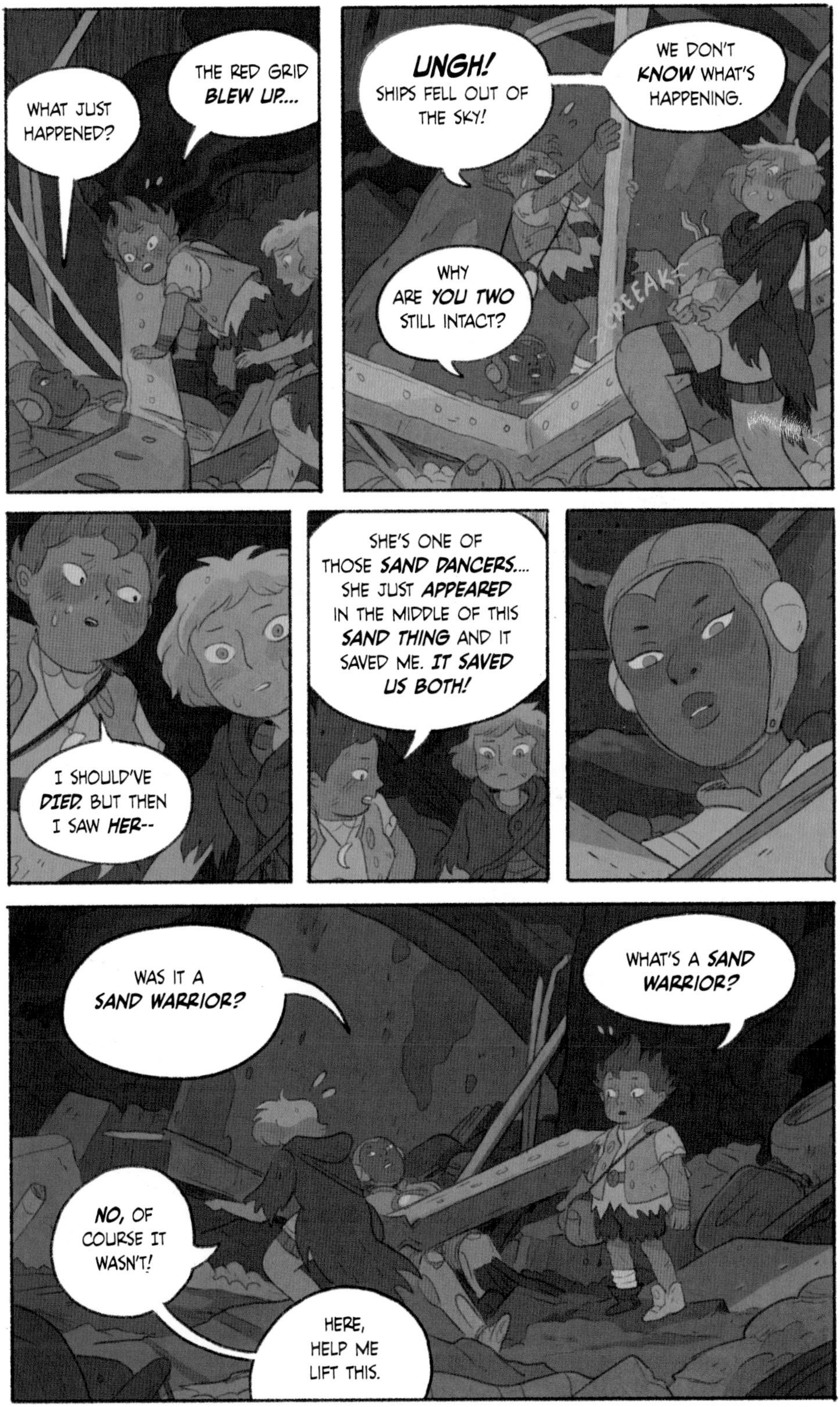
WHAT JUST HAPPENED?
THE RED GRID BLEW UP....
UNGH! SHIPS FELL OUT OF THE SKY!
WE DON'T KNOW WHAT'S HAPPENING.
WHY ARE YOU TWO STILL INTACT?
CREEAK
I SHOULD'VE DIED. BUT THEN I SAW HER--
SHE'S ONE OF THOSE SAND DANCERS.... SHE JUST APPEARED IN THE MIDDLE OF THIS SAND THING AND IT SAVED ME. IT SAVED US BOTH!
WAS IT A SAND WARRIOR?
WHAT'S A SAND WARRIOR?
NO, OF COURSE IT WASN'T!
HERE, HELP ME LIFT THIS.

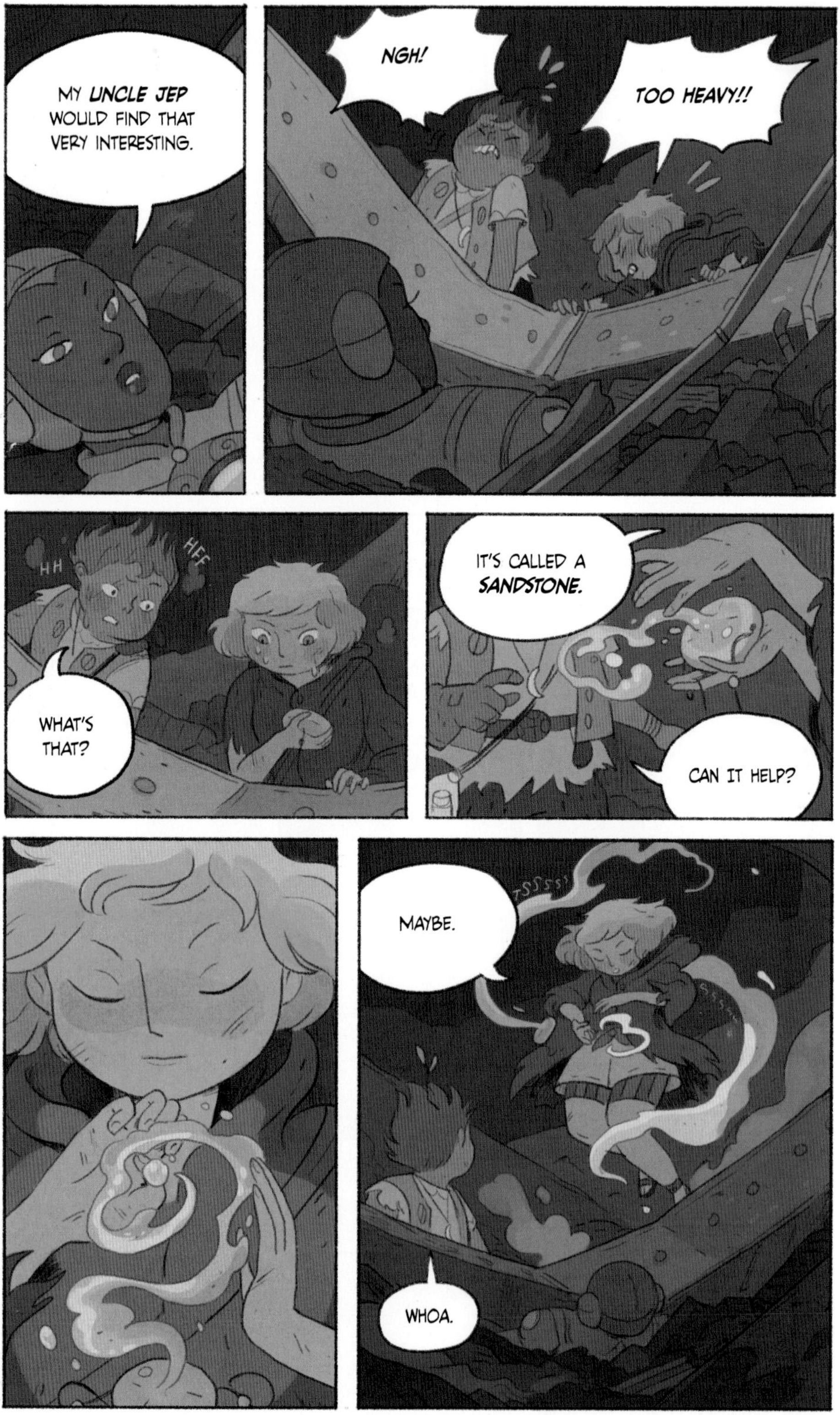

MY UNCLE JEP WOULD FIND THAT VERY INTERESTING.
NGH!
TOO HEAVY!!
HH
HFF
WHAT'S THAT?
IT'S CALLED A SANDSTONE.
CAN IT HELP?
MAYBE.
WHOA.

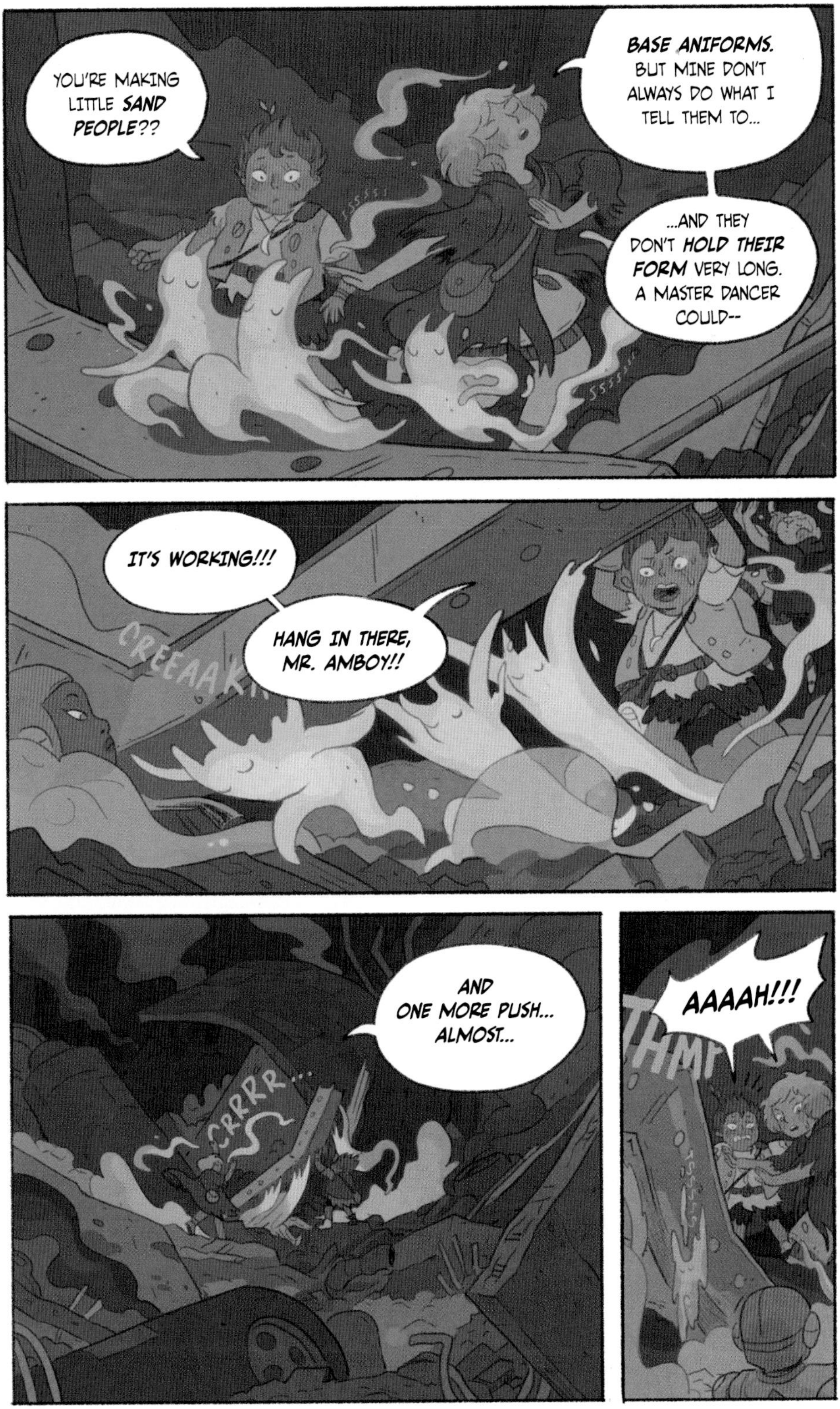
YOU'RE MAKING LITTLE SAND PEOPLE??
BASE ANIFORMS. BUT MINE DON'T ALWAYS DO WHAT I TELL THEM TO...
...AND THEY DON'T HOLD THEIR FORM VERY LONG. A MASTER DANCER COULD--
IT'S WORKING!!!
HANG IN THERE, MR. AMBOY!!
CREEAAK
AND ONE MORE PUSH... ALMOST...
CRRRR...
AAAAH!!!
THMP

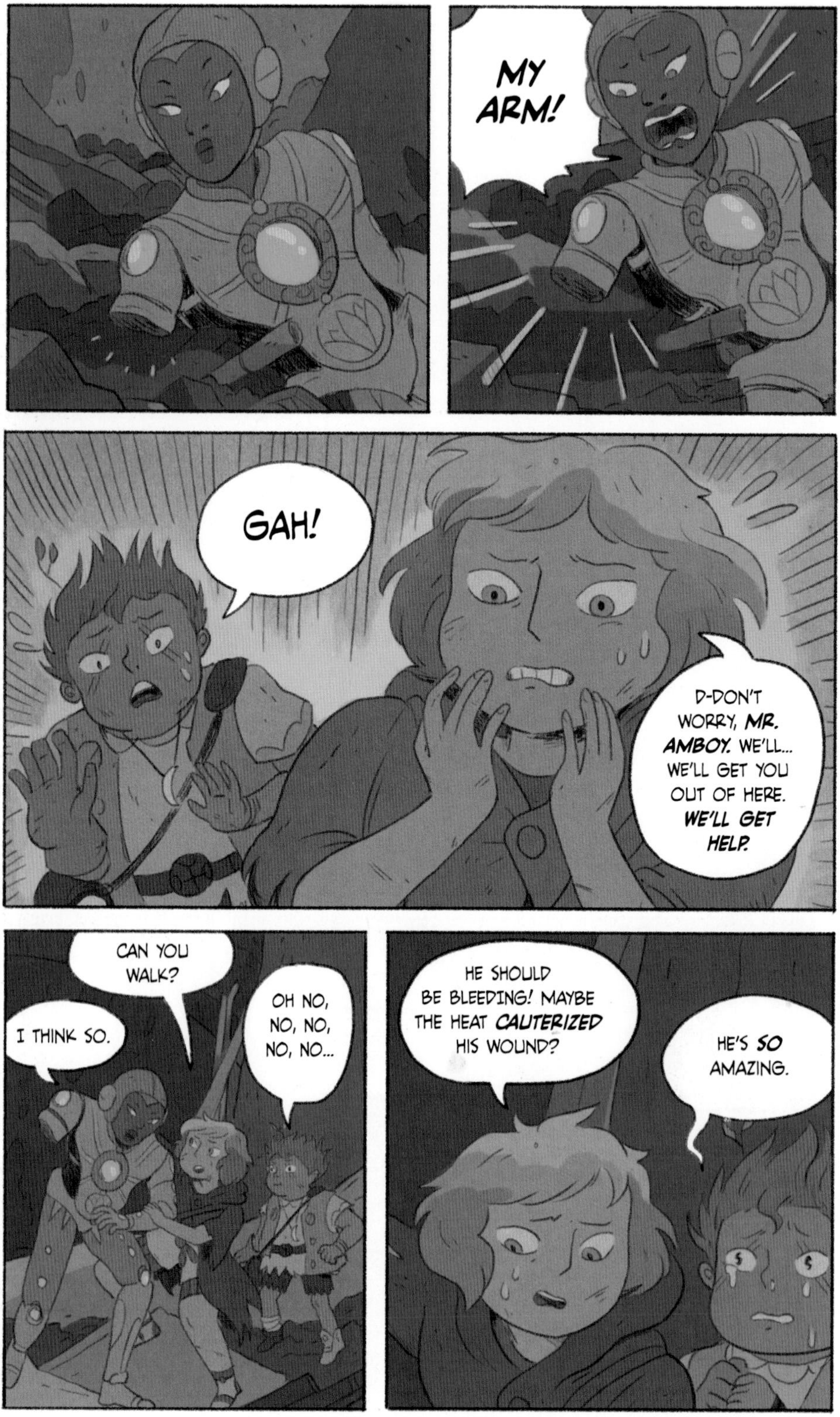

MY ARM!
GAH!
D-DON'T WORRY, **MR. AMBOY.** WE'LL... WE'LL GET YOU OUT OF HERE. ***WE'LL GET HELP.***
CAN YOU WALK?
I THINK SO.
OH NO, NO, NO, NO, NO...
HE SHOULD BE BLEEDING! MAYBE THE HEAT ***CAUTERIZED*** HIS WOUND?
HE'S ***SO*** AMAZING.

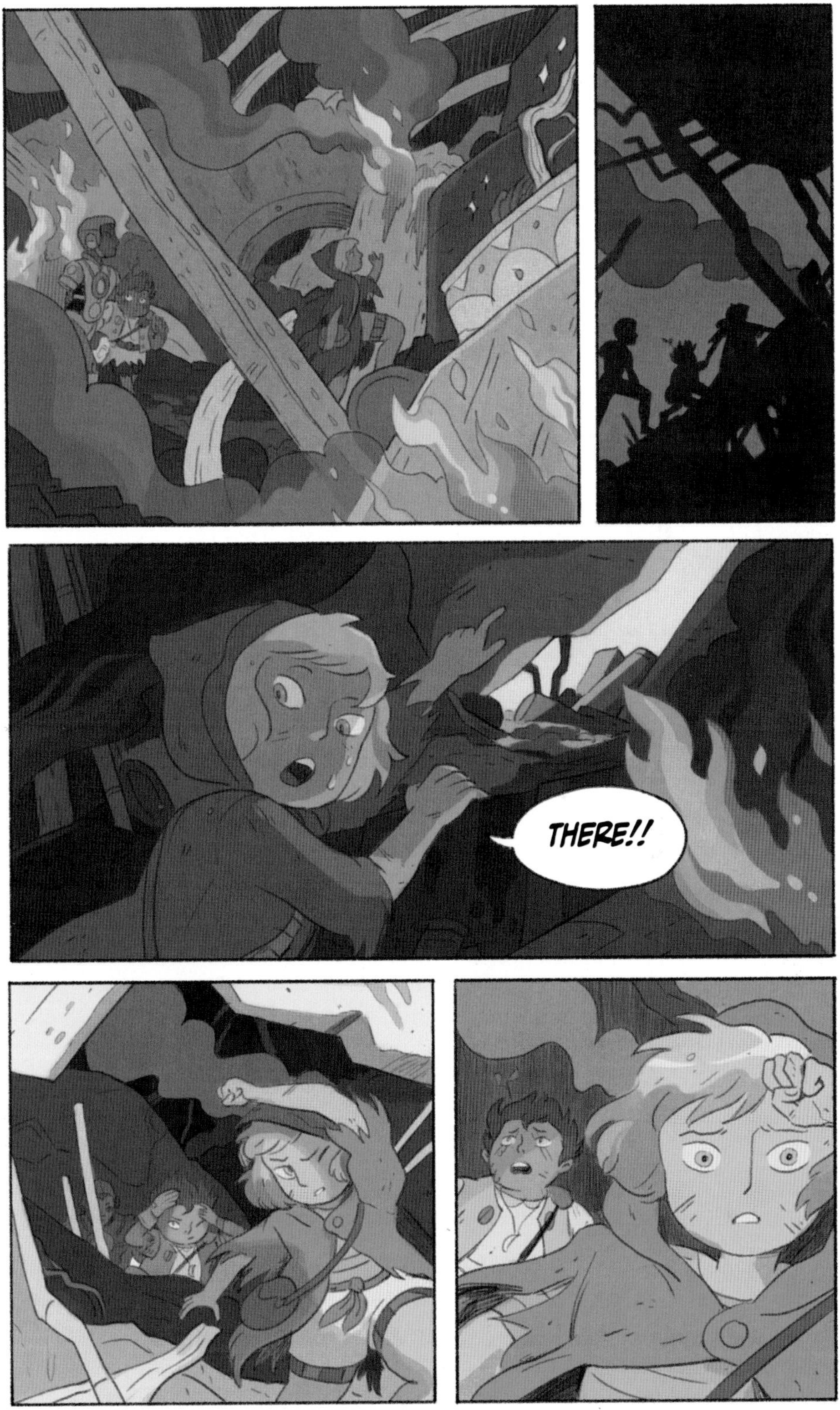
THERE!!

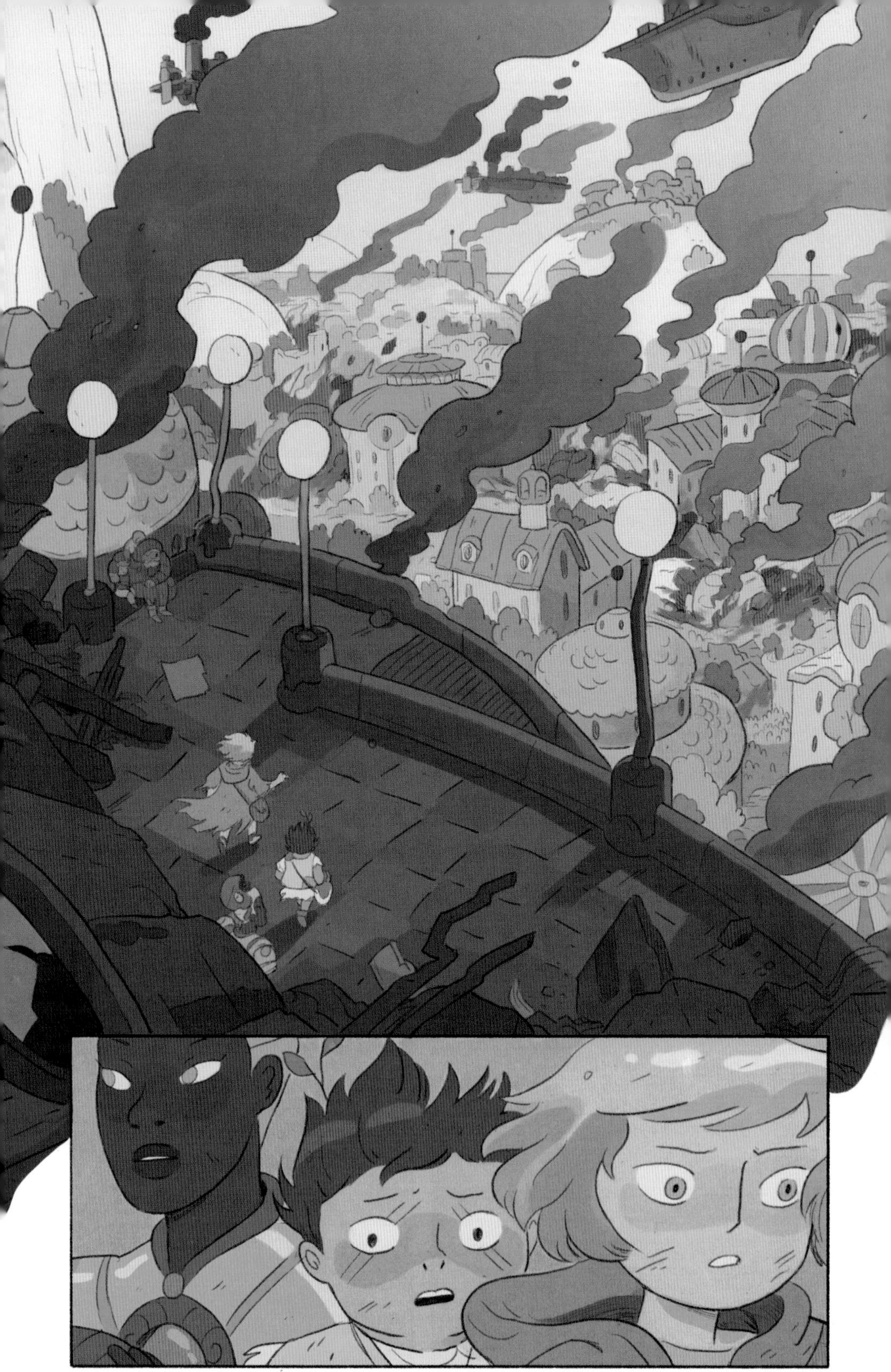

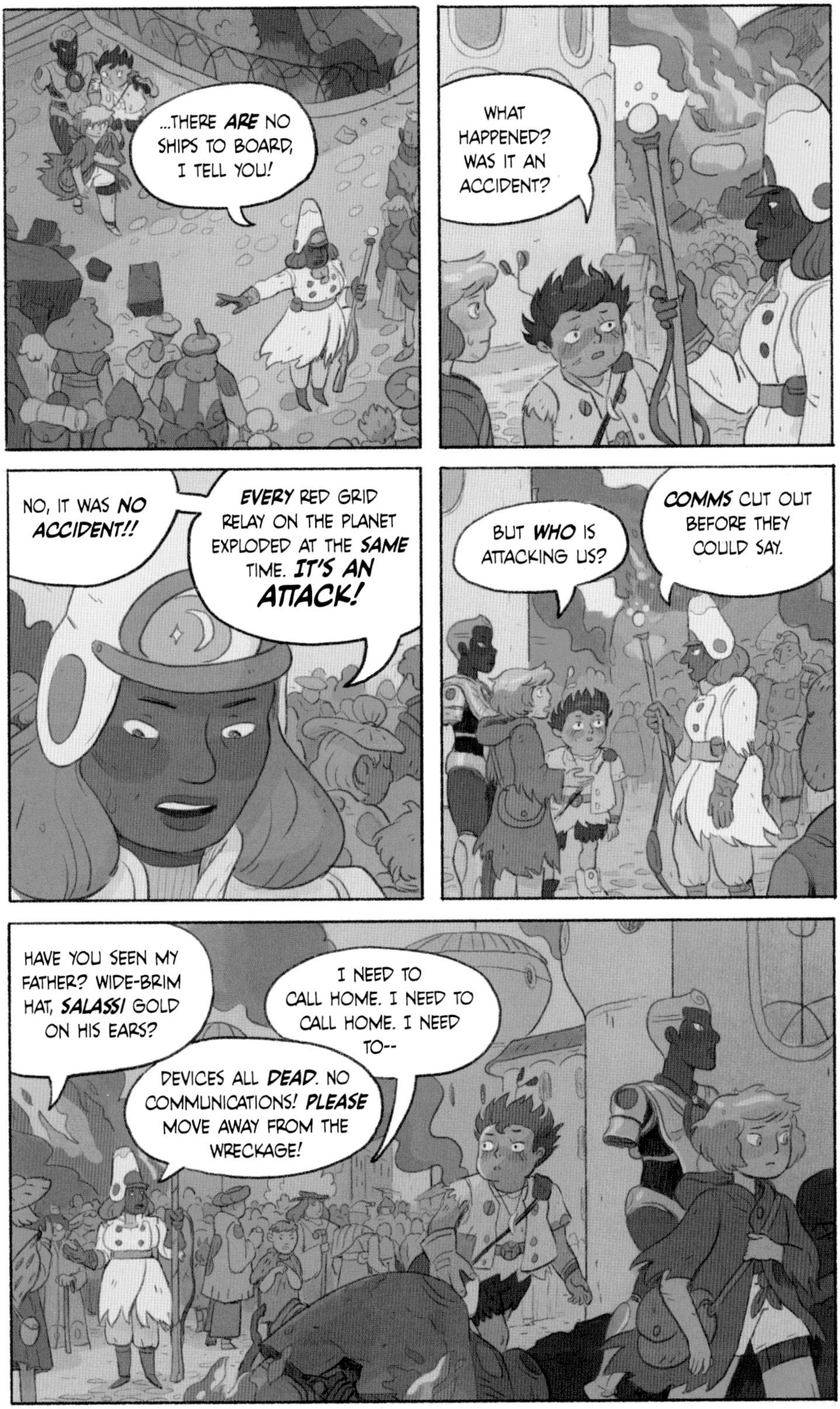
...THERE ARE NO SHIPS TO BOARD, I TELL YOU!
WHAT HAPPENED? WAS IT AN ACCIDENT?
NO, IT WAS NO ACCIDENT!!
EVERY RED GRID RELAY ON THE PLANET EXPLODED AT THE SAME TIME. IT'S AN ATTACK!
BUT WHO IS ATTACKING US?
COMMS CUT OUT BEFORE THEY COULD SAY.
HAVE YOU SEEN MY FATHER? WIDE-BRIM HAT, SALASSI GOLD ON HIS EARS?
I NEED TO CALL HOME. I NEED TO CALL HOME. I NEED TO--
DEVICES ALL DEAD. NO COMMUNICATIONS! PLEASE MOVE AWAY FROM THE WRECKAGE!

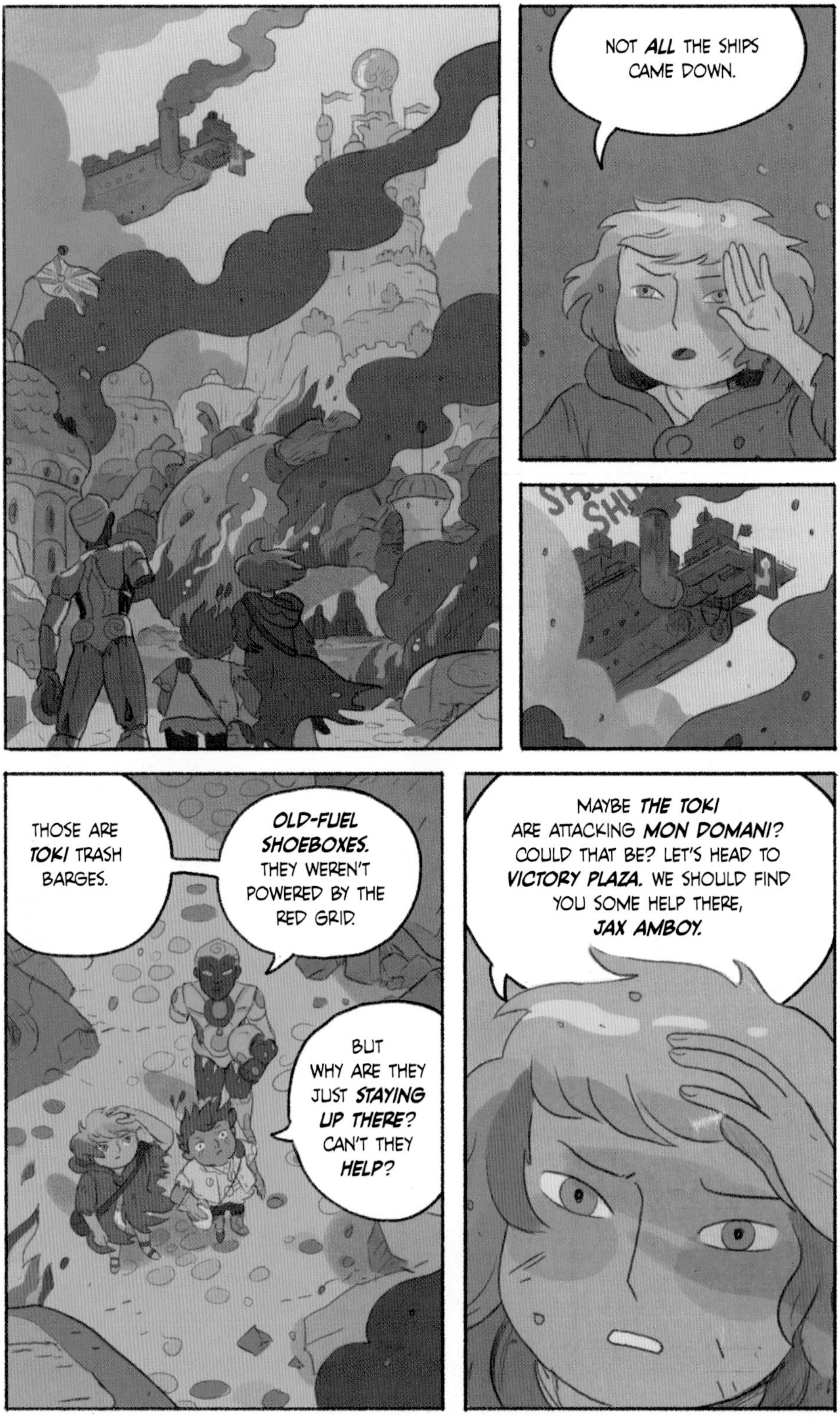
NOT ALL THE SHIPS CAME DOWN.
THOSE ARE TOKI TRASH BARGES.
OLD-FUEL SHOEBOXES. THEY WEREN'T POWERED BY THE RED GRID.
BUT WHY ARE THEY JUST STAYING UP THERE? CAN'T THEY HELP?
MAYBE THE TOKI ARE ATTACKING MON DOMANI? COULD THAT BE? LET'S HEAD TO VICTORY PLAZA. WE SHOULD FIND YOU SOME HELP THERE, JAX AMBOY.

Chapter 4

THE FALL OF THE SAND CASTLE

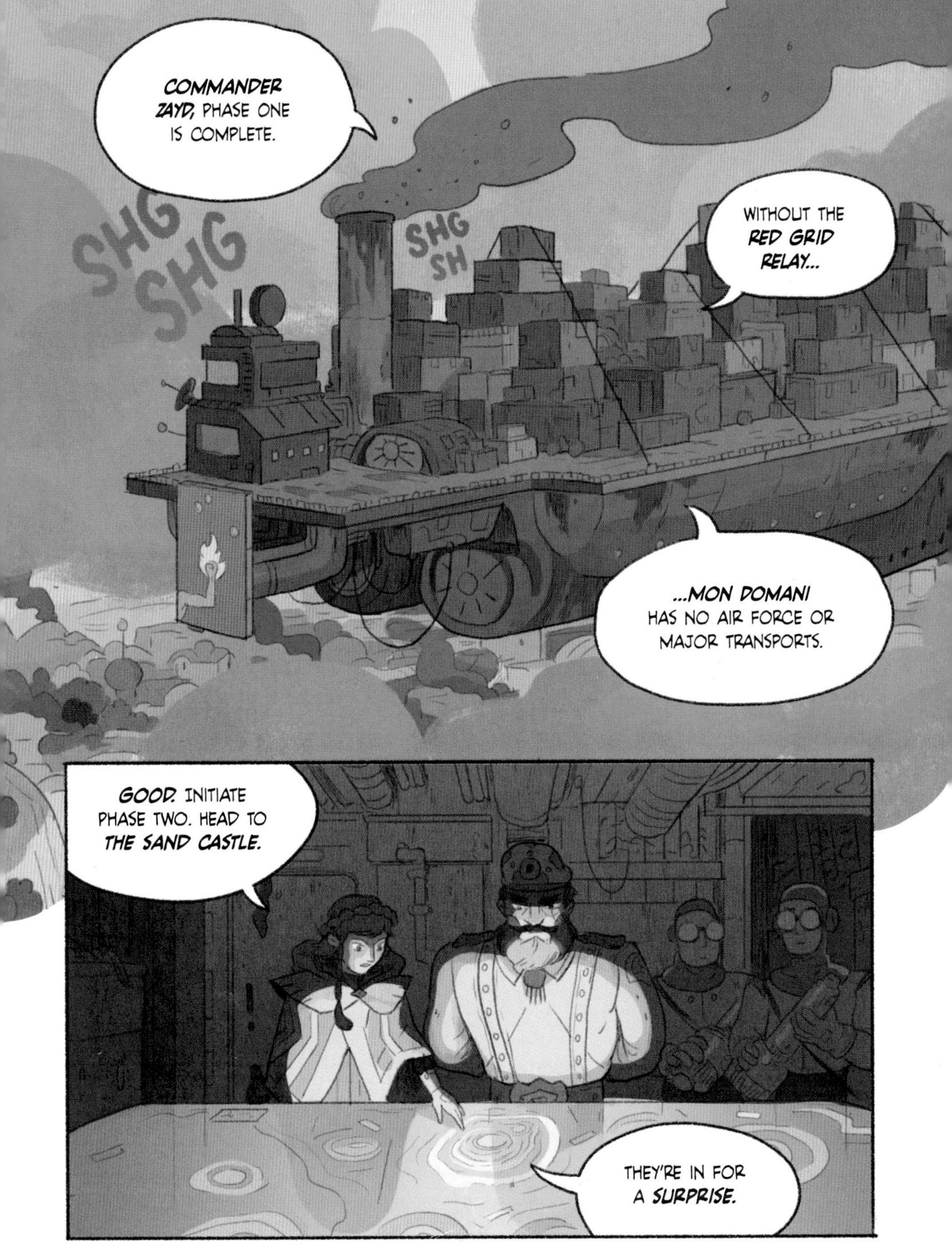
COMMANDER ZAYD, PHASE ONE IS COMPLETE.
SHG SHG
SHG SH
WITHOUT THE RED GRID RELAY...
...MON DOMANI HAS NO AIR FORCE OR MAJOR TRANSPORTS.
GOOD. INITIATE PHASE TWO. HEAD TO THE SAND CASTLE.
THEY'RE IN FOR A SURPRISE.

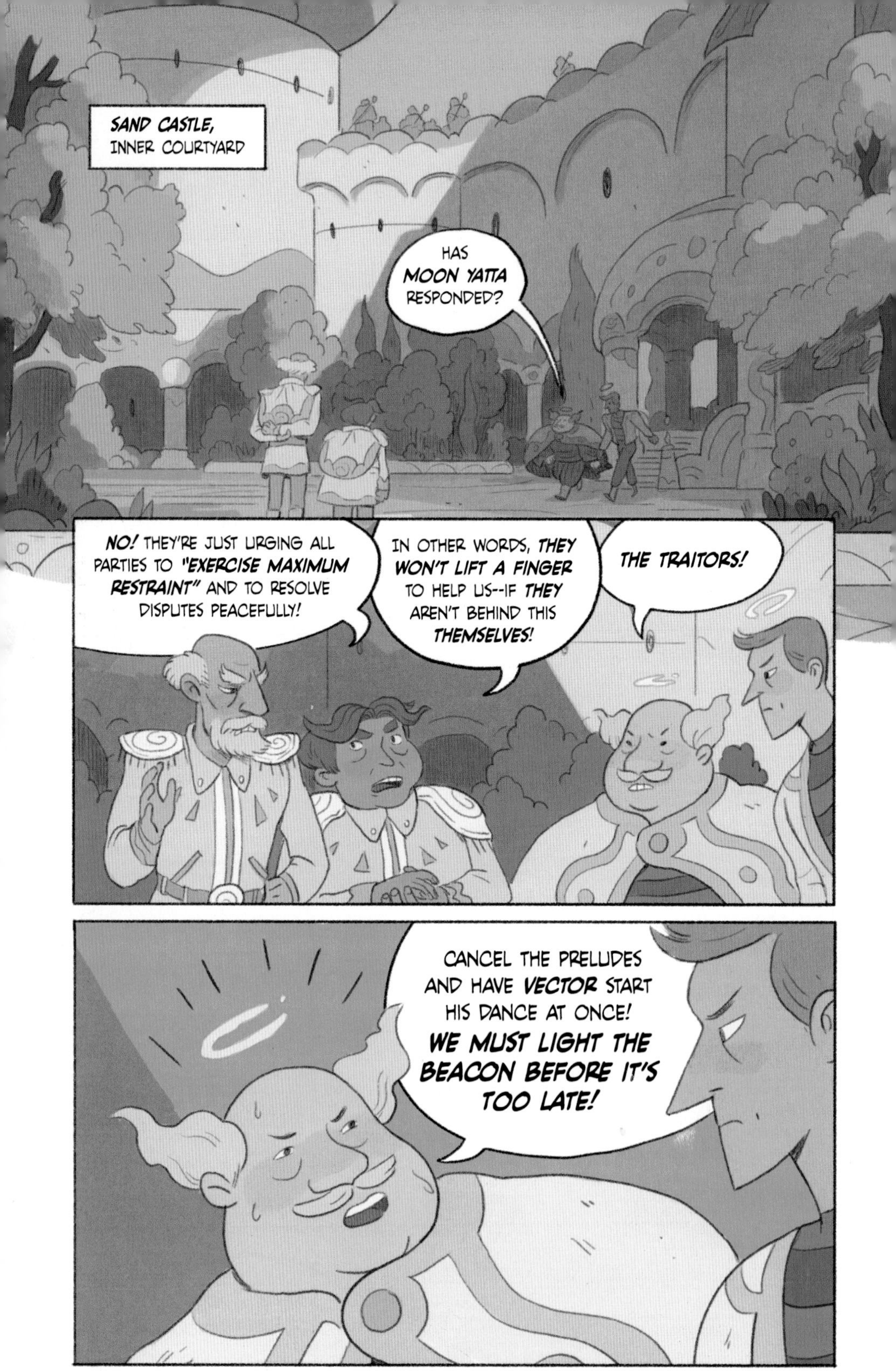
SAND CASTLE, INNER COURTYARD
HAS MOON YATTA RESPONDED?
NO! THEY'RE JUST URGING ALL PARTIES TO "EXERCISE MAXIMUM RESTRAINT" AND TO RESOLVE DISPUTES PEACEFULLY!
IN OTHER WORDS, THEY WON'T LIFT A FINGER TO HELP US--IF THEY AREN'T BEHIND THIS THEMSELVES!
THE TRAITORS!
CANCEL THE PRELUDES AND HAVE VECTOR START HIS DANCE AT ONCE!
WE MUST LIGHT THE BEACON BEFORE IT'S TOO LATE!

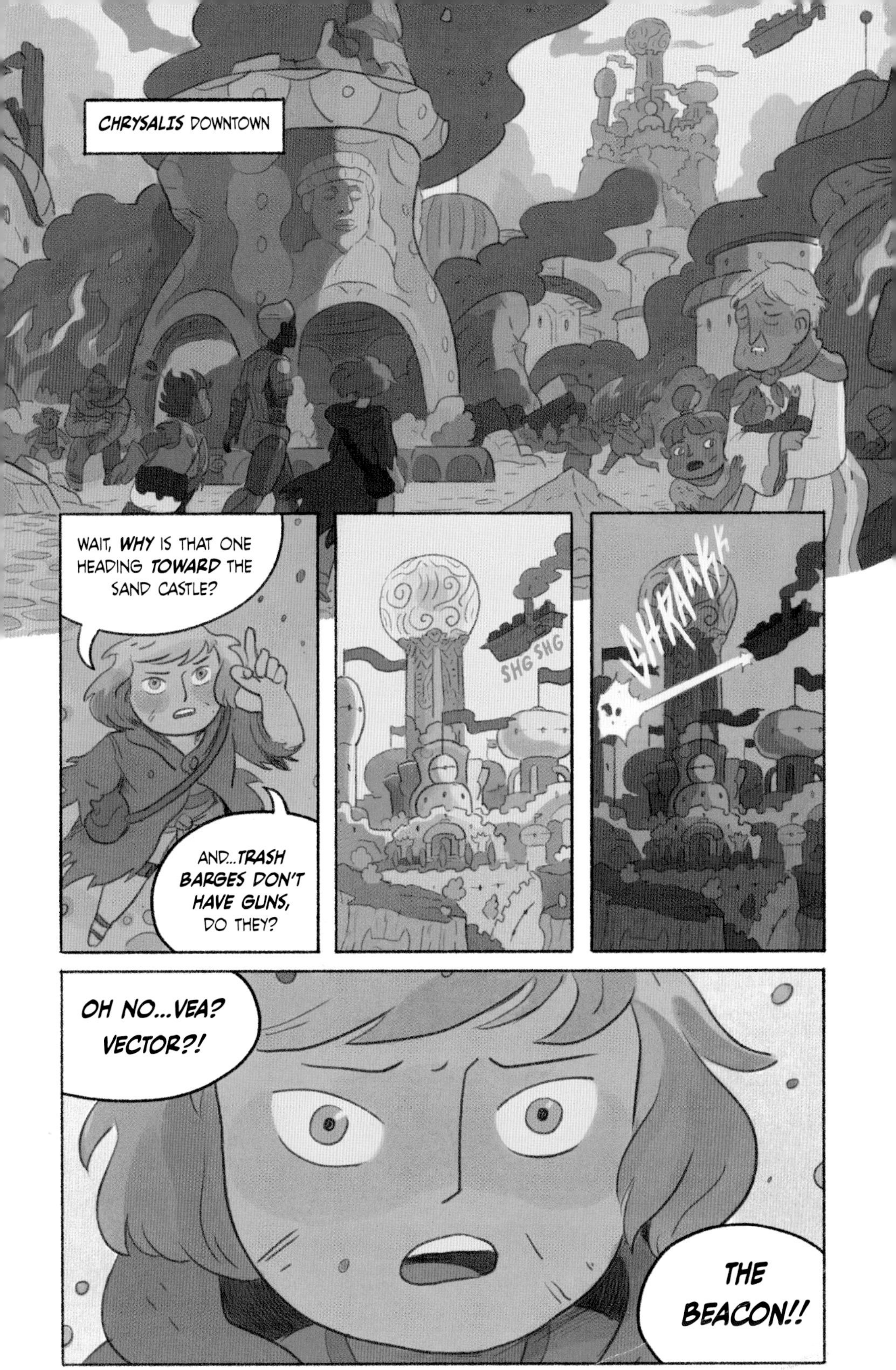
CHRYSALIS DOWNTOWN
WAIT, WHY IS THAT ONE HEADING TOWARD THE SAND CASTLE?
AND...TRASH BARGES DON'T HAVE GUNS, DO THEY?
SHG SHG
SHRAAKK
OH NO...VEA? VECTOR?!
THE BEACON!!

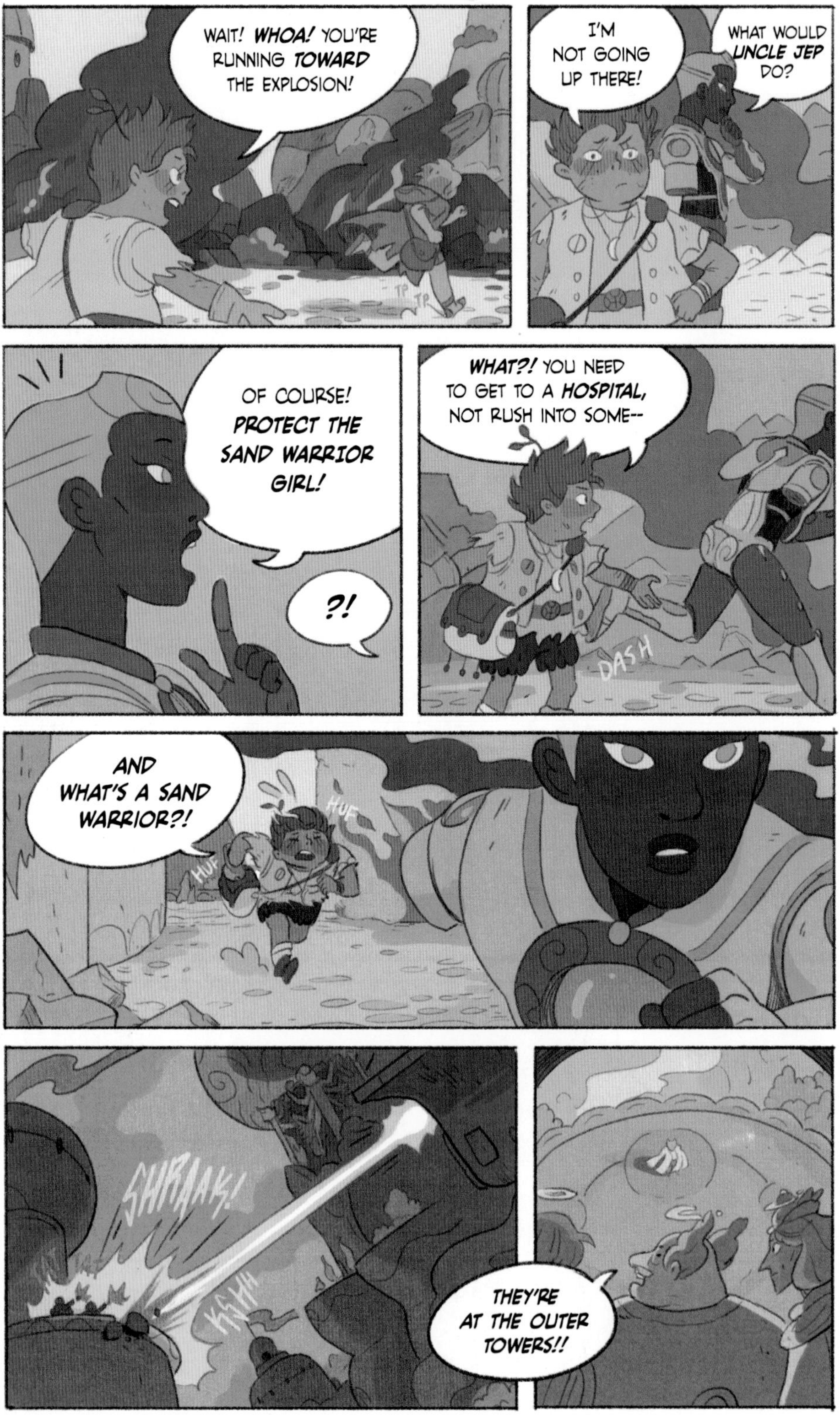
WAIT! WHOA! YOU'RE RUNNING TOWARD THE EXPLOSION!
TP TP
I'M NOT GOING UP THERE!
WHAT WOULD UNCLE JEP DO?
OF COURSE! PROTECT THE SAND WARRIOR GIRL!
?!
WHAT?! YOU NEED TO GET TO A HOSPITAL, NOT RUSH INTO SOME--
DASH
AND WHAT'S A SAND WARRIOR?!
HUF
HUF
SHRAAK!
KSHH
THEY'RE AT THE OUTER TOWERS!!

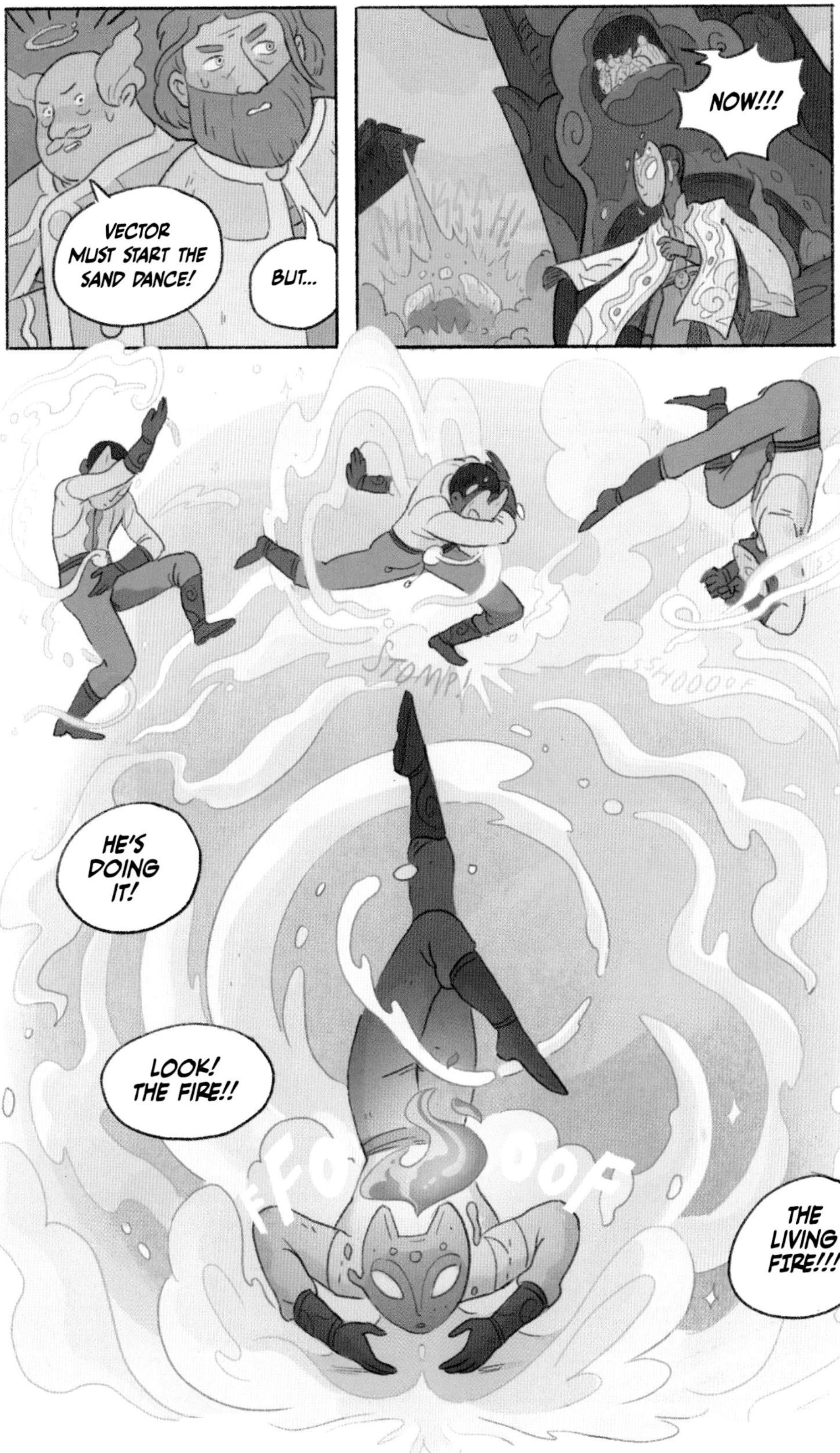
VECTOR MUST START THE SAND DANCE!
BUT...
NOW!!!
STOMP!
HE'S DOING IT!
LOOK! THE FIRE!!
THE LIVING FIRE!!!

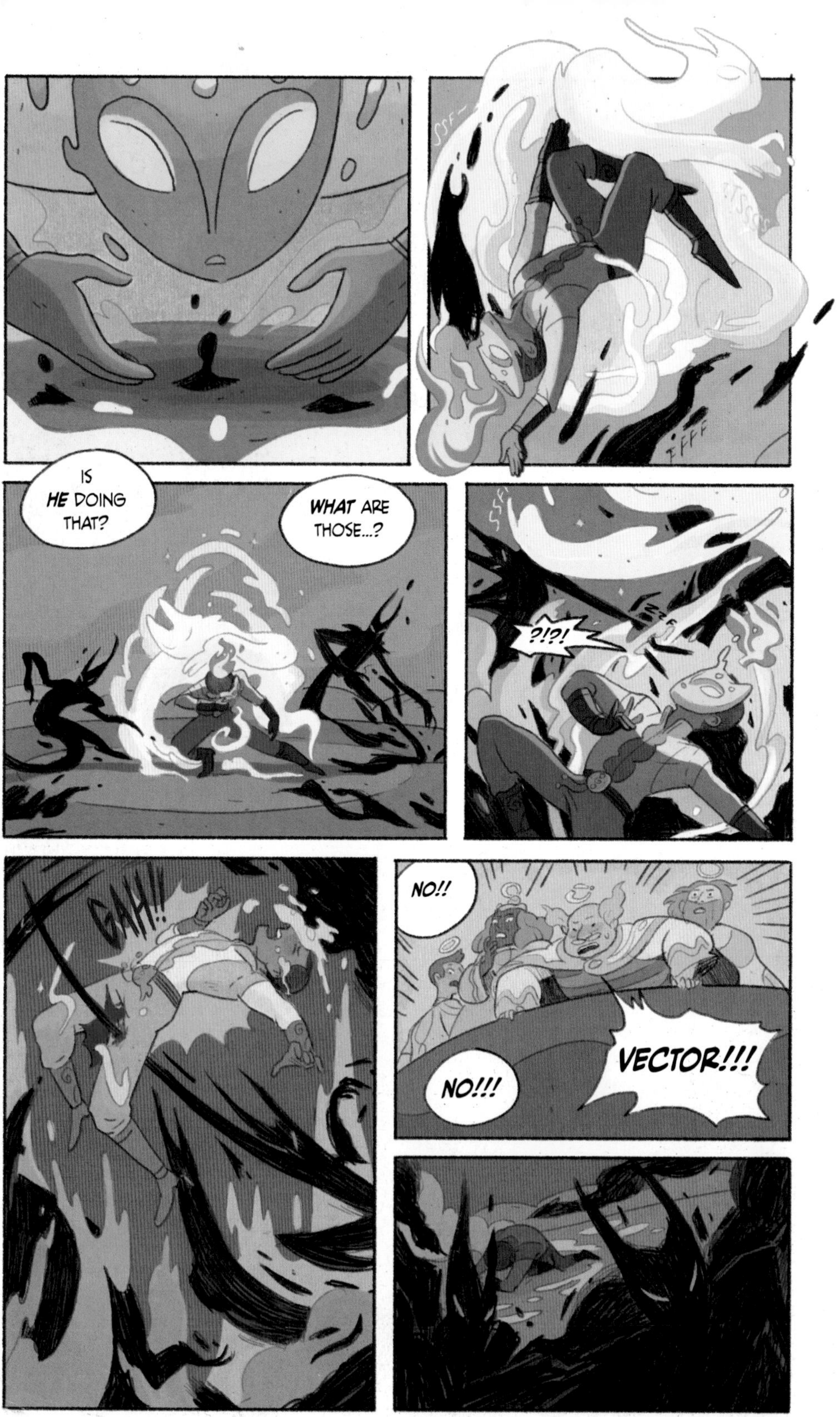
SSF–
TSSSS
FFFF
IS HE DOING THAT?
WHAT ARE THOSE...?
SSF
?!?!
GAH!!
NO!!
VECTOR!!!
NO!!!

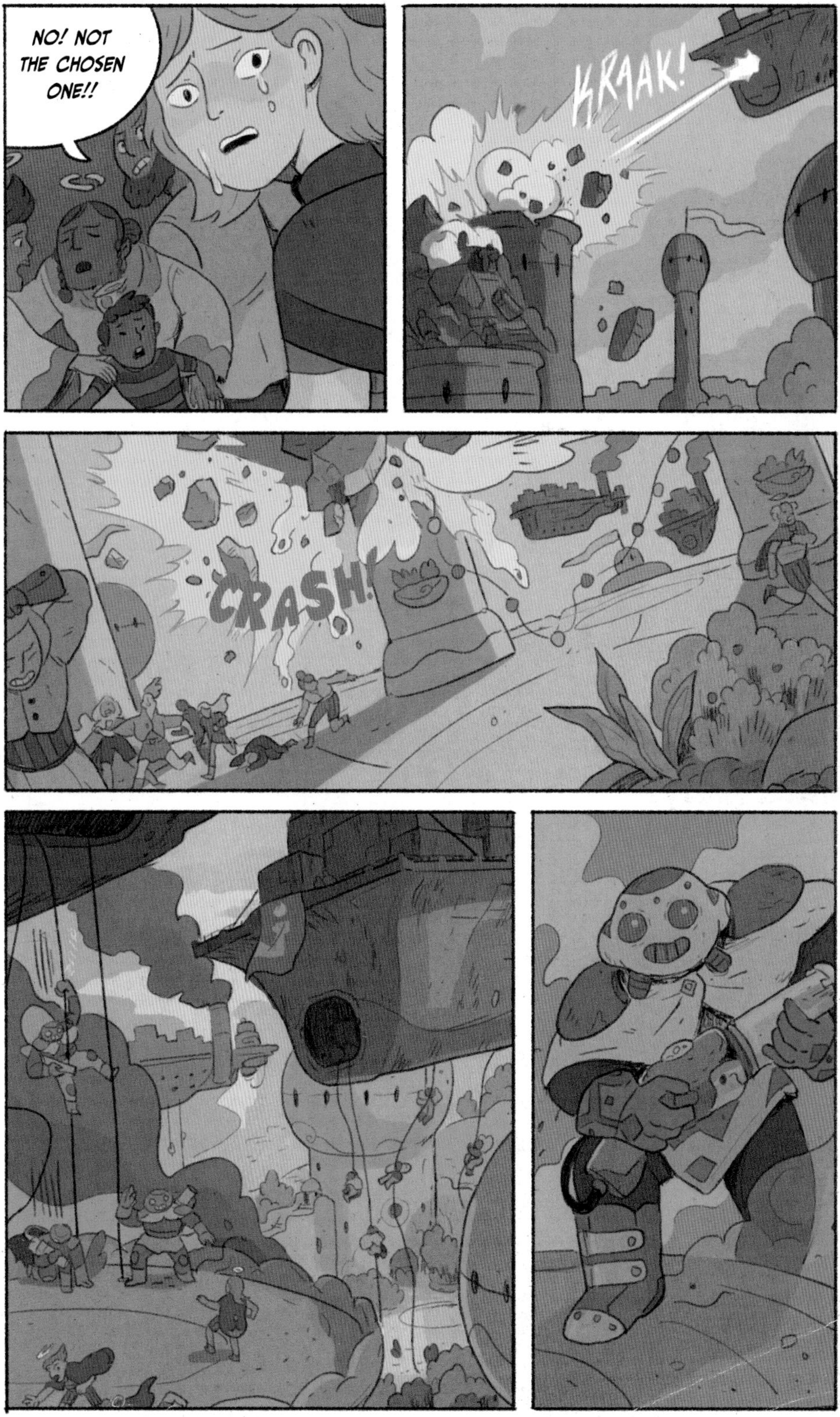
NO! NOT THE CHOSEN ONE!!
KRAAK!
CRASH!

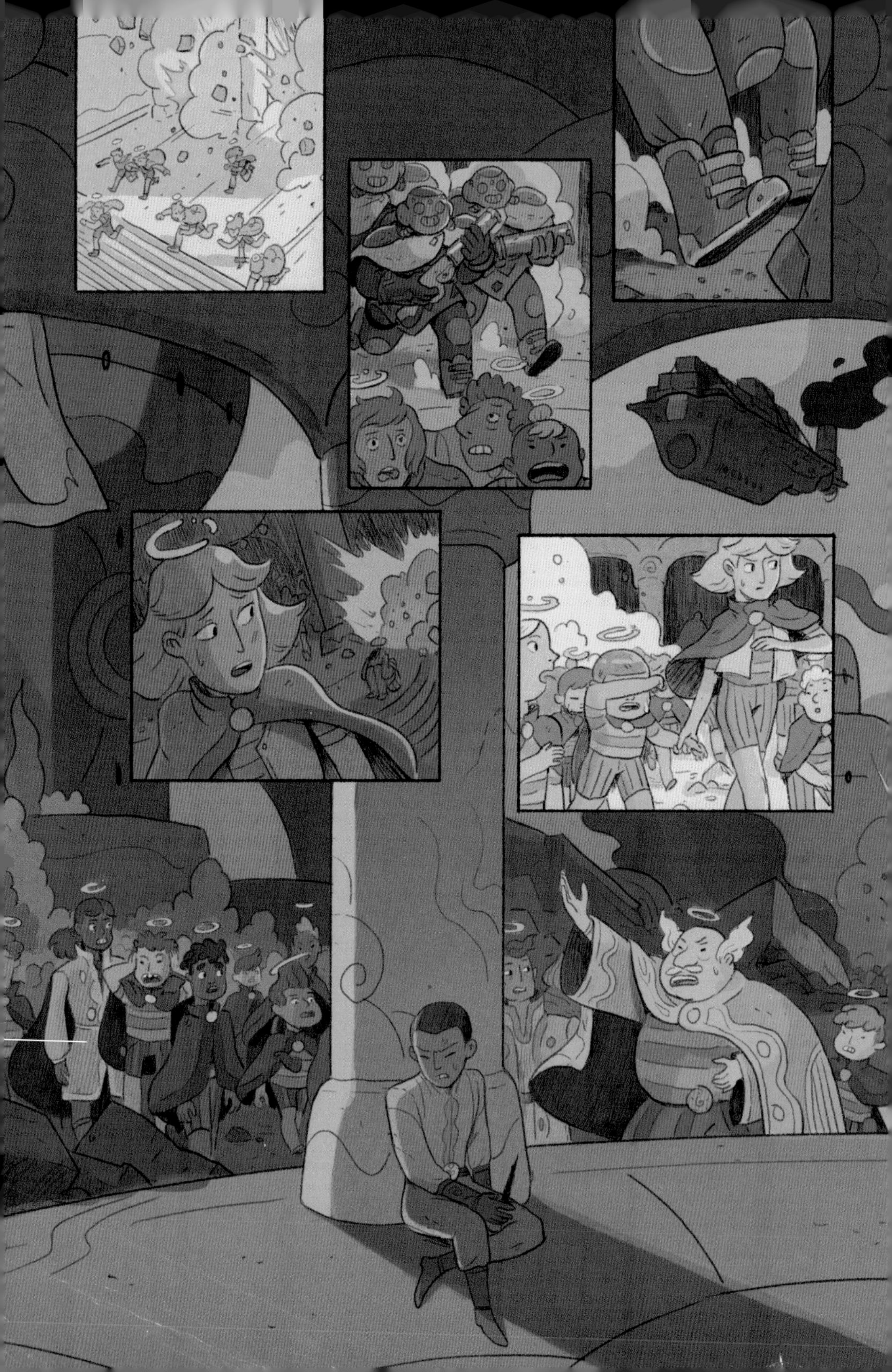

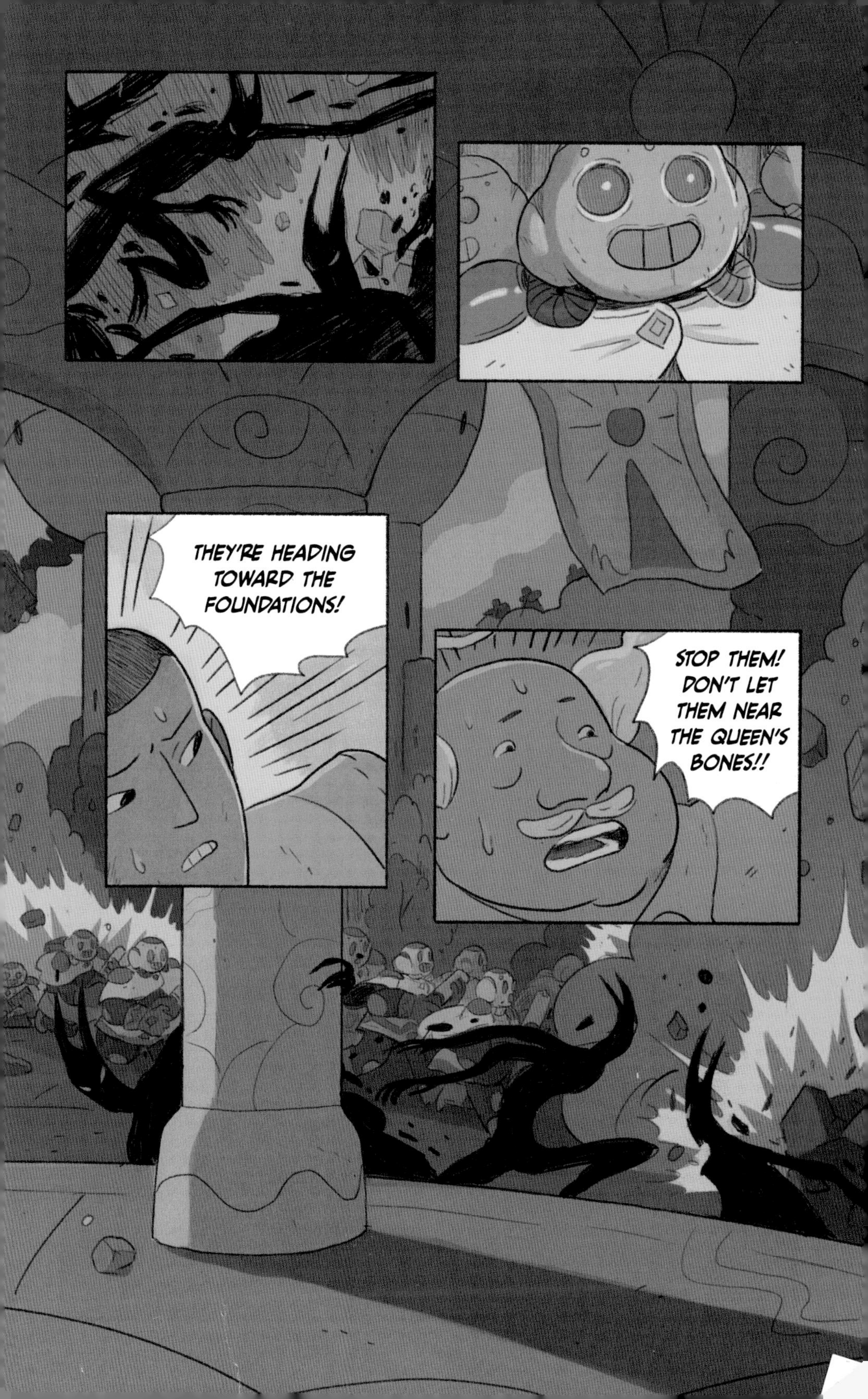
THEY'RE HEADING TOWARD THE FOUNDATIONS!
STOP THEM! DON'T LET THEM NEAR THE QUEEN'S BONES!!

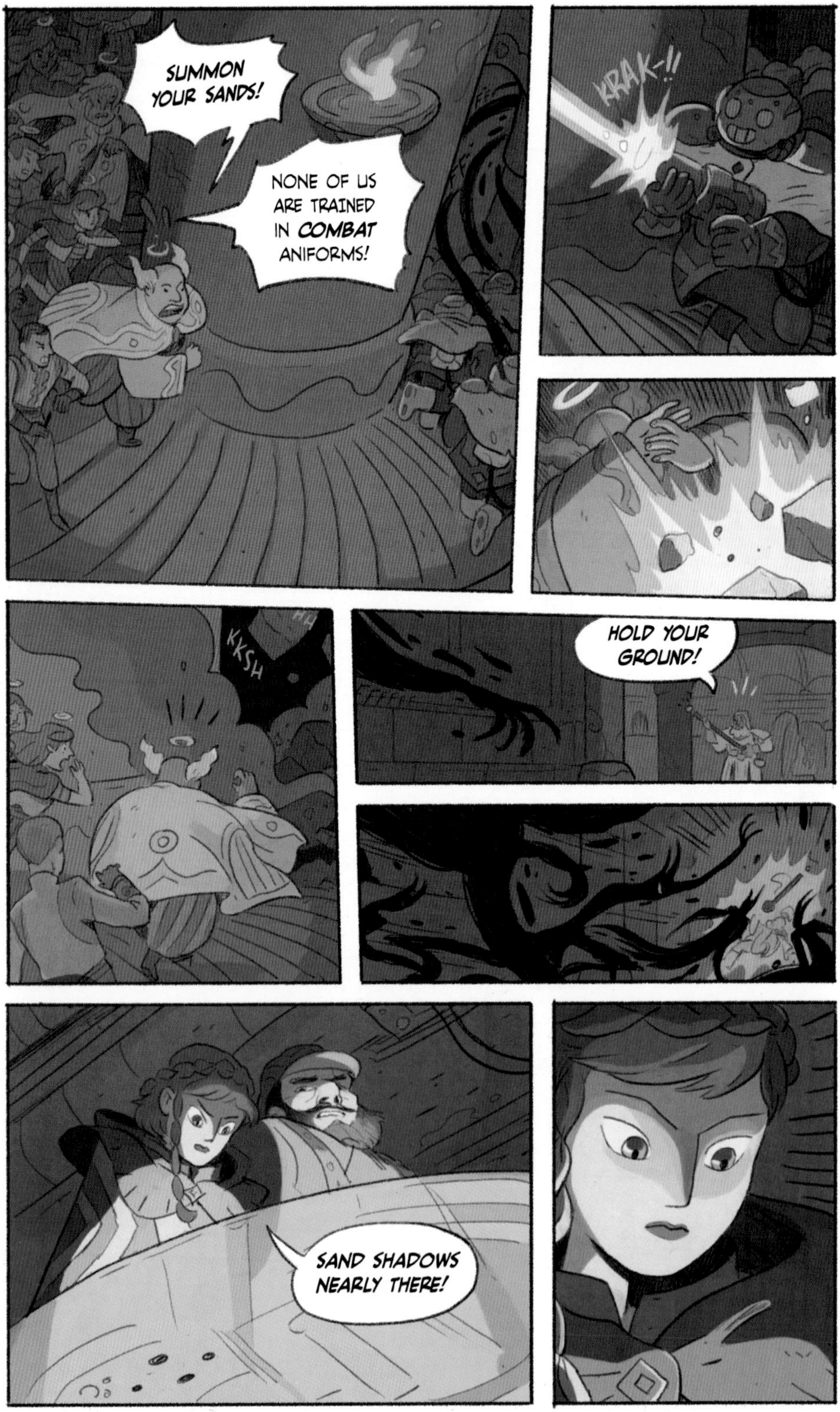
SUMMON YOUR SANDS!
NONE OF US ARE TRAINED IN COMBAT ANIFORMS!
KRAK-!!
KKSH
HOLD YOUR GROUND!
SAND SHADOWS NEARLY THERE!

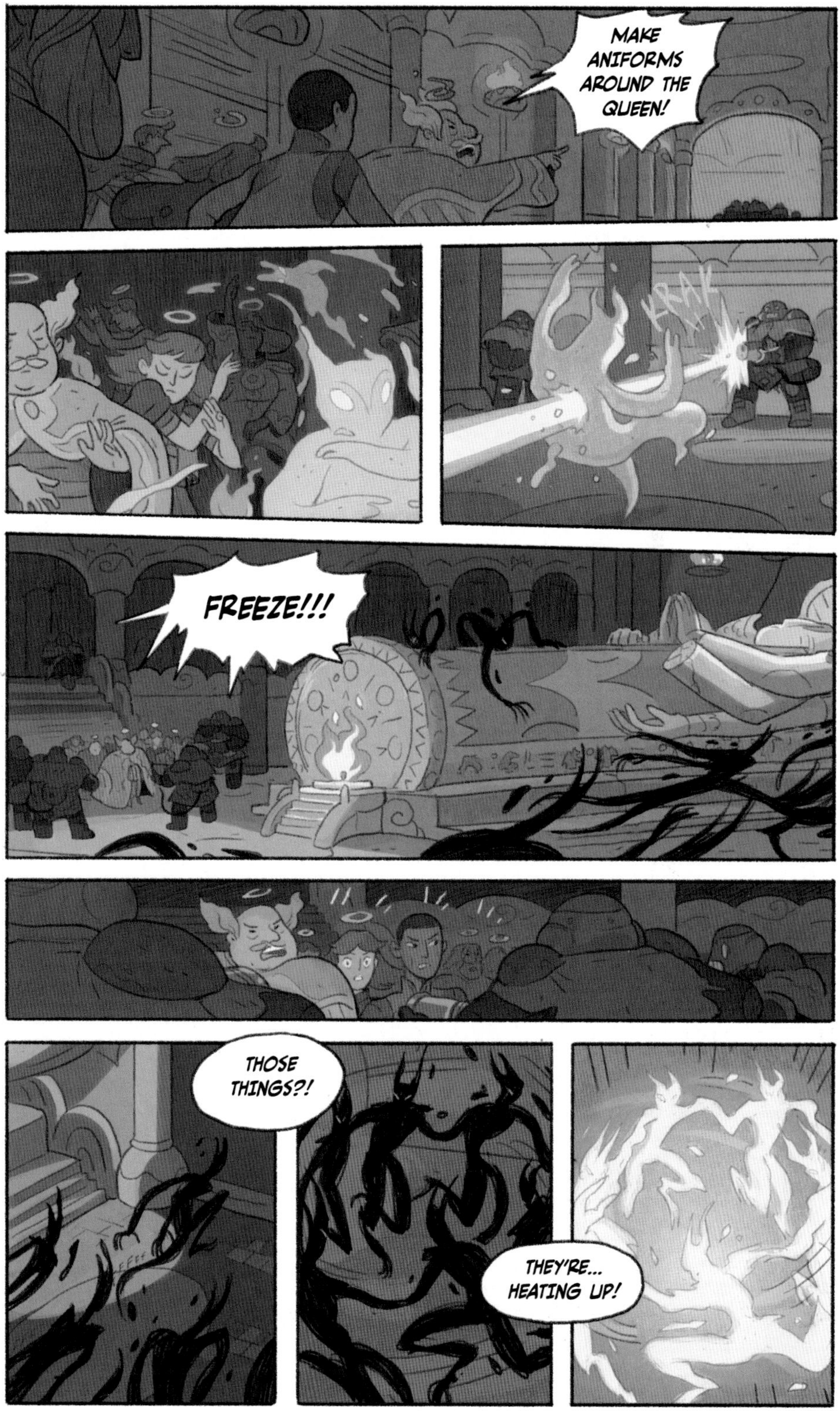
MAKE ANIFORMS AROUND THE QUEEN!
KRAK
FREEZE!!!
THOSE THINGS?!
THEY'RE... HEATING UP!

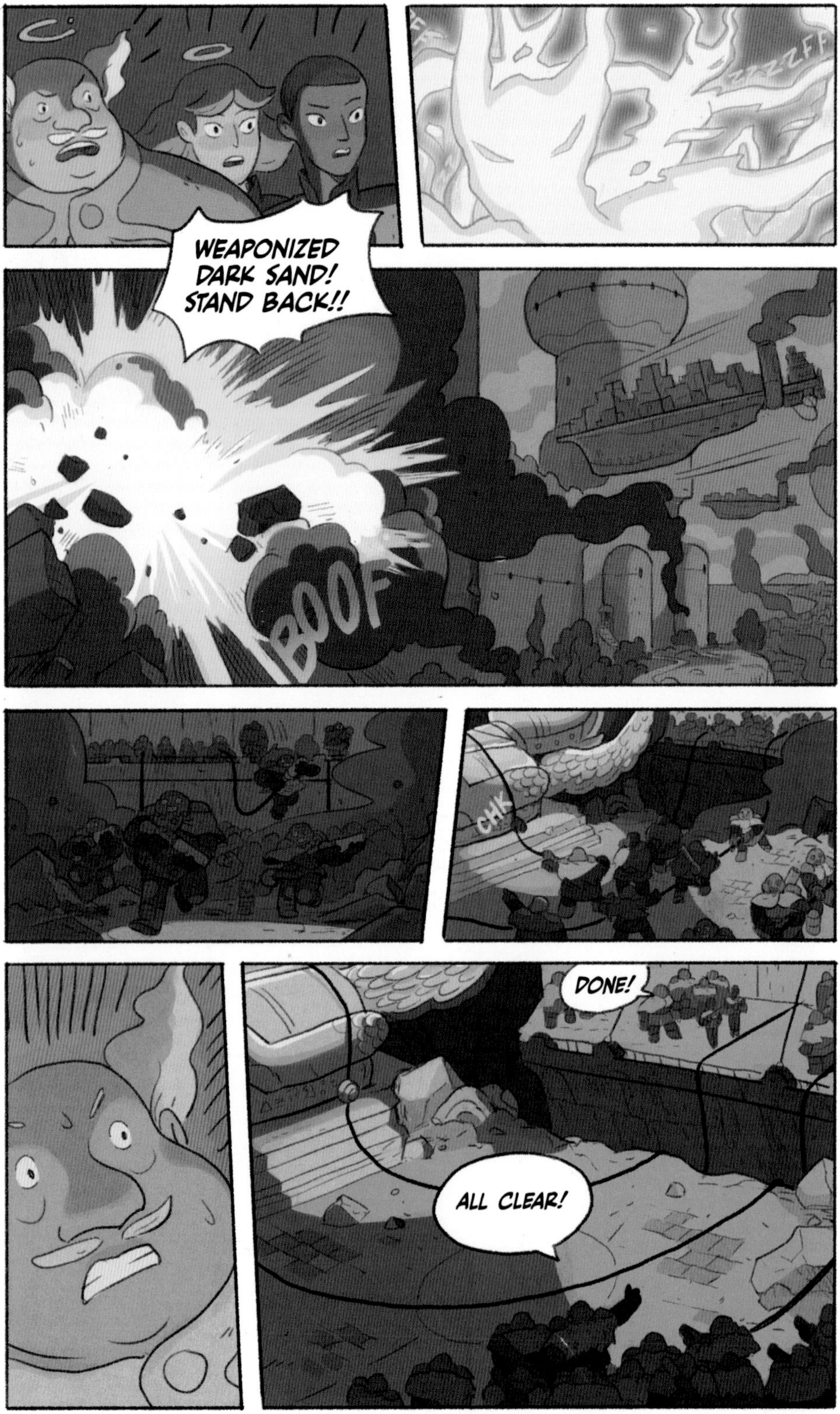
WEAPONIZED DARK SAND! STAND BACK!!
BOOF
CHK
DONE!
ALL CLEAR!

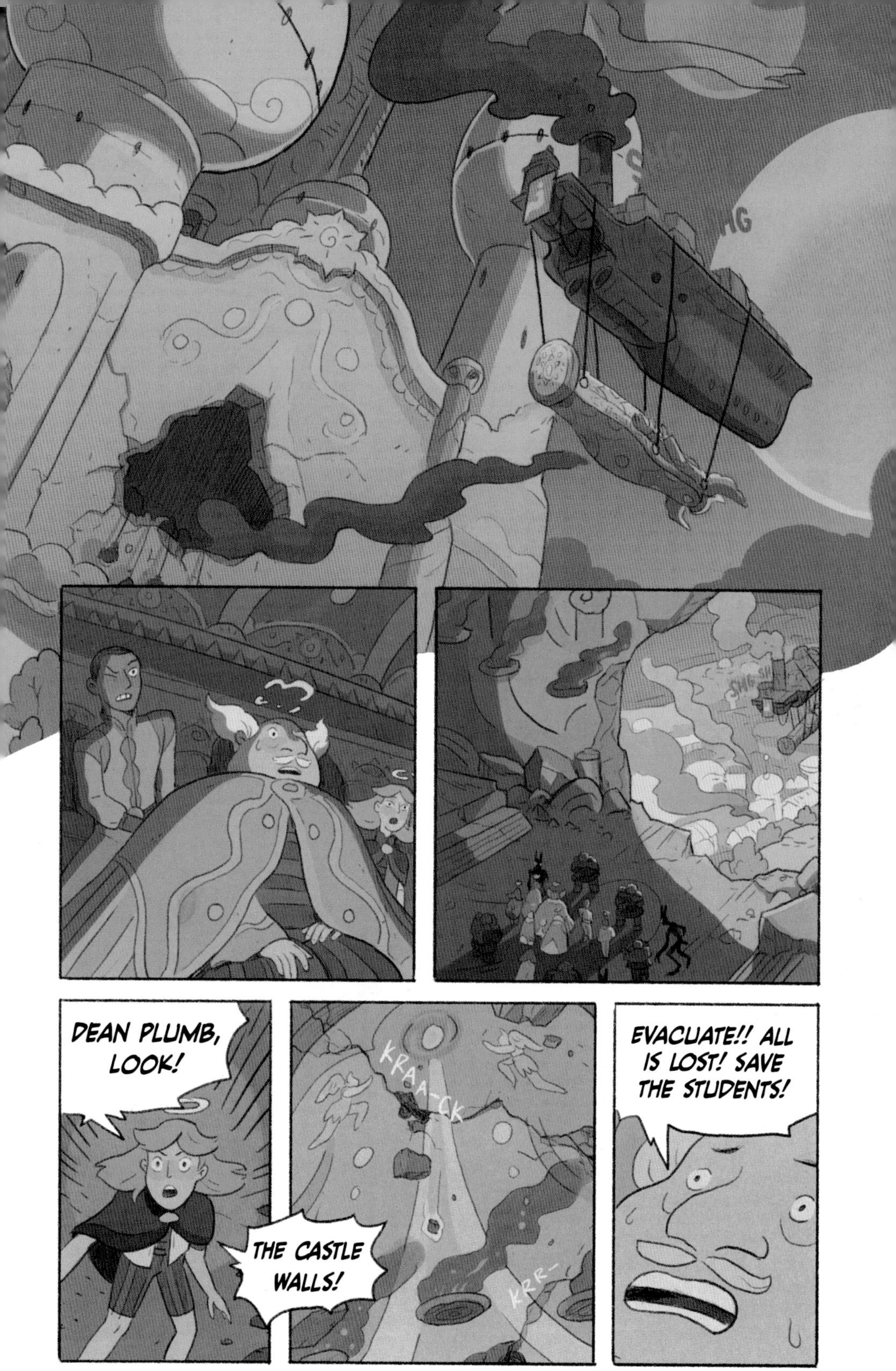
DEAN PLUMB, LOOK!
THE CASTLE WALLS!
KRAA-CK
KRR-
EVACUATE!! ALL IS LOST! SAVE THE STUDENTS!

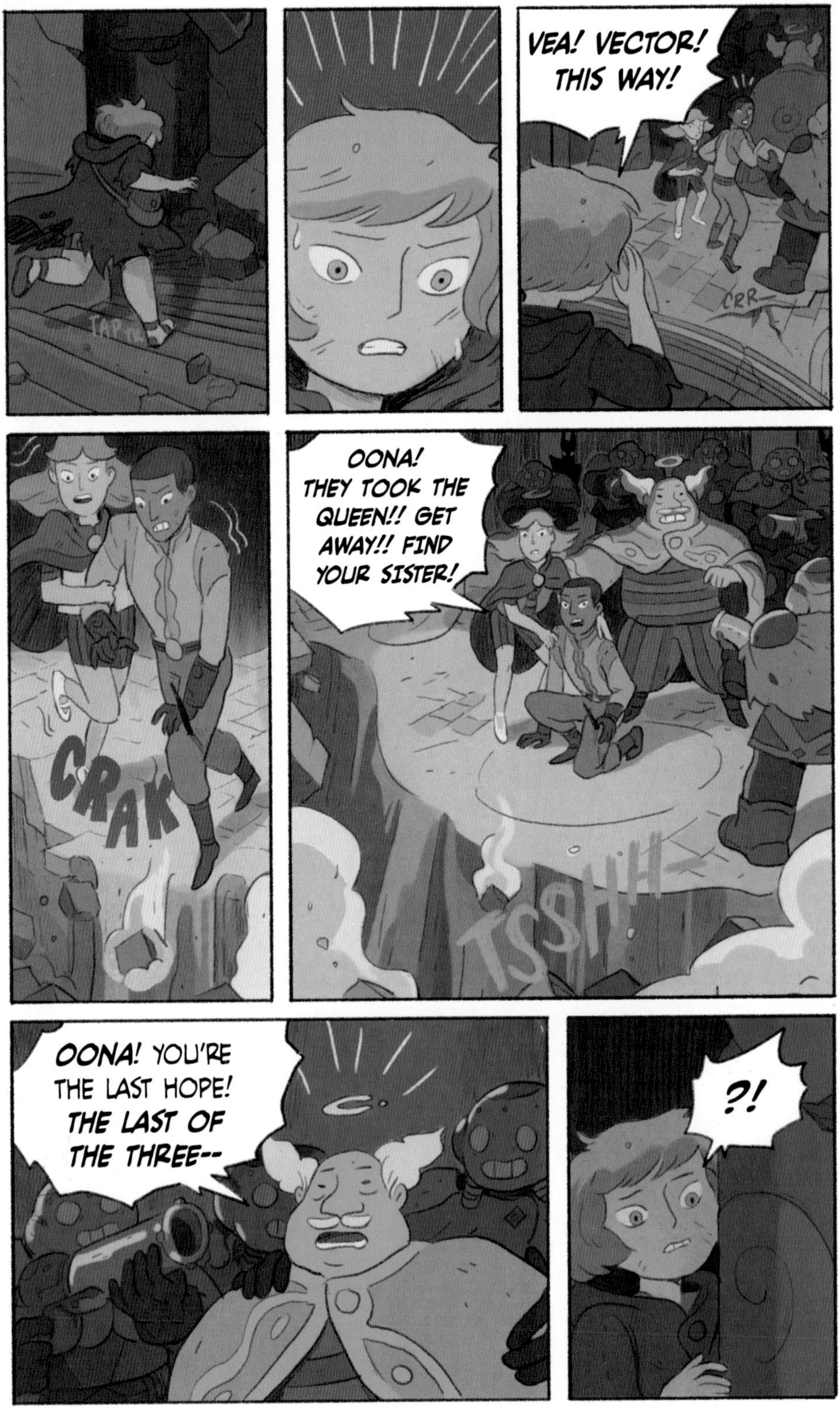
TAP
VEA! VECTOR! THIS WAY!
CRR—
CRAK
OONA! THEY TOOK THE QUEEN!! GET AWAY!! FIND YOUR SISTER!
TSSHH
OONA! YOU'RE THE LAST HOPE! THE LAST OF THE THREE--
?!

AAH!

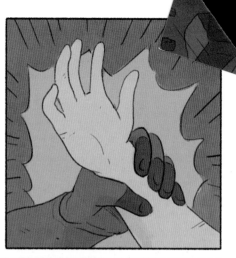

THEY'RE TAKING THEM AWAY!!

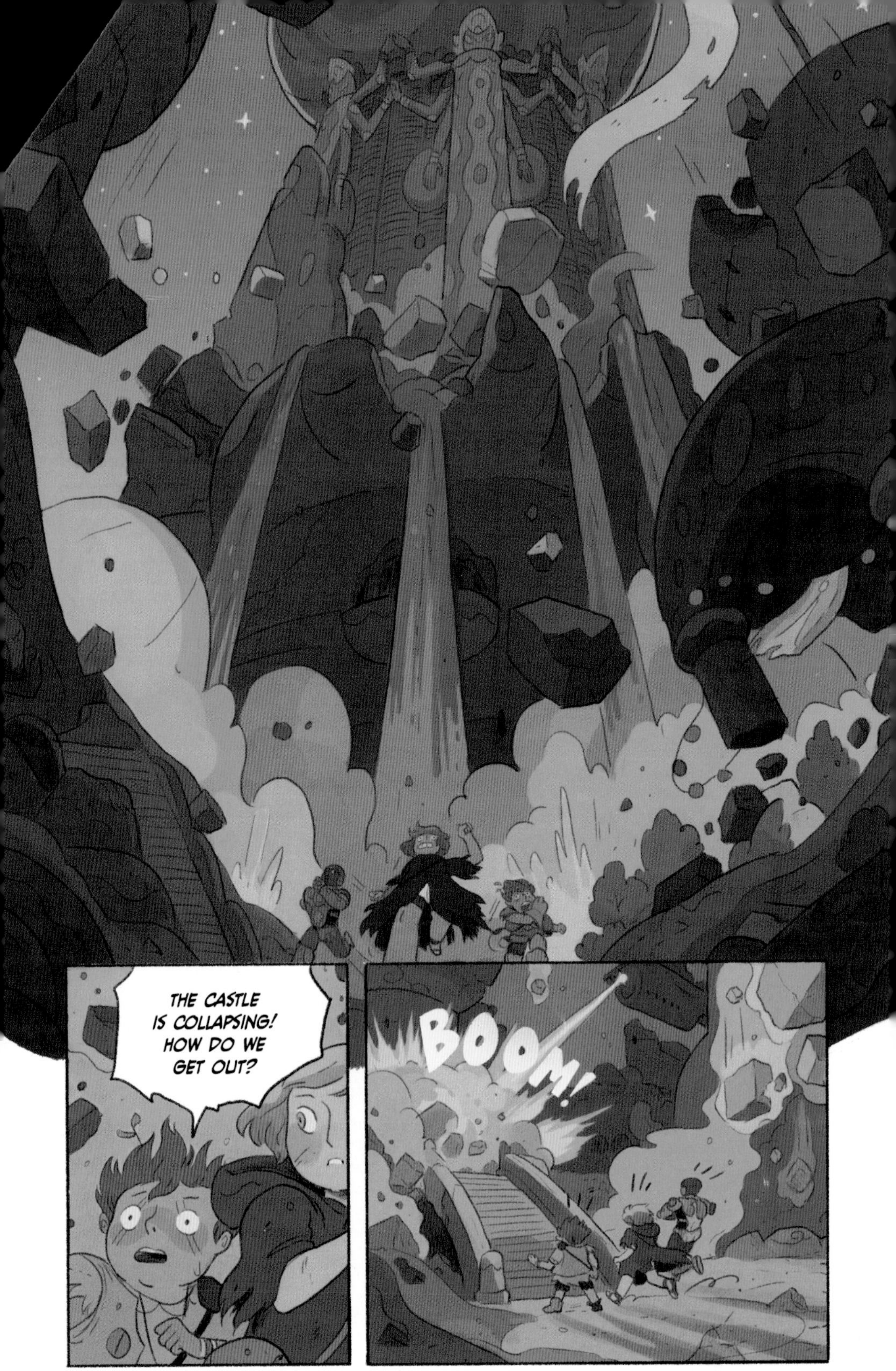
THE CASTLE IS COLLAPSING! HOW DO WE GET OUT?
BOOM!

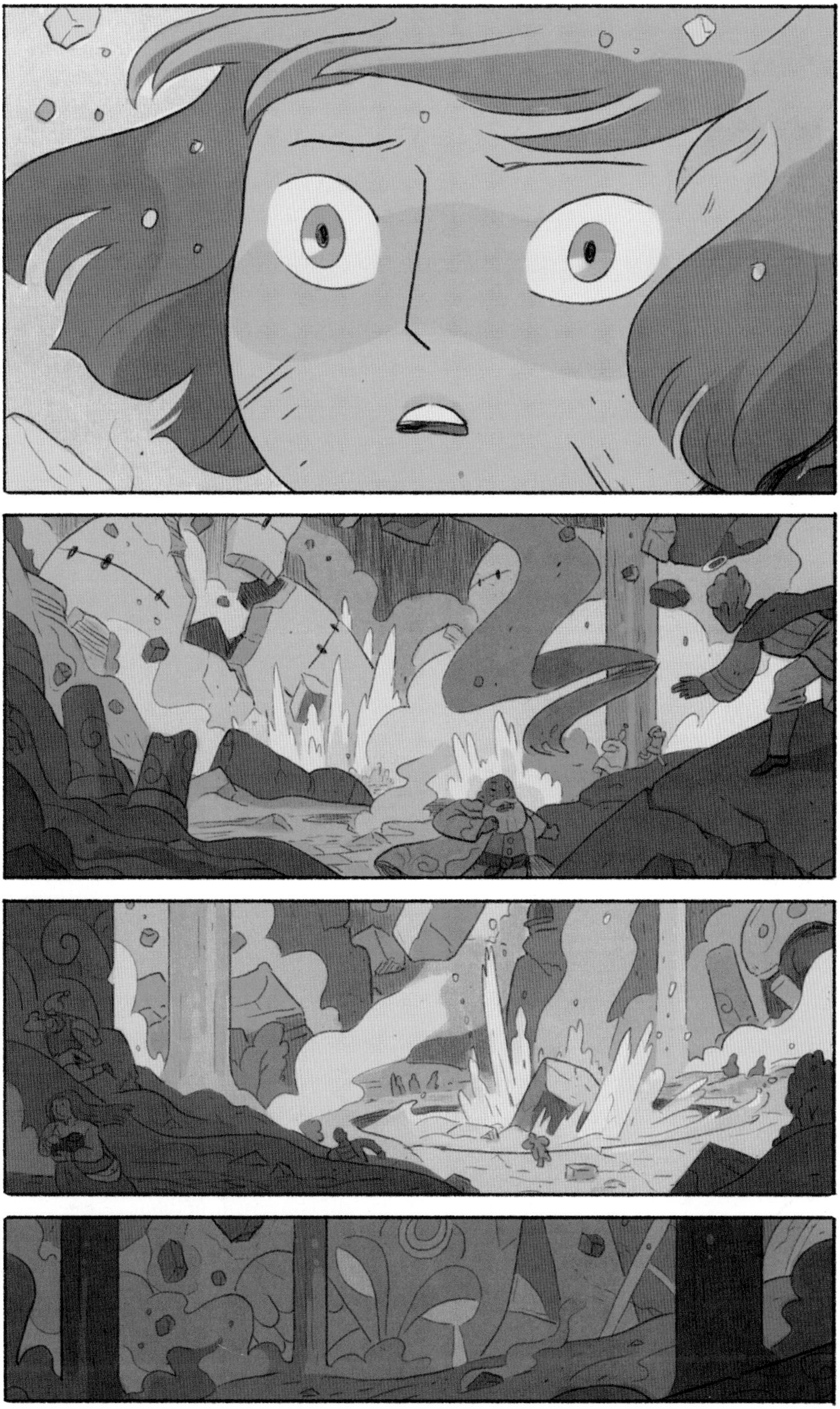

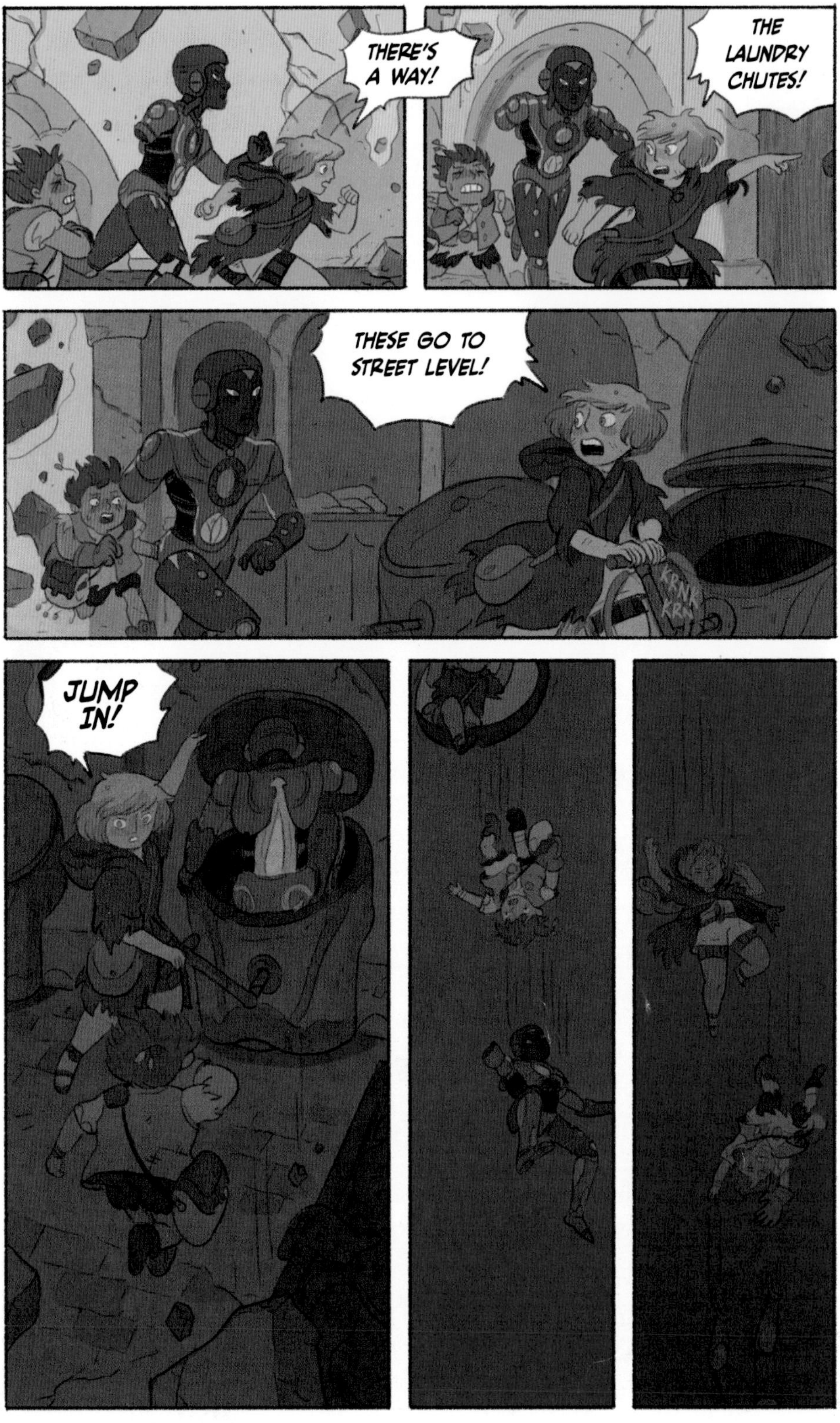
THERE'S A WAY!
THE LAUNDRY CHUTES!
THESE GO TO STREET LEVEL!
KRNK KRN
JUMP IN!

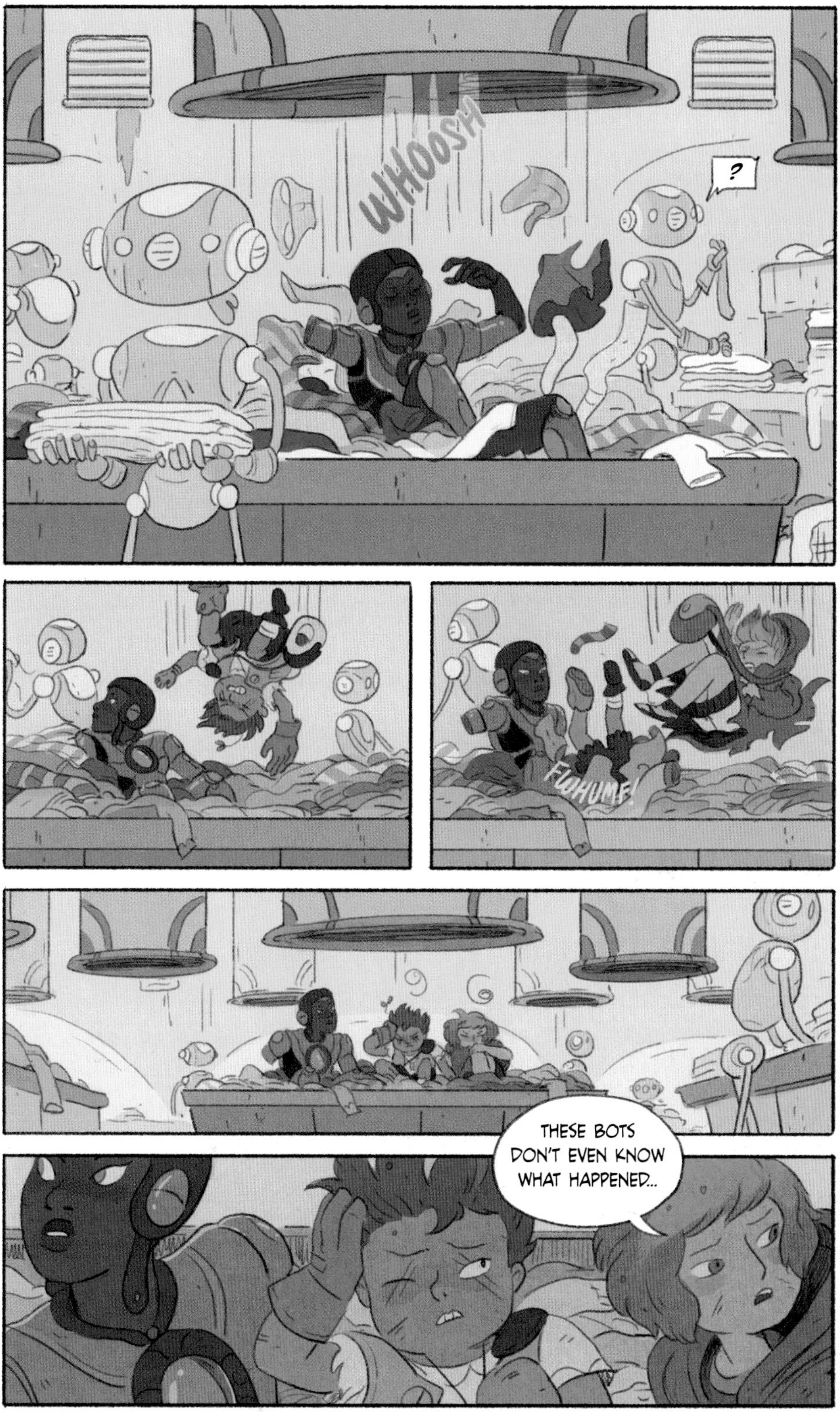
WHOOSH
?
FWHUMF!
THESE BOTS DON'T EVEN KNOW WHAT HAPPENED...

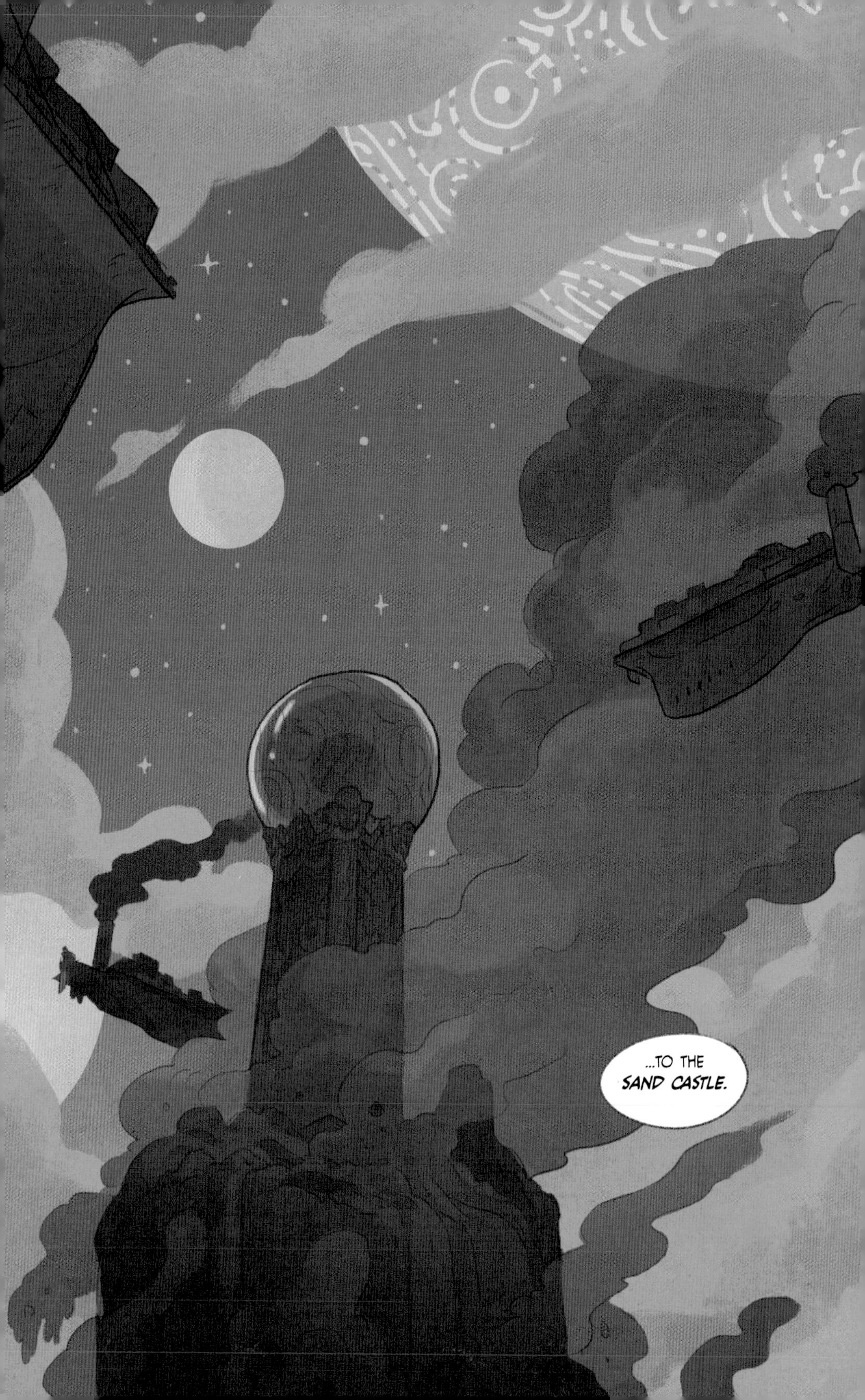
...TO THE SAND CASTLE.

Chapter 5
PASSAGE TO MAYAPOLIS

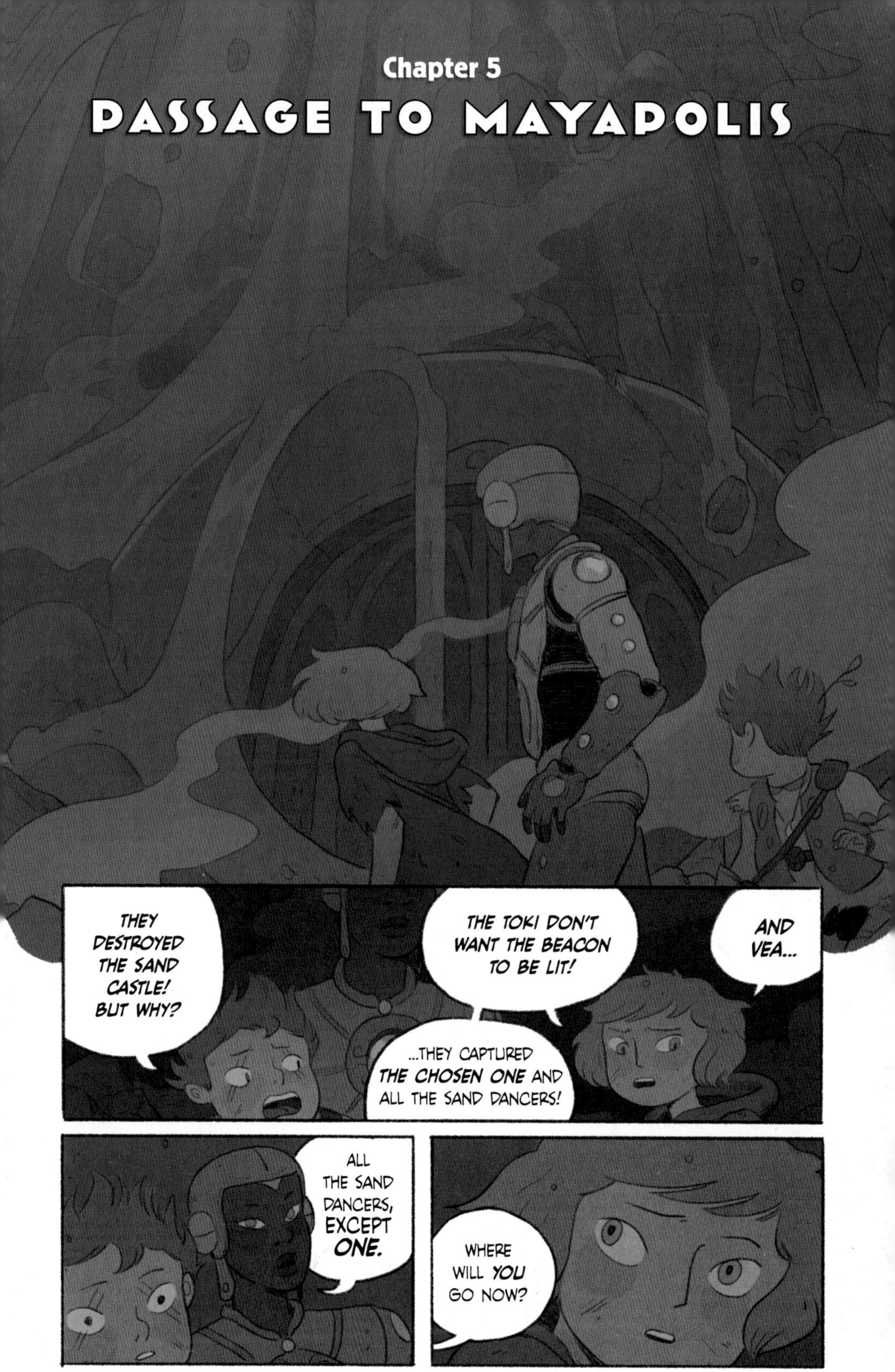
THEY DESTROYED THE SAND CASTLE! BUT WHY?
THE TOKI DON'T WANT THE BEACON TO BE LIT!
AND VEA...
...THEY CAPTURED THE CHOSEN ONE AND ALL THE SAND DANCERS!
ALL THE SAND DANCERS, EXCEPT ONE.
WHERE WILL YOU GO NOW?

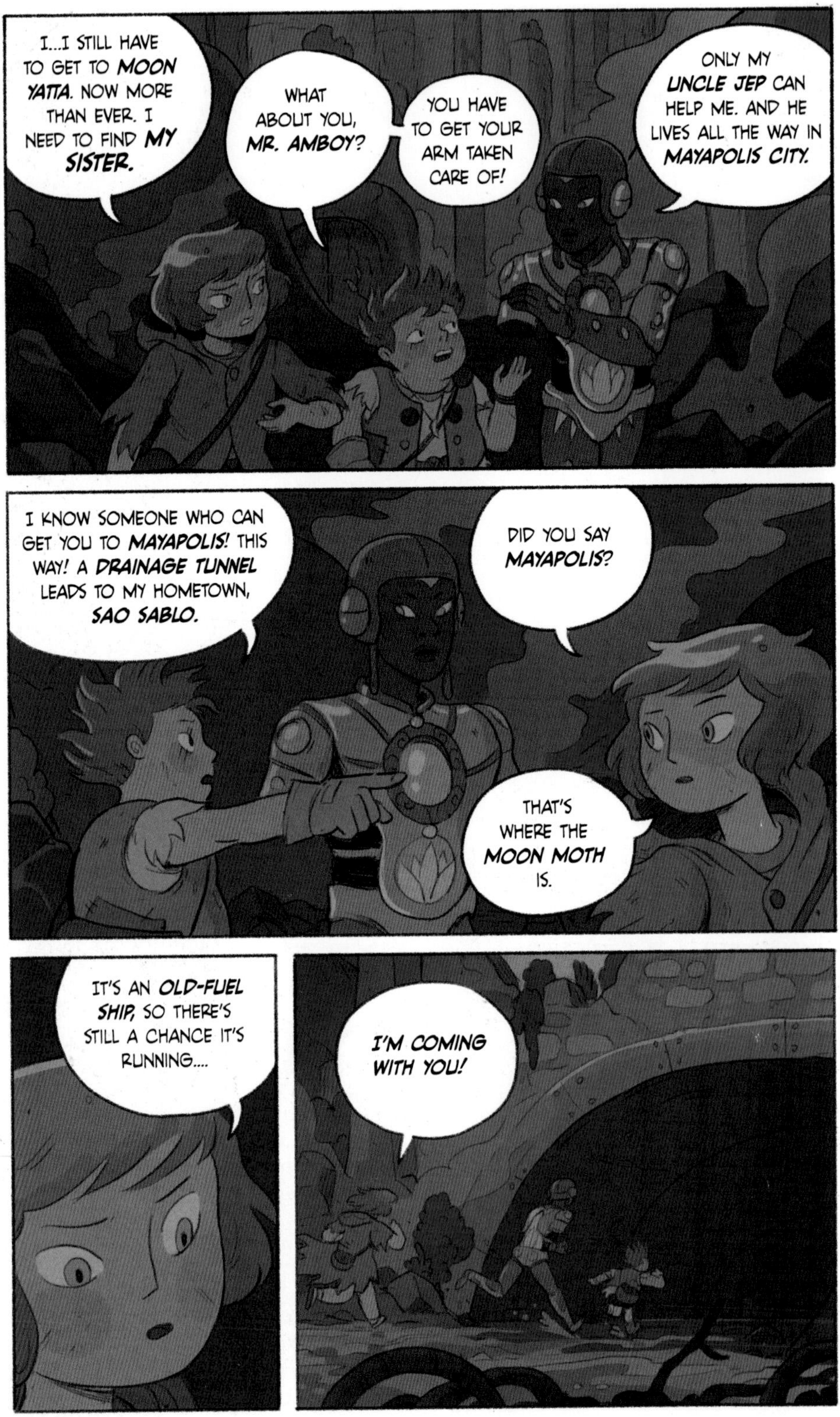
I...I STILL HAVE TO GET TO MOON YATTA. NOW MORE THAN EVER. I NEED TO FIND MY SISTER.
WHAT ABOUT YOU, MR. AMBOY?
YOU HAVE TO GET YOUR ARM TAKEN CARE OF!
ONLY MY UNCLE JEP CAN HELP ME. AND HE LIVES ALL THE WAY IN MAYAPOLIS CITY.
I KNOW SOMEONE WHO CAN GET YOU TO MAYAPOLIS! THIS WAY! A DRAINAGE TUNNEL LEADS TO MY HOMETOWN, SAO SABLO.
DID YOU SAY MAYAPOLIS?
THAT'S WHERE THE MOON MOTH IS.
IT'S AN OLD-FUEL SHIP, SO THERE'S STILL A CHANCE IT'S RUNNING....
I'M COMING WITH YOU!

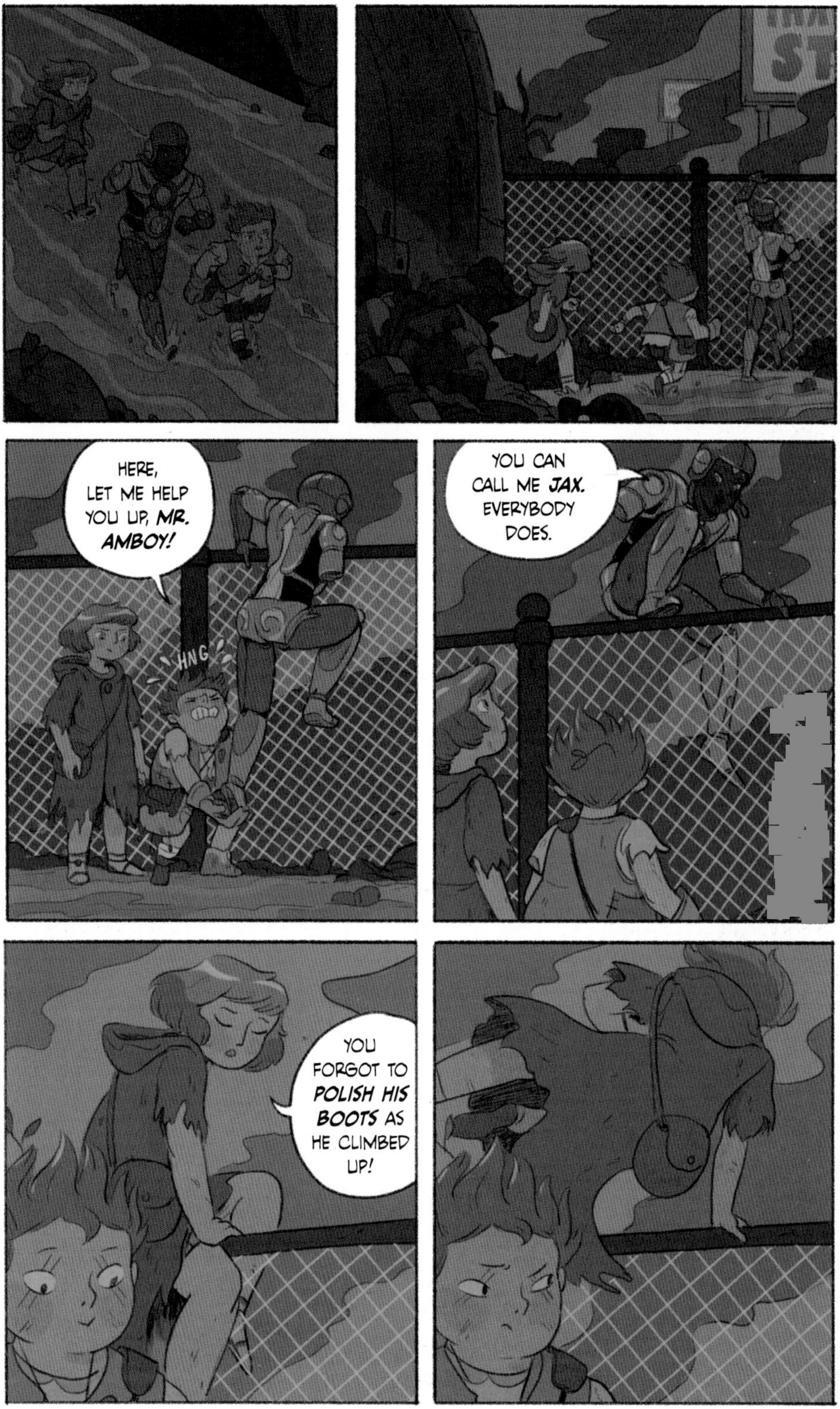
HERE, LET ME HELP YOU UP, MR. AMBOY!
HNG
YOU CAN CALL ME JAX. EVERYBODY DOES.
YOU FORGOT TO POLISH HIS BOOTS AS HE CLIMBED UP!

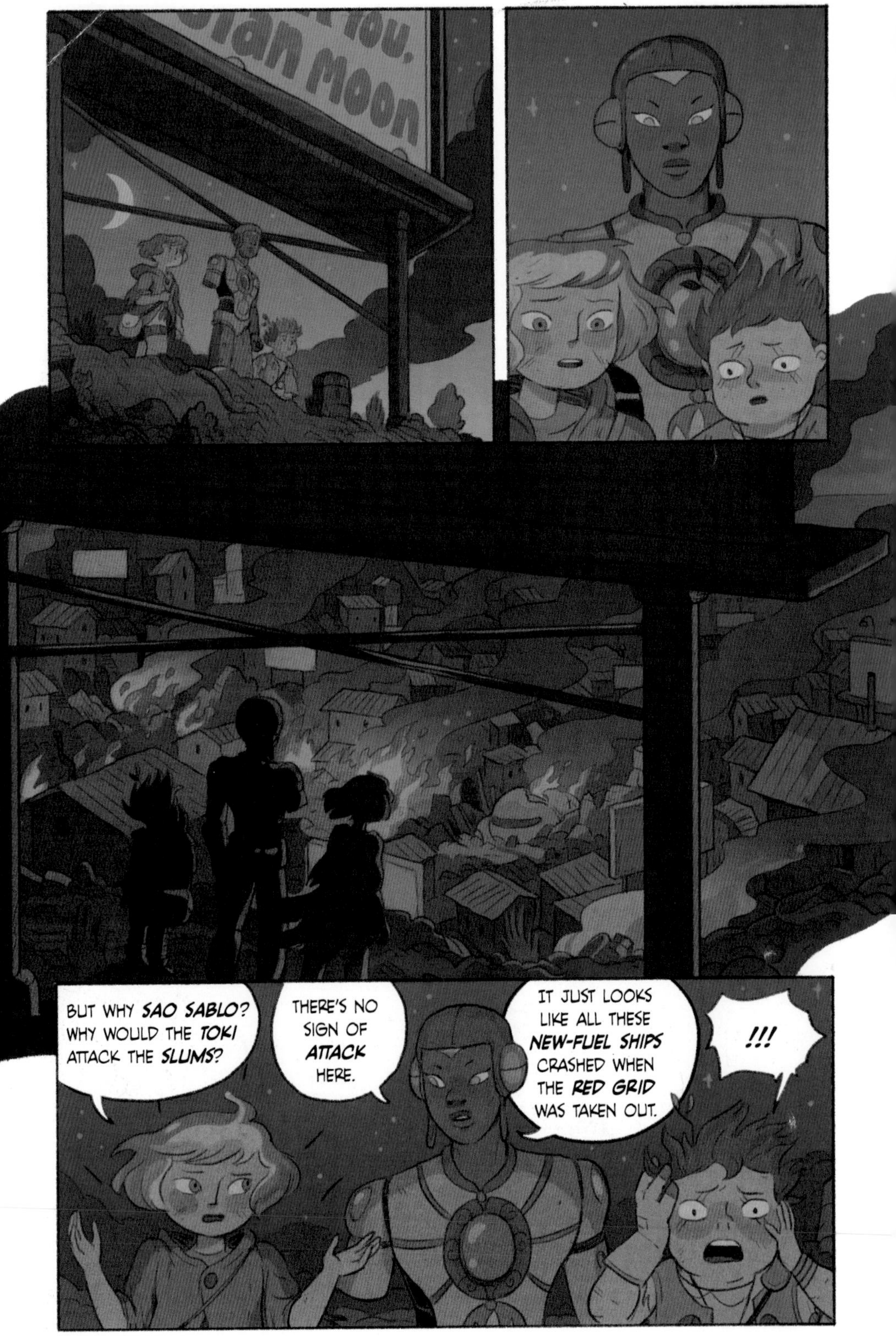
BUT WHY SAO SABLO? WHY WOULD THE TOKI ATTACK THE SLUMS?
THERE'S NO SIGN OF ATTACK HERE.
IT JUST LOOKS LIKE ALL THESE NEW-FUEL SHIPS CRASHED WHEN THE RED GRID WAS TAKEN OUT.
!!!

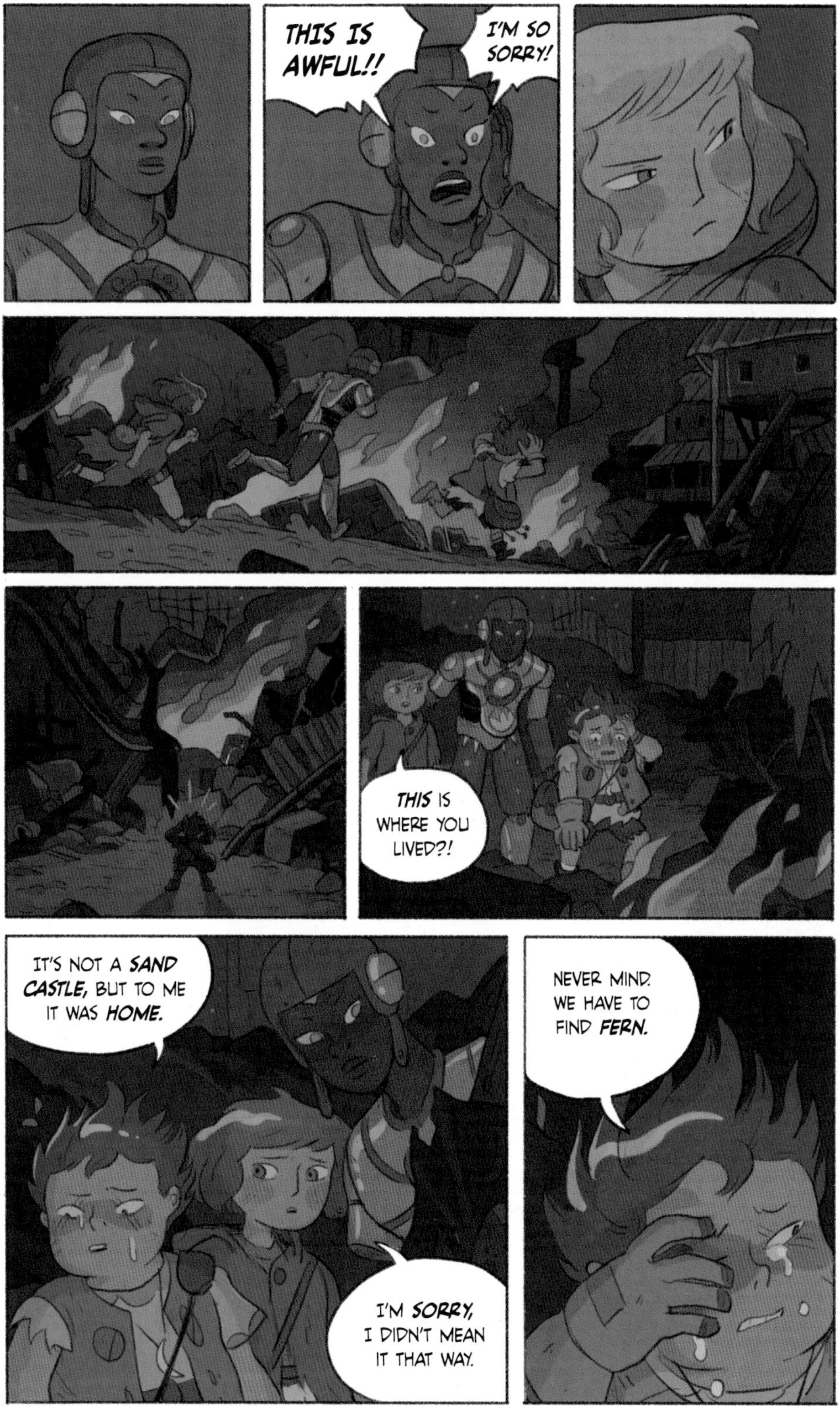

THIS IS AWFUL!!
I'M SO SORRY!
THIS IS WHERE YOU LIVED?!
IT'S NOT A SAND CASTLE, BUT TO ME IT WAS HOME.
I'M SORRY, I DIDN'T MEAN IT THAT WAY.
NEVER MIND. WE HAVE TO FIND FERN.

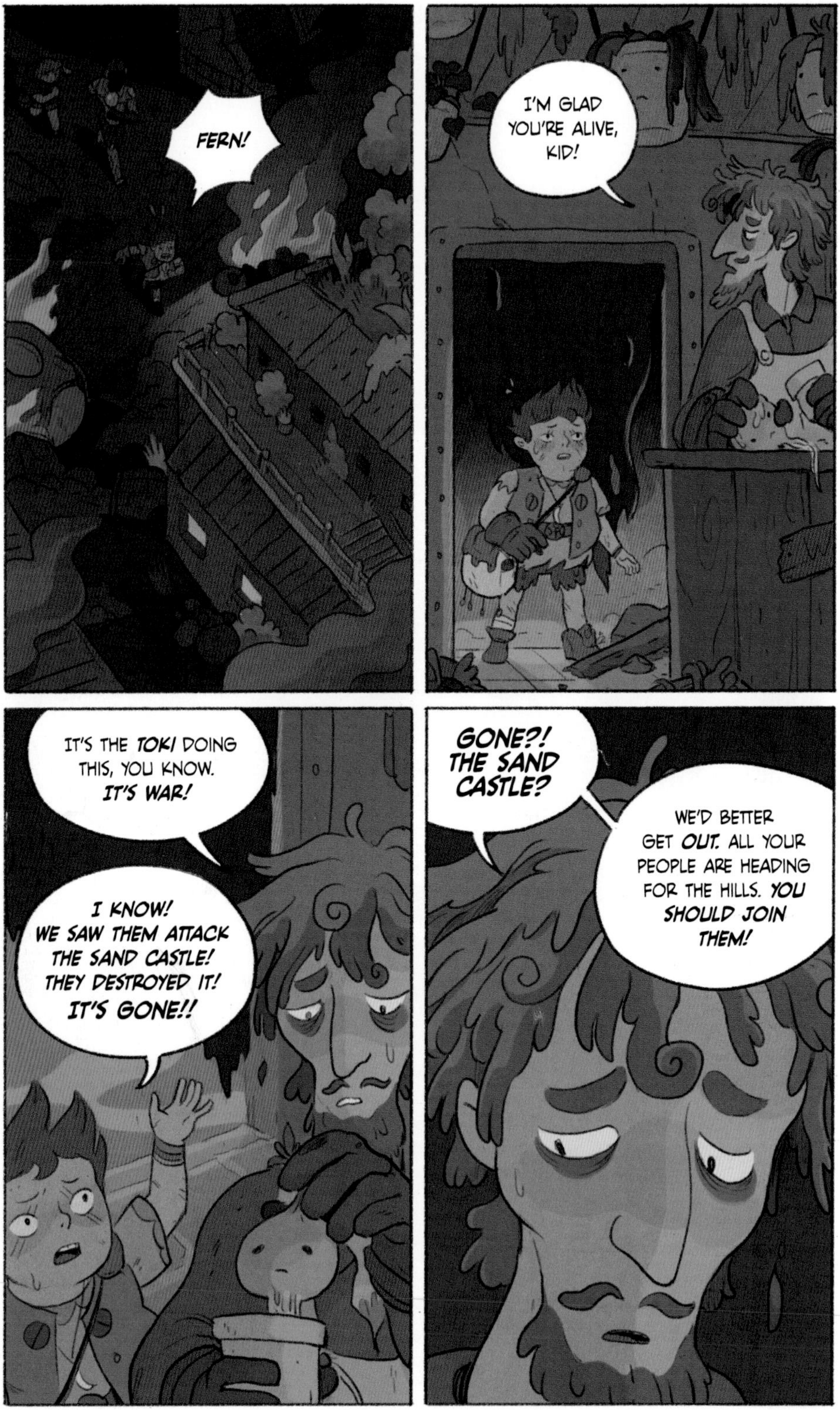
FERN!
I'M GLAD YOU'RE ALIVE, KID!
IT'S THE TOKI DOING THIS, YOU KNOW. IT'S WAR!
I KNOW! WE SAW THEM ATTACK THE SAND CASTLE! THEY DESTROYED IT! IT'S GONE!!
GONE?! THE SAND CASTLE?
WE'D BETTER GET OUT. ALL YOUR PEOPLE ARE HEADING FOR THE HILLS. YOU SHOULD JOIN THEM!

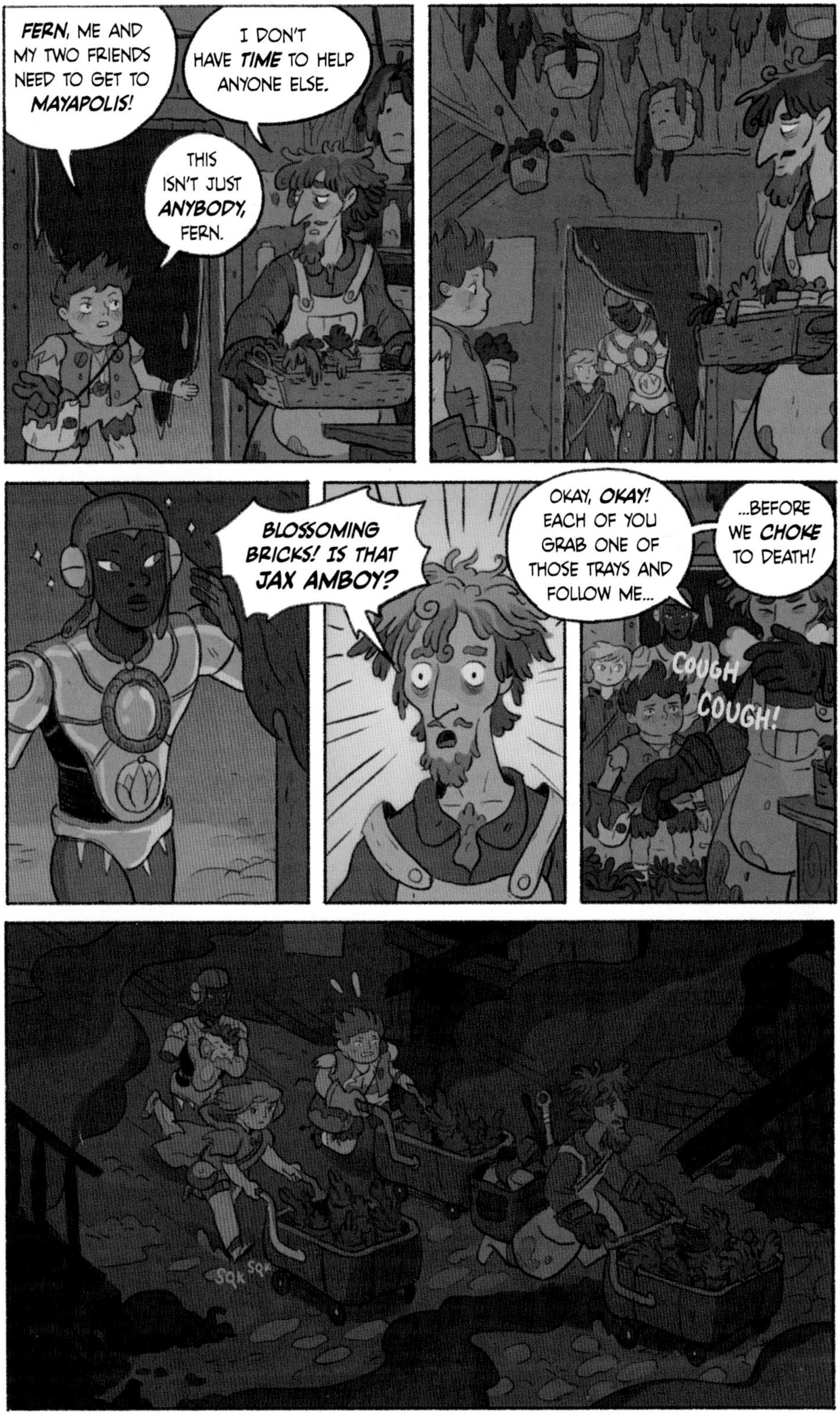
FERN, ME AND MY TWO FRIENDS NEED TO GET TO MAYAPOLIS!
I DON'T HAVE TIME TO HELP ANYONE ELSE.
THIS ISN'T JUST ANYBODY, FERN.
BLOSSOMING BRICKS! IS THAT JAX AMBOY?
OKAY, OKAY! EACH OF YOU GRAB ONE OF THOSE TRAYS AND FOLLOW ME...
...BEFORE WE CHOKE TO DEATH!
COUGH
COUGH!
SQK SQK

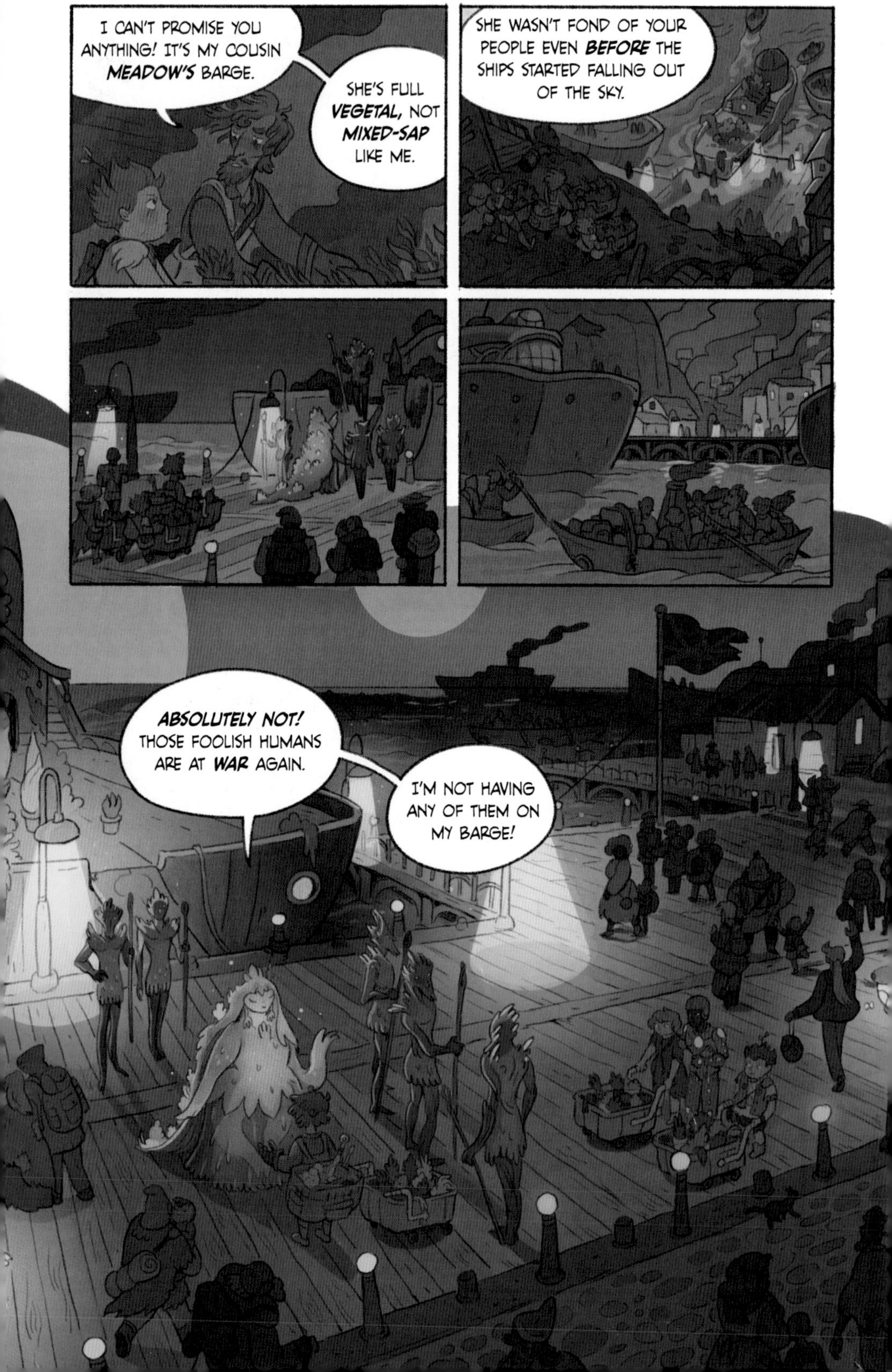
I CAN'T PROMISE YOU ANYTHING! IT'S MY COUSIN **MEADOW'S** BARGE.
SHE'S FULL **VEGETAL,** NOT **MIXED-SAP** LIKE ME.
SHE WASN'T FOND OF YOUR PEOPLE EVEN **BEFORE** THE SHIPS STARTED FALLING OUT OF THE SKY.
ABSOLUTELY NOT! THOSE FOOLISH HUMANS ARE AT **WAR** AGAIN.
I'M NOT HAVING ANY OF THEM ON MY BARGE!

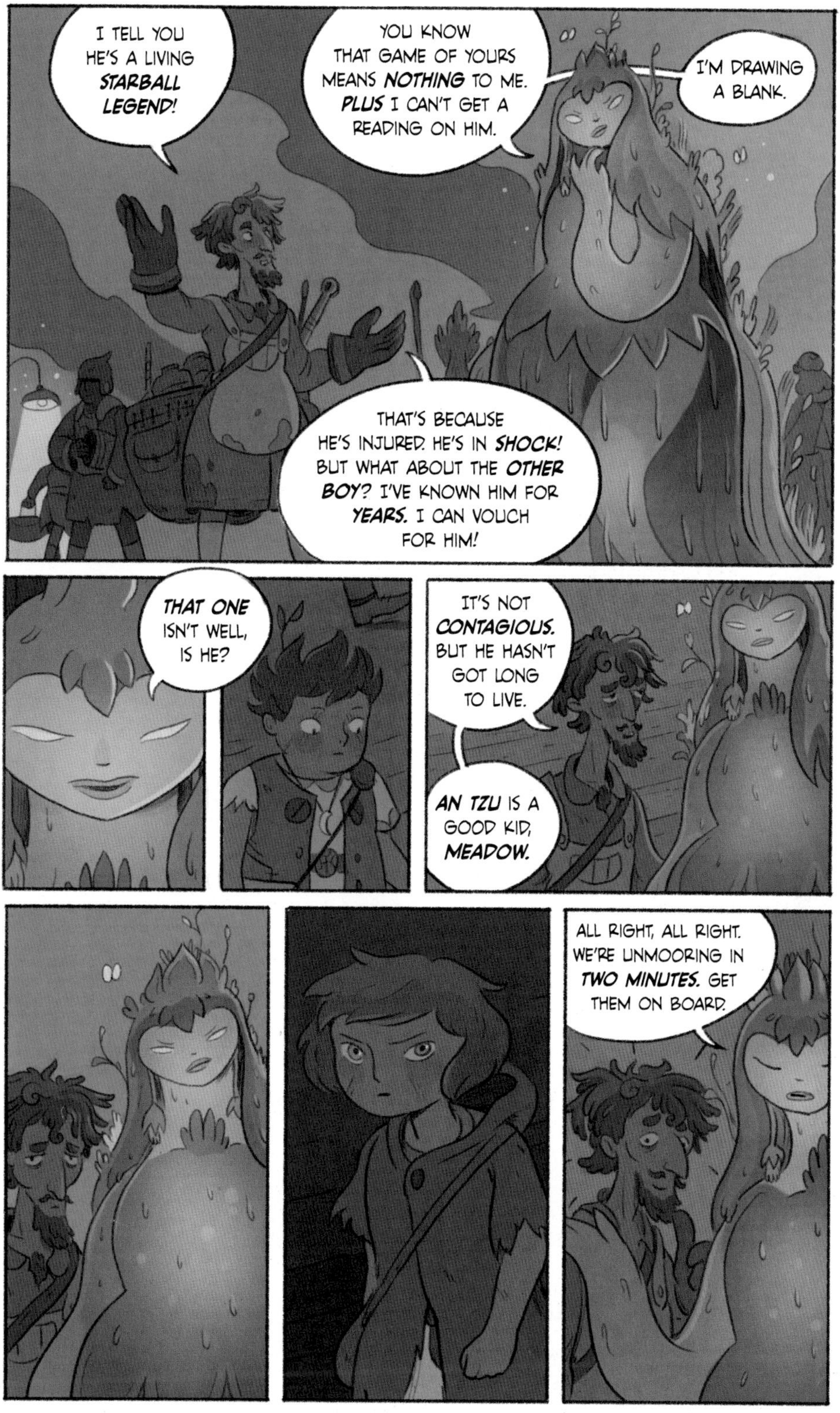
I TELL YOU HE'S A LIVING STARBALL LEGEND!
YOU KNOW THAT GAME OF YOURS MEANS NOTHING TO ME. PLUS I CAN'T GET A READING ON HIM.
I'M DRAWING A BLANK.
THAT'S BECAUSE HE'S INJURED. HE'S IN SHOCK! BUT WHAT ABOUT THE OTHER BOY? I'VE KNOWN HIM FOR YEARS. I CAN VOUCH FOR HIM!
THAT ONE ISN'T WELL, IS HE?
IT'S NOT CONTAGIOUS. BUT HE HASN'T GOT LONG TO LIVE.
AN TZU IS A GOOD KID, MEADOW.
ALL RIGHT, ALL RIGHT. WE'RE UNMOORING IN TWO MINUTES. GET THEM ON BOARD.

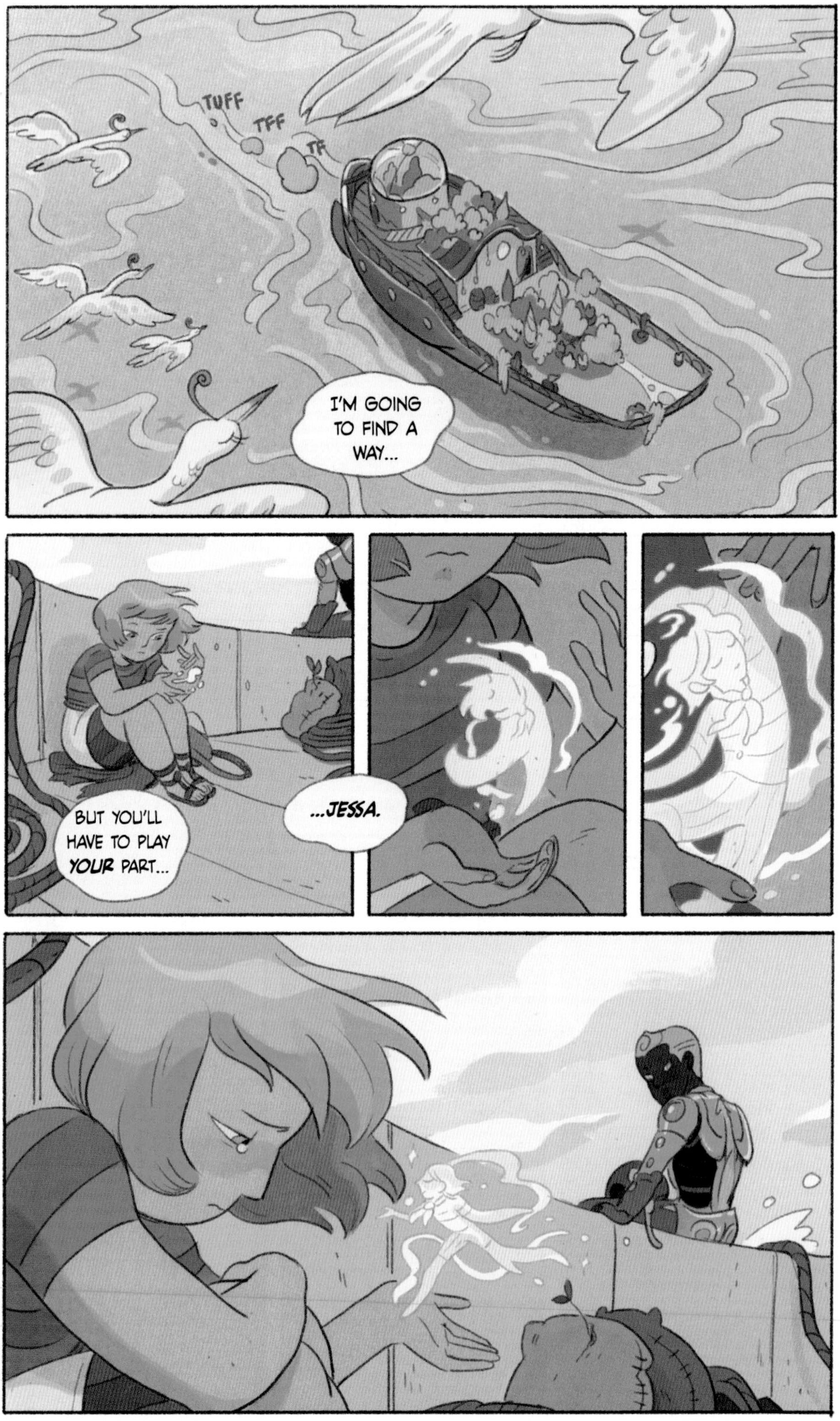
TUFF
TFF
TF
I'M GOING TO FIND A WAY...
BUT YOU'LL HAVE TO PLAY YOUR PART...
...JESSA.

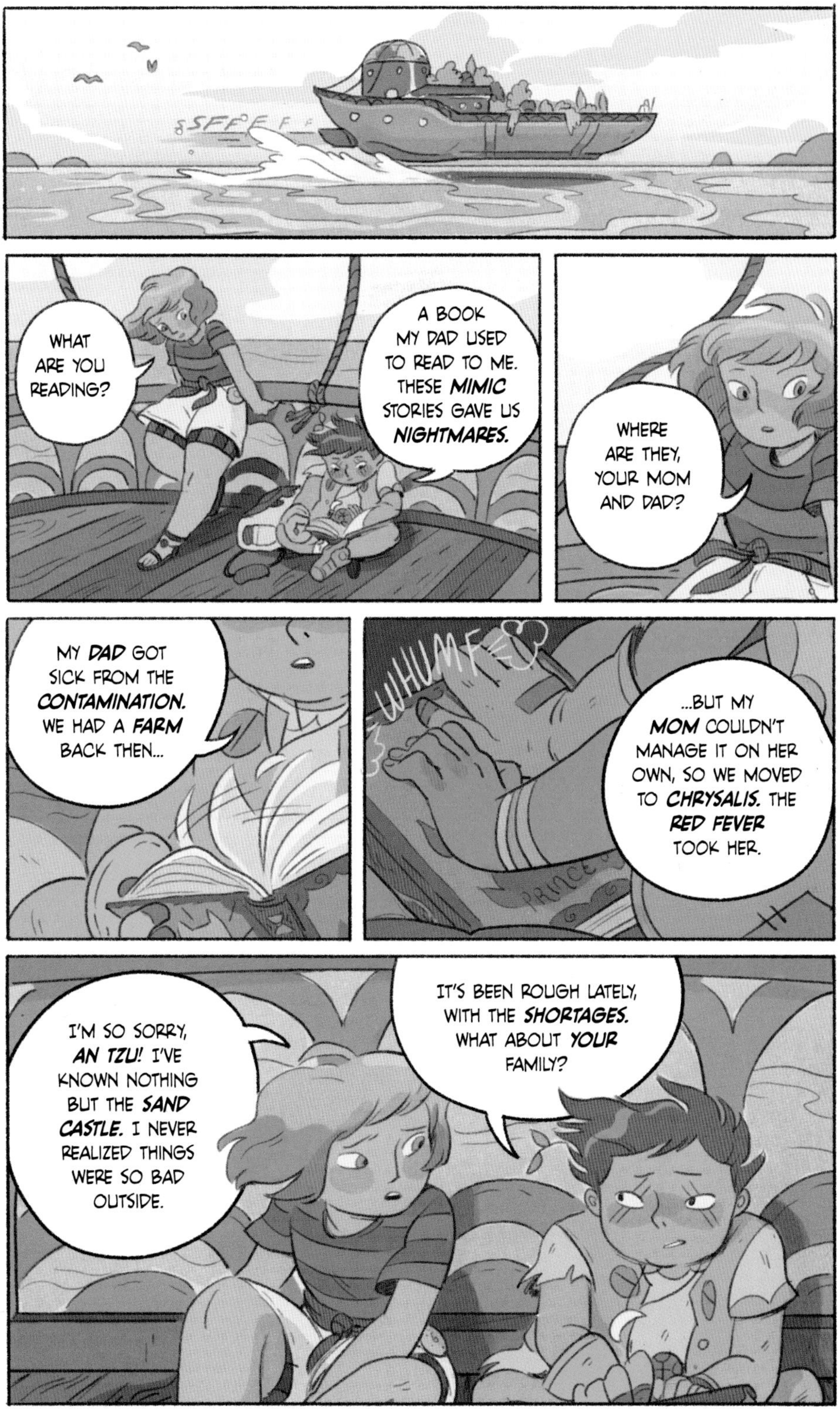
SFFFFF
WHAT ARE YOU READING?
A BOOK MY DAD USED TO READ TO ME. THESE MIMIC STORIES GAVE US NIGHTMARES.
WHERE ARE THEY, YOUR MOM AND DAD?
MY DAD GOT SICK FROM THE CONTAMINATION. WE HAD A FARM BACK THEN...
WHUMF
...BUT MY MOM COULDN'T MANAGE IT ON HER OWN, SO WE MOVED TO CHRYSALIS. THE RED FEVER TOOK HER.
IT'S BEEN ROUGH LATELY, WITH THE SHORTAGES. WHAT ABOUT YOUR FAMILY?
I'M SO SORRY, AN TZU! I'VE KNOWN NOTHING BUT THE SAND CASTLE. I NEVER REALIZED THINGS WERE SO BAD OUTSIDE.

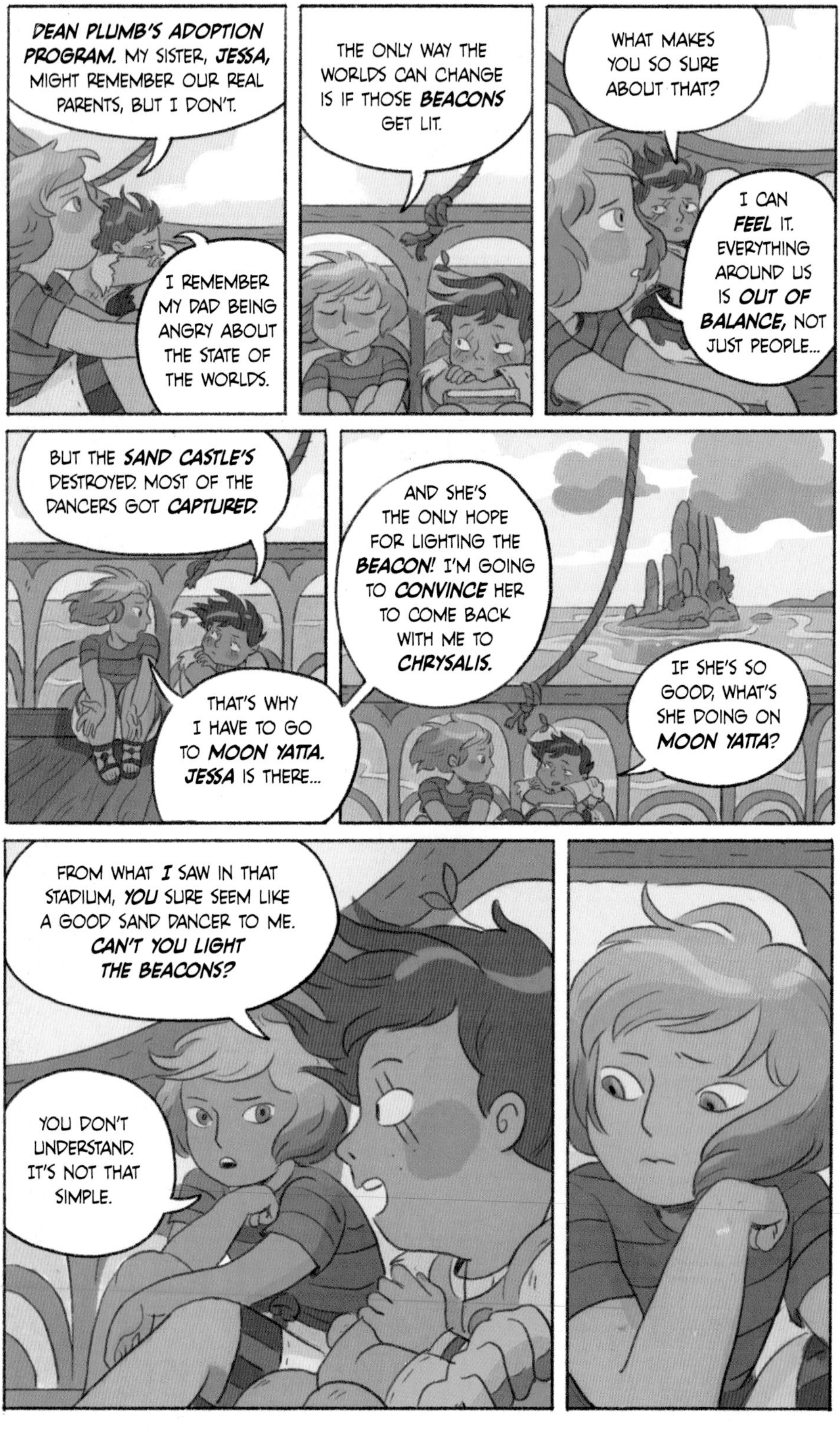
DEAN PLUMB'S ADOPTION PROGRAM. MY SISTER, JESSA, MIGHT REMEMBER OUR REAL PARENTS, BUT I DON'T.
I REMEMBER MY DAD BEING ANGRY ABOUT THE STATE OF THE WORLDS.
THE ONLY WAY THE WORLDS CAN CHANGE IS IF THOSE BEACONS GET LIT.
WHAT MAKES YOU SO SURE ABOUT THAT?
I CAN FEEL IT. EVERYTHING AROUND US IS OUT OF BALANCE, NOT JUST PEOPLE...
BUT THE SAND CASTLE'S DESTROYED. MOST OF THE DANCERS GOT CAPTURED.
THAT'S WHY I HAVE TO GO TO MOON YATTA. JESSA IS THERE...
AND SHE'S THE ONLY HOPE FOR LIGHTING THE BEACON! I'M GOING TO CONVINCE HER TO COME BACK WITH ME TO CHRYSALIS.
IF SHE'S SO GOOD, WHAT'S SHE DOING ON MOON YATTA?
FROM WHAT I SAW IN THAT STADIUM, YOU SURE SEEM LIKE A GOOD SAND DANCER TO ME. CAN'T YOU LIGHT THE BEACONS?
YOU DON'T UNDERSTAND. IT'S NOT THAT SIMPLE.

Chapter 6

CAT ISLAND

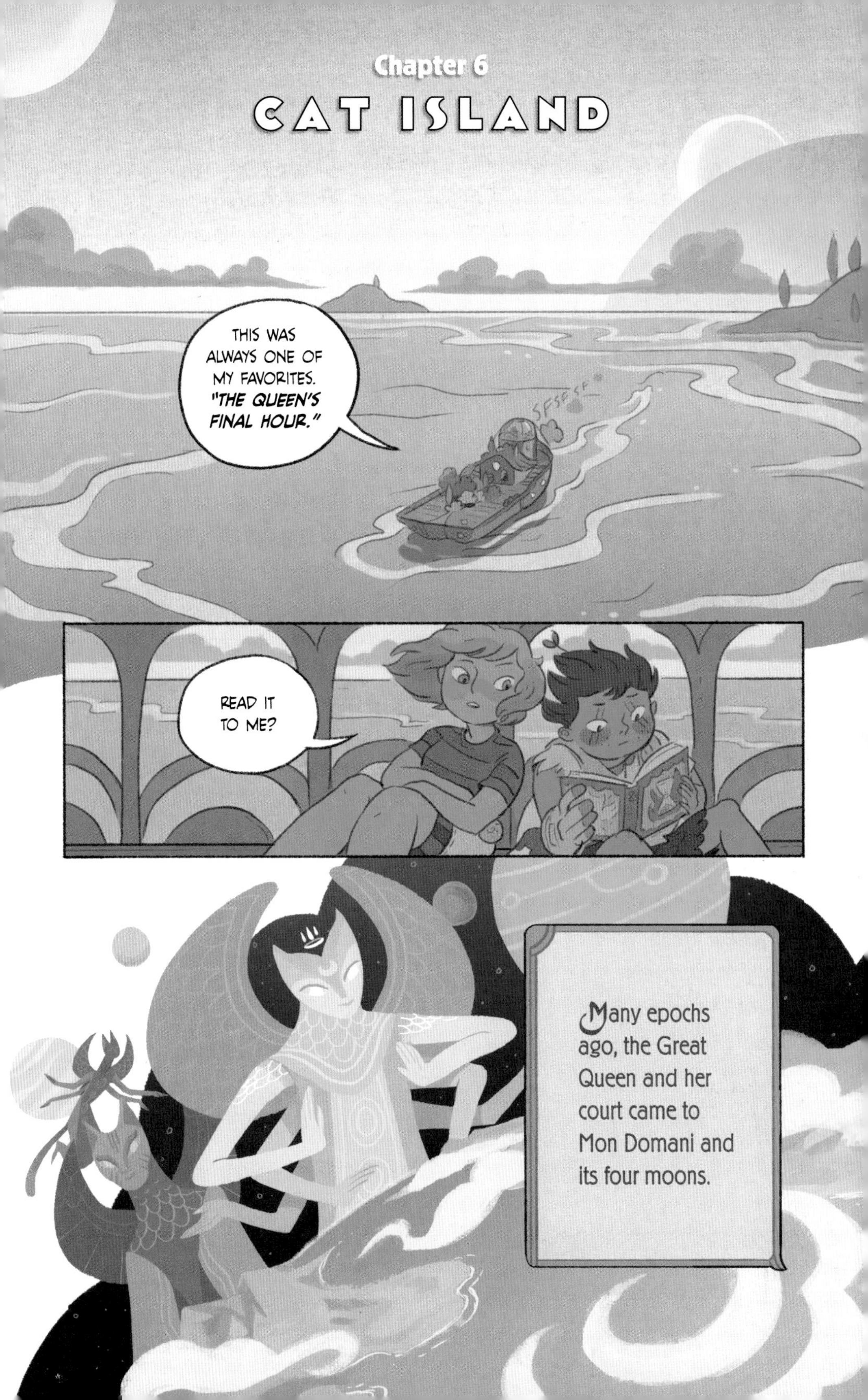
THIS WAS ALWAYS ONE OF MY FAVORITES. "THE QUEEN'S FINAL HOUR."
READ IT TO ME?
Many epochs ago, the Great Queen and her court came to Mon Domani and its four moons.

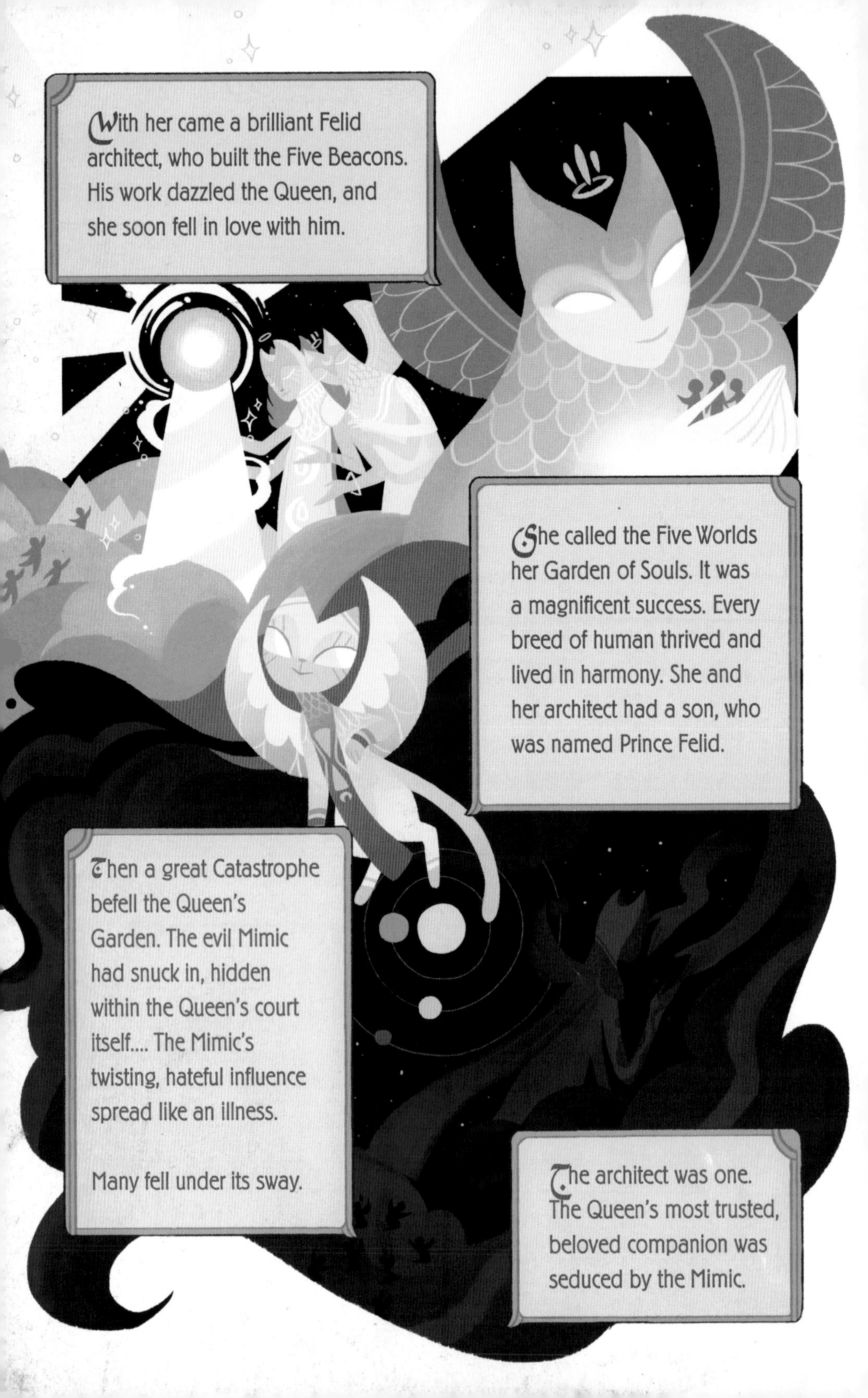
With her came a brilliant Felid architect, who built the Five Beacons. His work dazzled the Queen, and she soon fell in love with him.
She called the Five Worlds her Garden of Souls. It was a magnificent success. Every breed of human thrived and lived in harmony. She and her architect had a son, who was named Prince Felid.
Then a great Catastrophe befell the Queen's Garden. The evil Mimic had snuck in, hidden within the Queen's court itself.... The Mimic's twisting, hateful influence spread like an illness.
Many fell under its sway.
The architect was one. The Queen's most trusted, beloved companion was seduced by the Mimic.

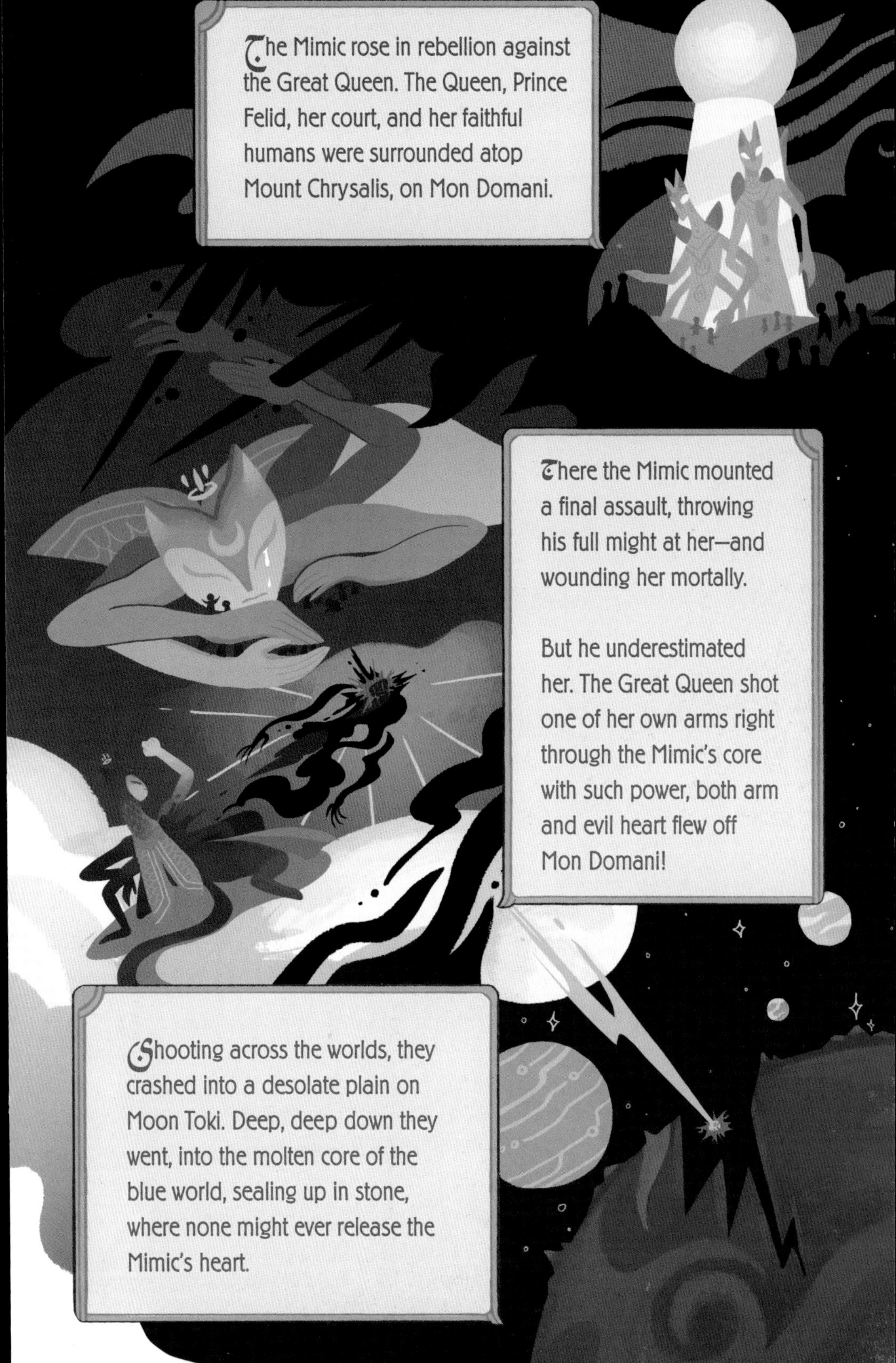
The Mimic rose in rebellion against the Great Queen. The Queen, Prince Felid, her court, and her faithful humans were surrounded atop Mount Chrysalis, on Mon Domani.
There the Mimic mounted a final assault, throwing his full might at her—and wounding her mortally.
But he underestimated her. The Great Queen shot one of her own arms right through the Mimic's core with such power, both arm and evil heart flew off Mon Domani!
Shooting across the worlds, they crashed into a desolate plain on Moon Toki. Deep, deep down they went, into the molten core of the blue world, sealing up in stone, where none might ever release the Mimic's heart.

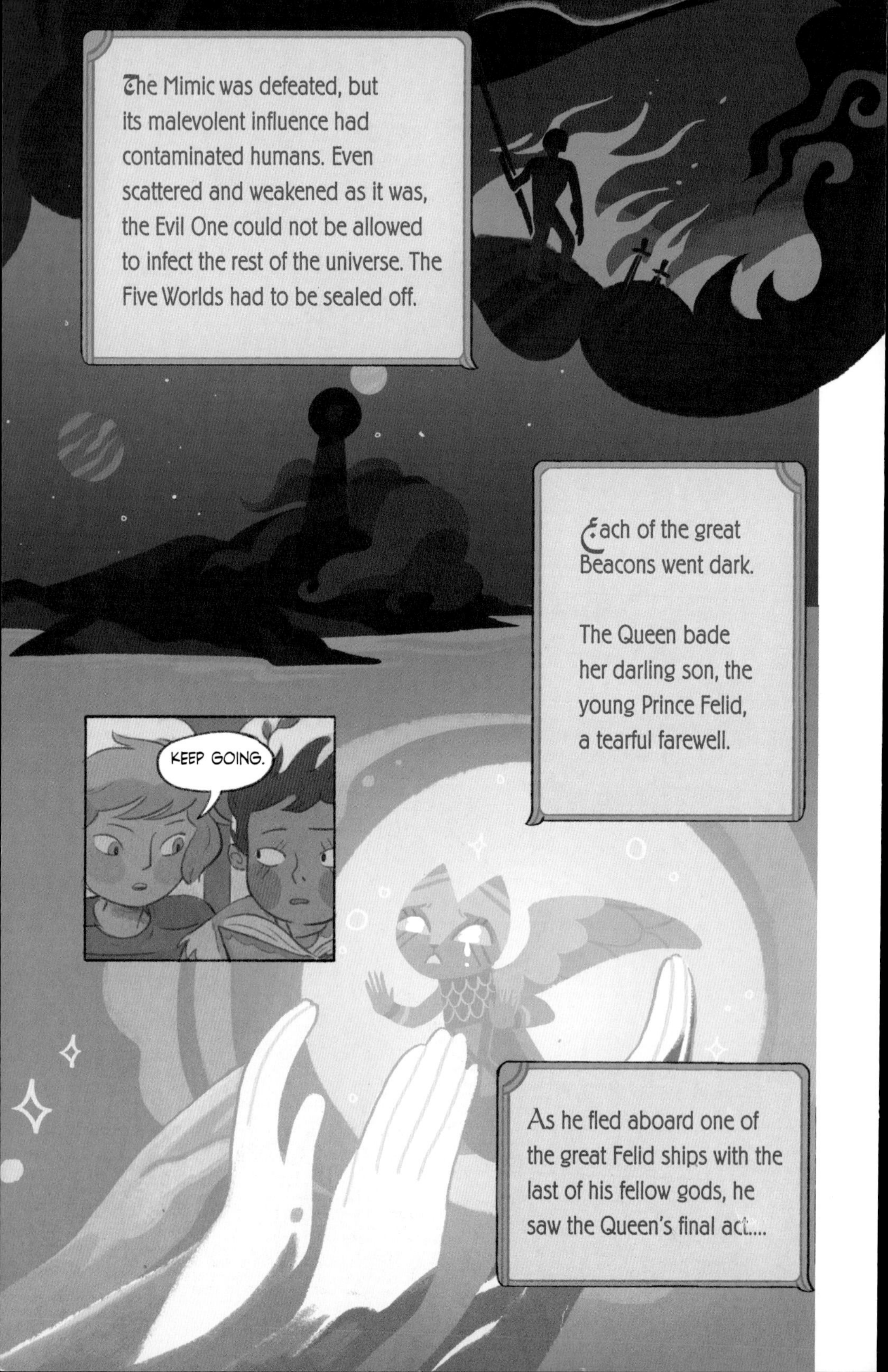
The Mimic was defeated, but its malevolent influence had contaminated humans. Even scattered and weakened as it was, the Evil One could not be allowed to infect the rest of the universe. The Five Worlds had to be sealed off.
Each of the great Beacons went dark.
The Queen bade her darling son, the young Prince Felid, a tearful farewell.
KEEP GOING.
As he fled aboard one of the great Felid ships with the last of his fellow gods, he saw the Queen's final act....

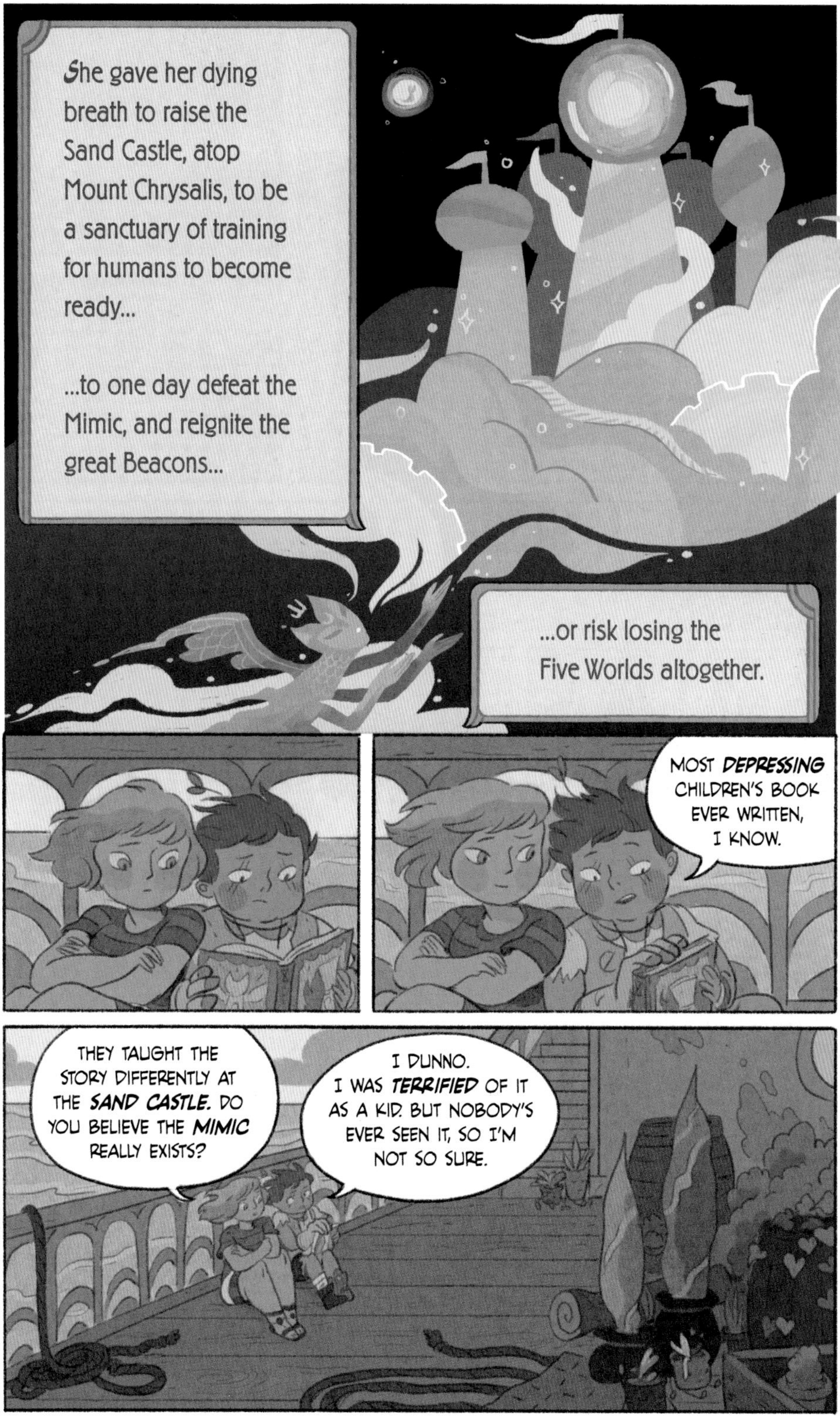
She gave her dying breath to raise the Sand Castle, atop Mount Chrysalis, to be a sanctuary of training for humans to become ready...
...to one day defeat the Mimic, and reignite the great Beacons...
...or risk losing the Five Worlds altogether.
MOST DEPRESSING CHILDREN'S BOOK EVER WRITTEN, I KNOW.
THEY TAUGHT THE STORY DIFFERENTLY AT THE SAND CASTLE. DO YOU BELIEVE THE MIMIC REALLY EXISTS?
I DUNNO. I WAS TERRIFIED OF IT AS A KID. BUT NOBODY'S EVER SEEN IT, SO I'M NOT SO SURE.

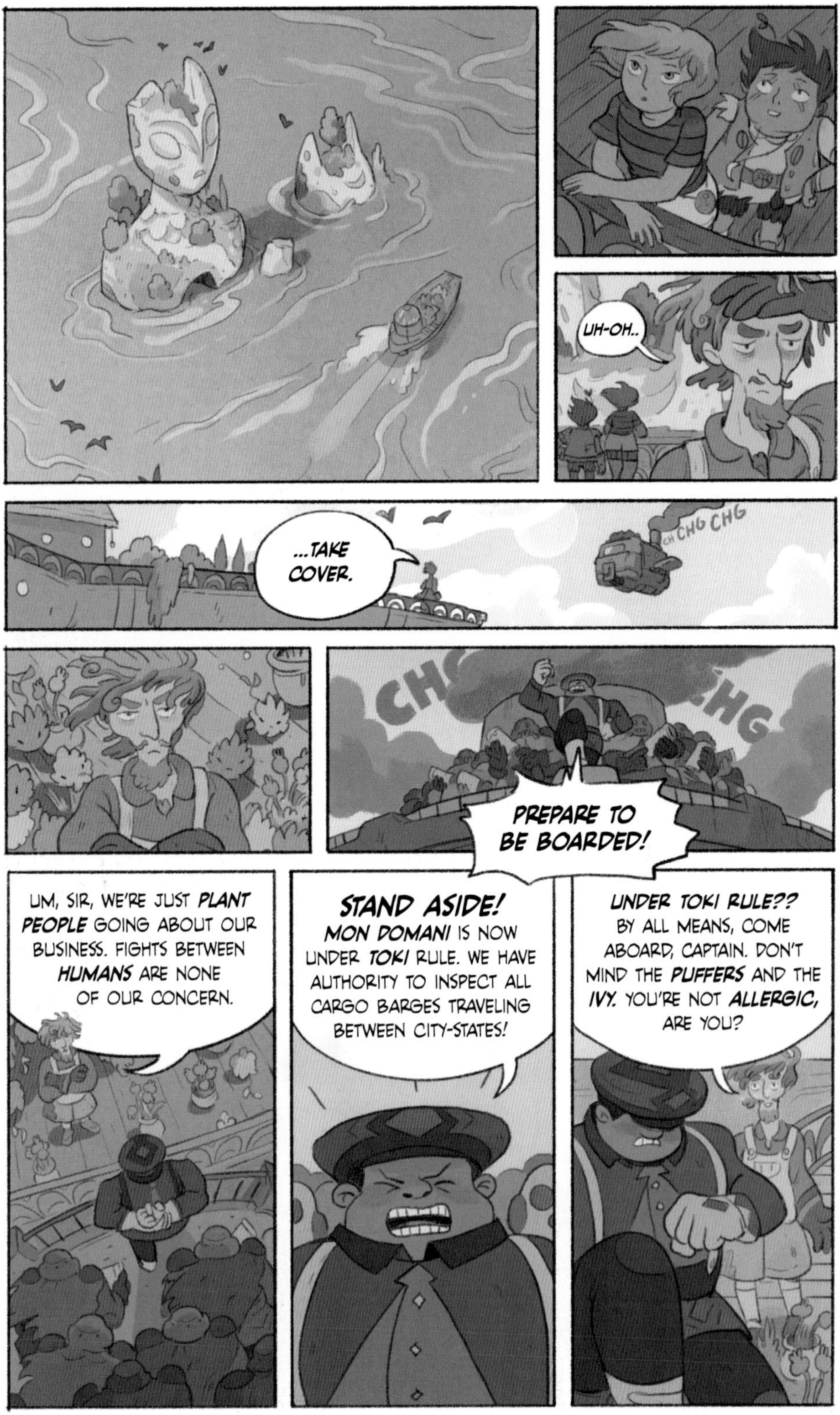
UH-OH..
...TAKE COVER.
CH CHG CHG
CHG
CHG
PREPARE TO BE BOARDED!
UM, SIR, WE'RE JUST PLANT PEOPLE GOING ABOUT OUR BUSINESS. FIGHTS BETWEEN HUMANS ARE NONE OF OUR CONCERN.
STAND ASIDE! MON DOMANI IS NOW UNDER TOKI RULE. WE HAVE AUTHORITY TO INSPECT ALL CARGO BARGES TRAVELING BETWEEN CITY-STATES!
UNDER TOKI RULE?? BY ALL MEANS, COME ABOARD, CAPTAIN. DON'T MIND THE PUFFERS AND THE IVY. YOU'RE NOT ALLERGIC, ARE YOU?

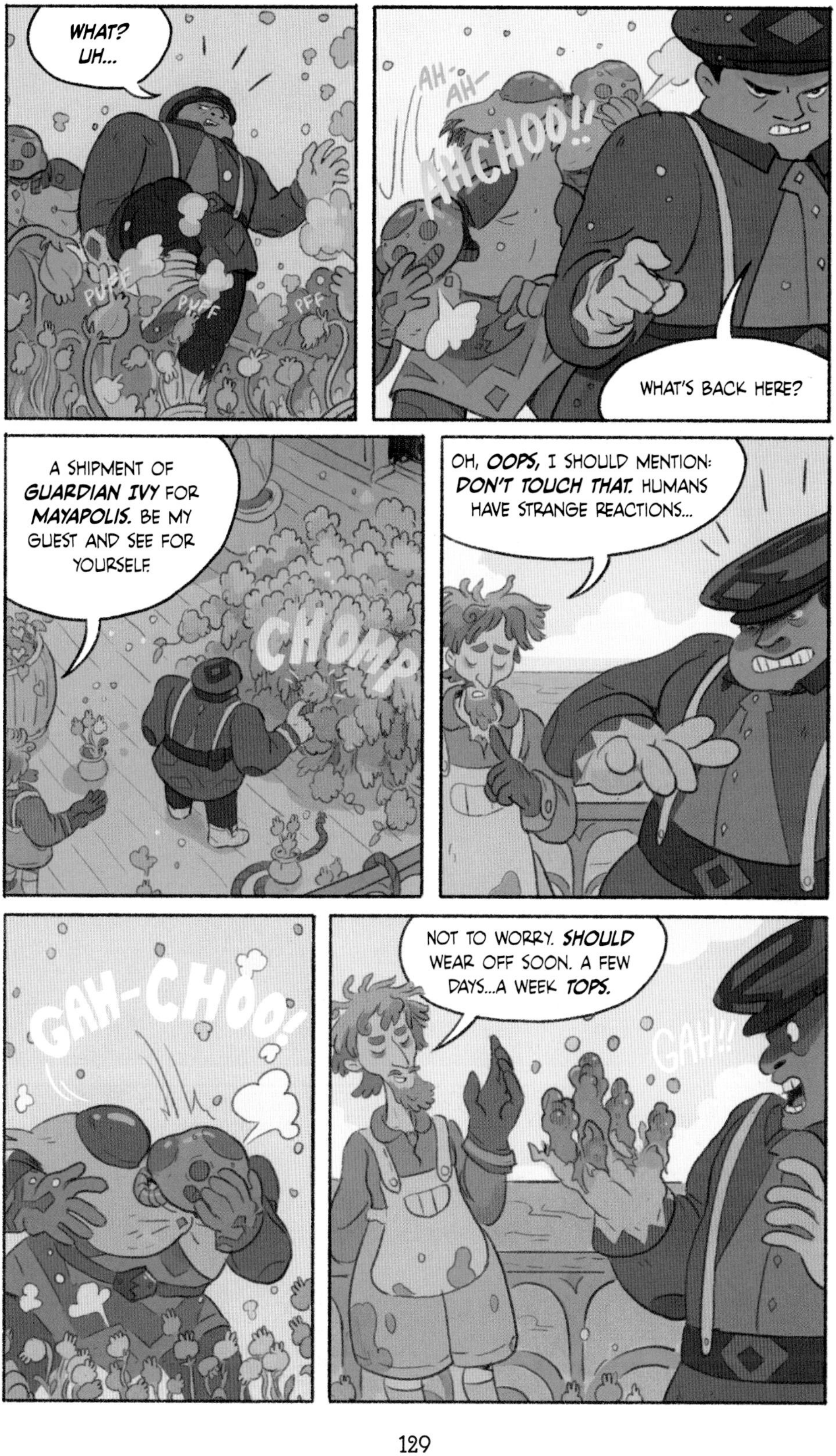
WHAT? UH...
PUFF
PUFF
PFF
AH-AH-AHCHOO!!
WHAT'S BACK HERE?
A SHIPMENT OF GUARDIAN IVY FOR MAYAPOLIS. BE MY GUEST AND SEE FOR YOURSELF.
CHOMP
OH, OOPS, I SHOULD MENTION: DON'T TOUCH THAT. HUMANS HAVE STRANGE REACTIONS...
GAH-CHOO!
NOT TO WORRY. SHOULD WEAR OFF SOON. A FEW DAYS...A WEEK TOPS.
GAH!!

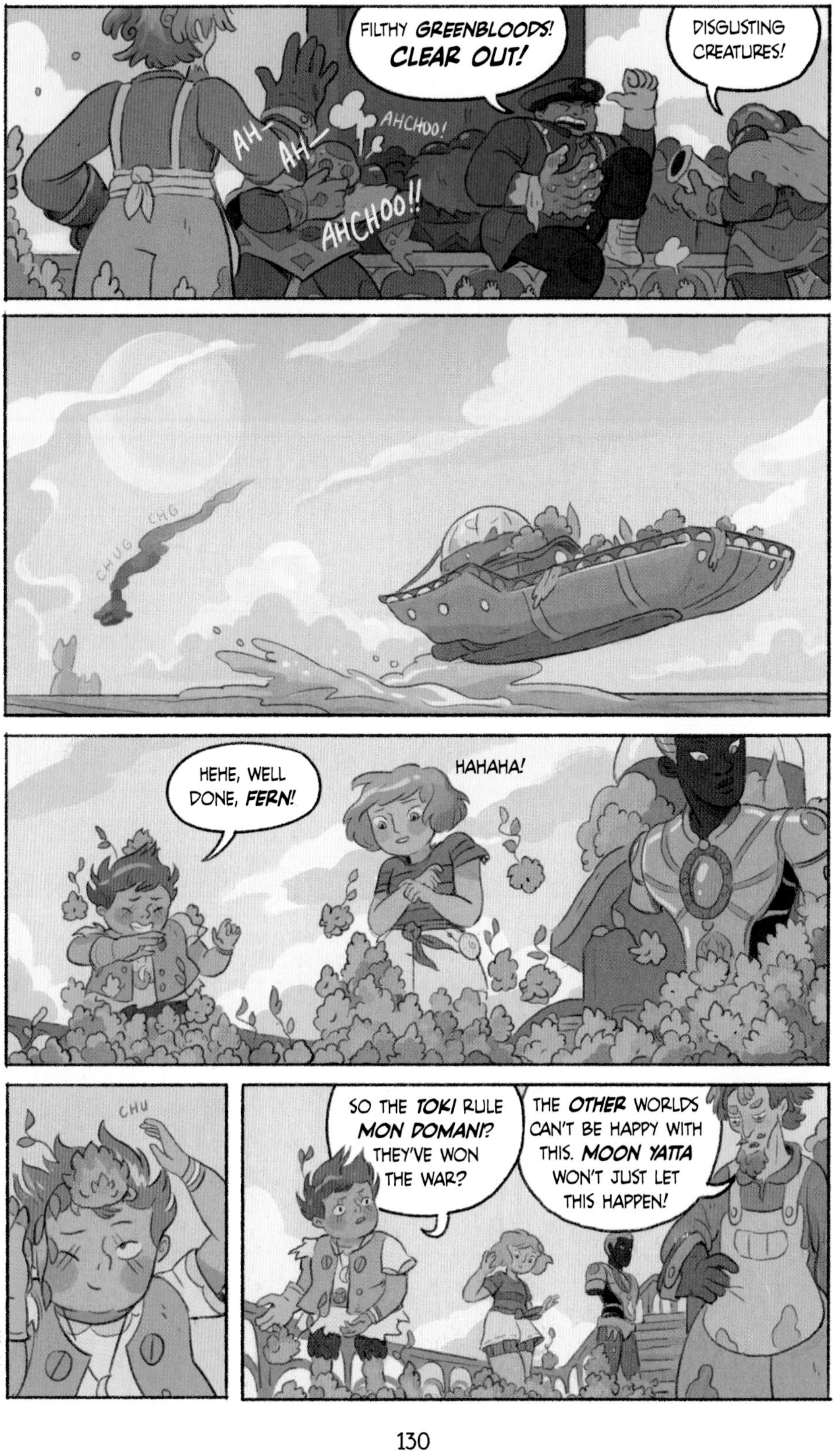
FILTHY GREENBLOODS! CLEAR OUT!
DISGUSTING CREATURES!
AH-
AH-
AHCHOO!
AHCHOO!!
CHUG
CHG
HEHE, WELL DONE, FERN!
HAHAHA!
CHU
SO THE TOKI RULE MON DOMANI? THEY'VE WON THE WAR?
THE OTHER WORLDS CAN'T BE HAPPY WITH THIS. MOON YATTA WON'T JUST LET THIS HAPPEN!

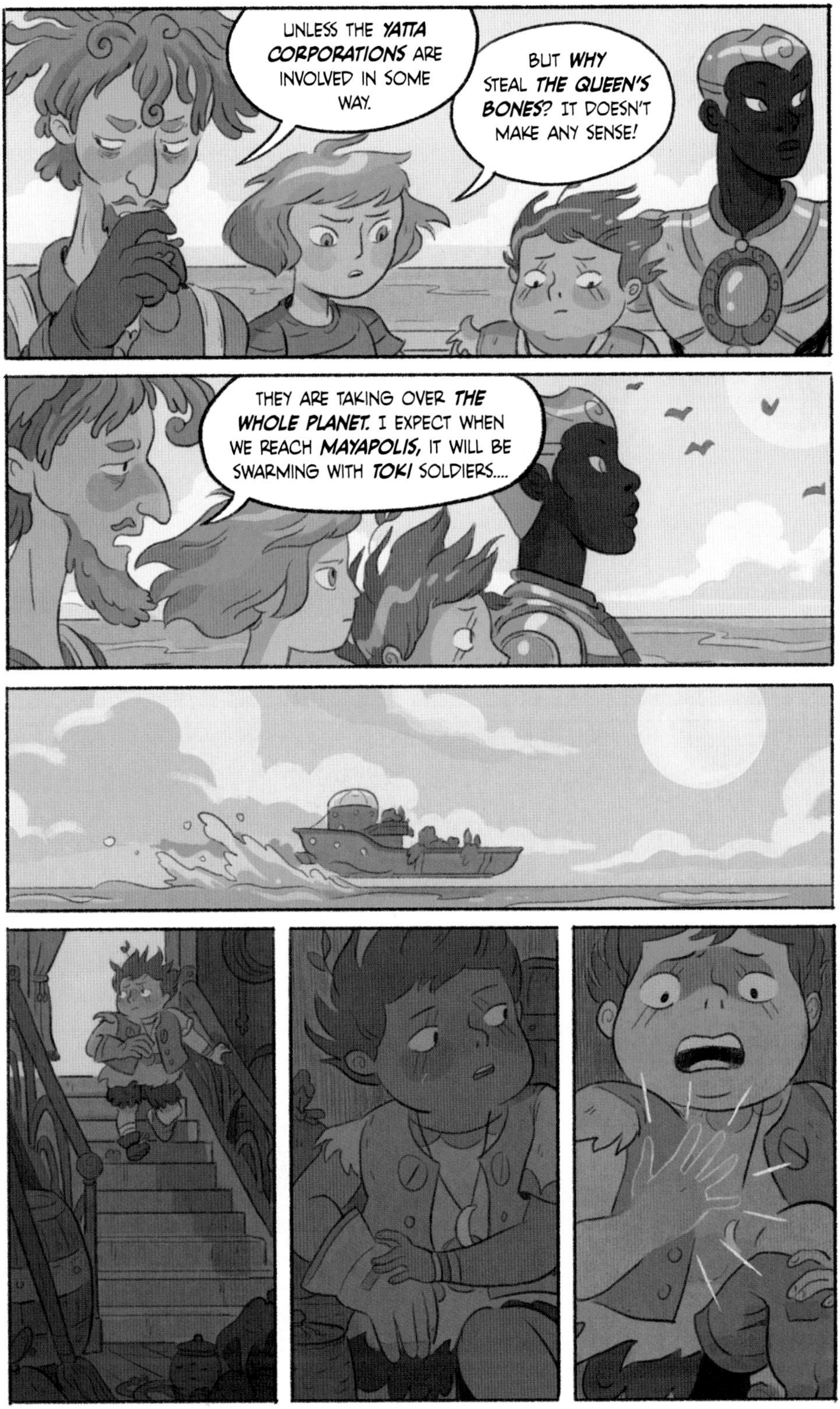
UNLESS THE YATTA CORPORATIONS ARE INVOLVED IN SOME WAY.
BUT WHY STEAL THE QUEEN'S BONES? IT DOESN'T MAKE ANY SENSE!
THEY ARE TAKING OVER THE WHOLE PLANET. I EXPECT WHEN WE REACH MAYAPOLIS, IT WILL BE SWARMING WITH TOKI SOLDIERS....

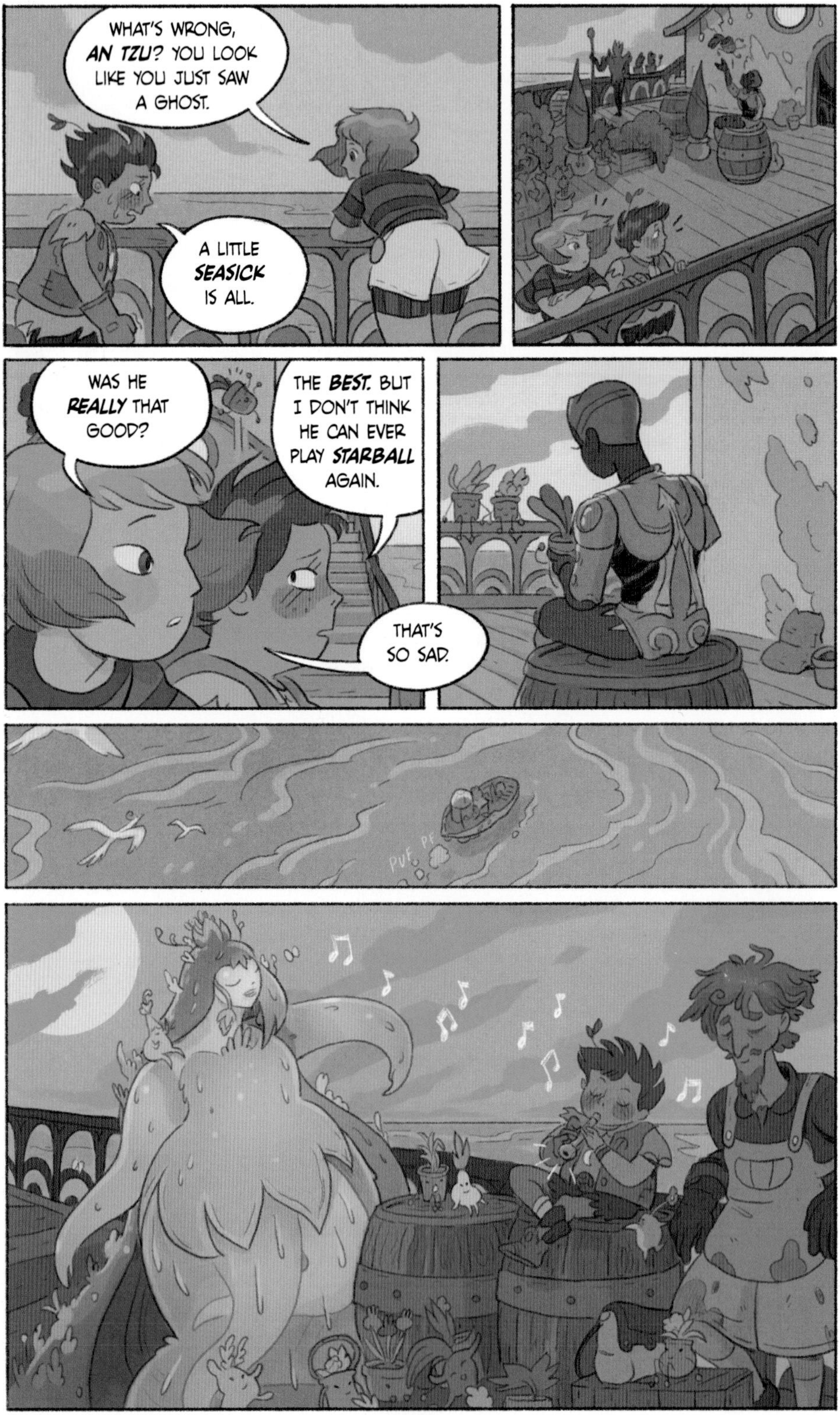
WHAT'S WRONG, AN TZU? YOU LOOK LIKE YOU JUST SAW A GHOST.
A LITTLE SEASICK IS ALL.
WAS HE REALLY THAT GOOD?
THE BEST. BUT I DON'T THINK HE CAN EVER PLAY STARBALL AGAIN.
THAT'S SO SAD.
PUF PF

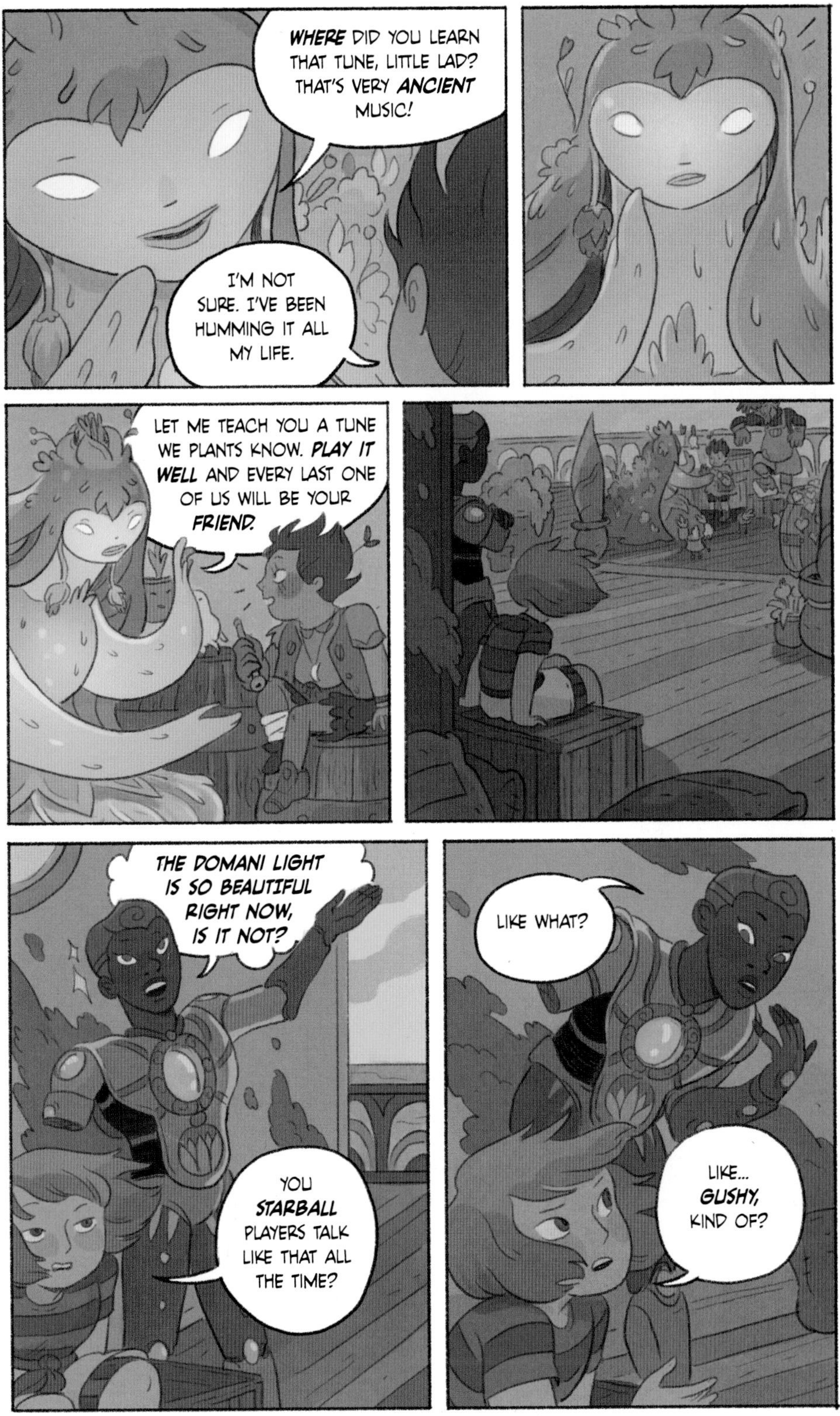
WHERE DID YOU LEARN THAT TUNE, LITTLE LAD? THAT'S VERY ANCIENT MUSIC!
I'M NOT SURE. I'VE BEEN HUMMING IT ALL MY LIFE.
LET ME TEACH YOU A TUNE WE PLANTS KNOW. PLAY IT WELL AND EVERY LAST ONE OF US WILL BE YOUR FRIEND.
THE DOMANI LIGHT IS SO BEAUTIFUL RIGHT NOW, IS IT NOT?
YOU STARBALL PLAYERS TALK LIKE THAT ALL THE TIME?
LIKE WHAT?
LIKE... GUSHY, KIND OF?

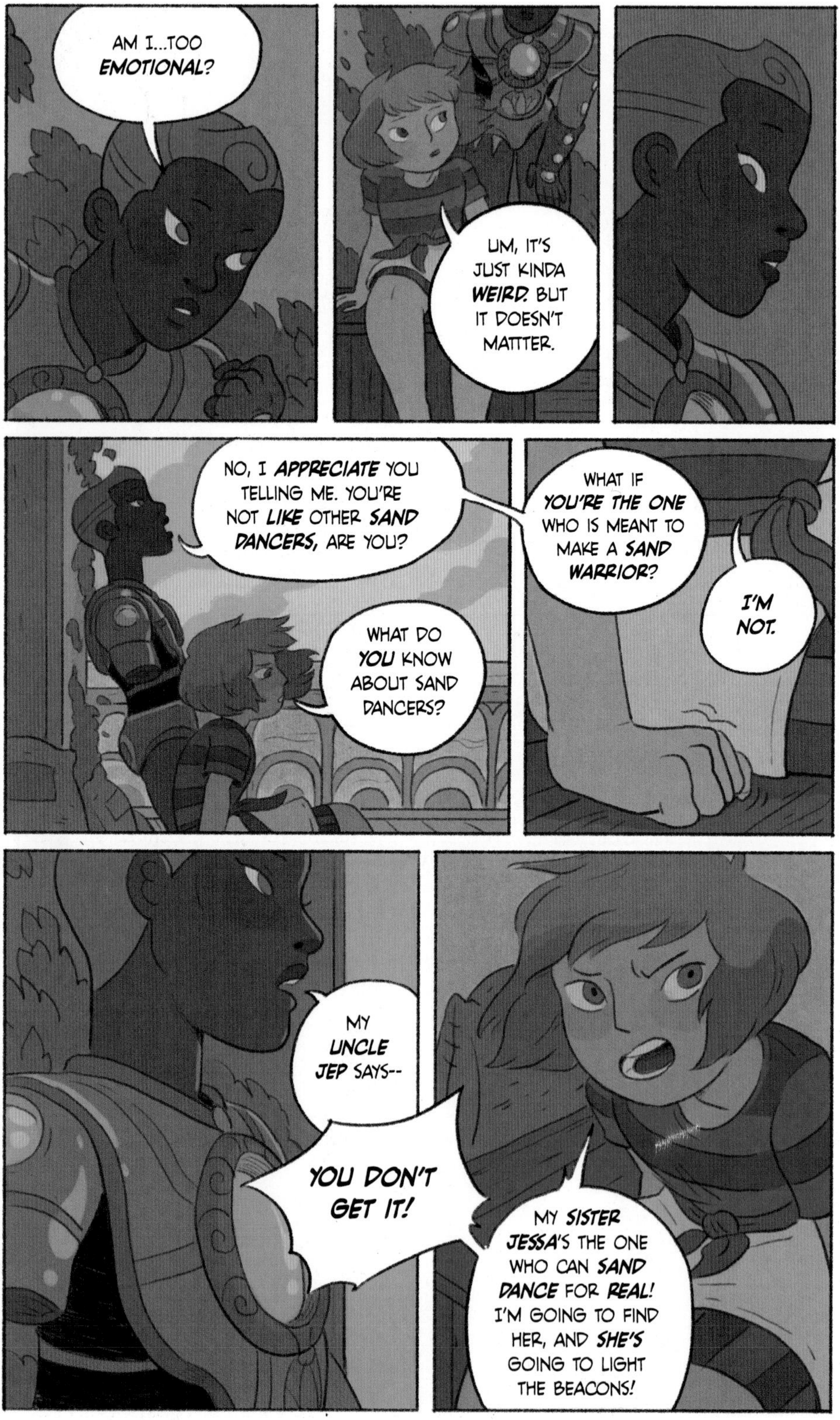
AM I...TOO EMOTIONAL?
UM, IT'S JUST KINDA WEIRD. BUT IT DOESN'T MATTTER.
NO, I APPRECIATE YOU TELLING ME. YOU'RE NOT LIKE OTHER SAND DANCERS, ARE YOU?
WHAT DO YOU KNOW ABOUT SAND DANCERS?
WHAT IF YOU'RE THE ONE WHO IS MEANT TO MAKE A SAND WARRIOR?
I'M NOT.
MY UNCLE JEP SAYS--
YOU DON'T GET IT!
MY SISTER JESSA'S THE ONE WHO CAN SAND DANCE FOR REAL! I'M GOING TO FIND HER, AND SHE'S GOING TO LIGHT THE BEACONS!

YOU CAN'T RUN FROM WHAT YOU REALLY ARE, *OONA.*

YOU ARE SO WEIRD!! I'M GOING TO SLEEP!

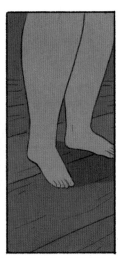

LOOK, I APPRECIATE WHAT YOU DID AT THE SAND CASTLE, BUT...

YOU *STARBALLERS* WERE HAVING YOUR *BIG GAME* RIGHT ON *BEACON DAY!* *LIKE IT WAS JUST SOME JOKE!*

SO DON'T TALK TO ME ABOUT "WHAT I REALLY AM"!

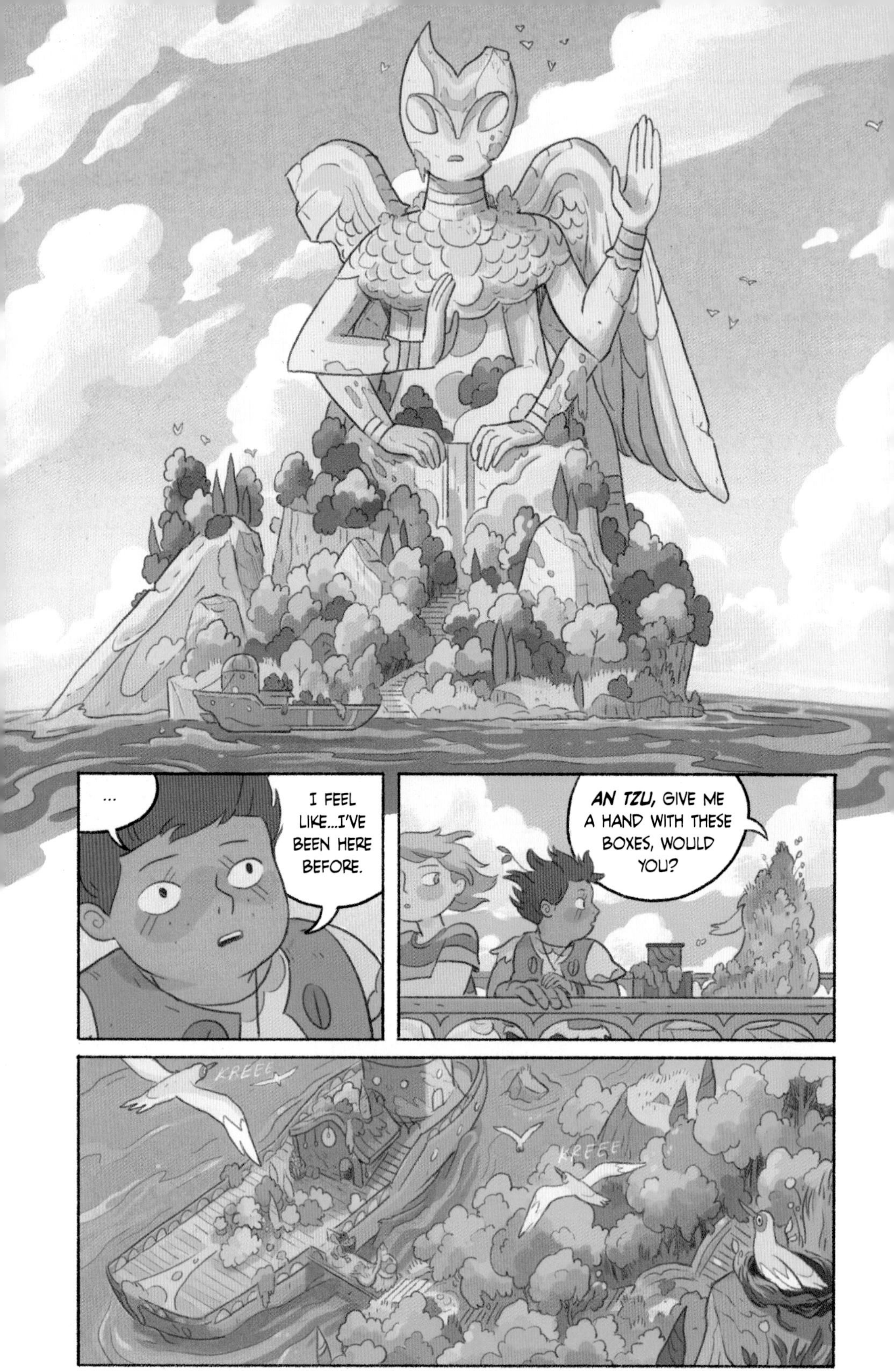
...
I FEEL LIKE...I'VE BEEN HERE BEFORE.
AN TZU, GIVE ME A HAND WITH THESE BOXES, WOULD YOU?
KREEE
KREEE

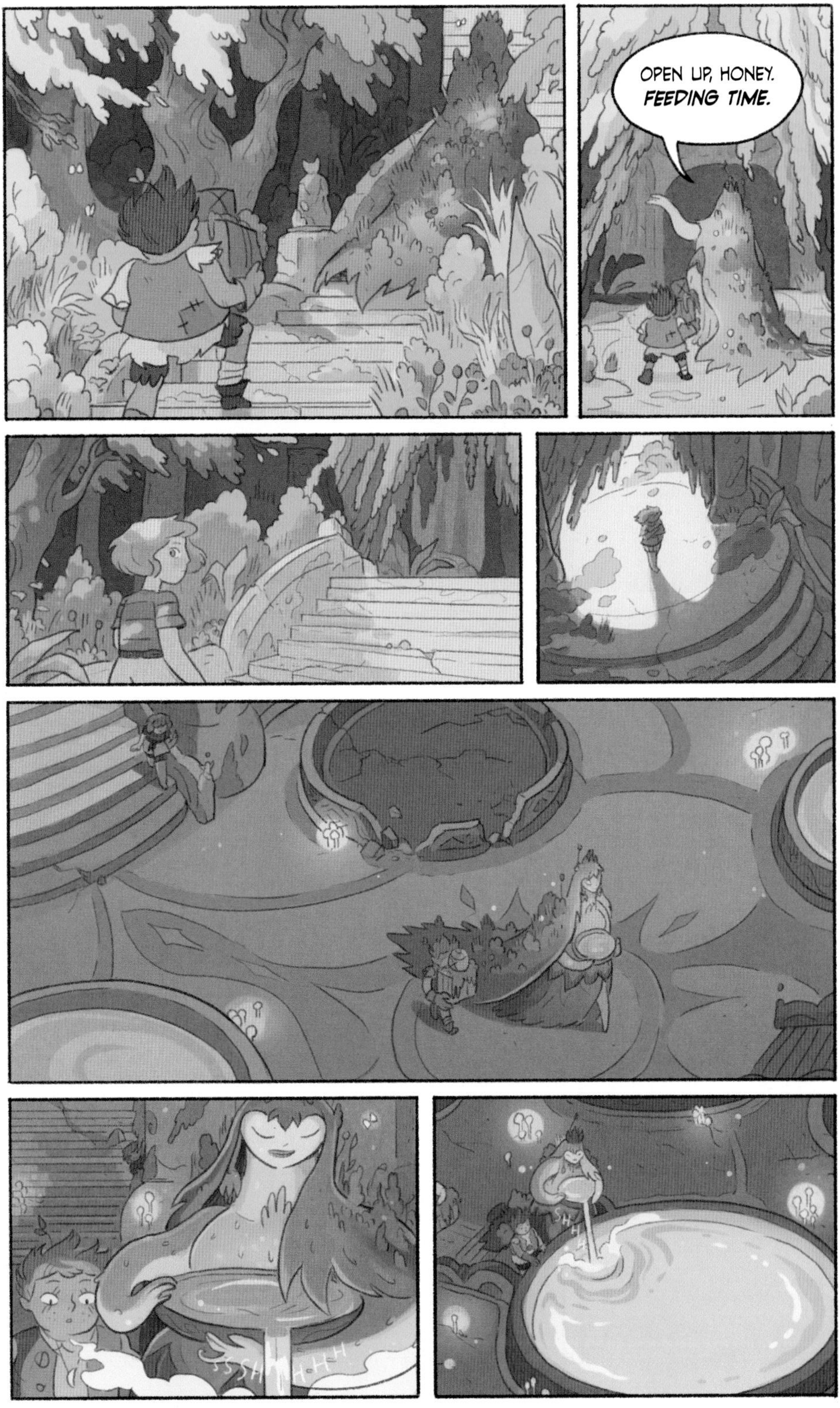
OPEN UP, HONEY.
FEEDING TIME.

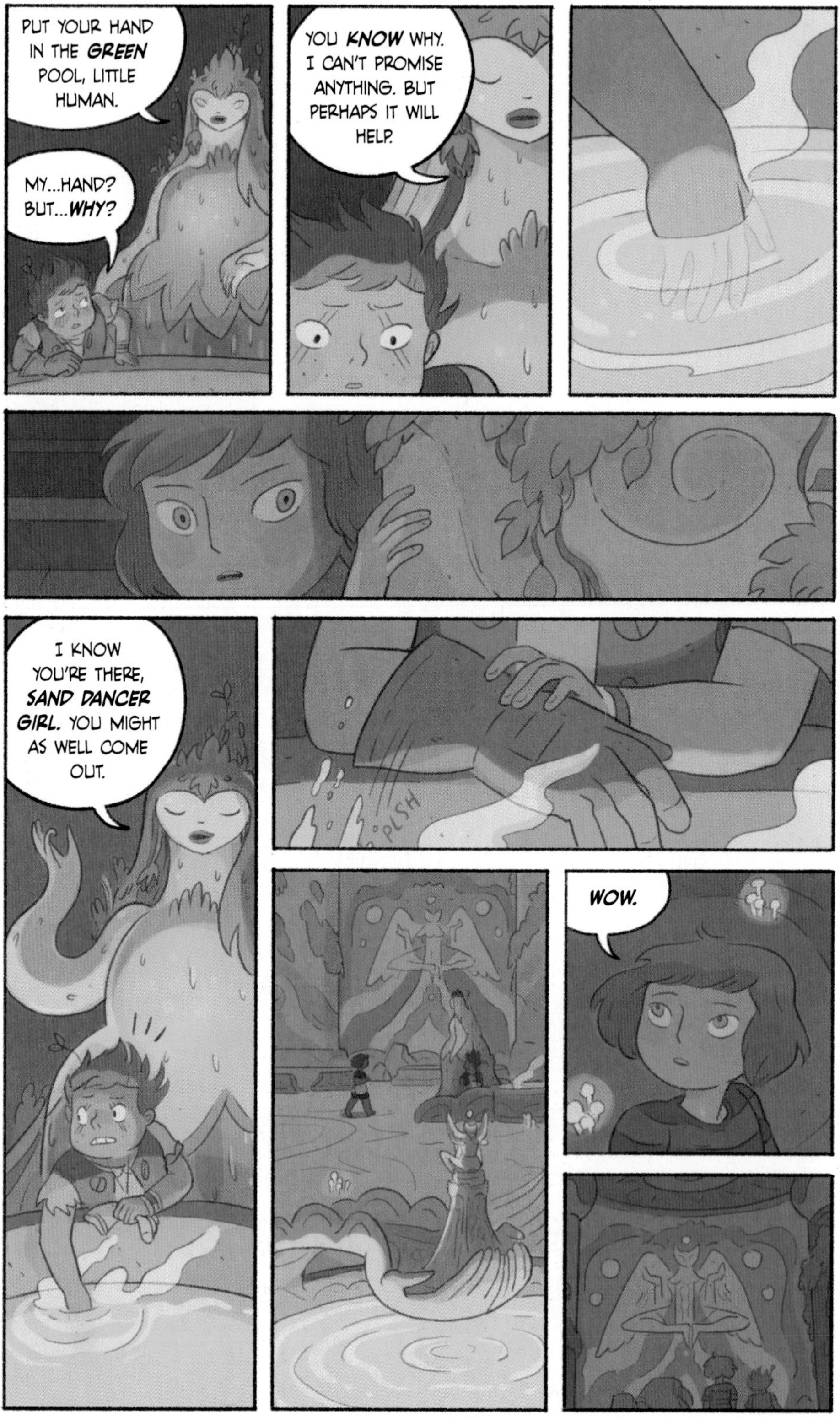

PUT YOUR HAND IN THE GREEN POOL, LITTLE HUMAN.
MY...HAND? BUT...WHY?
YOU KNOW WHY. I CAN'T PROMISE ANYTHING. BUT PERHAPS IT WILL HELP.
I KNOW YOU'RE THERE, SAND DANCER GIRL. YOU MIGHT AS WELL COME OUT.
PLSH
WOW.

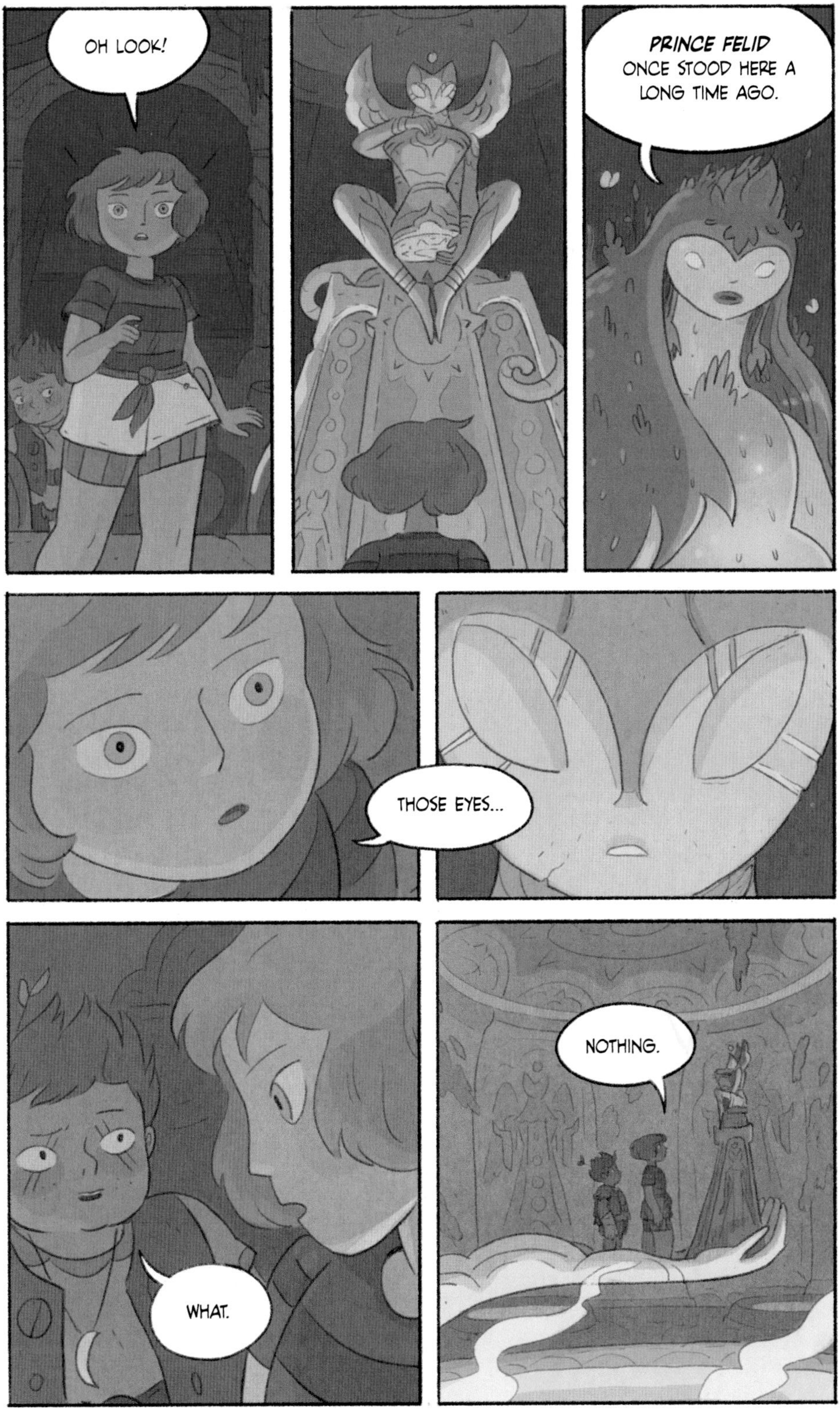
OH LOOK!
PRINCE FELID ONCE STOOD HERE A LONG TIME AGO.
THOSE EYES...
WHAT.
NOTHING.

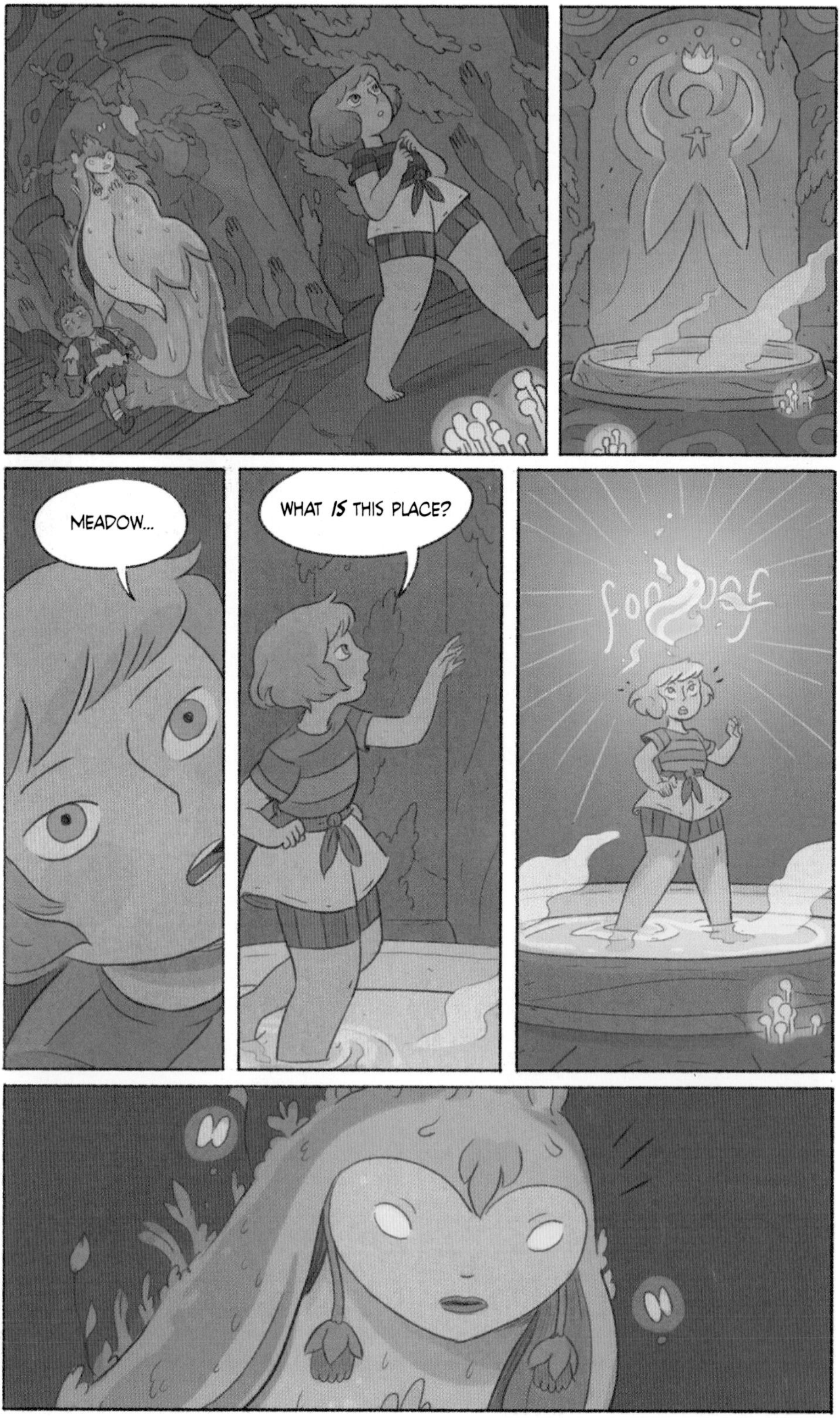
MEADOW...
WHAT *IS* THIS PLACE?

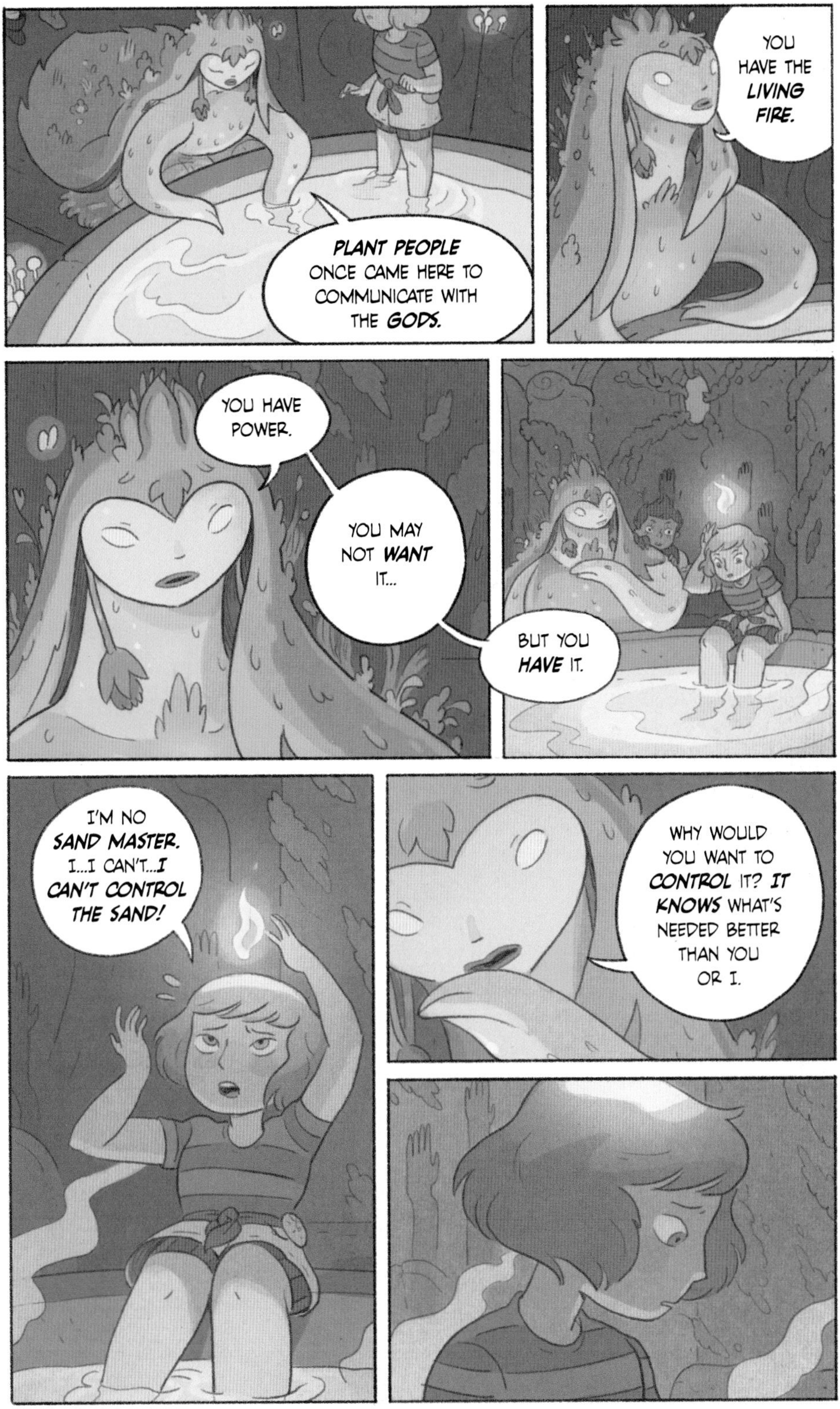
PLANT PEOPLE ONCE CAME HERE TO COMMUNICATE WITH THE GODS.
YOU HAVE THE LIVING FIRE.
YOU HAVE POWER.
YOU MAY NOT WANT IT...
BUT YOU HAVE IT.
I'M NO SAND MASTER. I...I CAN'T...I CAN'T CONTROL THE SAND!
WHY WOULD YOU WANT TO CONTROL IT? IT KNOWS WHAT'S NEEDED BETTER THAN YOU OR I.

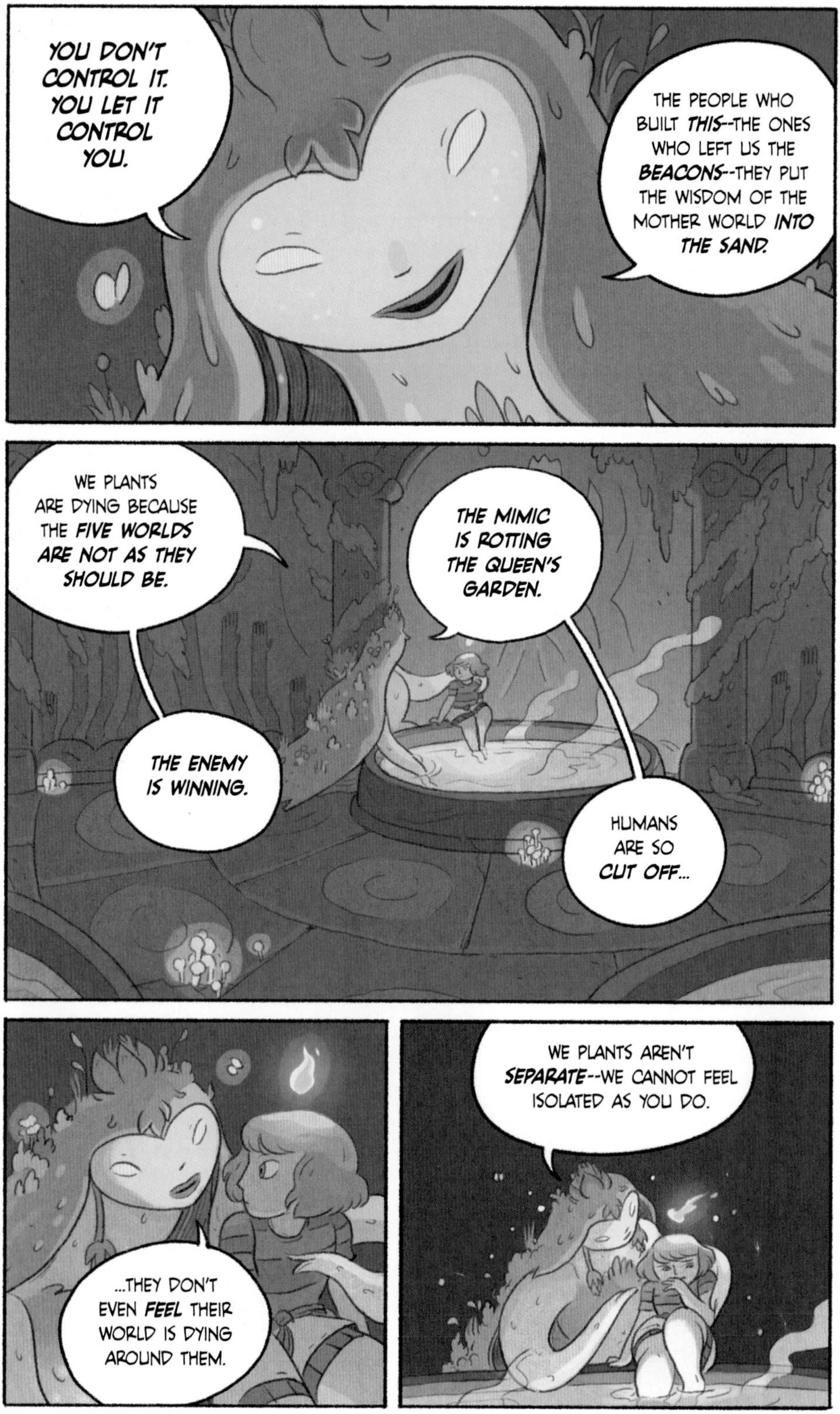
YOU DON'T CONTROL IT. YOU LET IT CONTROL YOU.
THE PEOPLE WHO BUILT THIS--THE ONES WHO LEFT US THE BEACONS--THEY PUT THE WISDOM OF THE MOTHER WORLD INTO THE SAND.
WE PLANTS ARE DYING BECAUSE THE FIVE WORLDS ARE NOT AS THEY SHOULD BE.
THE ENEMY IS WINNING.
THE MIMIC IS ROTTING THE QUEEN'S GARDEN.
HUMANS ARE SO CUT OFF...
...THEY DON'T EVEN FEEL THEIR WORLD IS DYING AROUND THEM.
WE PLANTS AREN'T SEPARATE--WE CANNOT FEEL ISOLATED AS YOU DO.

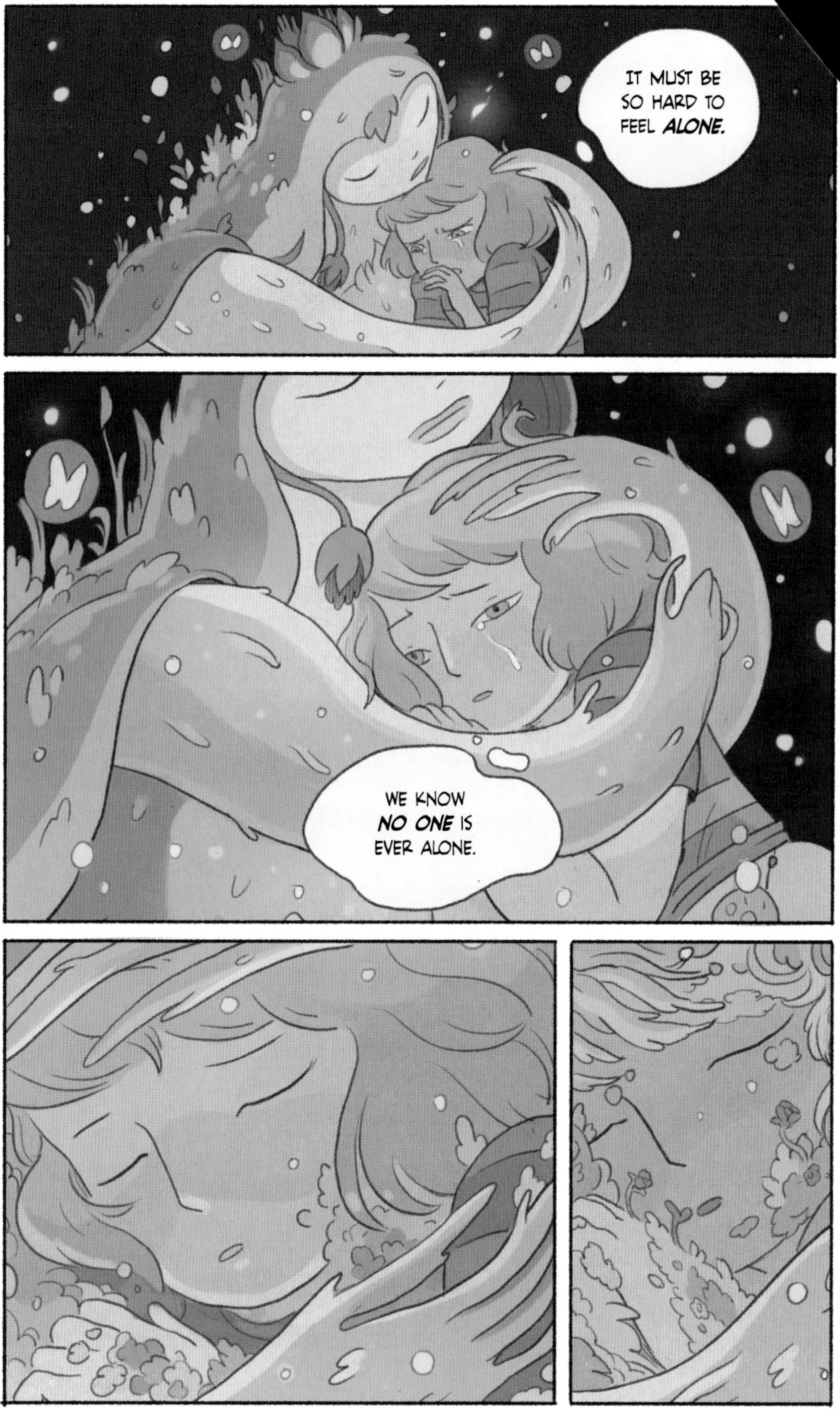
IT MUST BE SO HARD TO FEEL ALONE.
WE KNOW NO ONE IS EVER ALONE.

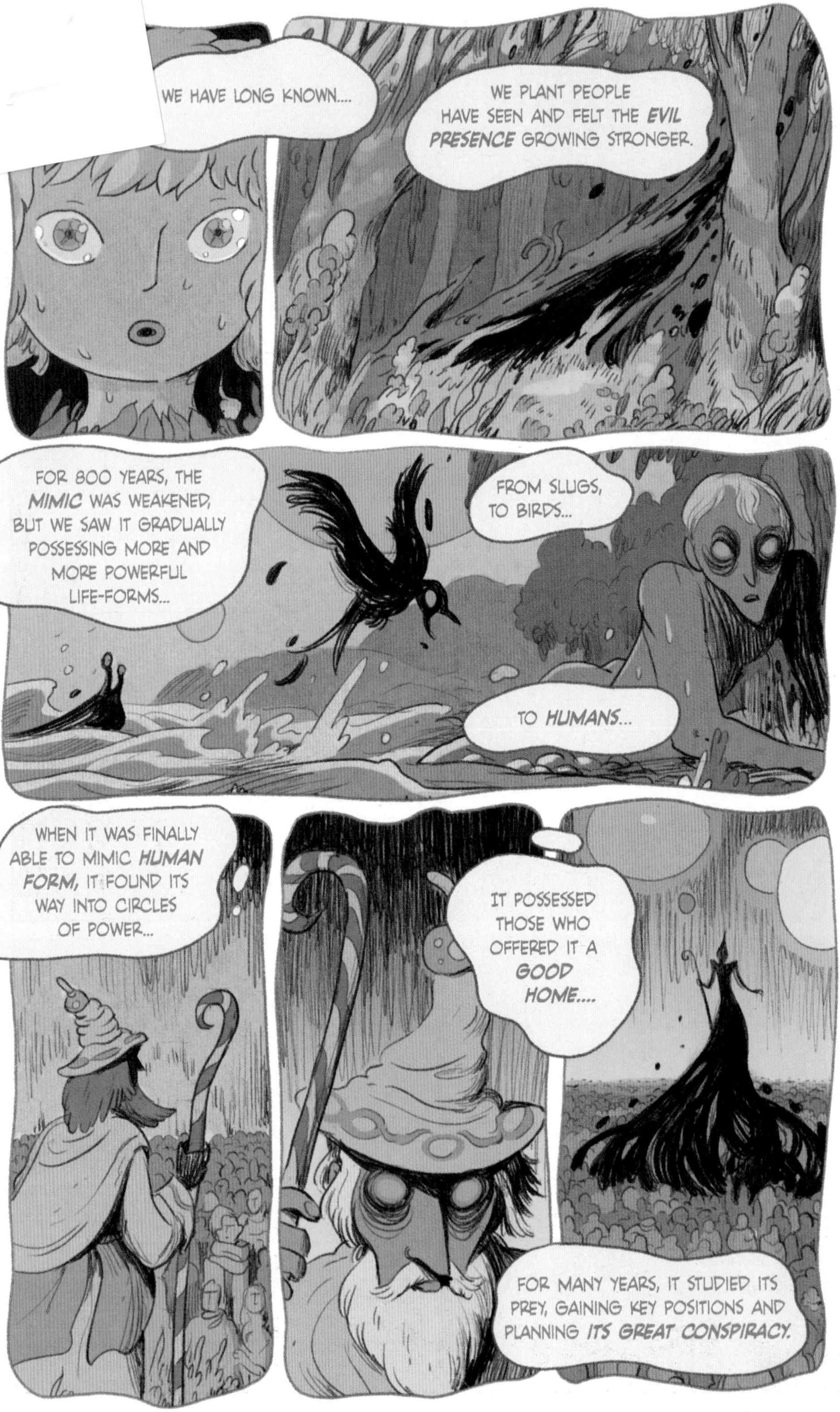

WE HAVE LONG KNOWN....
WE PLANT PEOPLE HAVE SEEN AND FELT THE EVIL PRESENCE GROWING STRONGER.
FOR 800 YEARS, THE MIMIC WAS WEAKENED, BUT WE SAW IT GRADUALLY POSSESSING MORE AND MORE POWERFUL LIFE-FORMS...
FROM SLUGS, TO BIRDS...
TO HUMANS...
WHEN IT WAS FINALLY ABLE TO MIMIC HUMAN FORM, IT FOUND ITS WAY INTO CIRCLES OF POWER...
IT POSSESSED THOSE WHO OFFERED IT A GOOD HOME....
FOR MANY YEARS, IT STUDIED ITS PREY, GAINING KEY POSITIONS AND PLANNING ITS GREAT CONSPIRACY.

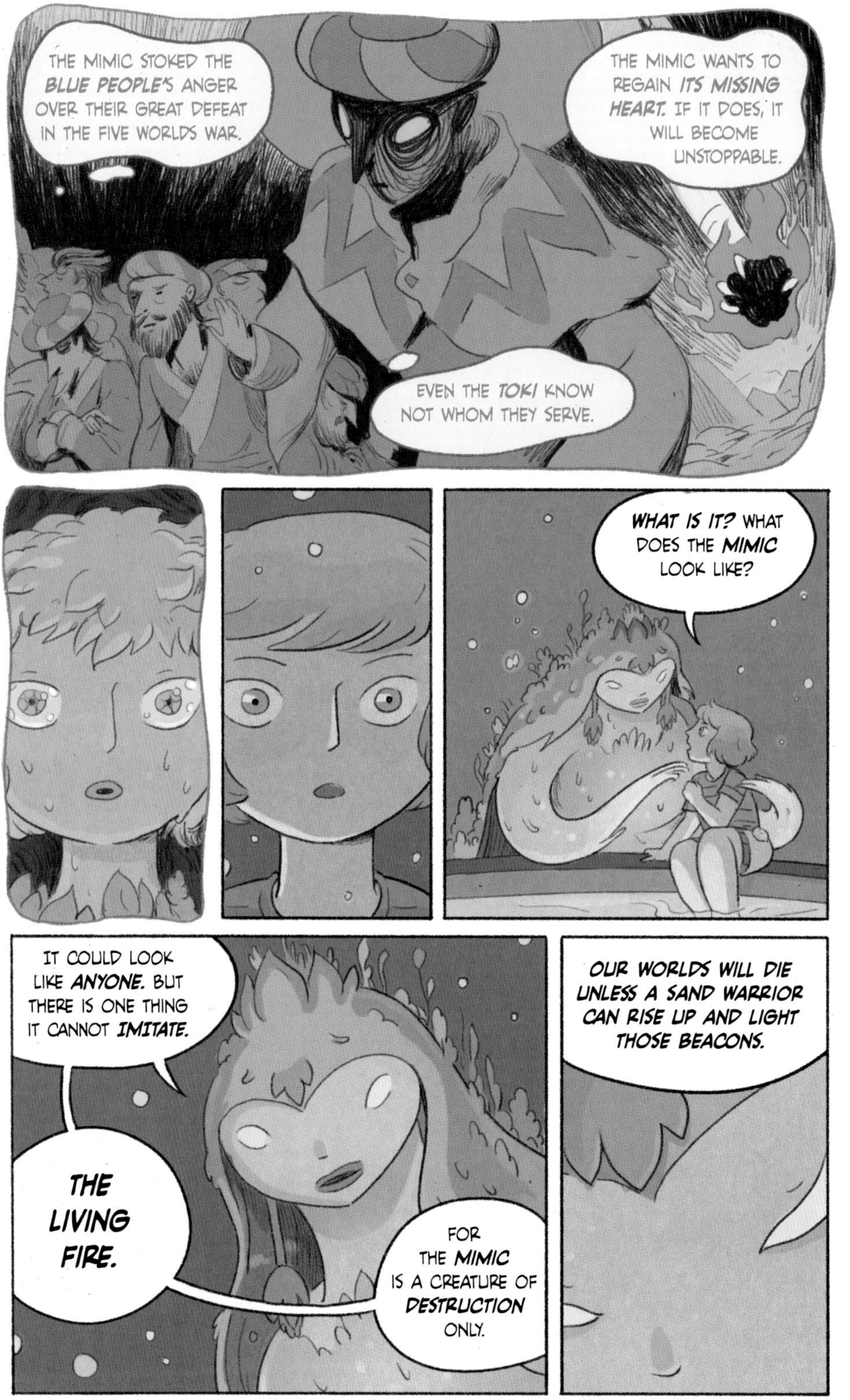
THE MIMIC STOKED THE BLUE PEOPLE'S ANGER OVER THEIR GREAT DEFEAT IN THE FIVE WORLDS WAR.
THE MIMIC WANTS TO REGAIN ITS MISSING HEART. IF IT DOES, IT WILL BECOME UNSTOPPABLE.
EVEN THE TOKI KNOW NOT WHOM THEY SERVE.
WHAT IS IT? WHAT DOES THE MIMIC LOOK LIKE?
IT COULD LOOK LIKE ANYONE. BUT THERE IS ONE THING IT CANNOT IMITATE.
THE LIVING FIRE.
FOR THE MIMIC IS A CREATURE OF DESTRUCTION ONLY.
OUR WORLDS WILL DIE UNLESS A SAND WARRIOR CAN RISE UP AND LIGHT THOSE BEACONS.

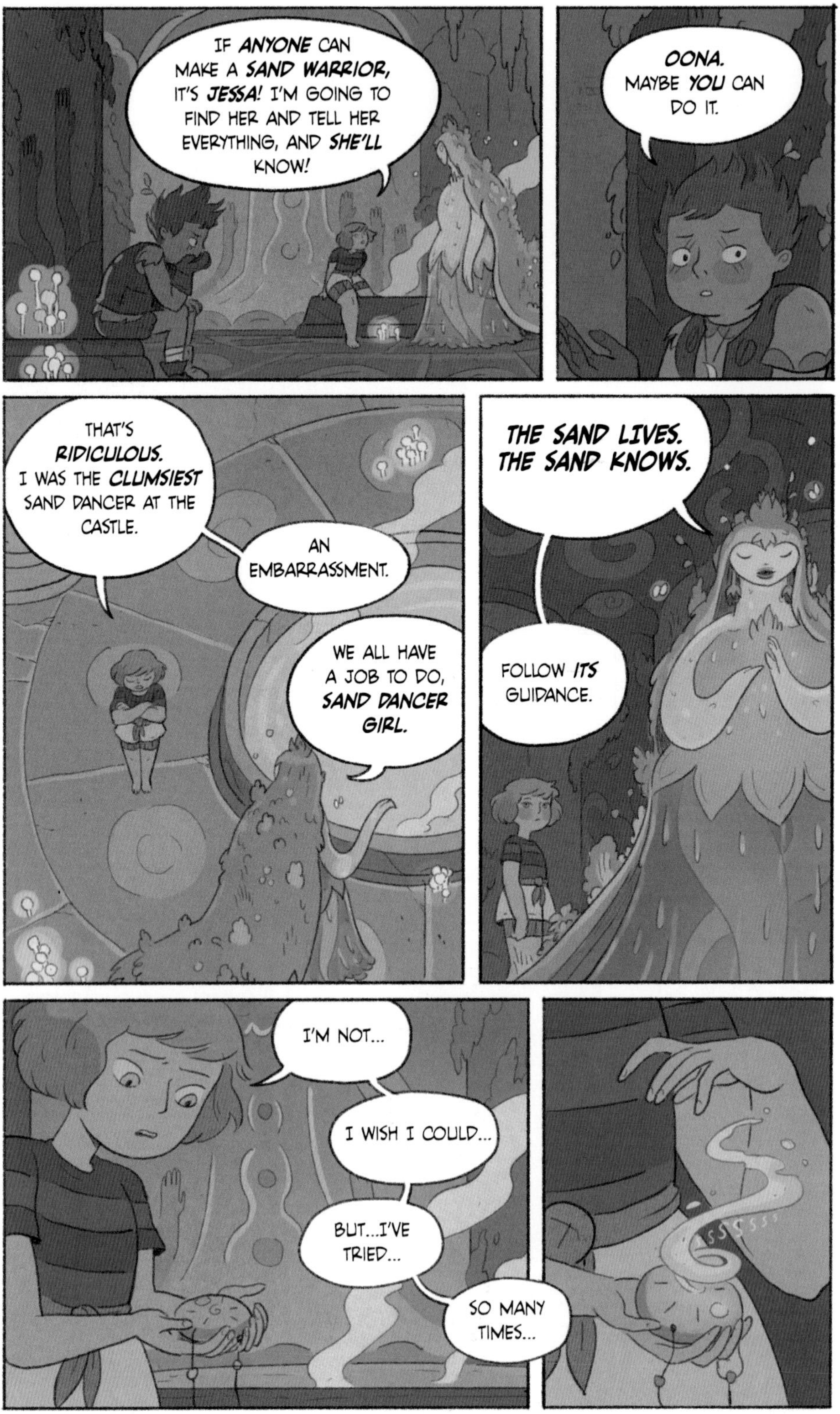
IF ANYONE CAN MAKE A SAND WARRIOR, IT'S JESSA! I'M GOING TO FIND HER AND TELL HER EVERYTHING, AND SHE'LL KNOW!
OONA. MAYBE YOU CAN DO IT.
THAT'S RIDICULOUS. I WAS THE CLUMSIEST SAND DANCER AT THE CASTLE.
AN EMBARRASSMENT.
WE ALL HAVE A JOB TO DO, SAND DANCER GIRL.
THE SAND LIVES. THE SAND KNOWS.
FOLLOW ITS GUIDANCE.
I'M NOT...
I WISH I COULD...
BUT...I'VE TRIED...
SO MANY TIMES...
SSSSSS

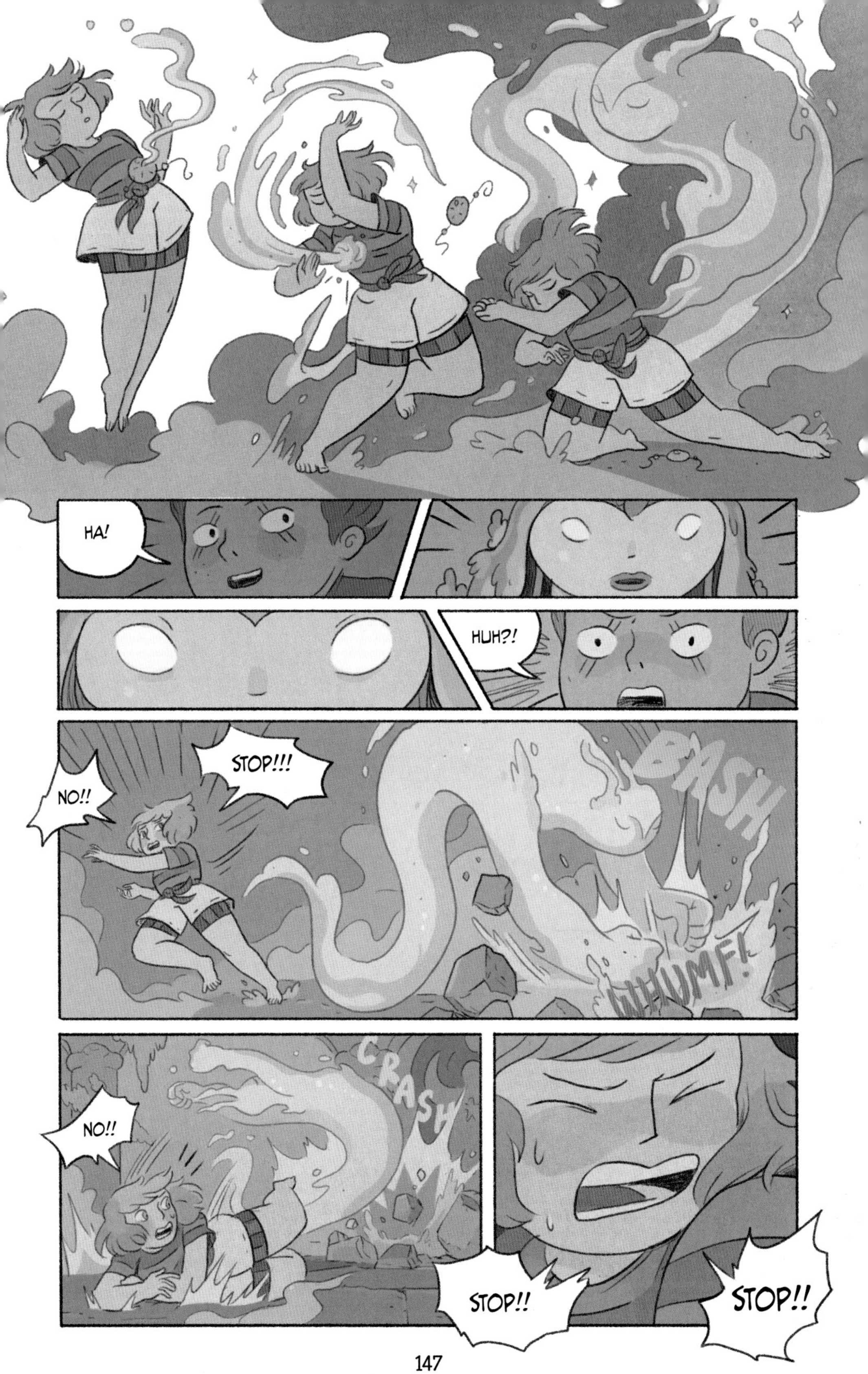
HA!
HUH?!
NO!!
STOP!!!
BASH
WHUMF!
NO!!
CRASH
STOP!!
STOP!!

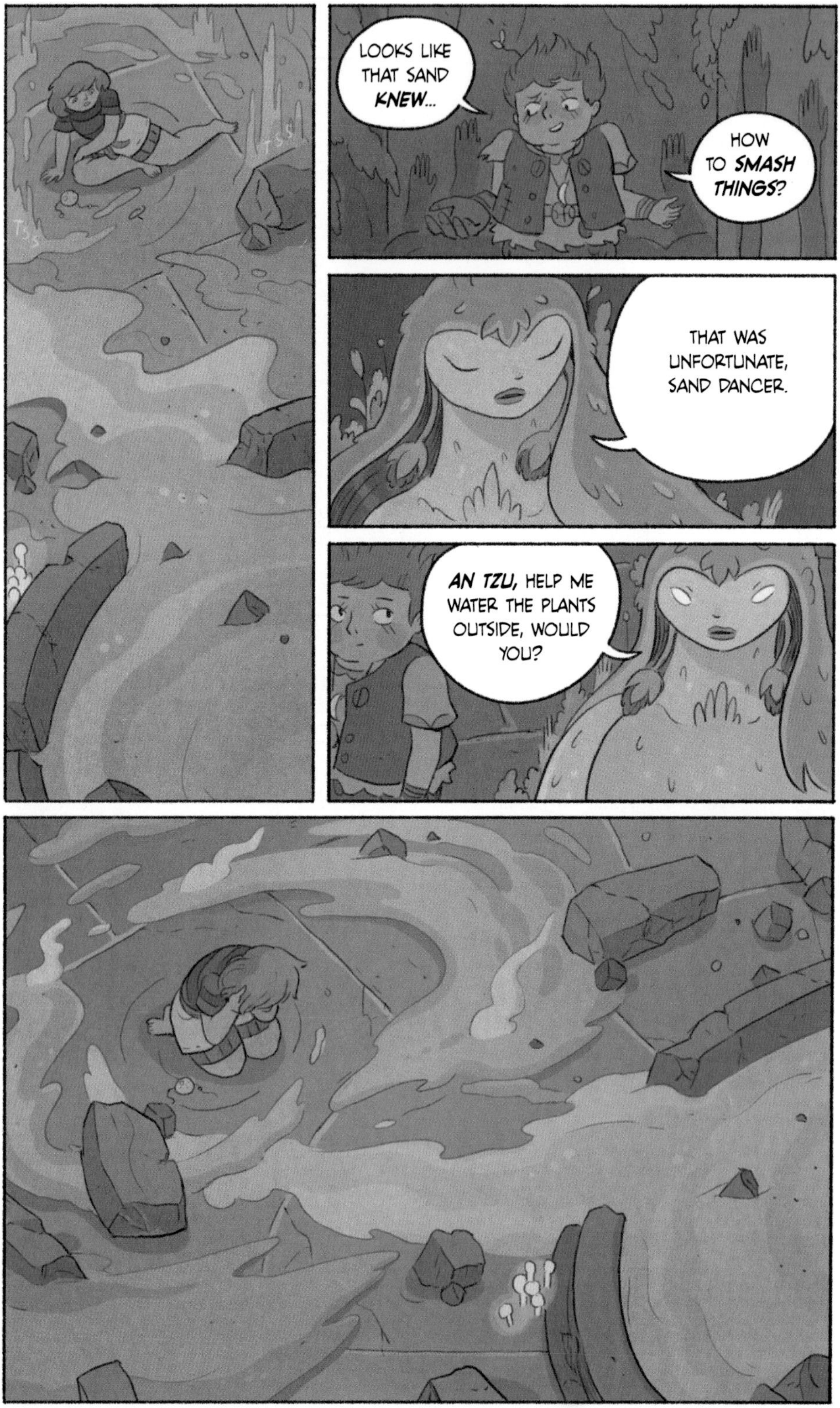
LOOKS LIKE THAT SAND KNEW...
HOW TO SMASH THINGS?
THAT WAS UNFORTUNATE, SAND DANCER.
AN TZU, HELP ME WATER THE PLANTS OUTSIDE, WOULD YOU?

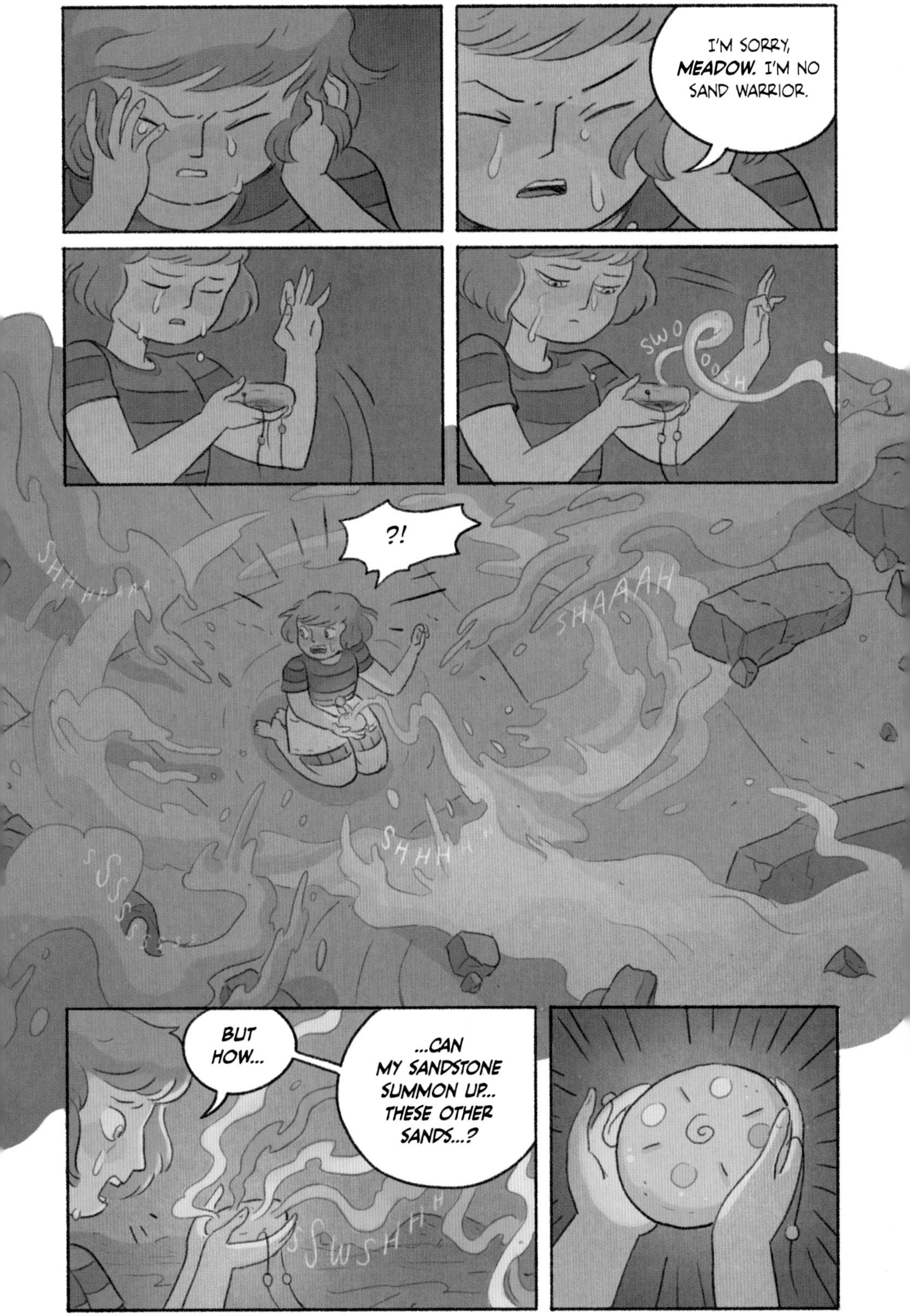
I'M SORRY, MEADOW. I'M NO SAND WARRIOR.
SWOOOSH
?!
SHHHHAAA
SHAAAH
SSSSSSS
SHHHH
BUT HOW...
...CAN MY SANDSTONE SUMMON UP... THESE OTHER SANDS...?
SSWSHHH

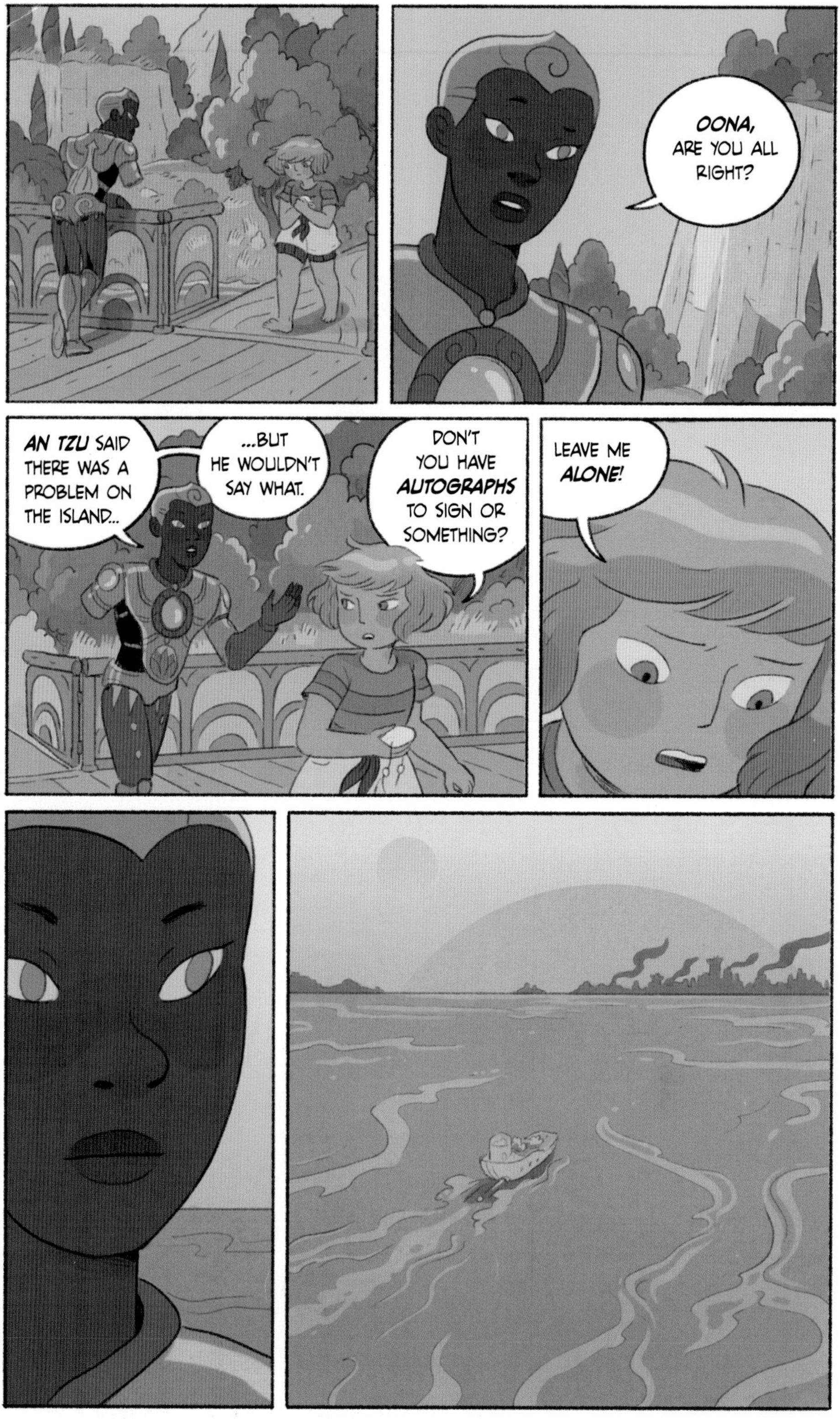
OONA, ARE YOU ALL RIGHT?
AN TZU SAID THERE WAS A PROBLEM ON THE ISLAND...
...BUT HE WOULDN'T SAY WHAT.
DON'T YOU HAVE AUTOGRAPHS TO SIGN OR SOMETHING?
LEAVE ME ALONE!

Chapter 7

THE SAND KNOWS

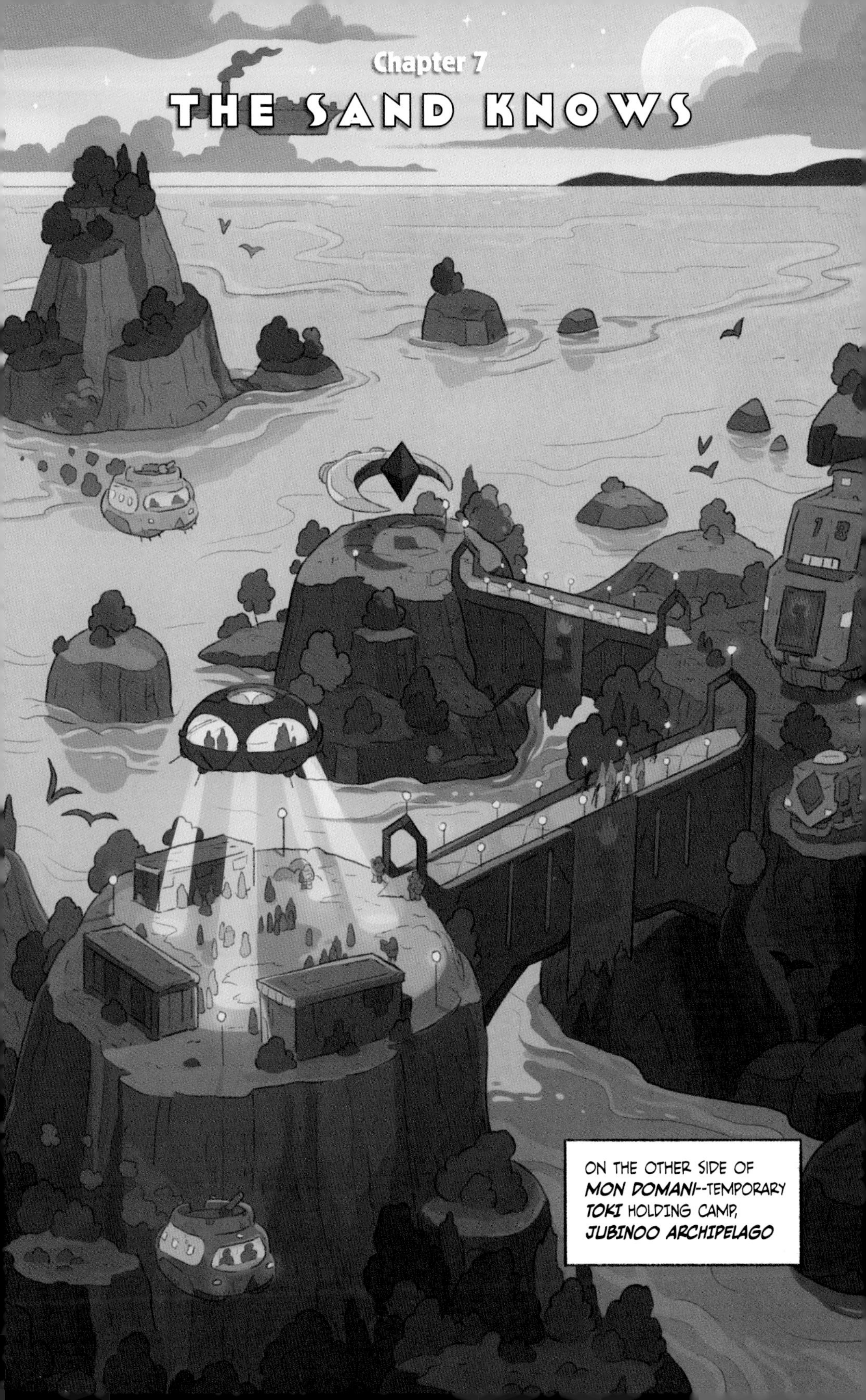
ON THE OTHER SIDE OF MON DOMANI--TEMPORARY TOKI HOLDING CAMP, JUBINOO ARCHIPELAGO

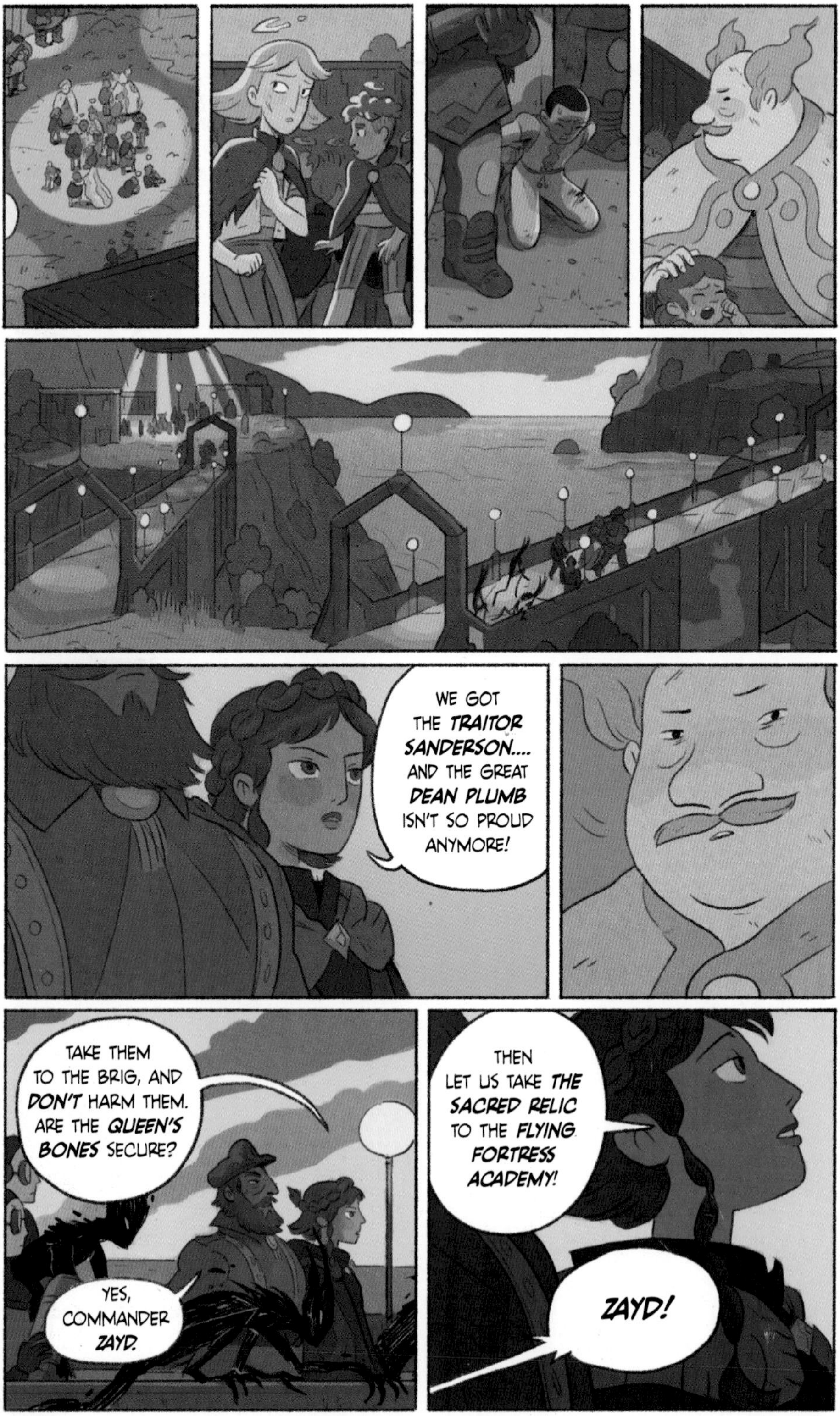
WE GOT THE TRAITOR SANDERSON.... AND THE GREAT DEAN PLUMB ISN'T SO PROUD ANYMORE!
TAKE THEM TO THE BRIG, AND DON'T HARM THEM. ARE THE QUEEN'S BONES SECURE?
YES, COMMANDER ZAYD.
THEN LET US TAKE THE SACRED RELIC TO THE FLYING FORTRESS ACADEMY!
ZAYD!

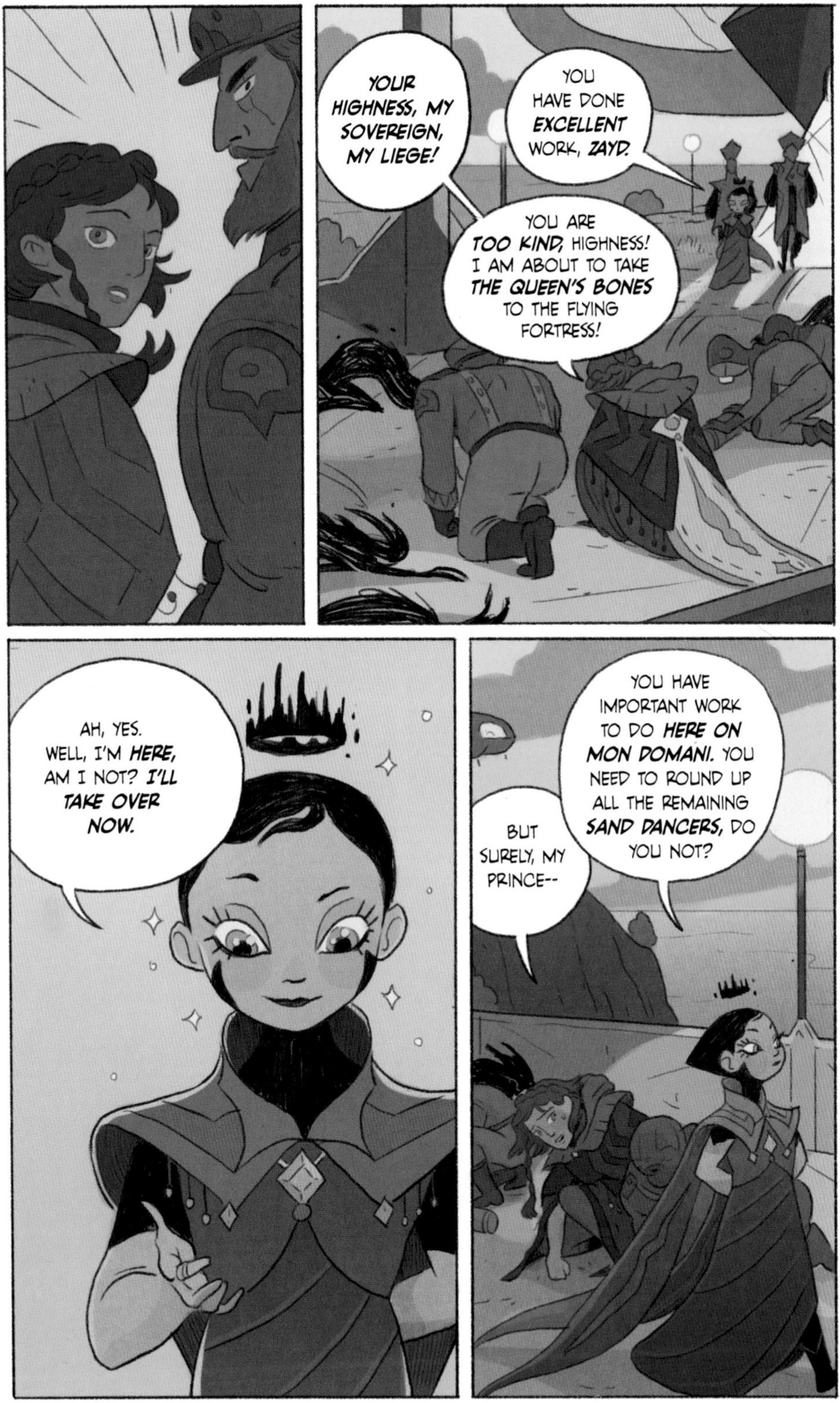
YOUR HIGHNESS, MY SOVEREIGN, MY LIEGE!
YOU HAVE DONE EXCELLENT WORK, ZAYD.
YOU ARE TOO KIND, HIGHNESS! I AM ABOUT TO TAKE THE QUEEN'S BONES TO THE FLYING FORTRESS!
AH, YES. WELL, I'M HERE, AM I NOT? I'LL TAKE OVER NOW.
BUT SURELY, MY PRINCE--
YOU HAVE IMPORTANT WORK TO DO HERE ON MON DOMANI. YOU NEED TO ROUND UP ALL THE REMAINING SAND DANCERS, DO YOU NOT?

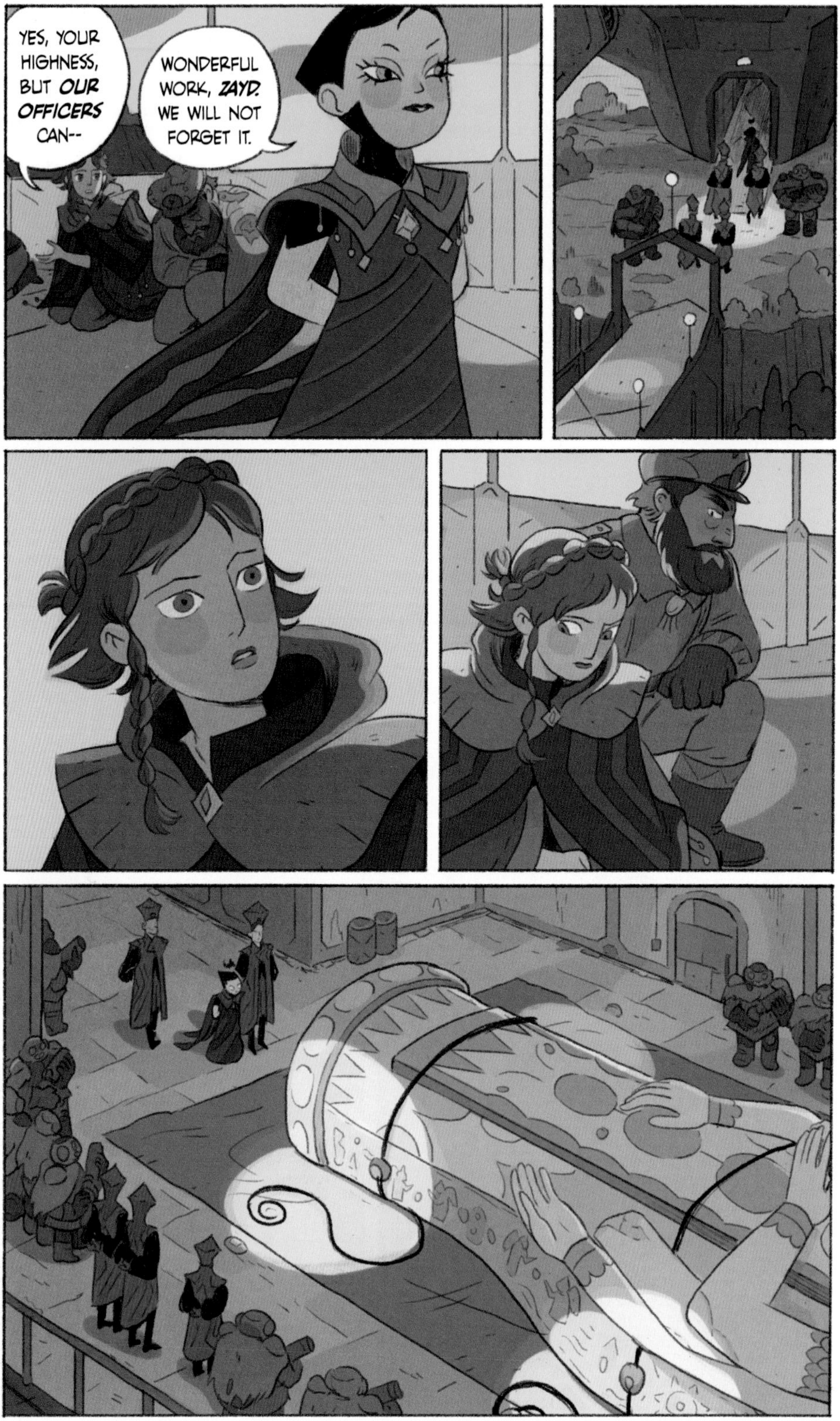
YES, YOUR HIGHNESS, BUT OUR OFFICERS CAN--
WONDERFUL WORK, ZAYD. WE WILL NOT FORGET IT.

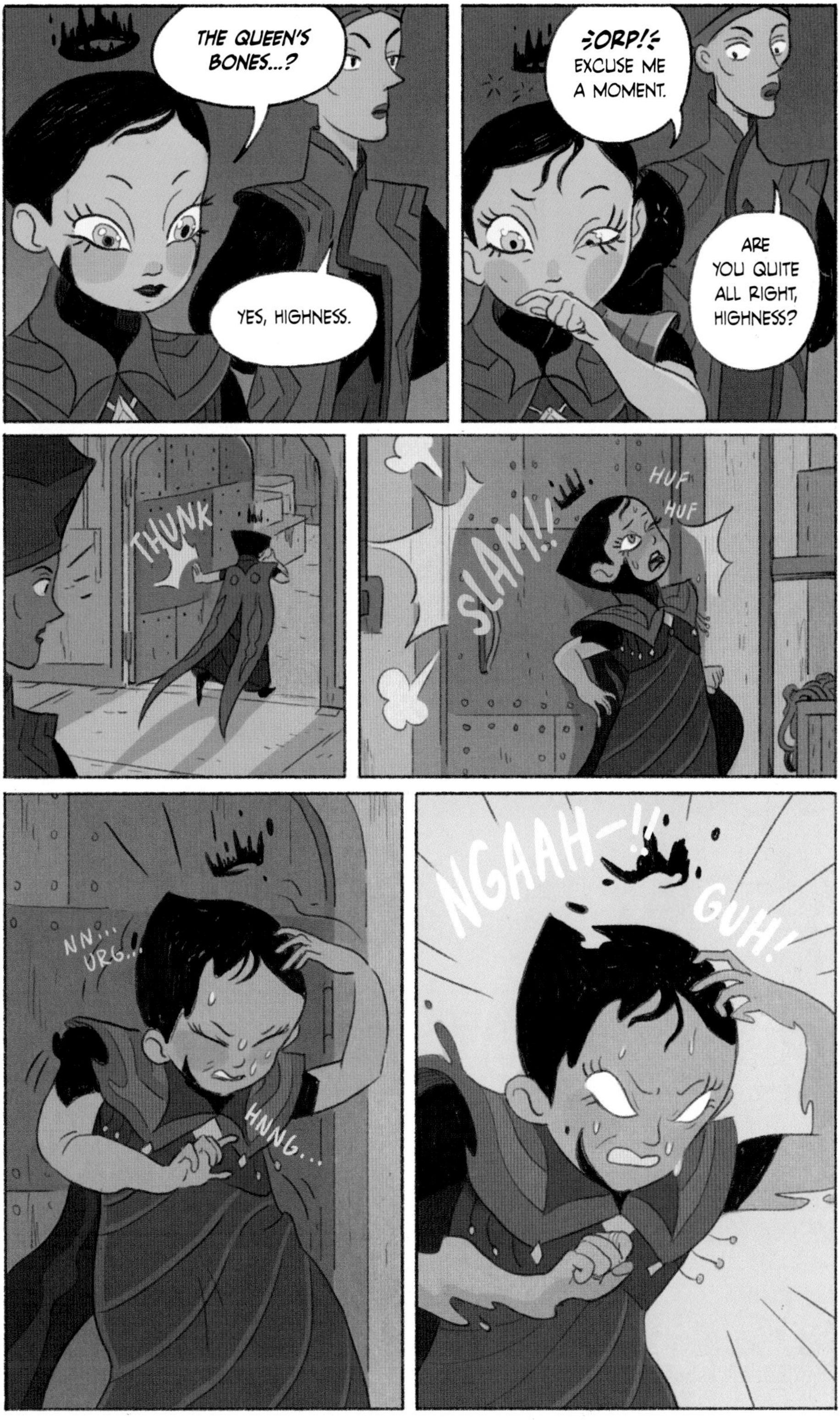
THE QUEEN'S BONES...?
YES, HIGHNESS.
ORP!
EXCUSE ME A MOMENT.
ARE YOU QUITE ALL RIGHT, HIGHNESS?
THUNK
SLAM!!
HUF HUF
NN... URG...
HNNG...
NGAAH-!!
GUH!

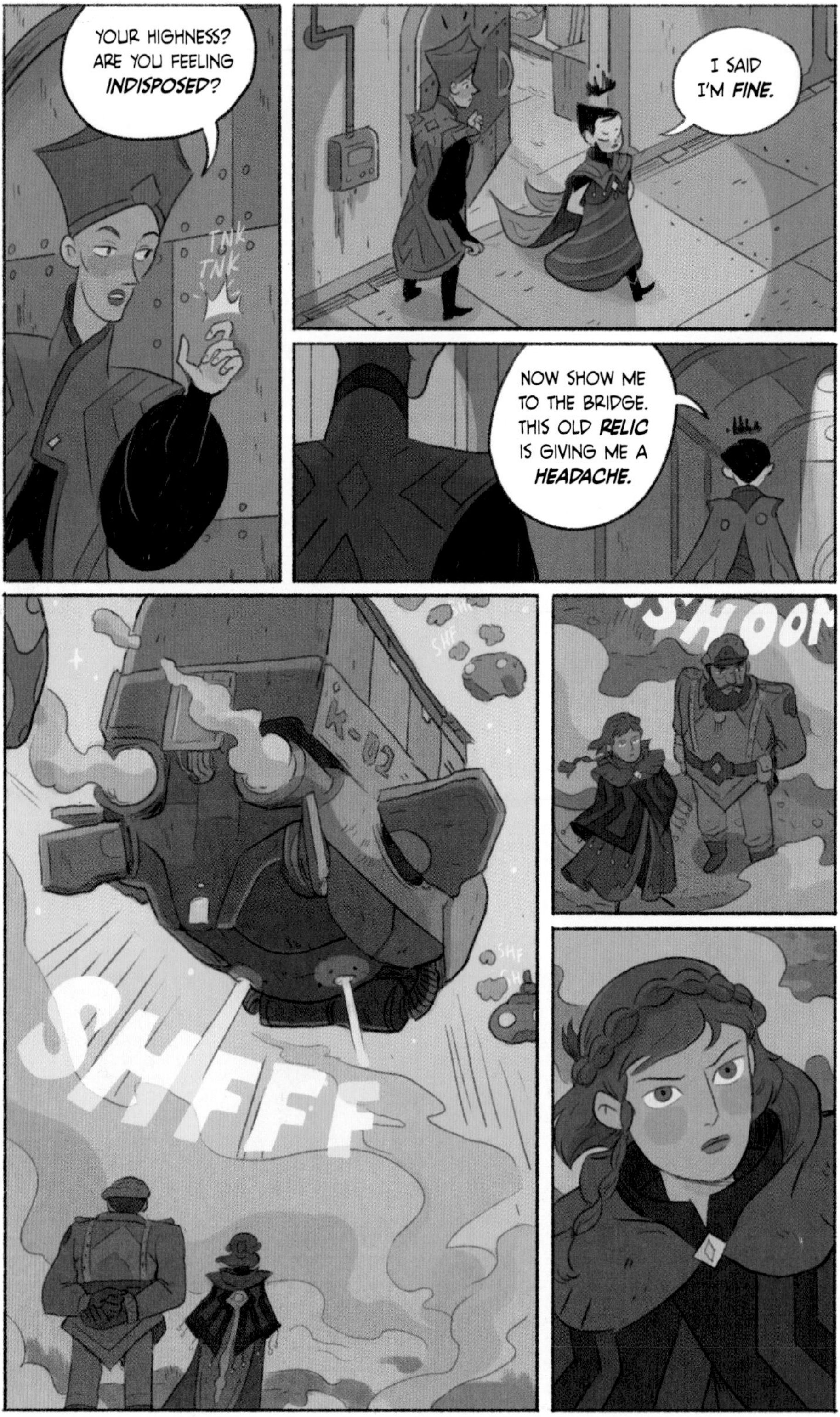
YOUR HIGHNESS? ARE YOU FEELING INDISPOSED?
TNK TNK
I SAID I'M FINE.
NOW SHOW ME TO THE BRIDGE. THIS OLD RELIC IS GIVING ME A HEADACHE.
SHFFF
SHF
SHF
SHOOM

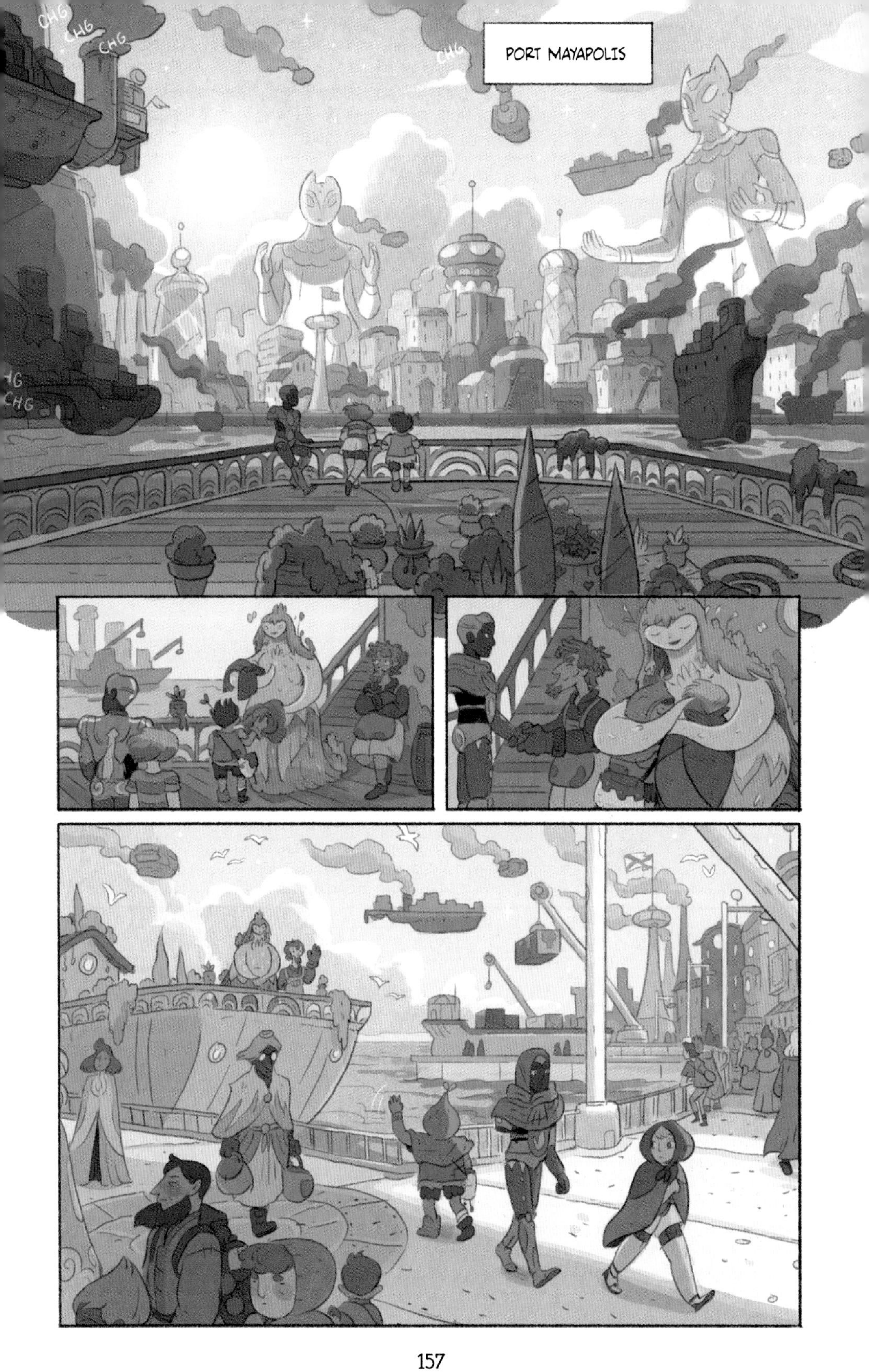
CHG
CHG
CHG
CHG
PORT MAYAPOLIS
HG
CHG

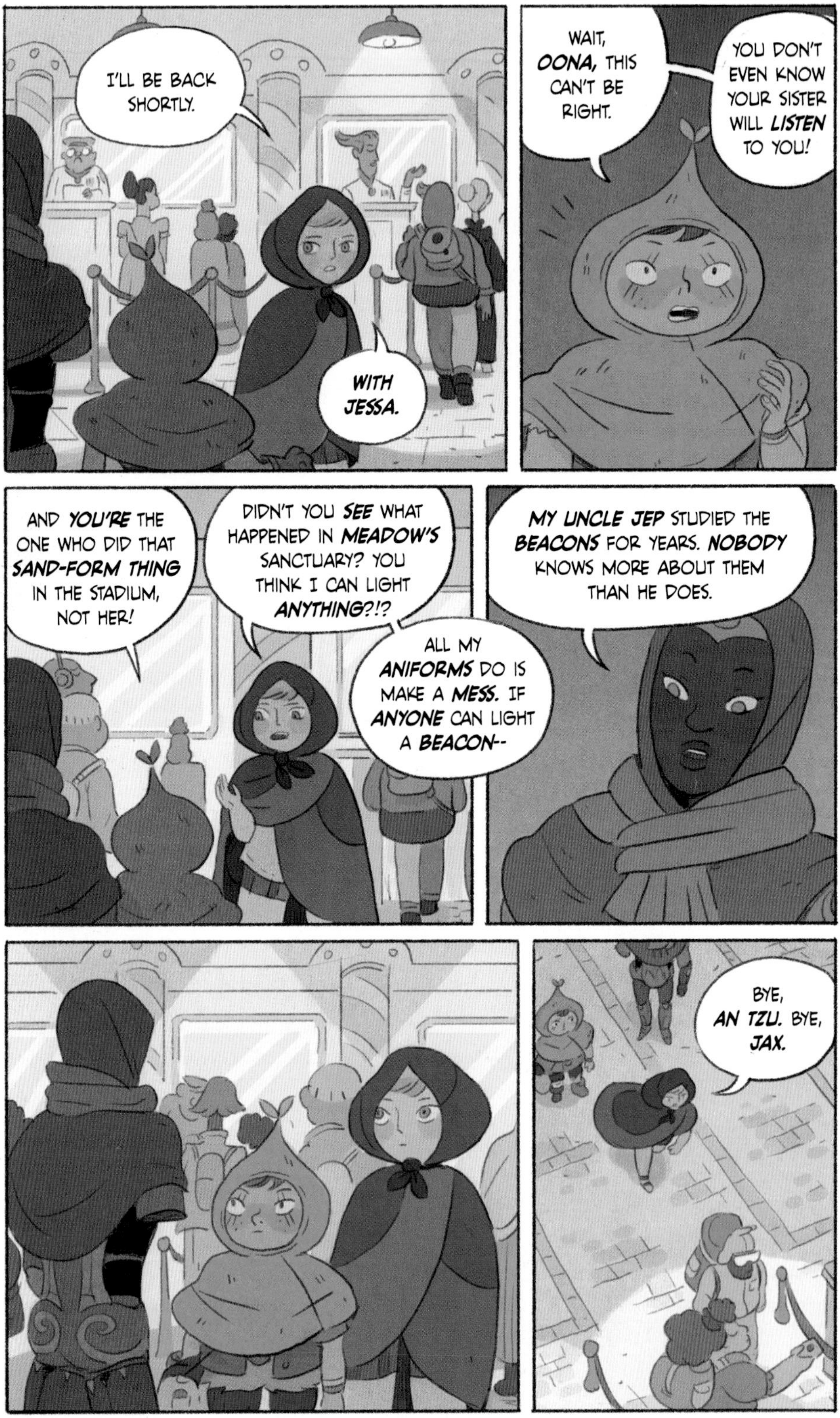
I'LL BE BACK SHORTLY.
WITH JESSA.
WAIT, OONA, THIS CAN'T BE RIGHT.
YOU DON'T EVEN KNOW YOUR SISTER WILL LISTEN TO YOU!
AND YOU'RE THE ONE WHO DID THAT SAND-FORM THING IN THE STADIUM, NOT HER!
DIDN'T YOU SEE WHAT HAPPENED IN MEADOW'S SANCTUARY? YOU THINK I CAN LIGHT ANYTHING?!?
ALL MY ANIFORMS DO IS MAKE A MESS. IF ANYONE CAN LIGHT A BEACON--
MY UNCLE JEP STUDIED THE BEACONS FOR YEARS. NOBODY KNOWS MORE ABOUT THEM THAN HE DOES.
BYE, AN TZU. BYE, JAX.

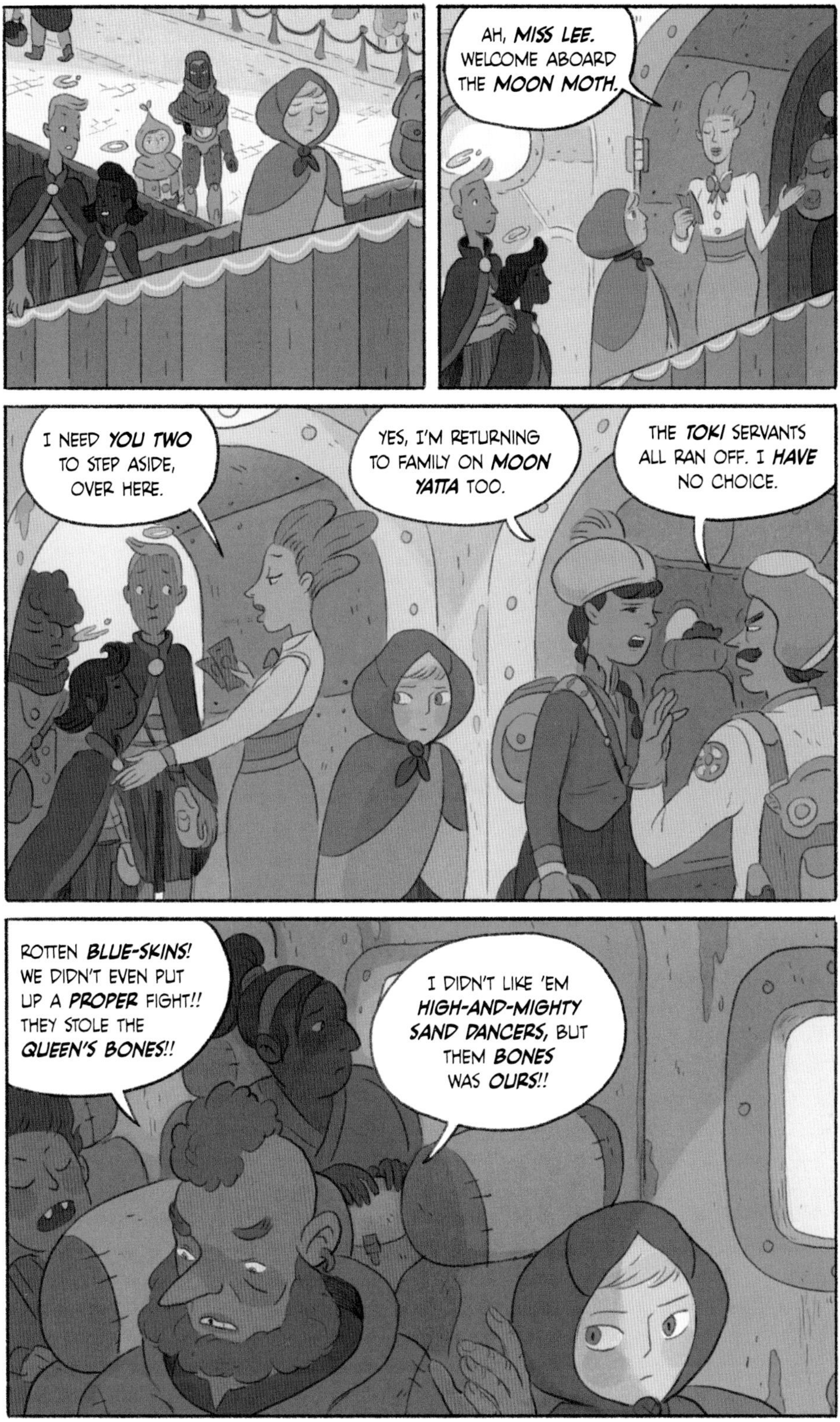
AH, MISS LEE. WELCOME ABOARD THE MOON MOTH.
I NEED YOU TWO TO STEP ASIDE, OVER HERE.
YES, I'M RETURNING TO FAMILY ON MOON YATTA TOO.
THE TOKI SERVANTS ALL RAN OFF. I HAVE NO CHOICE.
ROTTEN BLUE-SKINS! WE DIDN'T EVEN PUT UP A PROPER FIGHT!! THEY STOLE THE QUEEN'S BONES!!
I DIDN'T LIKE 'EM HIGH-AND-MIGHTY SAND DANCERS, BUT THEM BONES WAS OURS!!

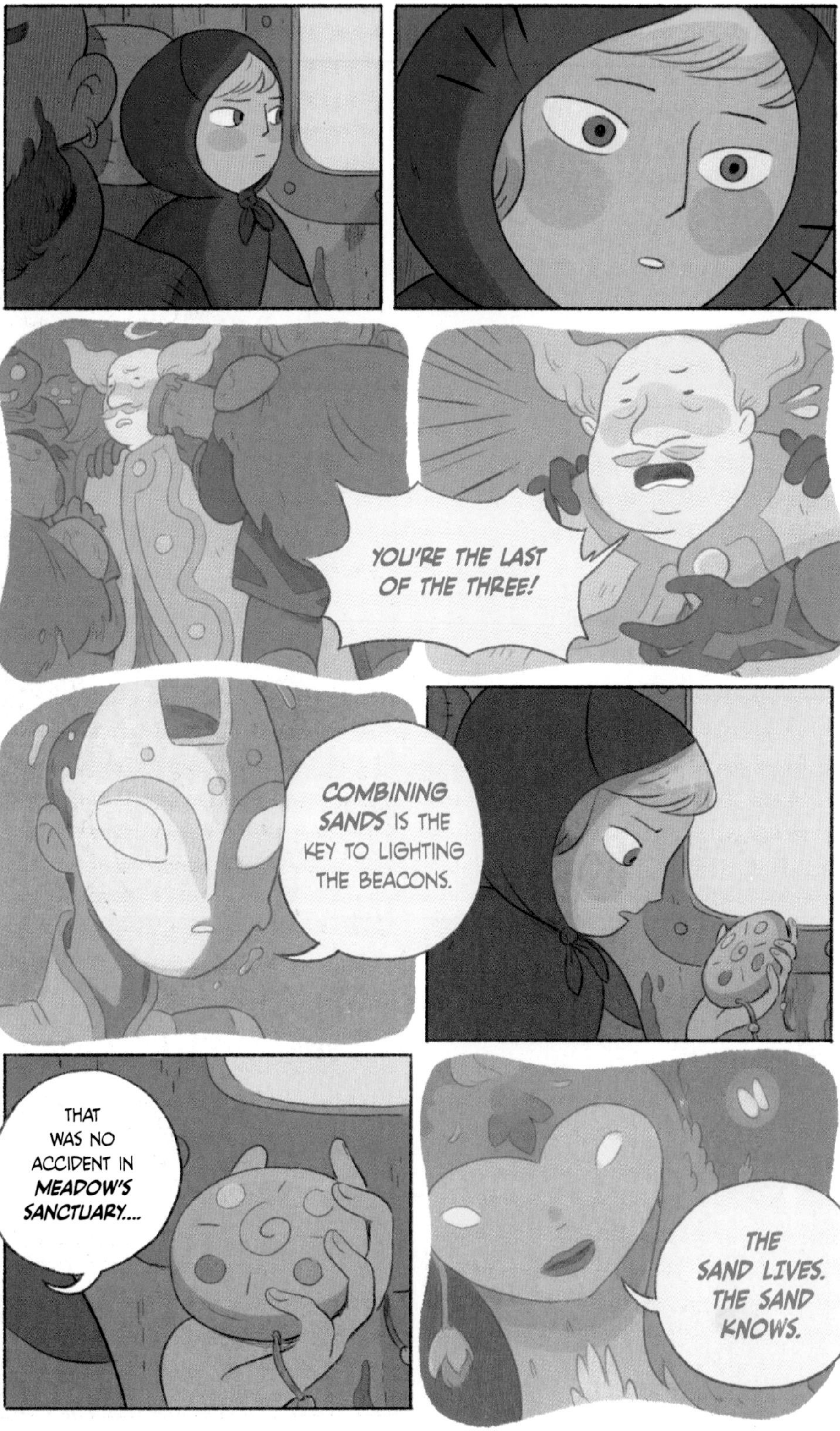
YOU'RE THE LAST OF THE THREE!
COMBINING SANDS IS THE KEY TO LIGHTING THE BEACONS.
THAT WAS NO ACCIDENT IN MEADOW'S SANCTUARY....
THE SAND LIVES. THE SAND KNOWS.

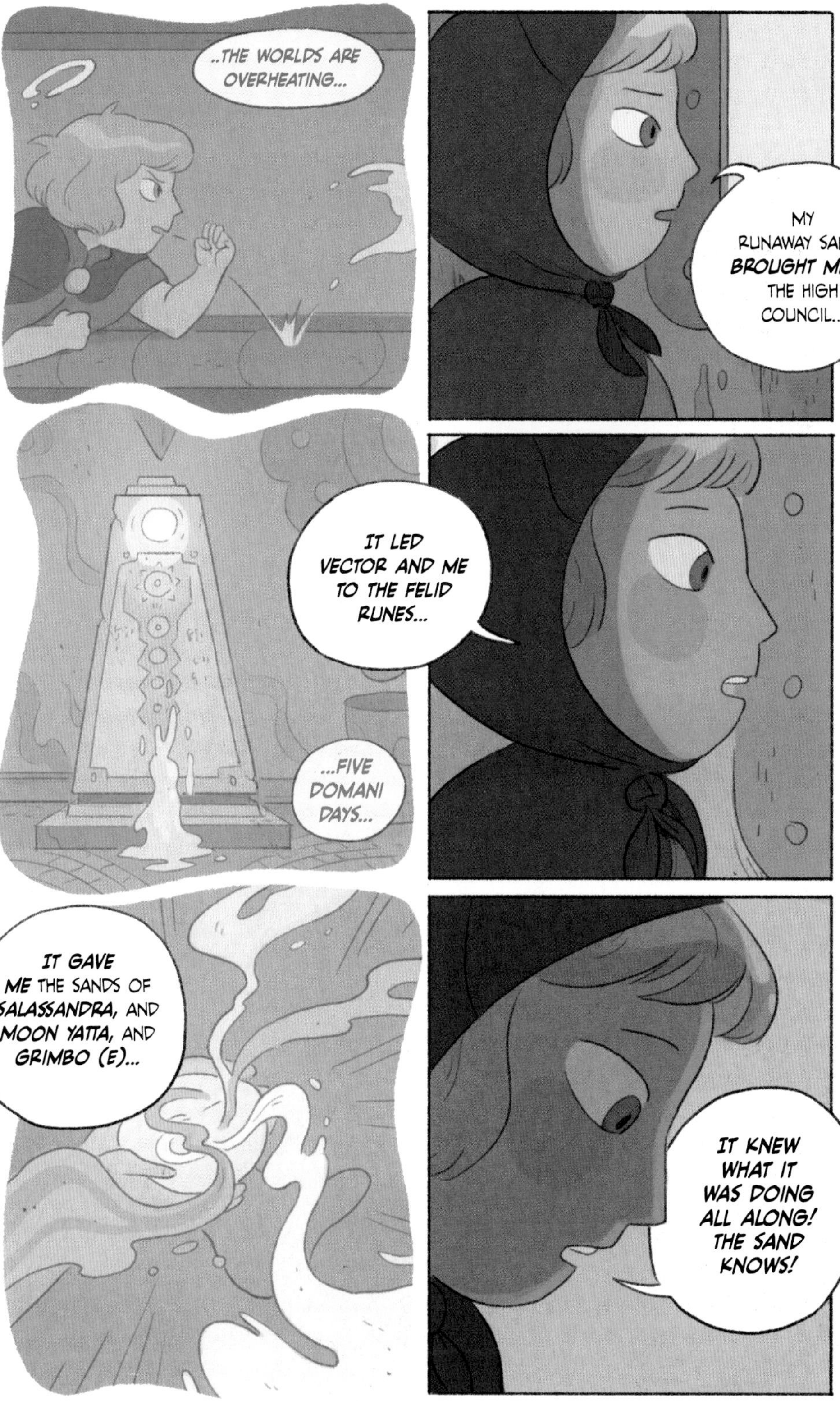
..THE WORLDS ARE OVERHEATING...
MY RUNAWAY SAND... BROUGHT ME TO THE HIGH COUNCIL...
IT LED VECTOR AND ME TO THE FELID RUNES...
...FIVE DOMANI DAYS...
IT GAVE ME THE SANDS OF SALASSANDRA, AND MOON YATTA, AND GRIMBO (E)...
IT KNEW WHAT IT WAS DOING ALL ALONG! THE SAND KNOWS!

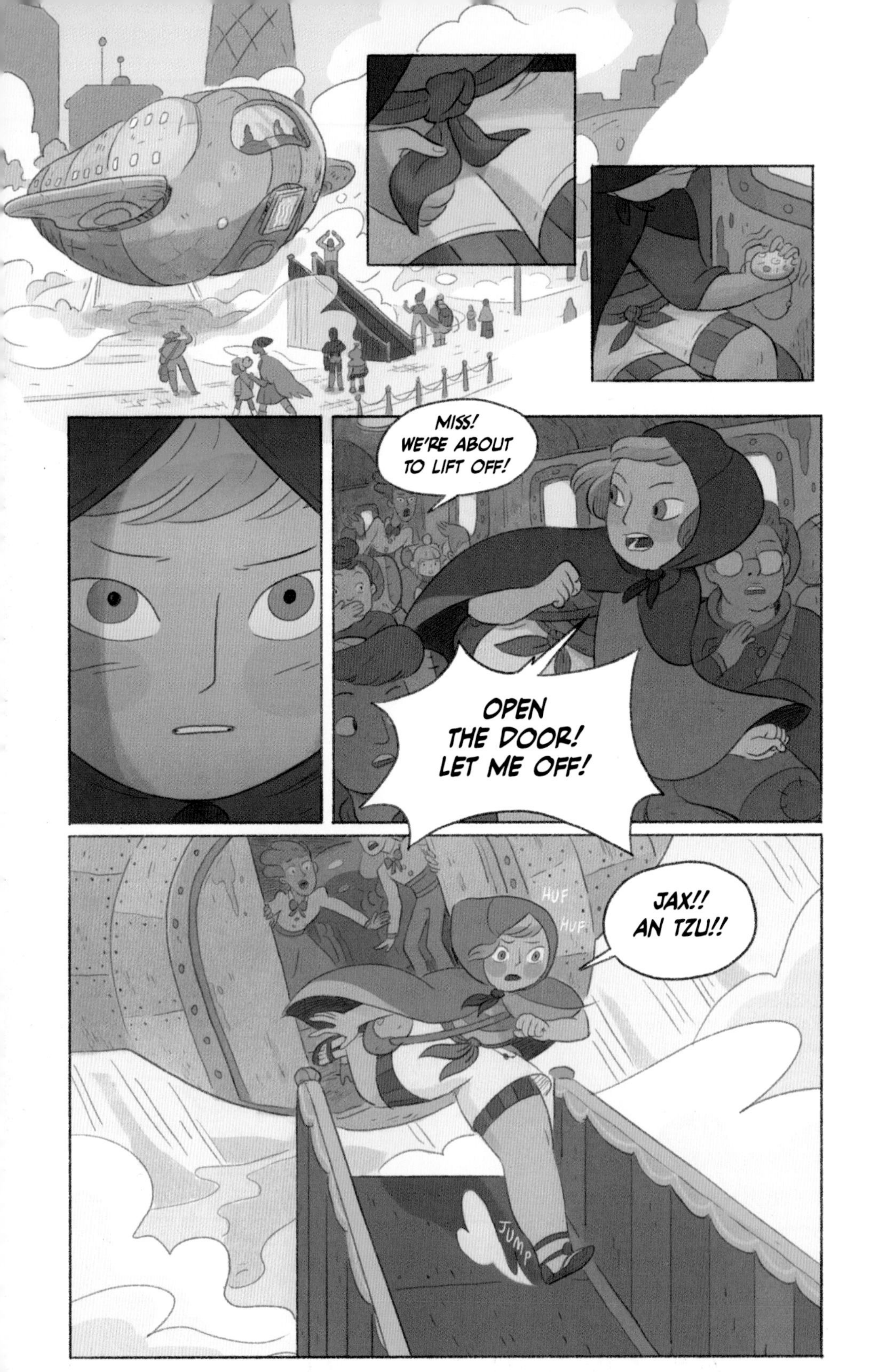
MISS! WE'RE ABOUT TO LIFT OFF!
OPEN THE DOOR! LET ME OFF!
HUF HUF
JAX!! AN TZU!!
JUMP

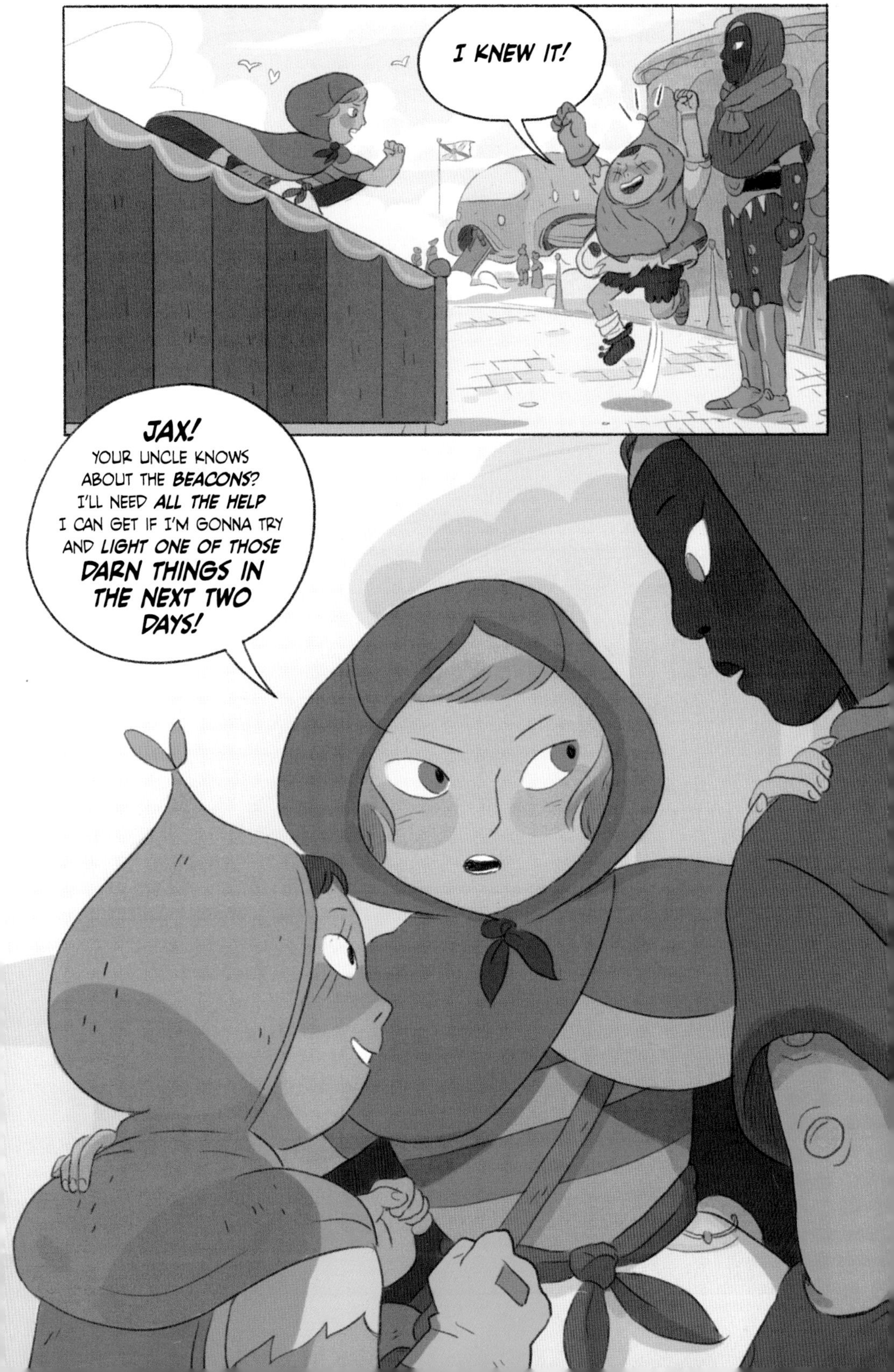
I KNEW IT!
JAX! YOUR UNCLE KNOWS ABOUT THE BEACONS? I'LL NEED ALL THE HELP I CAN GET IF I'M GONNA TRY AND LIGHT ONE OF THOSE DARN THINGS IN THE NEXT TWO DAYS!

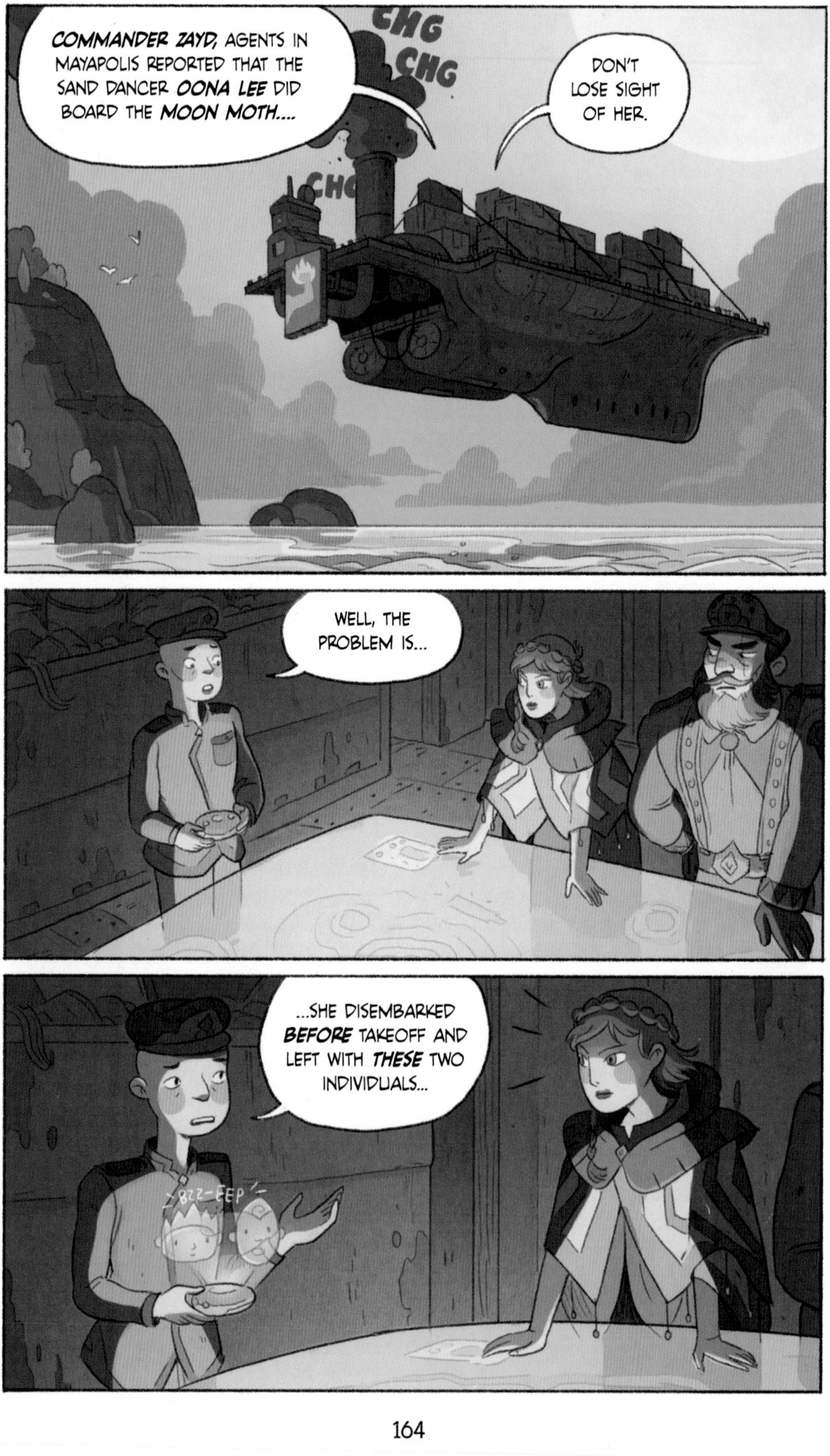
CHG
CHG
COMMANDER ZAYD, AGENTS IN MAYAPOLIS REPORTED THAT THE SAND DANCER OONA LEE DID BOARD THE MOON MOTH....
DON'T LOSE SIGHT OF HER.
CHG
WELL, THE PROBLEM IS...
...SHE DISEMBARKED BEFORE TAKEOFF AND LEFT WITH THESE TWO INDIVIDUALS...
BZZ-EEP

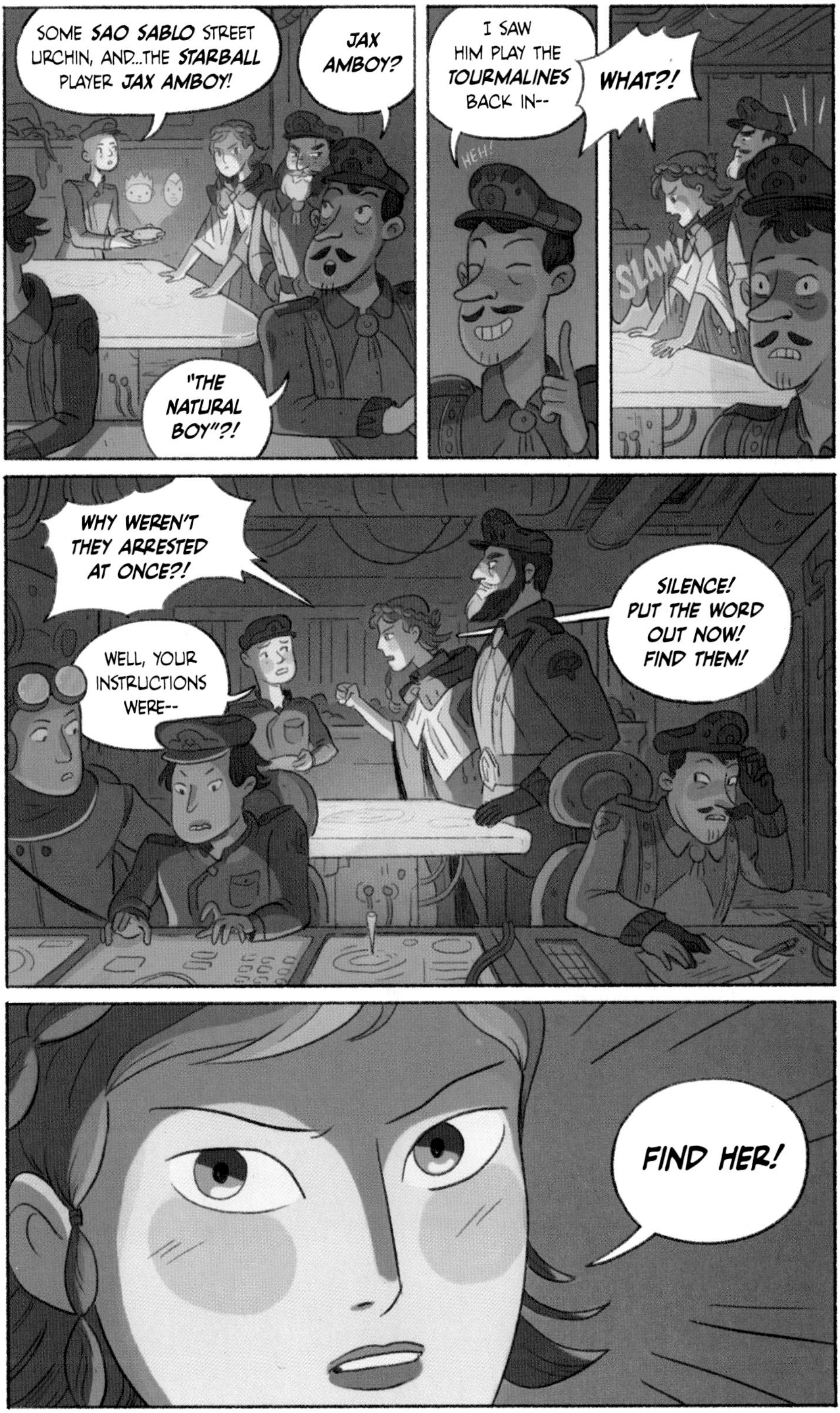
SOME SAO SABLO STREET URCHIN, AND...THE STARBALL PLAYER JAX AMBOY!
JAX AMBOY?
"THE NATURAL BOY"?!
I SAW HIM PLAY THE TOURMALINES BACK IN--
HEH!
WHAT?!
SLAM!
WHY WEREN'T THEY ARRESTED AT ONCE?!
WELL, YOUR INSTRUCTIONS WERE--
SILENCE! PUT THE WORD OUT NOW! FIND THEM!
FIND HER!

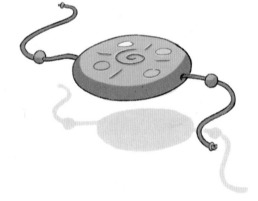

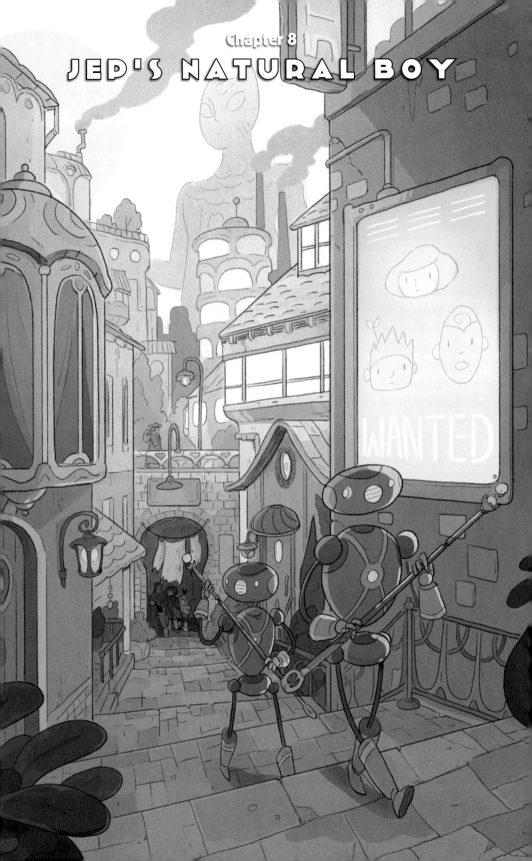

Chapter 8
JEP'S NATURAL BOY

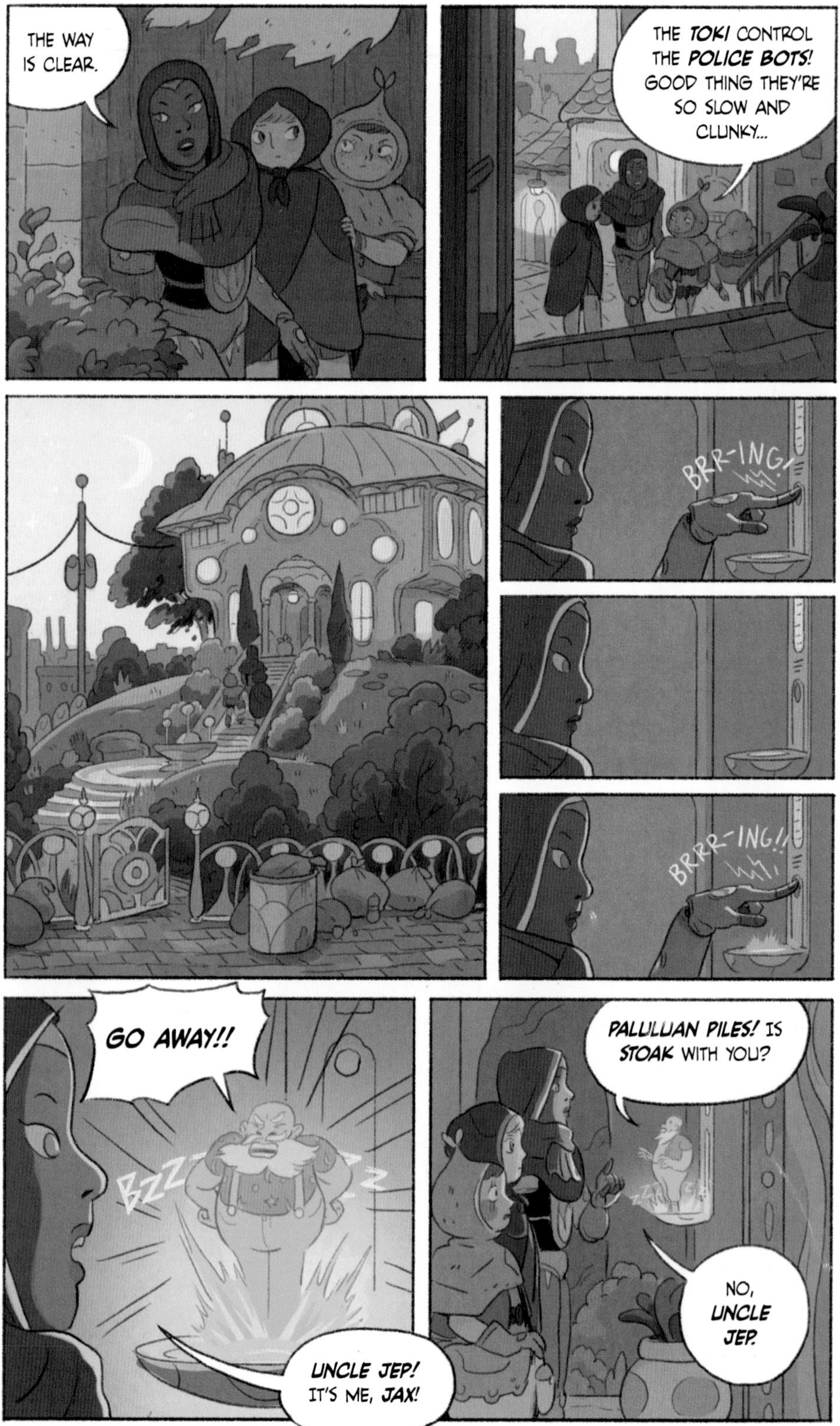
THE WAY IS CLEAR.
THE TOKI CONTROL THE POLICE BOTS! GOOD THING THEY'RE SO SLOW AND CLUNKY...
BRR-ING!
BRRR-ING!!
GO AWAY!!
BZZZ
UNCLE JEP! IT'S ME, JAX!
PALULUAN PILES! IS STOAK WITH YOU?
NO, UNCLE JEP.

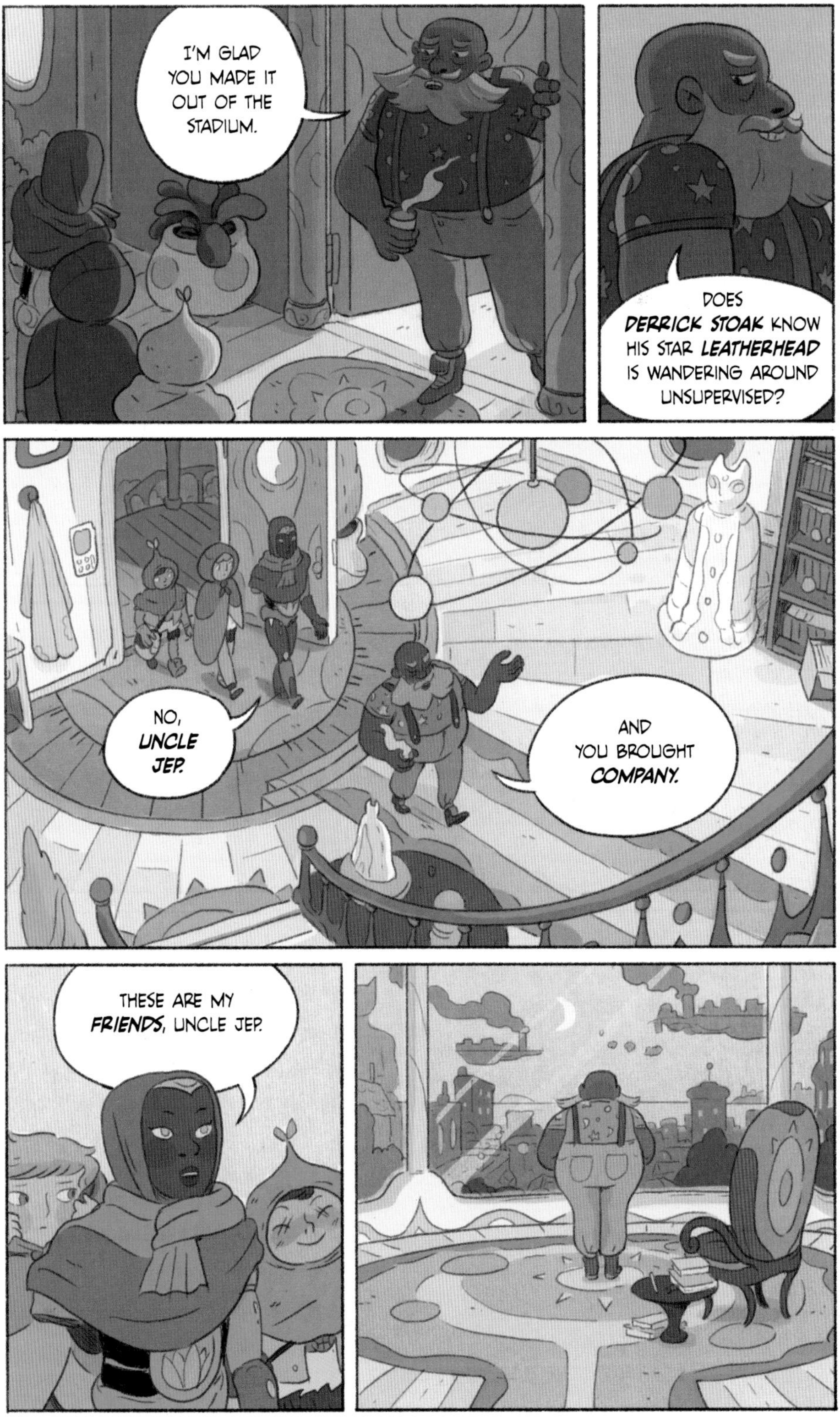
I'M GLAD YOU MADE IT OUT OF THE STADIUM.
DOES DERRICK STOAK KNOW HIS STAR LEATHERHEAD IS WANDERING AROUND UNSUPERVISED?
NO, UNCLE JEP.
AND YOU BROUGHT COMPANY.
THESE ARE MY FRIENDS, UNCLE JEP.

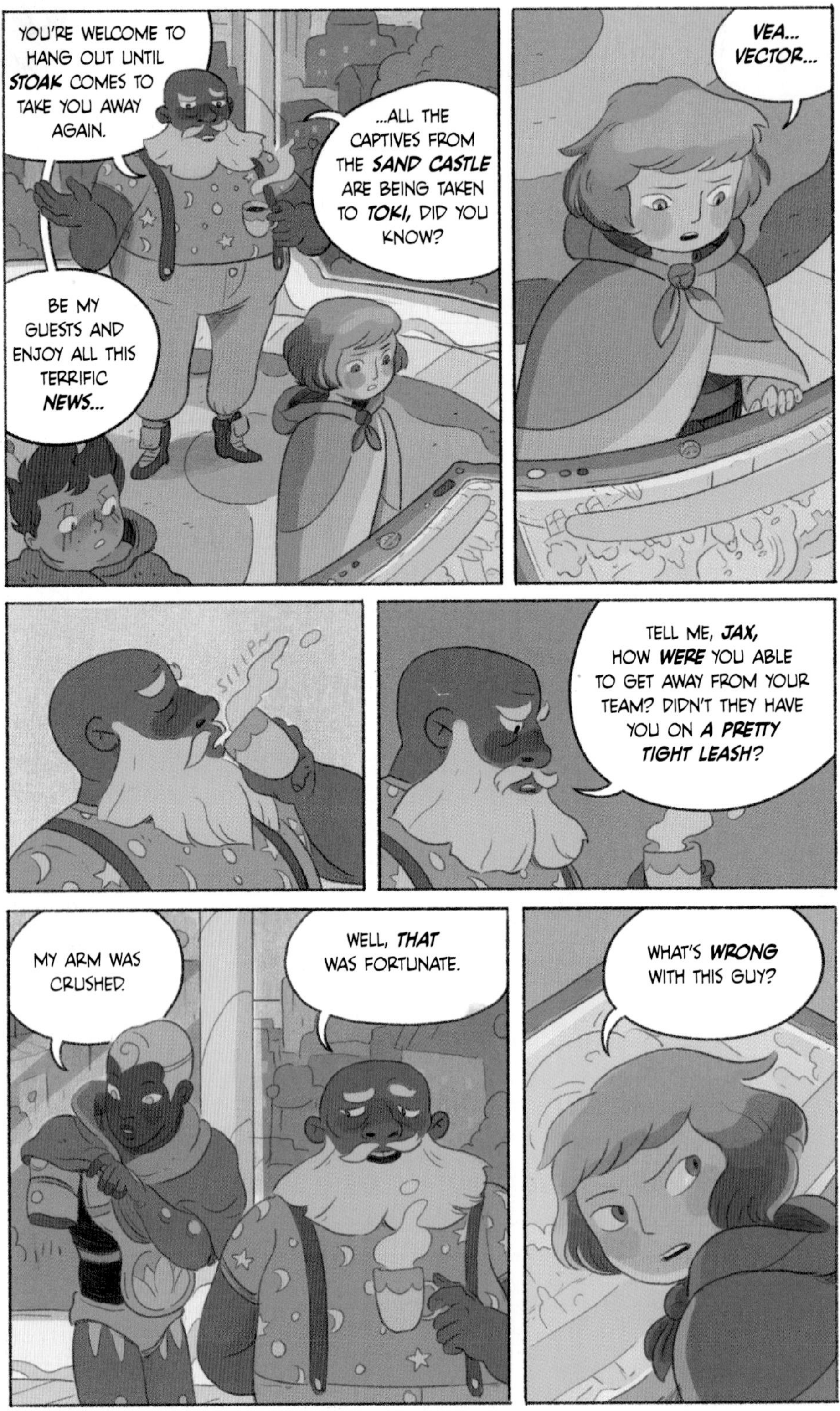
YOU'RE WELCOME TO HANG OUT UNTIL STOAK COMES TO TAKE YOU AWAY AGAIN.
...ALL THE CAPTIVES FROM THE SAND CASTLE ARE BEING TAKEN TO TOKI, DID YOU KNOW?
BE MY GUESTS AND ENJOY ALL THIS TERRIFIC NEWS...
VEA... VECTOR...
TELL ME, JAX, HOW WERE YOU ABLE TO GET AWAY FROM YOUR TEAM? DIDN'T THEY HAVE YOU ON A PRETTY TIGHT LEASH?
MY ARM WAS CRUSHED.
WELL, THAT WAS FORTUNATE.
WHAT'S WRONG WITH THIS GUY?

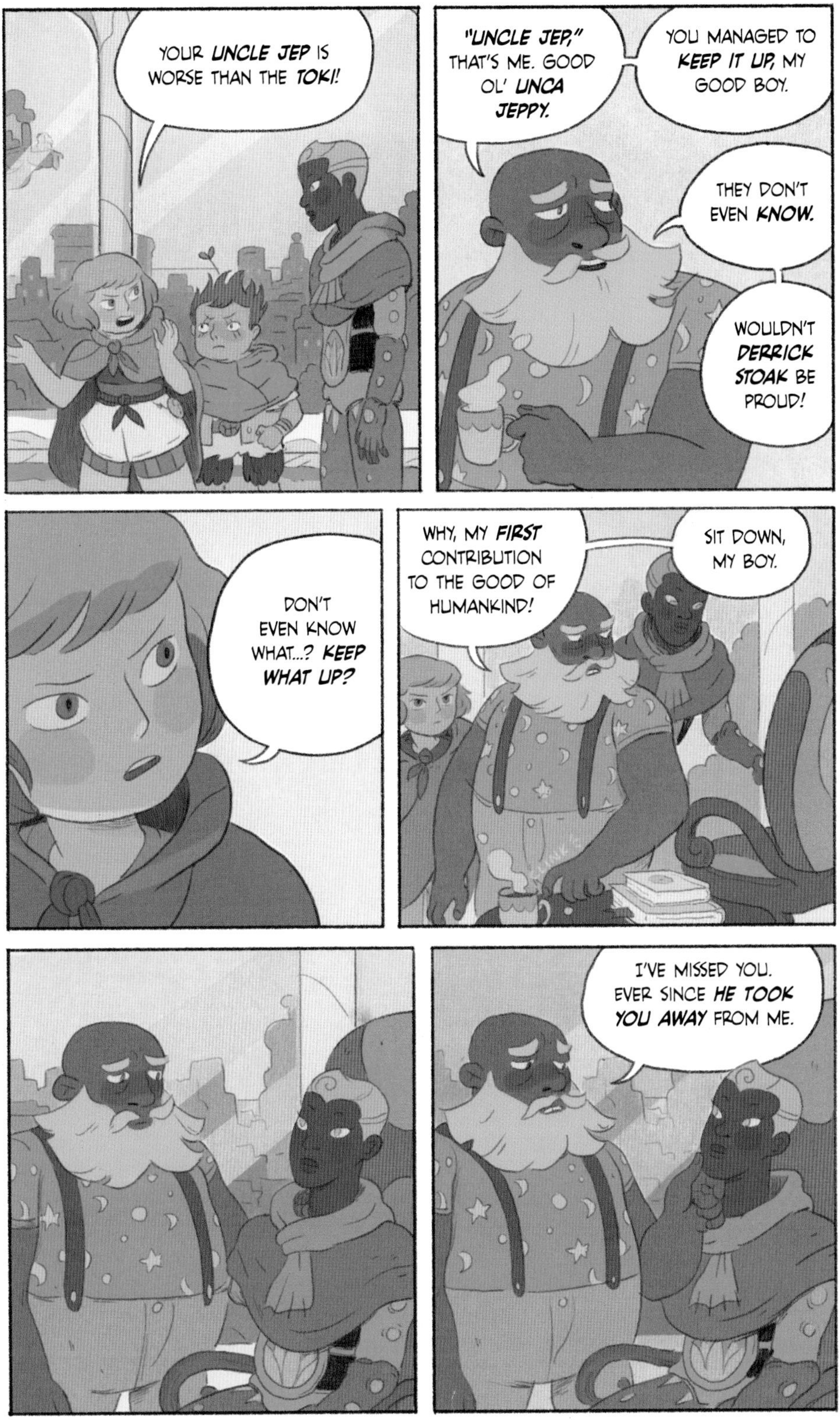
YOUR UNCLE JEP IS WORSE THAN THE TOKI!
"UNCLE JEP," THAT'S ME. GOOD OL' UNCA JEPPY.
YOU MANAGED TO KEEP IT UP, MY GOOD BOY.
THEY DON'T EVEN KNOW.
WOULDN'T DERRICK STOAK BE PROUD!
DON'T EVEN KNOW WHAT...? KEEP WHAT UP?
WHY, MY FIRST CONTRIBUTION TO THE GOOD OF HUMANKIND!
SIT DOWN, MY BOY.
I'VE MISSED YOU. EVER SINCE HE TOOK YOU AWAY FROM ME.

I'VE MISSED YOU TOO, *UNCLE JEP.* I NEVER HAD MUCH CHOICE BUT TO DO AS I WAS TOLD.

UNTIL THE *LINK* WAS BROKEN.

YES, THE *COMM-LINK* IN THE RIGHT HAND. HOW CLEVER OF THEM.

BUT NOW...THE *PUPPET'S STRINGS WERE CUT.* AND YOU CAME TO ME!

MY GOOD BOY.

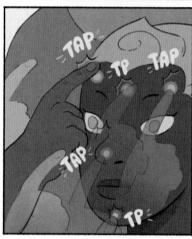

TAP

TP

TAP

TAP

TP

THNK

PSST

THUNK

PSST

WHAT?! NO! NO!!!

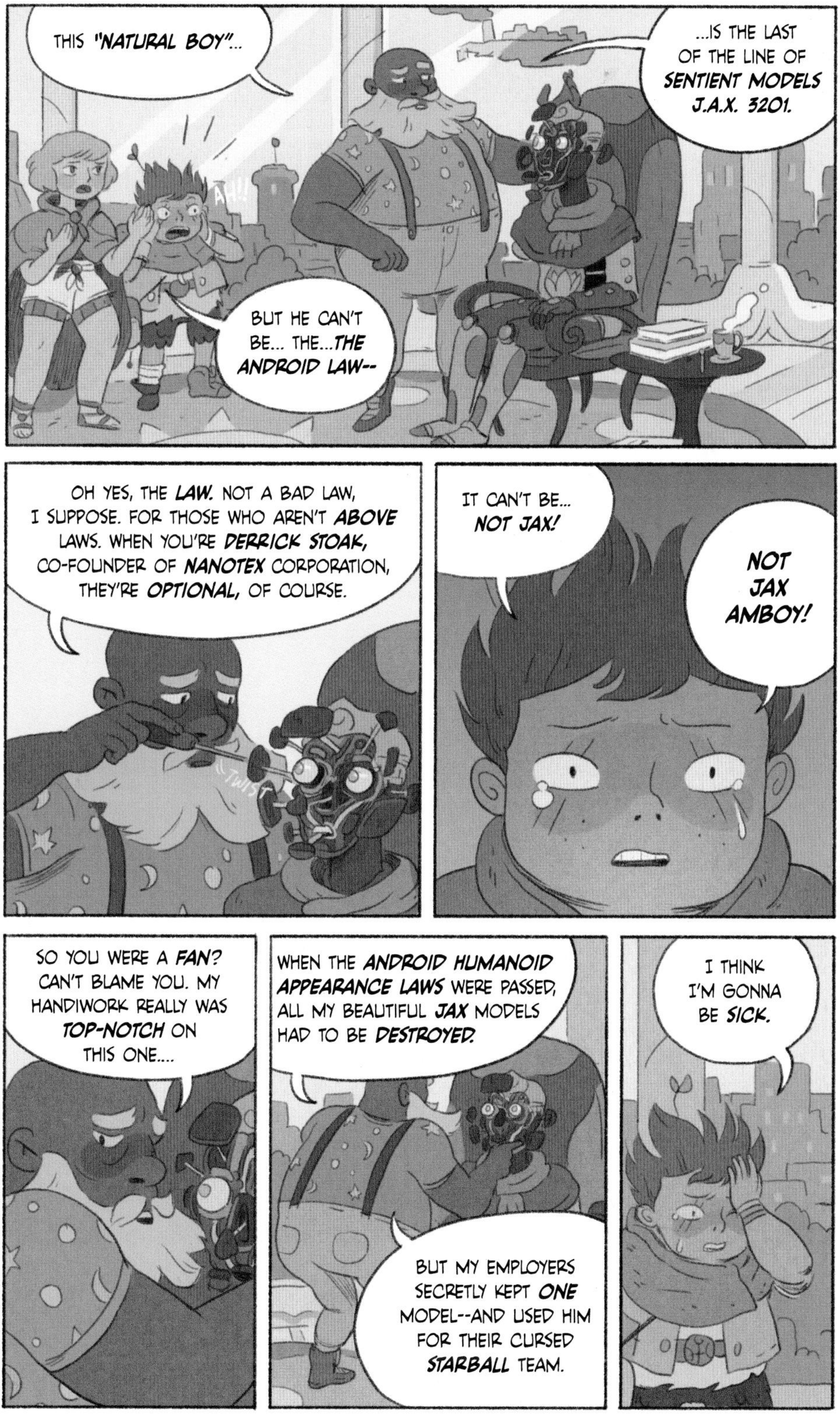
THIS "NATURAL BOY"...
...IS THE LAST OF THE LINE OF SENTIENT MODELS J.A.X. 3201.
AH!!
BUT HE CAN'T BE... THE...THE ANDROID LAW--
OH YES, THE LAW. NOT A BAD LAW, I SUPPOSE. FOR THOSE WHO AREN'T ABOVE LAWS. WHEN YOU'RE DERRICK STOAK, CO-FOUNDER OF NANOTEX CORPORATION, THEY'RE OPTIONAL, OF COURSE.
TWIST
IT CAN'T BE... NOT JAX!
NOT JAX AMBOY!
SO YOU WERE A FAN? CAN'T BLAME YOU. MY HANDIWORK REALLY WAS TOP-NOTCH ON THIS ONE....
WHEN THE ANDROID HUMANOID APPEARANCE LAWS WERE PASSED, ALL MY BEAUTIFUL JAX MODELS HAD TO BE DESTROYED.
BUT MY EMPLOYERS SECRETLY KEPT ONE MODEL--AND USED HIM FOR THEIR CURSED STARBALL TEAM.
I THINK I'M GONNA BE SICK.

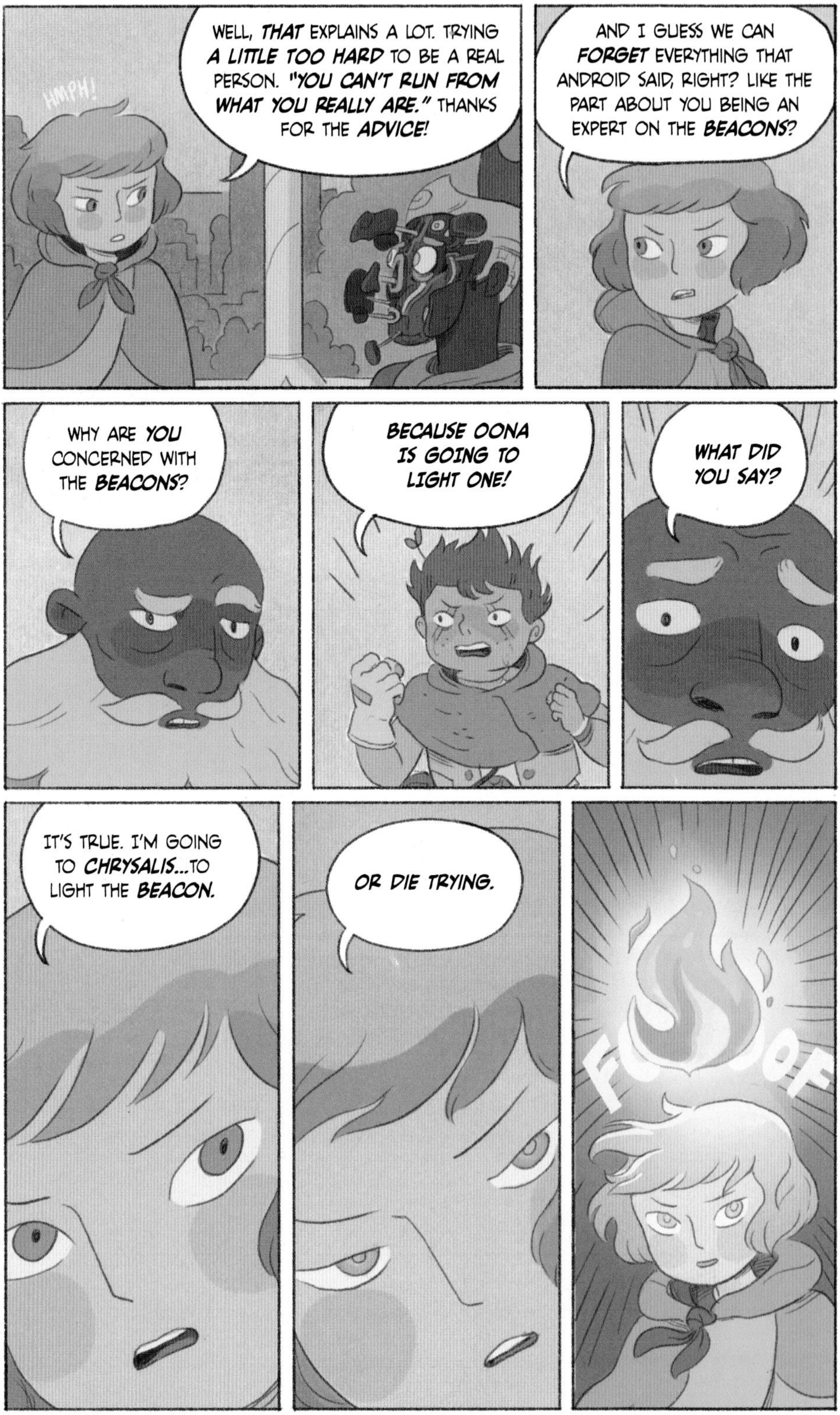
HMPH!
WELL, THAT EXPLAINS A LOT. TRYING A LITTLE TOO HARD TO BE A REAL PERSON. "YOU CAN'T RUN FROM WHAT YOU REALLY ARE." THANKS FOR THE ADVICE!
AND I GUESS WE CAN FORGET EVERYTHING THAT ANDROID SAID, RIGHT? LIKE THE PART ABOUT YOU BEING AN EXPERT ON THE BEACONS?
WHY ARE YOU CONCERNED WITH THE BEACONS?
BECAUSE OONA IS GOING TO LIGHT ONE!
WHAT DID YOU SAY?
IT'S TRUE. I'M GOING TO CHRYSALIS...TO LIGHT THE BEACON.
OR DIE TRYING.

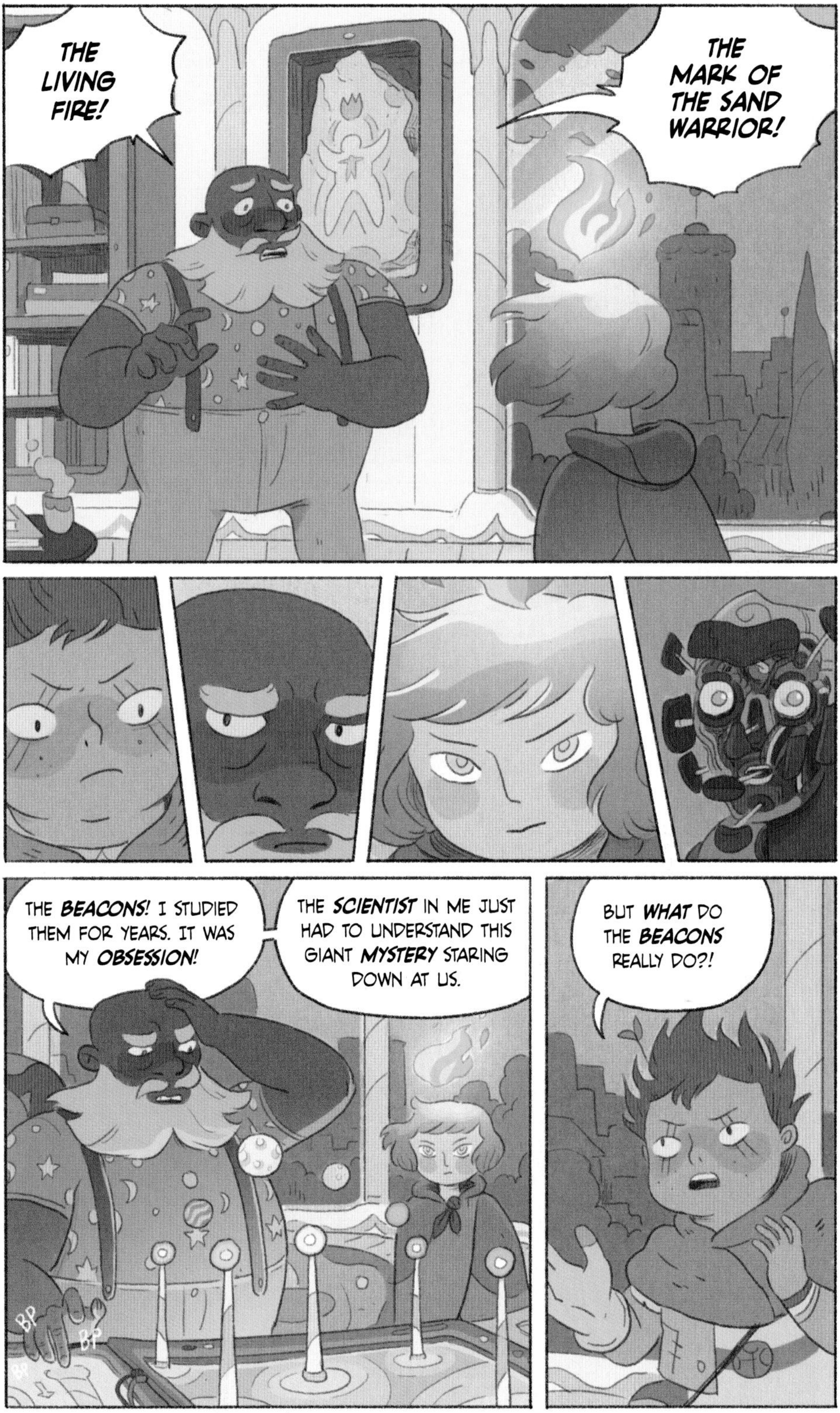
THE LIVING FIRE!
THE MARK OF THE SAND WARRIOR!
THE BEACONS! I STUDIED THEM FOR YEARS. IT WAS MY OBSESSION!
THE SCIENTIST IN ME JUST HAD TO UNDERSTAND THIS GIANT MYSTERY STARING DOWN AT US.
BP BP BP
BUT WHAT DO THE BEACONS REALLY DO?!

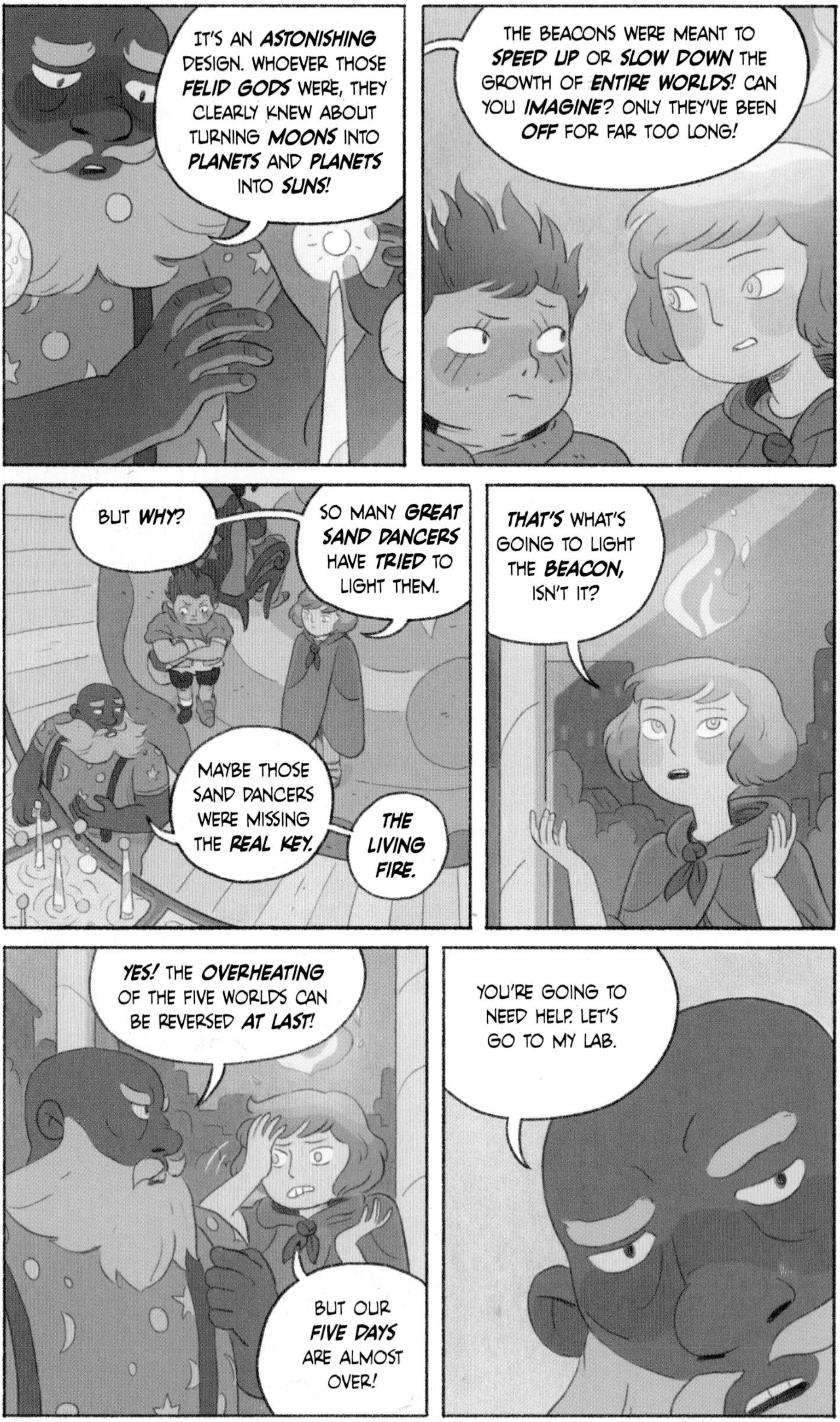
IT'S AN ASTONISHING DESIGN. WHOEVER THOSE FELID GODS WERE, THEY CLEARLY KNEW ABOUT TURNING MOONS INTO PLANETS AND PLANETS INTO SUNS!
THE BEACONS WERE MEANT TO SPEED UP OR SLOW DOWN THE GROWTH OF ENTIRE WORLDS! CAN YOU IMAGINE? ONLY THEY'VE BEEN OFF FOR FAR TOO LONG!
BUT WHY?
SO MANY GREAT SAND DANCERS HAVE TRIED TO LIGHT THEM.
MAYBE THOSE SAND DANCERS WERE MISSING THE REAL KEY.
THE LIVING FIRE.
THAT'S WHAT'S GOING TO LIGHT THE BEACON, ISN'T IT?
YES! THE OVERHEATING OF THE FIVE WORLDS CAN BE REVERSED AT LAST!
BUT OUR FIVE DAYS ARE ALMOST OVER!
YOU'RE GOING TO NEED HELP. LET'S GO TO MY LAB.

Chapter 9
ALTERATIONS

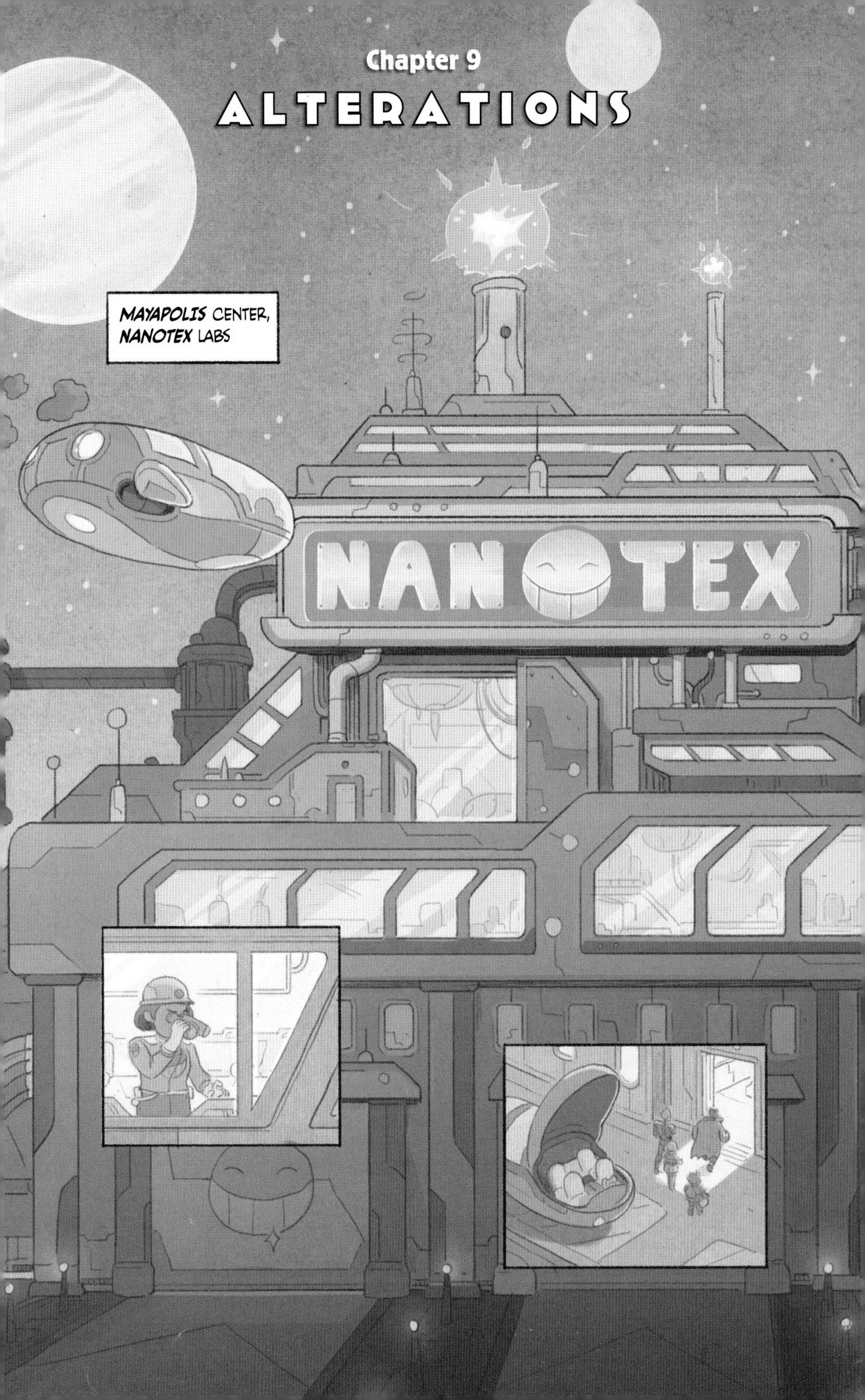
MAYAPOLIS CENTER,
NANOTEX LABS
NANOTEX

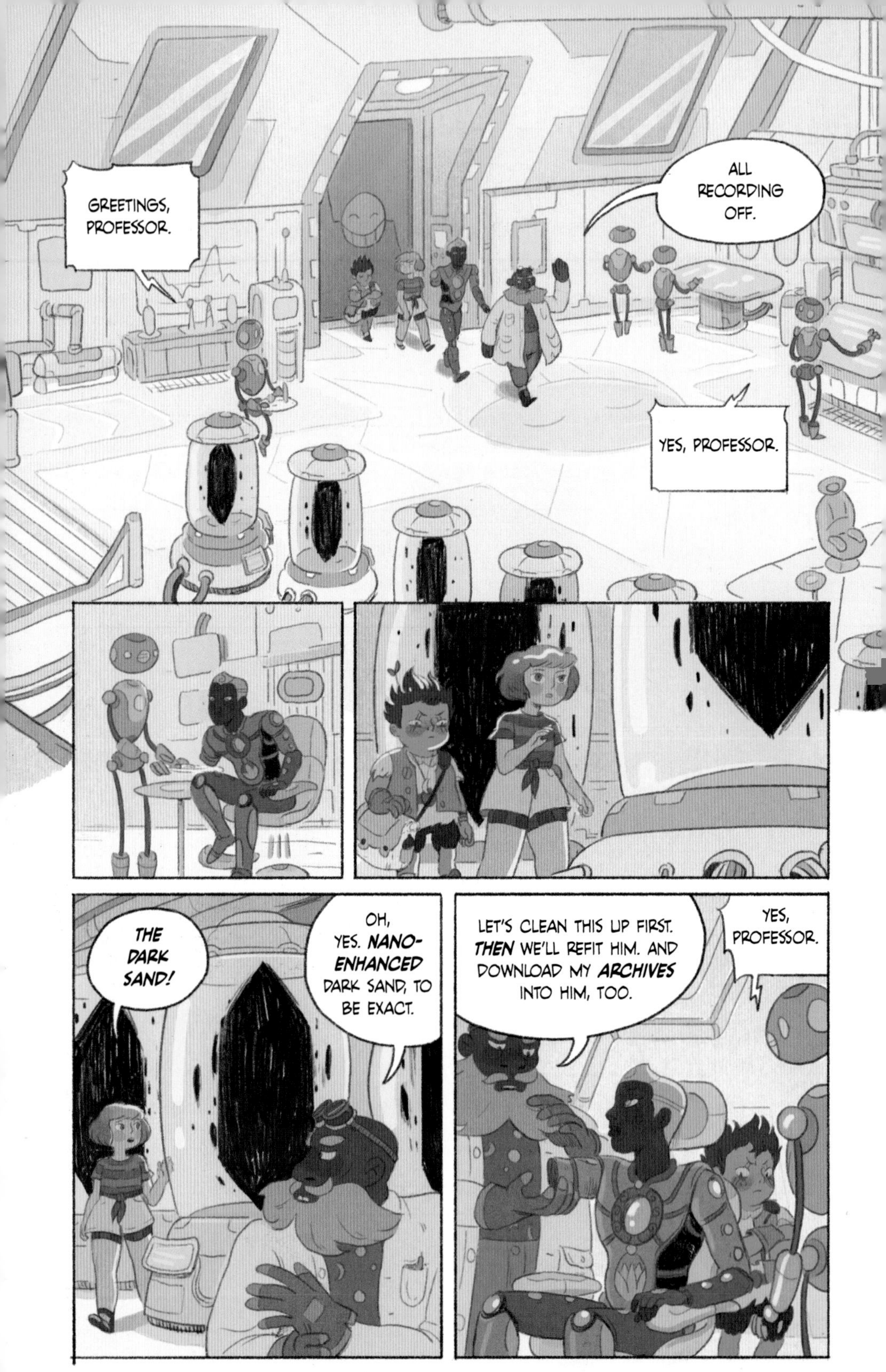
GREETINGS, PROFESSOR.
ALL RECORDING OFF.
YES, PROFESSOR.
THE DARK SAND!
OH, YES. NANO-ENHANCED DARK SAND, TO BE EXACT.
LET'S CLEAN THIS UP FIRST. THEN WE'LL REFIT HIM. AND DOWNLOAD MY ARCHIVES INTO HIM, TOO.
YES, PROFESSOR.

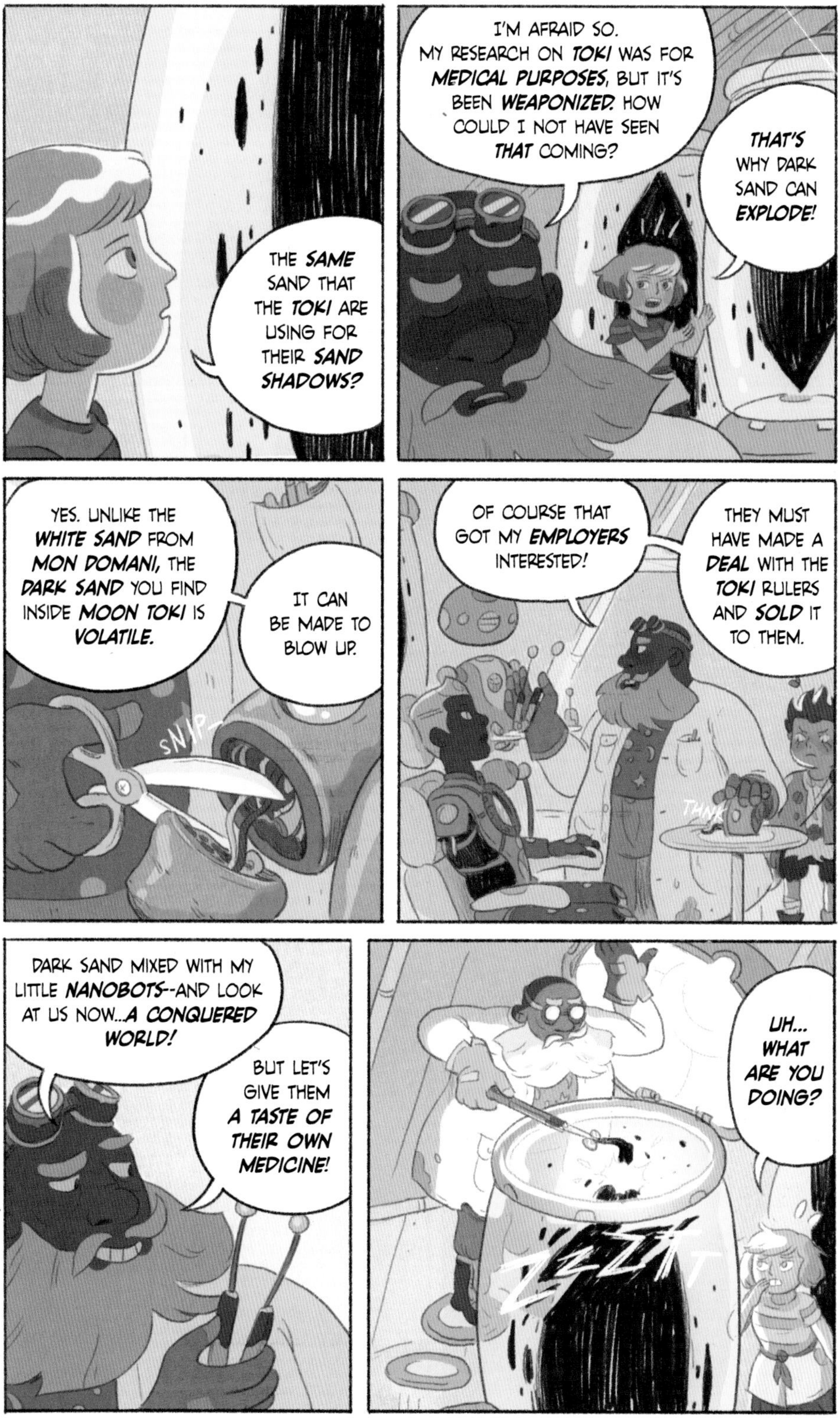
THE SAME SAND THAT THE TOKI ARE USING FOR THEIR SAND SHADOWS?
I'M AFRAID SO. MY RESEARCH ON TOKI WAS FOR MEDICAL PURPOSES, BUT IT'S BEEN WEAPONIZED. HOW COULD I NOT HAVE SEEN THAT COMING?
THAT'S WHY DARK SAND CAN EXPLODE!
YES. UNLIKE THE WHITE SAND FROM MON DOMANI, THE DARK SAND YOU FIND INSIDE MOON TOKI IS VOLATILE.
IT CAN BE MADE TO BLOW UP.
SNIP-
OF COURSE THAT GOT MY EMPLOYERS INTERESTED!
THEY MUST HAVE MADE A DEAL WITH THE TOKI RULERS AND SOLD IT TO THEM.
THNK
DARK SAND MIXED WITH MY LITTLE NANOBOTS--AND LOOK AT US NOW...A CONQUERED WORLD!
BUT LET'S GIVE THEM A TASTE OF THEIR OWN MEDICINE!
UH... WHAT ARE YOU DOING?
ZZZZT

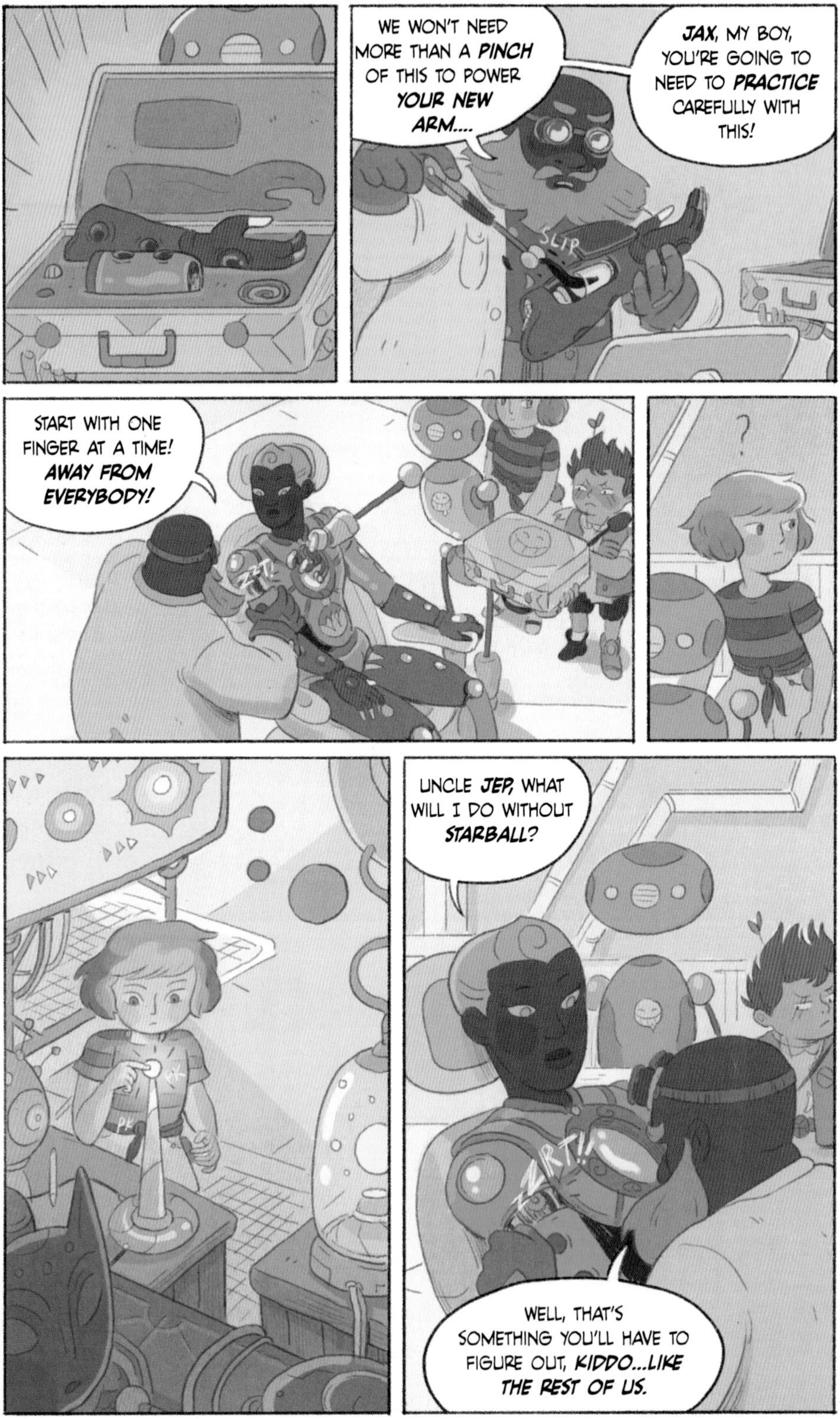
WE WON'T NEED MORE THAN A PINCH OF THIS TO POWER YOUR NEW ARM....
JAX, MY BOY, YOU'RE GOING TO NEED TO PRACTICE CAREFULLY WITH THIS!
SLIP
START WITH ONE FINGER AT A TIME! AWAY FROM EVERYBODY!
?
UNCLE JEP, WHAT WILL I DO WITHOUT STARBALL?
ZZRT!!
WELL, THAT'S SOMETHING YOU'LL HAVE TO FIGURE OUT, KIDDO...LIKE THE REST OF US.

BUT I'M NOT A REAL BOY.

BUT IT SEEMS YOU HAVE *REAL FRIENDS.* YOU CAN START BY HELPING *THEM, JAX.*

YOUR NEW ARM WILL GIVE YOU A LITTLE *EDGE.*

WELL, I *AM* A REAL BOY!

A REAL *DISAPPOINTED* BOY!!

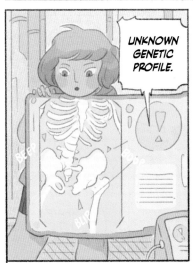

UNKNOWN GENETIC PROFILE.

HOLD ON A MINUTE...

WHAT'S THIS *CHROMOSOMIC WORK* HERE? WHERE DID YOU GET *THIS* DONE?!

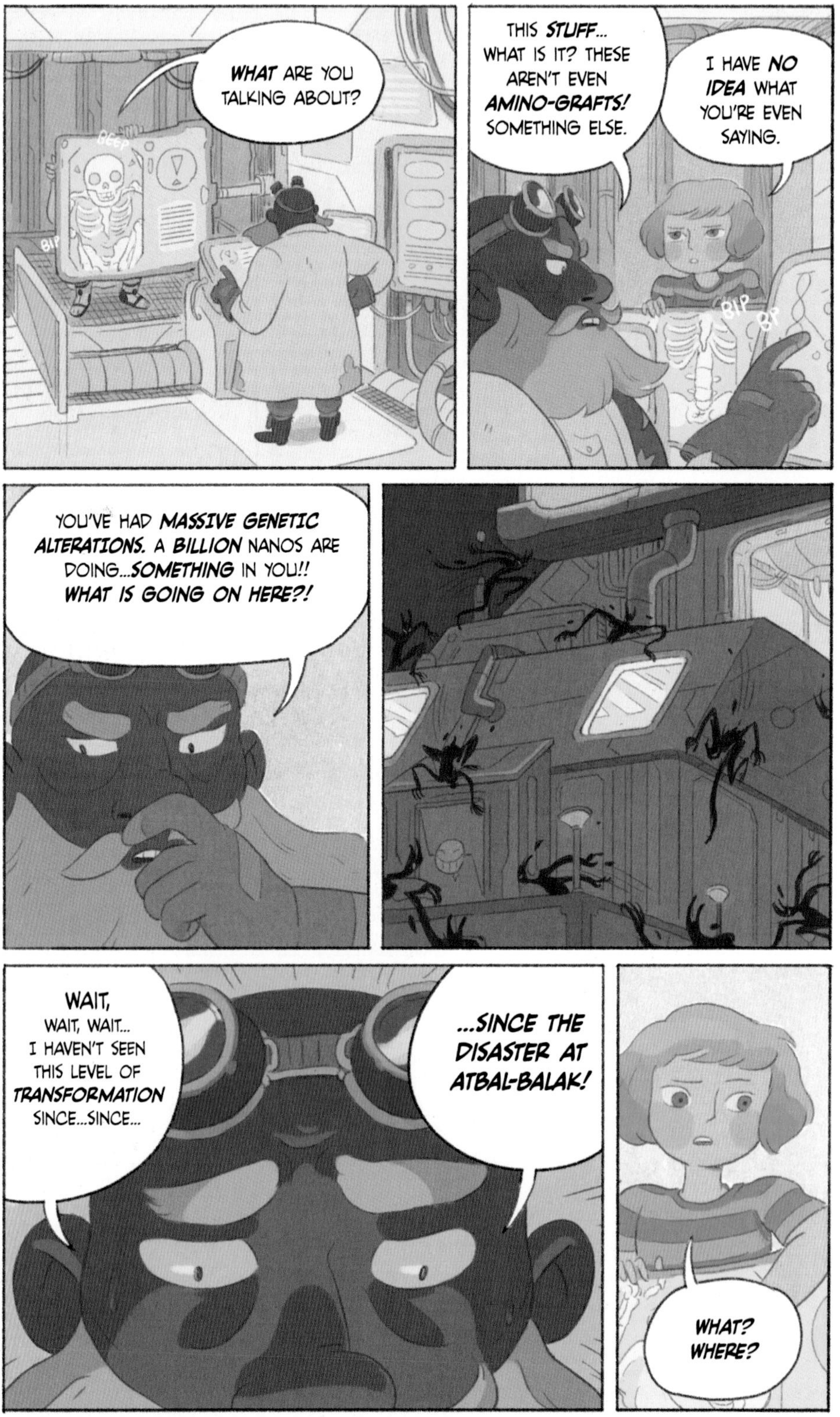
WHAT ARE YOU TALKING ABOUT?
BEEP
BIP
THIS STUFF... WHAT IS IT? THESE AREN'T EVEN AMINO-GRAFTS! SOMETHING ELSE.
I HAVE NO IDEA WHAT YOU'RE EVEN SAYING.
BIP
BP
YOU'VE HAD MASSIVE GENETIC ALTERATIONS. A BILLION NANOS ARE DOING...SOMETHING IN YOU!! WHAT IS GOING ON HERE?!
WAIT, WAIT, WAIT... I HAVEN'T SEEN THIS LEVEL OF TRANSFORMATION SINCE...SINCE...
...SINCE THE DISASTER AT ATBAL-BALAK!
WHAT? WHERE?

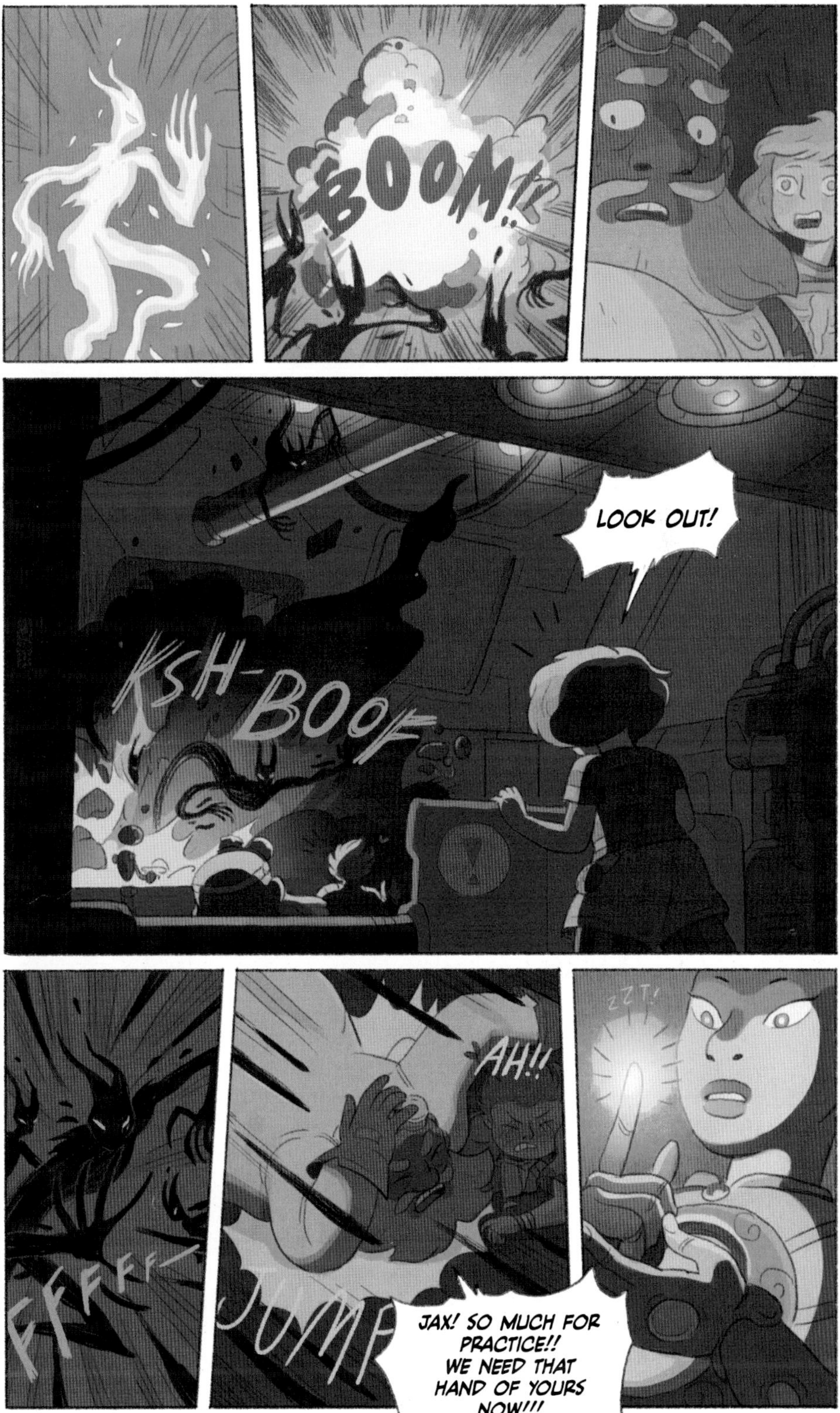
BOOM!!
LOOK OUT!
KSH-BOOF
AH!!
ZZT!
FFFFF—
JUMP
JAX! SO MUCH FOR PRACTICE!! WE NEED THAT HAND OF YOURS NOW!!!

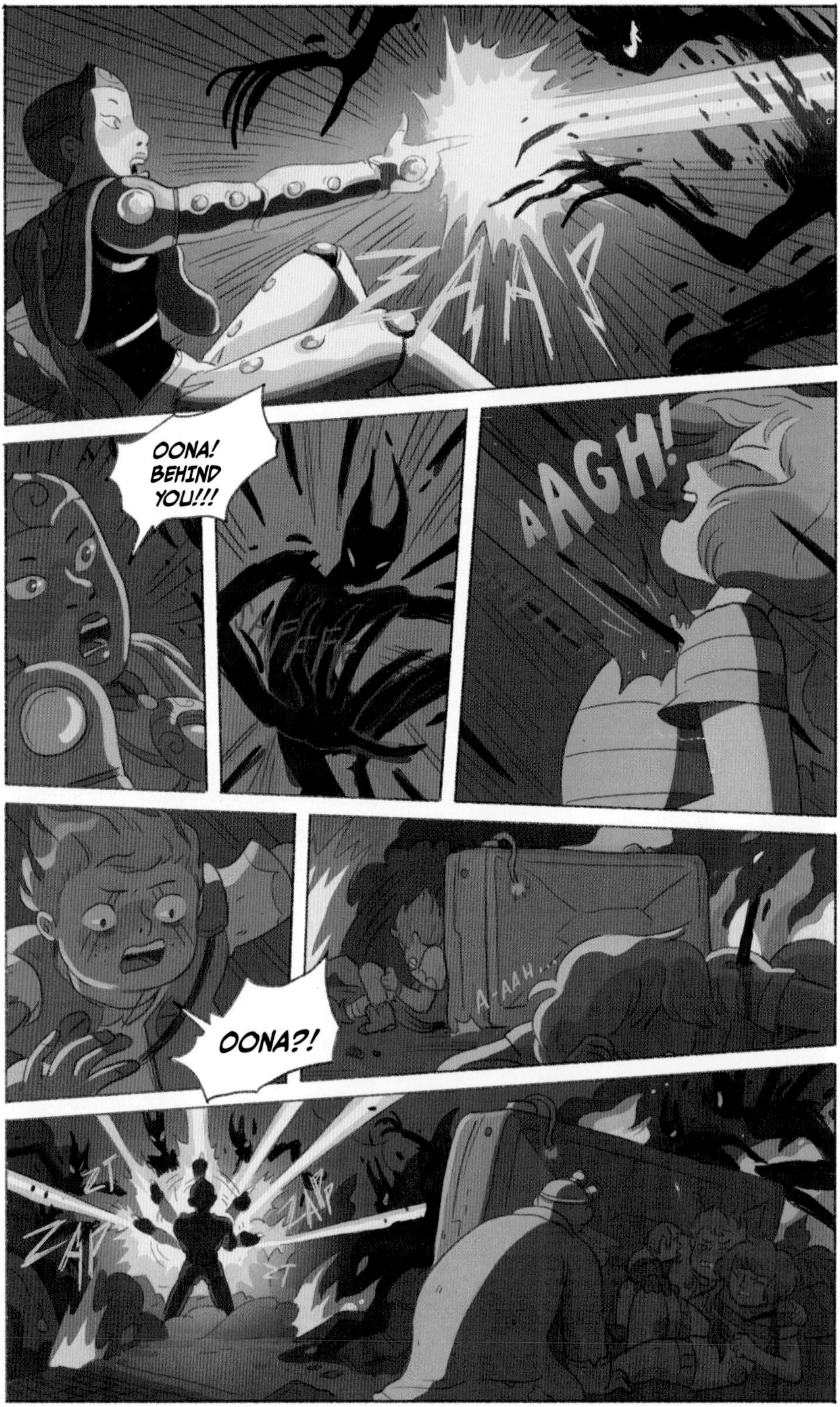
ZAAP
OONA! BEHIND YOU!!!
AAGH!
A-AAH...
OONA?!
ZT
ZAP
ZAPP
ZT

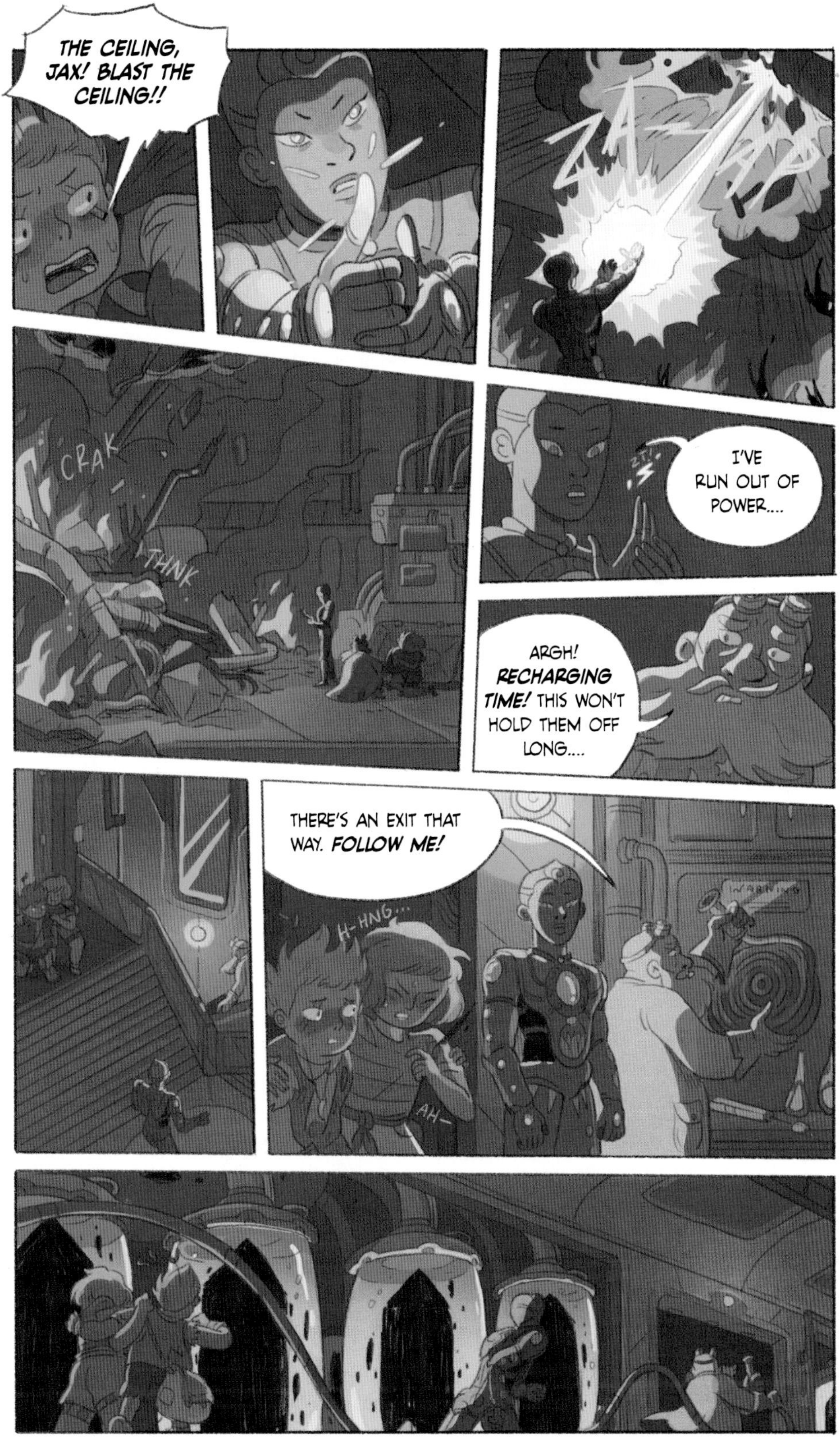
THE CEILING, JAX! BLAST THE CEILING!!
ZAAAP
CRAK
THINK
I'VE RUN OUT OF POWER....
ARGH! **RECHARGING TIME!** THIS WON'T HOLD THEM OFF LONG....
THERE'S AN EXIT THAT WAY. **FOLLOW ME!**
H-HNG...
AH-

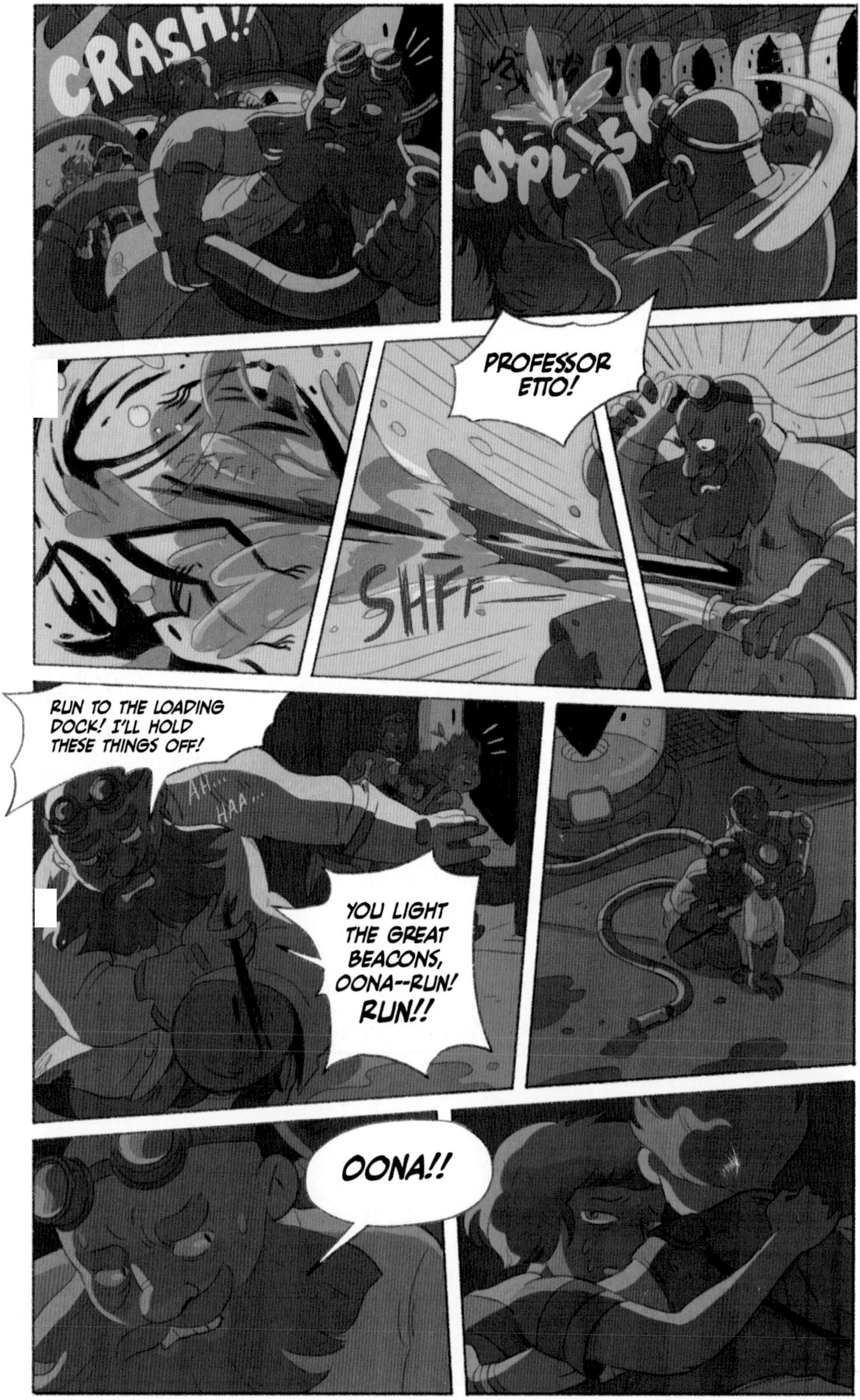
CRASH!!
SPLISH
SHFF
PROFESSOR ETTO!
SHFF
RUN TO THE LOADING DOCK! I'LL HOLD THESE THINGS OFF!
AH... HAA...
YOU LIGHT THE GREAT BEACONS, OONA--RUN! RUN!!
OONA!!

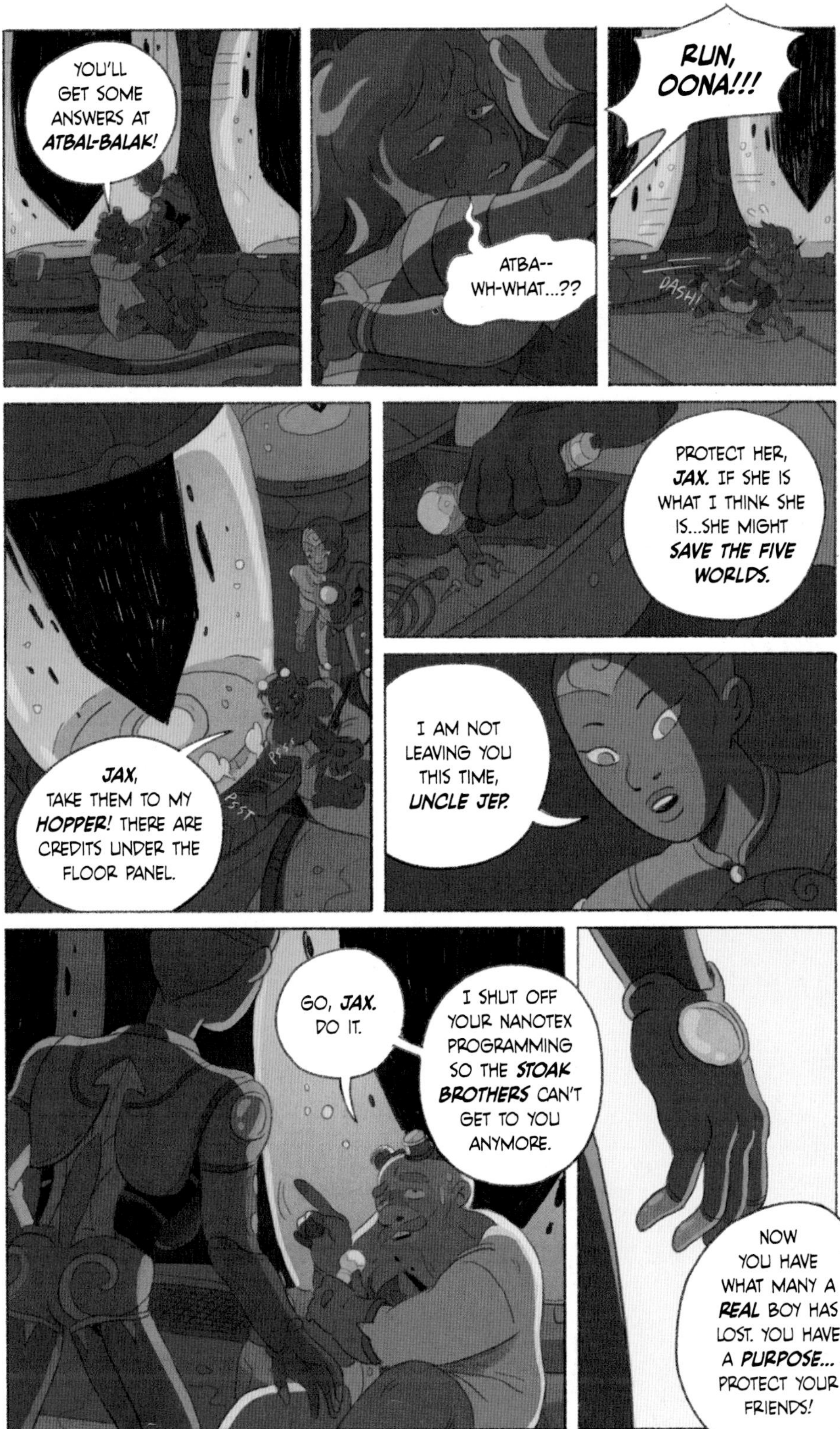
YOU'LL GET SOME ANSWERS AT ATBAL-BALAK!
ATBA-- WH-WHAT...??
RUN, OONA!!!
DASH!
PROTECT HER, JAX. IF SHE IS WHAT I THINK SHE IS...SHE MIGHT SAVE THE FIVE WORLDS.
JAX, TAKE THEM TO MY HOPPER! THERE ARE CREDITS UNDER THE FLOOR PANEL.
I AM NOT LEAVING YOU THIS TIME, UNCLE JEP.
GO, JAX. DO IT.
I SHUT OFF YOUR NANOTEX PROGRAMMING SO THE STOAK BROTHERS CAN'T GET TO YOU ANYMORE.
NOW YOU HAVE WHAT MANY A REAL BOY HAS LOST. YOU HAVE A PURPOSE... PROTECT YOUR FRIENDS!

BUT YOU...

YOU HAVE BROUGHT ME *HOPE*.

MORE HOPE THAN I'VE HAD IN A VERY LONG TIME... *GO, SON.*

HELP *OONA LEE.*

IS THAT MY NEW *CORE DIRECTIVE?*

NO. IT'S THE RIGHT THING TO DO.

THE *HUMAN* THING TO DO.

CRASH

TP   TP   TP

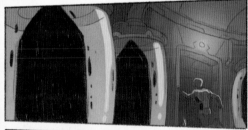

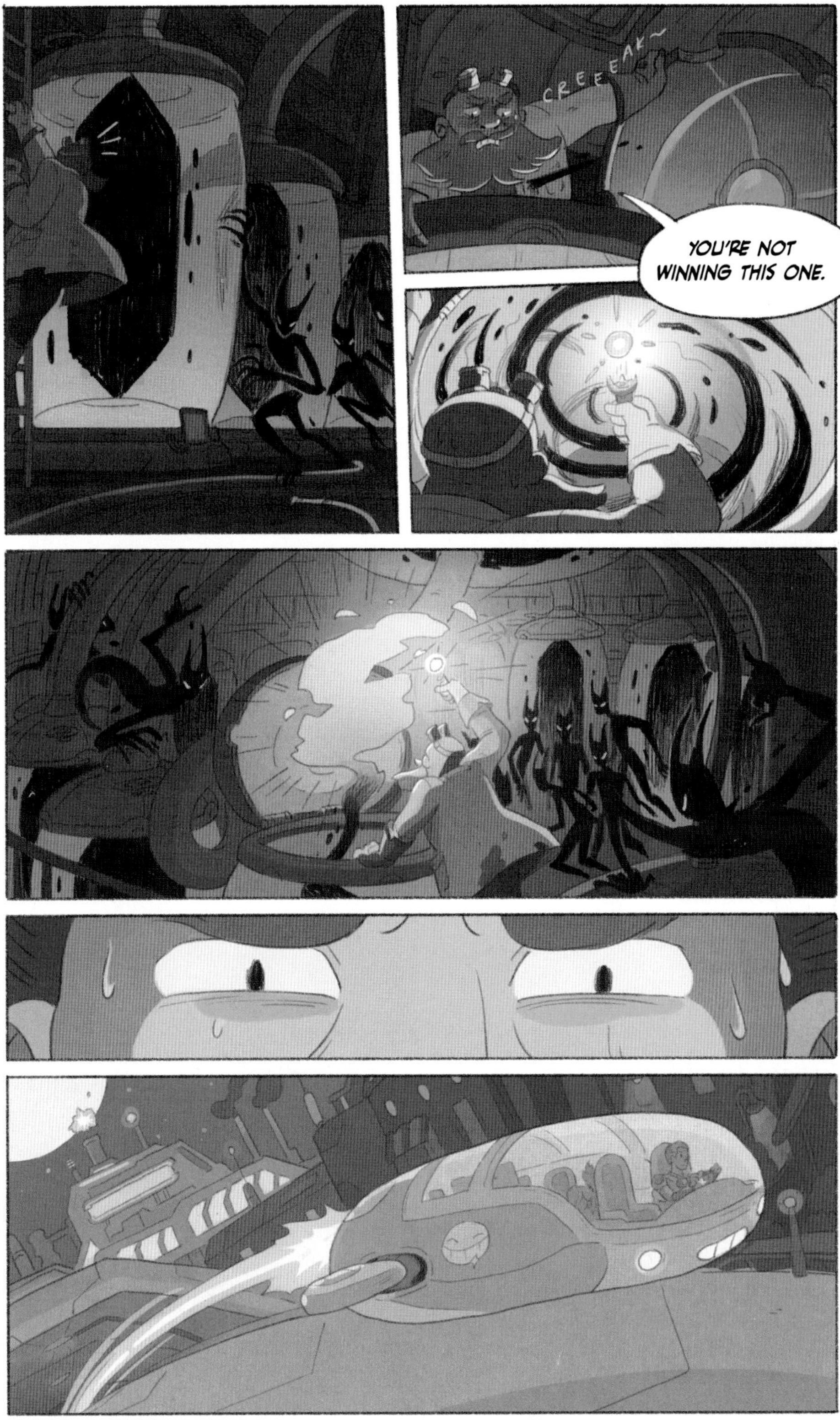
CREEEAK~
YOU'RE NOT WINNING THIS ONE.

KA BOOOM!!

YOU INCOMPETENT FOOLS! YOUR INSTRUCTIONS WERE TO CAPTURE THEM UNHARMED!

WE ARE ALMOST SURE THEY ESCAPED *BEFORE* THE EXPLOSION....

SLAM

SHE FOUND HER WAY TO *PROFESSOR ETTO'S LAB.* WHERE TO *NOW?*

CAN'T WE *CUT OUT* THE DARK SAND FROM HER SHOULDER?

WHOA, WHOA, *WHOA!* SHE'S A *LIVING* PERSON, REMEMBER?!

THE *DARK SAND* IS SPREADING IN HER. IT HAS A LIFE OF ITS OWN.

THE SAND LIVES...

THE SAND KNOWS...

STRANGE SANDSTONE. IT CONTAINS *FOUR* DIFFERENT SANDS.

SAND LIVES... SAND KNOWS...

SO WHAT?!

OONA IS DYING!!! DON'T YOU GET IT?!

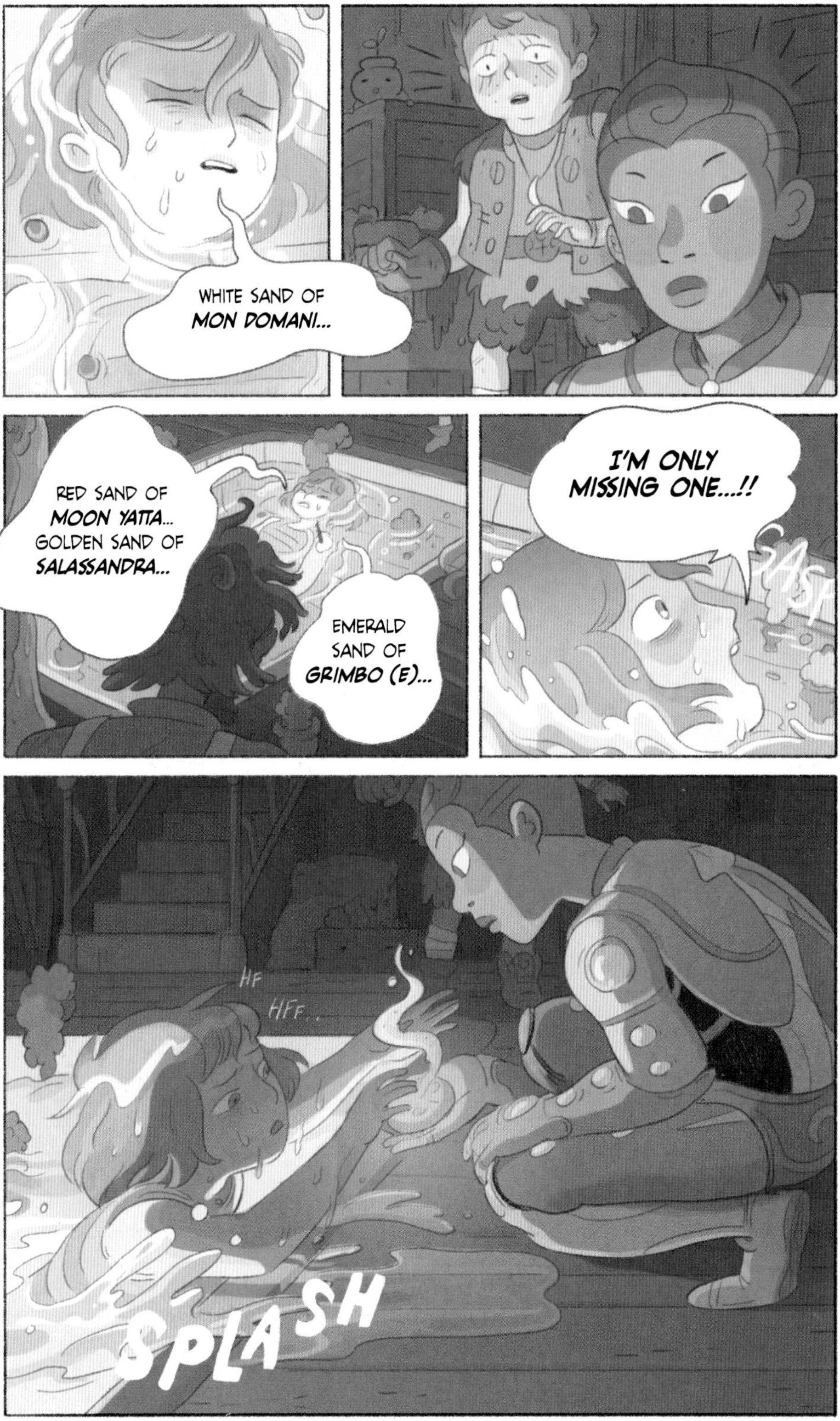
WHITE SAND OF MON DOMANI...
RED SAND OF MOON YATTA... GOLDEN SAND OF SALASSANDRA...
EMERALD SAND OF GRIMBO (E)...
I'M ONLY MISSING ONE...!!
HF
HFF..
SPLASH

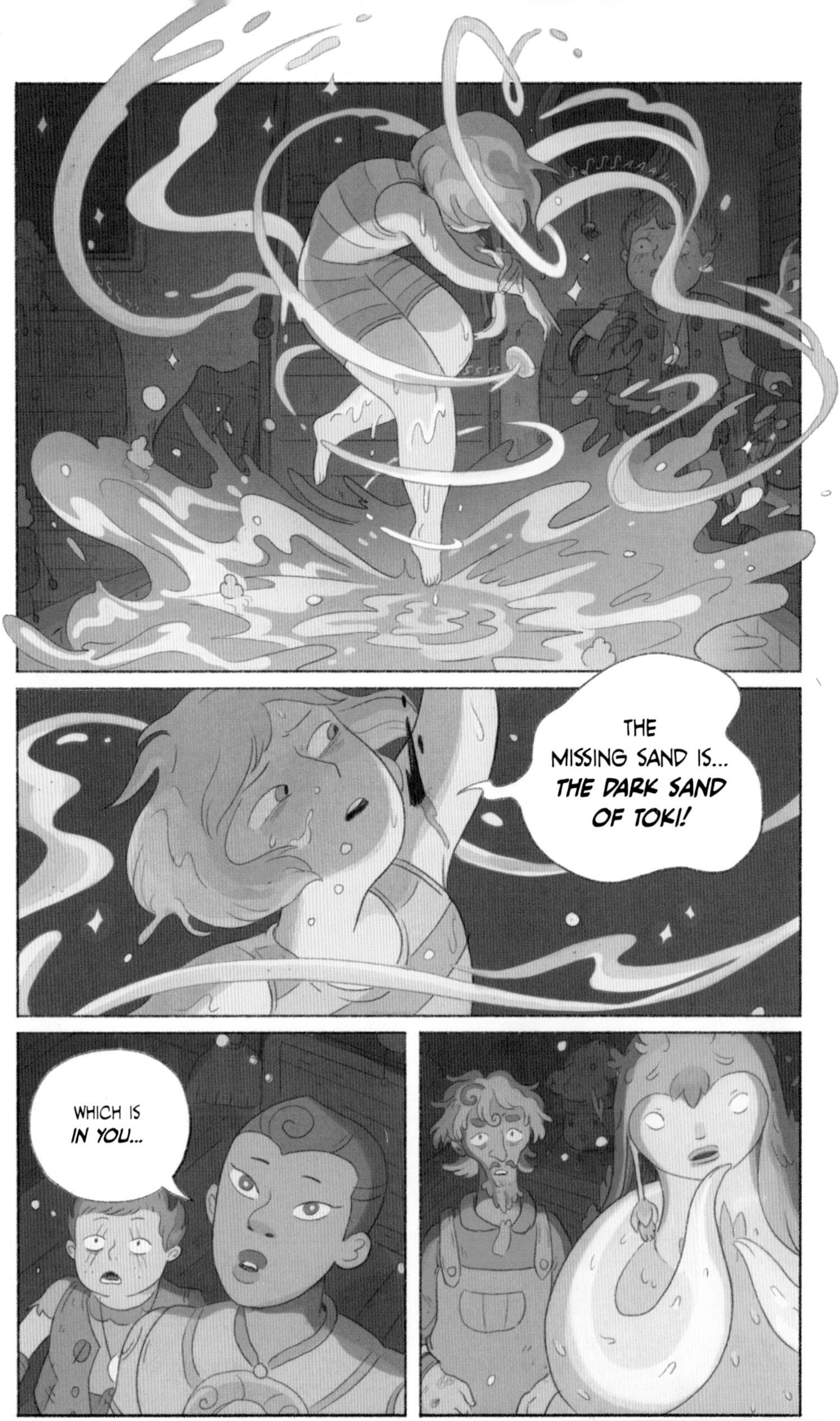
THE MISSING SAND IS... THE DARK SAND OF TOKI!
WHICH IS IN YOU...

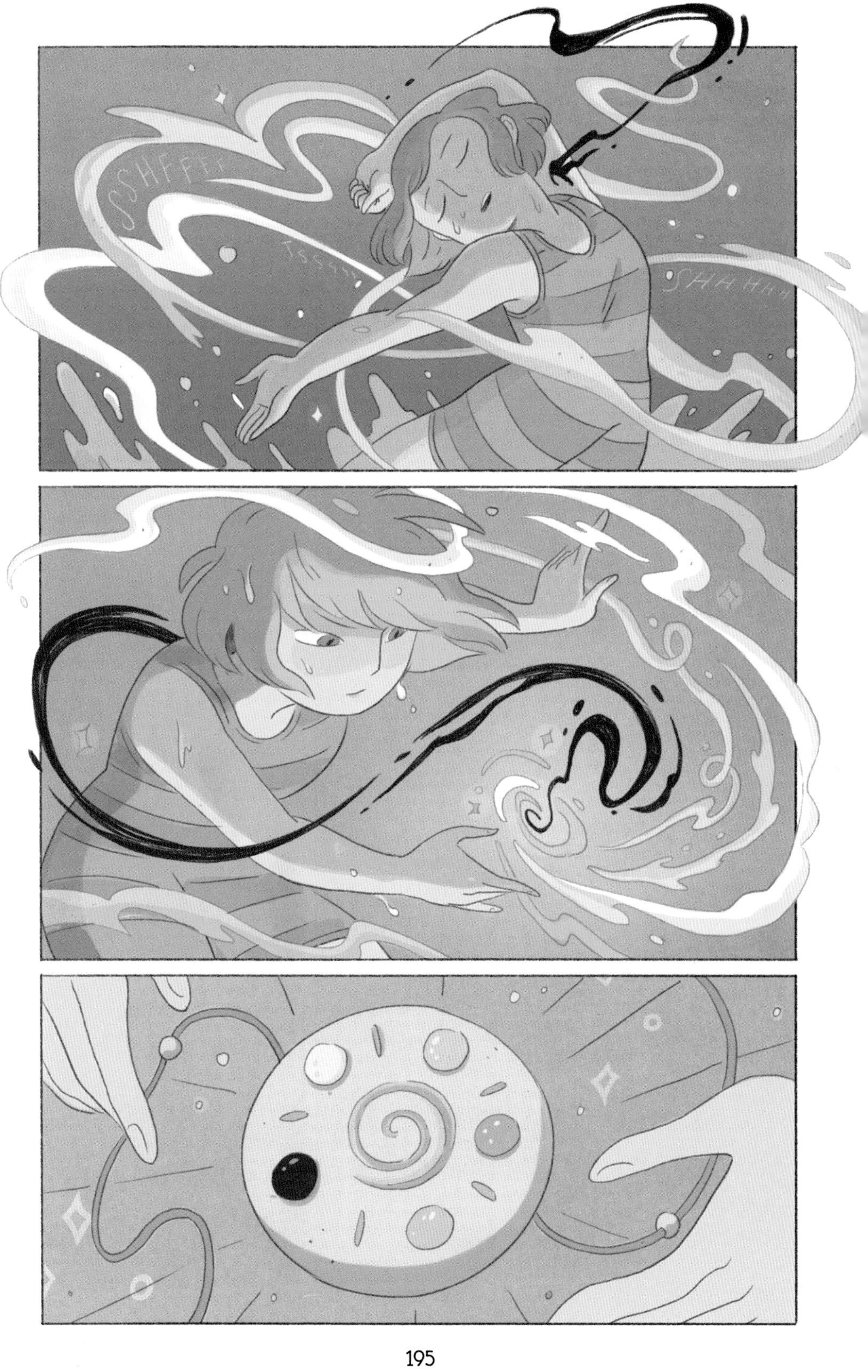
SSHFFFF
TSSSSSS
SHHHHH

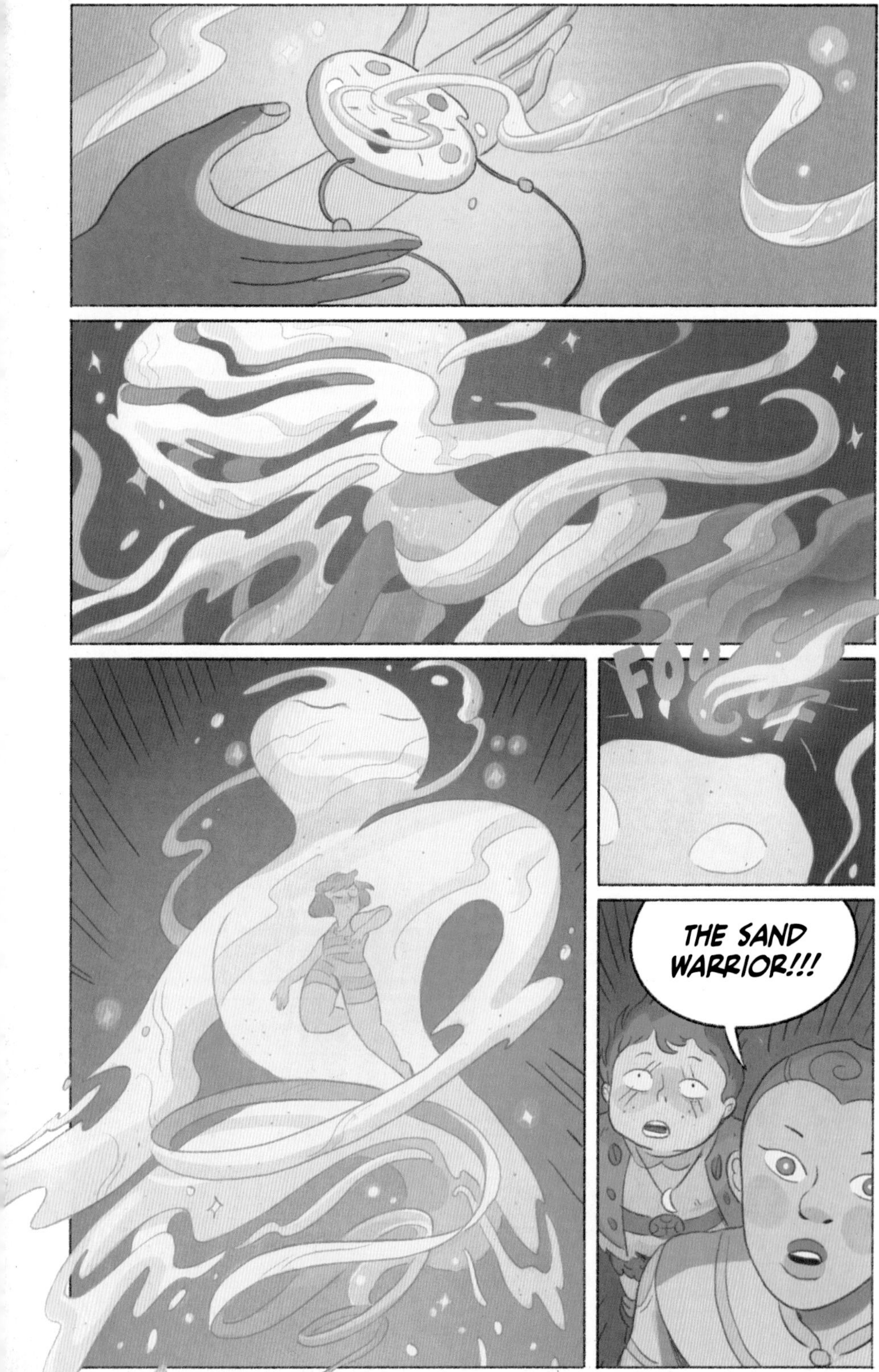
THE SAND WARRIOR!!!

Chapter 10
FIRE & RAIN

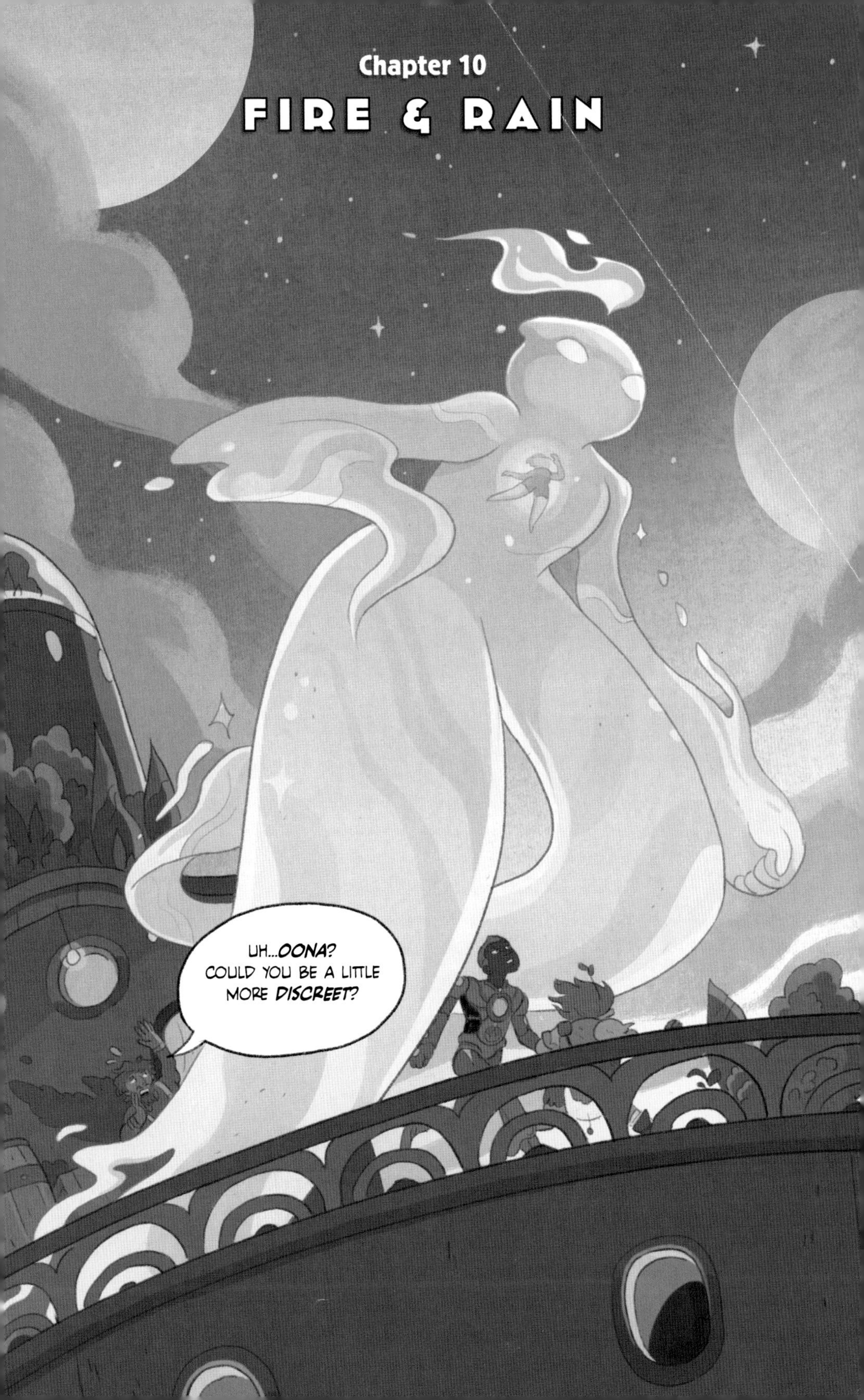

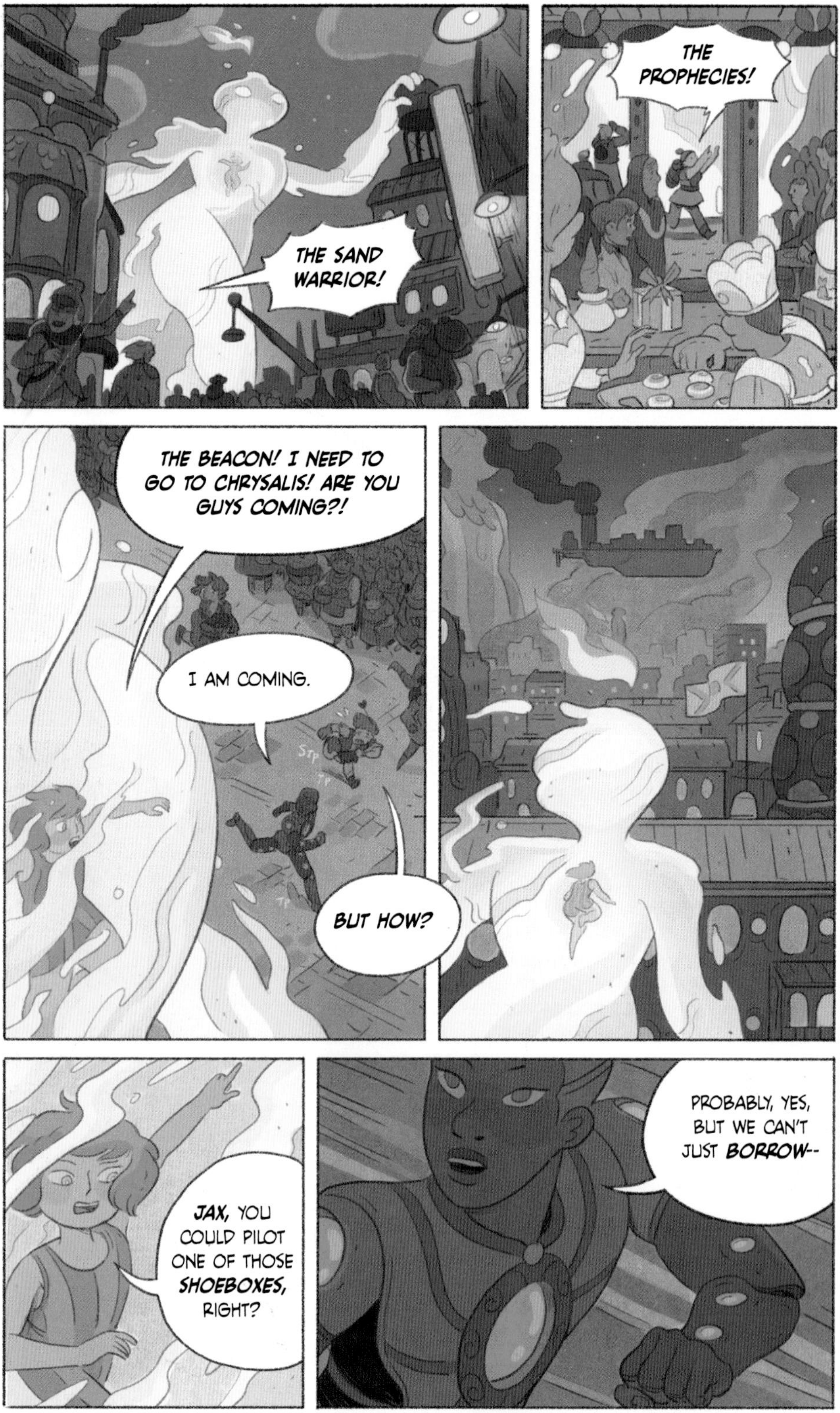
THE SAND WARRIOR!
THE PROPHECIES!
THE BEACON! I NEED TO GO TO CHRYSALIS! ARE YOU GUYS COMING?!
I AM COMING.
BUT HOW?
JAX, YOU COULD PILOT ONE OF THOSE SHOEBOXES, RIGHT?
PROBABLY, YES, BUT WE CAN'T JUST BORROW--

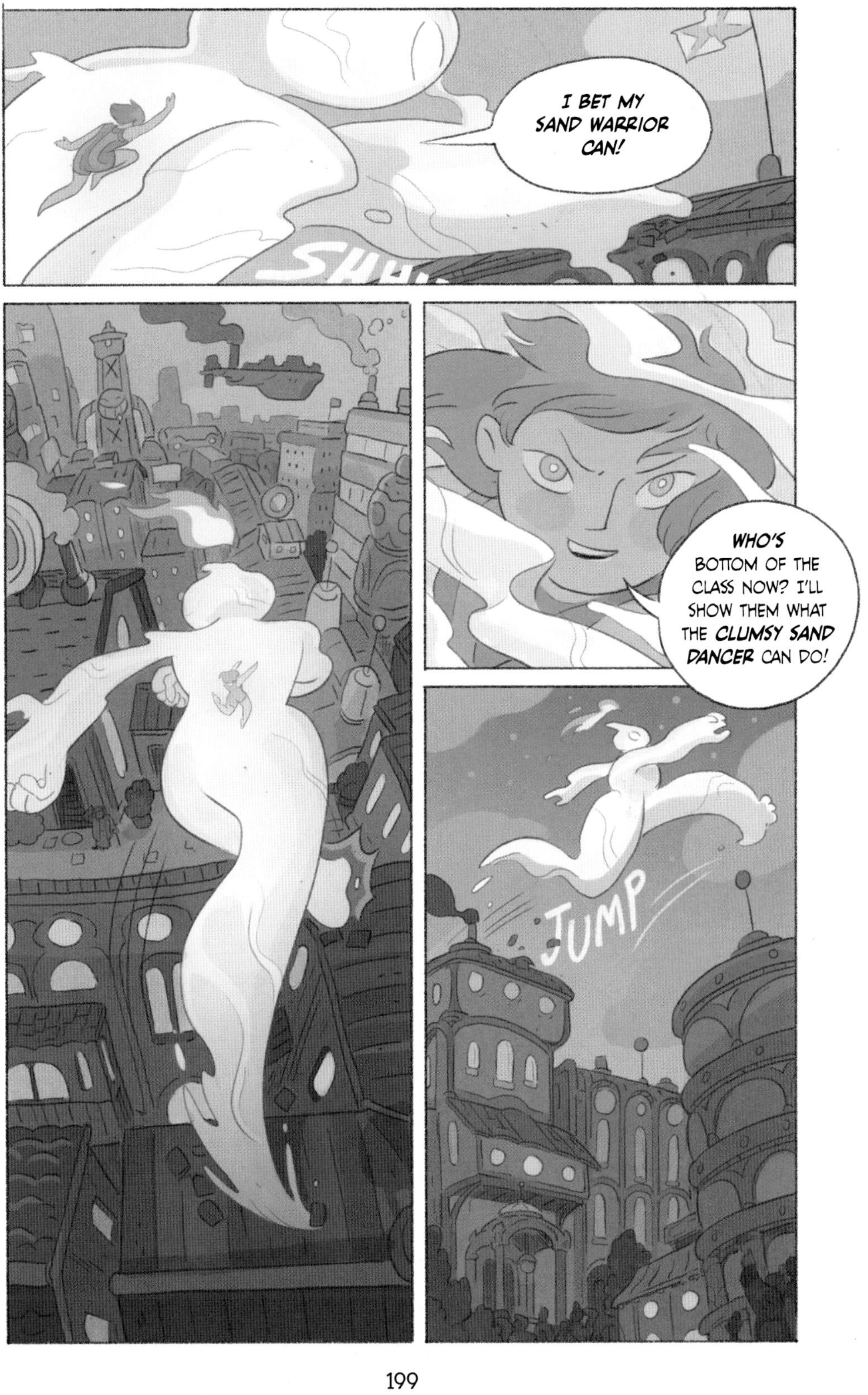
I BET MY SAND WARRIOR CAN!
WHO'S BOTTOM OF THE CLASS NOW? I'LL SHOW THEM WHAT THE CLUMSY SAND DANCER CAN DO!
JUMP

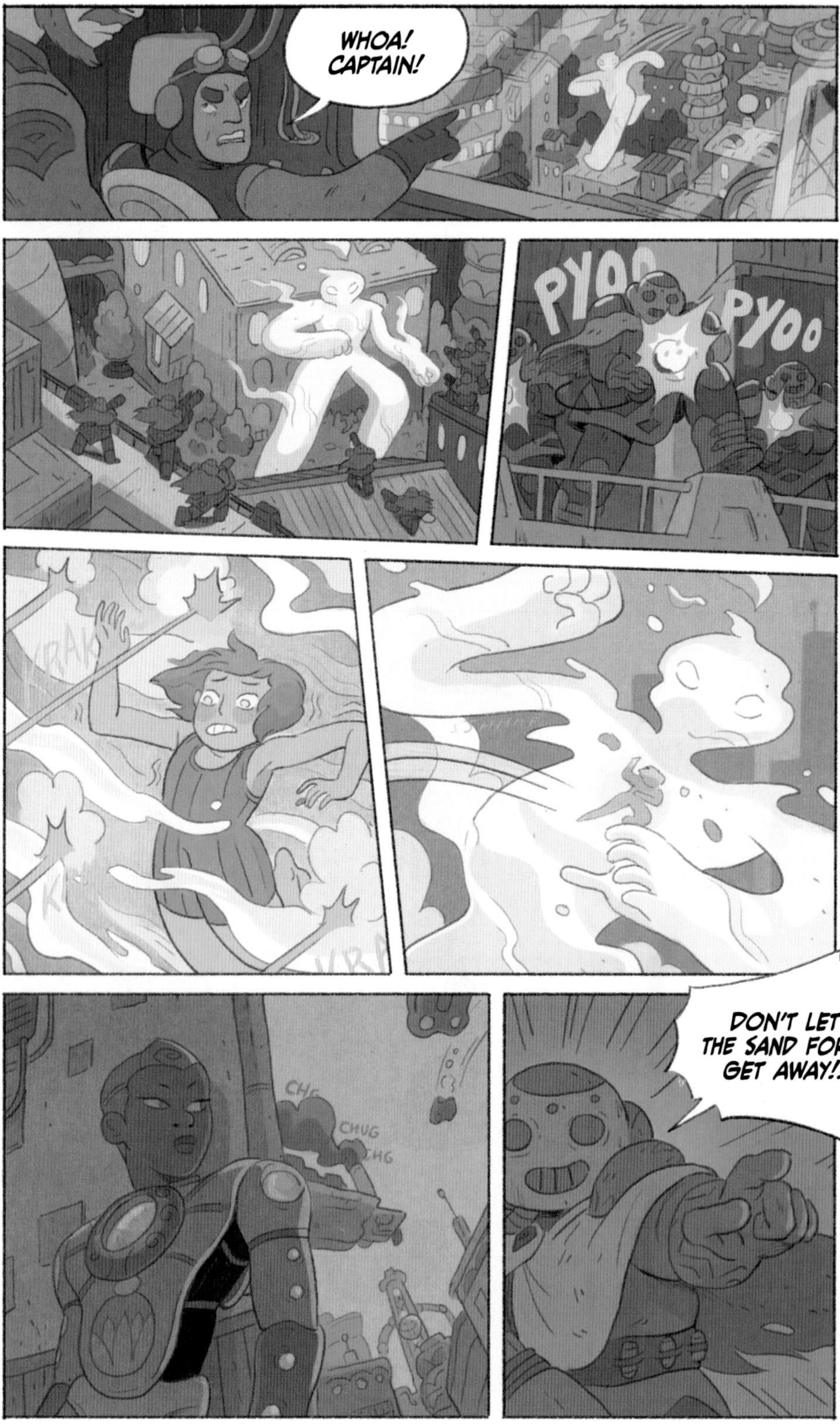
WHOA! CAPTAIN!
PYOO
PYOO
CHUG
DON'T LET THE SAND FORM GET AWAY!!

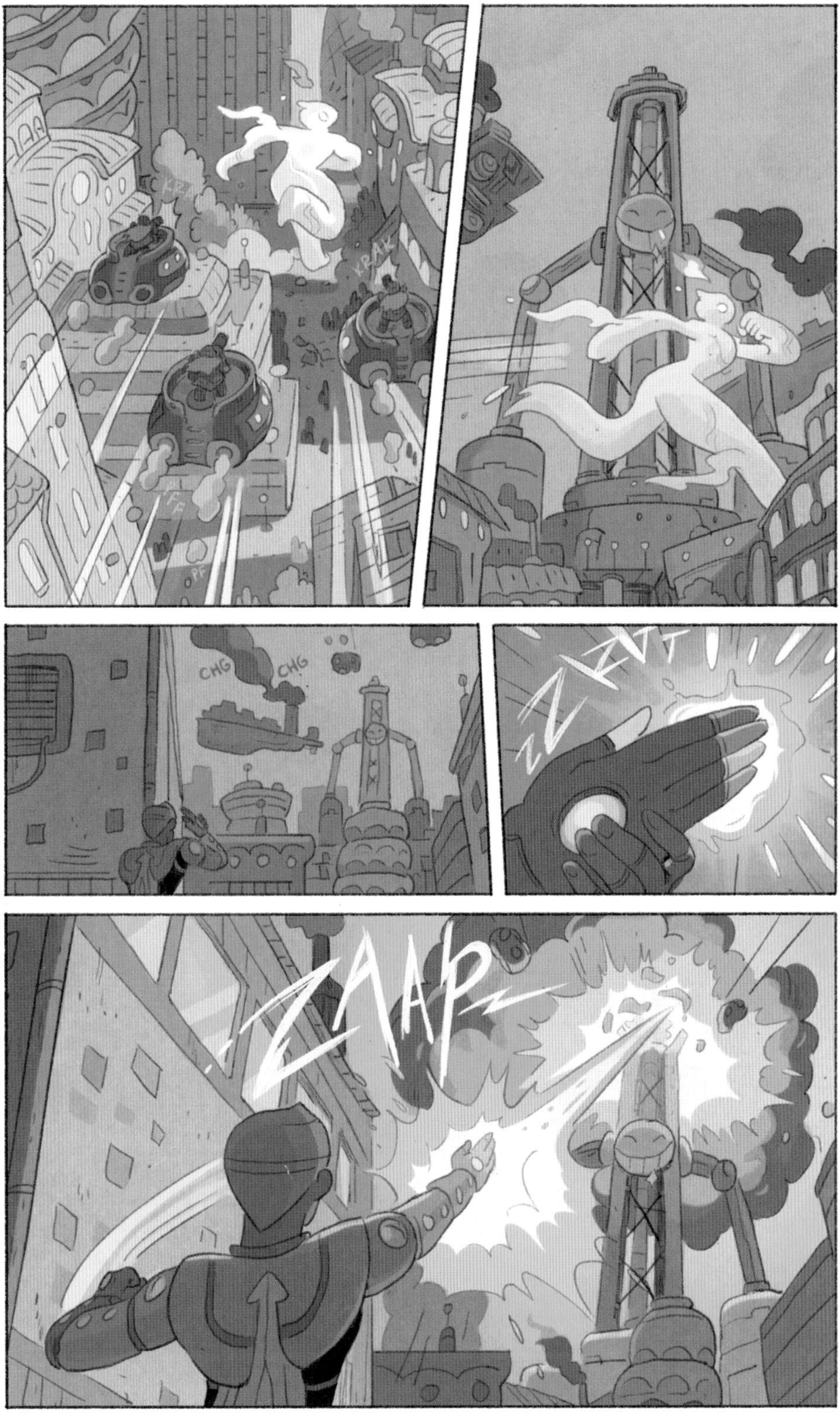
KRAK
PFF
PF
CHG
CHG
ZAAP

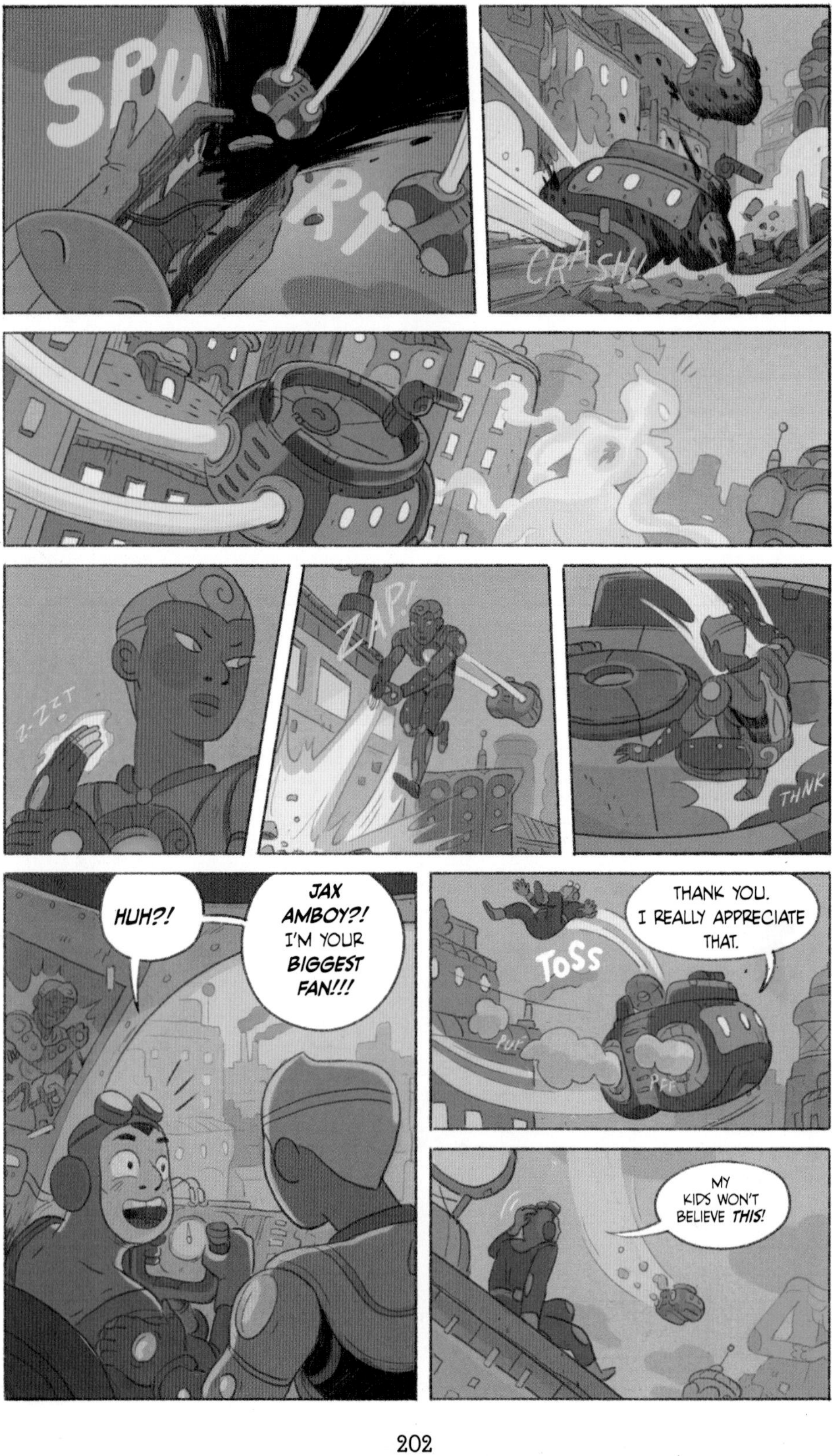
SPURT
CRASH!
Z-ZZT
ZAP!
THNK
HUH?!
JAX AMBOY?! I'M YOUR BIGGEST FAN!!!
TOSS
THANK YOU. I REALLY APPRECIATE THAT.
PUF
PFF
MY KIDS WON'T BELIEVE THIS!

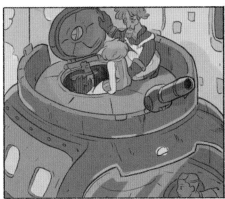

LOOK AT THAT. THE SUNS MAKE A PERFECT LINE!

WE HAVE MAYBE AN HOUR BEFORE OUR TIME IS UP.

STEP ON IT, ROBOT BOY!

WE'RE GOING FULL SPEED.... ACTUALLY, I *MIGHT* BE ABLE TO HELP.

SOMEONE TAKE THE WHEEL.

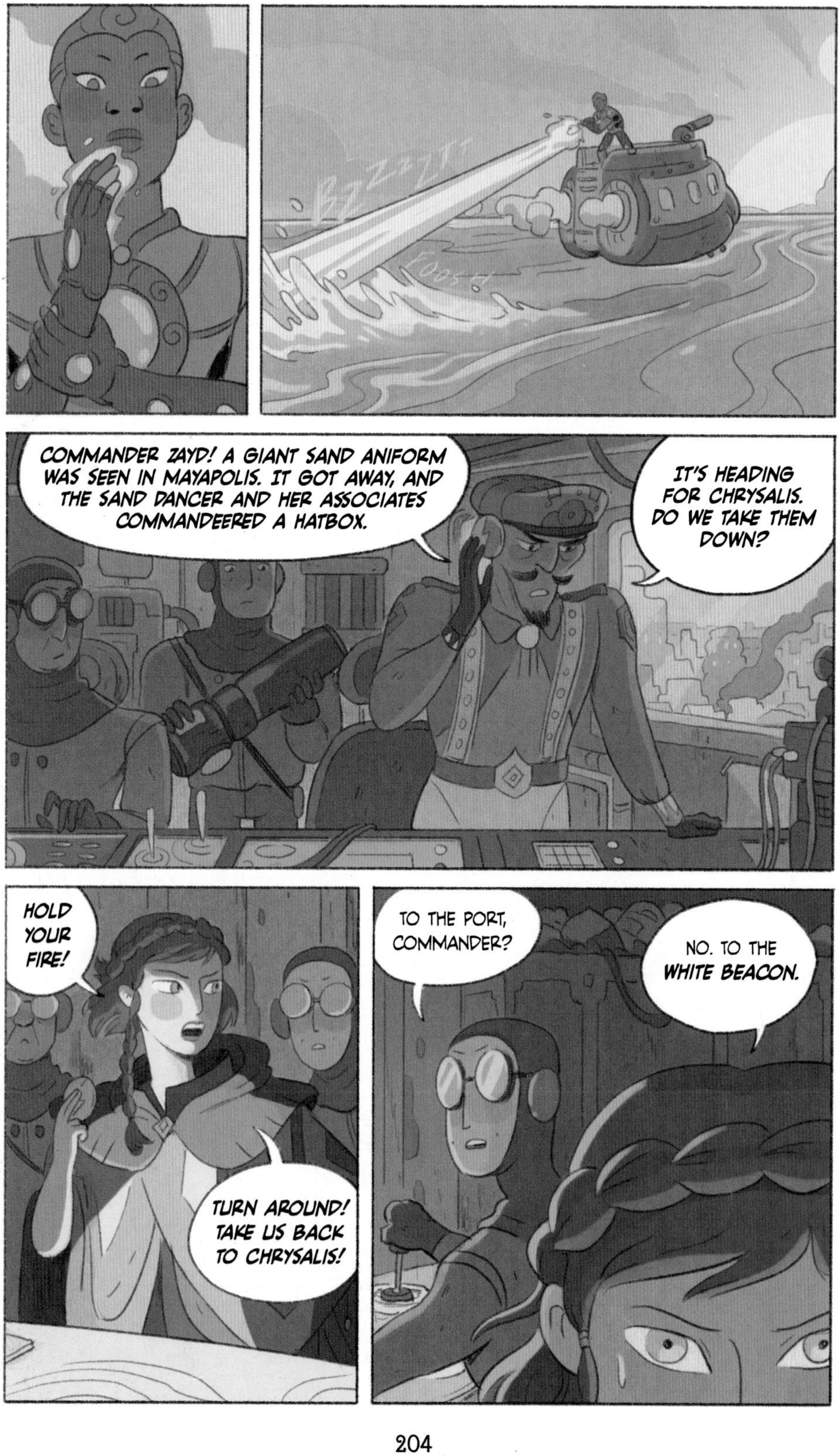
COMMANDER ZAYD! A GIANT SAND ANIFORM WAS SEEN IN MAYAPOLIS. IT GOT AWAY, AND THE SAND DANCER AND HER ASSOCIATES COMMANDEERED A HATBOX.
IT'S HEADING FOR CHRYSALIS. DO WE TAKE THEM DOWN?
HOLD YOUR FIRE!
TURN AROUND! TAKE US BACK TO CHRYSALIS!
TO THE PORT, COMMANDER?
NO. TO THE WHITE BEACON.

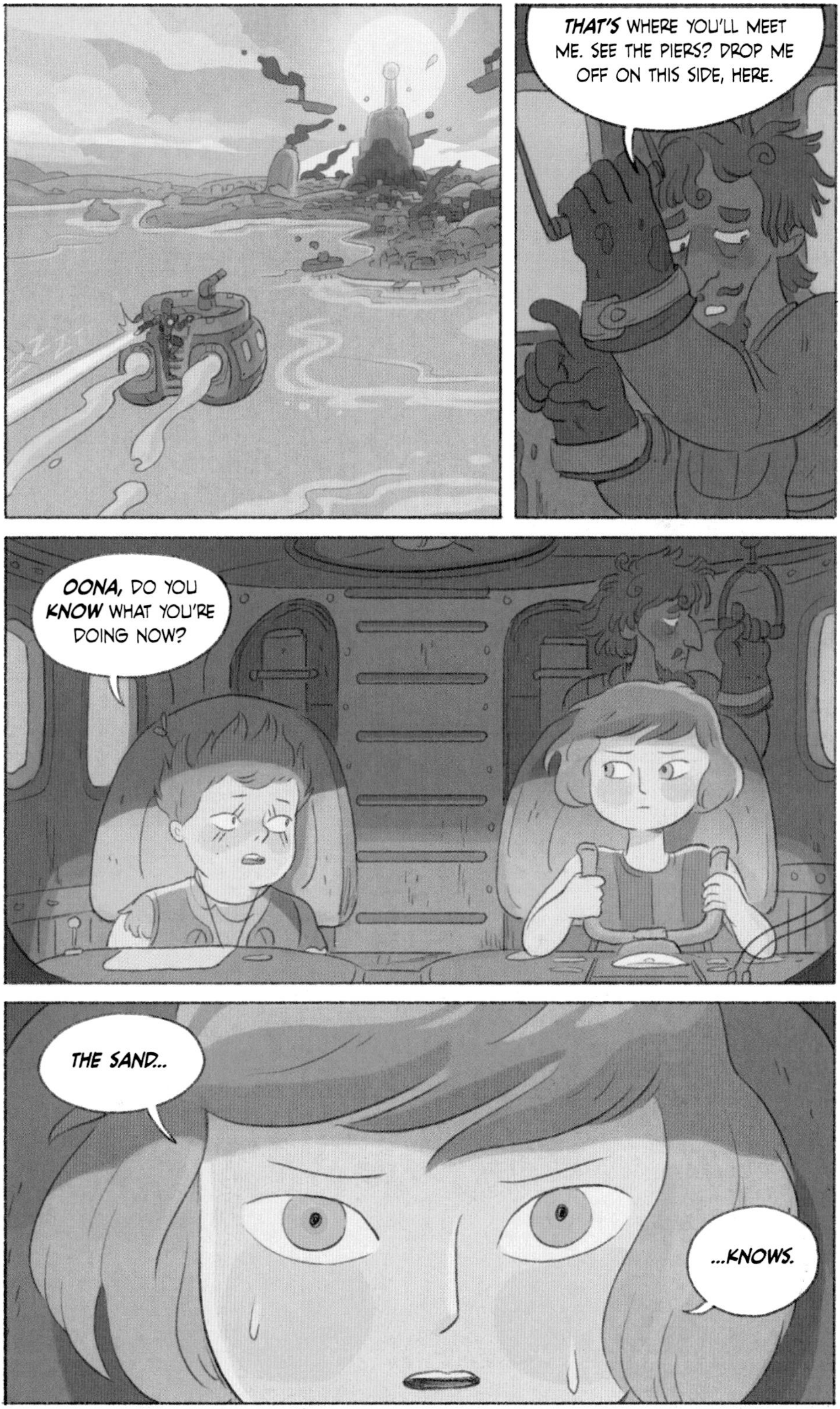
THAT'S WHERE YOU'LL MEET ME. SEE THE PIERS? DROP ME OFF ON THIS SIDE, HERE.
OONA, DO YOU KNOW WHAT YOU'RE DOING NOW?
THE SAND...
...KNOWS.

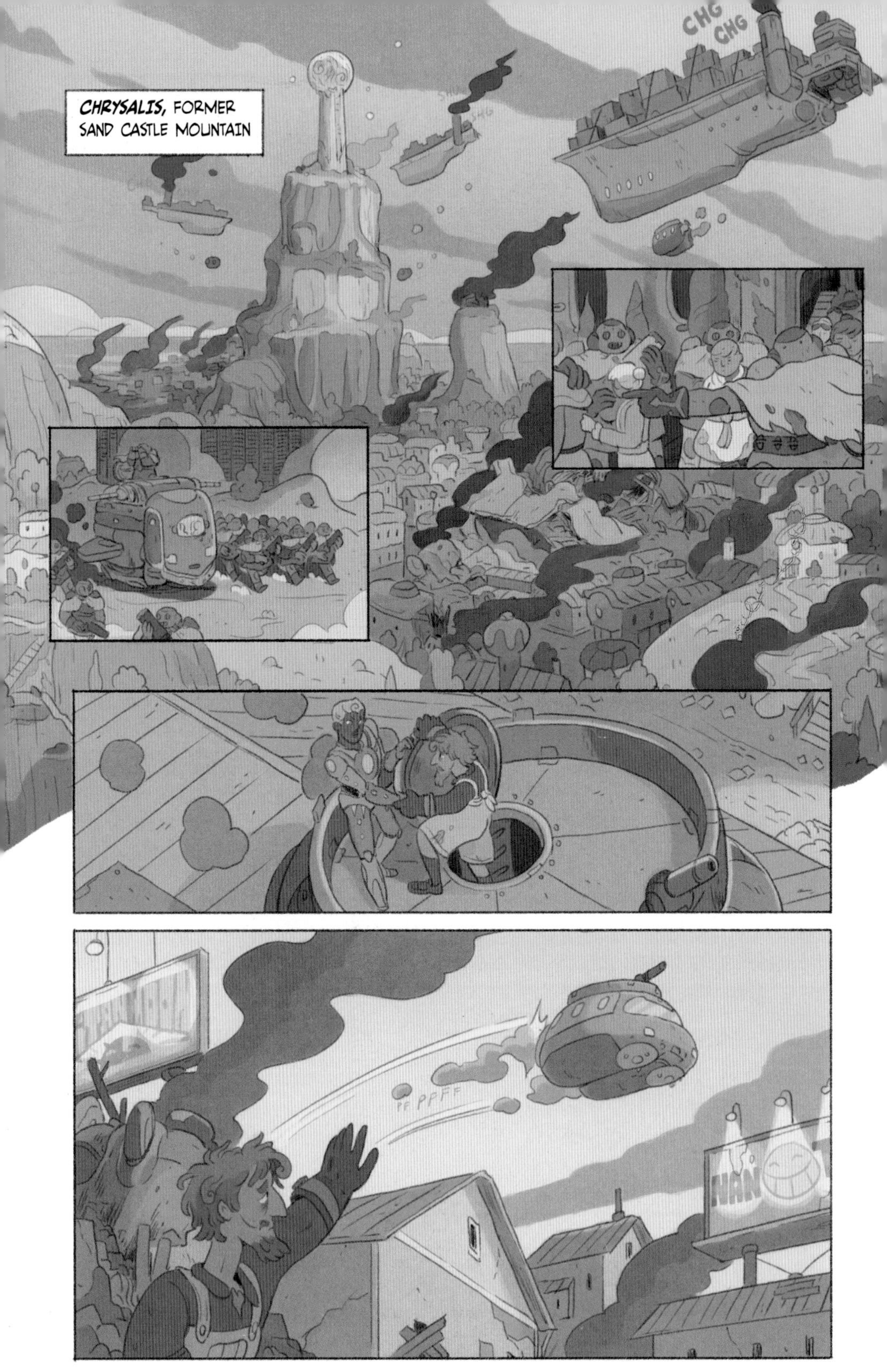
CHRYSALIS, FORMER
SAND CASTLE MOUNTAIN
CHG
CHG

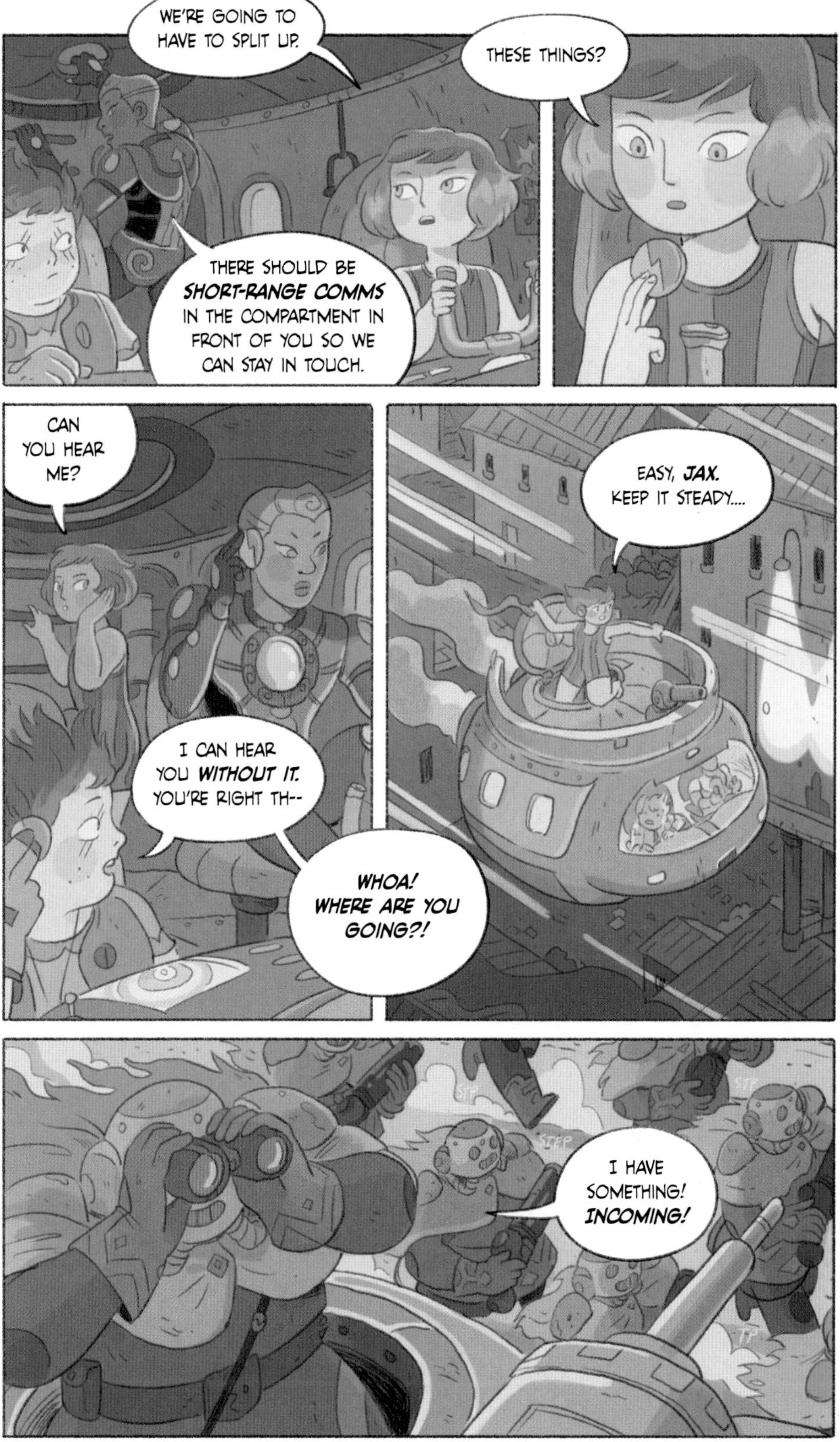
WE'RE GOING TO HAVE TO SPLIT UP.
THERE SHOULD BE **SHORT-RANGE COMMS** IN THE COMPARTMENT IN FRONT OF YOU SO WE CAN STAY IN TOUCH.
THESE THINGS?
CAN YOU HEAR ME?
I CAN HEAR YOU **WITHOUT IT.** YOU'RE RIGHT TH--
WHOA! WHERE ARE YOU GOING?!
EASY, **JAX.** KEEP IT STEADY....
STEP
I HAVE SOMETHING! ***INCOMING!***

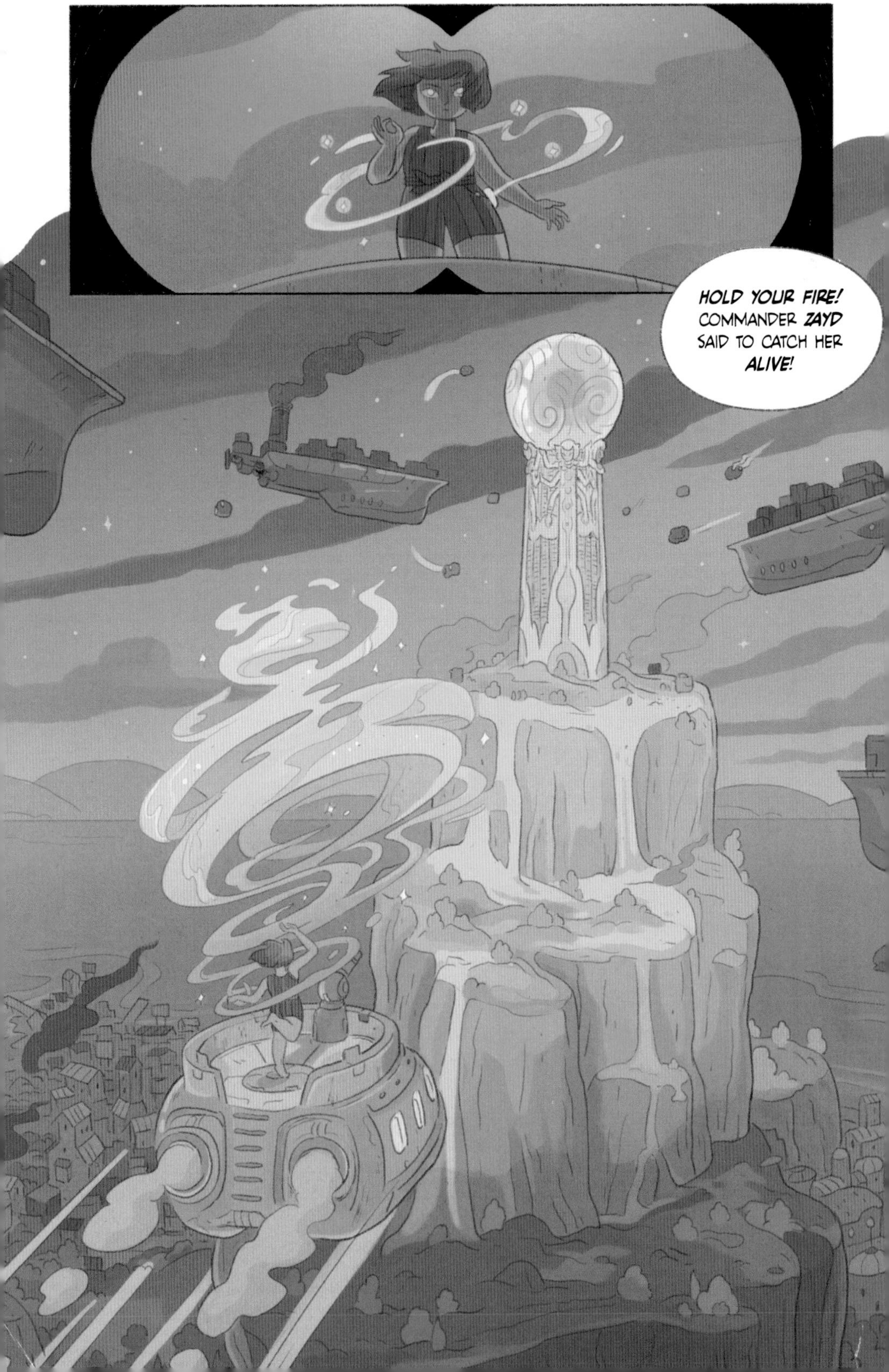
HOLD YOUR FIRE! COMMANDER ZAYD SAID TO CATCH HER ALIVE!

YOUR HIGHNESS? ARE THE *QUEEN'S BONES* IN THE *FLYING FORTRESS*?

PLANS CHANGE, *ZAYD*.

LEAVE THE *RELIC* TO ME.

WHAT OF THE *SAND DANCER*?

I WILL HAVE HER SOON.

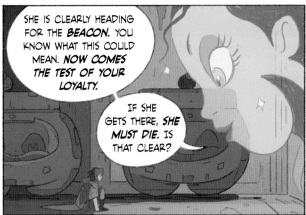

SHE IS CLEARLY HEADING FOR THE *BEACON.* YOU KNOW WHAT THIS COULD MEAN. *NOW COMES THE TEST OF YOUR LOYALTY.*

IF SHE GETS THERE, *SHE MUST DIE.* IS THAT CLEAR?

YES, CROWN PRINCE.

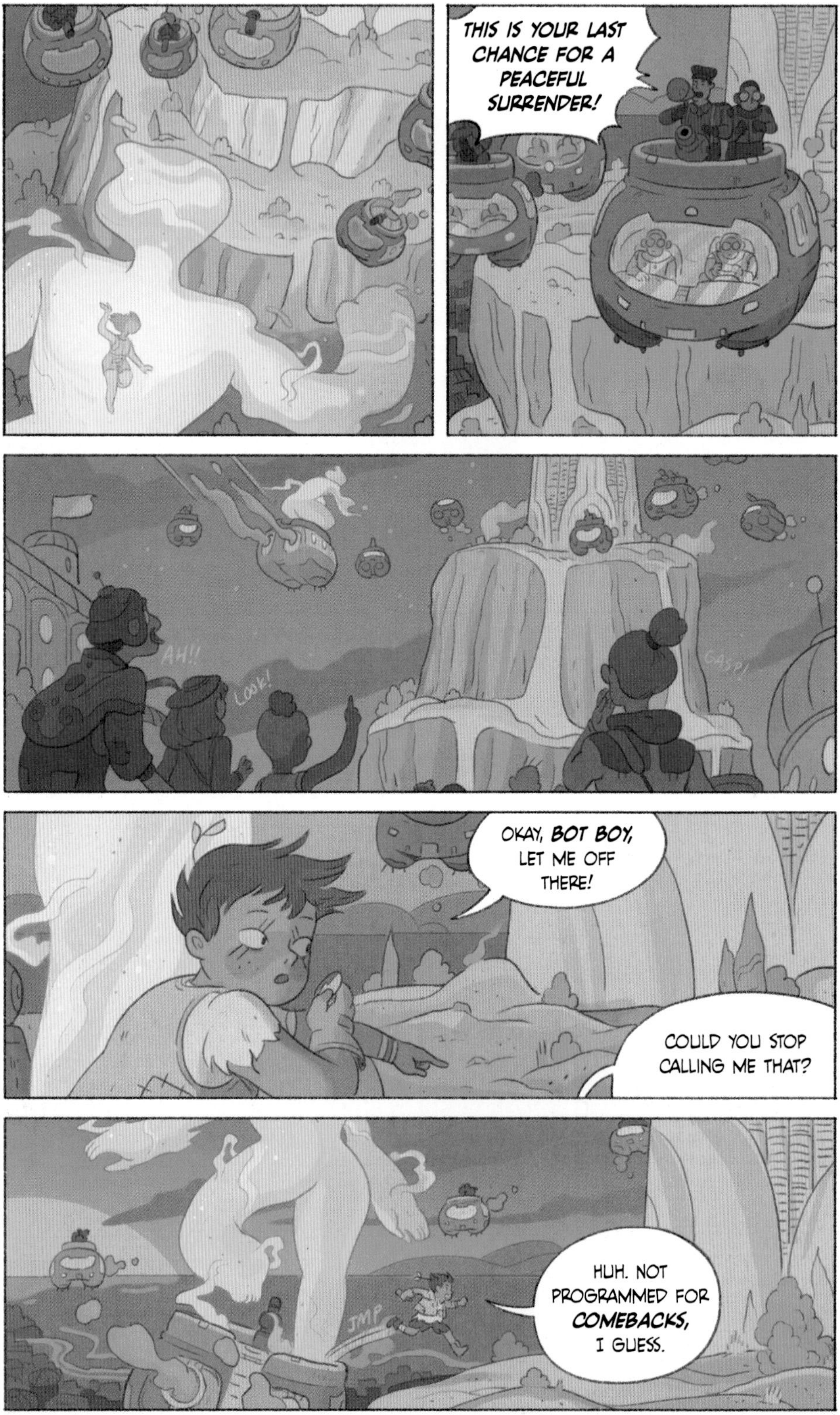
THIS IS YOUR LAST CHANCE FOR A PEACEFUL SURRENDER!
AH!!
LOOK!
GASP!
OKAY, **BOT BOY,** LET ME OFF THERE!
COULD YOU STOP CALLING ME THAT?
JMP
HUH. NOT PROGRAMMED FOR **COMEBACKS,** I GUESS.

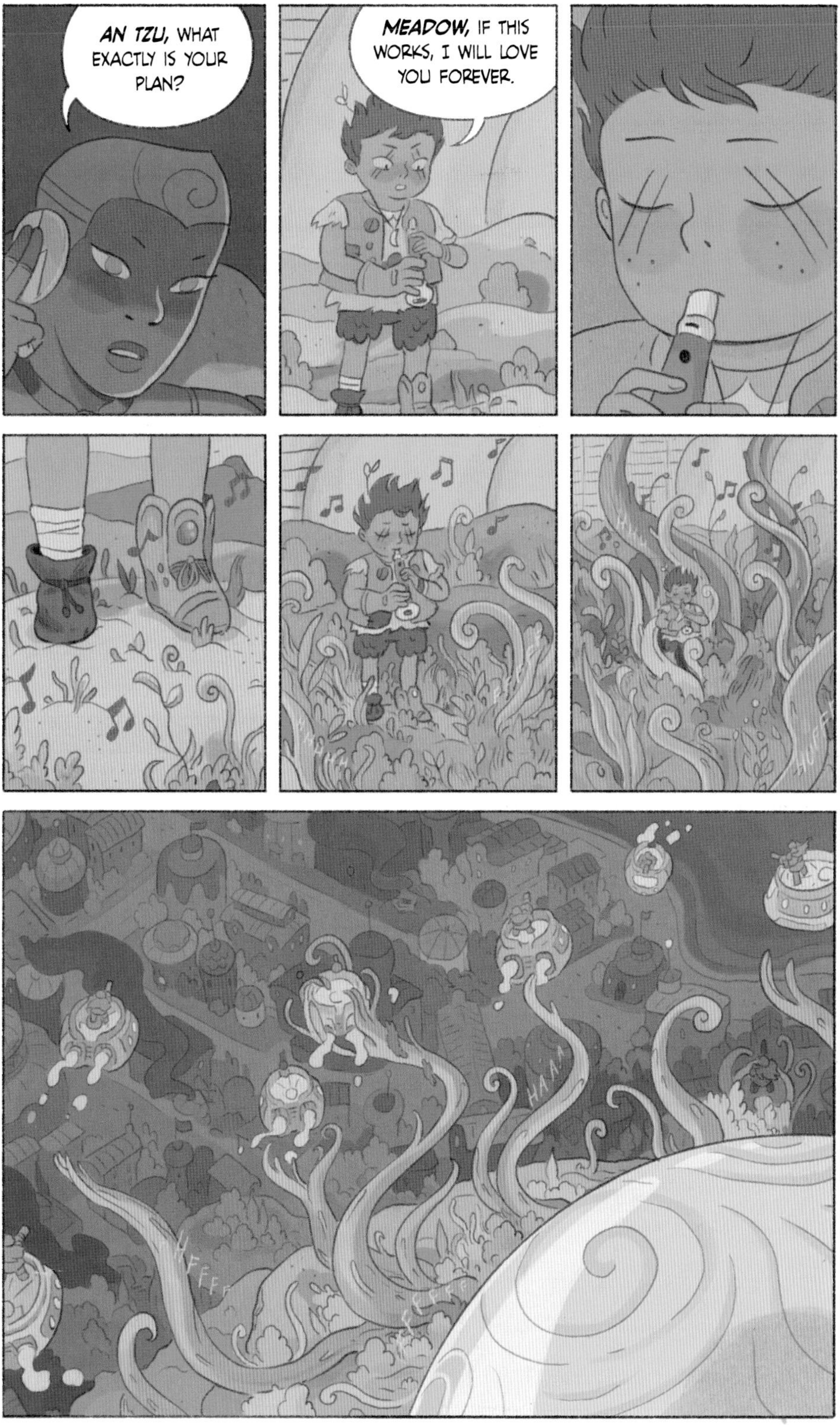
AN TZU, WHAT EXACTLY IS YOUR PLAN?
MEADOW, IF THIS WORKS, I WILL LOVE YOU FOREVER.

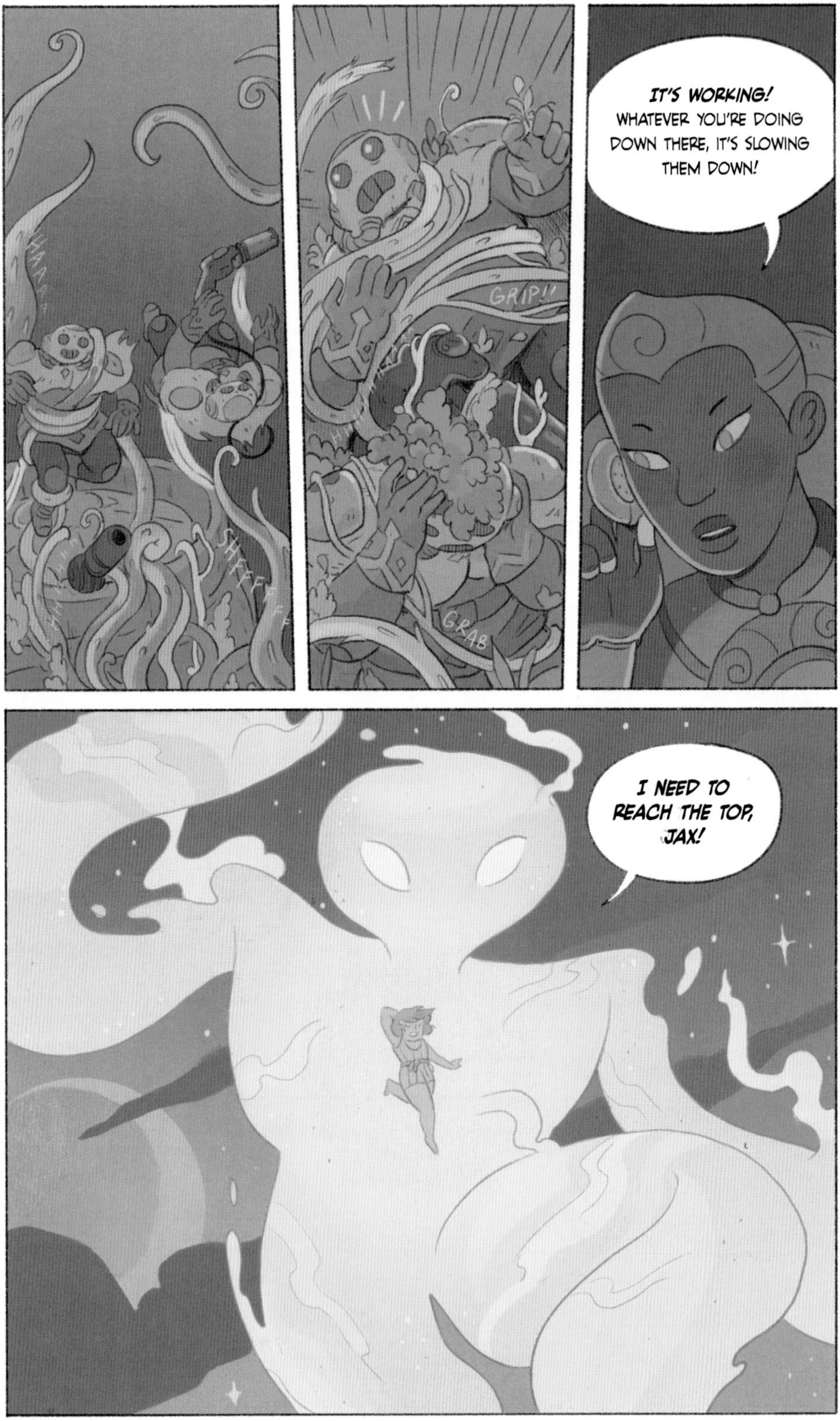
GRIP!!
GRAB
IT'S WORKING! WHATEVER YOU'RE DOING DOWN THERE, IT'S SLOWING THEM DOWN!
I NEED TO REACH THE TOP, JAX!

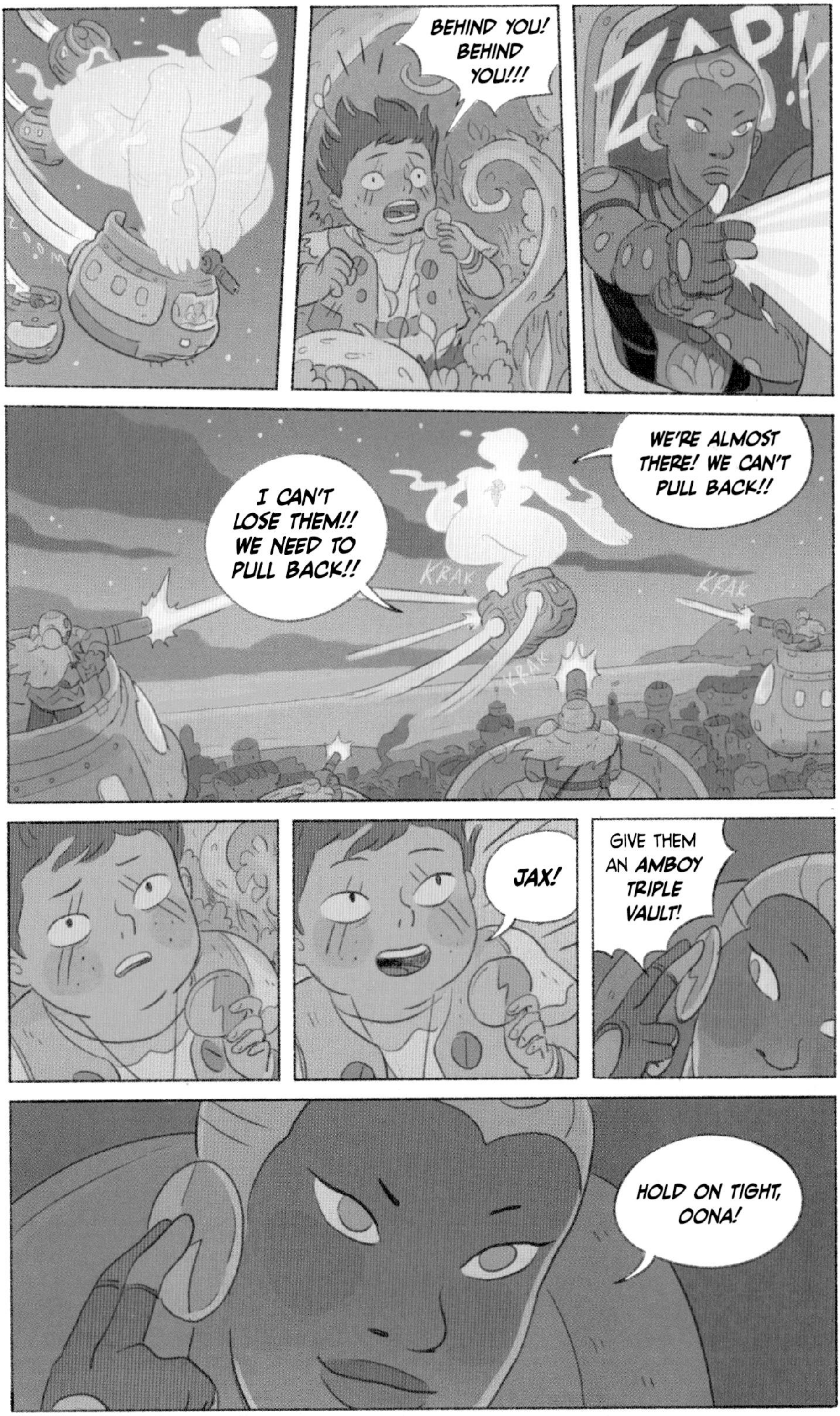
BEHIND YOU! BEHIND YOU!!!
ZAP!!
I CAN'T LOSE THEM!! WE NEED TO PULL BACK!!
KRAK
WE'RE ALMOST THERE! WE CAN'T PULL BACK!!
KRAK
KRAK
JAX!
GIVE THEM AN AMBOY TRIPLE VAULT!
HOLD ON TIGHT, OONA!

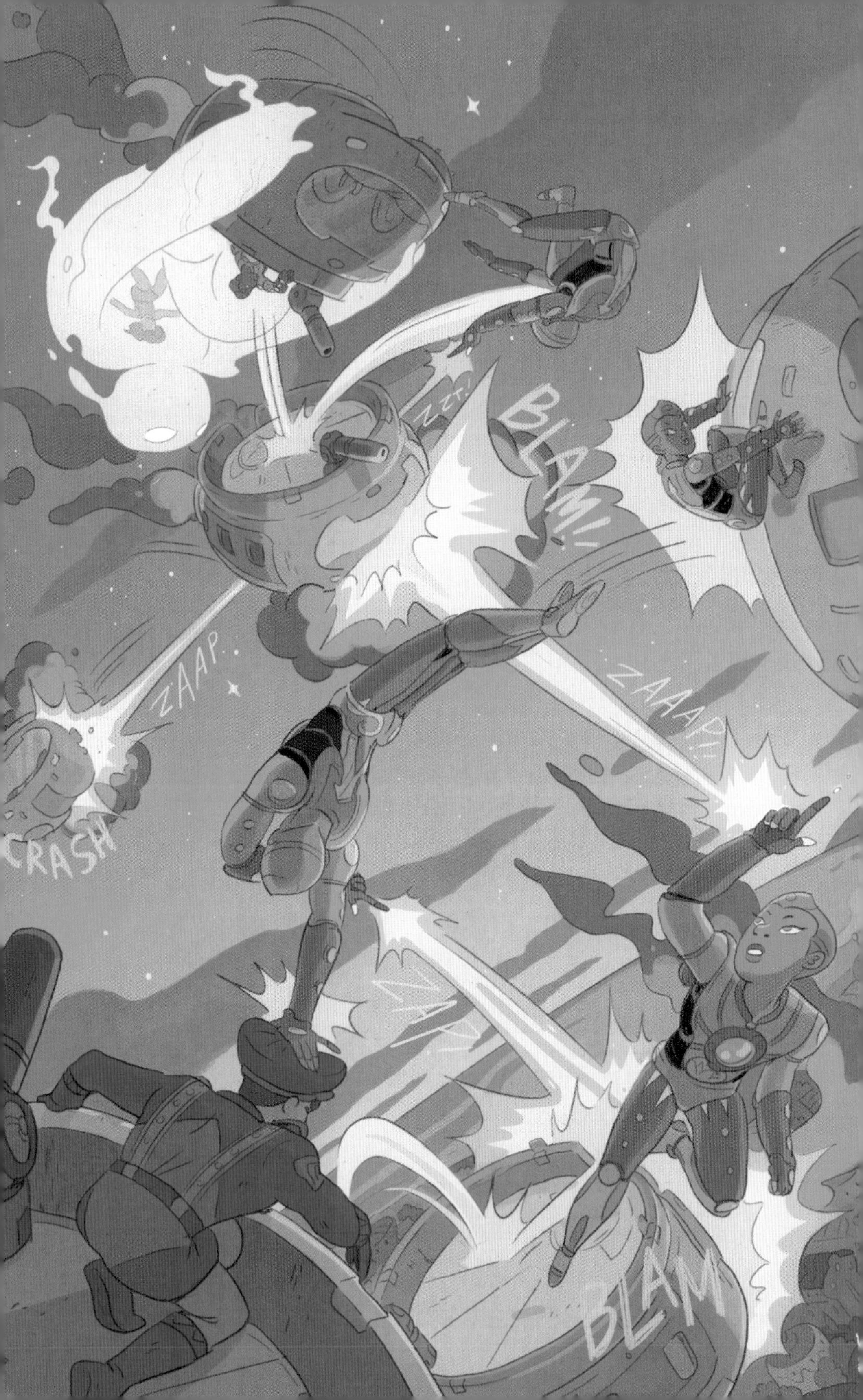
ZZT!
BLAM!!
ZAAP
CRASH
ZAAAP!!
ZAP!
BLAM

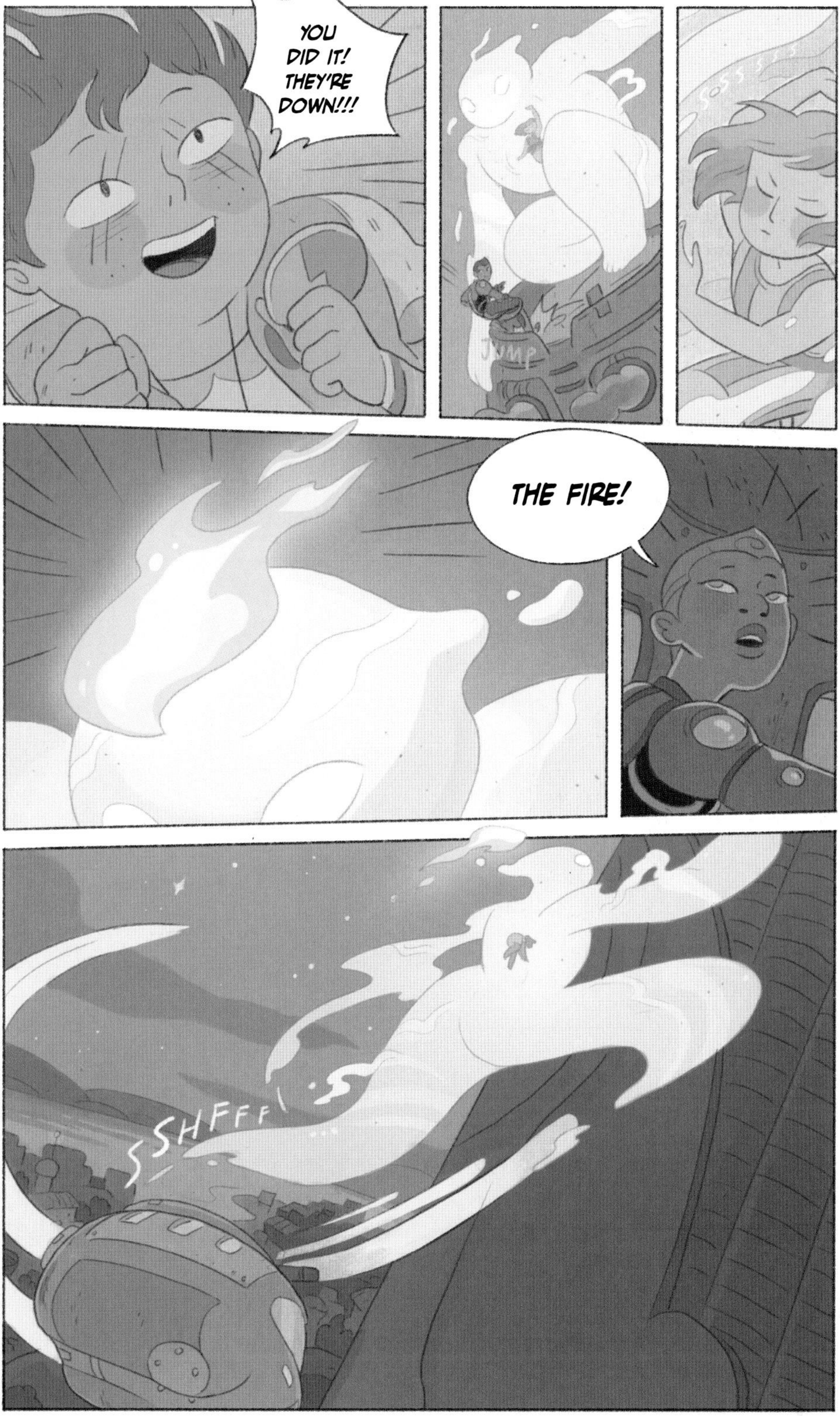
YOU DID IT! THEY'RE DOWN!!!
JUMP
THE FIRE!
SSHFFF

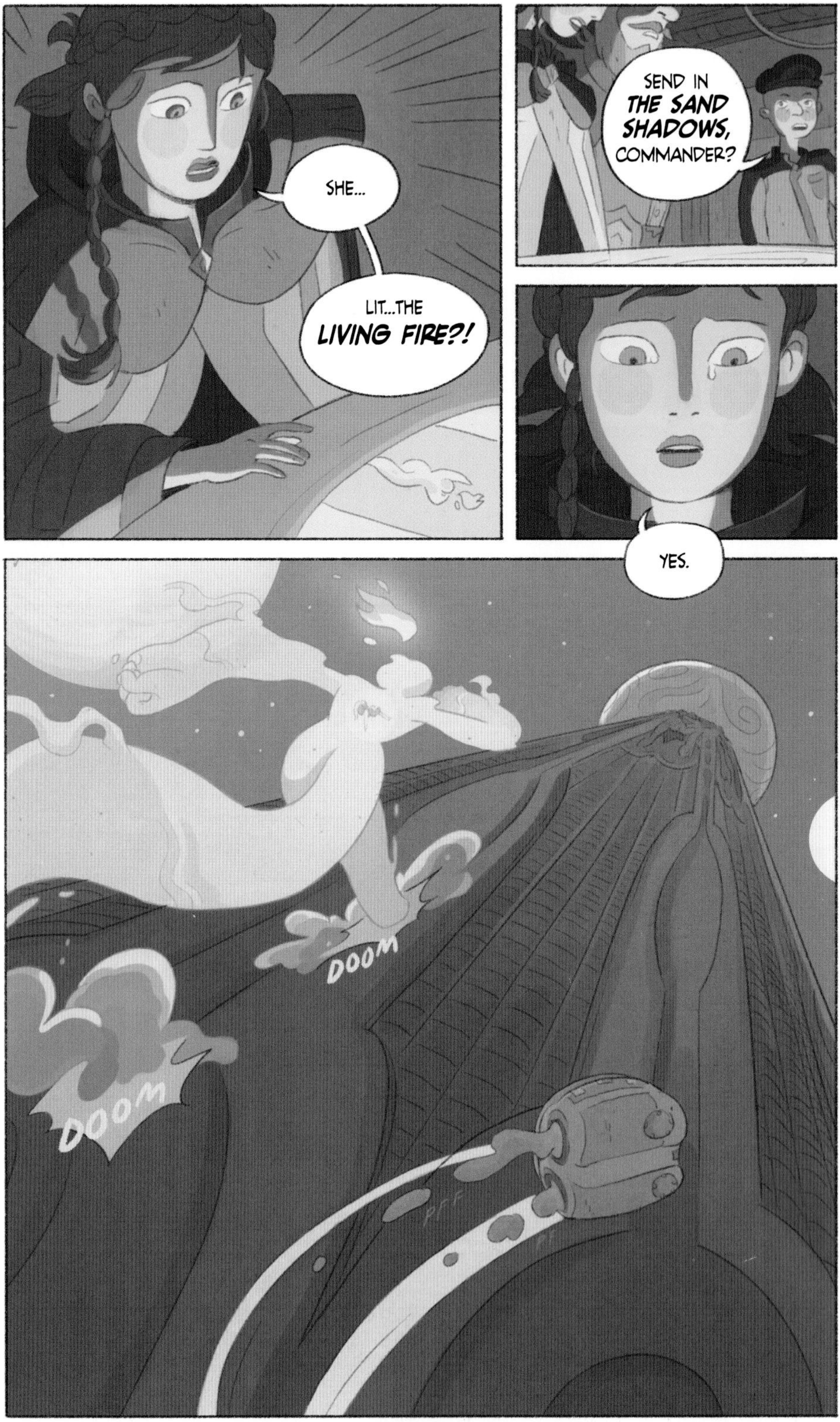
SHE...
LIT...THE LIVING FIRE?!
SEND IN THE SAND SHADOWS, COMMANDER?
YES.
DOOM
DOOM

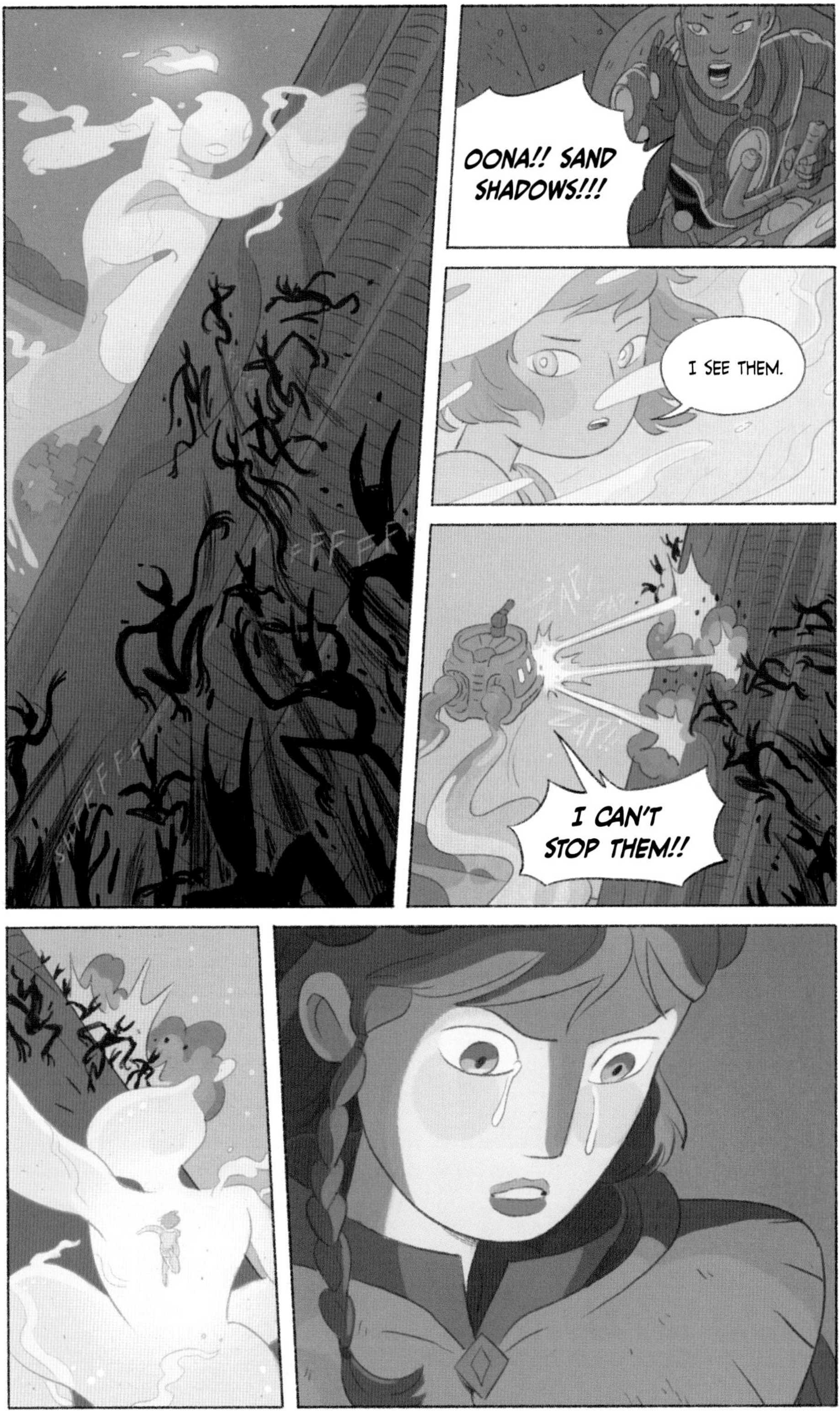

OONA!! SAND SHADOWS!!!
I SEE THEM.
ZAP!
ZAP!!
I CAN'T STOP THEM!!

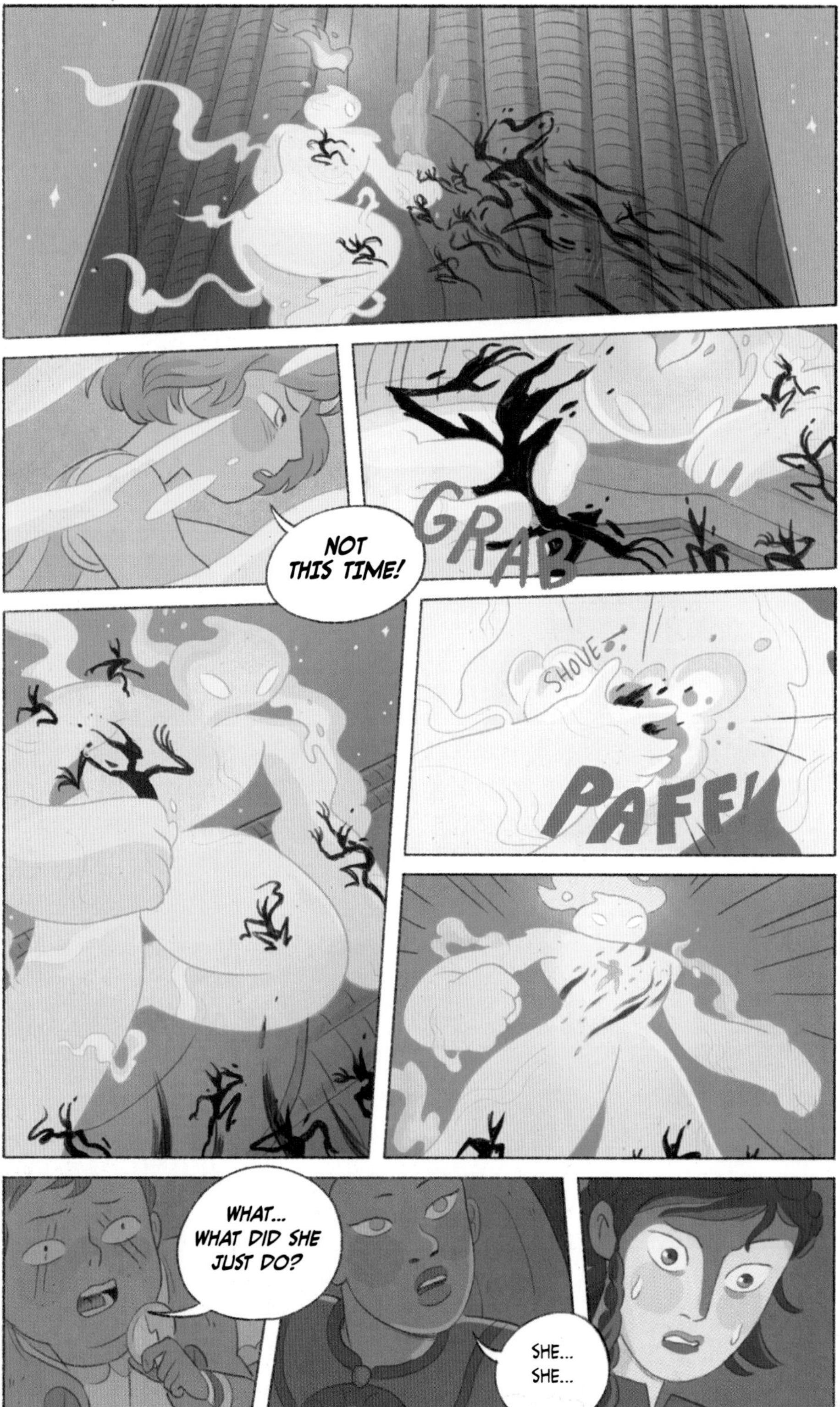
NOT THIS TIME!
GRAB
SHOVE
PAFF
WHAT... WHAT DID SHE JUST DO?
SHE... SHE...

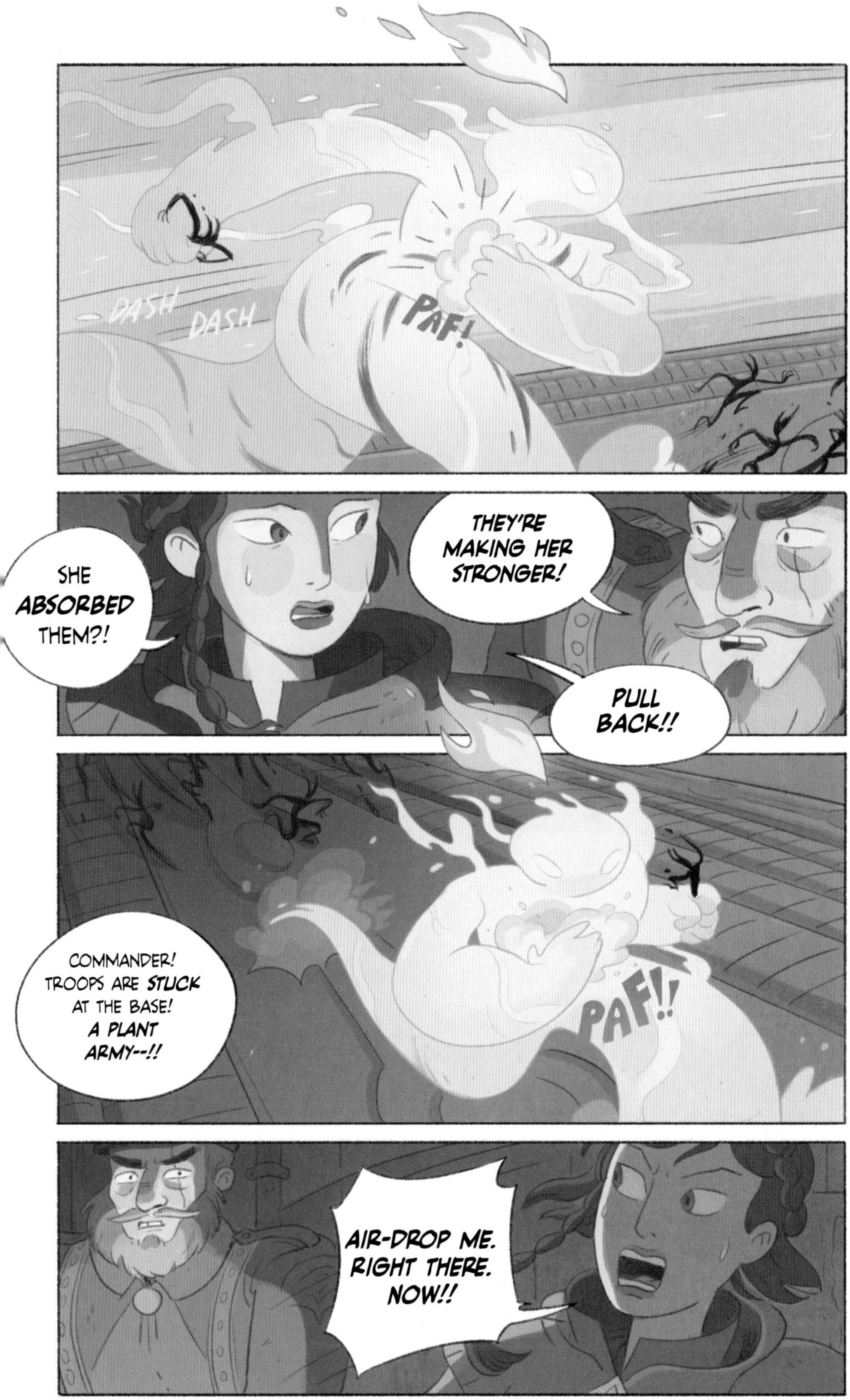
DASH DASH
PAF!
SHE ABSORBED THEM?!
THEY'RE MAKING HER STRONGER!
PULL BACK!!
COMMANDER! TROOPS ARE STUCK AT THE BASE! A PLANT ARMY--!!
PAF!!
AIR-DROP ME. RIGHT THERE. NOW!!

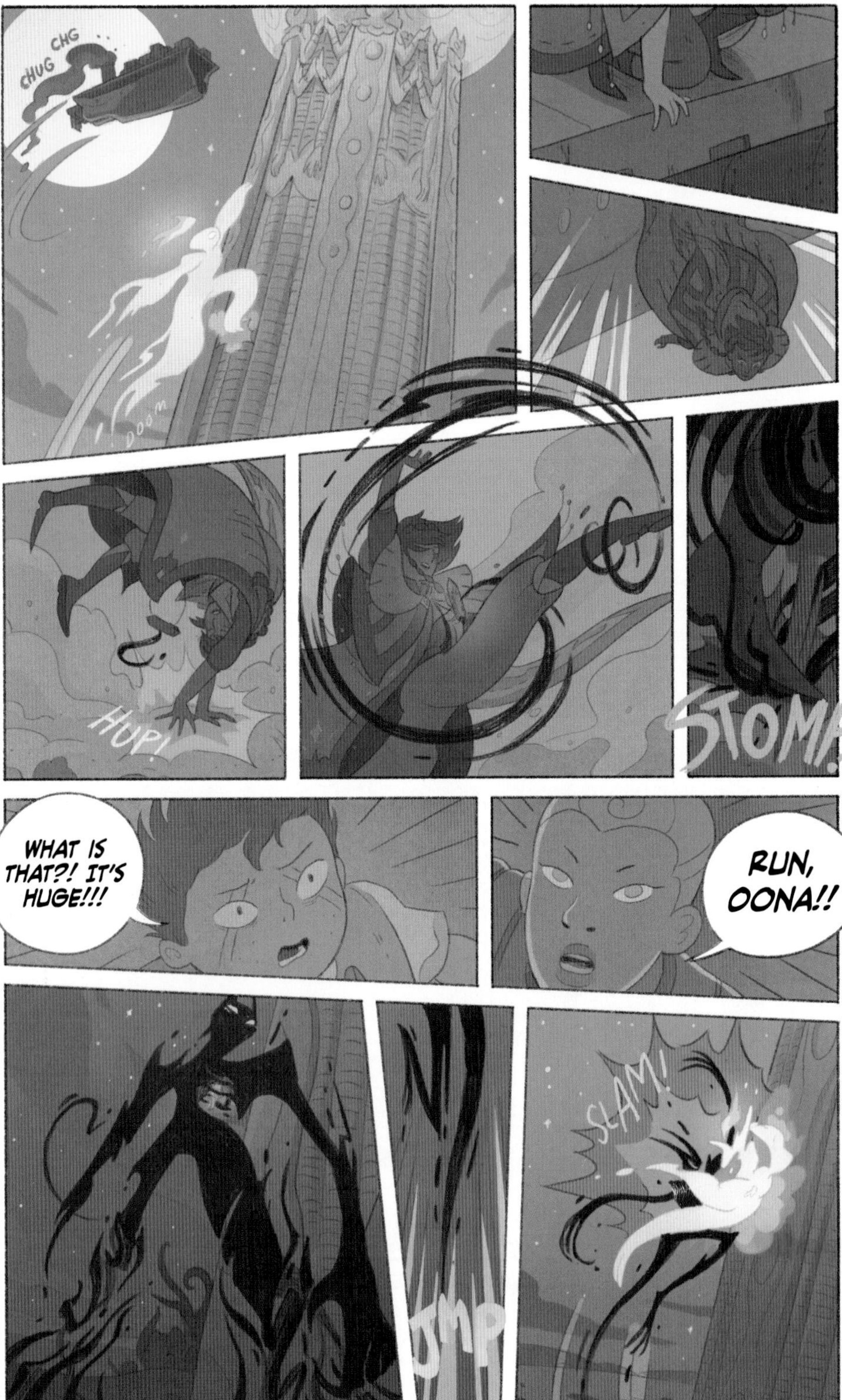
CHUG CHG
DOOM
HUP!
STOMP!
WHAT IS THAT?! IT'S HUGE!!!
RUN, OONA!!
SLAM!

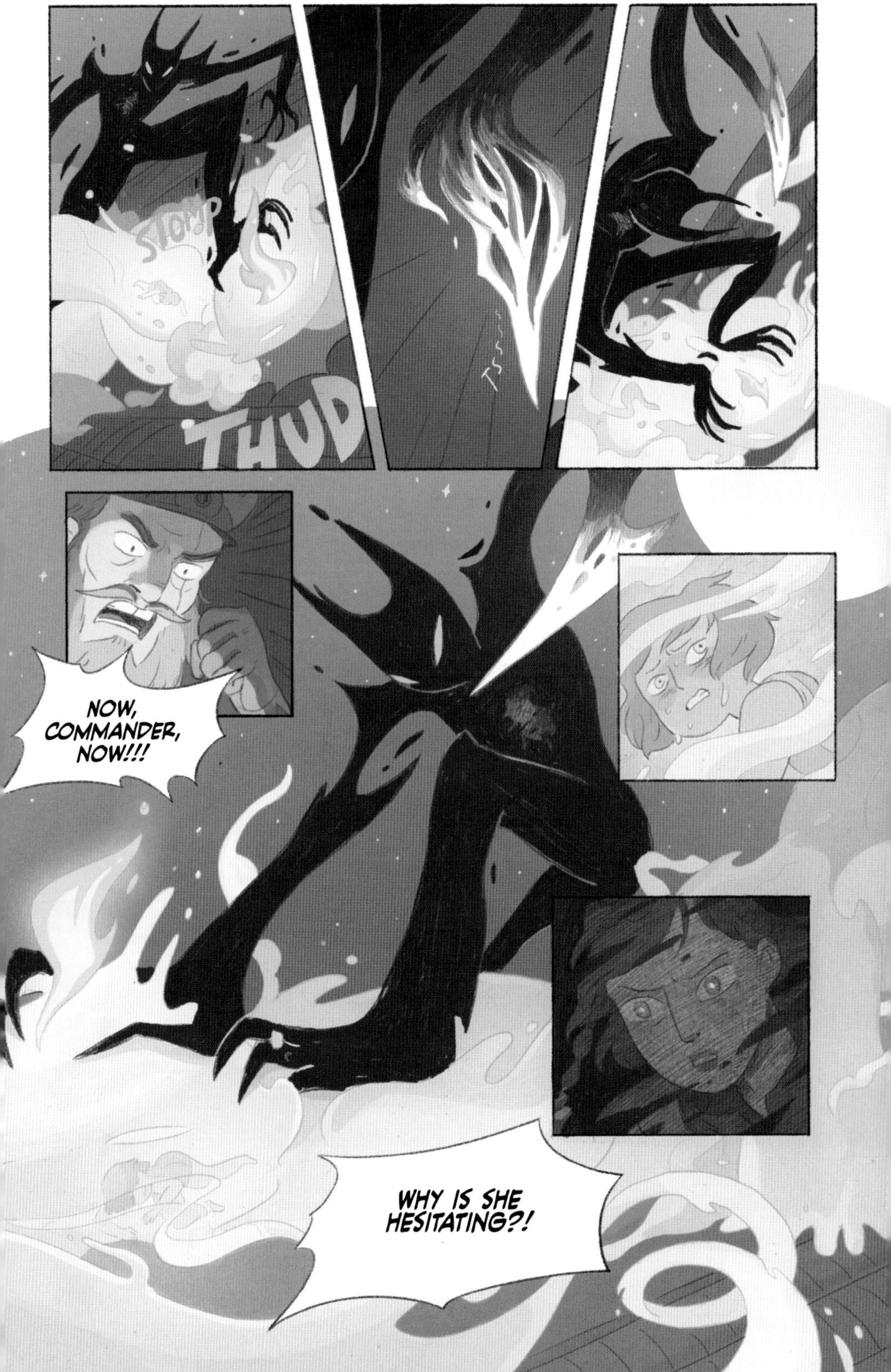
STOMP
THUD
TSSSS
NOW, COMMANDER, NOW!!!
WHY IS SHE HESITATING?!

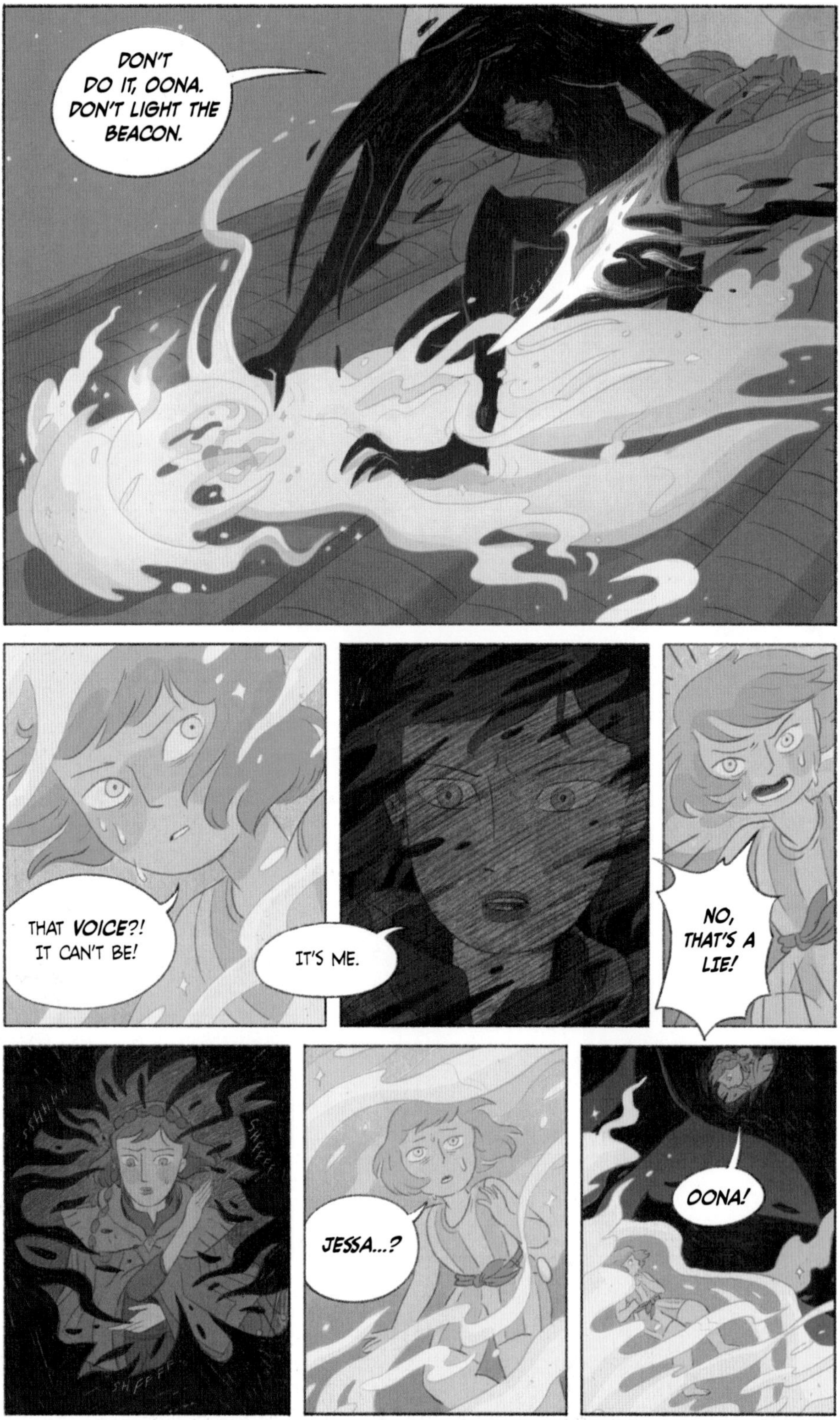
DON'T DO IT, OONA. DON'T LIGHT THE BEACON.
THAT VOICE?! IT CAN'T BE!
IT'S ME.
NO, THAT'S A LIE!
JESSA...?
OONA!

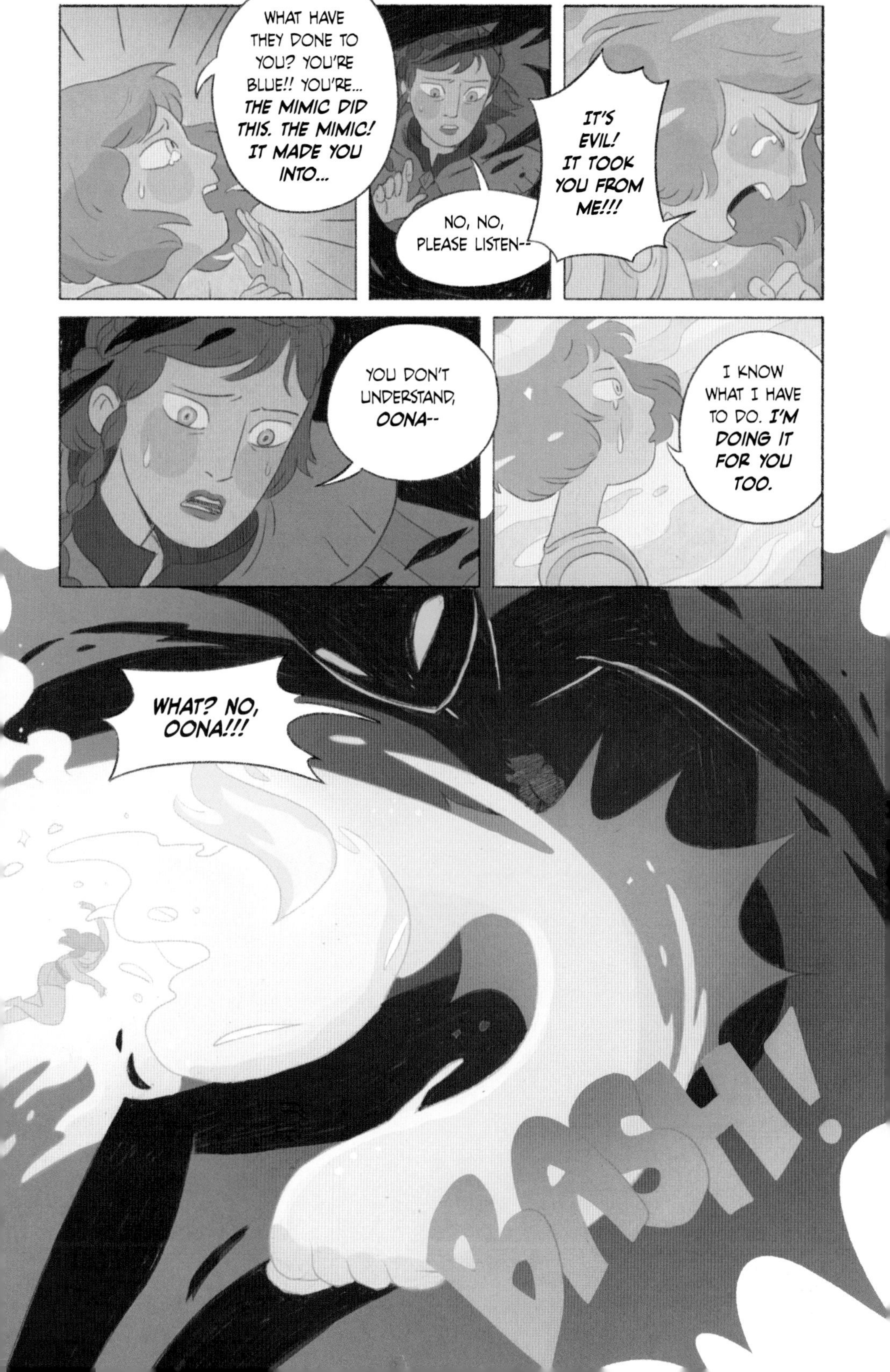
WHAT HAVE THEY DONE TO YOU? YOU'RE BLUE!! YOU'RE... *THE MIMIC DID THIS. THE MIMIC! IT MADE YOU INTO...*
NO, NO, PLEASE LISTEN--
IT'S EVIL! IT TOOK YOU FROM ME!!!
YOU DON'T UNDERSTAND, *OONA--*
I KNOW WHAT I HAVE TO DO. *I'M DOING IT FOR YOU TOO.*
WHAT? NO, OONA!!!
BASH!!

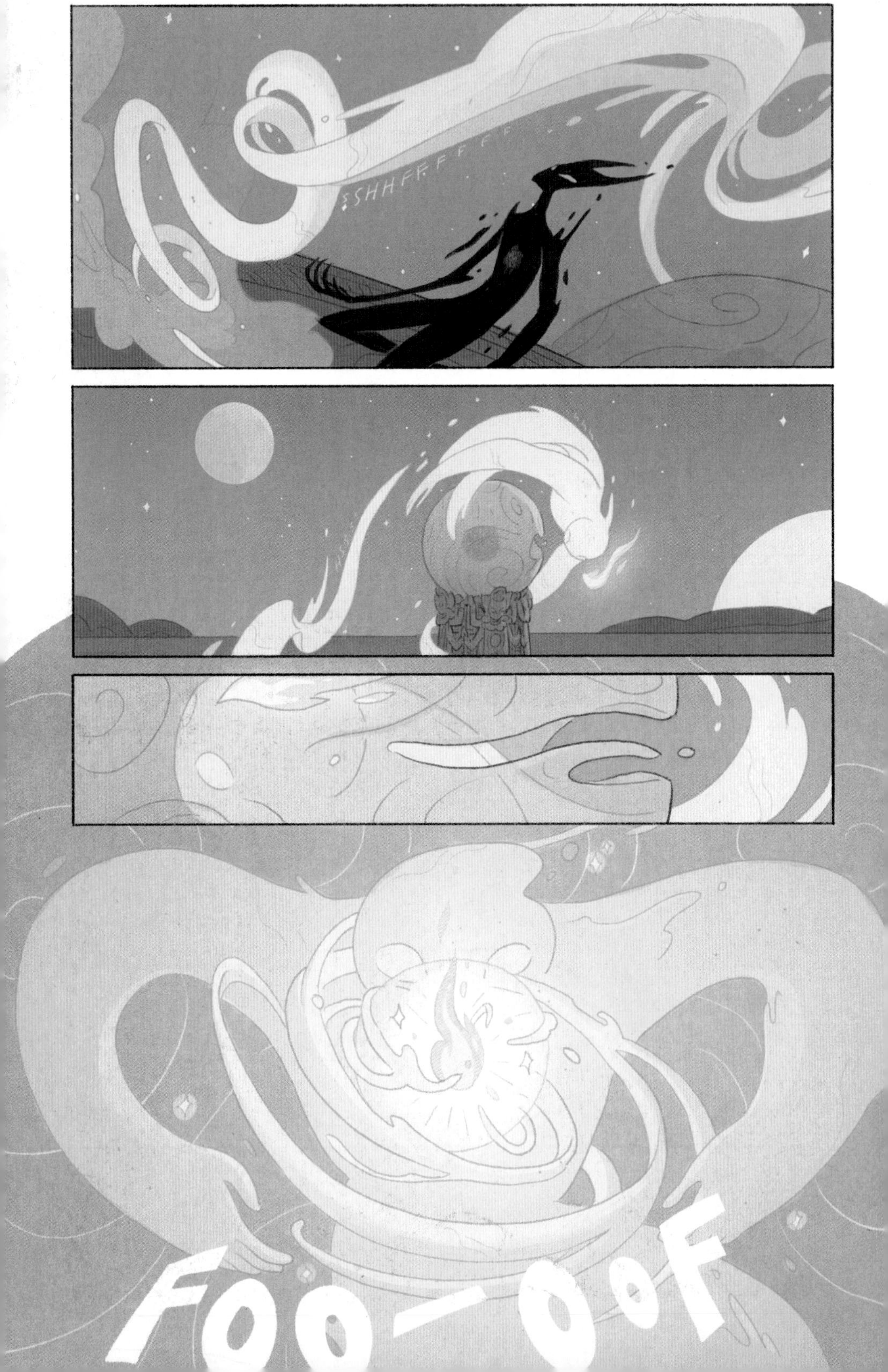
SSHHFFFFFFF
FOO—OOF

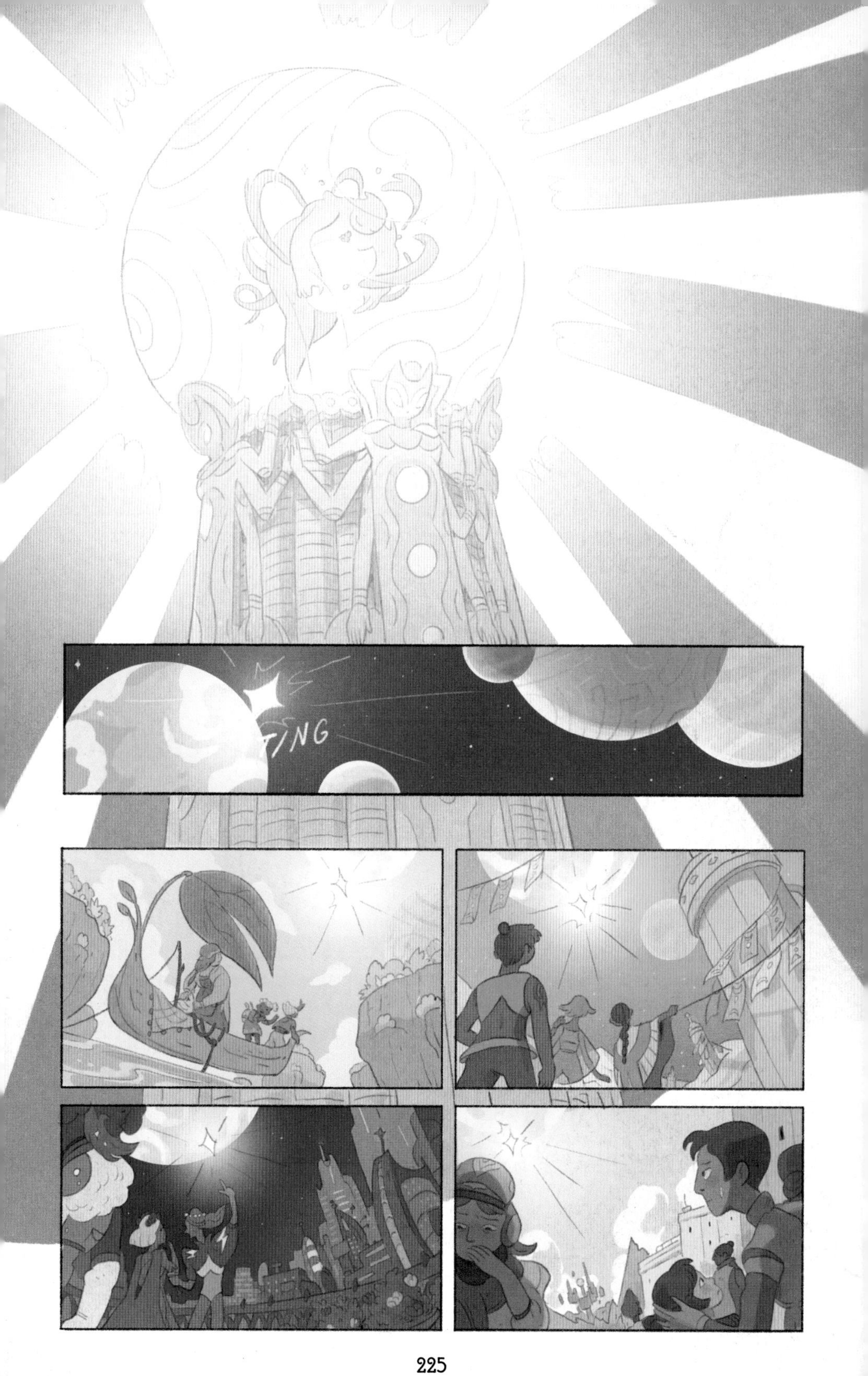
TING

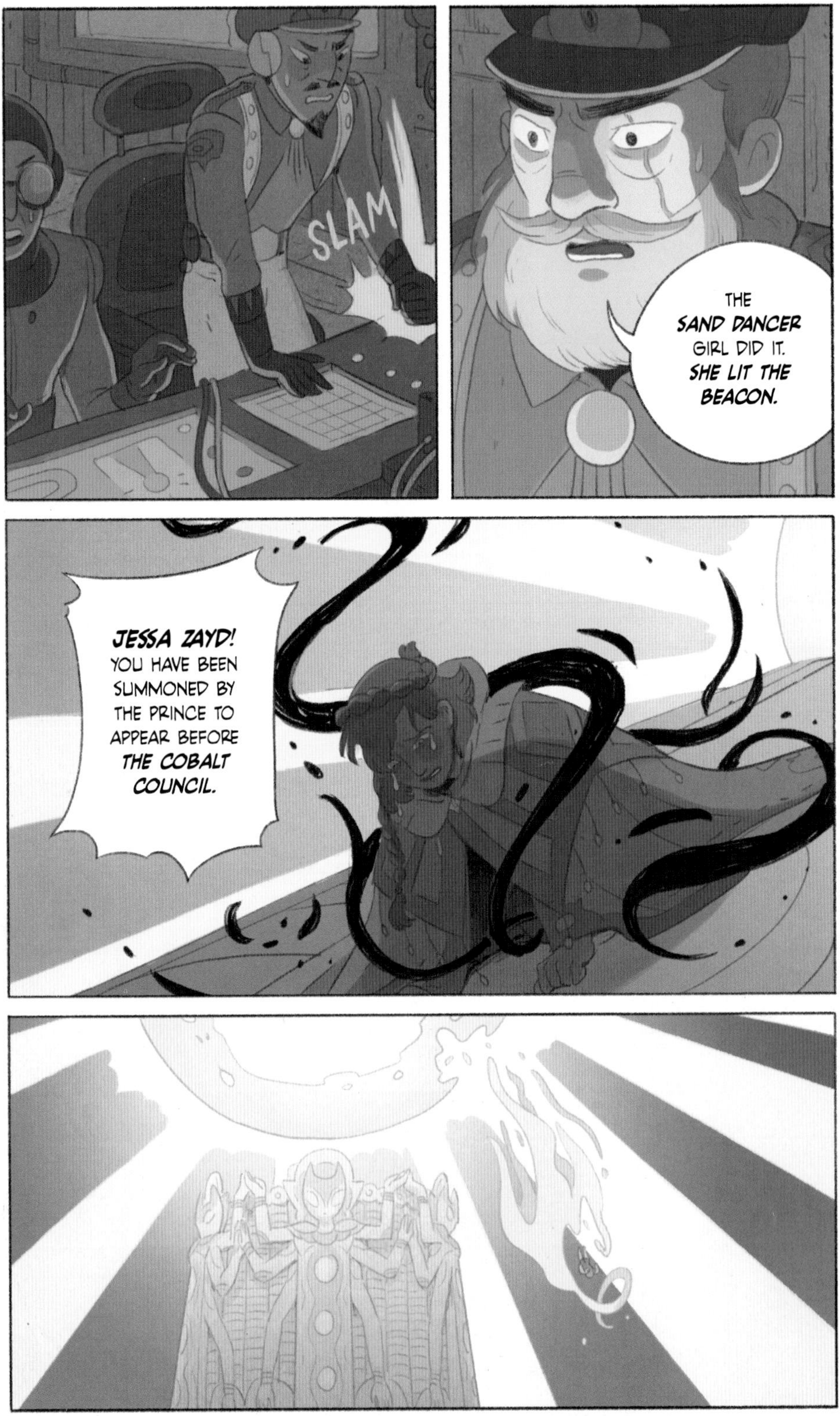
SLAM
THE SAND DANCER GIRL DID IT. SHE LIT THE BEACON.
JESSA ZAYD! YOU HAVE BEEN SUMMONED BY THE PRINCE TO APPEAR BEFORE THE COBALT COUNCIL.

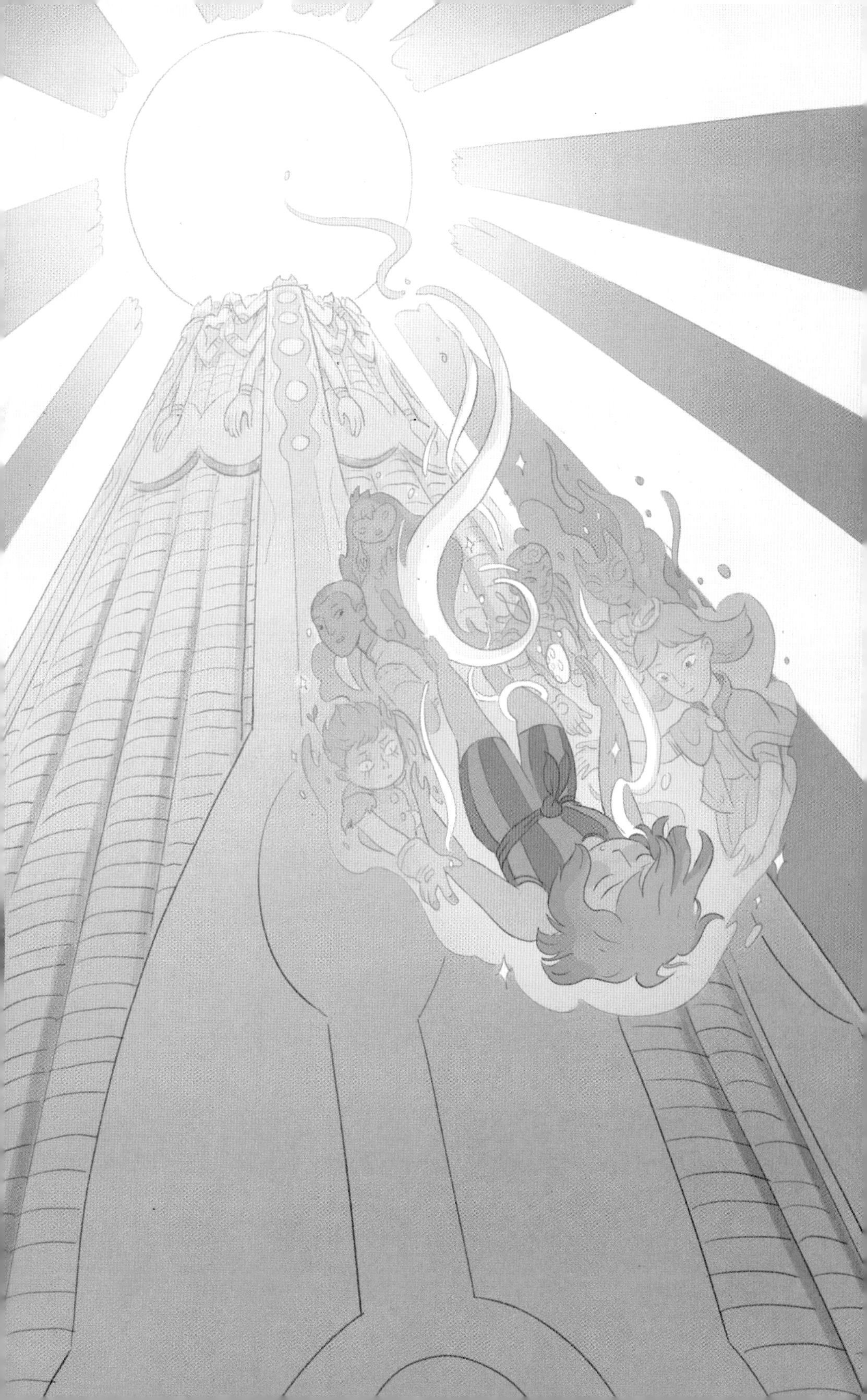

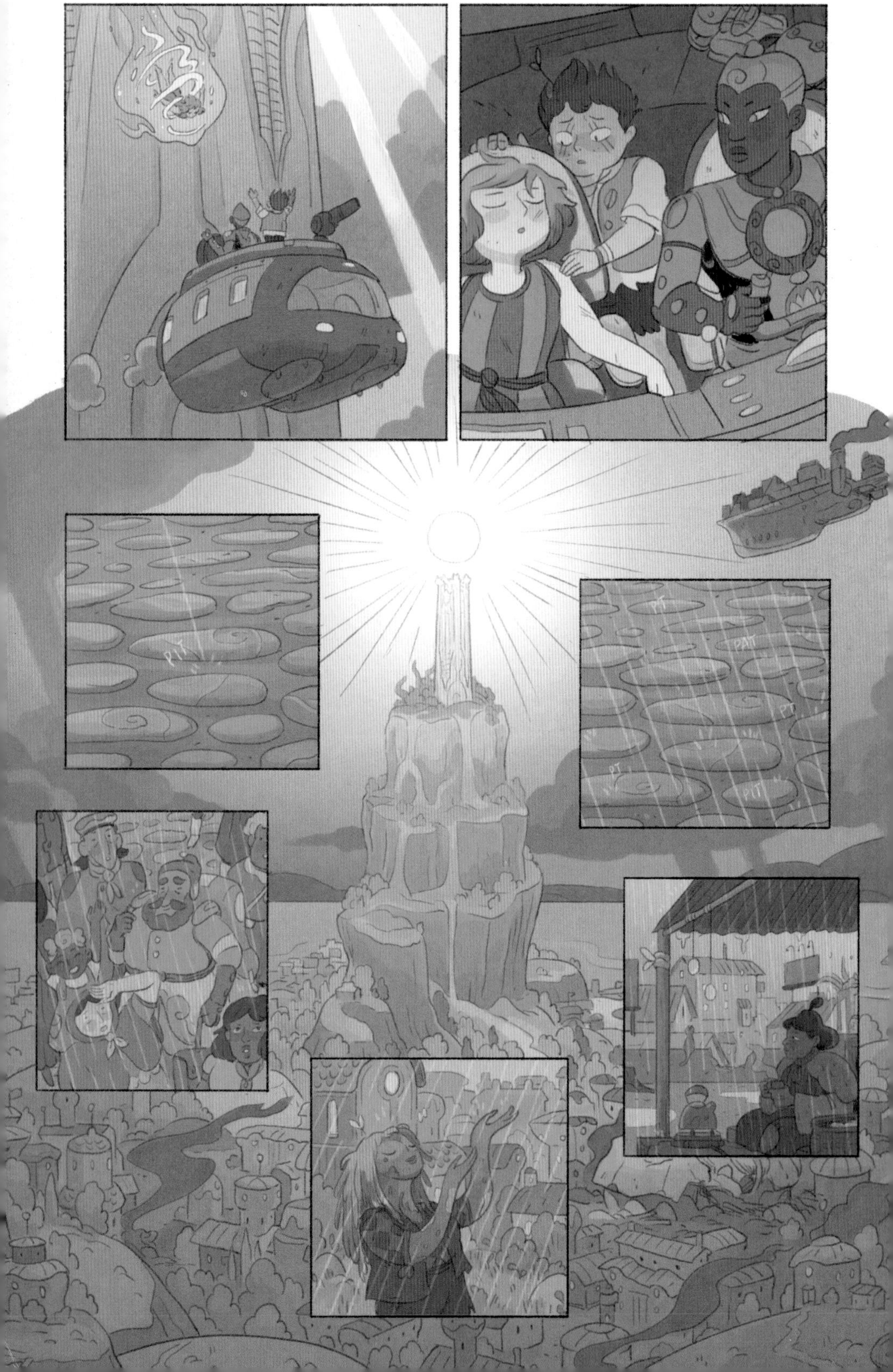
PIT
PT
PAT
PT
PT
PIT

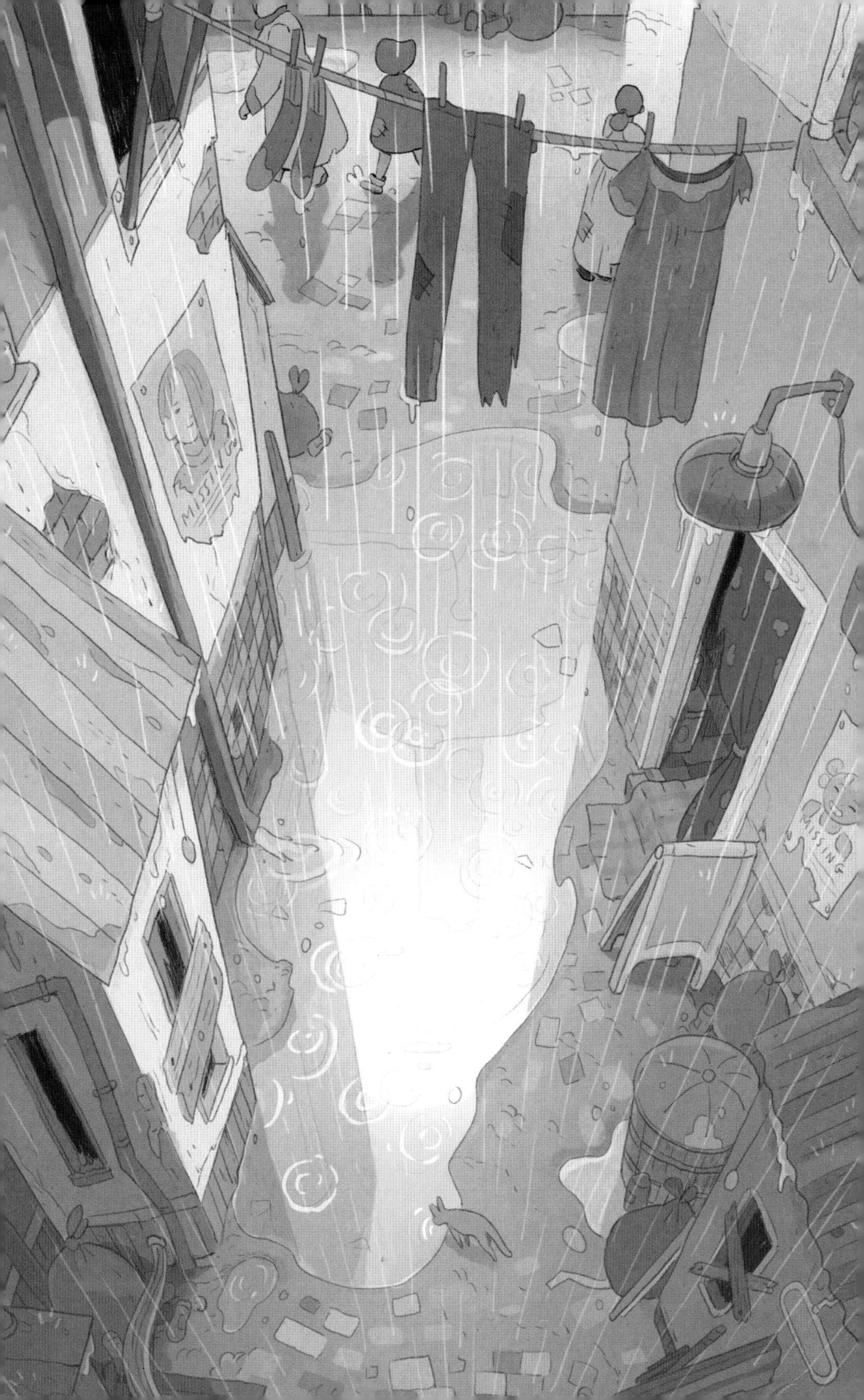
MISSING

Chapter 11

FLIGHT OF THE FLITORI

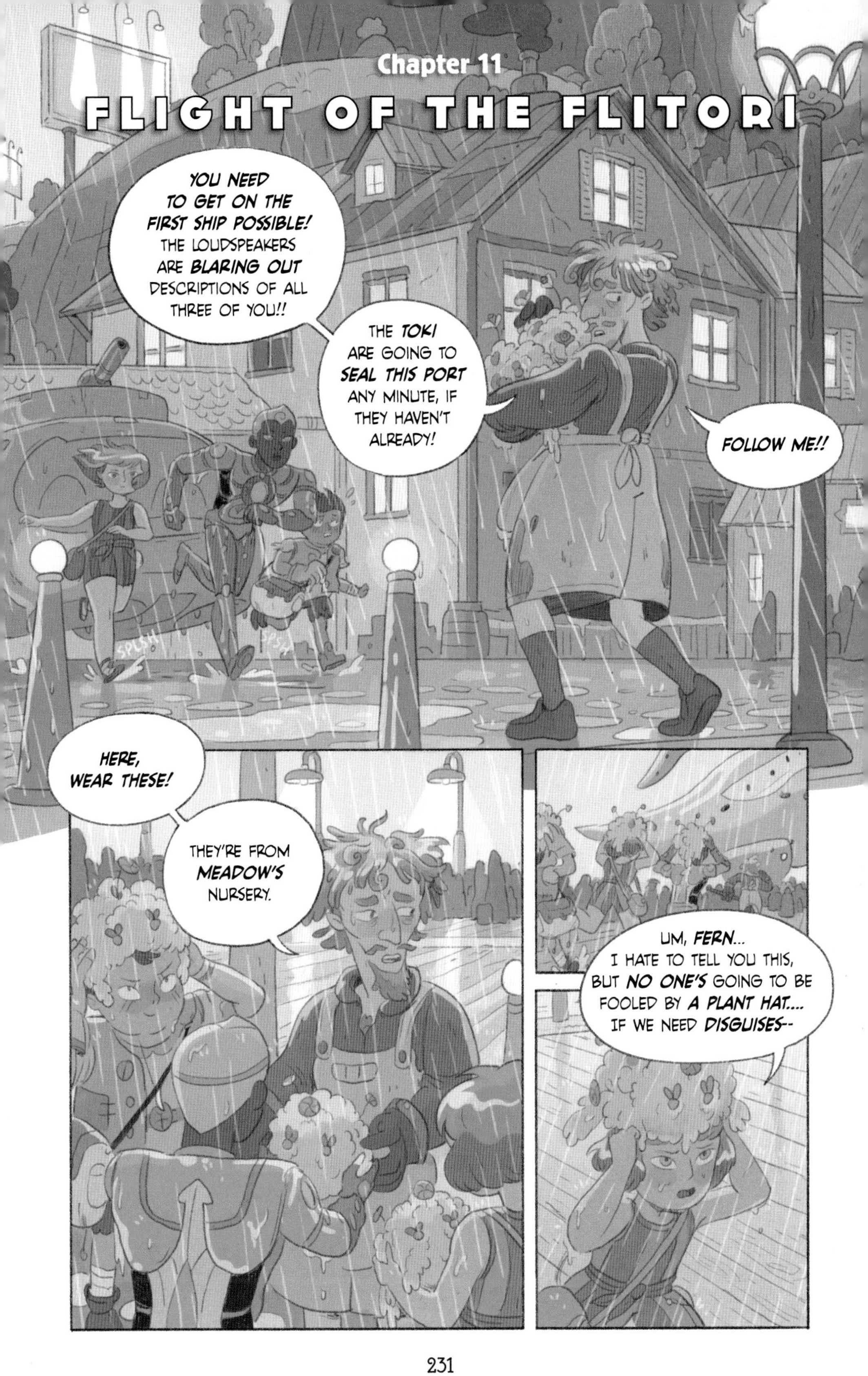
YOU NEED TO GET ON THE FIRST SHIP POSSIBLE! THE LOUDSPEAKERS ARE BLARING OUT DESCRIPTIONS OF ALL THREE OF YOU!!
THE TOKI ARE GOING TO SEAL THIS PORT ANY MINUTE, IF THEY HAVEN'T ALREADY!
FOLLOW ME!!
SPLSH
SPSH
HERE, WEAR THESE!
THEY'RE FROM MEADOW'S NURSERY.
UM, FERN... I HATE TO TELL YOU THIS, BUT NO ONE'S GOING TO BE FOOLED BY A PLANT HAT.... IF WE NEED DISGUISES--

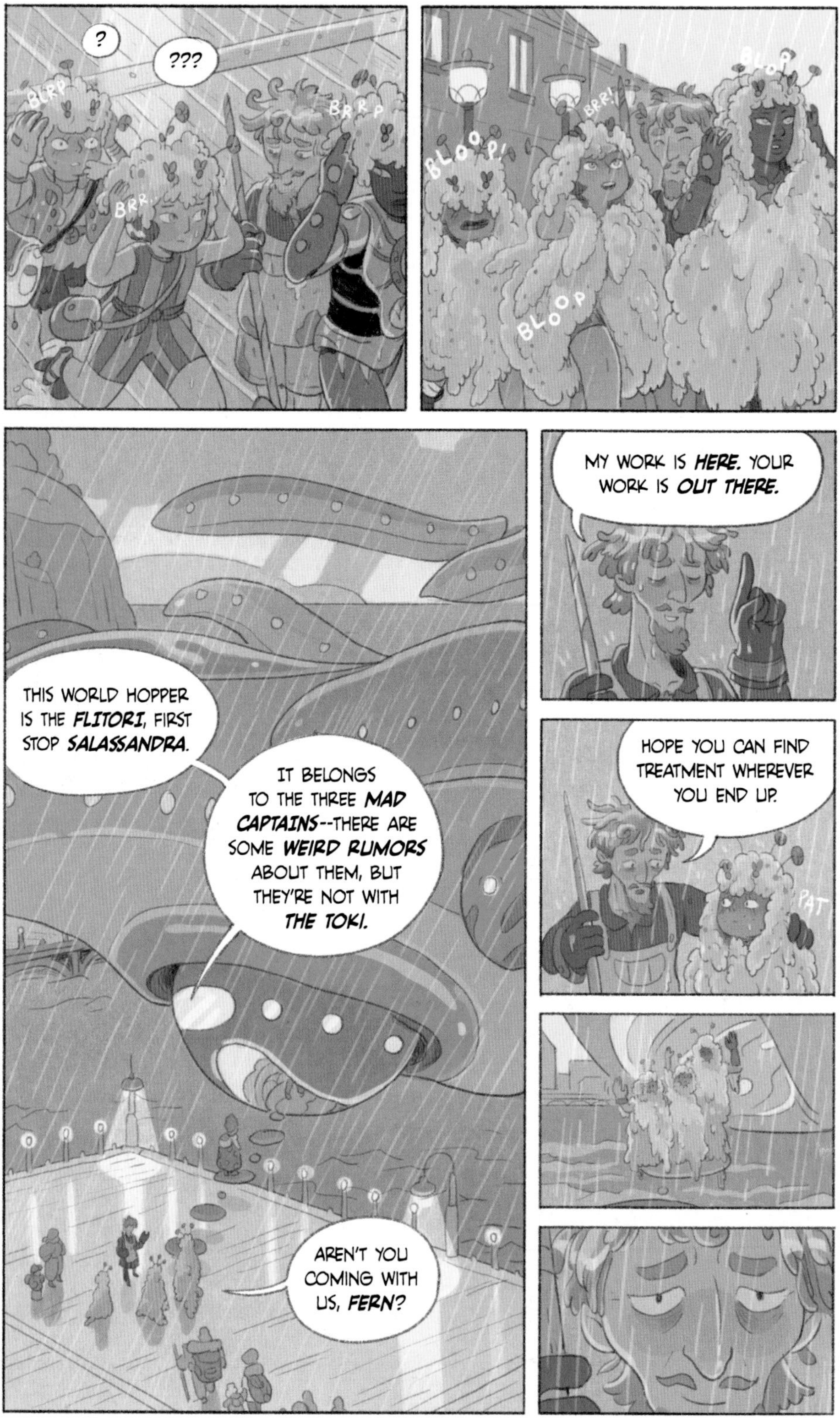
?
???
BLRP
BRR.
BRRRP
BLOOP!
BRR!
BLOOP
BLOOP
THIS WORLD HOPPER IS THE FLITORI, FIRST STOP SALASSANDRA.
IT BELONGS TO THE THREE MAD CAPTAINS--THERE ARE SOME WEIRD RUMORS ABOUT THEM, BUT THEY'RE NOT WITH THE TOKI.
ARE'T YOU COMING WITH US, FERN?
MY WORK IS HERE. YOUR WORK IS OUT THERE.
HOPE YOU CAN FIND TREATMENT WHEREVER YOU END UP.
PAT

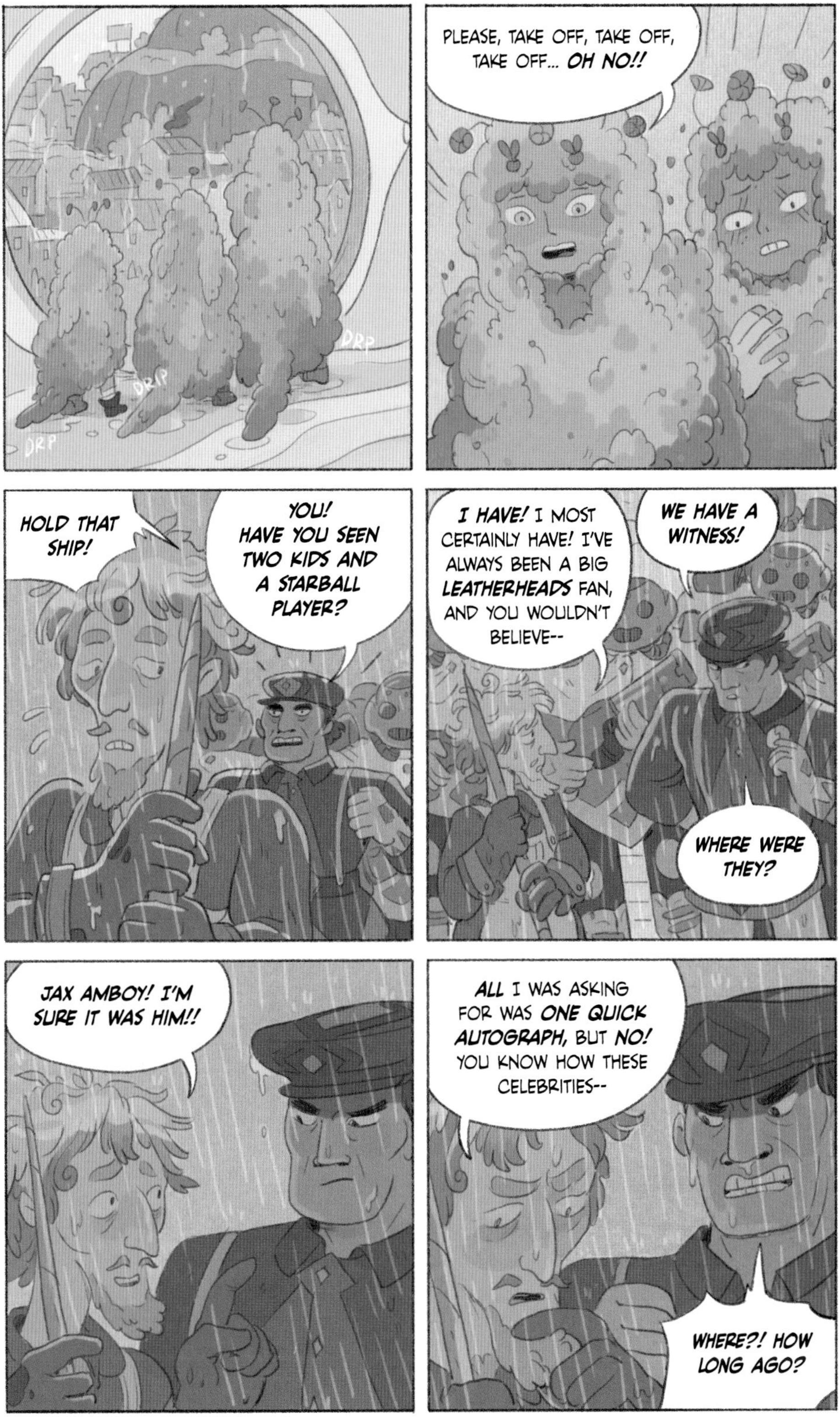
DRIP
PLEASE, TAKE OFF, TAKE OFF, TAKE OFF... OH NO!!
HOLD THAT SHIP!
YOU! HAVE YOU SEEN TWO KIDS AND A STARBALL PLAYER?
I HAVE! I MOST CERTAINLY HAVE! I'VE ALWAYS BEEN A BIG LEATHERHEADS FAN, AND YOU WOULDN'T BELIEVE--
WE HAVE A WITNESS!
WHERE WERE THEY?
JAX AMBOY! I'M SURE IT WAS HIM!!
ALL I WAS ASKING FOR WAS ONE QUICK AUTOGRAPH, BUT NO! YOU KNOW HOW THESE CELEBRITIES--
WHERE?! HOW LONG AGO?

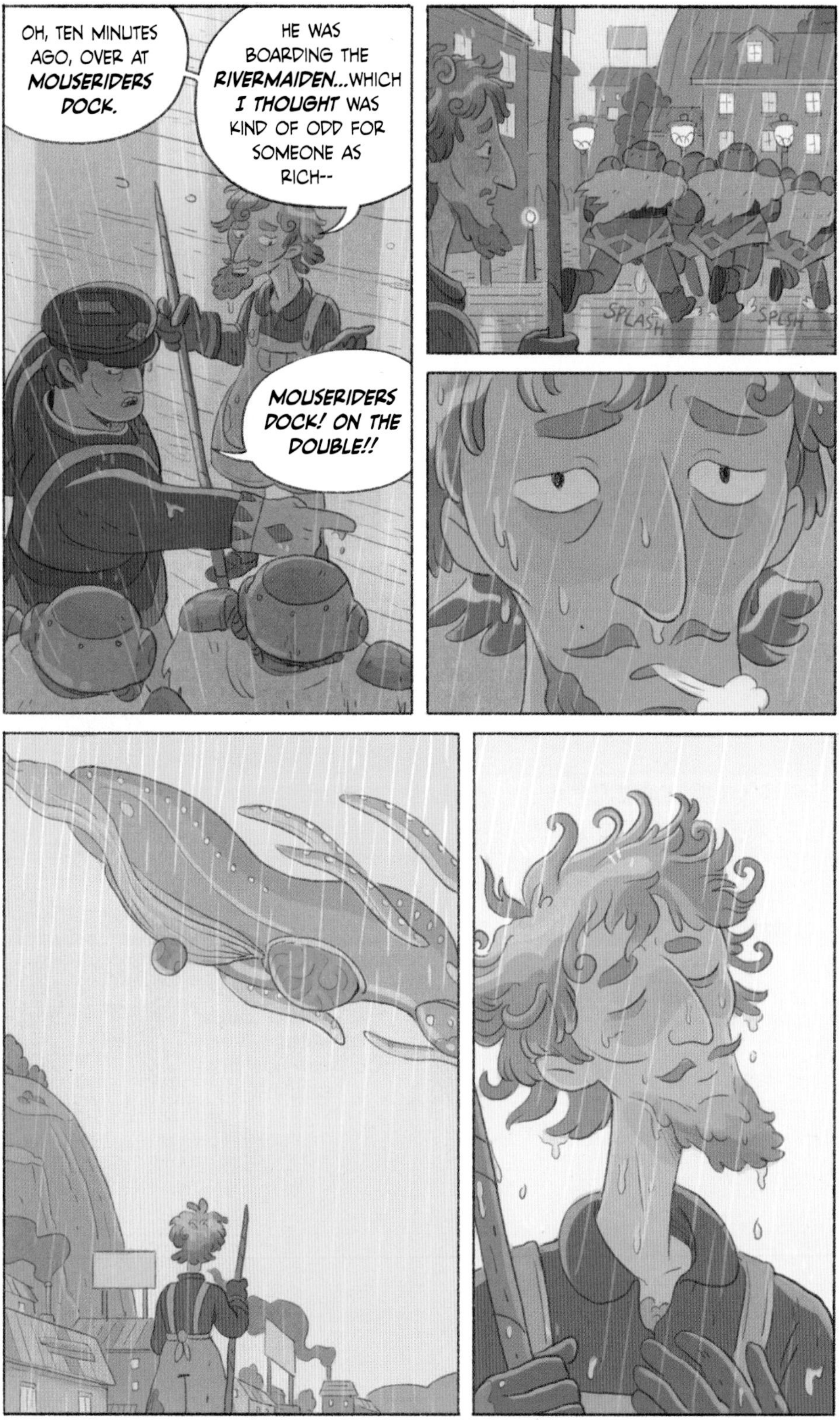
OH, TEN MINUTES AGO, OVER AT MOUSERIDERS DOCK.
HE WAS BOARDING THE RIVERMAIDEN...WHICH I THOUGHT WAS KIND OF ODD FOR SOMEONE AS RICH--
MOUSERIDERS DOCK! ON THE DOUBLE!!
SPLASH
SPLSH

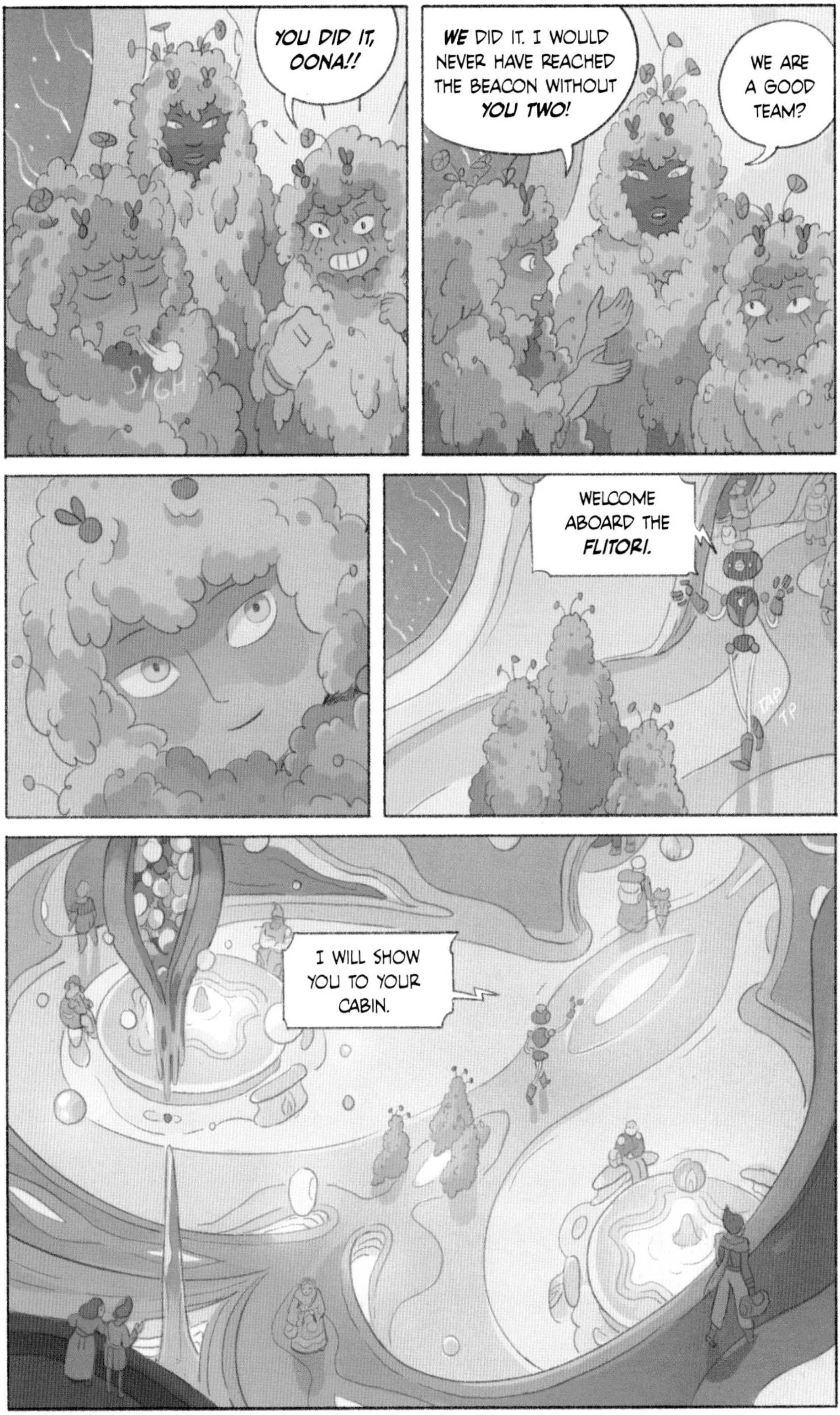
YOU DID IT, OONA!!
SIGH
WE DID IT. I WOULD NEVER HAVE REACHED THE BEACON WITHOUT YOU TWO!
WE ARE A GOOD TEAM?
WELCOME ABOARD THE FLITORI.
TAP TP
I WILL SHOW YOU TO YOUR CABIN.

WE REACH OUR FIRST PORT OF CALL, *MOON SALASSANDRA*, IN TWO *DOMANI* DAYS.

NEXT WILL BE *MOON TOKI*, THEN *MOON YATTA*, THEN *GRIMBO (E)*.

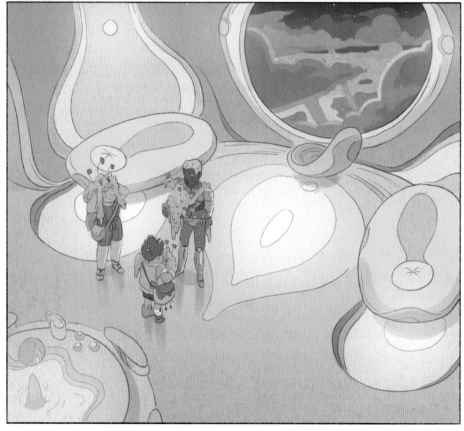

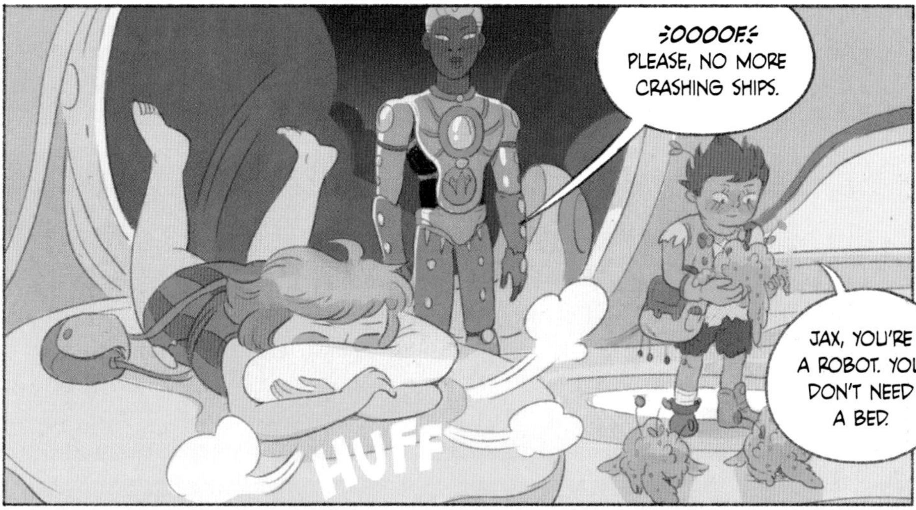
:OOOOF:
PLEASE, NO MORE CRASHING SHIPS.
HUFF
JAX, YOU'RE A ROBOT. YOU DON'T NEED A BED.

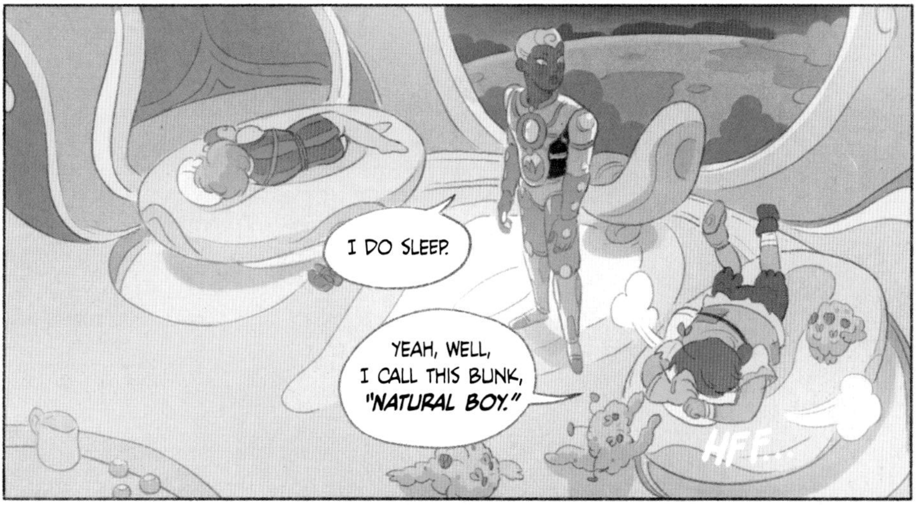
I DO SLEEP.
YEAH, WELL, I CALL THIS BUNK, *"NATURAL BOY."*
HFF...

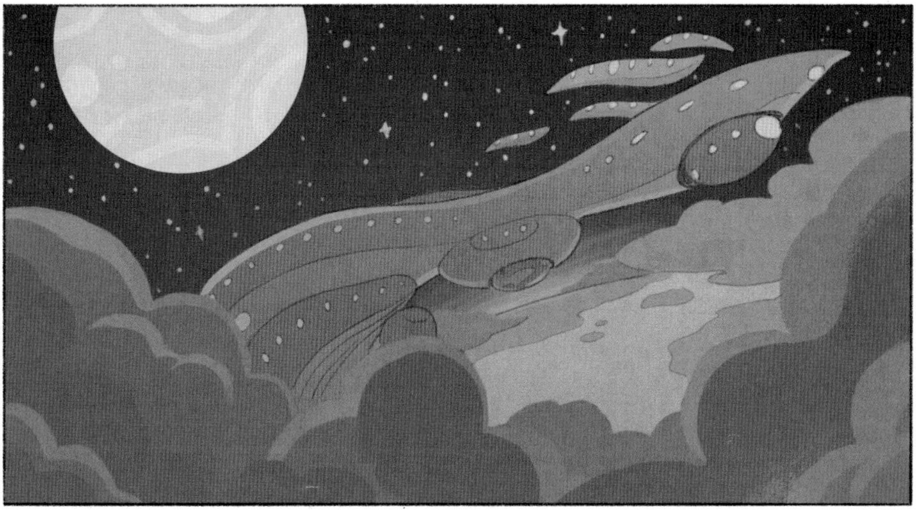

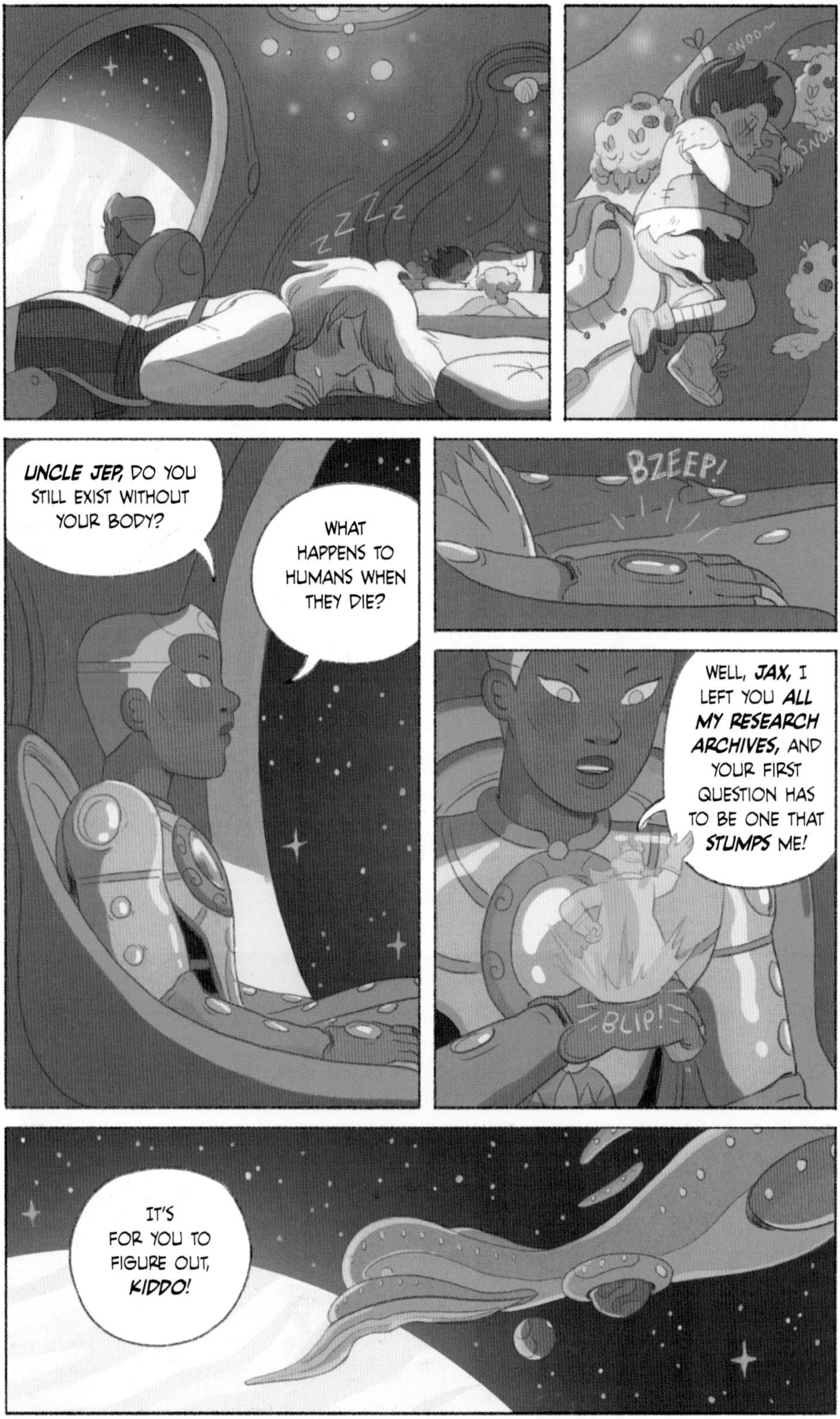
SNOO~
SNOO
UNCLE JEP, DO YOU STILL EXIST WITHOUT YOUR BODY?
WHAT HAPPENS TO HUMANS WHEN THEY DIE?
BZEEP!
WELL, JAX, I LEFT YOU ALL MY RESEARCH ARCHIVES, AND YOUR FIRST QUESTION HAS TO BE ONE THAT STUMPS ME!
BLIP!
IT'S FOR YOU TO FIGURE OUT, KIDDO!

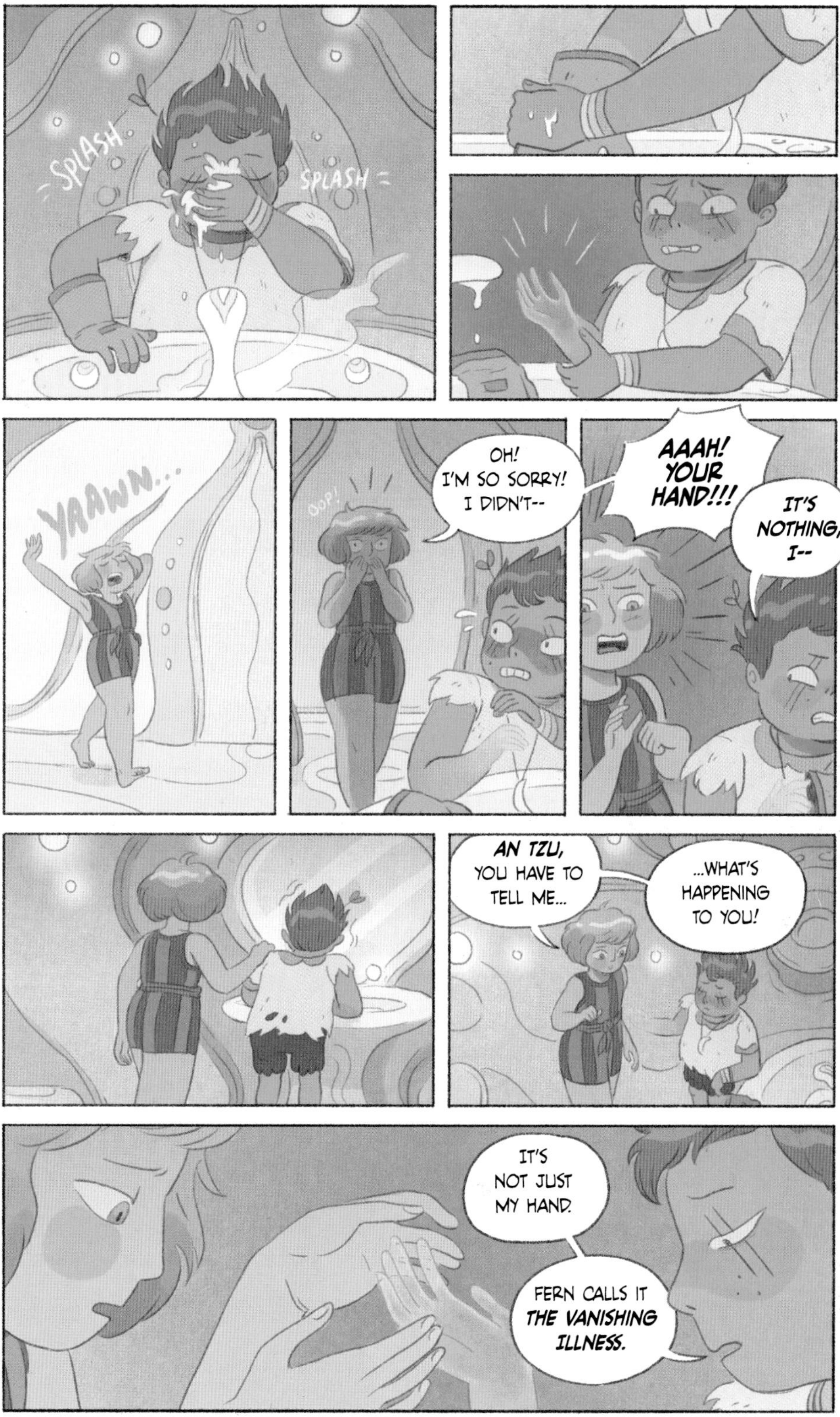
SPLASH
SPLASH
YAAWN...
OOP!
OH! I'M SO SORRY! I DIDN'T--
AAAH! YOUR HAND!!!
IT'S NOTHING, I--
AN TZU, YOU HAVE TO TELL ME...
...WHAT'S HAPPENING TO YOU!
IT'S NOT JUST MY HAND.
FERN CALLS IT THE VANISHING ILLNESS.

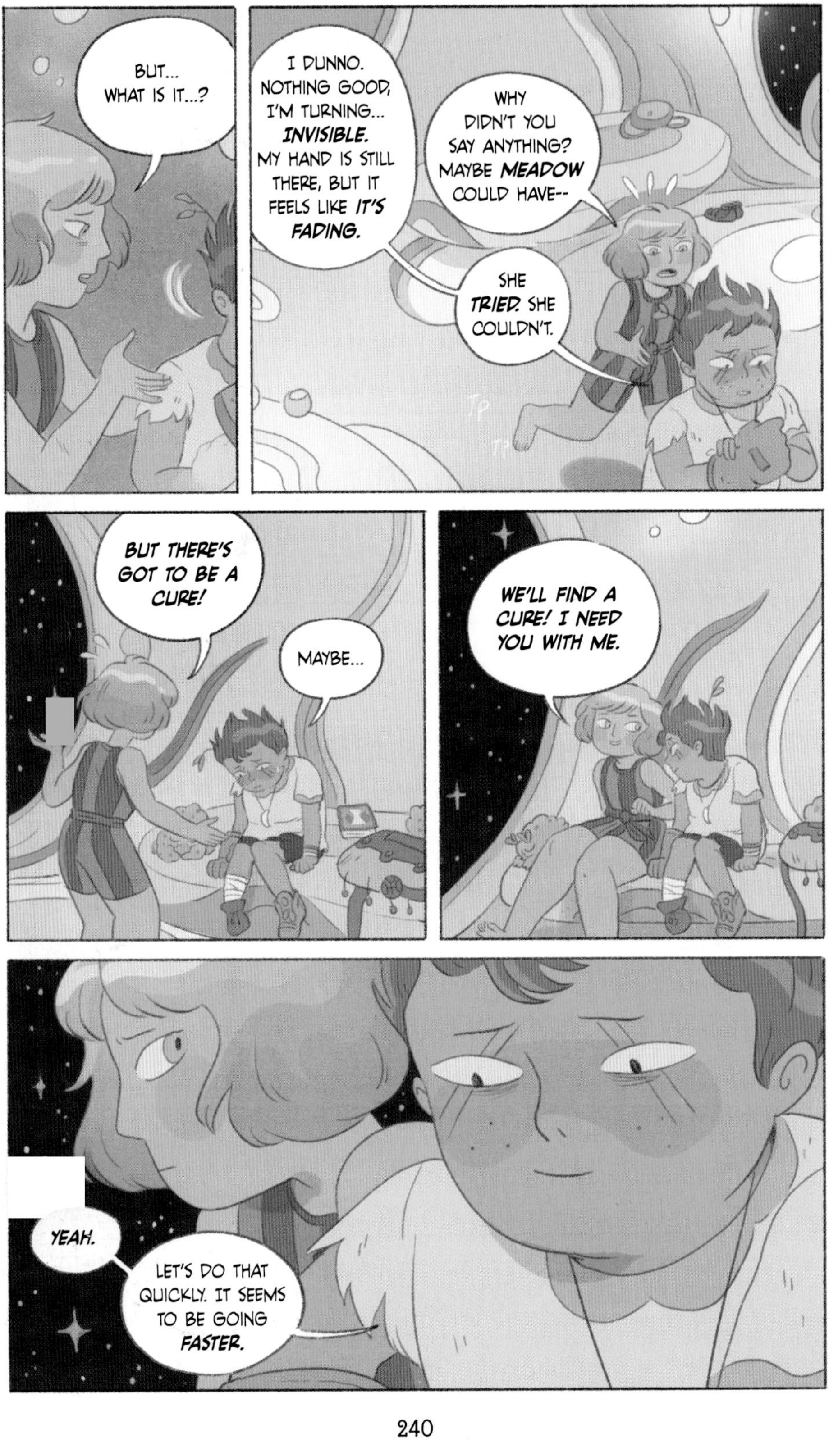
BUT... WHAT IS IT...?
I DUNNO. NOTHING GOOD, I'M TURNING... INVISIBLE. MY HAND IS STILL THERE, BUT IT FEELS LIKE IT'S FADING.
WHY DIDN'T YOU SAY ANYTHING? MAYBE MEADOW COULD HAVE--
SHE TRIED. SHE COULDN'T.
TP
TP
BUT THERE'S GOT TO BE A CURE!
MAYBE...
WE'LL FIND A CURE! I NEED YOU WITH ME.
YEAH.
LET'S DO THAT QUICKLY. IT SEEMS TO BE GOING FASTER.

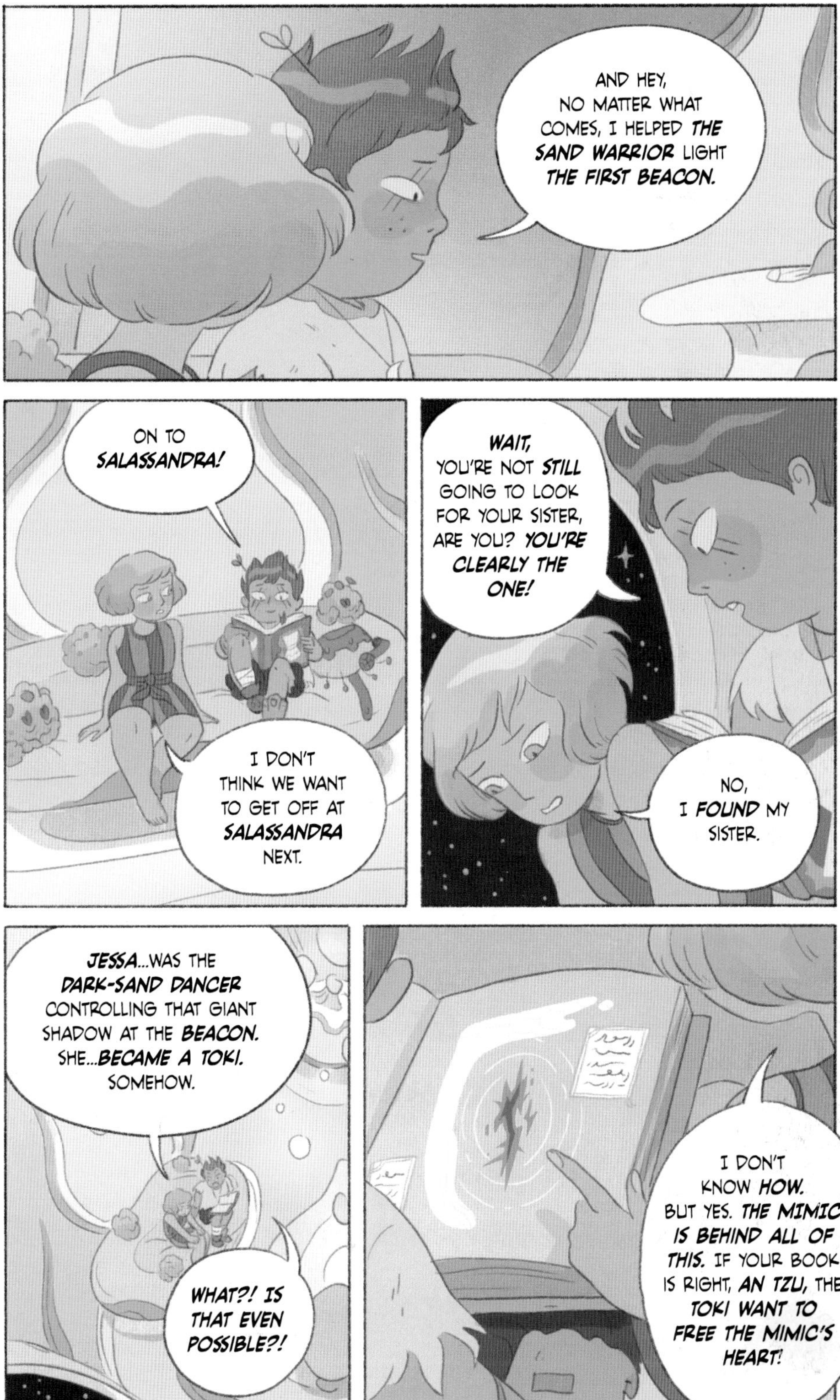
AND HEY, NO MATTER WHAT COMES, I HELPED THE SAND WARRIOR LIGHT THE FIRST BEACON.
ON TO SALASSANDRA!
I DON'T THINK WE WANT TO GET OFF AT SALASSANDRA NEXT.
WAIT, YOU'RE NOT STILL GOING TO LOOK FOR YOUR SISTER, ARE YOU? YOU'RE CLEARLY THE ONE!
NO, I FOUND MY SISTER.
JESSA...WAS THE DARK-SAND DANCER CONTROLLING THAT GIANT SHADOW AT THE BEACON. SHE...BECAME A TOKI. SOMEHOW.
WHAT?! IS THAT EVEN POSSIBLE?!
I DON'T KNOW HOW. BUT YES. THE MIMIC IS BEHIND ALL OF THIS. IF YOUR BOOK IS RIGHT, AN TZU, THE TOKI WANT TO FREE THE MIMIC'S HEART!

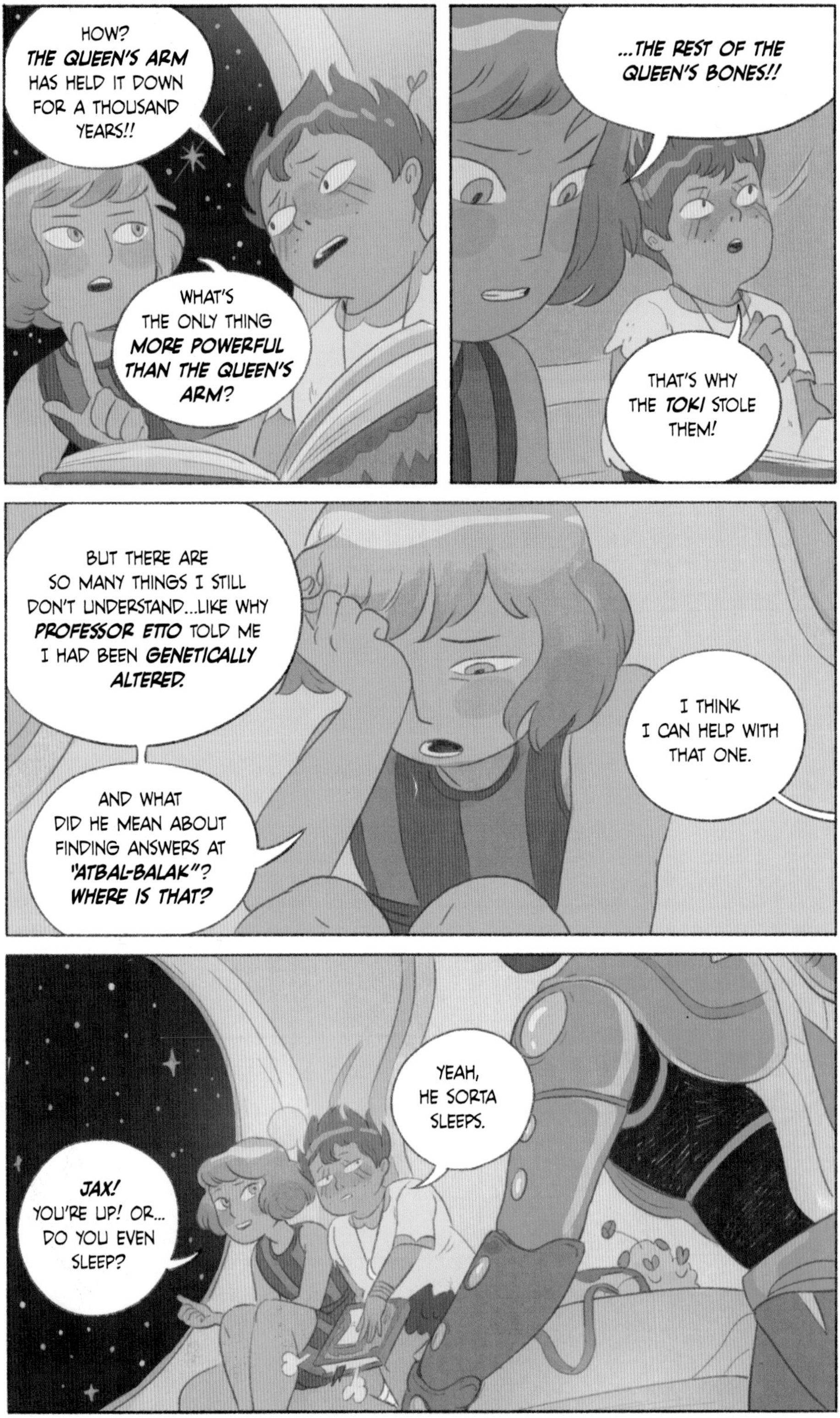
HOW? THE QUEEN'S ARM HAS HELD IT DOWN FOR A THOUSAND YEARS!!
WHAT'S THE ONLY THING MORE POWERFUL THAN THE QUEEN'S ARM?
...THE REST OF THE QUEEN'S BONES!!
THAT'S WHY THE TOKI STOLE THEM!
BUT THERE ARE SO MANY THINGS I STILL DON'T UNDERSTAND...LIKE WHY PROFESSOR ETTO TOLD ME I HAD BEEN GENETICALLY ALTERED.
AND WHAT DID HE MEAN ABOUT FINDING ANSWERS AT "ATBAL-BALAK"? WHERE IS THAT?
I THINK I CAN HELP WITH THAT ONE.
JAX! YOU'RE UP! OR... DO YOU EVEN SLEEP?
YEAH, HE SORTA SLEEPS.

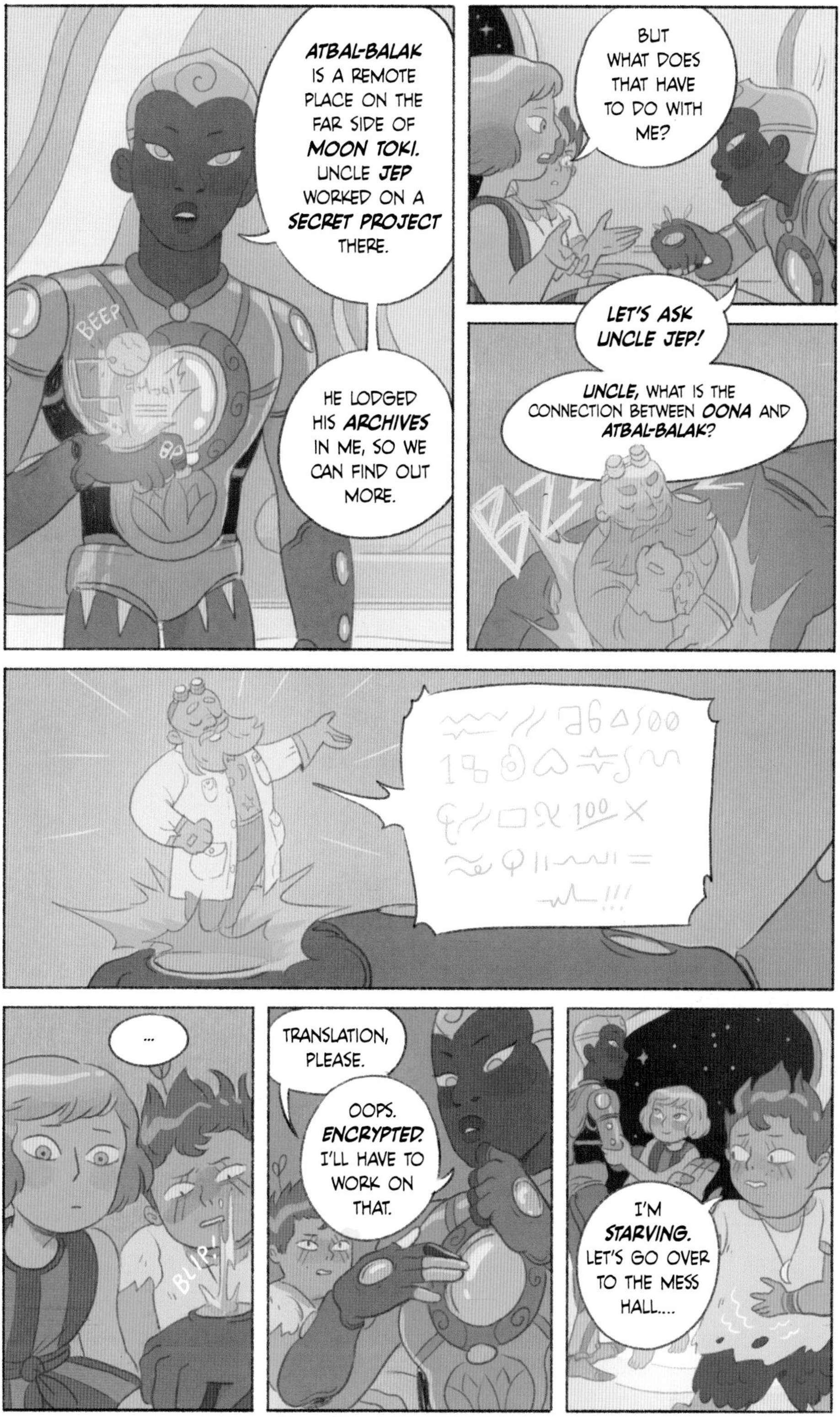
ATBAL-BALAK IS A REMOTE PLACE ON THE FAR SIDE OF MOON TOKI. UNCLE JEP WORKED ON A SECRET PROJECT THERE.
HE LODGED HIS ARCHIVES IN ME, SO WE CAN FIND OUT MORE.
BEEP
BP
BUT WHAT DOES THAT HAVE TO DO WITH ME?
LET'S ASK UNCLE JEP!
UNCLE, WHAT IS THE CONNECTION BETWEEN OONA AND ATBAL-BALAK?
...
BLIP!
TRANSLATION, PLEASE.
OOPS. ENCRYPTED. I'LL HAVE TO WORK ON THAT.
I'M STARVING. LET'S GO OVER TO THE MESS HALL....

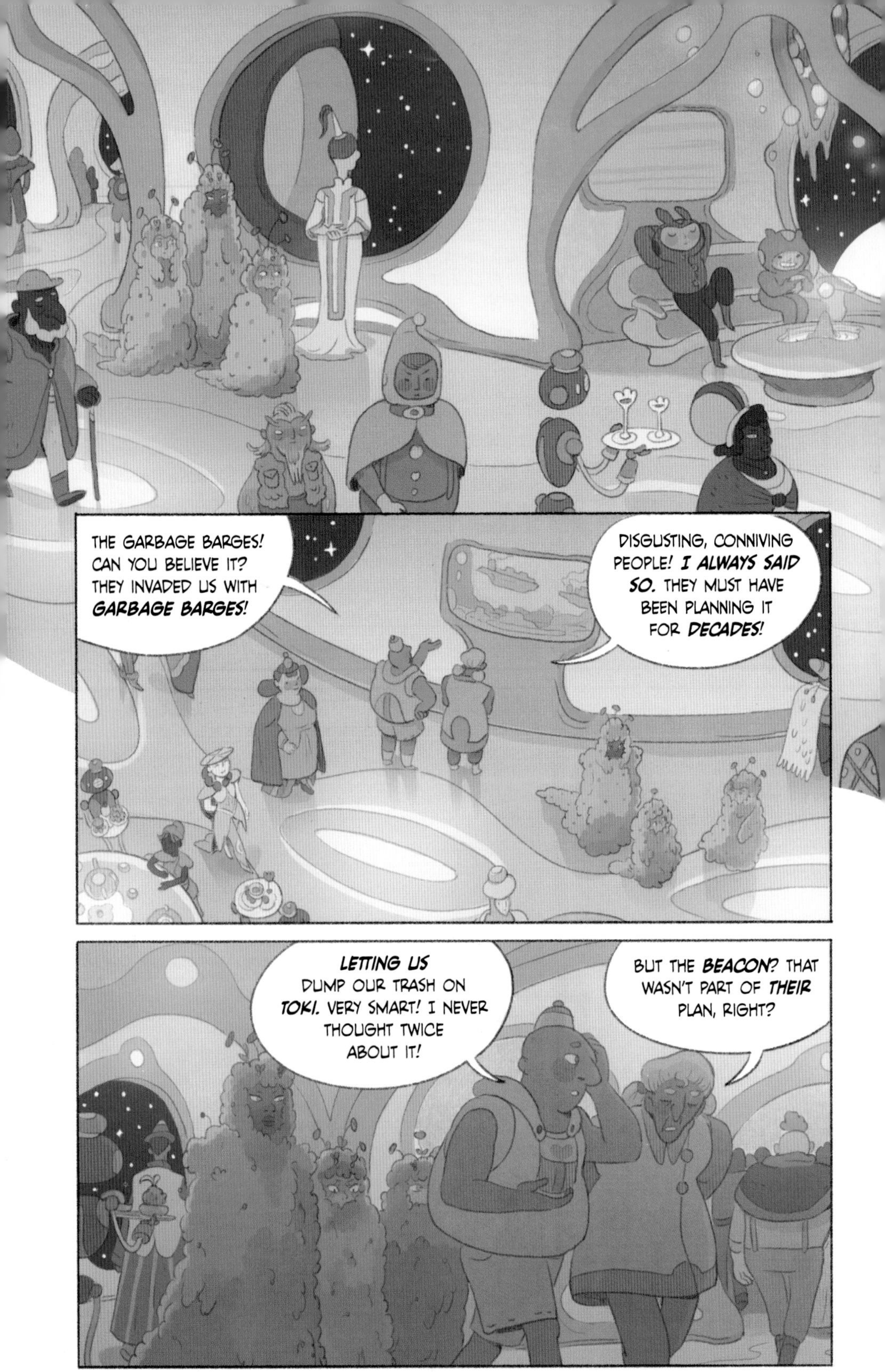
THE GARBAGE BARGES! CAN YOU BELIEVE IT? THEY INVADED US WITH **GARBAGE BARGES!**
DISGUSTING, CONNIVING PEOPLE! ***I ALWAYS SAID SO.*** THEY MUST HAVE BEEN PLANNING IT FOR ***DECADES!***
LETTING US DUMP OUR TRASH ON ***TOKI.*** VERY SMART! I NEVER THOUGHT TWICE ABOUT IT!
BUT THE ***BEACON?*** THAT WASN'T PART OF ***THEIR*** PLAN, RIGHT?

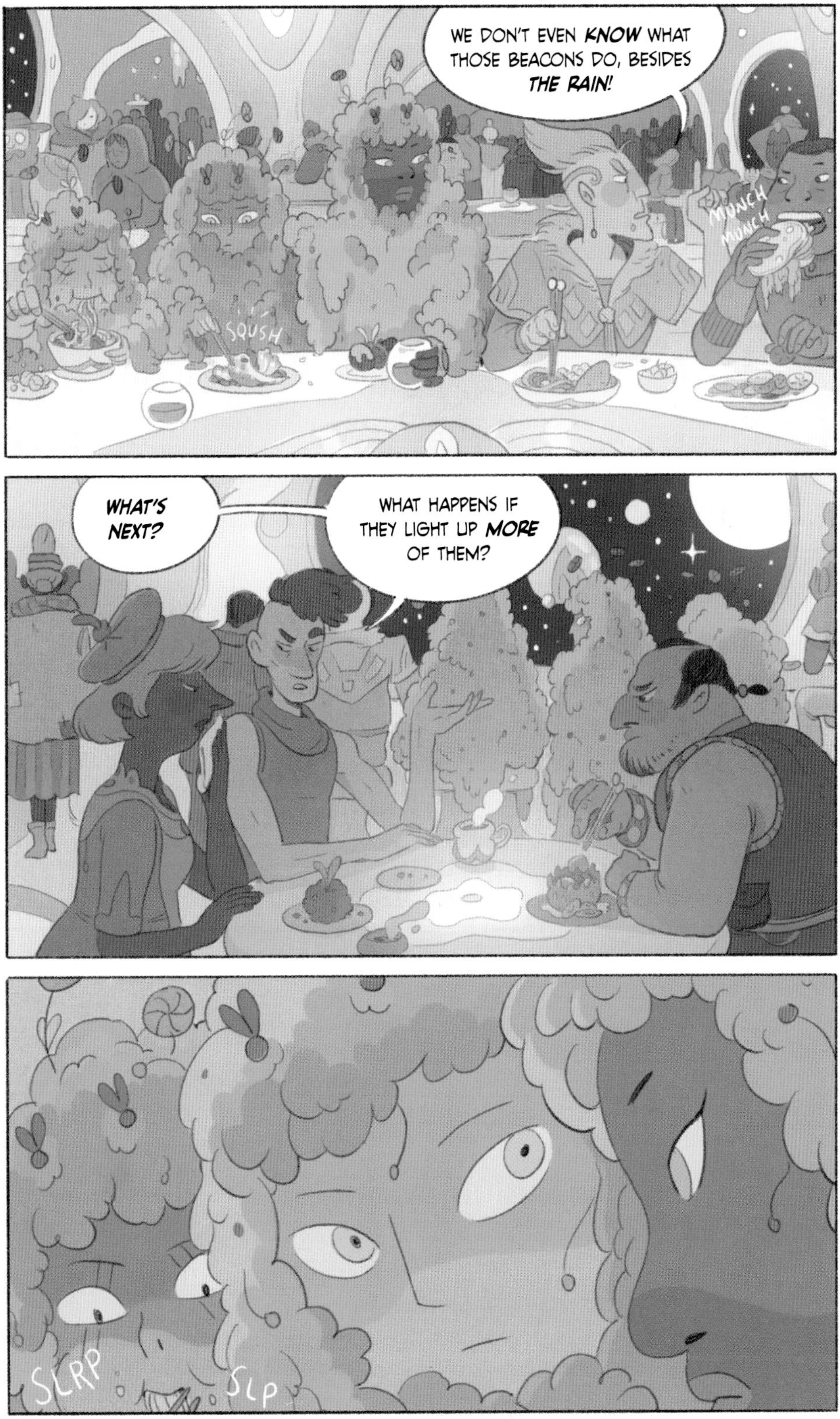
WE DON'T EVEN KNOW WHAT THOSE BEACONS DO, BESIDES THE RAIN!
MUNCH MUNCH
SQUSH
WHAT'S NEXT?
WHAT HAPPENS IF THEY LIGHT UP MORE OF THEM?
SLRP
SLP

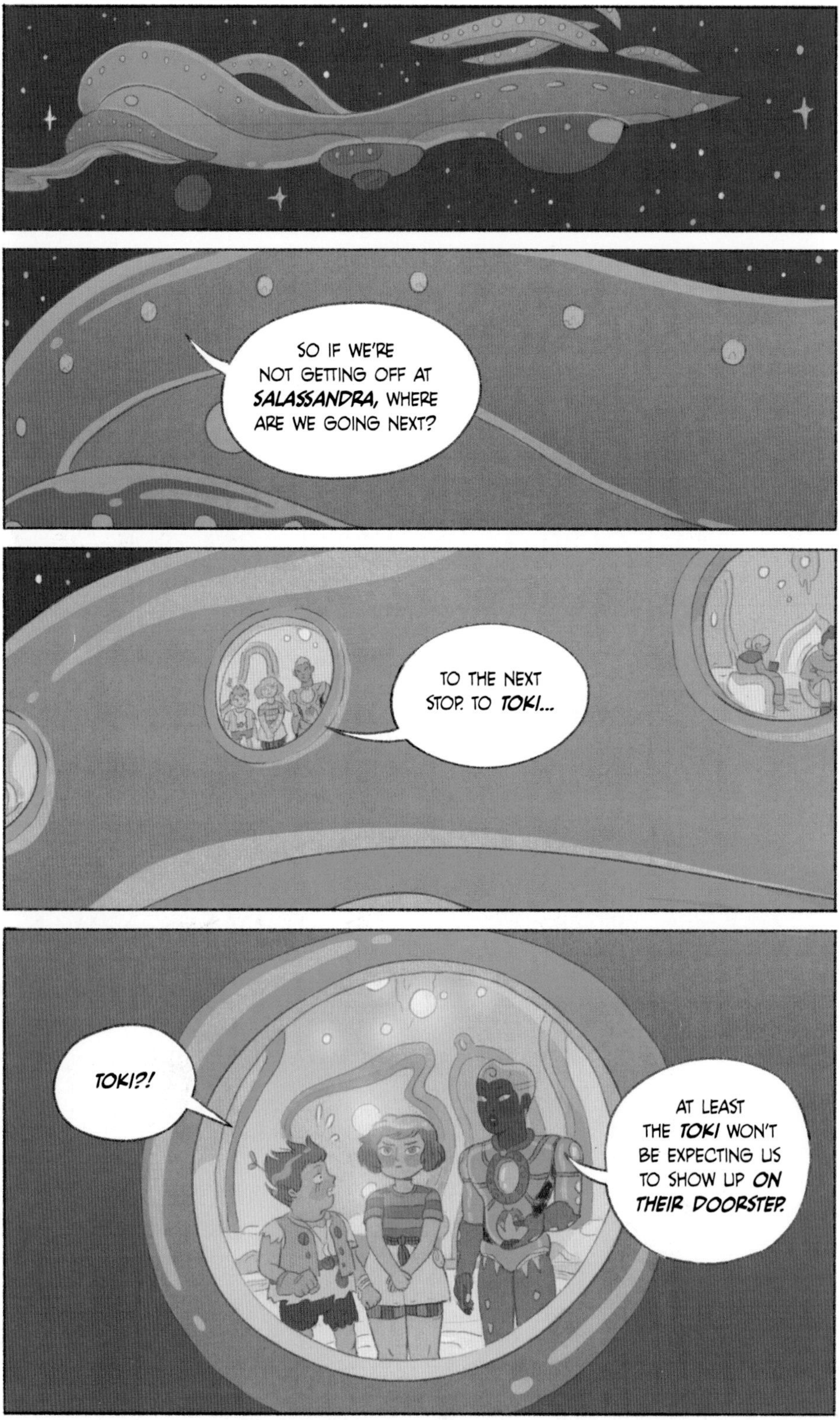
SO IF WE'RE NOT GETTING OFF AT SALASSANDRA, WHERE ARE WE GOING NEXT?
TO THE NEXT STOP. TO TOKI...
TOKI?!
AT LEAST THE TOKI WON'T BE EXPECTING US TO SHOW UP ON THEIR DOORSTEP.

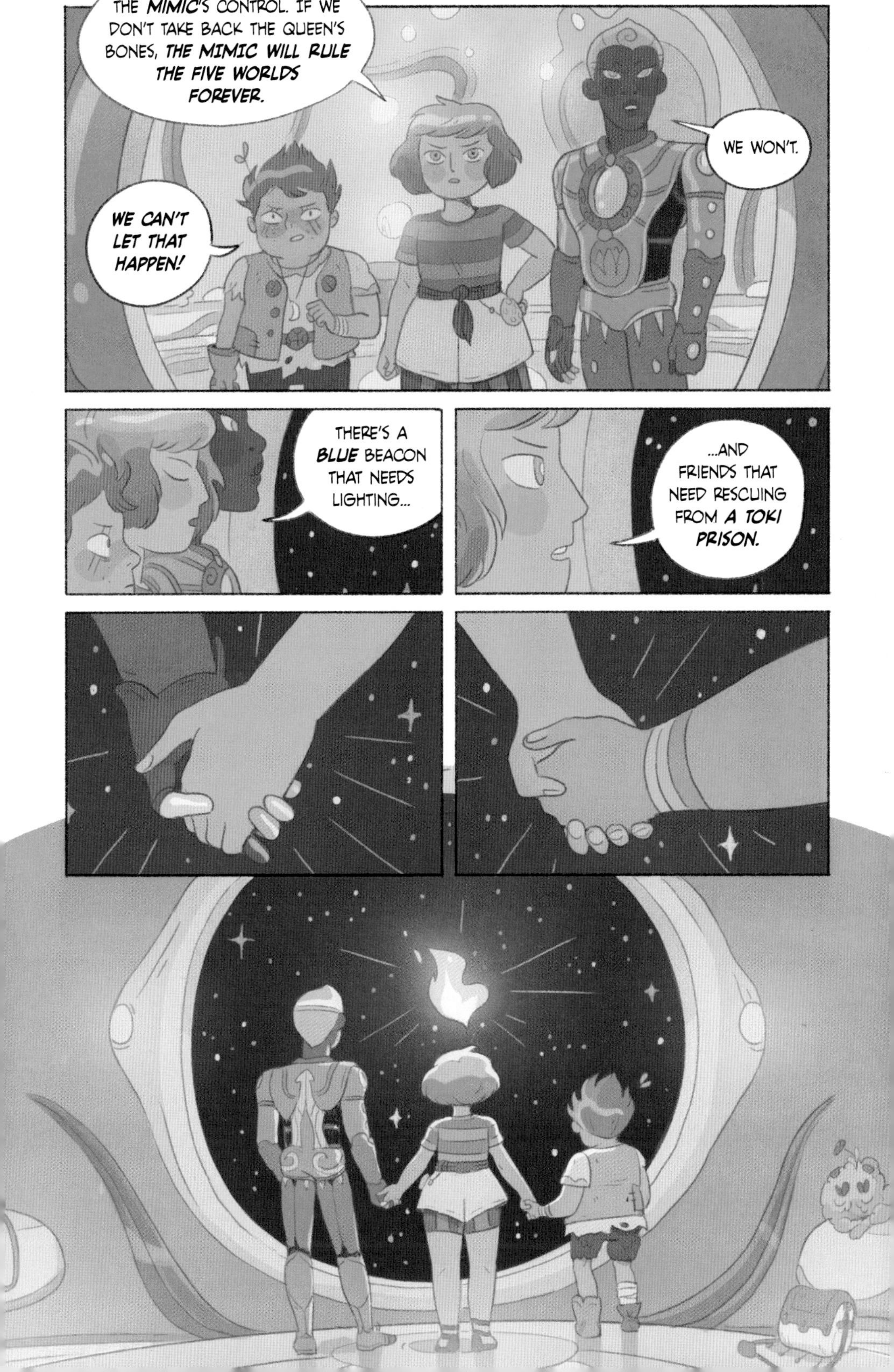
THEY'VE FALLEN UNDER THE MIMIC'S CONTROL. IF WE DON'T TAKE BACK THE QUEEN'S BONES, THE MIMIC WILL RULE THE FIVE WORLDS FOREVER.
WE WON'T.
WE CAN'T LET THAT HAPPEN!
THERE'S A BLUE BEACON THAT NEEDS LIGHTING...
...AND FRIENDS THAT NEED RESCUING FROM A TOKI PRISON.

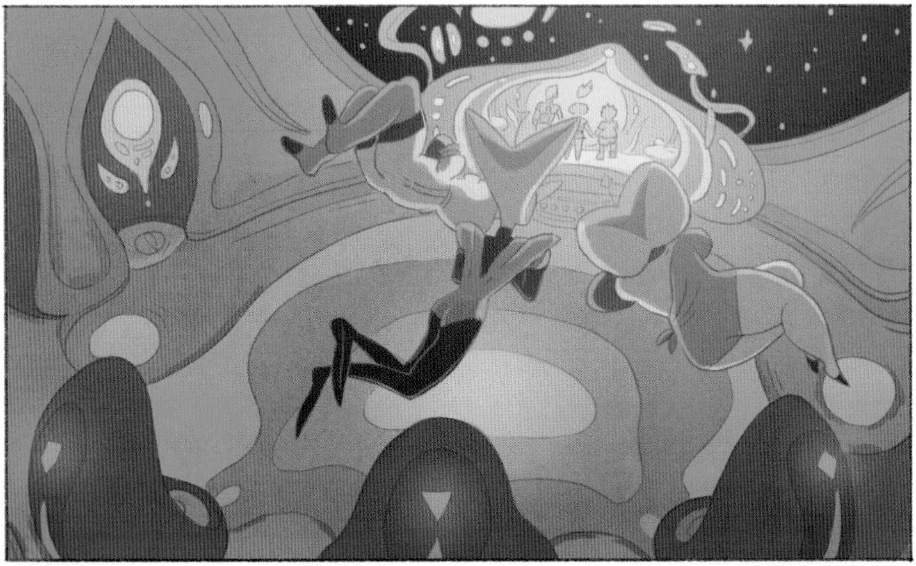

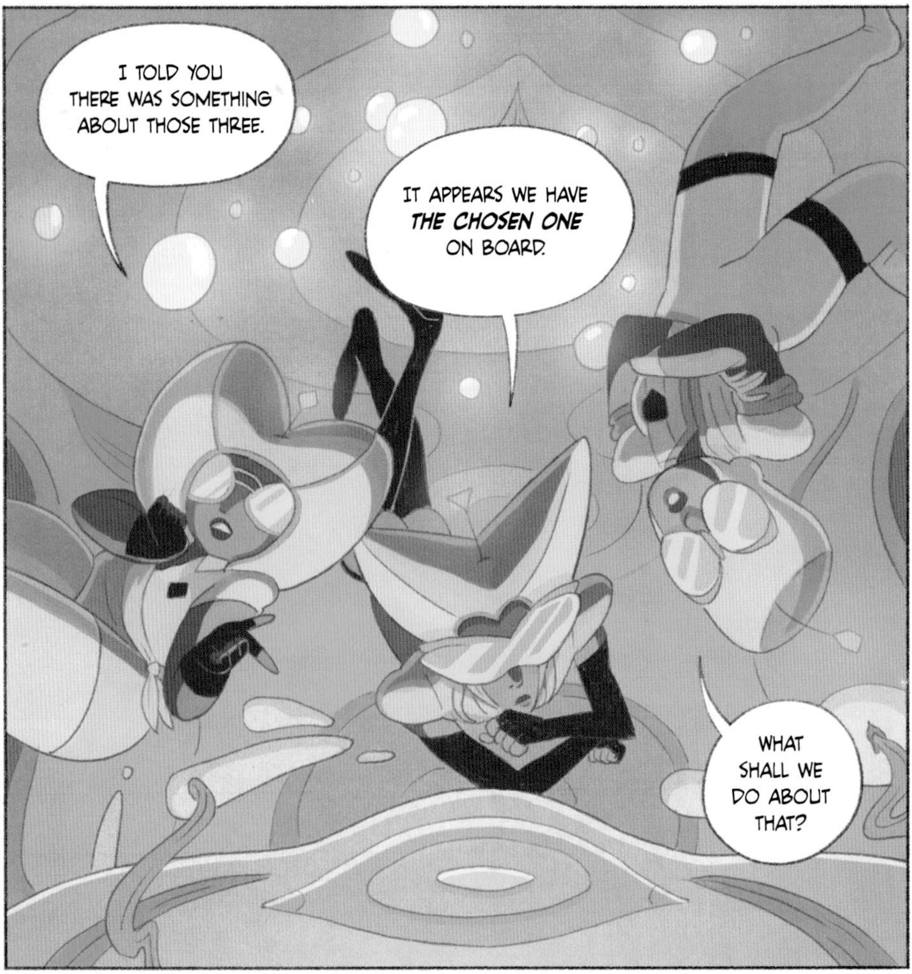
I TOLD YOU THERE WAS SOMETHING ABOUT THOSE THREE.
IT APPEARS WE HAVE ***THE CHOSEN ONE*** ON BOARD.
WHAT SHALL WE DO ABOUT THAT?

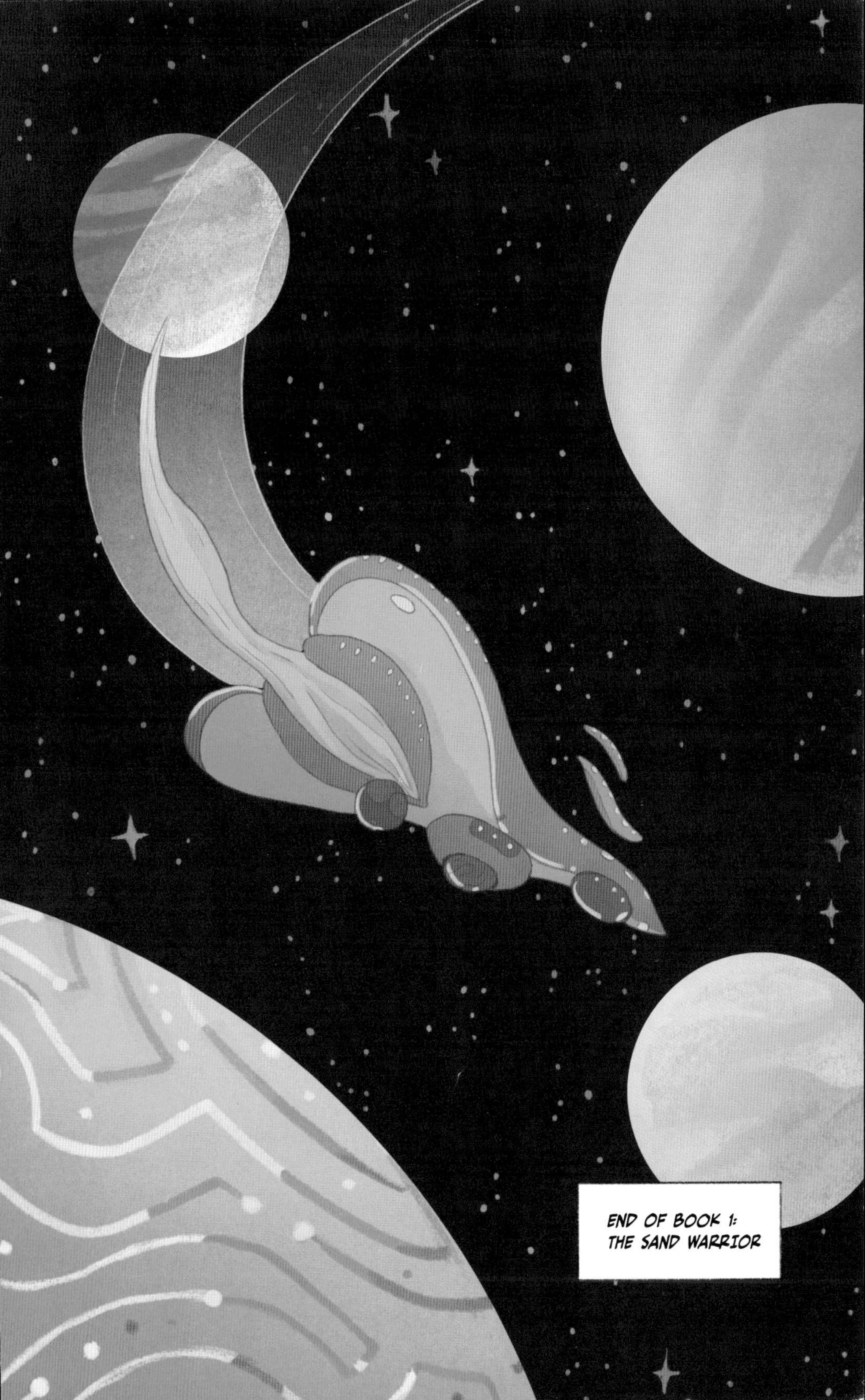
END OF BOOK 1:
THE SAND WARRIOR

To Julien and Clio—MS

To Shudan, Felix, and Elia—AS

To Mom and Pop—XB

To my friends and family—MR

To all my friends—BS

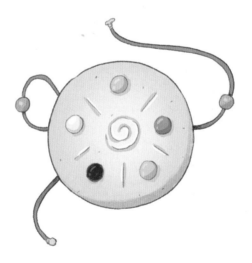

ACKNOWLEDGMENTS

Tanya McKinnon,
for support high and low, above and beyond

Our amazing Random House team:
Michelle Nagler, Chelsea Eberly, Elizabeth Tardiff, Kelly McGauley, Kim Lauber, Alison Kolani,
Dominique Cimina, Aisha Cloud, Lisa Nadel, Adrienne Waintraub, Laura Antonacci, John Adamo,
Joe English, Jocelyn Lange, Mallory Loehr, Barbara Marcus

+ Special thanks for added help, friendship & magic:
Siena Siegel, Sonia Siegel, Macarena Mata, Julie Sandfort, Gene Luen Yang,
Lee Wade, Sam Bosma, Kali Ciesemier, Noelle Stevenson, Carter Goodrich,
Moebius, Ursula K. LeGuin, Doris Lessing, Lois McMaster Bujold

Copyright © 2017 by Antzu Pantzu, LLC

All rights reserved. Published in the United States by Random House Children's Books,
a division of Penguin Random House LLC, New York.

Random House and the colophon are registered trademarks of Penguin Random House LLC.

Visit us on the Web! randomhousekids.com

Educators and librarians, for a variety of teaching tools, visit us at RHTeachersLibrarians.com

Library of Congress Cataloging-in-Publication Data is available upon request.
ISBN 978-1-101-93586-6 (trade) — ISBN 978-1-101-93588-0 (pbk.)
ISBN 978-1-101-93587-3 (lib. bdg.) — ISBN 978-1-101-93604-7 (ebook)

MANUFACTURED IN CHINA

10 9 8 7 6 5 4 3 2 1

First Edition

MARK SIEGEL has written and illustrated several award-winning picture books and graphic novels, including the *New York Times* bestseller **Sailor Twain, or the Mermaid in the Hudson.** He is also the founder and editorial director of First Second Books at Macmillan. He lives with his family in New York.

ALEXIS SIEGEL is a writer and translator based in London, England. He has translated a number of bestselling graphic novels, including Joann Sfar's **The Rabbi's Cat** and Pénélope Bagieu's **Exquisite Corpse** into English and Gene Luen Yang's **American Born Chinese** into French.

XANTHE BOUMA is an illustrator based in Southern California. When not working on picture books, fashion illustration, and comics, Xanthe enjoys soaking up the beachside sun.

MATT ROCKEFELLER is an illustrator and comic book artist from Tucson, Arizona. His work has appeared in a variety of formats, including book covers, picture books, and animation. Matt lives in New York City.

BOYA SUN is an illustrator and coauthor of the upcoming graphic novel **Chasma Knights.** Originally from China, Boya has traveled from Canada to the United States and now resides in the charming city of Baltimore.

What will Oona, Jax, and An Tzu find on Toki?
The adventure continues in

5 Worlds
THE COBALT PRINCE
Mark Siegel
Alexis Siegel
Xanthe Bouma
Matt Rockefeller
Boya Sun

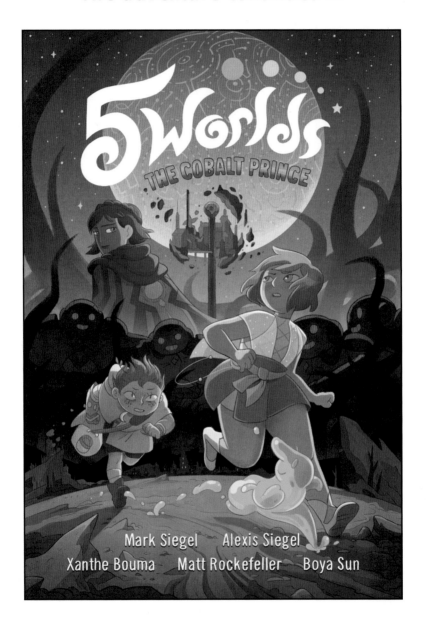

5W2:
THE COBALT PRINCE

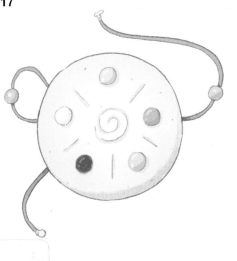

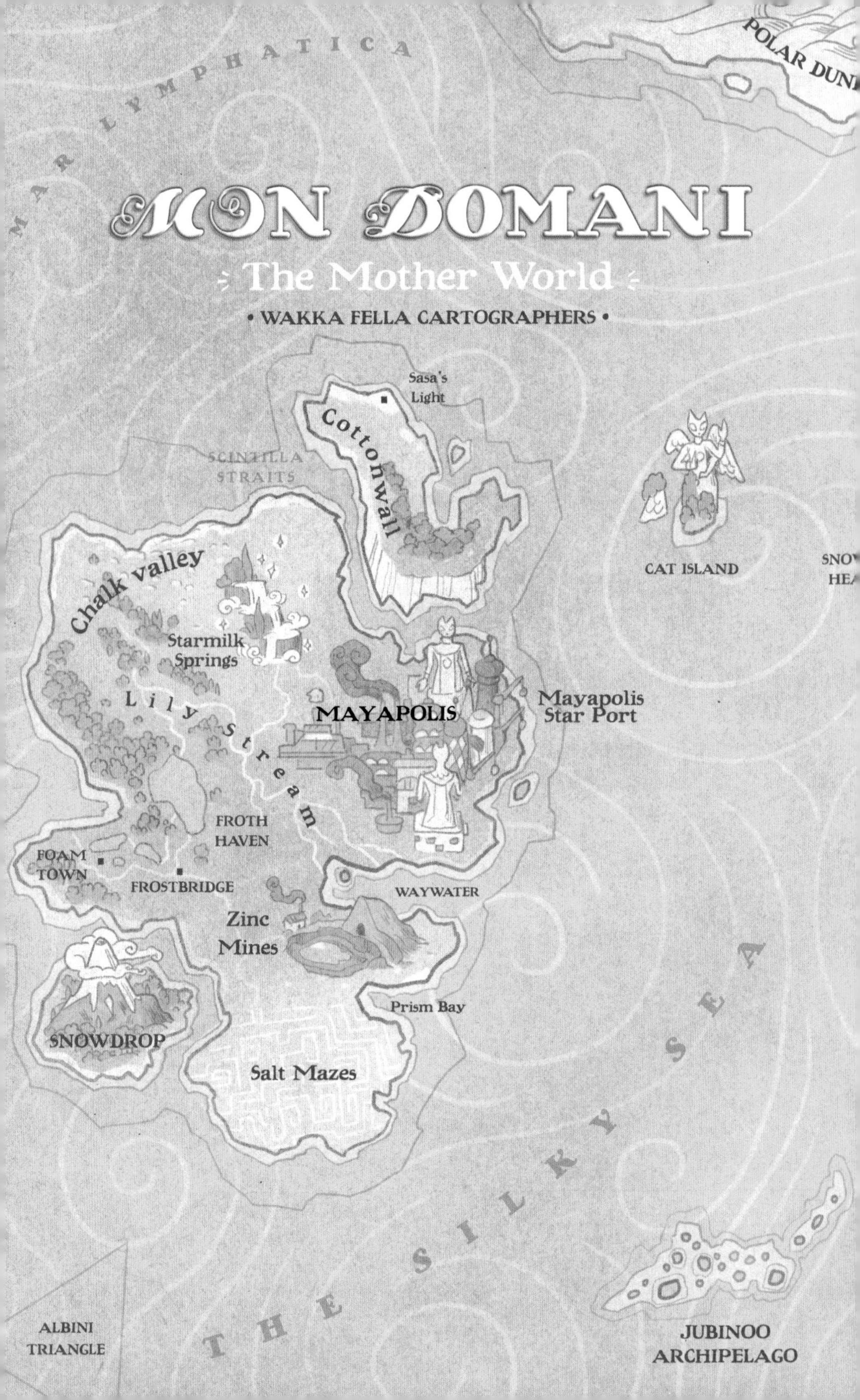
MAR LYMPHATICA
MON DOMANI
The Mother World
• WAKKA FELLA CARTOGRAPHERS •
Sasa's Light
Cottonwall
SCINTILLA STRAITS
CAT ISLAND
Chalk valley
Starmilk Springs
Lily Stream
MAYAPOLIS
Mayapolis Star Port
FROTH HAVEN
FOAM TOWN
FROSTBRIDGE
WAYWATER
Zinc Mines
Prism Bay
SNOWDROP
Salt Mazes
THE SILKY SEA
ALBINI TRIANGLE
JUBINOO ARCHIPELAGO